Captain Ty closed the door to his cabin. In the darkness he saw Angel's silken hair trailed over her slim arms and a blouse that rose and fell softly with each breath.

"Mmmm. Wha—" she mumbled, wakened from her sleep.

He removed his tunic and began to unbutton his tight, buckskin breeches when she cried, "I don't want to share a room with a strange man!"

With a deep growl he scooped her up into his arms and dumped her unceremoniously on the floor. Then he followed her down, bending one knee against her chest as he pinned her flailing arms high over her head.

She groaned when she saw the thick mat of crisp, curled hair so close to her face. Like a savage and foreboding beast, he emitted a strange animal heat—but his bright eyes sparkled as he lowered his head.

Now he would rape her, she thought frantically, searching for a means of escape. Her heart thumped crazily as she rocked from cheek to cheek to avoid his warm lips. She whimpered as he caught both her wrists in one hand while the other captured her chin, squeezing gently. He gazed deeply into her terrified eyes, and then, suddenly, set her loose.

Relieved and somewhat surprised, she vowed then to use her womanly cunning to make him think she was his slave—and one day, while his back was turned, she would flee and be forever free of this handsome devil!

YOU WILL ALSO WANT TO READ
WHITEWATER DYNASTY AND OTHER GREAT SAGAS!

PASSION'S PARADISE

BY SONYA T. PELTON

ZEBRA BOOKS

KENSINGTON PUBLISHING CORP.

ZEBRA BOOKS

are published by

KENSINGTON PUBLISHING CORP.
475 Park Avenue South
New York, N.Y. 10016

Second Printing

Printed in the United States of America

> *Forthwith the Devil did appear,*
> *For name him, and he's always near.*
> —Matthew Prior

Chapter One

1

The gentle wind seemed scarcely to stroke the sails of the *Fidelia*, yet slowly the ship glided lazily forward, leaning a little to one side as if weary after so long a voyage from England to the West Indies. The *Fidelia*, a two-master, square-rigged, with a fore-and-aft mainsail, was a weathered, barnacle-bellied beast with faded and chipped trim, that miraculously had proven seaworthy for several months. And so she rocked onwards in defiant security, with the luminous sea hissing beneath her prow and playfully tossing up pearls of foam that melted in the air before they fell. . . .

The *Fidelia*'s captain was usually not one to burden himself with the age-old superstition that women on board were bad luck, but he had been having second thoughts of late. Like now, as he studied Angel Sherwood with his watery blue eyes. He saw a pale slim beauty, a lovely demon who had bewitched him and his ship. Angel? He wanted to laugh out loud.

In the midst of wood and canvas and rigging, Angel's long, moon-white hair coruscated as if it flirted with the sun while she awaited Captain Warfield's answer. She had come to dislike him increasingly, especially his protruding eyes, which followed her about when she aired herself on deck while her parents napped below and the restless sailors were kept busy at task.

"Well, captain," she pressed. "Why *do* you fly the golden colors of Spain?"

The captain ran a stubby finger along a horrible scar that marked his sweat-curded face. He felt a great anger swell up in him and redden his face. Were Miss Sherwood a man he would

5

have her flogged for insolent behavior. But she wasn't, and her more than generous benefactor—a tall Yankee who went only by the name of Big Jim—had doled out extra coin in the assurance that no harm befall her or her parents, Lord and Lady Sherwood. Warfield would not have cared to displease the Yankee dressed in fastidious black, should he meet with him again. Hell's blisters! All he wanted now was to get this troublesome baggage off his back.

Warfield spat tobacco juice upon the deck and rubbed the glistening smear with his boot. "'Tis like this, missy. You see, the Trade sees to impose a fine to all British ships if'n they transport slaves," he began, stowing his spyglass under his arm. "So, I sail under false colors to save me precious coin." But not my neck, he was going to add, but thought it better not to. He was growing more vexed by the moment as this meddlesome young minx stood here on the deck of his ship questioning his intent.

Angel said nothing yet, but she gave a pondering glance upward. The sky was blue without a cloud, as if the Caribbean had never known a breeze, or a sudden storm. With no land in sight, with nothing but sea and sky to globe them, Angel realized more than ever how far she was from England.

"Slaves, in faith, captain?" Angel finally said, with a near giggle.

"Aye . . . they're here, black slaves down in the hold, missy."

"Oh? But I haven't seen any—" Angel waved a slim arm expansively. "Only the Negro boy Samuel have I seen aboard."

"That's because we picked them up couple nights back. You must have slept sound not to catch the shuffling up deck. Eyy, don't look at me through that storm cloud, missy. Ain't like it's illegal traffic. 'Tis just we pick' em up and transport them— that's all."

"That's all," she said mockingly. "And, captain, why haven't they come up on deck?"

"They get their air only at night. Tell you this, though, you'll hear them groan and holler when it gets hot enough for 'em down there. 'Specially if we sail into the doldrums."

6

"What about Samuel?" Angel dared ask.

"He's my biggest boy," Warfield almost spewed. "Use him for menial tasks above decks and below. You don't fool this old salt, missy. You know just about everything that goes on on my ship, save for the slaves."

Angel ignored that. "Captain, I've a feeling this tariff bothers you not at all. There is something else, something you are not letting your passengers in on?" Angel tilted her bright head.

Warfield blinked at the lass in disbelief, even though he should really be thanking her for reminding him of the danger of flying the Spanish flag. It had been said unwittingly on her part. He had sailed these waters for twenty some years now; and here were the privateers who preyed on Spanish vessels, and the danger would be heightened in the next few days, as they neared their destination. As he had in the past, he should have brought the flag down by now. His Majesty's navy hadn't been sighted even once during their entire journey. But, damn if he hadn't promised that Yank to let it fly all the way, the gold coins in his pocket reminding him he best do just that, even though it was a mysterious undertaking he should have avoided from the first. Warfield stowed his ponderings.

"In a few days, missy, we'll be coming up on Port Royal, and if there's any trouble . . . b'God! I'll bet me bottom dollar you could scare the britches off a band of cutthroats with your whip of a tongue. Go below now and say nothing to yer parents!"

"Cutthroats, Captain Old Salt? Really!"

Angel Sherwood grinned impishly when Warfield groaned and turned to stride violently away. She didn't go immediately as ordered but lingered quietly awhile longer, studying the tall, scrubby sails and the splintered decks, and smelling the salt spray of the deep blue sea that engulfed the brown beast *Fidelia*. Angel shook her head and sighed, thinking what a sheltered life she'd led before this strange voyage.

Coarse giggling strumpets, black slaves, and a cruel, unfeeling captain. What manner of ship were they on? Surely her parents could not have known the ship held so many evils, otherwise they would never have come aboard.

7

Angel now leisurely strolled back to the gloomy, barely livable cabin. She reflected back to the one particular morning in late February when the endless packing of trunks and luggage had begun. She had been amazed that all her gowns and frocks, her unmentionables and shawls, had been packed. She had been surprised at the time, too, how very few parties and balls she was permitted to attend. It did not worry her particularly because there were so many ways in which she could occupy her time. Never a day would pass that she did not go riding on her favorite mare, Echo.

Though she often wondered, Angel never once questioned the affairs of her parents' income or the new frugality they had practiced since the subject of the voyage first arose. Before their departure a number of the household possessions had been sold. Even odder was the fact that society life had suddenly begun to pall on her father; in the past Beldwin had held a large number of private affairs with his cronies in the Gold Salon at Stonewall.

Cards. It had been, ever since she could remember, the gambling fever with Lord Sherwood, first in the London house, then at Stonewall. They had rusticated to Stonewall when she turned eight years old. That had been in the year 1801.

Pertaining to the voyage, Angel had been determined that nothing interfere with her mother's and father's happiness. So she had closed her eyes to the strange goings on back home. Ah, but now she was finding it something of an effort to remain close-mouthed.

Just this morning her mother had mentioned, quite casually, that they were going to Louisiana after the Fair in Puerto Bello. Her father had said nothing, had looked upon Mama almost as if he hated her. Angel sighed dispiritedly. She had never heard them confess their love to each other. Was merely living a gay life and having a companionable mate enough? Mama and Papa seemed to think so. Was this to be her fate, also? Was this all there was to being happy?

I shall never get married! Angel vowed.

Yet beneath her reserve there lurked a most desirable woman, whose frosty nature could someday melt in the presence of the right man—a most virile man—who would

8

have to cut through layers of defense and fan the dormant fires in her, patiently, gradually.

But there had never been even one man who could fascinate her totally, nor had any stirred her blood to desire—the sweet madness she had heard romantics speak of had never come over her.

Didn't she believe the testimony of her senses, her deepest emotions, and the ache which had begun to squeeze her heart? Why was the male deepness of her dream-lover's voice a new searing fire in her blood?

Angel embraced herself dreamily as she hesitated before the little cubby of a room, making believe her phantom lover stood there beside her and would . . . she would bravely turn her head, close her eyes, and giving of her mouth, lift her head to be kissed, sweetly, then demandingly. She could almost feel her icy veneer dissipate, her mouth lusciously opening, desperately yearning at the same time for him to brush those lean fingers deliberately across her breasts. Arms slipping around his neck, body pressed close to his, leaning hard, clutching, waiting for possession . . . to lie yielding and naked. In a flash reality surfaced from lone desire.

Why fight fate? Come. You will soon be mine.

There! That unbidden voice again!

"I cannot understand. He draws me to him, this faceless, deep-voiced phantom," Angel breathed to herself softly. "Bah! I am an idiot! A dreamer! Sweet madness? Go away, randy voice, and play your tricks on another!"

Angel could not know until much later the significance of deliciously dangerous paths she had allowed her thoughts and dreams to enter during this long, idle voyage.

Shaking herself free of any further daydreams, Angel again heard her mother's voice as she had just that morning.

"I just know that you will like Louisiana, love," Christine had promised her, but Angel thought it had been spoken half-heartedly.

Angel lost count of the days. The fluttering from the hencoops on the deck above told her that daylight was near; another day that would drag by slowly, painfully. She was restless, and boredom reigned as never before.

Snuggled in her bunk with her old blanket of embroidered bluebells, Angel pored over the volumes once again that her Uncle Stuart had made her a parting gift of. The books were the only things that delighted her during these long days and kept her mind off the poor slaves down in the hold.

Angel glanced with growing distaste around the musty cabin she shared with Christine. The usual dull sight of two narrow wooden bunks, three rickety chairs, a rough-hewn table, and a washstand in one corner met her weary eyes. Barely visible in the gloom across from their crude beds were their trunks. A portable convenience was the only other fitting that vied for space in the crowded quarters; it was emptied twice daily by Samuel, giving Angel a chance to converse with the lonesome lad.

"If any more water finds its way into this cabin, I swear I shall mildew," Angel said as she bounded from her bunk to pace the confines.

"Yes, I know what you mean, love," Christine answered and fixed her gaze on a distant spot of hazy blue outside the porthole. She sighed. "But we are here and might as well make the most of it. Read to me again, daughter?"

Christine Sherwood's taut countenance and her youthfully trim figure belied her forty-odd years; it was the spattering of gray at the temples of deep gold that gave the tale away. Coming from a suitable station in life, Christine Littlington had married into the small but proud aristocratic Sherwood family. And after her father-in-law had died, toppling from his favorite thoroughbred ten years back, Beldwin had taken to the gaming tables, even going so far as to set one up in his own salon.

While her daughter read to her from the volume of Emerson, Christine reflected back to Angel's birth. The babe had already sprouted a thick batch of silvery-blond curls by the time of christening. Beldwin had stood firm on the French name which meant "angelic," and erelong, nicknamed her Angeline because of her lasting ethereal countenance. So she became Angel.

Little had changed as far as the cupid's-bow mouth and the fair coloring went, but her dimpled cheeks had been replaced

10

by high, aristocratic cheekbones. Spiky, dark amber lashes contrasted with pale waves of silken hair, that, when loosed, undulated to a tiny waist. Angel sometimes looked the seductive woman, but was yet an innocent so far as knowing a man went—Christine was certain of this one thing.

Though Angel had admitted countless gentlemen callers into the drawing room, and listened to proposals of marriage by the dozens in the moonlit gardens, as yet her interests didn't lie in the direction of total commitment. Oh, to be sure, Angel had had her share of girlish flirtations, but oftentimes Christine had witnessed the cool remoteness and the green eyes flash a warning when a dashing young swain became overly familiar. Woe be to the libertine who would ever try lifting Angel's skirts!

Christine was often of a mind to reveal to Angel the sad truth of their falling into debt, but more than one thing restrained her. Perhaps it was cruel holding out on Angel like this, but Beldwin demanded a waiting period, at least until they settled down in the new land. If they scrimped, eventually they could send for the beloved mare, Echo, and the offspring she was soon to give birth to.

One last adventure before settling down in Louisiana, Beldwin had said upon leaving Stonewall in the hands of the highest bidder. He believed the rebirth of his luck would occur in Puerto Bello, where they would be just in time for the spring Fair. There hadn't been all that much left after paying off just half Beldwin's mountainous gambling notes. She just prayed their meager purse would survive and not be gambled away before they reached their final destination. There just had to be enough for a down payment on a decent house. She bemoaned the fact that Beldwin would have to find himself a job for the first time in his life.

But why Louisiana, Christine had wondered out loud of Beldwin's plans to set down new roots there. He'd only shrugged, saying, "Why not, it's as good a place as any!" and had gone back to smoking his pipe. Christine had then had a strong feeling that he was running from the other half of those debts.

The days spent on the *Fidelia* passed, but not swiftly enough

11

for Angel. Her father sank lower into depression and stayed put in the cabin he shared with Warfield, hardly ever visiting Angel and Christine anymore. Her once handsome father was downing more and more of the cheap rum the captain kept on board. She knew he shared a few bottles with Warfield every day while they amused themselves with a deck of cards, and that he perhaps imbibed even more in the evening. Not only that, but on several occasions Angel thought she detected shrill laughter seeping out from the captain's door late at night.

One afternoon Angel was kneeling on the boards with Christine, sorting out the contents of a huge trunk. Angel silently watched her mother's still lovely hands caress a brocaded gown. Her parents had indeed drifted apart, and a disenchantment about the marriage vows had taken root in Angel's young mind.

"I am sorry, love," Christine began. "Things have not turned out so well, and I can tell that you would like to return home." She at once bit her lip.

Angel let that sink in, then said, very softly and a bit wistfully, "It is too late for that now, Mama. Look—" she made a sweeping gesture toward the porthole, "we have passed Port Royal days ago and are well into the Caribbeans. That nearsighted bumpkin of a captain would never heed our wish to hasten back to England!"

Angel sat back on her heels, thoughtfully regarding the arced trunk. She didn't want to disillusion her mother, and yet, she truly wished of late to be back home, surrounded by those things she most cherished.

"Echo must just now be foaling," Angel said wistfully.

"You can calm yourself that your uncle knows what to do when Echo's time comes, love." Christine's thoughts turned from the beloved mare. She really should confide in Angel that Beldwin needed desperately to go to that fair and win back some of the money he'd lost over the years. But she could not. She was growing cowardly in her old age, and now she worried what the future held for Angel.

Angel stood, smiling, and dusted off her hands. "Let's go see what has been prepared for lunch. We are both famished and this can wait, as we have all the time in the world for house cleaning."

With the noon meal of fresh fish and breadfruit partaken of, Angel went to find Samuel, ever on guard lest Warfield was about. It wouldn't be wise for the captain to discover that she had befriended Samuel. The lad would no doubt receive a severe lashing were he caught speaking to her in a friendly fashion. Sam was lonely, Angel knew, as she was herself, and she determined his age to be near her own. So young to be without some small measure of happiness; and there was not a soul that dared speak kindly to him. No one but herself. She doubted that he was even allowed to visit with the slaves below, his own kind.

She found Samuel at task. Assured that the second mate was not within hearing distance, and speaking quickly, she asked him point blank, "What will become of the slaves in the hold, Samuel?"

The black boy was getting used to Angel's friendliness. He had swiftly discovered at first meeting that the English girl didn't have a prejudiced bone in her body, and, strangely, she treated him like an equal. He even opened up to her occasionally, revealing facts that would have made the fainter at heart tremble with disgust. On his back were signs of a multitude of thrashings, lasting scars of the tortures of slavery he'd endured. His dark eyes brightened when Angel sought him out in conversation, but she often detected a certain underlying sadness, of suffering.

At first surprised at her question, Sam rolled his eyes about cautiously before he spoke, low. "They bound for America, Miz Angel. One day a slave ship'll pull up 'longside and then they be gone. If cap'n gets caught with um he'll drown um all to save hisself from prison."

Angel shivered with disgust at the thought of humans being murdered so heedlessly. "How awful for them!" she said. "But . . . how about you, Samuel, what will become of you?"

"Me, Miz Angel?" Sam snorted softly as he plunged his mop into a wooden bucket. "I belongs to the cap'n. He not too bad, beats me once in awhile when he gets drunk. If'n I does as told, allus okay."

Angel scowled at that. For some reason unknown to her

13

Samuel appeared fidgety this searingly hot day. He was obviously anxious about something, as was the captain himself.

"I can feel it, Samuel. What is wrong with this day? It is different from all the rest and frightening you. Am I right? Please tell me?" she begged, reaching out to touch a glistening black shoulder. She felt hurt when he jerked away and paid her no mind. In the next instant she fully understood. Samuel was looking at something behind her with dislike in his black eyes.

Angel whirled to face Ellen. She recalled when this woman, along with her two tainted companions, had boarded the *Fidelia* at the London docks. Angel had stood on deck, disbelief written all over her face. She had thought then that surely they were not staying, but they had, all the way. Where they were bound was none of her business, nor did she care to know.

Now the overly painted strumpet twitched up to Angel, one hand placed gingerly over her curvaceous hip. Angel thought how closely the rouged and powdered face resembled that of an overpainted doll she had once seen in a Paris shop window. It rankled her that Ellen might very well be entertaining not only Warfield but her father, too. Angel's lips pursed tightly as she watched Samuel mop down the deck, hurriedly working away from them.

"You wished to talk to me?" Angel queried huskily, slanting her frosty eyes at Ellen.

Ellen tarried as she leered down at the slightly smaller and younger woman, then peered up at the white-hot sky. "What do you want with that darkie, bright eyes? I know he's got a nice build and all that, but—"

"Hush up!" Angel snapped as she prepared to strike the other woman.

"Back off a bloody minute!" Ellen hissed, backing up herself in alarm at Angel's murderous look, seeing the clawed fingers of Angel's dainty hand outspread. "Forget it," Ellen drawled, trying to appear cool.

The larger woman began to stroll away but Angel snatched up the swinging arm. Ellen tried to avoid the grasp but Angel held on and warned softly, "Tonight when you sleep I shall slit your harlot's throat from ear to ear." She emitted a slicing

14

sound that caused the other to blanch.

Ellen steadied herself by clutching the ship's railing and rasped, "What the devil . . . and me thinking you was a lady of class. Nah. I'll bet you're a bloody gypsy from the Cornish coast. Blimey . . . a silver-haired Romany!"

"My, my. How did you guess. And it is not difficult to guess which side of the fence you come from . . . *Lady* Ellen," Angel mocked, unperturbed. "Yes, I was birthed near an old Norman castle where horrible witches yet stir their nightly potions in old black pots." Angel smiled inwardly at the horrified expression of the woman before her, adding, "Now, you seem to have a way of finding things out. Hmmm, I wonder how in the world you go about it." She tapped her chin in feigned thought.

"Ohhh," Ellen groaned. "My stomach's much too weak for the likes of you. I'd rather pass time with a bloody pirate. Hah! We just might have a chance at that. Heard that bug-eyed captain chatting with his fat old mate and—"

"Be still!" Angel demanded as she glanced out over the sea, then, swiveling her head to peer up at the sun while shielding her eyes, she said, "Of course—that's it! How silly of me to be so unobservant."

"Eh," Ellen smacked her lips. "You finally took your eyes off that darkie long enough to look around yourself. Yeah, we are drifting in a northwesterly direction. There's not a bloody thing that simple-minded Warfield can do about it, neither. He said as much. Better tighten your chastity belt, little witch. Your kind needs taking down a notch or two, and who better than a wicked-looking pirate with a nasty patch over one eye!" Ellen went hastily to her cabin before another word could be said.

A flickering of timid stars and a sickle moonrise engraved the incredibly dark sky. There was not even a surface ripple or a faint breath of wind to give a soul ease after the heat of the glittering day. The *Fidelia* haunted the waters like a slow-moving hunk of gray driftwood. Angel had found dining with Christine near impossible, and soon forgetting all about the succulent fish, she stood up and fastened her gaze outside

15

the porthole.

Sheets of moon-mirrored water held her stare as she thought back to the earlier rankling scene with Ellen. It had been for naught, and now even Christine had knowledge of their ungainly position.

Her eyes a gorgeous crystal-green, Angel escaped from the present to reflect back in time. After she had moved from the London townhouse near Hyde Park, Stonewall, with its foggy and muted moors, had held a special place in her heart. Her day-to-day life had been one big, glittering social whirl. She had been very happy, very gay. Then one day it all came to a halt.

The door to the past slowly widened further. She could see again the green baize table that had never failed to fascinate her, with its cards strewn wildly about, the group of men seeming dazed, in no way related to her mama, her nanny, nor her daytime papa. Always there had been young, well-dressed men in the house, always the roving eyes of the so-called gentlemen at parties, balls, and soirees thrown by her parents. Games the blueblooded played, like croquet on the lush lawns, had been Christine's favorites, while Beldwin ever drifted back into the salon as night fell, with his pack of bluebloods trailing. Often one of the young bucks would hang back and persuade Angel to change into her riding clothes and race across the moors.

She had learned well the studied ruses of the young men, knew that their lust-glinting gazes would ever play over her. Well into her teens there was not one who could compliment her expertly enough to persuade her into his bed. Many studied lovers had tried, and all had failed miserably. Offers of marriage there had been aplenty, but there had been no man special enough to win her maiden's heart. They had been blinded to all but the superficial.

All of a sudden a thrill shot through her. She stood for several moments, all trembly, as an unbidden flush rose within her. She held her breath momentarily, as she tried to set her mind on a different course. But as she had done during her nap that afternoon, again she was envisioning herself sprawled in an ungainly position, beneath the phantom of her dreams, in a green secluded place where she had wandered like a

16

moonstruck lass.

Now the full weight of what she had desired dawned on her. "Oh, no . . ." Angel agonized softly. She could not have wanted him to do *that* to her. This kind of thing was unheard of for her. He was not even real! A mere shadow! And yet, his fingers had burned her flesh tormentingly, as if he had been right there beside her in the bunk while she experienced a shaky quickening, then, tumbling to wakefulness, a trembling effusion she had only begun to taste but checked from going further.

Was she to meet this phantom in the flesh soon? She prayed not.

Angel sighed pensively before turning about to face Christine, whose nervous humming had abruptly ceased.

"What is going to happen to us, Angel? All of a sudden it's like we are on a ghost ship."

The captain and Beldwin had retired for a night's drinking, their meal left untouched. Their faces had registered annoyance at Christine's constant imploring. Now it was Angel's turn to be piqued. She paced back and forth over the splintered boards of the dining-cabin, her flounced skirts rustling and her beautiful but stern visage illuminated by the candlelight. She toyed with a wavelet of long fair hair while pondering the crisis.

There probably wasn't a thing to worry about. Cutthroats and pirates. Indeed! They more than likely would not run afoul of the fellows, she surmised, a scowl lining her fine brow.

"Angel. You are not hearing me," Christine chided. When her daughter faced her and stopped the pacing, she added, "Though the captain can't understand it himself, he says we are drifting north. How can that be when there is no wind?"

"I cannot explain the mysterious forces of nature, Mama. Perhaps we are riding on the back of some enormous sea creature, or an undercurrent is tugging us north." She shrugged. "I don't know. The captain is supposed to be the expert here. He should know what to do, at least show that he cares." She tossed up her hands, then began pacing again.

"Ohhh . . . that captain cares about nothing but his rum. He and his crew are all above getting intoxicated, and my Beldwin,

17

too. Listen. It sounds like people are moaning, too. There, you see, the vessel is haunted. A ghost ship."

Angel could hear it herself. The sounds of human suffering. But she tried putting her mother at ease a bit. "Mama, you are just nervous, hearing things. It happens when one is anxious and troubled."

"I suppose so. But what in God's name are we to do?" Christine almost sobbed.

Angel spun about, snapping, "I cannot believe that you are being the child, Mama!" Softening, her voice lowered. "You are going to wrinkle your face the more if you do not stop screwing it up like that."

Christine paled. "Daughter! Where did you learn such language? I've never heard you use such crude words. But then, we have all three of us undergone a personality change of late." She sighed deeply.

"I am sorry, Mama. But someone has to remain strong and keep the humor flowing." She laughed lightly. "A merry heart doeth good like a medicine; but a broken spirit drieth the bones."

Christine nodded absentmindedly but immediately started up again, while Angel rolled her eyes heavenward. "You know, that captain has been telling your father horrible tales while they sit over a bottle, about increasing attacks on ships in the Caribbeans and the Gulf."

Angel recalled hearing about these silly rumors from Pierre Le Naisse several months before they had embarked, but she hadn't absorbed any of the nonsense as important. She would not worry her mother further though, by relaying this; she would just permit her to ramble on, perhaps get some of the fear out of her system.

"Ships of all nations have been taken, but especially ones from Spain. And did you see, daughter, we are flying the Spanish flag? These pirates have been known to treat their women captives with barbarity. Oh, and you, my dear sweet baby." In the next moment Christine's eyes widened. "I am not frightening you, am I, love?"

"No," Angel said simply but tapped her slipper impatiently as she waited for blessed silence to creep into the room so that

18

she could think more seriously about their possible problem. But the silence was not forthcoming.

"Then your father says not to be overly concerned, while we are drifting ever closer into the merciless hands of those barbarians!" Christine sighed and sniffed. Then, poised with thoughtful expression, she exploded, "We shall hide you in the hold. They shall not ravish my baby!"

Angel wasn't listening to Christine's last words. She said to herself under her breath: "Of course. The Gulf of Mexico lies due north. Thank goodness for the tutor who urged me study my geography well. Can this be me, Angel Sherwood, beginning to believe all this frightful drivel?"

Suddenly Angel recalled Samuel's growing apprehension just this afternoon. My God, could there be some truth to it? Pierre Le Naisse had mentioned that these pirates sold slaves on the auction blocks somewhere south of New Orleans. The pirate-smugglers could be unpredictable. Pierre said that even Americans were afraid to send their children to France for their schooling as had been the custom for years. Piracy, he added, was again on the increase, being blamed especially on a madman sporting the name Black Falcon.

No longer able to stand the stifling confines of the dining-cabin and the distress in Christine's voice, Angel walked directly to the door, paused, and before entering the dimly lighted passageway, she faced Christine and tried to ease her plight somewhat.

"You needn't worry, Mama, as nothing ill shall fall upon us." I pray, she wanted to add in her new trepidation, but she pleaded, "Now, go get some rest after your tea. I'll join you in our cabin after a time. I'm going to check on Father, to see why he appeared of a pallor this night."

Captain Warfield was just stepping from his cabin when he beheld Angel Sherwood gliding toward him. She appeared like a beautiful apparition out of the night. His mood, sombered even more by drink, lifted as his gaze fastened on the graceful swing of hips and the full, ripe breasts adorned by the lace of her bodice. Her sweet scent wafted to where he stood and hovered in the air about him, heady, making his drunken senses reel.

19

Her attention slid from him to the closed door. Warfield selfishly wondered what it would be like to bed this fair young thing, then dashed the tempting thought madly away, reluctantly. Her father was ill, had taken a fever that had been in the making all day. Warfield was startled to recall that this young minx hadn't taken ill once in all the voyage, so far, and had gotten her sea-legs at the onset.

"Captain?" Angel tried and with a blink of her eyes bludgeoned his evil thoughts. "My father is ill," she stated.

"Aye, he sweats out a fever. Drink made him some worse. George, the cook and doc of sorts, has looked in on him and says it will pass," Warfield said gruffly, but he believed otherwise. The man was bad sick, something to do with his innards. Out loud he said, "Got to go see my mate now. Not to worry, missy."

Warfield took his leave brusquely, loosing his neckerchief as he went up the companionway. Angel made a mental note to demand the captain's secrecy about her father's illness as far as Christine went. At least, not until they were safely back on course could her mother deal with another affliction.

Opening and closing the door softly behind her, Angel tiptoed into the musty cabin that reeked of stale tobacco and cheap liquor. Eau de cologne assailed her sense of smell and she frowned while placing a cool hand to Beldwin's clammy forehead. He was so hot. He was gray and gaunt with dissipation, and he had become a sad old man. Angel felt her tears smart. There had been so little communication between them of late.

"Papa," Angel said in a hushed voice, "it is Angel. Your Angel. Remember?" She gulped hard, almost sobbing.

Eyes closed, Beldwin thrashed about and scowled and muttered incoherent words. He could not acknowledge his daughter's presence for he was insensible in his febrile sleep. He had taken on this illness with frightening speed, Angel thought alarmingly. He shivered and she tucked his blanket closer.

"I shan't bother you, Papa. You sleep now. Later when you awaken I'll have some broth made up for you," she said lovingly, but her words were more mumbled than clearly spoken in her fear of his dying.

On her way out Angel spied the captain's naked cutlass lying atop the wide table among long-nosed pistols that had been disassembled for cleaning and oiling.

So, the captain *did* expect trouble. She moved her gaze about the cabin, her eyes skimming over the bunk crudely squared against the bulkhead where Beldwin was now in blessed slumber. She glanced at a wooden chest, then spun about to exit when suddenly her head jerked askew and her widened eyes riveted to a dueling sword.

A foil! She crossed the narrow space to snatch it from the wooden rack above the chest. She stared down in horrible fascination at the sharp triple points attached to the tip. No button here, and why should there be! This was for protection—not merely sport.

Angel smiled secretively, wryly, while with one well-placed hand to her hip she slashed the air wickedly with the slim and flexible blade. It shivered, blue lights dancing along the naked, threatening silver edge and tip. The pale yellow flame of the candle leaned far. This foil was slightly heavier than a singlestick or a "waste," but with a little practice. . . .

"Step forward, Sir Pirate," she whispered huskily. "I shall now impale your randy carcass onto the bulkhead!" She straightened her sword-arm to make a direct thrust and lunged forward, envisioning red blood trickling down the invisible pirate's chest. A hairy chest at that. *"Touché!"* she hissed.

All she needed now to complete the picture were some breeches, boots, and a blouse. She recalled seeing an old bulging trunk stashed at the end of the corridor, and hurriedly rushed out to search among the old clothes for something to halfway fit her.

"Magnifique!" Angel soon said to herself, using Pierre's French as she discovered the needed items. She was exhilarated, her excitement fanned by discovering not only the foil, but these treasures, too.

Indeed, her exhausting fencing lessons for well over three years with Pierre Le Naisse—related to the fencing master La Boessière—would prove worthy of the pains she had taken to conceal the clandestine meetings in the old churchyard. No

21

more make-believe for her. She was in her own realm, an expert swordsman. Swordswoman! She would, if need be, fight off the whole ship of hairy fools herself!

Above, Warfield growled low to his mate, "It feels as if the ship's bewitched."

"Aye," breathed the mate as he crossed himself.

2

For days unreckoned the *Fidelia* had drifted off course. A diver had finally gone down to fix a damaged rudder that had clung miraculously by a mere sliver of wood. As if on cue, the wind took up and the craft began to slowly crawl southeastward under full sail. The crew and passengers all rejoiced, nerves settling down at the onset of movement in the proper direction. All but for Warfield, who grumbled about missing the slave ship, his harsh face blood-red with choking anger. He floundered about in indecision, finally agreeing with his first mate that he could get a weighty purse at the fair from a bondmaster instead of murdering such a healthy lot by drowning them.

At the crack of dawn, Angel first became aware that the ship had gained a curious new power. She lay in the half-dark of her bunk and smiled happily to herself upon hearing the flapping of sails, the timbers creaking and groaning with output, and the crew moving about after spreading the veritable clouds of extra canvas. Soon the sun would rise directly above them and hasten their voyage with sunbeams guiding the *Fidelia*'s bow.

Angel and Christine partook of breakfast together in golden silence. Beldwin was still abed, faring better, the strange fever having subsided somewhat. He displayed a weakened state and ate little when his daughter visited him. Angel was concerned that Christine didn't appear in such fine fettle herself. She told herself it was only the after effect, the possibility that they could have drifted into the hands of those villainous pirates.

Once back in the confines of the smaller cabin, Angel motioned Christine to the bunk and urged her to nap for a spell. Lady Sherwood gave in after token resistance and soon her soft snores filled the cabin. Angel applied herself to tidying up the place and when that was done she paced back and forth, trying to decide what to do next. She had the strangest feeling that something exciting and unexpected was about to take place, but thought it absurd in this place of reigning boredom.

With a devil-may-care attitude Angel began to dress as if she were going on an outing in the country. What else was there to do? And maybe it would cure some of her homesickness. She unbound the thick plaits of her hair and brushed briskly until the fair ripples shone like cornsilk. A green ribbon was fastened next to draw up the tresses on either side, leaving the heavy bulk of it draping gloriously down her straight back. A fresh frock donned, she went out, closing the door softly behind her.

Angel lingered unwatched on the deck of the time-worn sailing vessel, her long hair blowing softly about her rosy cheeks. She wore a kelly green spencer over a white muslin frock, with green embroidery throughout. The bolero, open in front, had long tight sleeves that hugged her slim arms. Several petticoats edged with frills showed beneath her skirts, and kid sandals with velvet ribbons crisscrossed her insteps and ankles. Her frosty-green eyes twinkled like the evening star, and a strange yearning expression played about her beautiful, fairyland countenance. Her heart hammered in her young breast as she gazed out upon the distant azure horizon. She was feeling invincible in this fresh morning air, and then the second mate's voice rang out loud and strong, shattering her dreamy state.

"Sail ho!" he hollered at length.

At the same stretch, the lookout man in the crow's nest joined in long chorus: "Ship sighted! Off the stern!"

Rooted to the spot, Angel stared around in tingling bemusement as a great commotion ensued. Warfield skipped by with such speed that he failed to notice her gaping about. She was already slipping carefully behind the bulkhead when the captain mounted the quarterdeck. She didn't want to be sent below—not just yet. Too, something held her mesmerized; watching, waiting. It was as if the time awaited had

23

finally arrived.

Peeping up around the obstruction Angel watched round-eyed as the captain snatched the spyglass from his first mate. Her heart fluttered as if it belonged in a bird's breast when the frenzied words drifted down to her.

"She sees us now, I think," Warfield croaked. "Yep, she's sailing into us. I—I can't make out her flag or kind just yet."

Her green eyes strained to follow the path the spyglass traversed, but could not see a thing. Wait! There it was—a black smudge on the northern horizon! The very direction they had been sailing away from since dawn.

"We seen lotsa ships so far, but this here's spooky all right," Warfield said. "She's tall-masted—ummm—and top-heavy, so we can outrun her if it's in her mind to overtake us," he added overconfidently.

"You kin make her out?" the mate asked in bewilderment.

"Aye, like I said—she's big. A real jim-dandy, too, by the looks of 'er."

The mate spat below and Angel ducked swiftly to avoid his spittle. She heard his answer: "Give it more time, cap'n. Sounds like just a merchant ship, and we're safe then. Here, lemme give it a look-see. I've keener eyes than you—" he added respectful address quickly, "sir!"

Warfield handed the glass over reluctantly, prepared to snatch it back at once. Suddenly there was a lump of fear in his throat. He recalled the last time he lost everything to those who called themselves privateers. They stripped him, right down to his black cargo, back then.

Warfield's worst fears were recognized when the mate gulped. "Aye, by golly, what's an Indiaman doing in these waters? She's hoisting another flag, but I can't—" His jaw unhinged, his forehead wrinkled. "Heyyy—what's that! Something's coming out from behind her, and it looks—like—a—a—"

"Here, gimme that glass, idiot!" Warfield snapped, and after taking a look he, too, wondered. "Pirate schooner?" He wasn't certain, and several hours passed as he asked himself this same question over and over, until his tongue felt like sandpaper. Finally Warfield blared, "India's flag—bones on black!"

"All hands on deck!"

"Roll out the powder!"

Then all they could do was wait, prepared. Hours ticked swiftly by and then, racing directly in front of the tall Indiaman that seemed now to loom ominously above the sea's horizon, was the form of a rakish schooner growing steadily larger. Coming fast, she was sleek, with a full brace of menacing guns showing. A weird excitement flooded Angel's strained limbs. She was mesmerized by the sheer size of the oncoming ship. Her legs stiff from standing, she too now caught sight of the great flag sliding up the mast of the smaller, speeding craft. It too was bones on black. She felt a sudden trembling in her cramped limbs as she thought of Christine and her ailing father and—"Oh, my God—Samuel!" she shouted. Where was the lad?

Whirling about, Angel broke into a run, almost tripped over a keg of powder and set it to rolling. Warfield at once noticed the commotion and the flying bit of muslin. He hurried after her, bellowing, "Go below! You! Damnit!"

"Captain, where is Sam? You must get him into the hold with the others—quickly!" she screamed over the din of the mates hollering and bustling about.

Warfield pushed her toward the bulkhead. "Damn your stupid crust, missy. We are in grave danger. If those pirates want—Huh! No hold is gonna stop them, they'll take the lot of them slaves if they get us—even Sam. Now, get your fluffy rump off the deck!"

Speeding below, Angel collided with just the person she sought. He grasped her roughly by the shoulders, black eyes terror-filled, mirroring the green eyes, as he breathed, "Miz Angel. You get with your mama, ain' nothin' we can do now. Me, I gotta get up on deck. I'se scared—hear?"

"Samuel," Angel begged holding him back, "you are talking frightened nonsense. Come into our cabin. We'll hide you in one of the trunks until they take what they want and go." She stopped, breathless.

Samuel pushed her at arm's length, his dark eyes like saucers. "Miz Angel, you'se the one who has to hide." He shook his head sadly, then snapped, "Now you git! Do it for me and your folks."

Feeling defeated after watching Sam go, Angel finally sped to her cabin and hurriedly rummaged through her reticule. Her hands shook violently as she pinned her hair quickly atop her head. She whirled about, but halted suddenly when the sound of soft weeping came from the darkness of the bunk.

"Mama!" Angel cried, going to her mother to shake her out of her dazed state. "Pull yourself together, Mama. Listen, I want you to go stay with Papa, he needs you now. Never mind what I am about. Please hurry. I've a plan that may save us all!" She shoved Christine gently out the door, and dumbly, Christine did as told.

A warning shot ordering the *Fidelia* to halt boomed and sizzled across the water, but it fell short of her side and sank into the sea. Buffeting the waves, the schooner gained rapidly on her prey, drawing closer with a yell of "heave to" sweeping across the *Fidelia*'s deck. Warfield hotly ordered the helmsman to "sail to the wind" and ordered the terrified crew to begin the cannonade.

The schooner was steadily drawing abreast of the vainly fleeing *Fidelia,* and her guns spoke once more and the crash of splintering wood exploded; the *Fidelia*'s side showing a jagged gap to the pirates who were whooping wildly at the damage created. All but one, who bellowed in a deep voice:

"Hold de fire! Capitaine Ty weel flog you for dees!"

Warfield did now concede. He was licked, even before he had a chance to fire back. He had wanted to fight for his ship and not give in this time, but again the odds were against him from the first. Before he had further time to consider his plight, grappling hooks were being attached to the *Fidelia,* and she was quickly being boarded by a disreputable mob of swarthy pirates who swarmed over the rail, carrying cutlasses and long, dangerous-looking pistols.

The diabolical pirates teemed like army ants. Not even pausing to look about, they broke into chests and hoisted heavy boxes over the rail, transferring what they thought of value to the black-hulled schooner. All the while, a burly, scarred, earringed pirate urged the seadogs on. He appeared to be French-Creole, and was for all to see—those who dared

26

glance his way—of ill-temper. He faithfully glanced back over starboard to watch the high-pooped ship approach.

As she came, the Indiaman drew tons of water that boiled about her handsome bow like flowing founts. Her tall, beautiful shrouds billowed like some enormous mountain, dwarfing both the limping tub and the schooner. A tall, rakish prince of a man stood on her highest poop, his hawklike eyes scouring the decks of the *Fidelia*. Captain Ty of the smugglers was thinking of Big Jim's warning—that the cargo aboard this *Fidelia* was precious indeed, and not to be harmed. He never said if it was human or otherwise—just like Big Jim to be mysterious. All he had said was: "You will know."

Across the way, recognition dawned dismally upon Warfield. Ten years back this Indiaman had been refurbished by an English lord, formerly belonging to the British East India Company; now he could see it had become the smuggler-captain's asylum on the sea, this monstrous truck-ship of the pirates'. When the schooner was loaded with as much goods as she could hold, the truck-ship would take the heavier swag and the slaves and the passengers. It was the way of these pirates of Barataria. Especially that one. Warfield smirked at the renowned Captain Ty, who towered above all with his spread-eagled stance.

Captain Ty was a Louisianian. He had inherited the cold calculation of the Yankee from his father, and the snobbish refinement of the South from his mother, whose ancestors boasted old English lineage. But Captain Ty hated this particular heritage. Warfield had learned this from a popular French whore in New Orleans. She had also said that the smuggler-captain was notorious for his savage indifference to women, but had added that he'd never paid her once, and she would have paid *him* if he had asked.

Warfield felt his bitter hatred for Captain Ty boil within his belly as he recalled that the smuggler had snatched black contraband from him before. This time, Warfield thought, he was going to give Ty a return gift for deforming him with this ugly scar. Warfield grinned evilly, feeling the pistols warming beneath his belt. His fingers curled.

The slight movement wasn't missed, however, as the burly

French lieutenant Blade took note of it. His smile was diabolical as his patois rang out with a nasty sound to it, his dark eyes slitting dangerously at Warfield. Blade had called something back over his shoulder, the warning carrying to Captain Ty. Now Blade directed his words to Warfield.

"You bad Engleesh. De capitaine, he should keel you dees time." He spat at Warfield's boots. "We are late," he stated, as if he was tardy to an elegant soiree. "But we catch up. Tsk, tsk, we bet you have de black slave like de last time? An' more? We are right, no?" He chuckled deeply at Warfield's murderous glare.

"You bastards! Not this time!" Warfield drew out the two loaded pistols—but too late.

Blade had stepped back to fire and the report had been like a thunderclap before Warfield could even cock his own pistols. Now Warfield was falling forward after the ball had first driven his torso back, and deflated, he slumped to the deck and sprawled in a pool of blood.

Blade stashed his empty pistol and peered about at Warfield's crew, inviting the next one to step forward and be taken down a whole peg. But they all stepped back cautiously while Blade fingered the second loaded pistol in his red sash lovingly, laughing wide and wicked.

"Ver' good," Blade said like a schoolmaster. "I t'ink I see what we 'ave below."

Making for the hatch, Lieutenant Blade was shoving the terrified men aside when he spied a black boy trying his best to remain inconspicuous. Samuel was crouching behind a coil of rope, his Adam's apple bobbing violently. He was thinking dispiritedly that he would rather go down with the ship when they torched it than let these cutthroats drag him back to the auction block. It had happened to him before; the last time he had been fortunate enough to escape from the *Temple* in Louisiana, but this time he wouldn't be as lucky, for they would remember him as one black who had escaped.

Only minutes had passed since the Frenchman and his band had boarded. Now Blade swaggered over to where Samuel had his dark head cast downward.

"Get up, black bo' or you sleep like a chile? Eyy . . . you

look familiare, bo'." Blade prodded him with the tip of his huge, curving cutlass.

Samuel peered carefully up at the dangerous pirate. He had sick fear in his belly as he recalled this pirate's nature. Samuel then begged for mercy, asking Blade to kill him. Appearing affronted, this pirate-lieutenant of the Black Falcon demanded that Samuel rise to his feet. But the lad crouched even lower as he realized his death-wish would go unheeded.

"Said get up! Moch bettair I t'ink for you," Blade warned. "But, you don' want to die, my fran." He suffered Samuel to rise to his feet, the cutlass nipping the lad under the chin and extracting a droplet of blood.

"Cutthroat pig! Leave him be!"

A youthful but huskily-lined voice shouted above the clamor of the buccaneers, and men's heads came about. Boxes and chests and crates clattered and thudded upon the deck. Contents spilled and spewed out. Chickens squawked as they flew about madly with a flurry of white feathers. Astonished, disbelieving eyes popped out at the furious, green-eyed lad who stood in quiet expectation. Blade turned slowly away from Samuel to encounter the new lad who had issued the daring command. Blade's eyes, red and veiny, roved over the small frame in loose-fitting tunic and cut-off breeches, the frosty eyes staring boldly and wrathfully back at him.

"*Mais oui*, de eyes, such a fire in dem!"

The pirate mob laughed expansively at the mocking quality in Blade's voice, and that one tossed back his huge, kerchiefed head to do the same. Angel lifted her chin defiantly against the mocking peals of laughter, snorts, and guffaws. She was now half-circled by strange, wild-visaged men, who were all curious at the outright display of sheer courage this dainty lad showed the ominous Blade.

Scarred beyond repair, the pirates were armed from their broken teeth down to bright-colored sashes. Their laughter grew until Blade swung a meaty arm to still them. He left Samuel and swaggered the several paces to the English lad. One bovine eye opened wide while the other squinted, and he spoke very gently, as if this lad were a mere babe.

"You are Engleesh, I know. Dat is bad. Capitaine Ty, he hate de Engleesh. De capitaine eats leetle bo's like you for his breakfas','" Blade announced, renewing his toothless grin when the sweet mouth before him opened and closed primly.

Angel lifted her chin proudly. "I *am* English," she snapped, her eyes taking in the congealing mass that was once Warfield, "and you are a ravenous, murdering pirate dog!"

All kinds of "Ohs" and "Ahhs" flitted amongst the crowd of interested buccaneers who were drawing closer yet to get a better look at the sweet-faced lad who stood with one arm crooked behind his back.

Angel's eyes were smoldering green, moistened from the heat of her fury as the laughter took up again. She backed up to keep them in front of her and they froze suddenly upon hearing a voice, their laughter dying down to a few titters. The voice sounded again—a deep growl of command coming across the decks. Angel looked up just in time to see the enormous Indiaman bumping up against the *Fidelia*, the schooner imprisoning the other side.

Angel gaped up over the high poop at the castle of clean, white, billowing shrouds. The *Fidelia* bucked and strained like a wild beast caught; Angel wondered for an instant if they would all drown as the huge grappling hooks crashed onto the deck.

The handsome ship's name caught Angel's regard for some odd reason—*Annette*, it read. Next, a blue flash of movement caught her eye, her gaze riveting to a rugged, lean-hipped but huge man with broad shoulders, just now swinging across on a knotted rope. He came down in the midst of the pirates, dropping easily to his feet like a graceful jaguar. With a commanding air he towered, just like his ship, Angel thought resentfully.

"What goes here?" he questioned brusquely, his glance sliding to the slim youth with the hating, crystalline eyes.

Angel felt more than saw those hazel eyes upon her, seeming to penetrate and burn through her disguise before he formed a light frown, thoughtfully. She noticed with a horrified glance, while he continued to study her, that his fawn-colored breeches were molded blatantly to sinewy thighs and spread-eagled legs. Blushing hot, Angel swiftly lifted her eyes from the

30

prominence there, but she met with a dark brow that quirked amusedly, with question.

All at once Angel experienced a new kind of fear. She had certainly became flustered at one cool look from this man. It wasn't to her liking. This had never happened to her before and she prayed he hadn't noticed her knees shaking. She had always had the upper hand when it came to dealing with men, and she was determined to get the best of this one too, pirate or not. With that thought foremost in her mind, her knees ceased their shaking.

"Ahhh-hh, Capitaine Ty, we 'ave here de leetle bo', angry like de black cat in de swamp," Blade said unnecessarily.

Captain Ty was still several yards from the unruffled lad when, to his surprise a slim and shining sword was drawn forth from behind unshapely breeches. The captain's dark brows arched and his hazel eyes flickered in thorough amusement. All present were stunned with disbelief and held their breaths, their curious eyes shifting between the captain and the daring English lad.

"Draw your wormy sword, captain dog!" Angel warned. "I have been awaiting your coming!"

"And I yours, foolish lad," Ty returned casually, curling his mouth.

"What?" She was thrown off guard again.

He shrugged coolly, rested his lean, brown fingers on the hilt of his sword. He was enjoying himself immensely, awaiting the outcome of this silly charade. Could this lad be the precious cargo Big Jim had warned him about? he wondered.

"Capitaine—" Blade interrupted, "de ship is begin to smoke." He expected no answer but thought it wise to warn the smuggler-captain just the same.

Angel too, ignored the warning. Her eyes snapped into frosty shards. "I see, captain. You would stand there and have me run you clean through, filthy pirate beast that you are!" She spat.

The crews stiffened and shot sidelong glances at Captain Ty. They knew his hot temper and his bitter hatred of the English. Even Blade, with some confusion and surprise, stared at the lad and his pointing sword. He had witnessed Captain Ty's black wrath and he wanted no part in this. He backed up several

31

paces, indicating with a wide sweep of his hand to several of his own crew to keep the fire in check.

Angel continued to glare unshrinkingly at the tall, handsome, and arrogant young man who moved forward with an easy stride throughout the band of pirates as if they didn't exist, so intent was his gaze on the spoon-fed youth who dared defy him. He stepped casually over the body of Warfield as if it was only a heap of filthy rubbish he wished to avoid. He snorted at the carnage that Blade had created out of one man, then measured the unwavering expression of the lad before him.

For the first time Angel noticed that his forehead bore a thin white scar running into his hairline. One ear was pierced with a twinkling gold ring and he sported a black beard. His shoulder-length tan hair was streaked burnished gold and swayed like thick silk. His tunic was open down the front to his leather belt, leaving her to stare at the wide expanse of muscled, furred, and scarred chest. She would glance no further down this time. She looked into his smiling, multiflecked eyes. He likewise studied her, believing he'd never met a more winsome lad.

"Enough of these ogling preliminaries, captain!" Angel snapped, bringing her sword up again. *"En garde!* I shall give you another scar to add to your collection—" she slashed out at his chest while he stepped back casually with arms folded across his chest, "before I kill you!"

Captain Ty's nostrils flared below a long, straight nose. "So, you really want to play—hmm?" He could not believe that this lad was for real. Either he was awfully damn brave, or terribly stupid. He chose the latter—the lad was definitely in for quite a surprise.

Captain Ty paused momentarily to bellow an order over his shoulder. "Get all of those powder kegs off this tub before they blow!"

Suddenly Angel was caught off guard as he came around with lightning speed. His blue-bladed sword was out and slashed through the torrid air with a deafening full roar. Angel gulped, feeling hot sweat trickle down between her well-hidden breasts. She watched, horrified, as he lunged forward, grinning wickedly, slashing to one side of her, then the other, testing,

32

thrusting, while she backed up, beginning to parry. She lunged deftly back at him with one weaponed hand, while the other hugged her hip.

Captain Ty's earlier thoughts of the lad's stupidity diminished, turning instead to amazement as his opponent carried on. The lad was graceful, untiring and fast—for a youth. It gave him cause to ponder the name and reputation of the lad's tutor. Still, Captain Ty played.

Despite the crew's tiring effort to check the fire, the *Fidelia*'s side was leaning fast and black smoke began to roil. But neither the captain nor Angel paid it any mind. For the nonce, Captain Ty was only amusing himself while the others worried the outcome. Ty could see that the lad was tiring from the heavy blows falling upon the lighter weapon; not once did the captain even come close to nicking the lad. He stepped back, winking his eyes aslant at the crews. They relaxed a bit as they recalled that Captain Ty had never slain a youth, nor would he ever.

Ty tossed aside his sword, and with a gesture to one of the men, he was again with sword. But this time he hoisted a lighter sword to match the lad's. In that split second that the thinner sword was clutched into his hand, he received a torn sleeve from his young opponent. He chuckled in his great surprise, and noticed the blood-lust in the green eyes before him.

"Ahhh, so you don't want to play around anymore," Ty remarked. "You are serious now."

Her cool green eyes now ringed with a darker shade of that color, Angel grasped the danger of his words. He had been sporting—thus far.

Ty's keen eyes narrowed, and his straight white teeth gleamed wickedly, clashing with his deep tan. Angel was breathing heavily from the exertion, but still she thrust at him in her determination to scar the arrogant countenance. Tears of frustration welled up over her eyelids and she began to trip in exhaustion, holding onto her seaman's cap with one hand.

Soon she was backed up expertly while he danced before her. She cried out as suddenly her sword went flying into the waiting sea. At the same moment he sniffed the fragrant air around the lad, Ty flayed open his opponent's tunic. The pirates gaped in sound astonishment.

Captain Ty stared hard, in disbelief. A second later his sensuous lips parted in humor as he said, "A perfumed and bosomed lad?" He stretched out a long finger to make certain, unnecessarily; Angel slapped the hand away and laid her hands across her revealed ivory flesh.

His manner changed. "What did you hope to gain, silly *girl?*" he drawled unpleasantly, reaching out to lift the delicate chin that had drooped in hope defunct.

Angel spat into his face. "Your death, bloody swine!" A tear sparkled in her eye and she swiped it madly away.

He softened. "Have you realized what a mistake this has been, as you should have from the beginning?" he questioned.

"I will never own to this—this mistake as you call it!" she said defiantly. "And you cannot make me!"

"Can't I?" He tossed his sword aside and the strident clatter caused Angel to flinch. He moved in on her swiftly then, grasped her shoulders with a biting grip as he pulled her roughly against his granite chest and flanks. "Can't I?" he repeated.

Angel's eyes widened in fear and she never once shut them as his lips came down to sear across her unyielding mouth, hurting, bruising, vested with power. She'd been kissed before, but never like this. He was ruthlessly demanding what she couldn't give. He jerked her even closer. His lips continued their burning and his tongue forced entry between her stiffly clamped mouth.

There was the strangest feeling of her body being consumed, drained of life's blood. She couldn't breathe; she believed he would end her life this way, crushing every bone in her comparatively frail body.

No! No more! She cried inwardly, squirming, and gnashing her sharp little shiv-teeth.

"Ouch!" Ty exclaimed drawing back in surprise, tasting the blood on his lips.

Angel watched him toss back his head, releasing her as he suddenly roared with laughter unbounded. She didn't think it all that hilarious, but then he was a complete idiot where she at least had some brains. Indeed! She must have misplaced them

34

this day to have been so foolish as to think herself a bloody one-man army. But never would she let him know this.

The shockingly shameful encounter was all over in two fleeting minutes after the captain had disarmed her. Infuriated, Angel listened while guffaws renewed as she fought desperately to conceal her bosom with torn shreds of the tunic. She spat venomous words at the captain's back as he swaggered arrogantly away, as if she was a child he'd grown weary of cavorting with.

Angel planted her hands firmly on her hips, and a courage grew with seething stride. "Barbarian!" she shrieked. "How could you dare! I shall see you behind bars for this. . . ." Her voice trailed off as she roughly swiped her mouth with the back of her forearm, sputtering his taste from her bruised lips. She smashed her seaman's cap tighter about her head, fair strands blowing around her scarlet cheeks.

"I'm sure you will," the captain drawled lazily over his shoulder. He fixed his regard as if in interest upon the painted tarts emerging from the bulkhead. "Look alive, lubbers!" he bellowed to the dumbstruck crews still gaping at the onetime lad.

While Angel hastily tucked the recalcitrant bits of the tunic inside, she noticed that she bled from a small wound between her breasts. She lifted her head, thankfully observing that she was forgotten in the commotion that ensued. Or so she thought. Captain Ty watched her every move from beneath hooded lids.

In the next moment Angel's eyes filled with a certain kind of horror. She had finally met him . . . the phantom of her dreams! He was an evil, seeking to possess her, body and soul. Indeed, he had been waiting for her; it burned into her mind with a clear awareness now.

A half-hour gone now since capture, the *Fidelia* was listing to one side fast, and gray-blue water seeped into cabins below. Timbers moaned and creaked like an evil demon, while barrels and scattered paraphernalia began to slide to starboard. The beautiful late afternoon sea glistened as it continued to slosh onto the decks unmercifully.

A crash of wood from somewhere below sounded and Angel

shook herself awake. She began to search about frantically for Samuel, but her most urgent thoughts rested on her parents. Samuel had most likely gone down to be with his kind, she thought as she dashed to find her loved ones, almost crashing into a crate from the sudden tilting of the ship.

The *Fidelia* would soon meet its fate in Davy Jones's locker, Angel thought desperately. Funny she would think that just now. And why did she feel so languid, almost at peace?

Angel's odd peace was short-lived. Her heart gave a sickening lurch when she heard the muted report of a pistol coming from somewhere below decks. Racing down, she almost passed by Christine and a swarthy bulk emerging from the smoke-darkened passageway.

"Papa! Where—" Angel screamed, then coughed as she tried pushing her way past the burly lieutenant.

Blade grasped her arm with gentle force to pull her along with them, all but lifting her off her feet. She kicked out at his shins and he howled when sharp teeth settled into the fleshy part of his arm. He reached out a hairy arm, and caught her easily when she would have flown.

"Ship's sinkin' fast," Blade snarled low. "You come along now, laydee green eyes."

"No! I want Papa. Let me go, you beast! Mama, where is Papa?" she screamed, then mumbled, "Is—he . . . ?" Her voice trailed off when Christine stared past her with a blank expression, then emitted a sorrowful murmur.

Christine shook her head in anguish while Angel resisted Blade's efforts to bring them up into the fresh air. When Angel was about to make a repeat performance of biting Blade, he shook her roughly.

"He's dead, was sufferin' bad from de fallen timber. You come now." Blade caught and picked Angel up to fling her over his back like a sack of lovely potatoes.

"You!" Angel shrieked. "You murdered my father just like you murdered Captain Warfield! You will all pay for this, your heartlessness, every one of you filthy rotten scum! Put me down! I hate you all, and in time I shall kill every blasted one of you bloody swine!"

With fruitless exertion, Angel pummeled the huge back and

36

tried kicking the gargantuan pirate in the groin. She was rewarded for her spent efforts by a hasty and healthy swat on her bouncing behind. She cried out, but more in outrage than in pain. She began next to fear loss of consciousness in the rib- and belly-crushing ride to the deck. Once above, she raised her head to suck in fresh air, sighting at once the young captain herding the wretched blacks out of the hold. Ty grinned widely at her tempting position and she hurled choking oaths in his direction.

Ty bowed mockingly while stepping up to give an order to Blade. "Take the princess—ah—whatever her name is, up the ropes to the deck immediately. We wouldn't want to see such precious cargo damaged."

"My name is—" Angel began hastily, then her eyes narrowed in suspicion and she snapped, "Ohh-ho no! You shall never have my name—never!"

"I shall learn it soon and from your own rosy lips," Ty promised. "You will see—girl." He turned on his boot and walked away with a swagger.

"Devil! Blackguard!" Angel said, shaking a dainty fist at the back of the tawny head. As soon as they were alone, she would beg Christine not to reveal her name to the captain, under any circumstances. He would learn fast that she would oppose him every inch of the way, wherever they were bound, whatever he would do to her.

Without any assistance, Christine carefully preceded Blade and his light burden up the rope ladder and onto the sparkling decks of the *Annette*. Later Angel would think how ironic it was to witness such cleanliness on this infamous ship, but for now, behind them, Angel could see her trunks being transferred and she thought of all the lovely frocks and gowns she would no doubt never wear again. Booty, to be sold like everything else, even Samuel. She prayed that wherever he was, he yet remained unharmed by the bloody beasts. His lot and the slaves' would be the worst of all of those captured this day. Or would it? Angel wondered dismally. And Christine—Mama would never be the same after this. And Papa—oh, Papa!

Shortly Angel was dumped unceremoniously onto the huge deck. Blade took his leave of them promptly to receive the goods being handed up to the *Annette*. Sniffing, Lady Sherwood shuffled up to her daughter, and Angel brushed back the graying hair from out of Christine's woebegone face, hugging her close to her side protectively.

"It is true, daughter," Christine began in a quavery voice. "Beldwin was crushed horribly by a timber—and I was spared. That man may be a thieving pirate, but he only put your dear father out of his misery—" Christine whined loudly, "Just like a horse with a broken leg. Oh, Angel, what are we to do?"

"Mama, there is no such thing as a merciful pirate," Angel admonished. "Were it not for him and his cohorts, father would be alive this very minute and we would be enroute to Puerto Bello. Merciful—Bah! How I would relish being back in England at the Tyburn tree and the head lynchman herding these all to its ropes. But Mama, do not call my given name out loud. Please!" she ended with a rush.

"I understand, love," Christine said. "Ohhh, Beldwin, my Beldwin," she mourned when the *Fidelia* groaned like a dying beast, slipping away fast.

One of the older strumpets sidled up to them, saying, "Aaah, don't be taking it so hard, dearie." She patted Christine consolingly on the back.

The one with the begrimed red locks joined in. "Sure ducks, after all one man's good asa'nother. And these buc'neers ain't so bad once they've had some fun, cocked you once 'r twice. Where we're going I hear it's nothin' but lovin', drinkin', and layin' about in the sun all day. We're goin' to have a corkin' good time!"

The first one, Peggy, turned to a fuming Angel, and gin-faced, grinned toothily. "Seen you tangling with that gorgeous captain when we snuck up. You sure got some guts, pris. Sure would like to be in your place tonight. Thank the Lord, I'd do. That hunk be all man and—what a man! Ain't never seen the likes of him before, no sirree!"

Sickened to the core of her being, Angel slammed her hands over her ears, wishing the threesome would go away, leave them be. She didn't want to listen to any more of their inane chatter and bawdy remarks. Suddenly she was wearier than she'd ever been in her eighteen years, and her right arm ached from the unaccustomed weight of the sword.

The toothsome Ellen remained silent, wearing a look that bespoke confidence in dealing with the opposite sex; each time a member of the crew passed by to wink boldly or pat her generously curving behind, she would very expertly snub him. But her gray eyes held promise of pleasure to come, in spite of her actions. Where the other two of her kind appeared bedraggled and slightly done in, Ellen still appeared fresh as a daisy. She was long of limb, coiffed curiously neatly, painted expertly, and her generous bosom bounced sensuously when she moved even the slightest bit.

Ellen Garth was nearing the age of twenty-five and desired more out of life than her present occupation offered. Even if it meant being the sole mistress of a handsome, generously virile pirate, it would be better than hopping from one bed to another.

When Angel and Christine thoroughly ignored the strumpets, the trio retreated to another spot, where they rummaged in their retained reticules to freshen up a bit. Ellen, though, chose to fix her gray gaze upon the tall, indifferent captain who ordered the torching of the *Fidelia* now. Ellen absorbed his every command, his deep voice resounding across the curiously immaculate deck. His body rhythm made her tingle all over warmly.

Angel, her mouth forming an enraged circle, tore herself from Christine's side and went to stand near the captain. She reached out a hand tentatively, then pulled it back as if he too were afire.

"Did you wish something of me, girl?" he asked, knowing who was close behind by the sweet scent that again assailed his nostrils pleasantly. He did not turn, though.

"Yes. Is that necessary, torching a ship that is already afire?" she questioned huskily with hatred lining her voice.

Still he did not turn but spoke low. "Certainly. Otherwise she will sink half-burned. We never leave a trace of that which we plunder, unless of course the ship is worthy of our needs—policy of the Black Falcon."

"Oh yes, the Black Falcon," Angel retorted. "And are you one of his also wise disciples?"

"Mmm, indirectly so," Ty murmured.

Angel hung her head dejectedly. "Did you know that my father was on that ship? And that one of your filthy swine murdered him?" She didn't know why she posed these questions to him, she guessed it was because he didn't seem entirely without feeling. Or, had she only imagined it when he had held her in that smothering embrace?

Now he turned to glare down at the little smoke-stained face, explaining, "Lieutenant Blade is not of my crew, though he may call me captain. These are my men, here on this ship. We are independent of the Black Falcon. True, Lafitte is the great teacher and leader of countless privateers. I am a smuggler. Let us just say that we work together, girl. It is much too involved for little maidens such as yourself to understand."

Angel swept her gaze from his smothering one and noticed the spot on the *Fidelia* where Warfield's body had been lying when the ship had first tilted. Forgotten in the pirates' haste was Beldwin's purse, just now sliding into the sea to be lost forever. Angel pursed her lips and unblessed Warfield. He had stolen her father's purse when he was sick, and that made Warfield as lowly as the beasts who now held them in captivity.

The Indiaman began to move, heeling to make the wide sweep to head back to the Gulf. Ty looked back to the blazing ship as it shortly became a fiery spot mingling with the deepening purple horizon. He felt the girl still behind him, watching the sea swallow the vessel that had been her home, he knew, for three months. And her father—who would find his watery grave at the bottom of the sea. Ty had made certain she wouldn't see the twisted and bloodied form of her father. When she was being carried aboard the *Annette*, he had aided with the wrapping of the body himself, securely binding it in canvas against the ravages of sea creatures and the constant movement of water.

Angel began to turn slowly to return to Christine when the captain's hand snaked behind him to grasp her wrist. He brought her around to face his brooding countenance.

"This of your father, it was not of my doing. He was put out of his misery—*coup de grace*," Ty said, shrugging leisurely.

Angel's teeth tugged at her lower lip before she spoke

40

venomously. "Stroke of mercy, you say? Hah! My father would be alive now if you had not intercepted the *Fidelia*. Not only are you in league with the Black Falcon, captain, but you are also a disciple of the devil himself. Pirate, smuggler—to my way of thinking, there is not a spit of difference!"

With a mocking bow, Ty released his grip on her, only to draw her back once again. "It might ease your mind to know, girl, that your father did not go down with the burning ship. He was wrapped carefully and my men rowed him a goodly distance away and there dropped him into the sea."

"Oh! How very kind of you!" Angel snapped before whirling away, leaving him standing to stare after her as she joined Christine.

Ty silently watched the graceful motion discernible under the baggy breeches. How could he have ever thought her stupid. Not only was she beautiful, brave, and fiery-tempered, but she was also wise for one so young. How young— seventeen? Eighteen?

Waiting to be ushered to their cabins, the English girl and her mother were last in line, preceded by the three giggling strumpets. Ty looked the women over thoroughly, thinking this younger one not to his usual taste when it came to having his pleasure. Rather, in the past, he had chosen women of more experience and nearer his own age. Someone like that comely tart Ellen.

A second later his eyes widened in pleasant shock, and his blood pulsed wildly throughout his system. Removing the seaman's cap and tossing her head back defiantly, the English girl revealed a superabundance of glorious cornsilk hair that swayed sinfully to her concealed waist.

Lord! A seductively beautiful young woman she is, he thought, pondering what other beauteous attributes lay beneath the loose-fitting attire. What would her name be— Leah? Perhaps Jennifer? Heather? How about Amber or Catherine? Something more like the name of a temptress— Rachel or Rebecca?

There was so much he would know, and he would hear it soon—from her own lovely lips. Not only that, but she would desire him as he wanted her, ever since the moment he had first

41

tasted those pouting lips. Their meeting had affected him poignantly. Swiftly this young vixen had entered his blood as none other had ever done. She would come to him soon, this green-eyed witch, and when he'd had his fill of her he would promptly release her.

A short time later the door to their cabin was opened. As he checked things out the pirate only smiled. His tall, powerful figure in the light of the fluttering candles threw a gigantic shadow on the ceiling.

Angel couldn't help herself, and said in a low, throaty whisper, "You are the devil himself."

"And you—an angel," he taunted.

Angel started, then relaxed somewhat. He hadn't guessed her name—or had he truly?

With that Captain Ty turned and left the cabin.

All's to be fear'd where all is to be lost.
                                        —Byron

Chapter Two

1

The sails turned deep silver as a tilted half-moon made an appearance. The handsome Indiaman slipped over the nocturnal waves as swiftly and gracefully as a bird to her destination. Angel stirred, hearing a strange sound pounding in her head. Floating to wakefulness, for a moment she couldn't get her bearings. She realized she was hearing the creaking of the ropes and the humming of the wind in the canvas, but the headache remained to remind her she hadn't eaten all day. Or had she? It didn't matter now as she remembered where she was and groaned, the hammock swaying beneath her.

The last thing Angel had viewed before being ushered below was the black-hulled schooner speeding on ahead, taking the ominous Blade with it. Much to her relief the captain had ignored her pointedly after their rankling conversation, and continued to stare out to sea, issuing an order now and then over his broad shoulder.

Rolling from the hammock to her feet, Angel felt the painful discomfort of her aching muscles. In the center of the huge cabin a single candle glowed on a roughhewn table, accompanied by a trencher of something still steaming. It appeared palatable enough, curiously smelling of hearty stew. Also, a loaf of crusty bread and a heavy mug of dark ale awaited her. It took her several seconds, still feeling disoriented, before she realized that only one place setting stared back at her.

Christine—where was she? She had been seated at the table, had promised to seek the bunk shortly. That was when Angel had fallen into deep slumber, giving in to the lull that surrounded her, the strange power that moved the macro-ship

43

like a fluffy cloud.

Angel now flew to the oaken door in a wild rage, and on finding it barred, pounded until she thought her fists would surely fracture if she kept it up. When certain that no one had even heeded her batterings, she whirled about to lean back against the door. With an exclamation of wrath she stomped her booted foot.

Did this imply she was to be imprisoned alone until the ravening beasts reached their destination? And, would the captain, who she decided was indeed unfeeling, actually take her to his bunk this night, as the strumpets had suggested?

Angel paced, fuming, as was her usual wont when perplexed. "I shall fight him tooth and nail—" she dictated to the bulkhead and crossbeams. "He cannot take me against my will!"

Skirting the table to go peer out the porthole, Angel knew bloody well the captain could do anything his black heart desired. He was bigger and stronger than she, by far. Already he'd treated her no better than a scullery maid in snatching that stifling kiss.

An abyss of shame engulfed her now when, touching a finger to her bruised lips, she recalled the torment of that long, searching kiss. What could she expect from a randy pirate? She was not in ignorance of the comportment of such knaves. He is worse than a knave! she decided. At any rate, she was now rested up a bit, and he would once again be met with a raging battle if he meant to rob her of her precious virtue. But this time she would not be defeated. There was really nothing to fear, she lied to herself.

Feeling a definite aloneness in this space, Angel stared out at the pendulous moon. She could hear above the captain's deeply masculine voice rapping out an order while urging his sea-dogs to resume their after-chow tasks. The sound mingled with the crackling of the topgallants in the meandering night breezes, and with it now there came approaching footfalls that suddenly halted outside her door. She heard with relief the sliding of a bolt before the oaken door was swept open wide. The sudden, whispering draught snuffed out the candle, and Angel's questing gaze riveted to the large, bedimmed figure

44

positioned just inside the doorway.

In the dim light Angel swallowed a surprised gasp at the sight of a huge, elderly pirate she had not seen before. After entering to relight the candle, he stood there eyeing her with malice, but chuckled low when seeming to recall something, the sound ending in a grunt. He wore a red kerchief bobbed off to one side, and his enormous, sweaty chest was bare down to the bright yellow sash at his thick middle that sported every weapon imaginable.

"Come along with me, lass," he was saying, "the cap'n wants you up on deck—on the double."

Angel relaxed a little upon hearing the deep Irish brogue, but held herself erect. "You inform the captain that I shall not move from this spot until my mother is returned. Also, if you will, inform him that if he wishes to speak with me he can visit my cabin." With that she sat gingerly upon the hammock to await the captain, and hopefully Christine.

"Arrgh," the man growled deep in this throat. Ty wasn't going to like this, not one bit. But rather than carry her up screaming and kicking like he knew this one would, Caspar decided to let Ty contend with this delicate matter.

Caspar shrugged, closing the door behind his huge frame, leaving Angel to wonder if she had put Christine in any danger by avoiding the captain's orders. The door, she knew, had been left unbolted this time, but it would be unwise to go now and search out Christine.

Angel took the time to study the spacious cabin. It differed from the much smaller confines she had become accustomed to on the leaky, musty *Fidelia*. Here, this vessel's wood was fairly new and had a good, clean smell to it, whereas the *Fidelia* had possessed an odor of rotting boards and even carried a stowaway rodent or two. If she didn't know better she would think they had boarded a fine vessel with reputable captain and crew.

There was a stack of neatly piled logs and hard-bound volumes in one corner atop a solid oaken desk; a huge sea-chest occupied the place opposite. There was a man-sized bunk and a sturdily built locker, big enough for a complete wardrobe. A masculine scent lurked all about, making her uneasy.

Angel waited. This one thing was certain: Once they landed she was determined to escape and go find the governor of that territory and turn them in. These pirate-smugglers would pay for their wicked crimes—once and for all.

A muffling of deep male voices and footfalls in the passageway reached her. A few seconds later the door was almost wrenched from its hinges. Behind the captain a lantern was held high, this time by a youthful pirate. The tall captain's shadow fell ominously on the boards and Angel followed it up to his handsome, bearded face. The irritation and rage clearly visible in the dimly lighted compartment shocked her. Gesturing his man back, the captain kicked the door shut with a booted foot, his lean, muscular arms folding across the wide expanse of furred chest peeping out. That mysterious ring-gem twinkled in his ear while his eyes sparkled with menace.

"Girl," he began slowly, "you've just forfeited the opportunity-to identify and secure your trunks. Too bad you didn't heed my command to come immediately, for at this moment all of the plunder is being securely repacked in large bales for convenient transportation and you'll not have another chance in acquiring your belongings. In those, lengths of silks are all that we deem salable. Unless of course some of the island women wish to have the worthless garments to amuse their lovers with, that is permissable."

Angel shot up from the hammock. "Worthless! Amuse their lovers! Ah-hh, no, not with my lovely gowns they shan't, as I haven't another set of clothes here, save what is on my back!"

Angel tried not to panic as he drew nearer. He peered down from his towering height at the tucked and tattered remains of the blouse she wore. Creamy mounds of flesh rose and fell as she tried shielding herself properly with trembling fingers. Long hair glowing fire-white trailed down over the crest of her bosom. The temptation seemed too much for him and Angel watched lean, tanned fingers reach out to fondle the silky texture. The hair curled around his fingers as he felt the girl loose queer shudders that slightly intoxicated his blood. Her scent was fresh, alien to him, unlike other perfumed women he'd known and bedded. Never had he seen such a fair, delicate coloring on a woman. He wondered if she realized just how

46

perfect she was.

"Your age?" he questioned, already sweeping away her despair over her possessions. His gaze of cool admiration lifted from her bosom to meet the ice-cold eyes.

"My age is of no significance at this moment, captain. My need of unspoiled apparel is foremost in my mind. Do you expect me to go about in a torn and filthy rag like a pauper?" she asked, slanting her lashes down at the lingering fingers. "I'm not used to this manner of dress," she added unnecessarily, shivering from his touch that now tingled lightly against her breast. Her heart was beating savagely fast. No man had ever been as bodily familiar nor as bold with speech in her presence.

"Where you are bound you'll need garments of some durability. You'll be given something suitable for the climate and ruggedness of the islands," he said somewhat harshly. "Until then, wear what you have on, or go nude if you wish. But, I must caution you. My men have lusty appetites where bosomed lads are concerned, especially ones with such rare beauty—" he snorted softly, "and—ah—a magnitude of talents such as you seem to possess would stir the blood of any healthy male."

A fresh protest broke from her quivering lips and the pale strand he had been fondling threaded through his unquenched fingers. He rested his hand on the hilt of his cutlass, surveyed the untouched meal that his cousin, Nikki Peroune, had set out earlier, and then his gaze wandered back to her, noticing her shrinking look of barely restrained fear.

"I see. You are not of a mind to release us," she uttered, but before he could answer she bit off, "My mother, where is she?"

Ty restrained a chuckle at her change of mood as he discovered the nature of her innermost fear. She was a virgin. She was his to take. With this revelation in his mind, the cabin was growing suddenly warmer, warmer than he'd ever known it to be.

He stood a moment looking down at her. "Your mother is fine, girl. Installed comfortably, sleeping like a babe. As for your first statement, I'll have to dwell on that one for a time. Then again, I do have need of a servant at my cottage on

47

Grand Isle."

"S—servant?"

"*Oui*. A servant. Healthy, youthful, and full of vigor, to see to my many needs," he answered smoothly, hazel eyes twinkling. Then, "*Ma petite*."

French? Angel frowned, pondering his game. "Captain! My name is—Oh! I am not a servant to any man, nor will I ever be. I was raised amidst a vast circle of the upper class, attended fine finishing schools and—"

"Yes . . . ?" he drawled, incensing her.

"I will be nineteen in two weeks, to ease your overly bold curiosity, and I am not a *girl!*" she rushed on hotly.

"I can see that for myself," he said smilingly, raking her boyish array. He had goaded her into giving her age, but the name he realized would not be extracted as easily. "Ahh-hh, but you are learning fast, *ma petite*. Much faster than I'd expected." Ribald laughter drifted down. "Now," he said briskly, "if you'll excuse me, my men grow restless and need a bit of chastening to keep them in line." He turned at once.

She viewed the broad shoulders and tapering span of back moving away from her. She didn't cherish the thought of being alone just now and muttered softly, pleadingly, "Wait—captain."

He halted, gazing askance over his shoulder. "Did you wish something more?" he wondered.

She affected a timorous plea. "I—I dislike being left alone—I mean especially on a strange ship. When may I have my mother's company?" She didn't relish the idea of pleading with the man, but decided it best not to anger him again. She'd learned quickly his methods of punishment in losing her possessions.

"In the morning," he announced lightly, reaching the door. "Don't torment yourself overly much in your longing for companionship. This is my cabin, sweet, and I'll return before long and tend to the small wound you received while dueling." He chuckled once, deeply. "Then I must seek my rest for a few hours."

Angel saw the door closing. Alone now, an incredible fear wound its way through every inch of her being. His parting words were disquieting. Now she feared the touch of a man, one man, and it was a desperate kind of fear. Certainly men had kissed and caressed her before. But this man here, he left her weak, spineless, at the slightest touch from his long fingers. Yet, at the same time there was within her a strange fire that made her whole being tingle with delicious thrills. He had knowledge of her fear, she thought with a new sense of dread. He would use it to his advantage, get her to heel to his every command. But it was up to her in the future to make certain that he never witnessed it again.

She felt weary, beyond caring, and the storm which had growled inside now settled in her stomach. She was hungry, but turning to the meal that had been lain out long since, she knew without tasting it that it was colder than millstone. Nevertheless, she sank down wearily at the table to pick at the crusty bread and sip the warm ale. As she did this she pondered the captain's manner of speech. It sounded unlike the usual jargon of an uneducated man, more like that of a fine, learned gentleman.

"Hah! Fine gentleman indeed!" She spat, sliding the cold fare aside.

Presently a peculiar languor overtook her and before long her head bobbed though she endeavored to remain alert. Stonewall; Echo. She had never been a rover at heart, for she loved the comforting warmth of the family hearth. This was all she thought of as she was lulled to sleep right there, bowed over her folded arms.

Captain Ty strode across the holystoned deck of the *Annette* and mounted the steps to stand beside the helmsman. His man nodded, indicating that they were directly on course. Aloft, another scanned the moonlit horizon, watching for coming changes in the weather by the look of the sky, the feel of the wind. The captain lighted a long cigano, scrutinizing the crew below, sprawling and slouching about in every direction, now that the booty had been securely lashed together to be loaded into pirogues upon arrival at Barataria.

The crew had partaken of the light meal of terrapin stew with new potatoes and spring carrots grown in the sandy loam of

Lafitte's pirate kingdom. They now shared several mugs of potent ale together as they bawled bawdy ballads of wine, woman, and a song or two of the sea. But mostly they sang of sirens.

Completely alone and ignored, Samuel slouched in one dark space. His ebony eyes reflected volumes of contempt for the crew. The tall captain had spoken to him but once to ask his name and order him to aid the others at their tasks. Finally submitting to his fate, Samuel knew where he was bound, but what would become of the Sherwood women he wasn't sure. He knew of these infamous men, and he prayed that Angeline Sherwood would be spared, and not be raped by each and every one of the men here.

"That cap'n looks like a light-hair Satan hisself," Samuel said under his breath, regarding the man above. He won't be gentle when he drags her to his bunk, if he ain't done so already, he thought. Samuel shuddered, but not so much for himself, anymore.

On the other side of the deck, Nikki Peroune shifted his gaze from his cousin Ty and leaned over to nudge Nash Mallory in the rib cage.

"Eyyy," Nash snorted. "I was dreaming about getting a bit of fluff. What gives—"

"Hold your randy tongue, Mallory. You know you aren't supposed to be snoozing on deck," Nikki muttered sternly.

"Bah! That's a crock of horsefeathers and ya know it, Prunes," young Mallory countered, feeling the precious warmth of his dream on the wane.

Nikki chortled with glee that he had gotten a rise out of Mallory. He slid his lean frame closer to the other young smuggler. "Where do you suppose, Nash, that the stormy English wench learned how to hoist a wicked blade? Certainly no dandy pup tutored her? Aha, what form! Such feline grace!"

"Yeah, what form!" Nash echoed, and saw in his mind's eye the captivating flash of white flesh.

"What do you guess is her age?" Nikki wondered out loud, dreamily.

Warming to the subject, Nash rolled to his elbow. "Eighteen; nineteen; twenty. Hard to tell. Yeah, she's a

50

picture of fresh youth and a dream to behold, even in britches! That hair, like white fire! Do ya think cap'n will keep her? He never before kept an English captive, usually dumps them out on the first bit of land we come across. Too, keeping women on the islands against their will won't be allowed by Lafitte." Nash turned thoughtful. "Don't think Ty meant to give her that nick, though. He was sniffing her out, forgetting how his blade moved."

"Sure, he didn't want to hurt her—him," Nikki said, grinning widely. He ran a hand through his dark hair and decided, "He'll keep her. Who wouldn't? Take me now, I'd be directing her to my pallet this instant if I was lord and master, not standing on deck like Ty sniffing the night air!"

"Never ya mind, lout. If she weren't so young and inexperienced-looking, she'd have more'n she could handle, and ya know it." Nash pondered something, rubbed his red-blond beard and said, "Can't understand him lately, though. He used to keep a woman for a few days, some even a week. But he hasn't even looked at a skirt. Ya know what I mean?"

Nikki considered this for a moment. "Hmm, yes, you sure would think my cousin hated a lay all of a sudden, the way he carries on. Rather, the way he doesn't. The beautiful quadroons can't even hold his interest anymore, it seems."

The conversation ceased as a huge dark shadow fell over the two engrossed. "What's this I hear?" the shadow asked. "Sure now, sounds to me like silly maids exchanging gossip, discussing love. Bah!"

"Caspar!" Nikki slurred, sipping from his sloshing mug as he stared up. "You old sea-dog. How long have you been listening in?"

"Long enough, pup. Sure now, I need enlighten you both of something. I been with Ty for over eight year now, ever since he turned twenty. Learn a lesson if you can, pups. Ty believes as I—that women are good for only one thing and that is this: Find them, if they don't find you first; play with them, bed them, and then forget their face. He has no mind if he breaks their silly hearts. 'Course, there are the exceptions and they know well what to expect, just a tumble and nothing more. The ones with running tears turn me stomach. All wenches are the same in bed, no difference. Turn them upside down and they all look the same. Ty loves them and leaves them, and that's enough for any man. Young pups or old sea-dogs like meself."

"Come now, Caspar," Nash chuckled leisurely. "Have you never been in love with at least one of your light 'o loves?"

"Tah!" Caspar spit bitterly. "They are all bitches and sluts, every one whorish and there for the taking. The devil take me if I ever tarry in that ungainly predicament—love! Bah!"

After his bitter tirade, Caspar picked his way through the lounging crew while Nash and Nikki tittered softly behind his back. Caspar was all pirate-smuggler, everyone knew, and his wenching days were long gone. He dedicated himself completely to his young captain now.

The captain, after speaking with Caspar and the men to stand watch, made his way to his cabin. He paused in the passageway to peer in on Lady Sherwood who still slept soundly from the sleeping powder he'd slipped into her cup of ale. The woman had been half-dazed with sorrow, and so needed something to help her sleep for a good many hours.

After closing his own door, Ty saw his cabin was dim. Dark shadows danced with his every movement, for the low stub of candle sputtered there on the table where the girl slept. His six-three frame moved carefully so as not to awaken her just yet. He took from a shelf a fresh candle to replace the one dying. When that was done Ty studied her at his leisure.

He saw silken hair whose long veils trailed over slim arms and blouse that rose and softly fell with each reposed breath. Lashes curiously like spun gold rested on flawless pink cheeks, reminding him of a healthy babe. She appeared vulnerable in her slumber and much like an angel, he thought. He wanted to laugh aloud. More like a little she-devil!

Even dressed as indelicately as she was, she had appeared more sensuously beautiful when awake and moving about than any woman he'd ever seen. And he had seen and been with the most beautiful women in the world—the creamy-tan quadroons of New Orleans.

It was not a customary action with him or Lafitte to hold English captives, nor to mistreat them or hinder them from fleeing if they wished. In fact, Ty demanded it, even handed them off where they could safely secure passage to their destination and with sufficient coin in pocket. But now that she was here. . . .

The flame on the candle leaned fast, threatening to snuff out from his sudden impelling movement to rudely lift the girl from her deep sleep. He shook her roughly when she would lean sleepily against his chest.

"Mmmm. Wha—?" she mumbled, blinked, shook her head to clear it.

Ty guided the drowsy figure to a shelf which contained ointments and sundries. She brushed unconsciously against his thigh and nodded her head on his chest.

"Come alive, wench, and see to the wound yourself. I've enough problems without that festering," he said icily, his eyes dipping to her bodice.

Slowly her languorous eyes took in every detail, wandering with curiosity as she wondered why he sounded so angry all of a sudden. He left her there hazily bemused, shaking sleep from her brain. She watched him obliquely, could see him removing his leather belt and weapons of infamous trade. His blousey tunic came off, ruffling his tan hair. He paused when fingering the fasteners of his tight, buckskin breeches, shot his scrutiny her way.

"Well?" he grated irascibly, "why don't you just turn about to fully survey me while I complete my disrobing?" He waited, but nothing happened. "Then, perhaps you need my assistance in applying the salve?"

Energized now, her head shook quickly, and she tossed her hair back from her hot face. She trembled as she held her back to him apprehensively. Then she halted her hands and stared straight ahead.

"Captain. Would it be asking too much for some fresh water?" Her words came out in a foolish rush.

"Fresh water?" he repeated, as if such a thing was nonexistent. Then harshly, "There is some, over there."

"Where—captain?" she stuttered, feeling a chill go through her. Would he come near her now? She prayed not.

"For God's sake, girl. The washstand. Where else!" he bellowed, his irritation increasing.

53

When the low creak of him climbing into his bunk reached her, she risked a swift scour about the room. There it was, with a full pitcher of water atop a porcelain bowl. She had missed the shadowy washstand in her earlier surveillance. Keeping her eyes averted from the bunk she went to the corner to bathe. She was thankful he'd not offered or demanded to minister to the scratch himself.

Not disrobing, she ripped part of the hem off the overlarge blouse to bathe the crevice between her breasts, then applied the slimy salve. The odorous stuff stung horribly, but she remained silent. She jumped suddenly when his deep voice filled the cabin.

"There are linens beneath the stand, if you would have bothered to look instead of further ravishing your only garments," he said gruffly.

"Thank you, kind sir," she mocked and bent to snatch a towel from the lower shelf.

With hooded lids, Ty watched the slim white arms move, knowing where the tapered fingers went, delighting in the way her hair rippled sinuously to her concealed waist which he knew a man's hands could completely encompass. Especially his own. He grinned at the tempting thought, but rolled to his back erasing the beauteous sight and stilled his irregular breathing. He'd been too long without a woman, he thought now, aroused.

It wasn't long before Ty was interrupted by the sound of the pitcher banging down with an angry thud. He muttered a low curse as he rolled onto his side, propping himself up on one elbow.

"What is it now, wench, an insect wiggling in your breeches, perhaps?" He scowled across to her blackly.

Angel whirled about, at once casting her eyes downward. She clutched the torn blouse to her. "I want to see Christine— my mother!" she demanded, her voice sounding strange to her own ears.

"Christine . . . hmmm? You forget easily, child. I said, if you recall—in the morning and not a second sooner," he growled with finality as he rolled to his back once again.

"No! Now! I do not wish to share a room with a strange man! Besides, what will the others think?" she added carelessly.

With a deep growl and a leap he left the bunk. He shrugged fast into his breeches, and in one swift movement crossed over to where she stood cowering at his coming. He swooped her up against his hard chest, bore her to his bunk while she squirmed and strained against him, squealing like a frightened piglet. He dumped her unceremoniously in the middle of the warmed bunk, then followed her down, bent on one knee as he caught her flailing arms and pinned them high over her head.

She tried not to see him looming above her, instead fixed her eyes on his wide chest, but then groaned upon seeing the thick mat of crisp, curling hair so close to her face. He filled the boundaries of her vision, nothing else could she see. He was like a tan-eyed lion, savage and foreboding, with muscles slowly flexing with every slight body rhythm—and he emitted a strange animal heat. His beautiful eyes sparkled as he lowered his head.

Now he would rape her, she thought frantically, searching for means of escape, but she saw none beneath his greater strength. Her heart thumped crazily as she rocked from cheek to cheek to escape being attacked by those warm lips. She whimpered as he caught both her wrists in one hand while the other captured her chin, squeezing gently. He gazed deeply into her terrified eyes, now vacant of the frosty glare.

"Do you think my men care if I lay you here and now?" he snarled, feeling her whole body stiffen beneath his. "And—why should you worry what they think? This is my cabin and what I do here is my business. We've had sufficient time to engage in several acts of mating—by mutual agreement or otherwise."

"Ohhh!" she gasped in shock over his crudely spoken words.

Arching her neck Angel tried shoving him from her as she brought her knee up dangerously close, unwittingly, to his groin. Bending a leg up swiftly to ward off the attack to his manhood, he murmured, "Ahhh, no, girl, you can geld a man like that, and especially at a time like this."

"Wh—what do you mean?" she asked, staring up at him innocently. "You are not a horse and—and—" The meaning of his statement hit her full force and she blushed profusely. "I—I didn't mean to—" she bit off her words and thankfully felt him release her.

Ty peered down at her after standing reluctantly, his eyes dark and unreadable. "You are a strange one, girl. I've not met up with your kind before and I am beginning to wonder if you don't belong in a sheltered cloister somewhere in the woods. A little nun in black habit with a wicked blade riding upon her hip, ha-ha. You would even tempt the devil if you chose to wear a long dark shroud, you know that?" He chuckled to himself at that, moving abruptly away from the bunk.

Crimson-cheeked, she shuddered at the thought of such a lonely life. Straightening her blouse and feeling a great relief after the terror greater than any she'd ever experienced before, she flung her legs over the edge of the bunk, bare feet cold on the boards. When had her boots come off, she wondered, then shrugged.

Ty began to peel off his breeches again while Angel clamped a hand over her eyes. She would rather not see what could happen to a man at a time like this. Isn't that what he'd said? She knew that men expanded when aroused, but had she truly felt it, or only imagined it?

"What are you doing?" she wondered out loud when he climbed into the hammock and yawned widely.

"What does it look like?" he asked, then changed his mind. "Never mind. Stay where you are. I will take the hammock tonight. Now, go to sleep or I'll have to teach you a lesson in obedience again."

Obedience indeed! she thought as she folded her legs beneath the rough blanket and snuggled down. So, he had been frightening her into silence and only because she desired her mother's company, and not his. How mean he was, and how stupid of her to have dropped her defenses so completely again. She increased her vulnerability twofold by stuttering and whimpering and struggling like a frightened child. But what else could she do in her position?

56

A convent—Me? She had to giggle softly undercover now at his outrageous statement. And tempt the devil? That shouldn't be too hard to accomplish if she wanted to. He was right here with her.

The lulling motion of the vessel riding the moonlit waves outside soon made Angel drowsy once more. Choosing to sleep fully clothed, she felt herself falling into that inevitable cocoon of repose. Her last thoughts were of the future, what it held in store for her under the ruthless hands of this captain. Whatever it would be, starting tomorrow she was going to show this beast she was a woman fully grown. She would activate her womanly cunning and make him think her his slave—up to a point. Then, she yawned widely, one day while his back was turned she would flee with Samuel and Christine. Island or not!

When Angel saw the flames she sat bolt upright, choking back a scream as she felt the wetness of her glistening skin bathed in sweat. It was morning, for the palest signs of dawn were at the porthole. She had been dreaming again, of the fire that had been a reality in that September of 1809. She had been strolling again through Covent Gardens near the theater; the blaze that broke out was so sudden and fierce that she'd been trapped on Drury Lane. She had felt the flames licking at her skirts as she ran blindly, heard the terrified people screaming. When she tripped and fell her pelvis had struck a loose cobblestone and she had bled.

A fireman had saved her from burning alive and just in the nick of time, but not before the backs of her thighs had been scorched. At first the superficial burns on her thighs had been scarlet; later, as they healed, they had turned pink. Now they were not so bad. However, they were still there to remind her, as were the nightmares, of the horrible scene of people on fire running from the buildings as she lay helpless.

A solid knock sounded at the portal and Angel's gaze flew to the hammock. He was gone. She bounded from the bunk in her wrinkled and soiled garments, but decided to disregard her manner of dress in the presence of such uncultivated, barbarous company. The knocking became insistent and she bade entry, poised demurely in the center of the room.

"Good morning to you, miss—umm—my name is Nikki, Nikki Peroune. The captain asked me to fetch you," this young man said, shuffling his boots and blushing from ear to ear.

"To my mother?" she tried hopefully.

"Certainly," Nikki returned, with a boyishly handsome grin.

Not giving her name, Angel sweetly returned the warmth with a captivating smile. She had seen this lad before, liking his looks at once. She thought him not much older than twenty. He had conversed on deck with the captain in a strange patois that seemed to mock French. Ruggedly lean, he was almost as tall as his captain. But this lad was friendly, aboveboard, and seemed to be one she could trust. She read it now in his amicable face that she had found a friend among these devils. Still, her name must remain secret, even to him.

A humble breakfast of crusty bread, oatmeal, breadfruit, and fresh water awaited her in Christine's cabin. The pabulum had been laid out neatly atop the table where Christine sat idly, nibbling a section of bread. She looked up with careworn eyes when Angel was ushered in by the gangly lad who had brought the meal beforehand. Christine at once held out her arms for her daughter to come into them. Angel cradled Christine close, pushing back loose strands of graying-gold hair. Christine searched Angel for signs of ravishment, noting the flushed cheeks.

"My Angel, are you—have you . . ." her voice trailed when for the first time she took in the tattered blouse. "Ohhh, no!" she gasped upon seeing the tiny healing wound.

Angel placed a hand over Christine's lips to still her, shook her own head to cancel out the older woman's worst fear. Angel twisted around to the young man still standing there shyly. Had he caught her name? There probably wasn't a thing to worry about. Angel could be taken as an endearment.

Nikki cleared his throat in embarrassment under the girl's searching gaze. "If there's anything you need just holler," he said. "If we got it on board, I'll return immediately with

58

it, miss."

"Yes, umm—" she was going to say Nikki, but that wouldn't be fair, "sir, I would like needle and thread, if it wouldn't be asking too much."

Nikki blushed profusely at the respectful term. "Certainly, and right away, miss," he said.

Angel thanked him, offering her most engaging smile as she displayed small white teeth. He blushed again and was gone.

Preoccupied, Christine too reflected back to that fire of 1809. She had fretted over her daughter's loss of blood, and perhaps something else. But she had remained silent, wondering all the time after the fire, and trying not to think what would happen should their daughter wed a man wanting a wife with her maidenhood intact. Perhaps this was the reason why she hadn't rushed in seeing Angel married off as other mothers did their daughters.

Christine sniffed the oatmeal then pushed the stuff aside. She wasn't feeling at all well and the congealing lump in the tin plate made her stomach heave. Her thoughts were jumbled. What a joke on the pirate had he taken Angel to his bed, thinking he was getting an undisturbed maid.

"Mama, you must eat something to keep up your strength," Angel said, trying to be as cheerful as possible. She was doing justice to her own modest fare when she noticed Christine hadn't budged. Angel sighed. "If we are to escape once on land, we must store now all the strength we can. So, eat everything given you, even if it's not to your liking. Please?"

"Not now, love," Christine began, staring at the door. "Perhaps when Beldwin comes I shall eat something. You know how I dislike dining without him. Do not cock your head at me, love, I've had a crust of bread and besides, I don't feel so well. Would you mind terribly if I rested for a time? You are certain they haven't touched you? You appear so dishevelled."

Angel shook her head firmly, and tried swallowing a hunk of bread that stuck in her throat. Washing it down quickly with water, she continued to stare at Christine, who had already stretched out full length on the bunk with eyes shut.

Christine, Beldwin is dead! Angel wanted to scream but held

59

it back. She listened wide-eyed as Christine rambled on.

"Don't you believe what those pirates tell you . . . Angeline . . . Beldwin will come . . . soon we will reach Puerto Bello . . . Louisiana . . . Beldwin, we have to tell . . . Stonewall . . ." Christine's voice drifted off, she slept. Angel feared her mother hovered on the brink of nervous breakdown. She had seen it happen to Uncle Winnie, as they carried him away while he mumbled inanities like a frightened child.

Rising on shaking limbs, Angel began to pace back and forth, everything around her taking on a dreamlike quality. This must be what it would be like to be committed to a dark cell, agonizing over the time when the gaoler would come to lead the death march. Or, as in her case and much much worse, total ravishment at the hands of that arrogant, unfeeling captain. That would be a fate worse than death, to have her flesh violated by him. They had to make plans, she and Samuel.

There was the sound of a knock before Angel could think further on where to search out Samuel. Nikki stood on the threshold, with one hand holding the needed items plus a piece of forest-green cloth.

"Mademoiselle Sherwood, I have brought you needle and thread, and filched a bit of material you can maybe use for something?"

Angel's laugh tinkled. "Indeed I can. It is just what I need to bind up my hair so that it's out of my face. Perhaps you could lend me your blade there so that I could cut it into strips?"

"Ah, I'm sorry but I can't do that, mademoiselle," Nikki said regretfully. His eyes lit up then. "But maybe you could show me what you want and I'll cut it here and now."

"Yes, yes of course," Angel said, hiding her disappointment at not being able to secure a weapon. "Come over here to the table, sir, and cut me some ribbons."

Later, after Angel had stitched up her blouse and bound up her hair, she went to make sure Nikki had left the door unlatched. He had! It hadn't been a very nice thing to do, but she had beguiled the poor lad out of his wits with her charm and he'd floated out the door with his head in the clouds, as many men, young and old, had done before him. She knew, however, that the captain couldn't be fooled as easily by her chicanery. She had not met up with his kind before either, and it ruffled her feathers maddeningly.

Coming up from the space below, Angel had to blink back the sudden brightness of hot tropical sunlight. Peering around, she could see the captain at the helm. His back was displayed to her. Good. Observing further, she noticed that part of the crew examined a sheet of canvas that had been spread out on the deck, while some worked with coils of rope. The ship heeled, taking a new tack, and the captain shouted an order which a young man with a thatch of red hair obeyed instantly, climbing up into a web of rigging. The tall shrouds flapped instantaneously, sounding like a clap of thunder, and the water astern foamed.

Before she began her search for Samuel, Angel viewed several of the crew dangling up above in the complicated tangle of webby ropes; all were sufficiently busy. Good. Moving cautiously, Angel espied Samuel near the stern of the ship, where he was washing down the decks. Goodness gracious, Angel thought, that lad sure spends a lot of time swabbing decks!

Angel crept stealthily to the rear, oblivious to the long strides being taken by the captain, who was coming catlike across the deck.

Almost to the rear now, Angel squeaked when a pair of hard hands grabbed her from behind, digging up into the soft flesh beneath the arms of her blouse. She knew without looking who held her in a viselike grip. She was yanked around to meet the full impact of those hazel eyes, noticing for the first time the green and gray swimming in the light golden brown. He was so near that she could feel his warm breath upon her face when he ground out his anger through straight white teeth.

"What in hell do you think you're doing up here without my permission!" He shook her once thoroughly and a pale strand of hair sprung askew from the forest-green ribbon. He regarded the strand as if it was an evil snake coiling toward him.

Angel slowly tilted her fine chin up. All of her resolutions of the evening past were rapidly fleeing. How could she act the

61

mature woman when she couldn't even stop trembling when he came near her? Suddenly she had discovered a new side of his rage and she felt her chin beginning to drop. But inside her mouth she gritted her teeth firmly. Be his slave? Never!

Angel could feel the stares of the crew and there were murmurs amongst them. Nikki detached himself from a group of men and she saw him sauntering up behind the captain. His look was surprised, then thoughtfully worried.

"It is hotter than blazes below, captain," Angel began. "And I needed a breath of air. Besides—" Angel stopped, noticing Nikki giving her a look that spelled "take care."

"Yes?" Ty drawled.

"Am I also forbidden to speak with my friend?" she asked, disregarding Nikki's warning to be silent.

"Friend?" Ty scoured the faces of his crew, each and every one of them. Then he regarded Samuel, who peeked up sheepishly. "Ahhh, of course, the black boy," he said, coming back to the girl, his one earring flashing, catching the sunlight to blind her as if summoned to do just that. "Perhaps it is, was, in your mind, girl, to escape once we are situated on land?" He blinked finally. "Hmmm?"

How could he have known! Angel stamped her bare foot. "Indeed, that is the first thing I intend doing. Then I shall pay a visit to the authorities of that territory and—"she quit. Oh drat, why couldn't she have kept her mouth shut! He made her so exasperated she couldn't think straight.

Ty had released her with such suddenness that it now left her stunned. He tossed back his tawny head to roar and the crew joined him in equal humor. She failed to see what all the hilarity was about and glared at them as if they had gone daft. Suddenly the chuckles died down and the captain gave her a mocking grin, his dark brows shrugging then falling into dark furrows.

"You face a gigantic task, girl. Governor Claiborne is by no means a popular figure, either in New Orleans or at the Baratarian settlement. There is no way to escape off that island, unless of course you take to the swamps. Ignorant of its twisting dangers, many have perished in the awesome jaws of a crocodile, or have gone insane hearing the hoarse croaking of alligators and the screams of the water fowl, have been known to wander—" he twiddled his fingers villainously near her nose, "and more horrors!"

"Oh!" Angel exploded, jumping back when he spooked her with a loud scary voice.

"Also," he went on, less sinister, "the authorities have little time for smugglers and privateers, much less a damsel in distress." His eyes laughed at her sudden helpless look. "Now! Go below and stay there until I give you permission to come up for air." He turned brusquely and went to ask Nikki why the door had been left unlatched.

Sniffing haughtily, Angel had whirled to enter the bulkhead when her breeches snagged a loose nail. She bent over to tug furiously, but bit a trembling lip when they stubbornly held fast. Glancing over her shoulder she saw the crew pointing her way, and, when the captain began striding again toward her, she worked swiftly, too swiftly, for a rending tear left the entire lower section of her breeches clinging to the nail. The men ogled a slim leg and part of a thigh that was displayed whitely to them.

Angel looked squarely at the captain and snarled, "Damn you!" and then to the crew, "And damn you bloody others!" and snatched up the ravished leg section of her breeches.

Now even Samuel could not help loosing a small giggle. Ty shook his head, clucking his tongue, encouraging the crew to guffaw loudly at the nonplussed female. Facing them directly, she appeared as if she had been in a battle with a score of mountain lions, so tattered were her garments.

She disappeared below while male laughter rang out aboard the *Annette*. Angel plied needle and thread once more, hopefully for the last time.

2

Snuggled on an arched chest, Angel drew a lugubrious sigh. It was stiflingly hot in the cabin that she and Christine had been largely confined to during the week that followed their capture. But stifling though the incarceration was to Angel, she did not venture above for air. She had been asked by Nikki to come up for a stroll around the deck; he would escort her personally, but she declined. The last thing she would be, she thought, was the object of the crew's diversion. It couldn't last though, for sooner or later they would need fresh air. Christine was already complaining about the lack of it, even though she too preferred to stay put.

Christine repeatedly napped, as if she had been given a sleeping powder to keep her in a torpid state. Angel noticed Christine hardly ever looked at food anymore, and no wonder. With provisions low, now it was the usual meal of sea rations— beans and hardtack. There was plenty to drink though, and Angel now lingered over a pitcher of cool tea that Nikki had brought to her earlier. She reflected back on their conversation of a week ago.

"I hope you didn't get into too much trouble, leaving the door unlocked. I'm sorry, truly I am," Angel had said to Nikki.

"Think nothing of it, mademoiselle. In fact, I kind of enjoyed it. We'll have to do it again sometime," he said jokingly.

Angel had been laughing at his humor, then she grew sober, thoughtful. He was so nice and she felt badly having to be secretive with him. But she couldn't allow her name to leak out, not as long as she'd made a vow and the captain held the upper hand.

"I thought you might like to know," Nikki had gone on, "that in a few short weeks we will be nearing the island stations of Lafitte."

"These islands, they are also home to you?" she asked, thinking of the captain as well.

"Yes, home," Nikki answered politely, not offering any more information.

He had gone out after that and Angel had the strangest feeling that he wanted to linger longer, tell her everything she needed to know to escape. But, she sensed there was a bond between the lad and the captain, and she didn't know just yet what it was.

It was on a sparkling morning almost two weeks later when Angel sat with a teacup balanced on her lap. The amber liquid sloshed onto her piebald breeches and she stood with a start as the *Annette* listed to one side. Male voices drifted down shouting "Ship sighted off the bow. Dead ahead!" and footsteps pattered repeatedly above.

She stood listening for a time, breathless, praying that a rescue would ensue. But peering out the porthole she could see nothing, and she only heard raucous shouts. That in itself was disheartening.

After what seemed an eternity—there it was! A flagship that at first appeared as a dark shadow on the edge of the world, now steadily grew larger as it advanced toward the *Annette*. Angel's heart sank when she saw the Bolivian flag fluttering in the breeze, a colorful banner bathed in sunlight. She strained her eyes further and saw that a black schooner, sitting low in the water, trim and rakish, followed the larger bulk. Both clipped smartly through the turquoise waves.

Her heart sank even further when she sighted a pack of grinning pirate rats beyond a squat man with broad shoulders. Standing behind the rail of the flagship, the predominant figure suggested power, his hair light and his tanned face like dark parchment. He was greeted by a welcoming committee above her, with Captain Ty's deep voice sounding loudly.

"Dominique!" Angel heard someone shout jovially.

"My frans!" the man called Dominique yelled, spreading his meaty arms to include one and all. Then, "Capitaine Tyro', eyy, I have a cargo of slave an' silk, Indigo, spices, an' all from India. But hey, de *joli* ladies. Ahh-hh, wait till you see dem, *sombre* and ooh—laah!" He made a curvy outline with stubby hands Angel could see from where she peeped out trying to see more.

"Dominique, *magnifique!*" Angel could hear Captain Ty shout as if he'd made this greeting a hundred times before, especially as concerned pretty women.

"Ladies—from India?" Angel thought, feeling funny little

65

butterflies start in her belly. They must be very beautiful, she decided, letting her gaze slip down over her clean but ravaged garments.

Straining her neck, Angel could see the exotic women now as they left the schooner to climb the rope ladder that had been rolled out as if to welcome royalty. She could see the amber-skinned women and girls as they latched dainty hands and bare, pretty feet into the rope squares, giggling, flirting from under silky black lashes.

Squashing her nose against the porthole, Angel saw the long, familiar arm reaching down to pull up a willowy girl with slanted eyes. Dark eyes, full of promise, and Angel could see in her mind's eye the captain's lust-filled countenance above her.

Angel flushed hotly when a pirate, hoisting a crate of foodstuffs, saw her and squinted an eye evilly. She whirled her back to the porthole and shuddered. He reminded her of something she'd read of once—an emaciated monster with a deadly glance—a legend.

Tinkling giggles reached her again. Ladies, pooh! Dressed in colorful and slinky silk, flirting outrageously. Indeed, exotic tarts was more like it. These so-called ladies were not boarding merely to take tea, but to spend the night merrymaking!

So true, Angel thought as a short time later she curled on her bunk, listening to the wild revelry and drunken laughter of both male and female above and in the passageway. No dinner was brought to them, but it was just as well, for she'd had her fill of beans and hardtack. Yet, had she seen them bringing various delicacies aboard the *Annette?*

Poor mama, Angel thought looking over to where Christine sat, idly humming to herself. What would become of her? First Beldwin, now this. Christine was growing apathetic and Angel had to make plans, had to get to Samuel somehow. Perhaps later when the ship slept in drunken stupor she would slip out and search him out. If only Nikki would come, maybe she could persuade him to leave the door unlatched, tell him she would take that stroll now.

Now more than ever, Angel was wishing she could bathe, not merely sponging off with a basin of brackish water, but in a full, luxurious tub-bath. This being her sole longing for now, she went back to gaze out the porthole, feeling somewhat unclean, soiled. Between the ships she could see a tan spot on the horizon dotted with waving branches of emerald. They had come to a standstill, must have anchored out, and that should be their destination up ahead, she determined.

Angel returned to her bunk and hours passed, then sundown, and a dark, starless night followed. She awoke to see ghostlike clouds flitting by the porthole, alight and eerie from the lanterns that were situated about the decks. She turned to see that Christine slept soundly again.

As she was lighting a candle, a knock rattled across to her. She called out and the door swung wide to reveal Nikki leaning against the jamb grinning happily, his lean face a ruddy flush.

"Princess Sherwood," he said bowing gallantly. "Mon capitaine waits your pleasure in the dining chamber. We have many guests, some exotic, a few disreputable—ah—let me rephrase that one, many disreputable smugglers and priva- teers. Among them you will meet the infamous Dominique You. But, don't let the man frighten you, he is actually very kindhearted, a Frenchman throughout."

Just like Blade, Angel thought. "I am not available," she said out loud. With that she began to push against the door but was met with a booted foot barring closure.

"Ah-ha, but you must, the captain demands it," Nikki warned. "And if you don't he will come and drag you there. It could prove to be very embarrassing for you, petite princess. So . . . you will come?" His warm eyes beseeched.

"No. I've only this outrageous rag to wear. I need a bath and besides, I am not a bit hungry," she lied.

Nikki was thoughtful a moment, his regard sweeping the tattered garments. "Ummm, yes," he murmured, tapping his chin. "Ah! I'll be back shortly after I speak to the captain on a certain matter. I'm sorry, princess, but I'll have to keep this door latched, what with the partying crew and visitors all roaming about."

Less than half an hour later there came a timid rapping, followed by a feminine giggle. Pushing herself up from the bunk and frowning in puzzlement, Angel went to the door. Nikki bowed then took his leave as Angel was staring into beautiful dark eyes. It was the young girl who the captain had helped up the rope ladder. Flung across her arm was a slinky dress much like the one she wore herself. Of watered silk, its color was a soft petal pink with embroidered apple blossoms shining throughout.

"You like?" asked the exotic, willowy girl as she held the thing up for Angel's inspection. "Tall man make me give it to you. I have more, no care. You keep. It is Chinee, like me. Other girl are India. We go to house in Calif-or-nia—" she giggled behind her free hand, "but no more."

Angel was about to mention that she, this Chinese girl, was fortunate to retain her belongings, but she bit off the retort. "Thank you," she said, not knowing what to call her. "But I don't think I can accept it. Besides, I am staying right here."

"Stay here?" the Chinese girl frowned lightly, then exclaimed, "Oh, so sorry. My name Kuai Hua. Mean blossom in Chinee," she announced, smiling cheerfully when Christine sat up rubbing bleary eyes, looking the slanty-eyed girl over.

"Very lovely, ah, Kuai Hua," Angel said perfectly. She couldn't fathom the insouciance of this girl, who had been set upon by a mob of randy pirates. "The woman over there is my mother—Christine," Angel informed Kuai Hua, who had been studying the older woman with interest.

"I like Chris-tine," Kuai Hua said and slid her regard back to the younger woman. "Your name please," she said.

"I—it is . . ." Angel paused, thinking this one over. "My name is Sherwood," she said quickly, but speaking the truth nevertheless.

"Is nice. Sher-wood," Kuai Hua tried, and with embarrassment shrugged sympathetically, then thrust the tunic at Angel. "You take. Come to party please?" she pleaded in a tiny voice.

Angel accepted the dress, more to delight in the slippery texture for a time than anything else though, realizing that only skilled fingers could have cut and sewn this delicate fabric to its sensual shape.

Kuai Hua was still regarding Angel expectantly when, much

68

to Angel's surprise, a huge hip-bath was carried in by a grinning Nikki and the huge man who had come to fetch her to the captain that first night aboard. She now heard his name and thought Caspar a fitting title for him.

Wooden buckets of warmed water from the galley followed, borne by strapping lads whose eyes roamed over Angel and Kuai Hua. The Chinese girl returned the stares, but Angel could only gaze in joyous expectation at the filling tub, the clean linens, and a bar of olive-green soap. Shortly the men filed out the door with Kuai Hua following. She had promised to return after Angel's bath and arrange her hair into a sleek chignon.

In no time at all Angel, excited now, rose like some splendid sea-nymph glistening in soft sunlight, while Christine handed her a coarse linen to dry herself. They were fortunate to have one brush between them that Christine had concealed in the folds of her skirts during the raid upon the *Fidelia*. Angel used it now after the streaming tresses had been towel dried. With another linen wrapped around her and tucked in at her breasts, she brushed briskly until her glorious hair shone with its own sunlit glossiness and was almost completely dried for Kuai Hua to arrange.

Christine hummed an old French melody while holding up the fitted silk tunic; it was a song she'd often hummed while Angel was a wee babe snuggled in her bright pink crib. Angel listened to it now and recalled that Christine had often mentioned that her maternal great-great grandmother had been a Frenchwoman.

When Kuai Hua returned she was full of flushing smiles. Angel decided that the girl must have been pinched somewhere and soon thought she knew exactly who had accomplished the deed by the ecstatic look that lingered on Kuai Hua's little face.

"Oh well," Angel sighed. "I guess if we have to join them we have to—or it's walk the plank!" she said gruffly, pretending to balance herself while crossing one foot in front of the other.

"Sher-wood funny," Kuai Hua said giggling at the English girl's antics.

Angel no longer thought of Kuai Hua as merely an exotic

tart, but she was actually having fun, enjoying herself for the first time in a long while in the presence of this delightful, unselfish girl.

Twisting this way and that, Kuai Hua soon created a sleek chignon that made Angel appear strangely exotic herself, with her slightly tilting eyes made even more so by the hair sweeping up from her face. The fitted tunic went on next over her head, buttoned up from the midriff by a mere three tiny buttons, widely spaced and pearly. Angel blushed at the unusual tight fit that hugged her youthfully curving hips, her slim waist, and made her nicely round breasts shapelier than ever.

Angel was wishing she could see herself in a full-length mirror, but as there was not even a tiny looking glass aboard she had to rely on the approving look that Kuai Hua was giving her. By the second-skin feel of the thing, Angel had the feeling that Kuai Hua's unvoiced compliment didn't measure up to what she herself regarded as decent.

Christine's eyes, usually dull of late, were now alight with something close to shocking disapproval mixed with a new awareness of her daughter's growth. She remained silent.

"Look beau-ti-ful, Sher-wood," Kuai Hua announced, secretly wishing her own dimensions came as close to the luscious form she saw before her. "Sher-wood look like girl now, not boy. Like *Mu Lan*, white flower of spring."

While Christine was taking her bath, Kuai Hua slipped out and returned a short time later when Christine was sitting with a towel draped around her and looking forlornly at her only faded dress that had been washed countless times in brackish water. Angel tapped her chin in indecision as she too, regarded the soiled garment.

"I shan't go if you stay here, Christine," Angel sighed.

"Why look so sad," Kuai Hua said, then proceeded to roll out a long piece of silk that the East Indian women wore. As Christine looked doubtfully at the length of silk, Kuai Hua took from beneath her arm a waist-length bodice of purplish-black silk. "All for Chris-tine!" she exclaimed and was rewarded when Christine finally smiled.

"That settles that. Ah, Kuai Hua, you are wonderful," Angel said as she went to hug the Chinese girl.

Fifteen minutes passed, and then, as if on cue, Nikki arrived to usher the Sherwood women to the dining-cabin. As she walked, Angel was feeling suddenly older, more mature, and she wondered why. Perhaps it was only the silky thing she wore.

Kuai Hua had already pressed into a small group of exotic young females at the far end of the oblong room when Angel entered. The women were laughing in their rambling, shrill voices, muttering a foreign language with snatches of English floating up now and then. Serving the hale and hearty group of variously garbed men around the table were the three overly painted tarts. They sashayed about as if they knew their business well here. Like alehouse women, flashed into Angel's mind.

Suddenly Angel found herself the recipient of many bold and some lewd stares as heads came about at the table. It was the privateer named Dominique You who stood up bowing lavishly while his tarnished eyes measured the English beauty from head to foot. His visual search ended where the long slits displayed a slice of long and shapely limb and he licked his thick lips before he spoke.

"Tyro', he tells me you are Engleesh," Dominique said, preferring to call the captain by just his name; the Black Falcon was his only captain, and he, in turn, was Lafitte's favorite lieutenant.

"Yes, yes I am," Angel answered, while her heart's pounding sounded like thunder in her ears. What else was she supposed to say? And where *was* the captain?

Then she felt it—the power of that smothering gaze riveting her to the spot. His awesome presence seemed to fill the chamber even as he stood in the shadows, titanlike, and in the smoke-filled crowd of faces he came to stand beside her.

"Ahh," Captain Ty said, "our tardy guests have finally arrived, last but not least. Right, *cherie?*" He guided them around the table. "Sit down, here. We have this night a delicious gumbo soup, thick and savory. Plantains, and a rare vintage of wine," he said thickly, and as if he'd drunk his share of the latter.

Feeling trembly while she tried to breathe normally, Angel found herself imprisoned next to Ty as he scraped up his chair to the table and sat down. The roughness of his trousers rubbed against the bare flesh of her left leg. He smelled not of wine but of potent brandy. He was dressed entirely in somber black, even the silk shirt with its blousey sleeves was a shiny black, showing off the burnished glints in his thick, leonine hair. His entire aspect bespoke cleanliness, the soap smell mingling with the brandy and that undefinable odor of masculinity. Her senses began to swim from his suffocating nearness and the continuous sidelong search of his lazy eyes.

"You grace dees banquet by your mere presence, cherie," Dominique said across to her, and her smile was slightly forced as she acknowledged his compliment.

Dominique reminded Angel unpleasantly of Blade, and she was thinking this just as the thick gumbo and plantains were being served by a black man named Rolfe. The one-sided conversation came to a halt. After tasting the gumbo, Christine proceeded to attack the meal with relish, while Angel only picked at it absentmindedly, even though it was thoroughly delicious. She was aware of the many lusty and sly pairs of eyes sliding her way, and especially of the hazel ones of the man beside her. Those particular eyes were upon her much too often.

"Don't you like it?" Ty asked his dinner companion just as Rolfe was about to pour wine for her.

"No," Angel said, holding up her hand. Meeting his frown, she amended, "I mean—yes. It is quite delicious." Then to the servant, "I'm sorry, could I bother you for some tea with lemon?"

Rolfe paused in mid-air with the wine decanter. Ty choked then spewed out his brandy while Nikki and the others chimed in unison "Lemons?" and peered at one another. Angel blushed crimson, not daring to glance around the table.

"Limey!" a man seated next to Dominique guffawed and earned a poke in the ribs from the lieutenant.

Rolfe straightened, saving the day. "Sorry mum. We's fresh outa lemons right now, used the last of dem up just yesserday. I sure get you some tea though, soon's as I can." He turned to face Ty's amused grin, the lifting brow.

Angel heard smothered giggles behind her chair, knowing full well that the three tarts were laughing at her unusual request. Ellen, gowned in a gaudy, taupe creation, lingered close behind the captain's chair. She had arrived on the spot shortly after Angel had been seated, and now Angel could detect the cheap eau de cologne that Ellen had liberally doused herself with; that and something else emanated from the woman, one scent unfamiliar and acutely disturbing to Angel's senses.

Ty glanced at Angel, seeming to know what bothered her. His teeth played with his lower lip thoughtfully as his lids fell, giving quick scrutiny to the bit of taupe just passing by in back of his chair. Angel's heart fluttered crazily when he stretched out long fingers and brushed them against her arm as if examining the texture of her skin, then gave his full attention back to the meal, letting his hand fall back to his thigh.

Dominique You leaned forward to speak directly to the English girl. "You seem ver' young to be fightin' pirates. You fight with de sword, I have hear. How do you come by dees?" he asked between bites of his plantains.

Angel was listening to the crew above, bawling a salty song of the sea, ribald laughter breaking out now and then, shrill feminine voices—and something else. Had there been a scream, or was she just imagining it?

"Mademoiselle Sherwood," Ty began. "Dominique has put a question to you." He almost laughed aloud when she started, eyes leaping from her plate. "He asked—how is it that you have knowledge of the sword?" He had often wondered the same but had never thought to ask her.

Angel swallowed the sip of tea she'd just taken hastily and glimpsed Christine on the other side of the captain, seeing that she was preoccupied with her wine glass and its contents. She began to speak low, chose her words carefully so she wouldn't be ridiculed again.

"A man . . . a Frenchman by the name of Pierre Le Naisse tutored me for three years," she began, hearing exclamations of surprise and admiration all around her. She went on, "I learned of this famous fencing master through an acquaintance in London, and when I met Pierre we automatically became fast friends—" She was suddenly interrupted when she felt the stiffening beside her.

In a surly mood, Ty tossed off his remaining brandy and swept an arm about the room. "And why not! I believe Monsieur Le Naisse is known·as the finest swordsman in all of France, and now England. Might I add—rogue? Rapacious womanizer?" His eyes raked over the fair-haired girl beside him, as if to include her in Pierre's library of conquests.

"Tsk, tsk, Tyro'," Dominique said, smiling playfully at his long-time friend. "Do you not have dees qualities, too? Why of course, all of us finer men, we do. And de leetle lady, you know what we mean? *Non*, surely you do not," he said decidedly.

"Oh, indeed I do," Angel quickly returned and then faced Ty squarely. "You are mistaken, captain, about my friend Pierre. He may be as you say a rogue, a mischievous flirt at times, but not this other, captain. Why, in my presence his conduct befitted that of my own dear father. . . ." Her voice trailed off as a look of sadness crept into her face.

Not believing her in the slightest, You said, "Loyalty is a good quality in a woman. Eef one could gain your trust dees man could 'ave himself a fine mistress." He peered directly at Ty, chuckling.

Captain Ty swiped the brandy bottle up from the table and brusquely poured a generous dollop into his glass, then settled back to nurse it as he studied the posturing females around him for the first time that evening.

"No, not my Angel," Christine piped up belatedly. "She does not fight with a sword, and not with such men." At once she fell silent as the entire table gave her queer peeks, some gawking over shoulders. She fell to studying the tattoos on Dominique's swarthy arms, tilting her head. Then she riveted her gaze to the portal, thoughtfully, as if waiting for someone.

Angel had checked her start upon hearing Christine mention

74

her name. But again, as before with Nikki, she decided that her name had been taken as an endearment, nothing more.

For the remainder of the evening, now pressing close to midnight, Angel was immersed in conversation with Dominique and Nikki. She found she liked Dominique. He was a satisfying conversationalist, curiously enough, as was Nikki. She had missed talking with people of late about interesting subjects; but she was not panicky about solitude and had in the past liked privacy at times, often walking, riding, and thinking, alone. She was snubbing Captain Ty now, having pushed his wandering knee aside with her own more than twice so far.

And Ty lounged back in his chair, voicing a comment every so often. He was surprised that Dominique, an avowed hater of the English like himself, was so wrapped up in what the girl was saying about the Duke of Normandy.

The topics ranged from Napoleon to His Majesty's navy, to the Louisiana Purchase, to the New England Federalists. Nikki fancied history, especially that of the wicked city of New Orleans where he had grown up.

"I do have some knowledge of New Orleans' past history," Angel said, catching Nikki's attention. "I have read the three volumes by Wilkinson entitled *Memoirs of My Own Times*. But just how much of it is truth, I'm not certain."

Ty leaned over to whisper in her ear. "You wasted your time, mademoiselle, poring over those bulky volumes. To get a better picture you should have had available for your reading *Connexion with Aaron Burr* by Daniel Clark, and *The Corruption of General James Wilkinson*."

"You—you read?" she asked incredulously.

"When I find the time," he shot back, looking down at her with a humorless smile.

How very strange, she thought, that a man of basest reputation should also be learned. It came to her now in the twinkling of an eye: There was much about this man beside her she didn't know. Did she really want to know more?

Ty too, was regarding the English girl with new interest, leaning far back one side of his chair and smoking a cigano, when suddenly the door burst open. Dominique had been telling the young woman something about the islands they were sailing to in the morning, when he halted in mid-sentence to greet a man of medium height with dark-brown hair. This new arrival had an arrogant air all about him, Angel noticed immediately, and the smile he gave was more a sneer.

"Pearce Duschesne," Dominique all but hollered. "Meet Lady Sherwood and her lovlee daughter—ah—why, of course! Mademoiselle Sherwood. They are Engleesh." With his hand waving circles in the air, he added, "But in dees case it does not matter, see, they are guests for the time being."

Angel caught the last words of the introduction. Indeed, tomorrow once more they would be prisoners. But now the Frenchman's impertinent eyes, dark like his hair, were boring a hole to the core of her being. She shifted in her seat, placing a hand to her bosom to ward off the rape in his eyes. He nodded politely to her, ignoring Christine thoroughly.

Half-intoxicated, Ty greeted the man coldly, and the other was equally cold to him. It was as if the two had a score to settle with each other and hostility crackled in the air all around.

Breaking the pressure, Dominique gestured Duschesne to a seat beside him. Dominique chuckled, thoroughly enjoying the hostile exchange as Pearce settled back his rangy frame into the unoccupied chair, reaching at the same time for a heavy mug that Ellen swooped down in front of him. His interest was more in the English girl than on matters at hand—like the men who had been caught thieving, tried to sneak off in a rowboat, and were to be keel-hauled come dawn. Never before had Pearce so openly displayed his lusting after a woman as he did now, his face a mask of desire. Then the chill, as of death itself, struck him, as he felt Ty's hazel eyes piercing into him.

"Daughter," Christine blurted suddenly, "I think I'll retire now. Are you coming?" She rose, and Ty immediately went to help her when she weaved unsteadily.

When Angel was about to do the same, Ty pushed her gently back down. "I'll see your mother to her cabin and then return shortly myself." As he was leaving he shot Caspar a meaningful look.

This time when Rolfe was replenishing wine glasses, Angel

held hers up to be filled. Soon the fiery liquid burned all the way down and she felt a warmth growing in her belly. She tried smothering a cough, but Rolfe smiled knowingly, shaking his dark head. The Madeira was too strong for her gentlewoman's taste. He would bring her a lighter wine after this, he decided.

As most of the pirates and smugglers and Dominique were situated at the far end of the table, now mingling with the exotic women and the strumpets, Angel found herself alone with Caspar and Pearce. The younger of the two men rose and moved around the table to seat himself next to her. They were well out of earshot of Caspar, and the clamor in the room made it impossible for anyone to hear what Pearce was saying, anyway.

"Well now, we seem to be almost alone, Mademoiselle Sherwood. That is, no one is paying us any mind." Pearce's arm swept casually around the room. "Except for that lout, Caspar. He does not matter though, does he. So, *ma petite*, are you Tyrone's new mistress?"

"Tyrone?" she said curiously.

"Mmm, certainly. Tyrone. Didn't you know?" he questioned with a wolfish grin.

She sent him her frostiest regard, making her eyes snap like winter pine needles. He was slightly taken aback by her repulsion of him, but pressed on nevertheless.

"I do not believe he has gotten to you yet, *petite*. Has anyone, for that matter?"

"*That* is none of your business," she snapped, and hoping he would go away after he'd heard her out, she added, "You know yourself that I am held captive, as is my mother, to these foul and bloody pirates. I am not mistress to anyone nor shall I ever be . . . *Mister Duschesne,* and I shan't be with your friends much longer. You see, I plan and I shall escape. There!" She made to rise but was met by Caspar's nod from across the table that ordered her to sit back down. She did so, not wanting to anger the huge man.

"Mmm," Pearce murmured. "You *are* what the men have been saying about you since I boarded the *Annette*—A little spitfire and a beauty to boot." He lowered his voice, causing

Caspar to bend an ear. "How would you like me to help you escape, my pet, hmm? Why is your first name such a mystery, also?" he fired at her confusingly.

"Never mind that!" Angel snapped. Then her head whirled to face him, caution creeping into her face. "You—you would do that? Hah! I do not believe you, and why should you, Mister Duschesne?" There was something infinitely dangerous about this smuggler under Dominique, yet he didn't frighten her half as much as the captain did.

Pearce was recalling the long ago night of a quadroon ball, given by the queen of that society, Jacinta Villerne, handsome, golden-skinned Jacinta, very talented in the bed. He had almost enticed her into that situation when Tyrone swaggered onto the scene. Tyrone had swept her out from under Pearce's nose, left him standing like a schoolboy panting after that nonpareil bit of fluff. Pearce had reason to snicker afterwards, though, for he did get to her and the Creole lady lived up to her reputation. She had been wild and completely insatiable, had left him dead tired by morning but not unhappy. Now, this English girl he had plans for. . . .

Pearce was about to answer her in the affirmative when he noticed that her attention was elsewhere. She was watching the buxom blonde, Ellen. That one. She had said snubbingly to Pearce that she was saving herself for the captain. No one else was to touch her.

Pffah! Tart Ellen couldn't hold a candle to this green-eyed vixen. But he might have something here in the way of jealousy, he thought with a wicked gleam in his eye, taking in both fair-haired women.

Ellen, her regard passing over them with a smirk, picked up her skirts, her face registering concern over the disappearance of someone, and hastened out into the passageway.

Angel was smothering a yawn and toying with the wine glass when Pearce again leaned toward her. Her head whirled from the wine she'd finished, now replenished by a lighter wine she should have rejected, and she had already forgotten that Duschesne had mentioned helping her escape. Had the captain forgotten about her, was he meeting Ellen now in the passageway? She wished he would come, not for his company but so that she could request leave and go seek her bunk.

"It is settled—" Pearce suavely broke into her thoughts, "then?"

Angel sighed, was just about to ask again why he should want to do this when Ty entered, looking provoked about something as he rested his gaze on the two. He moved into the cabin with Ellen following close behind, her frown matching his. Ty took his former seat and Ellen hung about nearby, glaring down at the nameless girl like a hissing cat.

"Well, so here is Captain Ty," Pearce made emphasis on the name mockingly, like a challenge. "Are you going to keep this fine bit of merchandise or are you thinking to release her upon reaching the islands?"

Ty brushed the silken arm with his fingertips, causing little shivers to run along Angel's spine. A possessive look stole into his eyes as she looked up into them, then at the lips curling into a boyishly crooked smile that lifted one corner of his sensuously carved mouth.

"I have never seen greater loveliness, and I think I'll keep her around for awhile, Duschesne. Why . . . did you have something in mind?" Not waiting for an answer, he added icily, "You may as well forget it. This molly-coddled suckling and her mama will be guarded well on Grande Isle and not one moment will pass that they'll be left unattended."

"I am not a pampered child!" Angel fumed out loud. "That you both could haggle over us as if we were just that—bits of merchandise! Oh!"

"Stay!" the captain ordered when she suddenly shifted uncomfortably and made to rise. He turned back on Pearce to continue. "You know my men well, Duschesne," he said simply, inclining his head toward Caspar, who bulged with drink, making his size now more appreciable.

"Umm, yes," Pearce muttered, rapping his fingers once upon the table and then scraping up to his feet.

With that Duschesne took himself to a thinning group situated at the far end of the table. There, Dominique had latched onto a little moon-faced woman and was leading her to the door. Dominique tossed a sidelong grin toward Ty and the younger man leaned back to chuckle warmly. He shifted back to Angel with a new light burning like a golden candle in his gaze.

Angel crumpled, knowing what request she must make now—or else!

"Captain," said Angel, ripe red, "could I—I mean—could I go—" She peered down at her sweating palms and blurted softly, "You know."

"Why didn't you say so sooner? My mistake, sweet," he confessed. "I should have acknowledged your discomfort a few minutes ago. Over there near the bar, and be quick about it before someone else has the same need."

On returning from the convenience, Angel was pulled up short by what she saw. Ellen had her arms wrapped around the captain's neck, and either he was trying to buss her while she was too excited to stay still, or Ellen was trying vainly to get him to do so. Whatever the case, it appeared very intimately playful as Ellen's legs were caught between his thighs, her head tossed back and her face flushed. Those long, tan fingers were caught in yellow-gold waves that cascaded down Ellen's back, giving her the look of a light-skinned gypsy. All of a sudden Ellen reached down between them and licking her lips wet she. . . .

Angel, whirling from the lewd scene, found that she was facing Pearce. He smiled knowingly while she couldn't bring her limbs to move away from him. She was wooden, horrified by something she couldn't name. Pearce reached out to touch her arm lightly and she recoiled, the contact making her skin crawl. She had to get away from these filthy vermin!

Shoving Pearce aside Angel fled headlong, but soon noticed she was going right back to the convenience. Confused she made an about-face, was fleeing toward the exit when a voice halted her slippered feet. It curdled her blood.

"Miss Sherwood!" Ty had barked, swiftly dumping his baggage.

In a few unbroken strides he was behind her and she quaked at what was to come. With brutal sureness he seized both her arms and spun her about to face his stormy countenance. She dared to tilt up her perfect oval face and defy him with chin jutting out. Her beauty stunned him, while a warm current of desire passed through his body.

"Now, for your next lesson in obedience, my sweet."

Those who remained in the cabin began to observe the couple with rapt attention; Ellen especially was taken aback by the scene, pursing her lips together firmly. She saw the wolfish look on Ty's handsome face as he very expertly bent the frightened girl into his arms like a willow twig and kissed her hungrily, then greedily, before Ellen left the room in a huff.

Angel tried wiggling out of this vise, but was met with hard thighs molding her ever closer as his hand at the small of her back splayed and pinched her waist. While he continued to kiss her probingly, her head spun round and round like fall leaves whirling, curling in the wind. She felt their hearts beating as one while she could hear wild whoops of revelry brushing her befogged mind as she tried surfacing. But the equatorial heat pierced her halfway between her waist and thighs, rising to the crest of her bosoms when this new, delicious pleasure washed over her and she was lost, drowning.

He lifted his lips and released her so suddenly, bursting forth with deep laughter as he tossed back his tawny head, that she was left on a merry-go-round of confusion. She felt as if over her face and neck she broke out in a scarlet rash, her lips felt sore, swollen, and her breasts felt oddly the same way. Next, she was galvanized into recognition of his seemingly cruel act.

"How mean and evil you are!" she spat at him and released a quivering breath of revulsion.

"Oho! Pardon me, but were you enjoying yourself, my sweet?" he asked, his gaze unchanging in its lusty warmth as it raked indolently over her soft curves.

Angel vibrated with fury, drew back her hand to deliver a stinging slap to inflict pain somehow on that beastly handsome smirk. But her effort was thwarted by a powerful buttress that at once folded her arms behind her back. A broken sound escaped from her throat and her fear grew that now he would carry on what he'd begun.

81

"Please," she whimpered, cramped up to him again.

"Please what?" Ty breathed into her ear hotly, his hand moving on her throat in a hypnotic fashion.

"Can I go now . . . please," she pleaded, near to tears of exhaustion.

Seeing this, he took her by the hand and brusquely led her out into the dimly lighted passageway where he brought her to stand before her cabin. He glanced toward his own cabin door, staying with his hand in hers as he fought with an inner conflict, the fierce, searing desire to take her there. Instead, he leaned indolently against the wall and smiled, the delicate crinkles at the corners of his eyes confirming his love of the outdoors and the sea.

She wheeled about. "I have no desire to linger here in this darkened hall with you any longer, captain, as one of your mistresses no doubt would eagerly do, namely Ellen, for one." Her hand was checked smartly at the knob. "Why don't you go back to her, she is certainly willing to ease your lust!" she tossed back to him.

"And you are not?" he asked, planting a kiss at the tempting curve of her neck.

"Why should I be!" she answered frostily, facing him to break free of the searing lips. "I find you not only ungentlemanly but an extremely vile person, Smuggler Tyrone. Even if you forced me I would not yield between your thighs. You could never make me perform like one of those . . . those tarts!"

"At least you have an idea of where I would like to put you," he said, chuckling. Then, almost angrily, "So, Pearce has been exchanging gossip with you, hmmm? And what did you offer in return for my name, my first, that is? Yours, perhaps?"

"Never, not even he shall have it," she declared, "and neither does your name interest me, he only told me, that is all."

"I'll have it soon, and not only that. I promise you, girl, it will prove to be a delightful pleasure for both of us when I break you in, show you that love has many joys."

"Love?" she said disparagingly as she wrinkled her nose. "You sir, distort the meaning and fail to arrive at the true

82

understanding of what should be a fond and tender feeling. Animal lust is not what a man and woman experience who are in love with each other." Angel suddenly couldn't believe she herself had said this, she who never gave love much thought.

He shrugged. "Lust is an overpowering desire and lovers feel this need to indulge with the opposite sex. What is 'being in love' and how do you know so much, have you experienced love, Miss Sherwood?"

"I—I just know there has to be something more than just animalism involved. Any living thing can want—want to—"

"Want to make love?" he asked gently, reaching out to lift her chin. "Is that what you were about to say, sweet?"

"Yes, yes, bloody damn. Is that all you can talk about, think about?" she all but screamed at him.

He was tempted to show her, very nearly did as he fondled her shoulder, itching to slip lower. "Tsk, tsk, such language," he murmured. Then, "Ah but what then would you like to discuss, sweet?" he laughed low.

"Going to bed!" she blurted unthinkingly.

"Meaning?" he asked maddeningly.

"Ohhh! I'm tired and I find this inane conversation doubly wearisome, that is all, nothing else."

He leaned back, chuckling, playfully thrusting his hips forward and causing little thrills to rush down her lower limbs. He felt her tremble against him and he cruelly continued to move sensuously. All at once tears glistened in her eyes.

"*Merde,*" he swore softly in French, reluctant to tear his hands from her shoulders that shook. "Go then, or I'll do you a naughty mischief and shame your mama's name for you," he ended cryptically.

She froze, expressionless, merely staring up into that cocksure countenance. Did he know or didn't he?

"Good night—girl," he finally murmured, giving her her answer.

He waited for the door to peep open and close as she quickly slid inside. He secured the wood and waited, listened for signs inside assuring him that she readied for bed. Voices stole under the door, mingled with the creaking of bunks.

"I forgot to tell you, love. Happy birthday, daughter,"

Christine sniffed sleepily.

The captain nodded, reassured that what Nikki had earlier informed him of was true. Today had been her birthday—actually yesterday—for it was well past midnight. Her eighteenth year was over, but the future lay waiting. He swaggered away from the door, smoothing the front of his breeches with his palm.

The rare and radiant maiden, whom the angels name
Lenore—
Nameless here for evermore.
—Poe

Chapter Three

1

After relieving his man, the captain took a spread-eagled stance at the helm, finding himself alone with his thoughts, save for a few bearable snores here and there below. His gaze lifted to ghostlike clouds flitting just above the tall masts. It was a beautiful night and the heavenly body made illustrious the smooth and glistening surface of his thoughtful face. He set it against going back down to awaken the young Sherwood woman, but his jaw twitched unwittingly.

To the contrary, Tyrone found himself forming an image of her—that fair maid—in his mind, and the immediate result was swelling desire. In his mind's eye he envisioned her lying naked, entwined in his arms, a blond cloud of hair spread around them both, fragrant, rousing his senses to madness. A painful longing began in his breast and spread to his groin, building with intensity. His wanting would find no surcease in these wee hours.

At last he asked the image of the moon on the inky sea: What am I waiting for? He already knew the answer to that. Oftentimes he yielded himself surreptitiously to the notion that she would soon beg for his pleasure, and then, just as often quickly cast the foolish thought away. Yet, he plumed himself on his skill as an unrivaled lover, shocking his women to the core with his expert performance. He chuckled low. In fact, they would seek him out time and again. But never before a youthful maid untouched. But was she really undisturbed? Sometimes he had pause to wonder. The fair one seemed worldly-wise enough.

How long *had* it been now since he eased the ache in his loins? Too long. In frustration he ran his fingers through his hair, raking it off his forehead. Since he had met this winsome maid he'd not desired another. His appetite hungered for but that one morsel—that so-called angel. Lord, but he was acting like a lovesick lubber.

Ellen. He could seek her out now and put an end to this sweeping fever. Ellen and *her*. It was like comparing a pebble to a scintillating diamond, the latter precious and rare. Still— Ellen was here and game, the release he needed. . . .

Angel woke at the peep of dawn, hearing shouts of heartiness from the crew above. She felt the bow turning and knew enough of ships by now to realize they were luffing the helm. She heard the thunderous flapping of sails as the ship heeled while catching the wind. The tilting cabin soon arighted itself when she came steady on course. The captain's voice came down stirringly deep, making her conscious of the evening before and her brand-new feelings. As a result, she flung away the suffocating blanket, and with a double-kick to the thing, leapt to her feet.

"Angel, come quickly!" Christine's voice piped from her position at the porthole. She indicated something directly off the bow.

Angel hurried to stand beside Christine. They viewed two long, slim, low-lying islands running parallel to the mainland, separated by a passage wide enough for deep-sea vessels. The longest island bent northward and sprouted long green peninsulas into another body of water in the background that looked to be a huge bay. They were still too far out to see what else lay beyond, but Angel thought it appeared to be a huge body of verdant land.

America! It had to be. Angel's heart fluttered with her first obscure sight of this alien earth. In the next instant she felt numbed, fraught with sadness that this occasion should have been joyous instead of what it was. Then a sixth sense nudged her. Perhaps, just perhaps, here happiness could be found somehow or another, and in time to come. After all, the future was only as bleak as a person made it. And Christine—

she had to think of her, as well.

Suddenly there crashed all around them an ear-splitting explosion, causing Christine to rush into her daughter's arms. They relaxed a bit when laughter abounded free and easy above them. They were not, Angel thought ludicrously, under attack after all. No, and why should they be in their own waters, she reasoned at last, feeling the vibration ebb away.

Just last night Angel had listened while Captain Ty casually mentioned that even reputable citizens of New Orleans and surrounding parishes carried on thinly veiled transactions with the smugglers at the Baratarian settlement which they called home. What was even worse, there were leading businessmen who were openly in league with him and this other—the Black Falcon, Lafitte. All the while the captain had slyly watched for her reaction, making sure she absorbed every word he spoke, but she had remained impassive.

Angel stretched in exercise—forgetting for now the explosion—bending from the waist to touch the floor with the palms of her hands, while Christine began her daily ablutions at the washstand. Angel straightened her spine. If this were the case, she continued to ponder, who did that leave for her to go to who would listen to her tale of abduction? There had to be *someone*, despite the captain's warning that her search would be futile. She decided here and now that it would be worth a try, that it had to be shortly after they set foot on these islands. A few days should give her time enough to get the feel of the place and its passable outlets. If she was caught, what was there to lose, anyway?

Directly in back of the macro-ship, Dominique's schooner followed at a safe distance. Both had hoisted their infamous banners to clearly display their colors: one Bolivian, two "bones on black." After swinging down from the mainmast spar, Tyrone strode up to the high poop, and placing his hands on his lean hips, tossed back his head, delighting in the wind ruffling his hair. His eyes were hues of the wild willow in the morning sun. They flashed into vigorous action with the help of his spyglass, counting and studying the dozen vessels, all sturdy sailors, that rode at easy anchor in the distance.

Sliding the glass to the right, Tyrone observed the smiling faces of the islanders that awaited their entrance, standing near the rude fort that boasted a full brace of cannons still smoking after their noisy greeting. Tyrone grinned in anticipation, shifting his glass from the lacy fringe of surf to the powder-soft beaches to beyond where palmettos and ferns and creepers merged with the vivid green of oaks and shrubbery.

The fort faced the Gulf, squarely erected on one of the shell mounds to give it a commanding position. These large shell heaps forming mounds and banks showed that the island had been inhabited since ancient times. The north side of the fort overlooked the Bay where the privateering vessels and rakish lateen-rigged feluccas had been emptied of their loot. The goods lay in the warehouses to be examined by merchants, some to be transported upstream. This would be his forthcoming task, enriched with danger as he wound his way through the swampland, making deliveries to clientele sworn to reticence.

Not only that, but smuggler Ty would make frequent stops to deliver surplus to needy families so that they could furnish their households with food, clothing, and needed sundries, trading back and forth amongst themselves. A nineteenth-century Robin Hood, Nikki often called Tyrone when in one of his clownish moods.

"Nik!" Tyrone shouted down from his perch, spying the lad below. "Have the Lady Sherwood and her fair daughter taken breakfast yet?"

"Aye," Nikki returned smilingly.

"Good. Escort them to the deck and on the double, mate!"

"Aye, aye, captain!" Nikki barked importantly.

As he sprang to do his cousin's bidding, a comical grin broke out on Nikki's face. He liked the jovial mood Tyrone was in this sunny morn. For one, Tyrone was highly pleased at the rich prizes taken this time out. Too, there would be plenty to go around, and for Tyrone's impoverished river-folk thrice the usual. Nikki smiled at the day as he slipped into the bulkhead. If his cousin could tame half-insane runaway slaves, soothe frightened black captives, take in all kinds of criminals to work

88

devotedly for him, and even tame a hound that was brought to him part mad, half-starved, so could he likewise tame the spitfire who was already showing signs of submissiveness. Yet, what would be the Sherwoods' final kismet, Nikki wondered as he strode through the passageway.

Taking in the spectacle ahead and just off the bow, Angel's eyes lit up, reflecting brightly the shimmering islands and the aqua Gulf. It was a sea in itself, this bay; of blue and green and tan lights with masses of banana trees, and further beyond, live oaks draped with silvery Spanish moss. Now as they drew nearer she could pick out ships of every size and shape. Red sails colored the bay and a delightful sound reached her—the advancing and receding of the great, creamy white surf against the broad expanse of beach.

Angel saw before her two islands growing steadily larger by the minute, lying close together, and further up the coast and toward the west, yet another. Gulls and pelicans playfully dominated these islands, while other smaller birds she could not identify soared and wheeled against the azure sky, looking as though they were related to the gull.

Here was adventure, Angel thought silently to herself. It was this too, that Christine would think if only papa was alive, the circumstances different. But Christine just gazed ahead silently, as if searching for that beloved someone to come walking along the beach waving a warm greeting to them. Angel's heart suddenly went out to her.

As a warm, fragrant breeze from the south whipped at Angel's tied-back hair, the mysterious scent reminded her somewhat of delicious oranges. She began to feel that someone was intently studying her every move, and looking up to the raised deck she saw that, indeed, the captain watched her with curious warmth in those moody eyes. She was having a hard time tearing her gaze away, as he held her mesmerized, reminding her of a wild creature of savagely passionate moods. Growing suddenly warmer than was the sun's doing under that magical gaze, Angel became thoroughly aware of the ragged, unfeminine outfit she had mended with needle and thread countless times. Consequently her cheeks flushed hot and red;

89

she looked away.

Tyrone, coming down with a feline grace, with the bright white sun shining along the edge of his cutlass, adjusted the nasty-looking pair of firearms he wore tucked to the ready into a wide leather belt. Before reaching her side he issued commands to which several deep voices came back with "Aye, cap'n!"

"Morning, girl," Tyrone said, as he brushed his hard knuckles over her softly flushing cheeks. "What do you think of this island paradise so far—beautiful, isn't it?"

Angel, battling that jarring, half-faint feeling, remained silent. Again his touch was leaving her without courage, giddy and lightheaded. She knew he waited with alert expectancy to hear her comment, but his muscular arm brushing her shoulder somehow kept her mouth from forming any. She could as usual detect the fresh odor of milled soap mingling with tobacco and the masculine scent he emitted. She could feel that sidelong gaze measuring her mood. She stayed still, not voicing her opinion of what lay ahead sparkling and beckoning to her. Here was adventure—and something else.

Mistaking her attitude for snooty disregard and with lingering anger over the events of the evening before, Tyrone took his suddenly brooding gaze elsewhere. For a moment he regarded Ellen strolling the deck with her companions, then, snorting softly to himself he dipped his head to Angel once, at last striding away to find more pleasant company elsewhere.

As Tyrone joined Caspar at starboard, Ellen came up silently from behind. The huge pirate had his eyes earnestly fixed on the undulating strip of sparkling sands ahead. He was watching for a bit of silver-tipped black to emerge from behind the backdrop of cottages and come racing along the beach to greet them.

Tyrone smiled knowingly. The pirate's interest lay solely in the hound. Caspar loved Noble as much as he did himself. The once mistreated pup had now grown into a large, healthy hound that policed his cottages day and night, permitting no one wearing an alien scent near. Both these men enjoyed the happy reunions with Noble immensely.

Feeling somewhat dejected but realizing it was her own

doing, Angel began to covertly study Captain Ty, noting the way the silky tan hair lay close at the nape of his neck, observing the long, lean back, slim hips and firm buttocks in taut breeches. How handsome and virile he is, she thought disturbingly. How. . . .

Abruptly she chided herself. She must stop this foolishness. It wouldn't get her anywhere except the one place she had no desire to be. Horror of horrors, if he touched her intimately she would simply die!

She flushed crimson for the third time this morning when, in the next moment and as if on cue, the threesome turned to stare directly at her. Tyrone said something to Caspar and the bulk of that meaty frame swelled and rolled with everything but circumspect mirth as he nodded furiously. Tyrone's visual search caressed every inch of her, setting her atingle and aglow. Just as swiftly as he had raked her form with his eyes he now presented his back once more to her, took up scanning the shores ahead.

"Pshaw!" Angel blew in a huff. "Robin Goodfellow and his blockheaded sidekick," she said under her breath. "How I would love to see them both fall overboard and swallowed up by sharks!"

Next, something caught her eye. Ellen was rubbing her hip against the captain's tight breeches and he didn't seem to mind in the least. Angel felt something tug at the strings of her heart and she wondered what it all meant. Why should this bother her?

What happened next surprised the skeleton crew on deck, and especially Angel.

"Would you mind not doing that!" Tyrone said, glaring askance to Ellen. "Your nearness offends my delicate sense of smell. Stand off from me, bitch!" He elbowed Ellen rudely aside when she hadn't shown any indication of leaving his presence.

Gawking at the captain as if he'd slapped her, Ellen finally ambled away, going to stand not far from Angel and Christine. The other two tarts, Tessie and Peggy, had taken in the curious scene also. Angel could hear what Ellen said to them now.

"Just like last night, shoving me off like I was some kind of

91

garbage. And him, he was supposed to be such a lusty lover, heard tell by some of Dominique's crew. Hah! and I suppose that nameless little slut over there smells better'n me." Then she tossed her head in the direction of Caspar. "I heard what the captain said to that lug about her having tender meat. . . ."

The last words were lost to Angel as Ellen bent to whisper something to the two, and they, after hearing the secret, regarded Angel with wonder. But Ellen only narrowed her steely eyes to glare at the English girl's form, as if she very much would like to carve up her most private parts. Just that look of Ellen's told Angel very much, and her ears warmed, then burned hotly.

At last, the tall vessel was passing between the two islands and the bulk of the *Annette* glided majestically as she entered the little harbor. The main island, Grande Terre, was alive with dark- and olive-skinned men, women, and shouting, cavorting youngsters, and crowded with many-sized ships that gave the impression of a busy, bustling seaport. Shouts of greeting echoed across the bay in Arcadian and Cajun patois, the same that Angel had heard the captain speaking with several of the crew and Nikki. Now, those fellows had already furled the sheets and were kedging the vessel, while some stood ready to load the longboats that just now were shoving off the beaches.

"Ladies," Tyrone gave Angel his most smiling perusal, "go below and ready what you must take with you. Shortly the pirogues will come to take you ashore."

"Captain, we have no garments, only a few meager items, if you remember correctly!" Angel wanted to mention their trunks but didn't see any need to. He knew exactly what she was driving at.

"Well, go pack what you do have, then," he drawled. "Too bad you saw fit to return that dainty little number to Kuai Hua this morning. I found it rather becoming on you." When he saw that she hadn't moved a muscle, he warned, "Go now, or you and your mother will be left behind to keep each other company on a vacant ship."

Angel shuddered at the thought of one more bloody night spent waterborne and made haste, pulling Christine gently but firmly along behind her, for her mother again displayed that bewildered expression she wore so often of late.

Sometime later, Angel climbed down with Christine to the manned pirogue that would paddle them ashore. She patted Christine's hand reassuringly, then scanned the crowd awaiting the longboats. She had glimpsed back over her shoulder once to the handsome ship and had seen Tyrone commanding a longboat laden to capacity. Vindictively, she began to hope that the bloody duffer captain and his contraband would sink in the bottomed-out boat and be strangled by pondweed. He deserved it, for being so nice one minute, then nasty to her the next!

That's it Angel, keep your spirits up, she thought to herself and resolutely straightened her spine like a starched general.

The still water mirrored their passage, the surface like a clear looking-glass. She was watching silver fish swimming in the water when a streak of gray and black caught her attention. It raced toward the water's edge as it leapt and barked and wagged a long bushy tail.

Oh, my Lord. A wolf! She had read of wolves before, and now they were going to be eaten alive! Still, he wasn't attacking anyone on the beach. The people there kept their distance, though, as if they feared that beastly hound. Angel prayed it wasn't strangers he craved for his dinner.

"Noble, come!" Tyrone's voice deeply rang across the bay. "Come on, boy!"

Angel emitted a horrified shriek when all at once the beast was swimming fiercely toward that voice. She clutched her mother's hand and cowered next to her as the beast, with mouth agape, displayed long, sharp fangs, a pink tongue lolling between. His golden orbs shot them a quick perusal, and determining them to be unknowns, he paddled on by, much to Angel's relief.

Behind them, the beast was greeted with cheers and soothing tones coming from the captain's longboat. To Angel, twisting around to see the scene, there was no mistaking whom the beast belonged to. He barked and licked that captain all at the same time, while grinning almost humanlike, the tall and pointed ears now resting back in meek submission.

Relaxing somewhat, Angel turned away from the happy

reunion. She should have expected to witness such strange creatures on this wooded isle of the smugglers. And this was only the beginning, she told herself.

When they stepped onto the sands of Grande Terre, she had no cause to feel ashamed of her state of dishabille, for the women who greeted them frigidly were donned in stained and filthy frocks of muslin and brocade, while some wore serviceable but faded calico. Angel read into it that the frocks and brocades had been part of the loot which the pirates had taken from formerly captured ships. Now her own belongings would become part of the pleasure these women sought in rummaging through the trunks and then cast aside the old for the new. To please their men, the captain had said.

A palmetto-thatched village scattered here and there in large clearings filled the backdrop beyond the bone-white shores. Robust men strolled with some of the women while others worked on small pinnaces; and smugglers and fishermen and rum-runners, they all milled about the village. Too, all smiled upon the captain and his crew, cheered them as heroes as they peered at the ill-begotten treasures and, of course, Dominique and Blade were not to be left out. Those two had done the dirty work.

Angel heard the clash of many tongues, and the sight of so many mixed races made her curiosity grow. Equally curious glances rested on her and Christine, while the people didn't seem to be as interested in the tarts who were climbing out of the pirogue in a most ladylike fashion, assisted by many grubby hands. No doubt, those here had witnessed Ellen's kind on numerous occasions, Angel thought with disinterest, because something else was bothering her suddenly.

A barefoot, bronzed man of indeterminate age, sporting a bright red kerchief round his head, spat onto the sand as he stalked her, his dark eyes rudely fixed on her slim legs where Angel had rolled up her breeches. She was in bad temper and was just about to tell him to scat when an idea struck her. The captain had been bending at some task when he glanced up and saw her being ogled by the man. She worked fast, smiling enticingly as she had in bygone days, deliberately allowing the pirate a peep of ivory shoulder as she let the blouse sag a little,

94

then more, making the man drool when the tops of her round breasts came into view.

Before she knew what was happening, Tyrone had dropped what he was doing to stride swiftly toward her, the huge beast loping easily behind his furious master. She reacted with a startled shriek when he shoved her rudely aside and confronted the man crossly.

"It seems we can't trust you out of our sight for one minute, Jerel. Where is your captain?" he asked all at once.

"Wh—where he always is this time of day, Monsieur Ty," Jerel stammered, not understanding the smuggler's anger. Then Jerel thought he knew, looking at the fair young woman in strange clothes. He said, "Monsieur Jean is resting on the veranda."

"He knows we have come then," Tyrone stated. "Go now, inform him that I've business to discuss and would like it to be this evening."

"Yeah, yeah, Monsieur Ty. I will go now as you say." With that the pirate swaggered away, after giving the beauty one last peep over his shoulder. He saw her snatch up the blouse with a jerk. He shrugged, confused.

Chaste maiden, hmmm? Tyrone pondered, seriously beginning to doubt it. His smouldering eyes bore into hers. "There is no doubt that your presence on this island will prove very taxing for me. I'll have to think of something. Perhaps a bodyguard . . . like Noble here."

"Keep that bloody cur away from me! He's scary, he frightens me half to death. I would rather have a human bodyguard, if you will. But must you demand this?"

"Definitely!"

"Someone like Samuel, for instance?" she said without looking at him.

"*That* is entirely out of the question."

She hung her head dejectedly. "I suppose he will be auctioned off like all the other slaves," she sighed, baiting him.

"You don't fool me for one minute, girl. Look at me! I'll tell you—I plan to keep Sam here, same as you. But you may as well forget it, as there is no way in hell a darkling like you, or Sam, can escape this island. Oh, yes, you may have already

95

heard the lad did escape once before. But that was from the Temple, where Lafitte auctions off the blacks, and it is quite a distance north from here. Unless you want to be eaten alive by crocodiles or raped in the swamps by half-insane runaway slaves or criminals, I would think twice before I venture out, if I were you."

"Rather than this!" she snapped back. "Anyway, I don't believe you." Though she put a brave front on it, she felt her chances of escape blown apart by those few and possibly true words.

"Believe what you will, but come along now. I've sent ahead a servant to clean out a cottage for you and your mother. I'll take you there now."

Still delighting in the feel of the powder-soft sand, Angel carried her old boots while Christine followed, Tyrone striding at the fore, like a barbaric lord leading his captives to their place of imprisonment. The beastly hound ran before his mater, sat and waited, then resumed his scampering when the party caught up. He did this over and over, and Angel could not help but find it rather amusing. Tyrone patted the huge head each and every time, pleased at the hound's antics. They shared a man-and-beast camaraderie that made Angel wonder if they were not truly one and the same—both beasts.

Christine slogged in utter weariness, stubbing her slippered toe on a pebble or a protruding rock, halting, then catching up, breathless. Angel had to say something to make the captain slacken his furious pace and listen to her.

"Wait!" she finally burst out, flushing instantly when he turned suddenly to fold his arms across his wide chest.

"Well—what is it now?" he growled.

"Just look at my mother, captain. She is in shock and needs care. This sudden exercise is killing her. Can you not see that? Or are you blind as well as savagely cruel?"

His countenance darkened, his gaze shifting between them. He could see that the younger woman had positioned her hands insolently upon her hips while she awaited his answer.

"You have barbs at the tip of your tongue, girl, and you are beginning to grow difficult once more. Why all of a sudden do you seek the medical attention of a physician for your mother?

96

In the many days past, you were the one who appeared without vision, for the lady has been in this state of mild shock for quite some time now." He hesitated, wanting very much to snatch up her wrists and shake her brutally. "As for my being savagely cruel, you have seen nothing of my wrath yet, and don't tempt me to punish you again, sweet. It was not you, but I, who found it most enjoyable last time, if short-lived. I would be thoroughly selfish this time and see you done my way. You do understand what I'm getting at?" he asked pitilessly.

"You need not explain any further, captain," she returned, half-petrified that he would carry out his threat. She waited, knowing there was more to come.

"On this isle you will address me as Ty, or if you want— Tyrone. Not captain. Jean Lafitte is captain here, or as many choose to say—king of Grande Terre. He doesn't care much for the name Black Falcon, nor 'pirate.' As I mentioned before, he prefers to be called privateer. Mine is a free enterprise, and I lead my own men, my smuggler-crew. They may call me captain here—all else not," he declared.

"My mother?" she reminded him. "Cap . . . Tyrone."

"Doctor Laporte will see to her shortly, after you are settled temporarily here. When my business is finished here in a few days we will go to the bordering island, Grande Isle, where I have my own cottages."

They had not gone far after starting off when Angel's eyes widened and she clamped a hand over her mouth. She was filled with alarming dread at the sickening sight that she saw before the gates of the village. Swaying in the wind, where a gibbet had been erected in the square, was the limp body of a middle-aged man dangling from a rope-end.

Tyrone had heard his followers gasp, knowing full well the reason. He shrugged off the gruesome scene as if this were an everyday occurrence, and continued on. He had not taken even ten paces when the girl caught up and tugged at his sleeve.

"Why is that man hanging there?" she dared to ask, trying to keep up with him.

Noble growled deep in his throat at the sudden contact that the stranger had made with his master. Angel started and jumped back. Tyrone glared down at the hound, making a

97

mental note to have it understood with Noble that she was to be protected, not the reverse.

"He is hanging there, girl, because he is obviously dead, and a definite reminder to all who might disobey the rules here."

"What has he done to suffer such inhumane torture?"

"No doubt about it, the man was very ignorant. But I prefer to call it greed. Any way you look at it, his deed was deserving of punishment."

"Punishment!" she blurted, horrified at his callousness. "An end!" she declared hotly.

"He fired on an American vessel," he declared, peering down at her with hypnotic eyes. "And I would have meted out the same—ah—end, were it one of mine who disobeyed my orders."

Tyrone knew he had frightened her, for she clamped her mouth shut immediately and fell behind him once again. Angel tried forgetting the grisly scene, but she knew it would forever haunt her.

Wending his way through a deep green thicket of shrubs, Tyrone soon halted before a cottage hidden from view behind oleanders and palmetto scrub. It sagged dejectedly, gray against this backdrop of greenery. But anything looked welcoming to Angel after residing aboard ship for better than three whole months.

"This is your home for the time being and until one of the larger cottages next to mine on Grande Isle can be evacuated of its occupants," Tyrone said lazily, studying her closely.

Much to her surprise, wild orchids and flowers of every color in the rainbow grew in clustered profusion before the sagging door of the cottage that was also shrouded from roof to floor in lush green vines and creepers abloom. Before entering she turned to Tyrone as a belated thought struck her.

"Do you mean to say that you would cast out a family for the sake of keeping us close by—I mean—to make yourself sure—if we tried to—Oh!" Blast it, but he befuddled her!

"Escape," Tyrone finished for her, a cold note of warning injected in his steely voice. Then, "It's not like that at all. The family I speak of is but a smuggler and his two comely wenches that he not only shares his meals with but his bed also. Not to worry, they'll take up residence elsewhere, my sweet."

Angel's sweet smile was one of affectation while she paused in a bed of wild violets as he flung back the creaking door and bade them enter. "I shall see to this door, order it repaired immediately—ahh—lest you try this foolish thing that busies your mind night and day," he grinned.

For how many times that day she couldn't count, her retort was stayed. Gliding past her oppressor to cross the threshold, Angel felt a shadow of fear enter her. He was going to imprison them again! And, when they became neighbors, would she be forced to share a bed with him? Or, then again, maybe he had other plans?

Would he seduce her against her will? she wondered next. All of a sudden strange sensations began to build inside her. She recalled flighty girls at school whispering of what a man and woman did when they were alone together. It was not pleasant for the woman at first, they had whispered, giggling behind their hands. Angel thought now—if it was anything like what the captain did to her emotionally when he grazed her cheek with his fingertips or bruised her lips with a searing kiss, she wanted no bloody part of it!

Once inside the cottage, Angel found that of the two dusty rooms one was smaller than the other. Heavy batten blinds covered the two main tiny windows. Roughhewn boards served as walls and streaks of light filtered through the wide cracks. Angel stared at a big cobweb in the corner of the room where a spider had just entrapped a fly in its finespun home. Bathed in slanting sunlight speckled with dust-motes, she appeared most forlorn in this strange country so far from her beloved homeland. She felt suddenly just like the poor fly.

Christine passed her hand over a crude table and three chairs that stood in the center of the room. She seemed relaxed all of a sudden, peering next into a wooden chest that gaped open but was void of any contents. At last, she paused near a large wooden-frame bed, mosquito netting draping its tall posts. It was wide enough for two.

A smaller room without curtain or door held a tiny, narrow cot that surely would deny a guest a whit of comfort the night long, Angel guessed. Her mother lingered in there now, staring around.

"The air is fustier here than in the larger room," Christine chirruped as if she were deciding to rent the place or not, "but it will do in a pinch," she added in a high voice.

Angel smiled at Christine's healthier mood, which brought her suddenly and strangely near tears. Mama puttering around Stonewall in royal blue silk. Stonewall, with its shelves lined with finely tooled books and glorious objets d'art that shared a wall with massive, gilt-framed paintings. She could almost hear the cut-crystal drops that tinkled musically in soft evening breezes and see the candles glowing whitely in the girandoles, complimenting snowy-white table linen.

All the while Tyrone watched the fine girl silently, thinking how very lovely, even in the masculine clothing, she looked as she paused in the shaft of sunlight peeping in. There was a penseveneess in the now softer green of her eyes, melancholy and haunted. Her softly pouting mouth was delicate in the hazy sundrops all around her; urging, tempting him to taste fully the sweetness of her youth. It came to him in a new burning heat that he wanted to crush her in his arms, console her, then make mad, passionate love to her. It had been too long since last he had known a woman, nor had he even had the desire to do so in the months past. But now his loins flared with desire so intense that it overwhelmed him with its throbbing ache.

In two easy paces he was beside her, all of his brawny height shielding out the pale shafts of light. She stiffened at his sudden nearness and turned away, swirling her hair around her like a pearly cloud, shrouding her face from his hot gaze. He stretched lean fingers around to cup the fine chin in his big hand, bringing her thus to face him. Panic mounted in her breast when she could do naught else but meet those beautiful eyes shaded by thickly fringed lashes.

"I feel you are a flower yet untouched by lover's hands," he murmured, as silken lashes shyly brushed her cheeks. "Yes, you are yet to unfold and become even more lovely under a lover's caresses." He laughed deeply in his throat when she quivered. "What is your name—Rachel? Catherine? Leah?" he fired so quickly that her head reeled.

Cocksure of herself, Angel's soft laugh tinkled and she

100

shook her bright head firmly. "None of those. But why don't you ask my mother, sir?" She challenged him to just try and find out.

"I know your game but not your name, my lovely," was all he said.

His warm gaze touched her face, her hair, and lingered upon the soft flesh above the V in her blouse. Her hand crept up under his full regard to shield that spot and he quickly captured it there as he caressed the small hand.

"Tyrone?" she breathed.

"Are you forever going to play games with me?" he asked, now brushing a thumbnail over the pulsating spot.

She was going to faint, she just knew it.

He sighed deeply. "What is it you wish?"

"Small needs for two destitute females."

"Speak up, sweet. What is your desire? A comb? A mirror? And perhaps fresh and clean unmentionables?"

"Yes, Tyrone, all of them. And a freshwater bath for each of us?" Her eyes begged demurely.

"You'll have them all," he said, running a tan finger along her breastbone as he pondered something deeply. "And what are you willing to sacrifice in return—your maidenhood, or your name?"

"How could you!" she breathed hotly, turning three shades of red. "My name is all that is left of my dignity, mine to keep from you forever. You have all those precious few items I had taken with me on this hapless voyage. What would you have me do now—strip off this ragged outfit and give you that too?"

"That will do," he said grinning, "for a start, which will lead us to this other you neglected to mention."

"You are a devil, indeed, a randy devil!"

With that she stepped back and her words were proven true, for as her eyes fell to his tight breeches the sight that met her glimpse caused her rapid alarm. Her eyes flew to his face and saw white teeth bared, lips curved sensuously in a smile.

"You are as curious as I, aren't you, my sweet?"

"No, no, I am not! Never!" she returned intensely.

"So, I am a devil—hmmm? Witches are supposed to be able to conjure up the devil. I've often been named the devil for my

101

ways. Are you perhaps my little witch, come to feed my wickedness?"

She tossed her head. "I am sorry, sir, I never trust a man who is full of superstitious beliefs!"

"Come now, let's not quarrel," he said cajolingly, "we were just beginning to get acquainted."

Like lightning he reached for her, but was halted when Christine drew between and splayed out her hand. "What goes on here! Lay hands off my daughter, sir. No one courts her without my permission."

"Go away, skinny nag, and leave us be," Tyrone growled, angry at the sudden intrusion.

Glaring at him, Angel tossed an arm protectively about Christine's shoulders. "Ahh, no, sir. It is you who should leave us be. Can't you see she has had enough excitement for one day?"

"Very well," Tyrone said, turning to exit. "Come Noble, the ladies want to be alone. You'll have all that you asked for, girl. Still, there is one thing left you must bargain for—" he left it dangling in mid-air.

"Meaning?" Angel wondered out loud.

"Sam's freedom."

"But—you said you were going to keep him," she said confusedly.

"A man can change his mind, can't he? I will send for you— later," he said and was gone.

Gray shades of evening fell about the tiny cottage. Inside a candle had been lighted and the single flame flirted with the draft, casting dancing shadows on the crude walls. Angel woke to a persistent, agitating humming about her head and slapped at a mosquito that had found its way beneath the netting. She could hear the sound of soft night breakers playing along the sandy beaches with a soft *whoosh* and a sighing. She could smell the delicate wild fragrance of the perfumed garden surrounding the small dwelling. Outside she could hear the gay laughter of men and women from afar. If she didn't know better she would have believed them to be on an island paradise. A green isle in the sea. . . .

Another persistent humming came from the chair where Christine sat contemplating stars through the tiny, bare window, stars that were just beginning to make an appearance in the darkening purple sky.

"How long have you been sitting there, Mama?" Angel inquired softly as she parted the netting and dangled her legs over the side of the feather-tick bed.

Christine sighed wistfully. "I have been watching the coming of night, Angel love, and wishing . . . wishing—ah, well, it is beautiful here, you know. While you slept a man came to fix the door, but he did not put a lock on like that bold captain said he would. I peeked outside and would have taken a stroll if not for the man seated outside the door." She shivered visibly. "A scarier man I've never seen, love. Are you hungry? I certainly am. I only wish that. . . ." Her voice trailed off again.

"Mama—" Angel bounded from the bed, tugging on her breeches, "you are overtired and you are rambling. Now, you get in that bed and rest as I asked you before. I am certain that someone will bring dinner soon and I'll awaken you at that time. Come now—into bed with you."

"Oh, all right. I am a bit weary but did not want to wake you before. I guess I'll rest a bit before dinner."

"That is what I said, silly goose." Angel shook her head. "Anyway, the bed is big enough for the both of us. I will see if I can tidy up this place somewhat. Whoever did so didn't do a very good job. Look, here is a broom," she said cheerfully as she began to sweep out the smaller room.

Soon, Angel had a pile of dust from each of the rooms, plus all crawling inhabitants, waiting at the door to be swept out in the morning. She didn't want to see what lurked outside their door until the morning shed some light upon the doorstep.

"Oh, daughter," Christine piped from the bed, "no one cleans house at nightfall. Not even servants. Why, back home the servants were abed by now."

Angel whirled to shake a finger at Christine. "Shame on you. I thought I told you to get some rest!" Then she thought of Christine's words and tears twinkled fiercely in her eyes. "Mama. We will get out somehow, just you wait and see. I shall

103

find a way to get us through the swamps to seek out the proper authorities. They will help us secure passage and we'll be back in England before the winter's chill nips the land. But, you must be willing to be left alone while I find my way around this isle—and Samuel, I must find him, too." And, there must be a way to get around the scary oaf outside guarding the door, she schemed.

It became apparent, even before Angel looked up, that Christine was asleep and hadn't heard her last words. She tried to decide what to do next when a knock rattled across to her. Walking soundlessly across the boards, Angel was hoping that the evening meal had arrived. She was so hungry that she believed she could eat an entire pig and then some.

The native Baratarian who stood there with head bobbing a greeting had his hairy arms loaded down with coarse-looking but fresh garments. Behind him, Angel could see yet two more islanders, each lifting an edge of an ancient wood tub.

"I am Bron and my woman is Thelma," the man with the clothes was saying. "And my woman cook for you now. Man outside will bring women to my cottage when youse all done with bath and change clothes. Here," he said, finally handing her the neatly folded pile, in which bright calico frocks lay in the midst of linens, yellowed chemisettes, and colorful kerchiefs.

"Thank you, and your woman, mister Bron," Angel said, liking this burly man instantly on sight. He had black, kindly eyes that smiled at her amiably. His coveralls were worn-out but clean, and she could detect a slight odor of fish, suggesting that he was a fisherman, not a pirate or smuggler.

He then handed her a basket of yellow plums, bananas, and oranges, and a small wooden box that resembled an ancient treasure chest miniaturized. Bron mentioned that the fruit was for them to munch on later if they became hungry during the night. On opening the box, Angel found two sets of combs, brushes, and mirrors, all tortoiseshell. Angel stared at them, thinking suddenly of Captain Ty. Him and his bargains! She snapped the lid shut viciously.

The water the men were just now pouring into the tub was sparkling clear and steamed hotly. It would be rainwater that the islanders caught in the huge barrels she'd seen along the way to the cottage.

"Monsieur Ty say youse to come to home of Cap'n Lafitte just after youse had your dinner," Bron said, handing her a bar of oatmeal soap his wife had made up the day before.

"Thank you again, Bron. But, tell me, how are we to get to this Lafitte's residence?" Angel asked the shy man.

"I will take youse there. Not so far, little one. Just on north end of island. After dinner we will go," he said, then left with the men.

Again Angel bathed but Christine stayed abed. As in the past, she muttered that too many baths caused a woman to wrinkle and age early. They donned fresh but coarse frocks and then were escorted to the home of Thelma and Bron. Angel tried not peeking at Christine's so-called "scary man," the guard, but she certainly could smell him, for he reeked strongly of cheap rum and sweat.

They were greeted warmly by the household, consisting of two small children and, of course, the parents. The small, svelte woman, even daintier than Angel, pulled them gently inside with one arm while she balanced a babe on her hip with the other.

"Oh, you come. I cook for you, you like. It is no good to eat on ship with men, no?" Thelma's voice was delightfully comforting and her shining eyes sparkled in merriment. As there were not many women on the island to her liking, Thelma at once liked what she saw in these newcomers.

Angel received the babe into her arms while Thelma bustled about contentedly, chatting about whatever came into her mind, but she tactfully ignored the word captivity. She dished out a fish stew consisting of terrapin and freshly dug spring vegetables, with fragrant herbs floating on top. A pitcher of fruit-water emitting a pleasant herbal smell was placed in the center of the crude table.

The fare here would sustain a small army, Angel was thinking. There was even wild amber honey, and Thelma mentioned that bees left hives in great numbers to be collected all summer long. Thelma added that she even owned a peat garden for growing roots, as she proudly placed a platter of sugar beets in front of the guests.

Angel and Christine did justice to the meal that Thelma had painstakingly prepared, and they felt fully satisfied at the conclusion of it. The meal of the evening before was not to be sneezed at as far as having been delicious,—Angel reflected back to it—but under those stifling circumstances she had only picked at it absently.

Bron belched ungraciously before excusing himself to go laze in his favorite chair in an adjoining room. All too soon Bron would take them to Lafitte's home, Angel thought dispiritedly, but only for a second. For now she played with the children while Christine wouldn't take no for an answer when Thelma declined the older woman's offer to help in clearing away the dishes and tidying up.

The setting was all very pleasant for the time being, but in the back of Angel's mind there still lurked an apprehension of what lay in store for Christine and herself at this Lafitte's residence. She was recalling Tyrone's parting shot about a "bargain." Perhaps Thelma could enlighten her as to what could be expected once they were delivered to the captain's home. It was certainly worth a try, even if Thelma and Bron were ordered to remain silent under Tyrone's orders.

"Thelma," Angel hesitated briefly. "Could you tell me what it is like—I mean—" She had to speak simply to make herself understood by the uneducated but sweet woman. "What do these men do at these gatherings? Are there other women there? And, this Lafitte, what is he like?" She wanted very much to ask if Tyrone had a woman there, but left it at that, hoping Thelma would catch on. But she hoped and prayed that indeed Tyrone kept several mistresses and would see fit to leave her be.

Bron chose to saunter back into the main room at that time and Thelma, doe-eyed from the questions fired at her, wiped her thin hands on a soiled apron and peered at her husband for license to speak. He nodded but his black eyes cautioned her not to reveal too much. Angel did not miss this.

"Oh," Thelma said, looking terrified for a second, "we never go there, not inside. Men play games with cards, drink very much, we know. Lafitte have a woman, very pretty, people

106

say, but I never see his woman before. Island people say Monsieur Ty have many woman and—" She bit off as Bron cleared his throat noisily, just when Angel wanted to hear more.

"Is that all?" Angel urged, dismissing Bron's warning to his wife.

Bron scratched his olive-skinned forehead in thought. He wanted to warn her that smuggler Ty took his pleasure where it could be most easily gotten, but he chose instead to cheer her up. "Cap'n Lafitte, he want to see all that men bring from the sea. He might even say to Monsieur Ty to let youse go. You be lucky, little one, maybe even go home," Bron smiled.

"Home," Angel echoed, her green, staring gaze faraway.

Thelma felt a mixture of compassion and joy for the younger woman, and she prayed that her yearning to be home would be fulfilled soon. On the other hand, Ty liked his women, and this one was a treasure he wouldn't part with so easily. Not until he tired of the poor girl, anyway.

A knock summoned Bron to the door and he slipped outdoors to speak with the guard, closing the door securely behind him. Angel and Thelma exploded into conversation at the same moment the door closed. They broke into giggles at their haste to gossip with the man of the house out. In the back of the room Christine played with the children as Thelma stepped closer to the girl to convey a warning.

"I will tell you, Missy Sherwood. You tell no one, please?"

Angel nodded her head promising secrecy. "What is it, Thelma?" she begged, her eyes feverishly bright.

"Monsieur Ty good to us, give Bron many treasure to sell and get good fishing boat. I like Ty, missy. But he bad one way. At first when he come to island he have many woman, different one every night. Some woman bad, too. Want to be with man too much. Too bad when woman have to chase man. I never chase man, Bron chase me. He catch me, too." She paused, and, philosophizing in her own simple way, went on. "Ty, him full of some hate. Someone done wrong for him when he was boy. God know it, and I see it in his eyes. Some sad in his heart, missy. Make him angry young man who take, never give. You be careful for if he make you love him, soon your heart be no

107

good for true man."

Angel choked back the lump in her throat. "Oh, Thelma, you are so wise for all your unworldliness. Thank you. I never realized that that could be the reason for his dark moods. I shall be careful and do not worry—a man who carries hatred in his heart and uses women as if they were lesser creatures, why, I could never love such a man. It's unthinkable," she ended, hoping that she'd gotten through to her new friend.

Thelma, her eyes full of understanding, reached out to squeeze the paler arm. "There be much talk of that man, missy. He grow tired of womans soon, growl to them. Be much careful when Ty have no woman now on island. Not here, but maybe in New Orleans where he goes soon. You lucky to be young. He like most woman older—much bigger." She caricatured the generous contour of a woman, before she grew serious. "Missy—woman get only what she ask for."

Bron entered just then, his black eyes sliding between them. He rested his gaze on the smaller form that shrugged innocently while the face smiled cutely at him. He couldn't help but return the smile, for he loved his spouse dearly, even though she was lonesome for female companionship and had it in her to gossip. Finally he gave his full attention to the English girl and steeled himself for the inevitable outburst of temper this one would display.

"Monsieur Ty send message to Sherwood women. Younger woman is to come alone, without mum. Lady will stay here with Thelma and rest till you come back, little one. Thelma will keep her happy with talk," Bron said, as his eyes twinkled with humor.

"No, I'll not go without her!" Angel said vehemently, but she had already known it would come to this.

Thelma gasped in horror. "Missy must. Monsieur Ty be very angry if you do not. Maybe you not even go home. You see Jean Lafitte . . . please?"

Christine ambled forward. "I've a headache, anyway, love. You are safe with Bron here, and perhaps Thelma is right and this Jean Lafitte will give us our freedom." She pressed fingers to her temple, frowning.

"Dr. Laporte is coming to see her," Bron whispered low, so

108

as not to alarm the older woman. "Soon he will come. We must go now, little one."

2

A ripe white moon glowed between night-etched flora and the island was cast into shimmering enchantment. Bron escorted Angel to the home of Lafitte; finally, but reluctantly, Angel had given in to their collective pleas, realizing it was expedient for her to do so. After all, she had to grasp this chance, as there might not come another after this night. Her longing for home was becoming stronger by the minute, and her self-will would see it to that end.

The lantern that Bron carried wheeled eerie spirals of light into the dark shadows and onto black patches upon the path where it was moonless. Angel realized with dread that they were coming upon the stockade she had seen earlier, and she prayed that by now the lifeless form had been taken away to be buried. She would never know, for as they passed that spot she kept her eyes averted, going between the construction of cypress logs and directly into the stockade. There loomed ahead the dark outline of the warehouse, its impressive dimensions sharing a square with another building nearby.

"Is that where they keep the contraband, in that huge building?" Angel inquired.

"Black contraband," Bron corrected. "That one is barracoon. Most time many captive in chains, sometimes hundreds. On island there are gambling houses and cafes. We passed some outside of stockade but too dark to see into trees. You see tomorrow."

Cafes? Gambling establishments? Angel wondered. She hadn't seen any earlier today. But then, she hadn't been looking, either. The sight of that dead man had sickened her to the point of distraction. But now, ironically, that it was night, she was getting a whole different picture. Why, this was almost like a little town. These bold and infamous men had carved out an empire all their own on these pirate islands.

How long before their secure little world would be destroyed

109

here? She guessed it couldn't go on forever—or could it? She was gladdened in this—that she would be safely home in England if and when this little empire should ever crumble.

Lafitte's residence was a long, low building at the very back of the stockade, with a palm-thatched roof, and bound by a capricious veranda that faced the sea. The facade was of brick on the outside, where a few torches had been placed to illuminate the entrance.

This Lafitte lives very handsomely, Angel thought, when she and Bron halted before the orange and blue brightness of the torches. A doorkeeper was letting them in when Angel turned to ask Bron a question and suddenly noticed he had already vanished off into the shadows. The doorkeeper also disappeared down a long hall, leaving her completely alone to stare around the spacious hallway that branched off into rooms speaking of opulence.

The floors were oiled to a luster of dark satin, the walls paneled in Santo Domingan mahogany, and damask hangings were everywhere. As she peered down the hall, a flash of brightly colored silk caught her eye as if floating on air coming to greet her; the magnificent gown belonged to a beautiful, golden-skinned woman with an air of voluptuousness.

"Welcome to our home, Mademoiselle Sherwood. I am Marie. Permit me to show you to the salon before Monsieur Tyrone and *mon cher* Jean have done with their business. We will have some sherry," Marie purred, as she was glancing back over her shoulder to make certain the young woman followed.

Lafitte's mistress. She looked like a glamorous courtesan. Angel suddenly caught a glimpse of herself and Marie in one of the many gilt-framed mirrors lining the wall. She was startled, horrified, at what she saw. Where Marie's gown was decidedly fresh from Paris and of the very latest design, her own simple calico made her feel dowdy next to this display of pure elegance. And where Marie's hair, a rich mahogany brown, was piled high in a fashionable upsweep, Angel's was looped simply into a single knot at the nape of her neck.

Marie herself was feeling somewhat embarrassed as she comprehended that this superb beauty was used to being seen in gowns comparable to her own. This one was too lovely to be dressed so plainly—so like a peasant girl—Marie decided.

"Here. Sit down on the settee next to the open doors," Marie said, as she gestured to the silk and wood creation, going to fix them each a glass of sherry. She returned from the rosewood liquor cabinet, handing the younger woman a dainty wine glass. "It is a hot night and the breeze off the Gulf feels good, no?"

"Yes, it does," Angel murmured. "Thank you," she added, watching the candles flicker in the girandoles, listening to the reminiscent tinkling that made her pine for Stonewall.

"Ahhh, these men," Marie sighed. "Business, always business. How to keep a woman waiting, they know. But then, it is worth it for a good man—no?"

Angel bristled. "I am not what you think, Mistress—umm—Marie. Tyrone is not my—my man, and I am not his mistress. I am his prisoner, as is my mother, and I am here tonight under the impression that Monsieur Lafitte will release us."

Not taken aback by this, instead Marie became thoughtful for a time. She had known instinctively that here, in this ravishing *petite*, were a courage and willfulness that would be very difficult for a man to break, to turn to willingness, to eagerness in seeking his bed. But this defiant little flower was going to have a time of it, Tyrone wasn't about to let her out of his sight, certainly not for quite some time to come. He had already made that quite clear to everyone. She was not his woman yet, in an established manner, that is. She will be, she is ripe and ready for the plucking, Marie determined. What Monsieur Ty wanted he usually got. And Marie was one among many persons on the islands who didn't hesitate to aid him in securing whatever it was he desired.

"Mademoiselle Sherwood," Marie began with a subtle smile. "May I call you by your first name?"

Angel's eyes darted at the woman. "No, you may not. I'm sorry," she said very simply.

The slightly older woman shrugged, hiding her disappointment. "Anyway, you may call me Marie. Now, if you wish to be persuasive to my man—ahh—we must fix you up a bit. Don't look so surprised, *petite*. Come with me to my dressing room and we will see." Marie gestured sweepingly for the guest to

111

follow her.

Angel, puzzling over the woman's intent, rose and went along until they stood in an elegantly appointed room smelling of exotic perfumes. Not just one scent, but a conglomeration of musky scents assailed her nostrils. Here the flatter pieces of furniture were of tortoiseshell inlay, decorated in elaborate patterns.

Marie crossed to a huge mahogany wardrobe, flicked aside the many glistening gowns, and whirling, held against her bosom a pale green one, empire-waisted and sprigged at the bodice and hem in a darker green silk embroidery.

Angel stared in wide-eyed wonder at the finely spun material and the daring décolleté cut of the bodice. The shining threads seemed to beckon her, to dare her to be so feminine and wanton beneath them.

"*Cherie*, you will be most irresistible to my Jean in this. It is you. Put it on, and you must hurry now. I will do something with your hair then," Marie said, carelessly tossing opaque petticoats onto the bed beside the chosen gown.

Marie left the room for a few minutes, returning with shears, and dainty slippers to match the gown. Angel hadn't moved an inch. Marie clucked her tongue at the girl staring out onto the moonlit veranda. Angel turned her head and contemplated the shears that Marie wielded. Somewhat wan, Angel reached up to touch her hair, sliding her hand unconsciously to her shoulders.

"Oh, do not worry, *cherie*," Marie reassured her. "I am only going to snip some hair off near your cheeks, make little curls to hug them. You will love it. It makes a young woman such as yourself appear older and—umm—more seductive."

But I do not want to look older and more seductive, Angel wanted to shout, and then flounce out of the room in a rage. But Marie was already reaching out to unbutton the coarse calico she wore.

"Thank you, but I can manage the buttons myself," Angel said as she began to disrobe. If this would get her home, she was more than willing to be the buttered biscuit at Lafitte's table.

Later when Marie had finished, she drew the young woman to the full-length cheval glass to let her peruse her chic

112

artistry. Marie herself could not believe what she had created. If this girl was gorgeous when she arrived looking the way she had, she was now a devastatingly magnificent creature. Marie was without a jealous bone in her body, and if her Jean delighted in what he saw tonight, it was good. Twofold, if Tyrone was pleased, more power to Marie. Jean liked very much to see his friends happy.

"Oooh, Marie," Angel breathed. "Is it me? I feel so strange." She then pursed her lips at her unconscious outburst. "It's unthinkable, so unladylike to appear like this. I mean, it is not decent. I cannot do it." Then she chided herself for her foolishness as she recalled Kuai Hua's little dress. Still, where that one had concealed her breasts for the most part, this. . . .

"Ooh-la, *cherie*," Marie purred, clapping her hands together. "I can see it in your eyes, you have already changed your mind. You will go—no? You will always get what you want, don't you know that yet? We charming and intelligent women, we always get what we truly want. Just so. You will see," Marie said slyly. "*Tout de suite*, mademoiselle, we will go now. *Mon cher* Jean is waiting."

As is Tyrone, Angel thought a bit nervously. She followed her hostess down a long hall bedecked with Spanish prizes, in her mind searching out Marie's remotest statement, the emphasis she had put on "truly want."

Marie, on the other hand, happily concluded that this English girl had overlooked the fact that the green gown couldn't have possibly been one of Marie's own. If Angel had noticed their dissimilar proportions, Marie would have been distressed in explaining where the gown had truly come from.

Marie smiled to herself as she rustled along. That devilish Tyrone, filching that gown from an oaken trunk earlier in the warehouse, having her maid Mona hurriedly press it. He was difficult to understand at times, particularly of late. He was acting very strange, almost as if . . . she allowed her thoughts to trail off. Ah, well, Marie shrugged. Ty needed something young and fresh to come into his jaded life right about now.

Angel paused just inside the portal of the huge somber room while Marie went directly to the men seated at a long, claw-foot table. She noticed that the hard floor on which she stood was blue- and purple-stone mosaic. More likely than not plucked from some merchant ship shrinking in mortal terror at being overtaken by these fellows, who sat now as casually as if they were some gorgeous playboys at His Majesty's Court.

She noticed at once, with distraction, that a lean man had stood up with an easy hawklike grace. Indeed, the Black Falcon himself. No wonder he had been given the name. His black, sparkling eyes matched the jet hair perfectly—unknown to her, it was styled in the current mode of New Orleans—long at the back and full over the ears. She had to admit that Jean Lafitte cut a romantic figure in his dark attire.

"Jesus! What a piece!" a man roared from the farthest end of the table.

"Silence, Nez Coupé!" Lafitte commanded the homely man known as Cut Nose, but there was an unmistakable tinge of humor in his voice. Lafitte inclined his dark head toward the young woman still standing tentatively by the door. "Come forward, Mademoiselle Sherwood. Here, so that I may see you better," he said.

Lafitte's broad smile evinced his pleasure when Angel stepped forward into the light playing from the massive stone fireplace. She felt suddenly as if she were indeed a piece on display at an auction, and there followed some moments of silence, when all seated there stared agog, in open admiration of her. All but for Pearce Duschesne, whose evil, brown eyes danced with an unmistakable glint of lust, as once before.

Angel had thought there would only be the four of them: Lafitte, Marie, Tyrone, and herself. She hadn't been prepared for this lusty crowd of men, some of them eyesores to behold. She'd be bloody damned if she was to be forever surrounded by such as these! Soon she would be away from here.

The debauched men witnessed before them a fair-haired temptress with skin creamy as ivory; cheeks flushing rosy with undeniable youth. Firm, round breasts were outlined in the taut bodice, and, at the crest, revealed perfect mounds of silken flesh. Sassy curlicues hugged flawless, delicately molded cheeks above naturally pouting pink lips. The sophisticated upsweep shamelessly portrayed an oval face and green eyes enhanced by the gown; these eyes tilted almost sinfully in a new manner created by this fashionable hairdo. Her amber lashes swept across her eyes, which, in rare defiance, considered every man at the table coming to rest hatefully a moment upon black-clad Tyrone, then switching quickly back to Lafitte.

This infamous captain hadn't missed the carelessly frigid, run-the-blood-cold look the young beauty slanted at his friend, his confidant. Shocking! It was enough to make a bolder man than he shiver in his boots.

In spite of this, Lafitte stared hard into the young woman's eyes and his own dark ones admonished: Take care, *ma petite.* You have whet the appetite of my friend. Under that great courage you possess, you still have a tender heart, and it is exposed to danger. Take care.

Angel's hand moved slowly along her breastbone, then to her throat, under this man's hypnotic stare. She had read a message clearly printed in those moments, in those jet eyes, when Lafitte had glanced to his friend and then back to her. Well! He didn't frighten her one bit, she tried convincing herself.

"Here. Sit down, mademoiselle. I will personally pour for you a delicate Moselle. You will like it," Lafitte said, with much authority in his pleasant tone.

Angel eased her body down slowly, and with demureness she received the wine glass proffered her by Lafitte, sipping carefully so as not to choke on the slightly bitter libation. She didn't want to disappoint him now. And, now was as good a time as any to entreat, she decided.

"Monsieur Lafitte. I have a favor to beg of you and if you will permit—as they say in France . . . I shall get on with it." Her tone was all sweet politeness, but inside she felt turmoil.

Merrily Lafitte's eyes twinkled. "Everyone here does, my dear," he returned cryptically. "But first, let us converse on more pleasantries for a time—*non?*" He reached up to his wide shoulder to lovingly stroke Marie's hand resting there.

With a touch of coquetry in her eyes, Angel took up the repartee swiftly. "Monsieur, you appear to be a Gascon with the blood of the Spanish Moors in your veins—*n'est-ce pas?*"

115

Lafitte's dark eyes flashed. "Parisian, my dear. I have often thought my countenance to be just as you say, and I must give you credit for possessing such intelligent observation. Do not think I am offended. To the contrary, I am rather pleased. Now . . . you too, have French ancestors, do you not?"

Tyrone shifted and leaned forward, wondering at Lafitte's game. He was very surprised and at the same time enkindled by what he heard next. It gave new life to this play of witticisms.

"Why, yes. But how did you guess, monsieur?" Angel breathed incredulously. She sat cautious now, though.

His chance had arrived sooner than expected, Lafitte thought. He was rather pleased at his guesswork, and before she could think on it further, he rapped out, "Your name, of course—the first one."

Jean Lafitte would never know how close he had come to the very truth, Angeline was to think later.

"My name . . . ?" Angel said now, dumbfounded.

Everyone present leaned forward expectantly.

Suddenly Angel wagged her finger sharply at Lafitte. "Ahhh, no, monsieur. Not that. I shall remain nameless while here."

As did everyone else, Lafitte sighed deeply, with disappointment. "You have beat me at my own game, *ma petite*. As quick with the sword—I've heard—as you are with your mind. Charm, beauty, wit, and daring. You possess them all. *Certainment*, you are a treasure, some lucky man's destiny."

Tyrone's brown fingers played across the table, rapping and tapping thoughtfully as the fair-haired one inclined her head graciously to Lafitte, a blush developing across her cheek-bones. There was something menacing in his manner as he sat trying to analyze her. She looked his way and their eyes locked as they regarded each other for a time. She felt hypnotized. He grew more handsome in her eyes each and every time she saw him—if that was possible.

Glasses continued to clink and gray smoke swirled all about from the tobacco the men used. Tyrone began conversing with an ugly-looking man whom Angel had heard addressed earlier as Nez Coupé. His appearance was not unlike that of a bulbous crab and his nose was only half there, giving her to believe that his opponent's sword had been quick. She shuddered, thinking how the other must have met his bloody fate while this one yet lived to tell the tale with his gruesome face.

Suddenly Marie clapped her beringed hands, commanding the attention of the room. "Let's play cards, my friends." She sat next to Angel. "You do not mind if we continue where the fellows left off, do you," she stated, rather than asked.

"You . . . you play cards?" Angel asked Marie, her eyes wide in astonishment at a woman's joining men in such play.

"But of course, and as usual, Monsieur Ty has been taking the winning hands tonight." Marie sent him a bold wink down the table, smiling secretively.

"You are running with Lady Luck again, Ty," Pearce said, quaffing his ale. "But say, are you willing to play for higher stakes now?"

"It depends on what they are," said Tyrone, blowing a puff of smoke above Pearce's head.

The men, peering back and forth between those foes, settled themselves more comfortably, as did Lafitte, to watch the coming action. Pearce half-shut his dark eyes, regarding the girl and then Tyrone. Leaning over to speak to Pearce in French-Creole, Tyrone's voice was rich and deep with this patois. Pearce nodded in answer to the question put to him as Tyrone, a hint of amusement in his hazel eyes, sensed the young woman's curiosity but kept his gaze steadily on Pearce.

"Perhaps then, Pearce, that delicate timepiece of yours I've often glimpsed?"

"*Oui*, Ty. The timepiece against the beautiful captive," Pearce returned with a fixed stare upon the one mentioned.

"Done," Tyrone said, snapping his lean fingers, at which signal a deck of cards appeared from Nikki.

Realization dawned upon Angel and she shot up out of her chair. "You wouldn't dare!" she shrieked. "Ohh, I have never been so humiliated. Let me out of here immediately, you bloody fools! I'll not be subject to your fun and games evermore!"

"You'll be anything I say, girl," Tyrone growled down to her. "Be seated and shut up or I'll have to paddle your fluffy butt in front of these gentlemen!"

117

Angel gasped. "You snake! I say not!"

The smuggler's chair scraped noisily as he stood looming dangerous, sure to mete out the punishment aforesaid. Angel held out a hand to stay him, supplication in her misty eyes along with sore regret for her words and actions. He nodded an infinitesimal degree, and she picked up her skirts with a twist of her wrist, and retreated to a safe corner to fume. Tyrone then sat to carry on with the game.

Angel's eyes were awash with hot, unshed tears as she lowered herself hesitantly, then dejectedly, onto a silk-cushioned chair, languidly half listening as cards were shuffled, flicked, and then played. Time registered slowly on the face of a tall clock ticking ominously loudly, seeming to foretell doom, in the midst of murmurs, shifting weight, and shuffling boots. Deepening gray smoke swirled, threatening to choke her. Marie, noticing her distress, crossed to the great french doors to push them wide enough to allow soft breezes to drift in off the Gulf.

Half-dazed, Angel noticed that Pearce Duschesne was breaking out in dots of perspiration, lighting up one black cigano after another, chewing more than smoking them, while Tyrone remained coolly unaffected. He was as relaxed as if he lounged bored in a box at the theater.

I hate you, I hate you . . . I hate you! Angel screamed inwardly at him. How could she have thought this horrible smuggler who'd brought her here handsome? He was ugly and sinful. He seemed to be keeping her from having a chance to speak with Lafitte. He didn't care if she just sat here and rotted, either!

Now the last hand was being played. Soon the game flicked to an end and Tyrone merely chuckled low when Pearce surrendered the timepiece, sliding it reluctantly across the table to him. Pearce's dark eyes registered cold resentfulness, as they fixed on that composed figure smoothly snatching up the watch. With one easy gesture it was tucked away in Ty's breeches' pocket.

Pearce steamed. "The timepiece should go very well with all your English spoils. So . . . does Lafitte know the tub was not

118

Spanish?" He shot a glimpse in the direction of the master of Barataria, but Lafitte only shrugged noncommittingly, unbothered by this last bit.

"Hmmm," Tyrone began, and went on mordantly, "I take it that you refer to the last tub captured—namely one *Fidelia*—and that unfortunate captain who saw fit to emblazon a Spanish banner upon her mast?" He halted here, wondering about that himself. Then, "Now, at the risk of seeming unpatriotic, I must say that even the British sail ships more seaworthy of their name, not lopsided leakers bearing Latin scrawls on her bow. Tsk, tsk, Pearce, you yourself knew she carried a bounty of slaves and a few ladies of unquestionable virtue. You even got a piece of each of those, heard tell." He snorted through his long, straight nose. "The *Fidelia* masked her illicit traffic by taking on passengers with little purse, or, as in most cases—people in a hurry to get to America, being unable to wait for more suitable accommodations. Nevertheless, she is no longer navigable . . . not from where she lies."

"No, I suppose not," Pearce answered bitterly. "Heard tell you were just waiting for her to sail into your hands. You lift your eyebrows? Why—even Blade knew about the banner, not to mention Big Jim, your—"

"*Merde!*" bellowed Cut Nose at Pearce's faux pas.

"Yeah, shit!" echoed Nikki, at once sorry, forgetting that ladies were present.

Boots scraped suddenly and Nikki wagged a warning finger at Pearce.

Tyrone stiffened, glimpsed the younger woman from the corner of his eye. He was puzzled. Big Jim knew about the flag? Why . . . that was incredible. But, was it indeed? Big Jim had stated that the cargo was precious—another mystery. And why was Big Jim consorting with those he felt were beneath him—the smugglers of the Gulf.

Now Lafitte did perk up, and making a church steeple with his fingers, he said, "Then that settles it—ah—this Big Jim is welcome here anytime."

"The day is becoming far spent, monsieur," Tyrone said all at once. "Shall we now hear what it is Mademoiselle Sherwood desires. She seems very downcast and eager to be back with her mama." His eyes went back to her like two fierce arrows; his voice was mocking.

At this point, Angel felt a cold twist in her breast, fear compelling her to remain silent and wait. Her hands shook, feeling bloodless. Now—the joy of knowing they could go home, or, the deathblow.

"Ah, I almost forgot your request, *ma petite*. Forgive me." Lafitte cleared his throat. "This business is wretched at times, I am sorry. You see, I know what it is you want, and I would personally be willing to release you. That is . . . if you were my captive. But, this matter is entirely out of my hands. Again, I am sorry." Lafitte rose to plant a warm kiss on the bloodless hand.

Now Angel peered up at him after he'd released her hand. Her eyes snapped forcefully. "That's it?" she almost choked out.

Lafitte nodded slowly, definitely. Then he smiled gently. "Now, *petite* mademoiselle, if you will excuse me I must go see what goods Dominique has brought me. Marie will remain for as long as you wish, if you want. Until you return to your cottage. You would like to go there soon—no?"

"Monsieur, you mean my prison, don't you?" Angel snapped, without thinking there could be dire consequences to follow.

Jean lazed against the door frame, casually lighting a black cigano before striding out the door. "Later, *mes amis*," he called back over his shoulder. "And mademoiselle . . . it has been a pleasure."

Pleasure . . . Oh! Angel had the greatest desire to scream at his lithe, retreating form, and take back every nice thing she'd thought about him. He was no better than the rest of these here—bloody buccaneers all! One and the same, these glutting French comrades, and not worth a damn farthing. And then there were Thelma and Bron who had befriended her and Christine. Had they lied to her, too?

Angel turned on Marie, not bothering to address her. "What is this all about? Has everyone only been plumping me up for the kill? Up to now I had the impression we were to be released." Her voice rose to a shrill. "You told me I would get what I wanted!"

Consequently everyone just ignored her, even Duschesne. Then Marie leaned over to pat her hand consolingly.

"Do not excite yourself so, *cherie*, sh-hh, I meant what I said. You will get what you want soon—do not forget my words. Now . . . enjoy. Have more wine and soon—"

Her last words were clipped short as Caspar suddenly leapt through the open doors, bringing the chipper affair to an abrupt end. His eyes were almost bugging out of his huge head and his meaty arms were full of threatening firearms, and Tyrone's cutlass.

"Trouble in the bay, lads," Caspar began urgently. "Think some slaves escaped. About nine men of color are heading out in the direction of the *Annette*, cap'n." He began to pass out the weapons and lancewood whips swiftly.

At the very same moment that Caspar finished his short speech, Tyrone overturned his chair and made a wild snatch to recover his weapons after fastening on a wide leather belt over his black breeches. Angel noticed belatedly that this had been the first time she had seen him weaponless, but not for long.

"Caspar, take the young woman back to her cottage. Come to the water's edge then—and post haste!" Tyrone bellowed, shivering the timbers.

With threats and crusty curses Tyrone and the others flooded out the doors, mixing Creole and American English together as if it were a potage. Tyrone shot back around the door to give Angel a thorough going over with his wild eyes. It was a hasty glimpse, but it said so much, at least to the sensuous and knowing Marie. Then he was gone.

Marie sighed as she lead Angel to the hall that would take them to the front entrance. "He has such eyes for you, *petite*," she sighed again over her shoulder. "You are lucky, for such passion I have never seen. You are a prize for Ty, and if you are sweet with him he will follow you like a lovesick puppy. I know." Then she lowered her voice for only Angel to hear. "No matter what anyone else says, *cherie*, what I have said

121

is true."

Angel shuddered at the thought of that tall beast tagging at her heels the rest of her life. He was a smuggler and this would be the last place on earth she would make her home. Furthermore, marriage was not in his mind, nor was living the life of a mistress in hers. Oh! Perish the thought of either one of them!

Angel paused at the door. "Marie, please speak to Lafitte. I—there must be something he can—" She listened, hearing bloodcurdling screams shiver across the bay. "Oh, do you think they will be hurt?" Her words had come too hastily.

Marie's laugh was husky. "No, no. Never. This is not unusual here on Grande Terre. Ahh, you worry for Monsieur Ty?"

Angel gave a sigh of exasperation, but before she could reply Caspar nudged her elbow impatiently. She left Marie with a tight smile and then stepped out into the island moonlight with Caspar close behind. All was silent now from the bay. All she heard was the sound of the wind among the thickets and oleanders. The nocturnal creatures chirped in her head—the "bargain" had been forgotten. So Angel thought.

A day passed, then a second. On the third day after their coming, Angel woke to the morning star twinkling in her window. Afterward an early morning haze possessively shrouded the island, and by noon the sun had burned away the mist, which surrendered to a heady sparkle in the air. Angel strolled idly in this sparkling atmosphere as she created a bouquet out of the rainbow wildflowers that grew in gay profusion all around the cottage. She added an orange blossom or two, never ranging far out of sight of the cottage. For there was that man, bloody homely, like something monstrous from out of the boggy swamp. His long, kinky beard was braided into pigtails that looped around his big ears, meeting a dirty red kerchief bobbed off to one side. An apropos black patch concealed one eye, the other followed Angel and Christine wherever they went. Angel could have sworn he was Blackbeard incarnate.

This man was none other—Angel learned from Thelma—than Rollo, and he was, as Angel named him, Terrible Rollo the Gaoler. Bodyguard. His presence promised lack of freedom day in and day out, except, of course, for a few moment's privacy behind the bushes for nature's calling.

"When does he take his rest and sup I wonder," Angel sighed resentfully, as she said this to Christine that morning. There was just no chance whatsoever to discover where Samuel was kept, much less to make a getaway, with this huge man just outside standing sentinel. She had this feeling, though, that Sam wasn't with the other slaves. He was somewhere off by himself, but still on the island.

And Tyrone had only stopped by once that she knew of to ask how the ladies were faring, greeting Rollo affectionately as "bonnie lad." Inside, she had heard him arrive, converse idly with Rollo, and then he was gone, whistling a bawdy ballad whose words by now were well-known to her. She blushed now again in remembrance of the second lewd verse.

Low spirits reigned as Angel thought increasingly of her native heath, and the hours hung heavy. Christine was now habitually crooning in a low tone, and was more silent than talkative when Angel tried to communicate with her. On that second day, Dr. Laporte, who was also Lafitte's bookkeeper, had spoken to Angel of Christine's condition, if it could be called that, he had qualified.

"There's nothing to fear, Mademoiselle Sherwood," Laporte had said with a friendly smile. He was a small, dark man, his eyes soft and warm, his total appearance seemly. No one could mistake him for a smuggler or a pirate, she thought.

"No particular kind of illness," he went on. "I would not make anything worrisome of this silence you speak of. She's had some misfortune befall her of late?" he asked in a few breaths, very businesslike.

Angel decided not to go into detail. "My father met his death not long ago, sir. She has been this way since."

Laporte had listened while she had spoken softly, forlornly, silver-hued strands of hair lifting from her shoulders in a short-lived breeze where they stood just outside the cottage.

This doctor-bookkeeper had never witnessed such pale beauty.

"I am sorry," he returned. "Time will be the greatest healer in this. It is temporary, but do not be overly anxious if it lasts six months, even a year. She has many ripe years left in her." He paused, then looked at her fixedly. "Perhaps a grandchild would help. They are such good medicine for the middle-aged and the elderly. If there was to be one in the near future?"

"Ohhh-nooo, doctor. There is no chance of that happy homey event occurring. That is quite out of the question, and especially in the near future. You see, I am not married nor do I intend to be soon. It might seem selfish in your eyes, but I have never given marriage much thought. At least, there is no possibility of ever meeting a likely mate here, to be sure."

Laporte smiled mysteriously. "Do not be too sure, mademoiselle, you may have already met him. Good day."

"Bah!" Angel blurted when Octave Laporte was well away, his form seeming to waver bluishly in the tropical heat as he blended into sand and sky. Then whirling, she almost bumped into Rollo as she tore into the cottage, slammed the door and leaned up against its roughness.

That had been yesterday. Now, blinking away the dimness as she entered the cottage with her fragrant and colorful bouquet, Angel was hoping to cheer Christine up somewhat. Her mother sat in her usual place by the oaken chest, staring as if she found something of interest in the rusty brass knuckles and the cracked leather straps.

"Mama, do you like what I have brought you?" Angel asked as she wiped an old dusty wine bottle with the hem of her frock, the flowers arranged prettily in it.

Christine was busy contemplating the calico frock her daughter wore. Angel had only one other besides this one, for she had returned the green gown to Marie, saying she had no need for it. Still, Christine had thought the gown beautiful on her daughter. Suddenly Christine smiled her pleasure at the gay centerpiece.

"Lovely, like you, daughter. You remembered how much I love flowers, didn't you?"

"Yes, Mama, and look," Angel exclaimed softly. "Never

124

before have I seen such a delicate pale purple shade, and these creamy little bells! Mmmm, aren't they precious?" She breathed deeply, tickling her nose in the center of the spray.

"Angel, love. Do you suppose that I could go visit Thelma now? I find it such a pleasure to play with the babes, bounce them on my knee." She made a motion as if she was doing just that.

Angel felt faint tingles of shock pass through her body. Buccaneers. Lovers. Babies. Oh! Was there no end to the romance? Even Christine was infected by it if she found babies a pleasure at her age. She recovered swiftly then. Well—why not? Angel asked herself. The doctor had prescribed babies as good medicine.

"Of course, Mama, you go. But tell Rollo the Terrible where you are bound so as not to arouse suspicion and have him following you. I'll tidy up while you have your visit. Tell Thelma I will come to help before the evening meal," Angel said, thinking how wrong she'd been in thinking them her enemies.

After Christine had gone her way, Angel looped and pinned her hair into a knot and set about her task, sweeping again with the sparse broom, shaking out the linens and hanging out the rough blankets to air on a leafy bower. She even persuaded numbskull Rollo to go fetch her a bucket and brush from Thelma's cottage, so that she could scrub the dusty boards. She had to keep busy. She waited. Thelma's and Bron's cottage was only a few hundred yards away, but hidden from view of her own cottage. More time passed, and she wondered what was keeping him. Perhaps the heat had caused him to linger over a jar of fruit-water, or, more likely, a jug of ale.

Angel began to tremble suddenly. Now! Now! Her chance had arrived. She was prepared to take the risk and find Samuel. The excitement in her veins was heady, making her shiver from head to toe. Galvanized, Angel heaved herself out into the bright sunlit patch, paused to peer around, then darted behind the bole of a shady oak. Her feet felt clumsy in her eagerness to flee and she lifted them with great effort, and as if in a dream. Soon she was panting hard but she was moving faster now through the low brush, heart hammering in her breast. Here and there she halted, leaned against a tree while trying to catch her breath, her cheeks a frantic red. She kept out of sight as she thrashed through the underbrush where bracken snagged at her skirts. High overhead gulls cried, startling her, but she knew she was nearing the stockade so she kept swift pace.

A few more yards and she stopped to part the leafy bower where it met sand and—and—something else. Her darting eyes picked up the scene before her and she swiftly shut the greenery to merely peep through some fronds. She realized that she had gasped and she bit her lip to keep from doing so again.

She now saw Tyrone looming ominously over a black figure that now lay face down and motionless in the sand. A puff of that sand was still blowing all around, telling of the fierce action that had just taken place. Samuel! She just knew it! She had seen the terrified but defiant face as he tried to run, was caught whiplash-quick and tossed bodily to the sand.

"You tried killing me, you black bastard!" Tyrone growled down to Samuel. Tyrone had distinctly seen the flash of blade held high under the sun's glare and felt the stealthy steps behind him. The dirk was now gripped tightly in his own hand, wrested from Samuel only moments before.

His feet planted firmly apart in the sand as he held himself in check, Tyrone continued to glare down upon his attacker. The young black had disobeyed orders time and again by outfoxing the guards and sauntering out of the stockade as big as you please. Tyrone had thought it clever of the lad the first few times, but now his brow continued to darken. He had a pretty good idea of what had prompted the lad to act so harshly. Samuel must have learned of his decision to hold the Sherwood women. The great dirk was familiar to him as he turned it over in his hand, studying the hilt. He couldn't be sure, but it just might be that Duschesne was at the bottom of this lad's actions.

At last, Caspar came puffing down the beach, his breathing ragged and dissonant. He peered closely at the captain and then at the frizzy head face down in the sand. Frowning, Caspar cast his gaze about the island and finally back to Tyrone.

"Humph! Rollo is out searching for the English wench. She left the cottage about an hour back. But, what goes here, cap'n?"

"Rollo?—What?" Tyrone snapped furiously, a second later whirling, his mouth slitted as he whistled shrilly through bared teeth, searching for the hound with his eagle-eyed vision.

Shortly Nikki and Noble, the hound, came running, six lean limbs stretching apace over the sand, sliding to a halt just in front of Samuel's head. Noble growled a warning, even though Samuel hadn't moved a muscle. Nikki did a repeat of Caspar's earlier puzzled actions.

"The English girl has escaped!" Nikki blasted after realization dawned that something other than what he saw here was amiss.

"No . . ." Tyrone expired with sarcasm as his voice fell a note. Then, "Caspar, take this savage to the barracoon. I see nothing left to do but have him shackled, give him bread and water only, until I decide what to do with him next." Suddenly he sensed something and stiffened, peering around. "Hmm, perhaps I'll just slit his black throat," he said loudly, "for I detect a conspiracy here." He heard a muffled gasp as he caressed the blue edge of his cutlass. He nodded his head slowly. "Take him away!" he ordered.

Tyrone backed up toward the gnarled trunk of a dwarfed oak tree, slowly, watching the others go. He began his whistling, waiting with arms akimbo as he alternately shined up his jackboots at the back of his breeches' knees. Noble cocked his head at his master's odd behavior.

"Ty—Tyrone?" the voice was tiny, hesitating.

"The very same," he answered the hidden voice nonchalantly.

"You knew bloody well I was here all the time!" the reply called from the brush.

"Almost," Tyrone said, and he quoted:

> "Some there be that shadows kiss;
> Such have but a shadow's bliss."

"What was that?" came the reply.

"Get your fluffy rump out here, girl!"

Gingerly she stepped out, shielding her eyes from the sun's sudden glare. "Y—you would bargain with me now, sir?" the last word was shivered out of her mouth.

"Ahh-hhh," Tyrone smiled into her eyes. "You do fear for your dark *confrère*. Still, this nasty act of his shouldn't go without some form of strict punishment." He rubbed his beard thoughtfully, pulling it into a dark curl. Her dewy eyes flirted shyly and he cleared his throat. "Then again—umm—I just might consider a slowly given kiss, a caress or two—" Here he splayed his big hands wide. "All for the lad's safety, omitting comfort for a time, of course, *cherie*. Here, let's go the way you have come, into the shadows, hmm?" Then to Noble, "Go to Nikki, boy!"

He watched the hound gallop away, and taking the small, cold hand, led her under spreading branches into a dense grove of live oak bearded with silvery Spanish moss. The sun filtered between trunks leaning away from the sea as it bounced down around where they stood surrounded completely by these gnarled woody figures. It was slightly cooler in this tropical wood where vernal green, rich browns, and deep orchids and pinks were all laced with the sun's softest kiss.

Immediately the smuggler encircled the young woman against him, lowering his head as he lambently kissed her flushed cheeks, lingering next on her pink rosebud lips. She kept perfectly still, though her pulses beat wildly and her shy protests were muffled within his mouth. His tongue wriggled between tiny teeth and her mouth was spread. Her stiffly sore muscles began to loosen and she relaxed unconsciously against him, her belly welded to the alien, hot, swelling fork of him. He swiftly and expertly undid the ties of her bodice and caressed the deliciously aching melons veiled only by the thin chemisette. He groaned his need for a woman and he wanted to know her. He shivered.

"Oh! No! No! What are you doing!" Angel cried out as her worst nightmares became horrible reality. He was becoming peculiarly ungentle with his hands, and his lips were sliding hotly down her throat. "Stop! Oh, stop this now!" She tried kicking out at him but her skirts were pinned between his legs.

Tyrone dropped his hands roughly behind her, sliding them down her stiffly held back as he drew her closer still, pinching her buttocks through her skirts. He snorted into her face, then pushed her roughly from him. He stared hard, almost hatefully.

"Green-eyed witch! Were you perhaps planning to have Samuel do me in? Then you three could escape—so you thought? And Pearce, what part does he play in this? Did he promise to cart you to New Orleans, then away to London merrily? Is that what you two schemed on my ship?" He didn't wait for answers but went on harshly, "Do you know what I've been up to these past days?"

"No, and how could I possibly? And I don't care to know, smuggler!"

"Well, I'll tell you anyway, my bittersweet vixen. Delving, that's what. It seems that Pearce has taken you under his dark wing. Don't tell me you had no knowledge of this. Ellen likes to know all, tell all. All gossiping whores do. In short, she listened in on your conversation with Pearce. The gathering on my ship, your birthday—recall?"

Angel had hesitated a moment, the telling moment, for she had given herself away and the look was one of a child caught with a dirty dress and mud-stained face. Her forehead puckered with a frown.

"Why not! What do you take me for—a senseless ninny? Or, a first-rate strumpet to sing joyful praises at being fondled? Blast it! All I want is to go home, back to England where there are no randy buck pirates that would try raping me at every turn. And Samuel—what he did was not planned by me, though I cannot blame the poor terrified lad for his deed here today. Can you blame him for hating you?—No, you cannot. I sought him out merely to—to—"

"To what!" Tyrone said pitilessly.

"How can you continue to hold us captive? You—you have no right!"

He smiled sardonically. "I can, and will continue to. My own

129

father has great influence in the city's governmental circles, so—"

"How nice for him. How nice for you, his infamous son!"

"Damnit! Let me finish," he growled after her interruption. "Needless to say again, my father takes care of his own. He is a big man in Governor Claiborne's book, as he is also a member of the Louisiana bar. If you are thinking to have me tossed into the calaboose, you should really think twice, my dear. As I've said before, the authorities have little time for a damsel in distress. Looking the way you do, if you but dare approach Claiborne in his study you may very well get hauled out with the dirty laundry."

That hit a sore spot in her. "Just what do you really want from me, smuggler Ty?" she asked wearily.

He affected the pose of a London fop, bent a knee and laid a finger along his nose as he said airily, "I hadn't considered it overly much just yet, my dear. But I shall, I shall. Until I decide, I shall keep you around—"

"Ooooh! Like bloody hell you will, you contemptible snake!"

Like summer lightning, Angel whirled and was thrashing through the bracken and brush before he even had time to realize she had fled his side. She heard him coming, springing just behind and groping madly at her skirts. A squeal cut loose from her as a gnarled stump jutted up from the ground in front of her, but she snatched up her skirts to nimbly clear it, thankful she hadn't lost any of her agility since her livelier days on the moors.

"Aha!" Tyrone exclaimed, pounding hard after her but failing to see the stump in his hot pursuit of her flying skirts.

Coming onto an orange grove, Angel exulted when she heard behind her a thud and a healthy *whoosh* of breath, followed by a bellow of pure rage; she smiled knowingly. How long it would take him to recover she couldn't know, but she was free now to run and she traveled like the wind on low foot, tearing her skirts free of dagger plant. She giggled upon hearing Tyrone's foul curses follow her, seeming to shiver the dark green, polished leaves of the trees.

130

She was moving well past the stockade, an indication that she was heading north and the swampland would be just beyond the vast blue lake. But how to cross it, and what if there wasn't an empty boat available to see her across? She ran until her lower limbs began to ache horribly. The calico, a faded indigo, began to stain again in her armpits and sweat trickled down between her breasts and slid down to her belly. Her speeding eye swept the wide swath of beige sand before her, searching for signs of a small fishing boat. Darting lacewings filled her vision as they hovered to glimpse the intruder then quirked away to be lost in the white radiance of sun and sand.

There it was! Two fishermen were just leaving their boat, smiling happily at the day's catch of dripping redfish and sea trout that streamed out behind them as they sauntered up the beach and disappeared around the peninsula.

Could she already hear the shouts of Tyrone's Nimrods in quest of her fleeing form as she paddled toward the blur that loomed ahead like a hazy nimbus? She shivered as she labored with the oars, wondering if she should lay up her plans—her sudden plans—to go north, follow the winding river to New Orleans and beseech this Claiborne to return for Christine and Samuel. But, what if! What if no one listened to her and what if what Tyrone spoke was gospel truth?

Desperately she paddled for what seemed ages and her arms ached horribly, until the boat bumped into a harder mass of grasses. Leaping out, and with all the physical strength she could muster, she pushed and heaved the boat to hide it in the house-high canebreaks, her flushed face distorted with the effort. She swayed, muddy and wet, for a long moment before climbing onto the unending plain of blue-green swaying grasses and winding streams and reedy marshland. Where did land and sky meet, she began to wonder, in this mystifying labyrinth?

An angry hiss pierced this new, eerie silence. She whirled to see a large monster with a long flat head and thick lumpy skin as it slithered below her with a horrendous toothy grin. Angel recalled the name—"alligator." She did shiver now, for only moments before she had stood in that same spot

131

in the shallows.

Only minutes had passed since she had reached the swamp, and full of eagerness, not discounting fear, she whipped herself into action and made her way through the great live oaks. Moss-draped, they arched huge branches over her, often completely shutting her off from the hot sun. These same towering stalactites saw themselves in the widening, serpentine watercourse she followed. Here and there the emerald water was dotted with lavender water hyacinths riding atop large green leaves almost a half-inch thick. Willows swept the water gracefully, and long-needled pines grew stately around her.

As Angel traveled at a more leisurely pace she felt she was in a green and blue world, swept apart from any she had ever beheld, and as all alone as Eve must have been in the beginning of creation when Adam was not at her side. She began to feel the swamp's inevitable dangers, the dangers Thelma and Tyrone had warned her of. She harkened to strange cries now and wondered shudderingly what marsh-creature she would encounter next as the sun climbed outside this boggy world to its zenith, causing haunting vapors to rise from the waterside.

"How far to this city on the river?" Angel whispered to the watery wilds, slapping off mosquitoes that had, along with gnats, learned of her presence, smelled her rich young blood.

Great blue birds with long necks associated with a relative of their kind—a great white bird with graceful, long plumage; they soared lazily along the bayous or loafed in the branches till she drew near, then flew off, but stayed ever nearby the lovely golden girl.

Angel came upon a maze of watery bayous, each of which twisted into a separate route, those water hyacinths blanketing the surface thickly here. Her fear of being lost increased when she realized she shouldn't have left the boat. Lord, she didn't even know the way back to it now. How stupid of her to have come by foot!

"Which route will take me to New Orleans?" she asked herself as she slumped against a huge live oak, feeling hunger gnaw at her belly. She wished now that she had snatched a few oranges to munch along the way and give her energy.

132

She was totally exhausted, famished, hot, and sought succor in the cool marsh grasses, moving languidly from the bole to doze in the lush, reedy green blades. Damp hair curled about moist pink cheeks in rich honey-spun ribbons while she dared to dream. . . .

A slip of the Foot you may soon recover,
But a slip of the Tongue you may never get over.
                                        —Franklin

Chapter Four

1

A hot siren song blew over dark sand. Shimmering silver
gulls wheeled over oyster-gray mounds. Silhouette-black
stallions stretched silken tendons, manes blowing black,
emerging through a blue mist with powerful stride. The dark
creatures were sucked up into an eerie foaming mist, a
princelike being appeared, foreboding, silken strands lifting
from bronze muscled shoulders, a gentle stirring in a soft,
sweet breeze laced with orange blossoms. Emerging liquid, he
strode forward steadily, broodingly, shimmering, borne from a
deep blue sea, uttering a strange patois across stretches of
metallic black sand. Wet and glistening the male beckoned; she
went, trembling. Eyes limpid pools, his brown fingers reached
out to mark her naked, quivering flesh, soothing, parting, now
withdrawing in a growing burn. Swimming in a sea of passion,
crying, curious, her young soul cried knowledge of his sleek,
silken flesh. Watery reflections of two entwined rippled, his
beautiful form dissolved; a bawdy poem was left her, her
breasts aching painfully, thighs sprawled, wanting to know.

Angel moaned, desiring the tall prince back. Eyes fluttering
open, she stifled a scream into the moist grass. She was a
confused mixture of fear and languid warmth. She knew this
prince of her dreams who had awakened her to his
lovemaking, then quit to leave her panting for an end she was
ignorant of. Wide awake now, the fulsomeness of the dream
left her shaking, angry that it had been he. Always he! No
prince but a beast!

"You cannot get me now, Captain Ty!" she chanted in a
singsong voice, stopped. A rustling in the shadows of dark

green and then . . . quiet.

She crouched on all fours like a hunted fox, eyes darting all around. She shivered, for her situation was not all that humorous. What would it be like when darkness came creeping over the swampland? Could she keep on? Should she try to find her way back?

She stood and as she walked, a wispy chain of the dream swirled in her brain. "Desire—Bah!" she said out loud, emboldening herself to trudge onward, choosing a branch of the river that the sun had begun to slant upon. North—to New Orleans, Thelma had mentioned offhandedly.

Later Angel realized she was trudging back to the exact spot she'd set out from much earlier. It couldn't be, and yet, the maze before her did just that—crossed and recrossed. She tried again, marking the spot this time. Again later, she agonized when returning to where a swatch of her torn chemise clung where she had secured it to a branch. She had made no progress, had been going in circles! She slumped down wearily upon a mossy log. With chin in hands she watched long, slippery fish shaped like snakes wriggle in the emerald water, causing little whirlpools to form. She saw herself in these eddies, wavering, becoming obscure—indeed!

She groaned, and how long she sat there she would never know. Lengthening misty gold streamers and gray-green shadows told her that soon she would suffer the Stygian night—eerie hisses, calls of swamp creatures, and the nocturnal swarm of bloodsucking insects.

"Lost! I am lost!" Fear nibbled at the core of her being. She shut her eyes tight, prayed that this was but a nightmare she would soon awaken from, find herself back in the safety of her bedchamber at Stonewall, garmented in her chiffon and finery.

Opening her eyes, Angel saw no flowery papered walls and downy bed, only felt herself helplessly vulnerable in this wild and treacherous marsh, sacrificed like a lamb led to slaughter. She did not welcome death yet. How could she? She was young, healthy, and there was so much of life yet undiscovered. . . .

She could almost see the hairy beast come to devour her tender heart now. It moved stealthily, gliding through the drifting swamp fog—No! It was a small boat and two men.

Indeed, they were ugly beasts of men floating eerily toward where she stood frozen with fear.

"Oh, God, no . . ." she breathed, recalling Ty's warning of criminals and half-insane runaways.

With a torrent of imprecations preceding him into the cottage, Tyrone all but ripped the door from its new jamb and leather hinge. He stood ominously tall as he raked with his eagle-eyes every corner for evidence, a clue as to where she might have gone. In his hand he clutched a red kerchief as he took in the domestic neatness of the place, spying the unused bucket and brush where Rollo had left them hastily after discovering the girl's absence. A delicate floral arrangement seemed to mock him with its sweet scent and bowing bells of pinkish-white dogtooth violets. He whirled darkly to Rollo then rubbed his sore knee where he had only just now bumped it again in his haste to be off searching.

"Where is her mother?" Ty asked callously.

Rollo tottered on the threshold. He smelled of sour ale as he lifted a grubby hand and rumbled in his deep voice, "The mam's at Thelma's. The little one's nowhere and I been all over the village. So've you. Only un'other she coulda gone. Where de 'gators be!"

Padding paws accompanying an excited bark met Ty just outside the cottage as the hound pranced up to mouth his master's arm. Ty patted the hound hurriedly and tossed aside the red kerchief the girl had worn the day before. He had repeatedly held the kerchief up to Noble's long nose to sniff, but to no avail. Now Noble was on to something!

"Ahh, Noble, good boy!" Ty praised the hound, who had retrieved the kerchief and now jumped about with it clinging to fangs as he begged to be followed this time. Ty ordered Rollo, "Go find your pallet, sleep it off!"

Man and cur loped easily along the late afternoon pinkened sand after Ty had checked the strap on his leg which sported his lighter weapons securely. Noble led the way, then leaped into the turquoise water of the bay. Ty nodded in decision and proceeded to shove off in a skiff. Noble joined his master inside the half-shell of the sturdy skiff and together they made the windy journey across the lake. Some time later, Noble left the skiff to wade into the soft morass, snapping and barking at a yawning alligator.

Would he find the fair maid alive? Ty brooded, spying the lazy creature that appeared to be without appetite. He grimaced, and then he spied the carefully hidden fishing boat. How she ever had manipulated it was beyond him. She must have a lot of hidden strength. Still, how had she even gotten this far?

He prayed to find her unharmed. If he did, he wondered, should he rid himself of the responsibility of caring for both women and speed them back to England's shores? They must have loved ones waiting their return? Still, he had desired that fair one from their first meeting. Would she always hate him, never yield to him? He cursed his craving of her tender flesh and pressed on in a feverish state, entering the tract of swamp familiar to him.

Marsh wrens called to man and dog queerly as they perched on branches in the late afternoon beauty of the fenny tract. The melodious music preceded them in a northeasterly direction. The birds stopped to await them, then flew on ahead. Noble knew the feathered creatures' game and tracked them as he also sniffed the daintily beaten path.

"What d'we have here. Will ya look at that, Les? Where d'ya s'pose she come from? Gal, what a puss for me sore eyeballs. A pure angel with green witchy-eyes! Heh!"

The two scrambled from their boat, countenanced like brothers of the same beast, Angel thought wildly, casting about for an escape route. But they were already circling in on her and she almost keeled over from the odor of long-unwashed bodies they emitted. She gulped down hard the bile rising in her throat. She had been prepared to flee and hide in a hollow somewhere till morning, but now if she ran they would surely catch her. She could only stand, frozen in fear.

The one named Les put a huge boot forward. "Yeah, Mitch. A wild and pretty swamp-witch. A fancy-lookin' wench, too." He stopped then and, like a man struggling for breath, pushed his next words out. "Where ya goin', sweetheart? Mitch 'n me, we ain't had a piece of fluff in a long time now. Lookee what she got there, Mitch. Boobs as purrty as ripe li'l melons."

Angel watched in horror as he wiped the drool sliding down his bristly chin with the back of a grimy fist. The other one took a step forward to make a grab at her, then halted, startled, at the foreign ring of her voice.

"Do not touch me, bloody pigs!" she had screeched, backing up to a willow.

Suddenly they broke out in raucous laughter. Angel knew she was on the brink of becoming thoroughly devoured by these brutish animals who thought themselves men. Long ago but not forgotten days in the sunshine of her youth sprang up before her eyes—sweet memories—as to one about to die.

"I'll take her first," said Les, grabbing her around her tiny waist.

Angel felt his pistol and dagger press mercilessly into her soft thighs and her struggles became helplessly ineffective against this vagrant who almost made her retch from his fetid odors. Les kept her in check with his shaggy lobster arms and gazed greedily at her while pulling the remaining coil of hair loose. Angel's vision dimmed by tears as he buried his fingers in it and twisted. But she wouldn't give him the satisfaction of hearing her cry out in pain.

"Please, let me go. You will be paid very handsomely if you bring me to New Orleans unharmed," Angel said in a hollow voice between breaths.

While exchanging a wicked grin with Mitch, Les squeezed her arms, his ferret eyes excited and sickly yellow as he spat an arching stream of dark spittle among the flounces of greenery. He watched until the spittle fell, frowned at it, then squinted at his armful.

"Crazy wench!" Les said. "Not as han'somely as what we're gonna get now. I ain't that dumb, either. You must've escaped from Pir'it's Islands, didn't ya, puss!" Long, grimy nails squeezed her arm again.

Angel fashioned quickly, "Yes! Yes! Smugglers, they kidnapped me. There is quite a reward if you bring me to Governor Claiborne. He is a very good friend of my father's. We—we live north of New Orleans," she lied.

"Crap! Yer a for'ner little bitch, and if I take ya anywheres it'll be back to them pir'its for some rum and coin. Mitch and me is wanted in New Orleans, anyways. And we ain't bringing you nowheres fer a long time. C'mere now!"

Horrified, Angel watched as he began to unhitch his suspenders. She stepped back, stumbling on a root, but Mitch reached out swiftly to bind her hands behind her back with a leather thong. He stepped back a foot to regard the green eyes envenomed with disdainful loathing.

"Why'd you do that, Mitch?" Les asked from behind a tree. He stepped out, not bothering to button himself up.

"Want 'er to scratch out yer eyeballs? Lookit'er, she looks like a cat ready to hiss an' spit fire. She ain't all that scared, either."

"Yeah. Push her down, Mitch. I'm ready. Lookit this one I got."

Les proudly displayed his flesh while Angel swivelled her head aside, dreading that which they grunted appreciatively over. She felt faint, and whirls of the fog off the water seemed to drift into her brain. An ugly scene was drawn before her as they advanced, one grappling her to the moist earth. She bit and kicked until she was cuffed across both cheeks. Their grunting voices came from afar as she heard one curse the other for his stupidity, saying she wouldn't be any good to them knocked out cold. She felt that her end was near. Already she was sinking into a great void from which return seemed impossible. Tyrone's handsome face seemed to mock her with the other two above her. She was dreaming once more—wasn't she?

As their faces distorted above her, she felt them tie a filthy rag about her lower face. Next she felt her skirts pushed up further, the feel of flaccid flesh against her thighs, the odor of rotting teeth, but when something slimy and wet dripped onto her fondled breasts, nausea flared up in her and her skin prickled revoltingly.

Angel kicked the man swiftly to ward off his penetration. Les groaned in pain as his manhood shriveled momentarily. He was preparing to cuff the girl himself and then continue, when a bloodcurdling growl shivered through the vaporous

139

atmosphere. He jerked up into his breeches, expecting to see a wild beast frothing at the mouth as it came.

"What's that, Mitch. Didja hear it?"

"Yeah. Sounds like a gerilla."

"Dumb shit, ain't no apes round here!"

"There's black panthers, though," Mitch gulped, whipping out his pistol.

First a rustle as green leaves stirred, then the lower branches parted and a black image emerged. Les and Mitch peered as one, down into the golden eyes of a huge animal who growled and displayed his long white fangs. Mitch's pistol swiftly cocked, and then halted as a tall figure strode nonchalantly into the open while whistling a merry but lewd tune. Puzzled glances were exchanged between the two vagrants, but they couldn't detect any danger in this gay chap's manner.

"That yer dog, mister?" Mitch drawled, his pistol aimed at the intruder. It came to him suddenly that this tall lad was searching for the fair one.

"Indeed it is, *mes amis.* Come here, Noble. Naughty dog! I've been wondering what became of you," Ty said, his narrowed gaze sliding to the sight of long, cameo-complexioned limbs exposed, a cloud of honeyed hair framing a harried little face. "And what have you got there, lads?" he continued in a high-pitched voice laced with indifference.

They all regarded her now, still lying in the sensuous sprawl, unable to mutter, nor barely move. She shut her lids against the open ravishment to her helpless person; finally, and with great effort, she maneuvered herself back with her heels dug into the ground, thus covering her naked and tempting thighs partially.

"Ya mean ya don't know her?" Les asked in disbelief, beginning to think the intruder a bit fluffy in the head.

"To be sure, *amis,* if I had she would be warming me bunk this *verrry* minute. Never laid eyes on the lass before now, though me wish is that I had." He had to stifle a chuckle at their openmouthed surprise in the change of his voice.

But Angel, furious now, thumped the earth angrily with her heels. She spat at the rag that wouldn't budge, narrowing her eyes murderously at Ty. She really should be glad that he had found her and just in time. But why did he deny knowing her just now? she wondered.

Mitch was preoccupied. His eyes lit up as he studied the gem dangling from the young man's lobe. He regarded the man as a dumb smuggler, decidedly a cuckoo, and said, "Eyyy, bucko. How would'ja like to have some fun—heh-heh—a trade?"

A dark brow quirked as the smuggler tugged at his earring with a thumb and a lean, brown forefinger. He carefully watched the other vagrant with the ferret eyes likewise licking his thick lips at the sight of the gem.

Ty crowed. "Sure now. What will it be then, lads?"

Eyeing the tall man warily, Mitch returned, "Give us the gem in yer ear an' you kin have a piece of that fluff over there. She's good. Jest had her, an' she was a virgin, too."

With eyes cold as marble, Ty jerked his head around to study the young woman. The dying sun empurpled her form, making it hard to read her face, but a few frenzied movements told the tale.

"Well now, I just might consider your proposal, gentlemen," Ty said.

"Huh? Eh, good," drooled Mitch. "Gimmee the erring an' you kin have a turn. Les here is next an' then me—ah—agin." He smacked thick lips over the fun to come.

"First the girl then the earring," Ty said tersely. "Otherwise forget it, lads."

A look of chagrin crept into Mitch's face, then he acquiesced with a nod as he realized the smuggler was adamant in his decision. He was also beginning to think of the man as dangerous, even though no weapon was visible on his person.

"I would feel more at ease if you stowed the weapons, mates. What do you say?" Ty asked lazily.

"Ah no, bucko," Mitch murmured. "This way or no, an' you do as we says or I'll put a hole in that hound's head fer ya. Now, let's get on with it. Never seen another man take a woman 'cept Les here. Heh-heh," he slobbered.

Ty shrugged and nodded. As shadows began to darken the glade, he strode to his captive and stood peering down at her. She rolled her head from his warm surveillance and he slid his regard back to the ogres.

"If you lads could scoot back over by that willow I'd get on with it. If you stand there breathing down my neck I'll not be able to do myself or the girl justice," Ty said smoothly as she whimpered in outrage. "Be still, girl!" he commanded, watching the vagrants settle themselves comfortably beneath said willow. Both were a little miffed at the smuggler's command.

"Hey, Mitch, don't they make a purrty pair? Him so good-lookin' and her so sweet 'n curvy," Les drooled, rum sliding down his bristly chin.

Ty pulled at his beard. "Hmm, I've been thinking, mates. You say that you've already had her. Well now, a virgin untouched would be more to my liking. Especially since this priceless piece I wear is much to be treasured. Surely, no female is worth that much, without virginity intact?"

Les scrambled clumsily to his feet. "He told you she was good, she's as good as a virgin. Mitch barely got 'em off before you come. Hurry on, we gotta be back to our camp soon." He plopped back down.

"Then there are more of you?" Ty inquired.

"'Course there is, an' if you don't hurry they'll be lookin' fer us," Les lied, directing his pistol at the smuggler. "You'll lose yer fluff an' yer earring, too, bucko." Even though he had his gun trained on the other, Les suddenly had a feeling the smuggler didn't give a hoot if he lived or died. Those were the most dangerous kind, he had learned.

The twin pistols urged Ty to ease his long frame down upon the girl's shaking, splendid form. She moaned as if she suffered pain when he lay with one leg tucked in hers, leaning upon one elbow with his free hand roaming over soft curves tenderly. His hand left her hips to slide down and make a motion as if he undid his breeches.

"Sweet—" he whispered low in her ear, undoing her binds, "do not fight me now, respond to my lovemaking."

Angel whimpered, shook her head firmly in the negative.

"Listen," he tried gently. "There is not much time, for, as they said, others will soon arrive. They'll all take their turns on you. Put your arms around me and yield to me now, girl."

"Heyy, he untied her!" Les hollered, making to rise, but the other held him back fast.

"Let 'em be, Les! She can't do nothin' with that big lug on her." Mitch grunted, then pulled at length from the bottle, scratching his lower parts at the same time.

Angel's arms crept up to the nape of Tyrone's neck. She heard him loose a husky murmur and she closed her eyes to the immediate scene, not knowing just what to do or where to put her hands. Tyrone made up for her lack of movements and very expertly caused a warmth to spread through her at his intimate rovings, his gentle touches. His eyes found hers in the twilight, boring deeply while his lean fingers moved swiftly to free her breasts from their cloth binds. Next he slid the filthy rag below her lips and turned once to survey the men who were verging on drunkenness. He came back to her with a low, throaty chuckle that further bewildered her. Now her breasts were caught between his linen shirt that was open to the waist and she gasped at the contact of her naked flesh on the furred mat. He lowered his head to cover her mouth with his searing lips.

Tyrone gyrated his lower half for effect, but forgot everything else in the following passionate moments. The fever rose and became a scorching flame as he crushed her madly to him, felt the silken curves he had longed to know. He drank in the sweetness of this nameless female, desiring to possess her completely.

Angel thought she could hear the hum of bees in the moss that draped over them, then realized the buzzing was within her own brain. Her earlier dream became a reality as his lean fingers moved leisurely, and with skill. They burned where they touched. She awakened to passion's first great dawning as a vortex of pleasure opened up to engulf her and she moaned hotly and without shame against his twisting, scalding lips. His fingers moved down, were hard between her yielding thighs. Suddenly her eyes flew open in surprise.

There! Tyrone thought deliciously.

Only a quarter of an hour had passed since his arrival to this place and now he released his hold on her lips, grinned into her face like the devil himself. Like a conqueror obtaining victory over a long-awaited prize, his manner told her that he had won, had evoked a response in her maiden's breast, between her thighs. She surfaced fast from her own blushing desire, realized he had been having a grand time, sporting again and using her like a pawn in his crude ploy.

He has a weapon! she raged inwardly. She could now feel the metal pressing against her knee!

"Oh! You! You!" Angel rasped. "Those pigs have not touched me—you knew!"

Suddenly Ty was all ablur as he leapt to his feet in one fluid movement, and, before he spun about, shot down to her, "Absolutely, my sweet. I was aware of it all this time!"

"Wha—" the audience slurred in unison, reacting slowly in befuddlement. Unsteadily they rose to the oncoming battle, jostling each other and all but falling back upon their odious rumps.

On command Noble sprang through the air, expertly avoiding the leaden bee that whizzed past his ducking head. In the strange glow invading the glade, Tyrone seemed almost to be in flight, Angel thought, and her blood ran cold as together man and beast met their attackers with relish and glee. By dancing about, leaping and hollering like a crazed Indian, Ty forced the second vagrant to carelessly unload his pistol. Hurling himself downward, Ty grasped a thick leg of each man, pulling them in together against his chest, feeling them topple backward as, first one, then the other pistol rode through the air like birds taking flight. Noble spared no time offensive to sink his long fangs into the odious flesh of Mitch's posterior.

Ty's dirk flashed out. "Forearmed is forewarned!" he shouted loud and clear, obviously enjoying this sport immensely.

Angel rose unsteadily and stomped her foot. "Forearmed—indeed!" she mocked scornfully.

Angel gasped in the next instant as Les, too, unearthed a long, gleaming dagger and went directly for Ty's throat. But Ty was ever so swift in meeting the onslaught that had momentarily caught him off guard. These vagrants were by no means any babes when it came to dirty, informal brawling and butchering. Still, they lacked the experience of a Gulf smuggler, and the expertise of fluid momentum that Ty dispatched with ease. One jump and the vagrant was dashed to the earth, breathless, as Ty hovered above him, straddling the puffing form with his long legs. Suddenly dirks clashed, one fell away, and Ty's dagger point went into Les's shoulder, and lifted, bringing red blood on its tip. Next Ty made his target the man's throat.

"Tyrone! No!"

The feminine shriek rent the new stillness of the glade and Ty started at the intrusion. He splayed a heavy hand over the man's face to stay him as he casually turned about to see his captive standing close behind. The look begged him not to slay the man. Ty grinned in devilment, but then grew sober, angry that she should intrude. A chill bore down upon her at the feral gleam in his eyes before she spoke tentatively.

"Please. Can you not see that the man has had enough? They are terrified now and will never bother us again. Just let them go—please?"

Tyrone saw the wisdom in her supplication and eased himself up to face her, while the vagrants cowered beneath the hound that held them at bay. Ty snapped his fingers and Noble sat proudly with a good portion of Mitch's breeches hooked on his fangs. Mitch sprawled in an ungainly position and a pained expression twisted his face as he painfully rubbed his aching backside.

Ty vigilantly bent to tug up a legging, withdrawing a pistol bound by a leather strap. Under her narrowed gaze deviltry gleamed as he tucked the weapon into his leather sash.

"You had two weapons!" she cried. "These bad men never threatened you for one instant. Double bloody damn, smuggler, you could have gotten us both killed!"

Ignoring her heated remark, Ty motioned the bad men to be on their way, and a great scurrying ensued as they pitched about to obtain the empty pistols lost in the fight. Ty pointed his drawn pistol at them.

"No-o-o, me buckos. Be off without your weapons," he said, waving them into the brush. Ty chuckled as the damp grass showed the quick passage of the hastening vagrants.

"Dumb shit, you and yer big ideas!" drifted back.

Confiscating the boat too, Ty shoved it off now with his boot, after gesturing for the girl to climb in. The strange glow

145

that had lingered now brought a deathly silence as Ty paddled swiftly downstream. Shortly he glanced over his shoulder to see her straightening the calico with angry tugs. Grinning, Tyrone continued his paddling, leaving her to glare at his dark back. *Here it comes,* he thought.

"Blast you!" she did blurt at him. "You are quite bloody mad, you know?"

"Are those the only delicate oaths you know, girl?" he called back. "I could teach you a few less feeble you most likely never heard of. Seeing that you've failed to comport yourself like a lady ever since our first shipboard encounter, I'll soon be of a mind to employ you as one of my crew—breeches, oaths, and all that goes along with it." He paused thoughtfully. "Then again, a wee time ago I'd the impression that just maybe and instead of acting the hoyden, you were beginning to show signs of emotion as a normal woman would. Now I see I was badly mistaken."

Angel glared at his dark shape. "Bah! You are no more a gentleman, Tyrone, captain of the *Annette!* And, who is she, perhaps some painted doxie you named your bloody ship after?"

"Beginning this night—" he began, his eyes all dangerous glitter, " you will share my humble cottage with me. Not only that, you will become my mistress as well, I promise. After you are a bit shopworn, you will be released, and the only thing you will be good for then is a toss—a doxie!"

"All I want is to go home, back to Stonewall and Echo and all that I held dear before this nightmare began. I hate you with all my being," she ended softly.

Tyrone swore softly under his breath, stabbing at the stormy water as a crack of thunder shattered all around them after a flash of lightning.

"What did you say?" she tried screaming over the whistling wind.

"A storm!" he said ferociously. "Sit still or you'll overturn the boat!"

His last words were lost to her as the blanket of heat was blown away by a fierce wind that shivered and shrieked like a banshee. Under a thunderbolt the island up ahead was lit up suddenly like a stage set for a play: the actors were twisting palms and banana trees in the flashes of lightning, their wide leaves like huge arms glistening from the salt spray. By now, Angel was snuggled up to Tyrone and holding onto his back for dear life, lest she be blown overboard by the gales.

The torrential downpour was in full swing by the time they reached Grande Isle. Ty pulled his human puppet along relentlessly as the rain rattled the frail houses and beat down around and upon them. They were both thoroughly saturated by the time the barely visible cottage was reached. Angel was pushed inside as Ty heaved the door shut against the tropical storm, setting a sturdy chair under the wood bolt to keep the door snugly shut. The wood floors were already wet halfway into the room.

Tyrone moved to light a thick candle and soon the large room was cast into flickering light. He then busied himself at a small dresser, rummaging through a lower drawer. When he turned he drew in his breath, his attention directed to the likeness of a beauteous stone marvel with firmly molded breasts and long firm thighs and legs. Motionless, she resembled a work of art, a Greek statue in the rain, plastered cloth clinging to her, rivulets streaming from head to toe.

Catching his perusal, Angel whirled about to busy herself in removing her sodden slippers and then she silently examined the cottage. Moist breezes more like tiny squalls squeezed through the cracks of the wallboards, breathing about her ankles as she walked across a circular straw rug that prickled her bare wet feet. She took in the masculine articles neatly piled here and there, surprised to find no signs of the magnificent plunder that she had witnessed in the home of Jean Lafitte.

"She even moves like a goddess," Tyrone said under his breath.

"Did you say something? I thought—" she bit off, turning about to face him. A length of material was draped over one arm, a shorter linen in his hand.

"I said—remove that wet thing and put this on. Don't stand there gaping at me, girl. Take it. You are dripping all over my floor."

147

When she reached out a tentative hand to receive the items into her shaking hands, she was very conscious of those all-seeing eyes upon her. She looked down at a puddle. Thankfully just then a scratching at the door made him leave her abruptly. It was the hound and Tyrone let him in.

Angel was struggling with the plastered-down calico and only had it pulled up to her thighs when Tyrone turned his full attention back to her. Pushing and twisting the skirt back down she fled to the back of the room there to struggle again, but this time with the latch of a door. Maddeningly she heard him chuckle at the futility of her motions. The door was locked and she snorted, turning around to see him briskly rubbing his tawny hair dry with a linen.

"Yes, it is locked, my girl. Only a storeroom for my weapons, books, and paraphernalia. There would not be room for even a babe to disrobe in there." He saw the droop of her fine shoulders. "Don't be disheartened, sweet, as Noble will not watch. A canine female would be more to his liking."

Green eyes flashed, glittering like precious gems as Angel clenched her fists into tight balls, and she stormed, "I am not your girl! And, I suppose *you* will survey me thoroughly as I disrobe, though your courageous beast may not!"

Settling himself comfortably into the wicker chair to light a cigano, he leisurely blew spirals of smoke into the moist air as he said with a well-fed smile, "Aye, that I will, lass."

Angel nibbled a thumbnail thoughtfully, then suddenly wrinkled a fine nose in distaste. Ugh! She detested men who used tobacco.

Tyrone contemplated the patter of rain pelting the palmetto-thatched roof as he leaned back, sighing noisily in content. Angel paused once to study the four walls around, then riveted her eyes back on the place occupied by an oversized feather bed draped with mosquito netting. Across the room, Tyrone grinned at her hasty surveillance of his furnishings and fixed her with an affirmative nod when her eyes questioned him. There was only one bed. Of course!

She clenched her teeth, and, without further hesitation, tugged up the cloth that was beginning to cause her itching and chilling misery. She didn't care anymore! She just wanted to get this bloody uncomfortable thing off. Another disturbing thought struck her then. She couldn't turn about, let him see her backside, for there were the marks from the fire, so she stayed as she was, facing him with a bit of nervousness and defiance.

Tyrone wondered at her immodesty of a sudden. It was not like her. He watched the slim arms drawing the frock along with the chemise, up over gently curving hips, and then she turned slightly to give him a full profile view of beauty unadorned. His breath caught at the sight of her smooth belly and the honeyed cradle of love between her thighs. Next he heard her moan softly to herself, then impatiently when the thing would lift no further, but was horribly twisted beneath the curve of her breasts. Not only that, but her arms were now entangled in the mess and she was making no progress in prying herself loose.

Angel twisted, turned, stomped her foot as she muttered simple oaths, and, finally whimpering like a frustrated child, lowered her fair head in defeat, jerking away tears with the back of one enmeshed hand.

Shaking his head with gentle mirth, Tyrone rose to cross the room and rescue the damsel in distress. He stood tall before this tiny woman and she kept her eyes averted from what she suspected was a mocking grin at her helpless situation.

"Here, let me help. The truth of the matter is, sweet, you are trying much too hard and too hastily," he said, bending over her to work at the material imprisoning her splendid bosom.

Angel shut her eyes tightly as hard knuckles brushed rosy tips, causing that strange tingle in them. The sodden garment was rolled down first then lifted up over her head. She quivered at the hot gaze raking downward as he didn't spare her, but stared boldly. He flung the thing aside, into a corner. When she wanted to reach down to fetch up the robe that had dropped, she felt his fingers slip to her shoulders firmly. He brought her up to face him, his eyes amber flames as they peered down to scald her with intensity, causing her knees to shiver.

"What do you conceal on this your naked thighs, my beauty?"

He spun her about to see but Angel squirmed so that he saw nothing but a tempting buttocks above long limbs. He was about to hold her close, press her back to him when a knock rattled across the floor, breaking the spell of the moment. Angel jerked into the robe as Ty muttered a dozen oaths while striding to the door and all but unhinged it.

"Hi there," Nikki said with a sheepish grin, peering over Tyrone's squared shoulders. "I see you are back, you found the young lady. We've been searching all over, then I saw the light here and I just came to—uh—see if I could do anything . . . something?" A raindrop clung to the tip of his nose and he blew at it ineffectually. "Say, is everything all right, Ty?"

Tyrone dashed away the raindrop with a flick of his finger, then stepped back to bow elegantly from the waist, and with a wide sweep of his hand bade his cousin enter his humble domicile.

"See for yourself, laddie," Tyrone said, a bit too cheerfully, making his cousin wonder if he really should or not.

"Oh, do come in, Nikki!" Angel blurted, gliding forward while toweling her hair. She felt so good being in warm and dry clothes, even if it was only a robe.

"So, it's Nikki now," Tyrone muttered, eyeing her up and down.

Angel avoided his comment and smiled happily at the boyishly handsome face. Nikki blushed, softening her heart with his gentle, comical manner. Tyrone regarded them, supplying Nikki with a fiendish, withering glare.

"Well, well, I see you two have met before," Tyrone pressed on. "Why don't we break out the bottle and renew old acquaintance, hmmm?"

Angel swept grandly past him, disregarding his inane statement. She gazed sweetly up into Nikki's dark brown eyes while she rested a hand on his forearm. Nikki glanced at that dainty hand as if a sparkling diamond rested there.

"How is my mother? Is she worried terribly?" Angel asked the lad.

As she as about to question him further, Nikki interrupted, "Whoa, princess. I was there a short time back, but almost

150

sunk my ship coming over here." He delighted in her little giggle at that. "Your mam was frightened of the storm and she was at Thelma's. I mean, Thelma fetched her back there before it broke good. Lady Sherwood thought maybe you went for a walk and got lost. She said wherever you are she believes you to be safe. Storms don't frighten you, she said, only fire does." Nikki peeked over to where his cousin stood stroking his beard in deep thought. Nikki snatched up the fair hand to kiss it gallantly. "I am ever at your service, dear princess. . . ." He peered around the robe to see Ty's boot tapping a puddle.

"Begging your pardon, sir—" Nikki looked up into the dark face, "but you should really have a change of clothes, you're dripping all over your floor."

Angel smothered a giggle, recalling Tyrone's exact words to her earlier. Nikki was trying to remember which sentence could be so hilarious when Tyrone joined Angel in gay laughter, now more at Nikki's bemusement than anything else. Angel bent at the waist, trying to still the tickly spasms with a hand spread over her belly.

All at once the gaiety was arrested as the tall smuggler and the fair maid gazed deeply into each other's eyes. Time hung suspended as Angel suddenly straightened the robe with nervous fingers while Tyrone continued to stare into her eyes. There seemed to be only the two of them in the room.

Nikki watched the long, warm exchange pass between his cousin and the sweet young woman. Oh, yes, she was undeniably a woman; and something was happening between the two of them. It was wild, wonderful, and strangely beautiful. His cousin would be a damned fool if he broke this one's heart! The other women hadn't mattered, but this little lady was very special.

Nikki coughed and Tyrone finally looked around himself. Everything was so fresh and new, it seemed. And as it was the first time she had completely relaxed, let down her guard, he was at an unusual loss for words. Her little face lit up in joyful abandonment had shaken him greatly.

"Sir, I've not had a morsel since the dawning of this day and I fear I shall soon faint from hunger," Angel said, squelching Tyrone's passionate bewilderment.

Nikki leaped to her aid, speaking up before his brooding cousin could. "The men are still dallying with their meal at the public house over on Grande Terre. What would you prefer, princess—creamed roe to start? Then wild swan and roast goose, some West Indian preserves? Shrimps? Oysters?"

"Yes, yes, all of it. I'm nigh onto starvation!"

Nikki smiled. "How about—*du chocolat?* Mmm, I'm sorry—*ne parlez-vous pas français?*" Nikki asked her if she didn't speak French.

"Bien peu, Monsieur," she answered, after pausing first. This dialect of French was strange to her, but she was catching on. *"Oui, du chocolat, merci."*

Tyrone finally broke up the conversation. "I'll accompany my—ah—Nikki to the public house. I'm needing a strong drink right now and the company of my crew. Caspar will return shortly with *le diner* to ease your famished state, sweet," he ended mockingly.

"But your clothes, you are still dripping wet." As soon as she'd said the words, she regretted them. An embarrassed pink spread across her cheeks and she studied the floor when they turned back to her.

At the door, Tyrone smiled amusedly. "I've a change of clothes at Nik's. Don't worry, sweet, I've never caught cold yet."

Angel presented her back to him, and after a moment she heard the door close softly. She suddenly felt a forlorn sadness creep over her and she yearned for Christine's quiet company. She walked over to peer between the wide cracks in the batten blinds. As quickly as the storm had come on it now abated, and the low moon made an appearance, setting the wide leaves of the tropical trees glistening like pretty silver ribbons. From the south, soft breezes rustled warmly about the colony and tall palms were once more arighted, dripping like delicate, trickling founts.

Alone now, Angel wondered what would have befallen her in the glade had Tyrone not come along. Perhaps it was better this way. Indeed, it was somewhat, for she could not have withstood the filthy vagrants who had been about to maul her to death. At least Tyrone was not unclean and always had a good smell about him that she liked. He would not hurt her—would he? She had detected some small bit of tenderness in him—hadn't she? He wouldn't be tender when he found out how much she detested him when he finally raped her! For it would have to be rape. Of course she hated him . . . men who made their living by defying death, by plundering and preying on helpless women, were not number one in her book.

"Oh, Christine. What is left to us?" Angel said, peering at the moon. She breathed deeply and pressed a cool cheek to the robe, smelling that heady masculine scent.

All she wanted was to go home, back to when she had been that nonpareil female, with fops and dandies following and fawning at her feet. She had enjoyed being the Pied Piper of the town and the country bucks, foiling them at their own games of love and courtship. Still, she had never viewed even one of her admirers as future bridegrooms. She had never been an ordinary girl, panting for "the inly touch of love" and all that happy stuff that came before betrothal.

What do I want? she began sadly to wonder. She had never given much thought toward the future. The past's fantasy had ended brutally. But now she felt some new emotion growing inside her, a reality she could not check. It grew with terrifying speed, and she could not give it a name. She was afraid to.

2

Captain Ty slackened his swift pace to enter the stand of oleanders that served as protection from the Gulf wind and marked the entrance to the cafe, better known to the privateers and smugglers as the public house. Shouts of roistering men and gales of shrill laughter from bold women, rose to reach Ty in the entrance where he paused with Nikki momentarily. Ty listened to the bawdy language being bantered about, not only by the men but the women also. Ty wondered what the English girl would think of this place, and he smiled, moving forward into the room.

The bacchanalian songs bawled here were lusty, though somewhat haunting in times of passionate moods. Ty felt the songs reach his heart's core as never before. Cups and goblets and plundered crystal banged noisily along the wooden table when he entered, and as if he were lord of a realm, they hoisted the sloshing vessels up to salute him and his good health.

A spirit of camaraderie never failed to exist between these lawless men, one hundred of whom Captain Ty led as smuggler-captain, and he received, for the most part, obedience, even affection. It was the same with Lafitte's outlaws, more than one thousand strong. So it was that Barataria prospered as never before and the coffers of Lafitte bulged and clinked with Spanish coin. The storehouses were filled to the brim with goods of English manufacture, while shiploads of prize silks and spices were brought into port bearing Indian stamp.

These seafaring brigands plundered only Spanish vessels—so it was rumored, and no one was the wiser. For they had many powerful connections in Louisiana, and public opinion was overwhelmingly in favor of the smugglers' firm establishment.

Once again men of the crews rested between voyages as they slept and drank and caroused or lusted after the women they had brought there, or the ones already installed on the islands. Most of the island women were quiet and submissive, obeying the men blindly, women who had little thought beyond their men and their children. There were men of every race and nationality. Life had been filled with adventure and the wildest kind of excitement as all took part in smuggling. And all received their measure of coin, the dividing of the spoils, and Lafitte was fair.

Captain Ty took his usual place between Nash and Caspar while Nikki filled the empty seat across the long table from them. Ty motioned one of the barmaids over and instructed her to prepare a tray immediately.

"And put everything on it, Alma," Nikki said. "Even some of that red stuff." He indicated the wines of rare vintage being passed about carelessly, as if they were mere tankards of alehouse brew. Nikki leaned back to watch the voluptuous redhead twitch away from the table, then turned his regard back to the men. "We'll need a strong arm to tote the tray back to the English girl. What do you say, Caspar?"

Caspar grunted his assent while watching his captain

proceed to take his own meal from the steaming platters of shrimp, oysters, and wild rice. Before Ty had even taken two bites he received a curious nudge from Caspar, who was grinning like a gargoyle, his eyes glued to Ty's plate as he munched his own portion of meat.

"How goes it with the English spitfire? Is she faring well after her trek into the swamp?" Caspar asked, wiping goose grease off his mouth with the back of his meaty hand.

Ty chewed his food thoughtfully and washed it down with a heavy draught of red wine. "She's fine," he said. "A bit damp and downtrodden, but that is to be expected from a silly wench who thought escape into the treacherous swamp a simple matter. We had some unexpected visitors but they are footing it back to wherever they came from. Without a boat, they'll have to do a little swimming, too, I'm afraid," he chuckled.

Alma entered the hall just then and placed a huge tray down for Nikki's inspection. After Nikki had checked under the spread napkin for the chocolate Ty had ordered, Caspar whisked the tray away, going out the door like a swaggering headwaiter.

Leaning over while feeding generous scraps of wild swan to the hound, Nikki glanced up and cleared his throat noisily to gain the attention of his cousin, who was conversing rapidly in French with Nash. He cleared his throat over and over, until finally he became hoarse and the last sound emerged as a loud croak. He soon shrugged, then bent back to feeding Noble.

All this time Ty had been hearing Nikki and ignoring him pointedly, but he now gave him his undivided attention as he clasped lean fingers over his sash and booted Nikki hard on his rump under the narrow table. Nikki yelped and straightened fast.

Ty chuckled low. "Well, let's have it, Nik. Something has been splitting the tip of your tongue ever since you arrived at my cottage door with your winsome face."

After rubbing his backside to ease the ache there, Nikki said, "I was just wondering, Sir Robin—" he grinned impishly, "if you were going to deliver merchandise at Donaldsville sometime this week?"

"Umm, sometime this week?" Ty scratched his beard,

making his cousin squirm uncomfortably. "I think so. There, and along the Bayou Lafource. You know yourself it should take approximately six days, at the most. You can come along or you can remain behind . . . whichever," he said, studying his neatly trimmed fingernails.

The younger man shuffled his booted feet beneath the roughhewn table, opened his mouth to speak, then ran dark fingers through brown shoulder-length hair nervously. Ty's brow quirked as he sat back to light a cigano. He waited. After a space, Nikki finally blurted out his request—and fast.

"Again I was wondering, cuz, someone should keep an eye on the English girl, I mean just in case she should try escape or something like that."

Ty's deep laughter had resounded in the hall and now he leaned forward to peer at Nikki. "Ahh-hah! So that's what has been itching your britches, dear cousin. Well—I promise you that the tyro has learned her lesson well. She'll not trod that way again nor part with these islands for some time to come."

"You'll have to relate that to me sometime, Ty. Now if you'll tell me—"

"You can stay, Nik. Escort the princess around the islands. If you wish, be her bodyguard, as Rollo forfeited that position earlier this day, and that leaves an opening for a spunky lad!"

"I'll say I'll stay!" said eager Nikki with a merry twinkle in his eyes, relishing the friendship to come between him and the girl. He bent to studiedly remove burrs from Noble's thick fur, relinquishing the conversation to Nash.

Pearce Duschesne chose to swagger in just then with a pair of women, one on each arm. One was Lola, a pretty, dark-haired girl with creamy skin and black, teasing eyes that instantly searched for that certain tall figure. She was twenty-five now, formerly from Santo Domingo, and had been residing on Grande Terre since the age of nineteen. She possessed a seductive magnetism which Ty had found irresistible, and she had enticed him—for a short time. Her reputation was not that of a lonely woman, though.

The threesome headed straight for them. Nikki groaned inwardly when he saw that the blonde was Ellen, and that she was wearing the green gown Miss Sherwood had given up!

There was only one gown that petite in size on the islands, and the doxie looked as if she had been poured into it, and was about to explode any moment now.

Indeed Ellen was feeling quite smug knowing who had worn the gown before her. She had obtained possession of it from the hulking oaf Rollo. She shuddered now remembering what she had had to give in exchange that day when Rollo was delivering it back to the home of Lafitte. After her curiosity about the garment had been satisfied, it had been an easy persuasion. Ellen had lied that it had originally been her own, and promised that if Rollo gave it back to her he would sample her charms more than once. He was searching for her, even now, she knew.

Ty had been entirely lost in his musing, bewitched by the memory of Angel's long limbs, her firm, round breasts and cameo complexion glowing softly by candlelight. But the vision vanished when he flicked a casual regard over the newcomers who were seating their strongly perfumed bodies at the table. Seated next to Nikki now, Pearce was suddenly aware of the hound's disturbing grumblings. The inhospitable greeting wasn't lost on Pearce, for they had been mutual enemies from the first. The man shifted nervously before he ventured to speak.

"How about a game, Ty, same stakes? Or are they too high now?"

"Why, Pearce, do you have another timepiece as precious as the one in my pocket?" Ty shot back softly, nursing his favorite brandy now.

"No . . . but I do have another. German-made."

"Then why ask," Ty answered tersely, his preference for English-made timepieces made apparent. He was suddenly aware of Lola's knee pressing against his thigh, but he remained impassive, thinking she would get the message and quit.

"When you tire of the wench send her my way. A little shopworn does not matter to me," Pearce said meaningfully. "In truth, I can't understand your interest in one so—ah— inexperienced and young. It is just not like you—Tyrone," he ended emphatically.

"Nor you, Pearce Duschesne," Ty returned, boredom lining

157

his deep voice.

Pearce was peeved, once more taken down a notch by Ty. The tall smuggler always seemed to best him, be it at a game of cards, women, or just idle conversation. He sat back, obsessed with a plan of revenge.

Nikki beamed down into his foamy cup of ale while his cousin remained apathetic to all. All but for Lola, who was becoming bothersome. She kept up the pressure of her well-padded knee until Ty loosed on her a glare that would surely have curdled milk. Put down, Lola rose to join Pearce on the other side of the table. Emboldened, Ellen stood to take the vacant seat.

Rollo entered just then and spotted Ellen immediately, seated beside Captain Ty. He decided not to interfere, but took a bit of bench nearest the door to quaff his ale. Ellen sat like a cat licking her fur, content to have Ty to herself, so she thought. She allowed for a full view of spilling flesh by leaning forward over the table.

Indifferently, and for the first time tonight, Tyrone regarded Ellen as he dropped a sideways glimpse into her bodice. Ellen sidled closer as Ty's heavy-lidded eyes suddenly grew wide, and he stared hard. Her face lit up.

At last there came a swift, rending tear and the green gown was separated all the way down to Ellen's waist. Flustered at first, Ellen was now thrillingly surprised as she was scooped up by her seducer and borne in strong arms toward the door. She was ecstatic and blew a kiss over Ty's wide shoulder to the revelers in the hall who had begun to shout encouragement. Finally, Ellen was thinking, Ty was hot for her.

Confusion reigned once more in Ellen as she was unceremoniously dumped into Rollo's thick lap. Blackbeard's likeness smiled largely at this good fortune come his way. His meaty hands were instantly on her waist when she squirmed to be away.

"Hear, hear," Ty's voice thundered down the hall, "I give Rollo the object of his heart's desire!" Then he lowered his voice, speaking only to Rollo. "See that you keep your new mistress in your hut and hold the raunchy slut from my sight. And, if Mademoiselle Sherwood ever sends you on an errand again, which I doubt, make certain that it's fully carried out!"

Eyes twinkling like blackberries in the dew, Rollo's head bobbed in answer. Ellen wriggled and squawked at this outrage committed against her and railed against the lasting imprisonment to come. Rollo cuffed her on the head and pinched her naked, bouncing breasts. Though bemused from their captain's actions, the crew arose with a great hullabaloo when Rollo proceeded to make love to the already half-naked woman. Tyrone then motioned for Nikki to accompany him out the door.

Caspar had heard the clamor from outside, and entering, hoped to find a dueling bash in full swing. He met the cousins' widespread grins, which added to Caspar's bewilderment, until his vision was filled with the object of the men's roistering. The doxie was spread-eagled on the floor, eyes now shining lustily at Rollo, who was unbuttoning his bulging breeches. Immediately all eyes were fixed on the beginning of the couple's copulation.

Caspar snorted as he turned to follow the other two down to the beach. He understood now the reason for the swift departure of the cousins. These impromptu functions were not his cup of tea, either. Too, they lasted overly long. Something else Caspar had forgotten, as usual, of late. His memory was not the same as it used to be. He must tell Ty that Big Jim had sent a message. Relayed word had just come in this afternoon by schooner *Fleet*. Aye. Ty would see the schooner when he strolled the beach tonight policing the harbor.

Caspar went along faster when he viewed the two tall silhouettes up ahead. There were two things that wouldn't sit well with his young captain. Number one: The Sherwood women would be penniless, for the lady's husband had carried in his purse all that was left to them after the sale of the Stonewall Manor. No home to go to, that meant. Number two: The only living relative was sickly, pressed with a mountain of doctor bills and himself destined to rent a room in a waterfront flophouse.

Caspar searched his mind for the rest. Ah, sure. There had been the gossips in the village bordering Stonewall. They had unabashedly told Big Jim that Miss Sherwood was a slanty-eyed vixen who cast spells over all the eager young males. But what was it she had done? *Laying abed* with bucks from Twickenham to Buckhurst Hill? Yes, he guessed it went something like that. Anyway, it was close enough.

To be sure, the captain had wanted the cozen wench and there would be no ridding himself of her and her mama now. When Ty tired of the poor girl, who would have her? Her sick uncle? Bah! Caspar doubted it. Just what was in Big Jim's mind, and why did he want Ty to know all this?

Hoping he had it all straight in his mind, Caspar went over it once more, mumbling to himself. He bumped smack into Ty, the deed to Stonewall fluttering from his sash to the sand at his captain's feet. Tyrone bent to snatch it up and the words were barely readable in the pale moonlight. He tapped the paper with an impatient gesture.

"And what is this?" Ty wanted to know.

Caspar explained the piece of paper and gave the relayed message, passed from mouth to mouth for the third time. He had Caspar repeat it once more, but the second time sounded crazier than the first to Ty. Suddenly his face lit with realization. He spoke slowly.

"So . . . mademoiselle is this *precious* cargo my father spoke of!"

The first blanket of twilight gray lifted to present the pink curtain of dawn parting with a glorious lamina of gold awakening, sending blades of yellow morning into the rosier hues. Upon opening her eyes, Angel was stimulated by this newness, this gentle aureole encircling the cottage, as if a magical spell were woven tight about it. From her curled up position in the wicker chair, she stared longingly at the big featherbed. She yawned widely. She would not have had the captain find her vulnerably asleep in that bed. Then, had she dreamed it, or had someone truly slipped by outside the window in the twilight past?

Shrugging tiredly, Angel lifted her hair languidly, and permitting it to sift through her fingers, let it fall halfway to the floor behind her.

"Why are you curled up in the chair when you know there

is a comfortable bed awaiting you?'' the deep voice grated as its owner stared at the sweet, reposed profile through the woven wickerwork.

Startled, Angel spun out of the chair and stood unsteadily in the middle of the rough floor. She had risen so quickly that a splinter had lodged itself into her foot, but she paid it no mind, just stared dead ahead.

"How long have you been standing there?" she breathed across to him. "I did not hear you enter. Last night—I must have fallen asleep in the chair—and—oh! I needn't explain my actions to you, you know very well why!"

"Do I really?" he sneered.

"You needn't appear so angry!" she stormed.

Tyrone regarded the bed suspiciously, then came back to her. "Couldn't you prevail upon Pearce Duschesne to stay a little longer? Or, were you merely making hasty plans for a clandestine meeting elsewhere, like when I am gone this week's end, for instance?"

Angel searched for words to answer him. She was thoroughly confused at his manner, his scornful scrutiny of her person. Pearce Duschesne? What was this? Was it Pearce who had slipped behind the batten blinds like a thief in the night and Ty had seen him? Why, she wondered, all these questions?

She stood closemouthed as he went to the back room, and unlatching the door, dragged out a large copper tub which he swung up easily and carried to the center of the straw rug. After ridding himself of his burden, he strode to the window, peered between the blinds, and waited. He paid her no mind for a time until, finally, he spoke with a bit of curiosity.

"Tell me, *naivétée*, did you find pleasure in your mischievous circulations in and about London?" He spun to face her squarely, noting the sudden discomfort.

"I—I have no idea of what you refer to," she said cautiously.

"Twickenham? Buckhurst Hill?" he questioned roughly.

Angel gasped and paled. "How—how could you possibly know about that?" she breathed. Then, "You could not!" She stared about the room as if she'd lost something of

161

great import.

"Village boredom does have a penchant for gossip, does it not, sweet?"

"But—but I did nothing to be ashamed of. In fact—" she lifted her chin a notch, "I rather enjoyed myself, and they were gentlemen—all the way. If you know so much about the circumstances, you also know that I was not alone. There was the cousin of one of the gentlemen along for the ride. In fact, it was she, Katherine, who planned the whole affair and with the best intentions in mind. But, we did—"

"Damn! You really had me fooled, you know that?" he said, and burst out into chest-heaving chuckles. How foolish of him to have thought her unsullied! Even in the glade when she had cried out her virtuousness, he had believed her. His humor quieted, he stared hard at the guiltless expression that was beginning to show signs of confusion once again.

Angel jerked away from his watchful inspection, but after a few minutes she asked, "Please . . . how do you know all this? You must know my name, then?" But he was already going out the door when she lifted her starry gaze up from the floorboards.

Angel chewed her lower lip as memories came flooding back to her as she stood bathed in the hazy morning sunshine pouring in through the door Ty had left open. How could he have learned of those times which seemed so long ago now? Not even her parents had had knowledge of the two separate, scandalous occasions when she should have been installed with relatives in London—an aunt and uncle who were long dead now—and instead had travelled with Katy Upchurch and her two young and rather handsome friends—one had been a cousin. Once to Twickenham on the Thames; once to Buckhurst Hill. She had become acquainted with several more young men along the way during their stops at inns to have a bite to eat and rest up a bit. That was what she had been about to tell Tyrone, but he hadn't given her the chance.

Her and Katy's escorts had been gentlemen, yes, but adventurous just the same. The villagers had called her a bold vixen on several occasions for her mild flirtations, but everyone had known she avoided doing anything really bad—

hadn't they? Of course, many had said this very same thing. It had been purely innocent and, yes, audacious fun, but it had set jealous tongues to wagging when Katy had told the younger villagers about the unchaperoned adventures. Angel had never joined them again and Katy had had the pretense to wonder out loud when she had declined.

Perhaps she shouldn't have allowed her tongue to slip with Tyrone, she thought now, for he might just take liberties because he thought her sluttish for her escapades.

Angel began swiftly to braid her hair for something to do. Flies were already buzzing in and swarming about the congealed mass of her half-eaten meal of the evening before. Tyrone suddenly returned, clutching in each hand a bucket of steaming water. Caspar followed with a pair of the same and they proceeded to fill the copper tub. Appearing sheepish, Caspar straightened, murmuring a "Good morning" to her, and she returned the greeting.

"Caspar," Tyrone began, "when you return to the kitchen with this clutter on the table here, see to it that Rolfe prepares a breakfast tray for one immediately."

Angel suddenly sensed that Tyrone was used to doling out orders as if . . . no, that couldn't be. He was a ruthless smuggler, no gentleman of refined living such as she was accustomed to having around her—before this!

Angel was completing the task of braiding her thick hair while Ty sat on the edge of the bed hauling off his tall boots and Caspar was just making his exit with the tray. She searched the room visually for something to secure the ends of her hair with, but there was nothing that would do the job that she could see. Much to her surprise Ty rose from the creaking bed to rummage through a tall dresser, and when he found what he had been searching for, he tossed the items carelessly onto the wicker chair and nodded for her to make use of the silver-painted wooden hair pins.

As she pinned the braids into a glossy crescent around her head she took time to wonder who had worn, possibly owned, the pins before. When that was done she eased herself back down into the wicker chair and faced away from him. She did not wish to watch him while he bathed. She had never seen a

163

man in a complete state of undress, nor did she wish to. She would await the completion of his bath and then ask when she would be allowed to rejoin Christine back on Grande Terre. But for now. . . .

"Could you perhaps fetch me one of the volumes that you keep in the storeroom? You did say you read? I would like very much to read while you take your bath . . . Tyrone?"

"I have already bathed and breakfasted earlier at Nikki's cottage. The bath is for you, *naivétée*," he answered, stretched out fully on the bed.

"M-Me?" Angel breathed, hugging the robe tighter about her.

"Yes, you," he returned in a sleepy voice. "Do you see anyone else in the room besides us?"

"Nooo," she almost whispered. She did so desire a bath, but not here, not now.

"You may see the volumes tomorrow, perhaps. As for now, get in that tub before it cools," he drawled with one eye on her. When she did not make a move to obey, he swiftly rolled off the bed and stood rigidly, his big hands planted firmly on his hips. "Would you care for my assistance? I've caught a glimpse of your charms by candlelight and would not be displeasured to witness more, and in broad daylight."

When he took up staring at a spot on the ceiling, Angel hastily shed the robe and made a little splash as she stepped into the tub. He had already climbed back into bed and, when he rolled over, his sounds of slumber softly filled the room. Shortly Angel snatched up a bar of soap, insolently flicking water in his direction. She scrubbed until her soft skin chafed, and again the perplexing question invaded her mind.

How had he come by his knowledge of her escapades in and about London? True, a man like him must have countless woman in several ports of the continents. But who in the village near Stonewall? Surely not freckle-faced Katy Upchurch! She giggled softly at the thought, then went on to scour her mind. She tried to recall each and every one of the women who had been escorted to the social affairs at her home, but their faces became as a blur in the bright lights of the social chamber where they'd sometimes danced till dawn.

Angel sat up suddenly, sloshing water onto the straw rug at the foot of the tub. She caught her breath, eyes sparkling. Had this smuggler met her before—a masquerade ball perhaps? Or—she sank back into the water, small and bewildered, looking as if hypnotized—Tyrone might have had all this planned, to set her family up, halt passage to their destination. To what end? she wondered. Maybe it was only his uncanny knowledge of everything and everyone that made her think this way. And sometimes she had the strangest feeling that she had met Tyrone before, long ago, many times. That was often said of lovers who were destined to meet in each lifetime. But they were not lovers and she didn't believe in such nonsense anyway!

With eyes averted from that lean form stretched out upon the bed, Angel stood to dry herself, then slipped briskly back into the coarse robe. She was crossing the room to examine the damage done to the frock when a quiet but firm rapping interrupted her. She called softly for the knocker to enter.

Caspar brought in her breakfast while she visibly scanned the tray for something cool to drink. Not only were there pitchers of fresh water, a jug of chicory coffee, and hot buttered rolls, but also dark amber honey. And searching further, she saw two large omelets filled with what looked like white meat and green vegetables, and a pastry of some sort!

Her mouth set to watering when Caspar swung the tray down. Her eyes widened at the small feast, once again, and she wondered if she could put even a fraction of it away. Well, she would certainly try. She would need all the fighting strength she could muster if Tyrone was still bent on keeping his word. Mistress or not, she was bloody starved!

"Miss, can I get you anything else?" Caspar inquired.

Angel liked Caspar's deep voice; he didn't frighten her with his immense size anymore. "Oh, yes, Caspar," she began, "will you see about getting me some fresh and clean clothes to wear? I'm afraid my frock is beyond reparation." She indicated the rag draped over the dresser.

"It's been taken care of, miss. Cap'n Ty gave orders earlier," he smiled, looking at the same time across the room to where his captain slumbered peacefully. He went on, "The clothes should be coming soon. You better eat now, you'll need your strength, sure."

With mouth agape, Angel stared after Caspar's retreating form. As he closed the door, she could see his smile had grown considerably larger.

An hour before noon Angel was donning the fresh but rather snug green-blue madras that the trusted black slave had delivered to her. She sighed now in resignation as she tied the straps in back. Her made-to-order frocks and silk gowns had been mostly of apricot, amber, peach with white, and pale green shot with silver for evening wear, all colors to compliment her eyes and hair. She couldn't impugn Tyrone on that score—those materials would not have been suitable for the consistently hot, muggy climate of these islands. For sure, she had seen the last of her beautiful clothes.

As a result of her hasty trek into the swamp the day before, her black slippers were completely ruined. The chemise, though, had been salvaged, and she slipped outside now barefoot to lean over a bucket of fresh water to scrub it clean. As she worked, her eyes kept straying back to the cottage and she saw in her mind's eye that cool recklessness that Tyrone displayed even in deep slumber. Before shutting the door softly behind her, she thought she had heard him murmur a woman's name; it had sounded like a soft caress. What did she care if he dreamed of another woman or not. She was outdoors and was feeling light and unguarded in the radiant glow of high noon.

After draping the rinsed chemise over an old chair, Angel, feeling slightly daring in her new freedom, decided to wander a bit. Everything was a salty blue, the air salubrious, and shedding all her cares, she became nimble of foot, wandering in and out of tall grassy patches, sighting the wealth of bright sails out in the bay. Tawny sand winked up at her and after a time she was drawn into the cooler sanctuary of twisted live oaks. Here the magical silence greeted her, and here she would be safe, for out on the shores she had viewed the crew busy mending nets and gear, and the unloading of schooners; the latter were being constantly repaired.

Feeling revived after the nourishing fare, she was enchanting as she stooped in her gaiety to collect some purple plum flowers nestled at her feet. She straightened and whirled with the sweet bouquet, pressing the soft petals against her warm cheeks. Lying back upon a bowed palm with spiny trunk, she peered up at the cerulean sky through the large, feathery leaves. Time seemed to come to an abrupt standstill and she closed her eyes, her back conforming to the bend of the trunk, her arms dangling over the sides. She permitted her mind to concentrate, to flow with the low sounds of tropical creatures and the distant shrieks of gulls diving for their nooning. Nothing else shook her repose.

A minute passed, then two, and a strange sensation began to course through her limbs, generating a warm flush which crept over her. She was suddenly afraid to reopen her eyes, knowing full well that someone was watching her—very near. Her breath quickened and her blood surged as she cautiously lifted her amber lashes. She could not gasp nor could she cry out. Her body went unbearably limp with shock, the sweet bouquet falling to the ground.

The dusky hazel eyes above her were intoxicating, the golden flames alive with vital force. Upside down they appeared evil.

"I told you, my beauty, that you would give me pleasure . . ." Tyrone murmured, ". . . and the time is come."

Galvanized into action, Angel rolled off the trunk and fell to her knees and palms, peering up at Tyrone standing nimbly upon the highest curve of the spiny trunk with his arms akimbo. Angel cocked her head at him in a curious manner, thinking that if she wasn't so afraid she would have found this scene most humorous. As she stood she tried to sound angry while exercising her courage.

"How did you get up there without me seeing you? At this I wonder—are you a monkey or a magician?" But her voice did quiver slightly.

"Neither," Tyrone replied, dropping catlike to the ground. "'Tis only I, m'lady, thine hood of thy Sherwood Forest come to claim my lady love. I repeat—the time is come," he ended, on a serious note.

"You said no such thing!"

He shook his head. "Tsk, tsk, your childish temper is

showing, sweet. Recall, less than a day has passed since I said it. As my mistress you will give me much pleasure, and you shall receive it as well."

"No! I shall not be a smuggler's mistress!" She stepped back to make ready to flee, but was caught in a merciless grip of steel.

"Am I so different from the others who have made love to you?" he asked as he stroked her arm, slid his fingers up to her shoulder beneath the cloth. "I too, can play the gentleman for you, just like your fops and dandies. If it is my infamous bearing that frightens you now, I'll put your fears to rest and show you that all such men aren't so bad—if you respond."

"I—there were no others. You know that as well as I do," she said, eyes leaping from his warm gaze.

"Do I now," he said flatly. "Oh, come now, m'lady, don't play the innocent with me again. Moral certainty of virtuousness has died. You knew that this very morning You see, torturing thoughts of retarding this union have fled my imagination completely, and, now that I have knowledge of your make-up—" he paused, shrugging wide shoulders, "let's just say it will not pain my conscience to see you through this time."

"Conscience! You have none to speak of!" she cried defensively.

Before she could retreat any further he hooked her waist with an arm and she was swooped up easily into a bundle. Her head spun wildly as he bore her to a green secluded place of high grasses where she struggled in vain, only to be nestled into the mossy cradle beneath. He came down in fluid movements, at the same time stripping off his blousey tunic and flinging it aside sharply, restricting her movements with a straddling imprisonment. He made slow, gentle murmurs deep in his throat to calm her round-eyed look of fear. She tried to rise and bolt when he took a moment to unfasten his sash, but the results were damaging. The madras came away with a gaping split from bodice to hem and she was sent gently back to the moss. She wrenched her head away from his unsparing regard of her quivering, glorious nudity and closed her eyes tightly against further visual assault. But still she knew he feasted his gaze upon her. Tears of utmost shame and bitter revulsion wetted her burning cheeks, while at the same time a strange languor began to steal through her limbs.

Tyrone, now unclad, stared at the masterpiece of womanhood and he swelled as never before. He muttered a curse at her coldness, but the hunger within would not be stayed this time. Instead, he strove to warm her as he tenderly nuzzled her damp cheeks, her ears, and the slim white column of her neck. The gesture went unrewarded as Angel arched her back and, drawing back her hand to beat at his chest, was checked as both arms were pinioned above her head with one large hand. Pressing his face to hers, Tyrone captured the sweet lips in a savage, searingly hot kiss. His free hand pressed and played between her thighs, slid up over her belly to the taut nipples, then slowly, painstakingly, inched back to the honeyed cradle of love. He was obsessed with a quenchless desire that only this woman could satiate, and it flashed for one quicksilver moment in his mind that from this time onward it would be thus.

"Ahhh, you are a nameless witch, a sweet tormentress," he murmured.

"Devil—" Angel returned in a breathless reply, "I hate you."

Laughter welled up from deep within his throat, indeed sounding demoniac to the writhing girl beneath him. He crushed her to him and was breathing hard and fast when she cried out at the contact of his hard, probing flesh. She pitched about, scattering the pins from the glossy crescent of her hair, and his lean fingers raked through the silken length to spread the flaxen cloud about them, while at the same time his lips brushed a rosy aureole.

"Please, please don't," she panted when he strove to push apart her knees with one of his own.

"I can't wait anymore, love, I must know you now," he groaned huskily as he mounted her. "Hate me, but don't close your thighs to me—you are ready, in body if not in mind. Relax, damnit!"

Angel dazedly felt his mixture of ruthlessness and deepening passion as he boldly nudged her clamped thighs apart. He pressed to gain entry, angry, as still she stiffened. His palms found her buttocks and he lifted her to him. In a moment of slightly crazed need she met him and he penetrated savagely. It was too late now, and she exclaimed out loud at the surprising, burning, swordlike pressure she was fleetingly experiencing in the fusion.

"Why the pain?" he asked hoarsely, almost inaudibly in her ear.

She heard his voice as from far away. He kept up the rhythmic strokes he had begun and could not end, not yet. He took her along smooth, shaded paths and enticed her to enter where the bewitching music and enchanting rhapsodies would unite them in one glorious flame. Suddenly her eyes flew open and she checked herself from going any further.

"No," he breathed, his voice crackling. "Come back to me. Damn!"

Angel only rolled her head from side to side as he began to take her more roughly, thrusting, singlemindedly fulfilling a long-awaited need to be satisfied. She glimpsed him through a blur but once, to see him covered with a thin, wet sheen. A moment later he stiffened, shivered, and tossed back his tawny head with a painfully ecstatic look coming over his handsome face.

When it was all over he brusquely left her, fell onto his back and would have released a deep sigh, but instead cursed low. He glanced down at the ivory-sleek thighs he'd just violated and she snatched up the tatters of the madras and rolled into it. She wanted to shield herself from any further ravishment by him.

She looks like a child filled with grief over the loss of some cherished possession, Tyrone thought. Really—had he ruptured a virginal membrane? From his hasty observance he had noticed no sign of blood, though, none whatsoever. Was the show and utterance of pain all a ruse then—or fear? To put an end to his lovemaking? Hah! He felt like an animal after the heat of a bitch!

Perhaps she had lost token virginity another way—a fall? He laughed shortly and bitterly at that. Highly unlikely, he thought, as Caspar's words rang in his ear—"laying abed with bucks from Twickenham to Buckhurst Hill."

Tyrone cursed himself for a jealous, crack-brained fool, and he stood to jerk into his breeches. All women were conniving bitches, panting after anything in tight, bulging breeches, unfaithful, and not to be trusted. And in due time, this one, too, would pant after his attentions, brazenly clench her thighs about him, as all the others who had come before her. She was his now and would serve his purpose well when trained to be his mistress, at his beck and call. Until he tired of her. That was inevitable. . . .

Tyrone peered down obliquely at his beautiful captive. She stirred slightly and protested when he bent to snatch away the madras. His warm regard roamed over the sweet curve of hips and thighs, slim arms pressing childlike against round, up-tilted breasts. Sun-kissed strands cloaked her tear-streaked face from his view while the mass of hair twined about bare shoulders and cascaded down past a slim waist. Even the bare feet were a marvel of pink, flawless perfection. Retracing his measuring regard, Tyrone felt himself stir below his sash once more. He drove away the urge to know her again and bent to drop the madras over the disturbing sight of her miserable quivering.

"Get up!" Tyrone commanded dispassionately as he turned away from her, the winking mystery of his pirate's ring blazing in slanting sunlight.

"I shan't," Angel began. "I'm staying right here, thank you!"

"Well then. We'll just go another round?" Tyrone suggested, coming back to her while toying with his sash.

Angel rose so swiftly that she forgot the madras. She bent now swiftly to retrieve the thing and wrapped it about her in a most disorderly fashion, to disguise the more intimate parts of her person.

Tyrone would have chuckled at her haste were it not for his foul mood. He strode along, confident that she tracked him back to the cottage. She did, glaring at his long, lean, and muscled back. In one hand he carried his tunic and it trailed along on the ground at the side of his tall boots. She was feeling intense hatred for this suddenly disgruntled man who had shamed and degraded her and spread apart her thighs as if she

171

was less than a strumpet!

If Angel had found the idea of marriage repulsive before, it was now a thousand times more so. She would never, ever, give her heart to a man now, never let down her guard and expose herself to the risks of love—not even as a mistress!

Chapter Five

1

The sunset melted like a great crimson candle, setting the island ablaze with splashy, deep-toned hues. A screeching gull appeared over the cottage like a powerful white spirit, its squalling overture mingling with the mellifluous chirpings of insects and night birds of paradise. Angel stood in the open door, encased in a lifeless form of melancholia after Tyrone had departed without a single word. She waited for night to fall.

Now in the calm splendor of moonlight, Angel stared at that lunate shape and started when a young owl, trying to look wise, perched on a bough of a spindly tree and peered round-eyed at the young woman from under his horny ears. She responded to the cute, feathery creature by smiling feebly, showing her loneliness, after he greeted her with an echoing hoot. The owl blinked one eye after a long pause of staring attentively; he seemed to heed her as she spoke hollowly to him.

"Oh, wise little owl, I wish that you could grasp the meaning of my words and answer me true. Still, if you could but form the humanly words, would they be powerful enough to gain me insight into this perplexing, tormenting emotion?"

The owl responded with an echoing hoot that sounded very much like "I don't know. . . ." and Angel had to smile genuinely at that.

Feeling all at once silly for speaking to the little creature, she went inside. Anyway, she wanted to escape the mosquitoes that were beginning to become a thorough nuisance. She was just about to shut the door when a dark shape moved steadily toward the cottage. Angel waited for the form to grow larger and become visible beneath the moon.

It was Ellen, looking all flushed and beside herself about something. Her gray eyes were glassy in the faint light as she peered behind Angel to see into the shadowy interior of the cottage. Angel began to ponder this unexpected visit when Ellen suddenly blurted out the reason for her coming.

"Hurry, you must come with me!" Ellen said breathlessly. "I've just crossed the pass by myself. It's your mother, she's very ill. I came to fetch you."

Angel's heart pounded wildly as she thought of Christine's odd behavior of late. Yet, a sixth sense told her to beware. She paused uncertainly, then cast the feeling aside and hurriedly followed Ellen a few steps. She halted short in her tracks. She peered down at the long robe. She couldn't make headway dressed as she was, so she told Ellen she would be back in a minute. She whirled into the cottage and fetched the tunic she'd seen earlier hanging on a nail. The blousey tunic went over her head in less than two seconds after she'd discarded the robe. There was no time to worry if Tyrone would mind her borrowing it—her mother needed her now.

Angel followed the fast-moving form in front of her, down to an unbeaten path which shortly led to the moonlit sands where, unaware that Ellen had purposely guided her away from the beached pirogues, Angel stopped directly in back of the stationary figure that paused as if uncertain of the way. The smirking strumpet turned.

"Well, miss prissy puss!" Ellen hissed, pointing a loaded pistol at the younger woman's heart. "How do you like being a smuggler's whore? That is what you are now, you know," she said and paused, delighted at seeing the other woman flinch. "Oh, always so innocent, aren't you! The little minx and her lunatic mama!"

Angel clenched her hands into fists. "How dare you! My mother never sent you to summon me to her bedside. Just what do you want and why are you pointing that pistol at me?" Even if she wished for a sabre now to defend herself with, what good would it do. A gun was by far the swifter and deadlier in any opposing situation.

"Why, to kill you, naturally," came Ellen's reply. "But

first, I want you to hear a few things, watch that angelic face of yours cringe. Strange, how you always appear so innocent, even with that blooming body and those tilted eyes of yours. I bet you've been laid a hundred times, haven't you? Tell me, is Captain Ty good? I wouldn't doubt it, from the woman talk around here. Did you know that Ty has another whore besides you? Ah! Well, her name is Lola and she and I talked about how horny that smuggler is. And, she's not the only one. He has sampled every bit of fluff from here to New Orleans and right on up to Donaldsville, wherever the hell that is!"

"How about you?" Angel parried, feeling strangely brave even though the pistol was aimed steadily at her breast.

Ellen drew herself up, her countenance an evil mask of hatred. All of a sudden she appeared pale and ghastly in the moonlight, like a specter of death. Angel held her ground while clutching the hem of the tunic tightly in her hands. For some odd reason the idea of death was not quite as frightful as being mauled by that smuggler. In fact, if not for Christine and Samuel she would welcome death this night.

"I've found out much from that drunken slob Rollo," Ellen went on spitefully. "Not to mention Pearce Duschesne. Did you know that the captain's mama had an aristocratic flow of blood in her veins—just like you, puss?"

So, Angel thought, Tyrone preyed on his own kind. She knew him to be Louisianian, but now she knew the reason for the odd mixture of unstudied Creole patois and mocking English diction. Yes, Ty hated the English, but why? Thelma's words came back to her: "Ty, him full of some hate. Someone done wrong for him when boy. In his eyes. Some sad in his heart. Be careful, he make you love him. You be no good for true man."

Feeling some triumph that she'd hit a sore spot in the other woman, Ellen went on. "You know, I used to enjoy all kinds of men before Captain Ty came along. That tawny-haired devil has made me forget them all, with his lean body and bulging crotch! Shees! I've bedded down with more men than you could ever even hope to meet in your lifetime."

"But not with Captain Ty?" Angel parried again.

"Bitch. Take your clothes off!" Ellen ordered, her gun

poking the air.

Angel's stomach lurched at the evil tone in Ellen's voice. She was feeling that same nausea as in the swamp when the filthy vagrant had almost succeeded in violating her flesh. Still, when she spoke it was in a wonderfully level tone.

"Why, Ellen, whatever for?"

"Never mind, just take off that silly blouse you've got on, and make haste, bitch!"

Suddenly Angel saw something move in the shadowy brush behind Ellen. Whoever, whatever it was, it was being stealthy, hushed. To keep Ellen's attention on herself, Angel tugged off the tunic and dropped it casually to the sand. In the face of death, Angel thought, there was no room for modesty.

Ellen's face hardened when she feasted her gray eyes on the beautiful and glowing bounty of womanhood that stood deathly still, like a naked sculpture in the light of moon. Crazed by jealousy of such perfection, Ellen backed up slowly to outstretch both arms, fingers pressing lightly upon the mechanism.

"What the devil!" a voice broke from out of the shadows.

Ellen was taken aback, half-turned to shift the bore of her pistol at the fearless intruder leaping out into the open, but the ball had already been released, the explosion a loud thundercrack in the still night air. Angel did duck swiftly and the ball landed several feet in the sand behind her. Ellen cursed the distraction, and glared at the young man who had deprived her of the morbid pleasure of blowing a hole in the younger woman's chest.

Nikki, brown eyes full of concern, strode at once to Angel's side. Bending a knee, he lifted the tunic to slip it over the naked, shivering form. He pulled her close into the security of his sinewy arms and turned a dark look upon the crazed countenance across from them.

All at once the beach was swarming with ready pirates and smugglers, all alert to the sound of trouble. By the light of the moon they ran, their sashes fully armed. Caspar had been the first one to witness the strange scene, and without further ado, now lowered the wickedly gleaming cutlass. He watched as Nikki lifted that dainty chin with a forefinger and peered down

176

into the pale face of the girl.

"Are you all right?" Nikki murmured, caressing her back with a gentling hand.

Angel stopped her shivering and nodded, feeling wonderfully warm and secure in the handsome young smuggler's arms. She pressed her face into the folds of his clean-smelling tunic, delighting in the youthful hardness of his chest and the gentle strength he gave her. She knew again, even more so, that she would always reserve a special place in her heart for him. He was like a brother, something she had yearned for while growing from child to teen to young woman—a young man close to her own age who she could go to, ride with, share her doubts and fears with, and, most of all, a protector.

"I will always be here when you most need me, princess," Nikki said, as if he'd read her innermost thoughts. "Never fear, as long as you are with us." He cleared his throat gruffly, holding her back from him as he added, "Not that you really need protection, little minx. But you were lucky tonight with me around." He shifted back to Ellen with a frown. "Now, what is this all about, hmm?"

Disgusted by the tender scene, Ellen snapped, "I'll tell you, you nincompoop! Captain Ty would have preferred me if she hadn't swished her rosy butt in his face, her and her phony innocence!"

"You?—Hah!" Nikki expostulated fiercely. "You, Ellen, are nothing but the lowest slut! Excuse me, princess, but it's true. She's already been laid by every horny smuggler here— those who'd have her. I only hope she hasn't spread disease here!"

Ellen pulled an ugly face. "The only disease here is stupidity. If you hadn't come along, that silly bitch would be lying here right now with a hole in her. You, big lad, won't always be around. I'll get to her yet!" she spat.

Nikki narrowed brown eyes, his voice was hard. "I think not, slut! Gentlemen! Take this baggage, chain her in a nice dark cell—the one next to the black boy's. Captain Ty will take it from there. Likely he'll send her to New Orleans—Lulu's House—where she can peddle her tarnished wares. I doubt if Lulu would even have her, though." He shrugged, dismissing the subject.

After several pirates had half-carried, half-dragged the screeching, kicking strumpet off down the beach, and the others had again shrunk back into the shadows of scrub, Nikki turned to escort the young woman back to his cousin's cottage. She laid a hand softly upon the dark arm and slanted a worried frown up at Nikki.

"You mentioned Samuel—is—is he all right?" she asked, afraid of the one answer she would not like to hear—that he might be sent to auction.

"I'm afraid not, princess," Nikki answered. Knowing that she cared for the lady's welfare, he treaded more cautiously. "He received twenty lashes earlier today, by Captain Ty's own hand. Don't look so scared, princess. If it had been Rollo's hand meting out the punishment instead of the captain's, he would've been more than likely dead by now. Rollo's lust for blood, among other things, is well-known here. Don't fret, princess, Samuel won't die." Nikki shrugged matter-of-factly. "The captain wouldn't allow such a thing to happen, mean ogre though he seems to be."

Angel heaved a weary "Yes," and let her shoulders droop. Not for herself, but for Samuel this time.

"Princess, you know that the black boy tried to stick my cou—, er, Ty, with a hasty blade, before you vanished into the swamps."

Angel was suddenly confused again with her feelings as they continued up the regular path to the cottage in silence. It was not the unbeaten path that Ellen had led her along earlier—almost to her death.

The young couple walked slowly, like disembodied spirits in the creeping haunt of evening fog that came like separate beasts across the bay, from out of the black bogs. Nikki was awfully quiet, and Angel didn't ask about the captain's whereabouts, though her mind dwelt on that question somewhat confusedly. But then, the captain was Samuel's nemesis and it irked her to think of the poor boy's bloodied back. Well, she didn't care if the ruthless smuggler ever returned!

If only Nikki would aid them in escape; it was not entirely

impossible, or, was it? Before she could open her mouth to find out, she noticed that Nikki had considerably slowed his easy swagger. He finally stopped to study her bare feet and she followed his eyes down, wondering.

"Princess, why are you walking lamely? Ah. You were hurt. Why didn't you tell me?"

Angel frowned momentarily, and then remembered something. The pain returned and she wet her lips before she spoke. "Yes, Nikki. It is just a sliver that lodged in my foot this, morning. It's all right, though." She then shrugged it off as nothing to be concerned over, and continued along the path.

She didn't get far when she was suddenly swooped up into strong arms, as Nikki said, "Silly girl. Why didn't you take it out? It has more than likely festered by now."

Nikki kicked open the door that had been left open a crack, and bore her to the wicker chair where he placed her down gently and then proceeded to strike flint to a candle that had gone out long ago. Nikki's huge shadow leaped across the ceiling as he rummaged in the dresser drawer. He picked up a pitcher of water and a shallow basin, going to bend on a knee as he ministered to the girl's discomfort. She only flinched once as he drew out the long splinter of wood and swabbed the swollen heel carefully.

A dark lock of hair had fallen over Nikki's forehead as he worked and Angel longed to push it back, to tell him how much his caring meant to her. He applied a sticky salve next and when he was done he sat back on his heels to study the sweet, weary face. She shook her head in answer to the question in his lovely brown eyes.

"It doesn't hurt—sure?" Nikki asked, despite the shake of her head. "It is festered, you know. It must have been terribly painful to walk, princess. I admire your bravery." He breathed a laugh through his long, straight nose. "You should have been a pirate or something like that. But, matey, you should have removed that hunk of wood a long time ago. Naughty girl!" His eyes twinkled in the soft candle glow.

"Nikki, I—" Angel bit off when he looked up to peer intently over the back of her chair.

Angel shifted around to see Tyrone leaning indolently

against the wall, a narrowed gleam in his hazel eyes. As he pushed away from the wall, his princelike body moving into the circle of light, Angel noticed his clean buff breeches. She read that he had been visiting the home of Jean Lafitte, otherwise he wouldn't be dressed as neatly as he was. His dark print, calico tunic was open to his waist and he smelled strongly of brandy even from where she sat. She saw in her mind's eye a repeat of that afternoon's performance and she blushed profusely when he came to stand over her. He saw the stuff at her feet and was visibly alarmed at the size of her once tiny heel.

"What the devil!" he repeated Nikki's earlier words on the beach when Ellen had been about to accomplish her deadly deed.

Bending to survey the bulging red heel, Tyrone's fingers were gentle as they clutched about her lithe ankle. Angel struggled without success to ward off the sapping sensations creeping into her limbs. His hair, ruffled like Nikki's, fell over his wide forehead and she at once pondered the likeness between the two, though Nikki's hair was dark and Tyrone's tawny. Yes, he reminded her of a huge lion, with eyes just as lazy green-gold. He was a king—a king among beasts of prey. She shivered from his tingling touch, the power vested in it, but a tiny flame of rebellion was nourished in her breast.

Tyrone read the shiver as dislike of his touching her. He snorted and his nose flared at the nostrils. "Well, it does seem to be well taken care of, though it is infected." He looked from one to the other, and stroked his beard as he added, "Nikki, could I have a moment with you?"

They went to the corner nearest the door and Angel heard them conversing in that French patois, presently hearing Tyrone's astonished "What!" that ended in a mouthful of imprecations. She realized that Nikki was relating to Tyrone the horrible incident that had taken place that night, for Ellen's name and "the princess" were muttered often.

The day had been a taxing one for her and soon the voices became indistinct and all ablur. Someone knocked, there was the odor of food, the clatter of a tray being set down, and a third deep voice entered the conversation. Caspar. Angel felt her hunger gnaw, but when no one called her to the table, she gave in to her weariness. She fell sound asleep, nestled in the wicker chair like a child too tuckered out to care about food—or anything else.

Languorous gray waves licked the shores in the later hours of morning, creating a soft rushing sound to permeate the palmetto and wood of the cottage. Rain pattered softly as the young woman in the bed tossed with the gentle murmur of the indraft and snuggled deeper into the rough blankets. She blinked beneath the covers as she wakened to the strange warmth in the room, despite the sounds of a cooler, moist wind blowing outside.

To Angel's dawning dismay she realized that she was stripped naked. But how! She couldn't have slept that soundly that she didn't know she was being divested of the tunic? As she sat up she clutched the blanket to her naked bosom and blinked and flushed in the glow coming from the brazier set directly in the center of the room. She glanced down to the foot of the bed and saw the tunic she'd worn the night before. It trailed carelessly onto the floor and the mosquito netting had been drawn back to catch the warmth into the bed. A further glimpse about the dimly lighted room evidenced that she was completely alone. The meal had been cleared away, causing her to wonder if in truth there had ever been one placed there the evening before.

Oh no! Angel thought, perhaps Tyrone could see fit to disrobe her and place her body in his bed, but he wasn't going to find her here, smiling sweetly, awaiting his pleasure. No sir!

Flicking back the blankets, she stretched to fetch up the tunic, when a long arm shot out from behind her and back she went. She shrieked in surprise as instantaneously a low chuckle sounded in her ear. She snapped her head sideways on the pillow to meet the flecked eyes head on.

"Oh!" she breathed into the leering face, "you've been here all this time, silent as a sleeping cat—just waiting to spring on me!"

"Mmmm-hmmm . . . and just as content, too, my beauty. You are most tempting when you slumber. If I didn't know better, I would believe you to be a highborn princess from some splendid castle. Still, you *are* a blueblood, aren't you?" Tyrone looked strangely disturbed and grave as he played with a wisp of hair shining with silver-blond highlights.

She tried to rise again but her progress was retarded as flexing muscles drew her mercilessly back. Halting her struggles, he allowed himself the privilege of studying her naked torso, placing a hand on either side of her, his lean, hard form barely touching her belly before she realized he too was fully naked. She stifled a cry as he pressed closer and she felt the silken object of his desire grow.

"Please—please don't do that," she begged, twisting against him.

"Shhh, my beauty. Give me a kiss and stop struggling like a tigress."

"Your beauty I am not!" she breathed, rolling her head aside to escape his lowering lips, pretending not to feel his heat and steel. "Smuggler, you are a *diable!*" she hissed hotly.

"Your French is exquisite, sweet. Though naming me a devil leaves me with a distressed pain in my breast." He affected a pained expression.

"A fleeting pain, no less," she returned mockingly.

He laughed heartily, then, sensing something, he lowered his head to cock an ear. Another growl of hunger rose, causing her to blanch in horror at the loud, embarrassing sound. She looked quickly aside to escape his knowing grin and his peaked brow.

"Mmmm, methinks the Lady Sherwood hungers not for love this morn, but a morsel to break the fast," he murmured, grazing her cheek with a kiss. "Sorry, sweet, I'd forgotten that you fell sound asleep when your dinner was on the table last night. Say . . . how is your dainty little foot this morning?" He dug it out from under the covers, studied it, and said, "Ah, it's fine, just fine, and shrinking fast. Thanks to Nik's doctoring."

Looking thoughtful suddenly, he let go of the healing foot and surprised her completely by leaping from the bed. Snatching up his buff breeches, he donned them in easy jerks. Angel had kept her eyes averted as he was leaving the bed, but still she had caught the white flash of lower limbs, contrasting boldly with the tan darkness of his upper half.

"Today is the Sabbath, and all of the islanders will soon be to church," he said in a muffle as he yanked the blousey tunic over the silken bunch of his thick hair. "Too bad you have nothing to wear. That is, as I think of it now, nothing on such short notice. Otherwise I would escort you there myself to worship beside me. As I have postponed my trip upstream to deliver merchandise, we will have all day—alone," he said, chuckling evilly. "So . . . I will return shortly with a liberal breakfast to ease that nasty grumbling in your little tummy."

When he turned back once to survey her mood before going out the door, he had to smile at the hastiness in which she had found and donned the white robe. Catching him staring, she whirled about, showing him flying blond waves rippling down to her tiny waist that was made even tinier as she jerked the ties waist-cinching tight.

After he was gone, Angel thought: How dare he! He knew why she didn't have anything to wear. He just delighted in rubbing it in, that was all!

Later, and true to his words, Angel shared with Tyrone a generous breakfast of fluffy crepes filled with berries, hot biscuits dripping with honey, chickory coffee, and her favorite herbal English tea.

As they lingered over their tea, Tyrone recalled her earlier surprise when he had mentioned the piousness of the island folk, and he now informed her that yes, the natives were very religious. He had also attended the primitive services now and then, and had been thankful that the sermons had been short ones, for he could never sit still for very long, even as a boy.

Tyrone watched covertly as she began to relax and loose her guard somewhat, conversing more than usual as she related like events from her own childhood. Soon she was animated, charming, and never did she realize that an ominous cloud was steadily approaching to spoil everything.

"It is not the folk here that surprise me, Tyrone, but you. I cannot for the life of me imagine you attending a single church service, even that of the most simple in nature. Should I apologize, sir?"

"To be sure," he began tersely, dabbing his beard with a

183

linen, "I've not always been a smuggler of infamous bearing."

She drew puzzled brows together. "Which one of your parents was English—or still is?" The words were out before she could snatch them back and she now regretted having been so tactless.

Tyrone tapped the roughhewn table with a forefinger. "Ah, my mother . . . was." He peered in cool detachment at the bowed head across from him and asked a question of his own. "Tell me, what else did that deceased harlot fill your head with?"

Her head snapping up, Angel gasped. "De—deceased? But how—could that be? Surely, you are jesting, being cruel?" she said hopefully.

"I forgot. How could you know," he growled, rising sharply, his chair scraping noisily on the boards. He disliked the turn that the conversation had taken, and gusts of anger had seized him and he could not sit still. "No, I am not jesting. I received the ugly report just this morning after dawn."

"But, you were here all night . . . weren't you?" she asked fearfully.

Tyrone expelled a breath. "I left with Nikki shortly after putting you to bed last night, then returned to crawl into bed with you late this morning. Ellen was murdered in her cell, and going by the warmth still in her body, the boys said it must have taken place shortly before dawn."

"How awful," she said in a small, trembling voice.

Tyrone snorted. "You say that so painfully for one who had all the reason in the world to hate her. Ellen almost murdered *you* in cold blood last night, and now you almost break out in tears over the harlot's death!"

"Oh stop! You are being sadistic about the whole thing."

"Me! Ellen wasn't being sadistic when she had to see you stripped naked before she could even pull the trigger? Mademoiselle whatever-your-name-is," he ground out, more irritated that he hadn't found out her name by now than anything else.

She wasn't listening. How strange it all was—her life had been spared and another's ruthlessly taken. To her Ellen had been only a confused woman; perhaps she had given much of

184

herself, received nothing in return in the way of happiness.

"It was because of you that Ellen sought to slay me, did you know?" Angel flung at his back.

Tyrone, ignoring her pointedly, went to let in the hound and fed him from the plenitude of leftovers. His emotions under control, he spoke to Noble as if no one else occupied the room.

"You, you don't care about anything or anyone!" she spat at the rugged bending frame of the man. She felt extreme loathing for his coldheartedness at this sorry time. "For all her jealousy and outspoken desire, she must have loved you deeply to want to slay someone she thought stood in her way. Poor woman," she added softly, "she was horribly miserable and at her wit's end—I realize that now, and I should have been more of a friend to her."

"Who?" Tyrone said with mock curiosity. Then, keeping his back to her, "Good Lord, Noble, where have you been to pick up such stubborn burrs!"

"Oooh! You are disgusting! A woman is dead this morning and all you can do is sit there and pluck burrs from that beast's coat. You've a heart of flint, Captain Ty, and I pity the next poor wretch who might pin her hopes on your cold heart." She shook so badly she had to sit down to calm herself, and once on the bed's edge she couldn't be still. "You may attract many with your—your animallike virility and your magnetic personality—" She stopped. What am I saying? she wondered.

Tyrone spun about. "Yes? This *is* beginning to become interesting. Do go on, go on."

"You did not let me finish!"

Tyrone bowed his head and tossed his hand in the air. "Do, do go on."

"Humph—I was about to say . . . you could never attract me, never make me a willing mistress. You are a randy beast, unfeeling, in my book!"

His face hardened into rock as he came to loom above her. "There are many eager ladies who would be willing mistresses to this randy beast, as you call me. Whether you believe this or not does not matter to me—I have never before, not even once, had to resort to rape in the past, my dear. Women come to my bed at the snap of my fingers, and, just as swiftly, they go. And

185

this is the truth—you will be no exception as far as the latter goes!"

She glared up at him, hissing, "I will never come to your bed willingly, nor will I beg for your favors. You will have to rape me the rest of my life, and even then, on my deathbed I shall spit in your rakehell's face!"

"When I finish with you, *ma petite*, you will want me. I promise you that, and recall—you will be no better than a strumpet, alone and peddling your wares after I tire of your charms. I *might* make an exception."

"Meaning?" she asked, not really wanting to know.

"Perhaps I will keep you longer than usual before I deposit you at the local bordello in New Orleans."

With that he turned on his booted heel and strode stormily across the room, almost upsetting the brazier on his way to the door. The slamming of the door echoed in the new stillness of the cottage. Still seated upon the bed, Angel slowed down her breathing that had become rapid during his bitter speech. She thought about what he had said, and all at once she found herself laughing. She stopped as she sighted the madras that Tyrone had ravished the day before. Crossing the room she picked up the torn garment and went to search out all the drawers. Among the contents she discovered exactly what she had been looking for—a needle and some strong thread.

Now and then there sounded a distant grumbling of thunder as the rain clouds moved westward and puffs of warmer air blew across the wet sand. The moisture of the morning rain sparkled as it dripped from thatched roofs and a young afternoon saw the coming of the sun, nestled like a glowing white ball beneath the blankets of blue-gray, foretelling a late orange sunset.

With the hound at his heel, Tyrone entered the public house and bellowed out loud to stir Rolfe from his labors in the kitchen. Rolfe scuffled out from the back room where racks upon racks of excellent wines, liquors, and ale were stored. He was wiping his black fingers on a fresh linen apron, the palms and fingers of his huge hands pink and shiny from hours of toiling at the stove.

Tyrone was just about to inquire as to where he might find Lola or one of his other past bedtime favorites, when Rolfe's black eyes danced with merriment as he peered around the broad shoulders of the captain and nodded to a darkened corner of the expansive hall. Tyrone quirked an eyebrow rakishly, while at the same time one corner of his mouth cracked in the beginning of a knowing grin.

He turned to view Big Jim lounging on a long bench to appropriate his tall frame. His legs were stretched out before him as he blew out a thick cloud of blue smoke that drifted up into his graying light brown hair. He looked the distinguished gentleman with his salt-and-pepper sideburns and his curling, black English pipe held deftly between his lean fingers. This time he was dressed neatly in dark buff trousers and a cream silk shirt with wide ruffles at his dark throat and tanned wrists. His blue uniform had been packed long ago.

In 1792 Big Jim had been instrumental in establishing a regularly organized police force under Corondelet—the Civil Guard in New Orleans. Big Jim had been strikingly handsome in his full uniform with cocked hat, blue breeches and frock coat, and breast straps of shiny black leather supporting a cartridge box and a bayonet scabbard. His ornament had consisted of a short sword and a flintlock musket. Later, and this time under Daniel Clark, he became commanding officer of a battalion of three hundred men to protect the city from the rioting and looting which had become rife among the lower classes. The *garde de ville* was composed mostly of Creole, American-Louisianian, and some born Yankee like himself—all residents of the city. A strict company of militia was formed soon after, and Big Jim had dropped out of the *garde de ville* in 1806 and hadn't returned since. Real estate was his main interest now, and he owned quite a collection of older southern homes, which he loved renovating, and which took up most of his time. When he could vacation, England was his destination.

With a lopsided grin Tyrone swaggered over to greet Big Jim. "Well, I should say—what a pleasant surprise this is, sir—but Caspar has already informed me beforehand of your coming."

Swinging his long legs around, Big Jim's jade-green eyes

sparkled and his face was tense with a strange excitement. Unusually, he now greeted his handsome son with a deep chuckle and a strong grip to both elbows. This surprised the younger man, for his father had never been one to display his affections openly.

Rolfe brought a dusty bottle of rare brandy while the older man continued to pull on his long pipe. The bottle was wiped clean, uncorked and set upon a table between the two men. When Rolfe took his leave, Big Jim leaned forward and a serious look came over the taut places of his sun-darkened face, leaping into his eyes.

"Did you get it?" Big Jim asked, the skin crinkling at his eyes.

Tyrone leaned back far, avoiding the question. "You shouldn't be here you know. The Bos' *Blacksails* is on her way here, and I might add—heavily laden with great chests of jewels, Spanish coin, and—ummm—yards upon yards of—ah—somewhat bloodstained silks." He stopped here, already thinking ahead to the green winding waterways and hidden mazes known so well to him. The great warehouses were already bulging with booty and it was up to him to see that the "top merchandise" got transported soon. He chuckled mentally here: Once more "Robin Hood" would unclench his gold fists, and the peasants awaited his coming. He could already see the smiling faces of the peasants as they traded the gold and jewels with the discreet merchants of New Orleans. Again, he would keep nothing for himself, except maybe this time some unstained gowns for Miss Sherwood.

"Well?" Big Jim tried again.

Tyrone watched his father gulp down a dollop of brandy, seemingly uncaring that he courted danger every time he visited these islands. Lafitte had knowledge of his visits, and knew also that Big Jim was a casual acquaintance of Governor Claiborne's.

Tyrone finally answered. "Yes, I have the deed here in my pocket. But are you sure it was the Sherwoods' manor you purchased, I mean the very same Sherwoods that are here?"

"Stonewall Manor, one and the same. In fact, I saw the family off at the London docks. Recall, it was I who informed your men and the lieutenant's of the *Fidelia*'s passage? I should be tossed in the calaboose myself for aiding pirates and smugglers. Sometimes I wonder what in hell I've gotten myself into."

"Hmmm, this is becoming more interesting by the minute," Tyrone said, and, "Is Stonewall another gift, sir?"

"Call it whatever you like. You can hold on to it, or give it back to Mademoiselle Sherwood and her mother." He watched closely as Tyrone tilted his glass, intent on becoming more than a little mellow. There was a striking change in his son, now twenty-nine, a transition that made him wonder if it had anything to do with Angeline Sherwood. He said under his breath, "Now that you have her, I suppose you wonder just what the hell you are to do with her?"

"What was that?" Tyrone began, "there is such a clamor outside that I missed what—"

"Said, it's too bad about Lord Sherwood and his unfortunate accident," Big Jim cut his son off. Everything had come off better than he had planned, but for that one thing.

"Wait a damn minute," Tyrone explained. "Lord Sherwood was not put out carelessly. It was an awkward situation and before I could get to him, Blade had already put the old man out of his misery. He was already dying, for he was broken badly, and sick in the gut besides. You could tell that by his sickly green pallor."

"You got what you wanted, didn't you, my son?" Big Jim questioned too quickly. Suddenly he knew what the change in Tyrone was: There was a bright new color in his eyes—the color of jealousy and possessiveness. It had been deep in Tyrone's temperment as a child, but had been lost somewhere along the way from boyhood to adulthood. It was good, for Tyrone was feeling again.

Tyrone ran his fingers through his tousled hair and answered somewhat tipsily, "I'm not so sure, anymore. Miss Sherwood is the most damnable wench I've ever been saddled with. I have a strong inclination to cart her and that whining mother of hers to New Orleans and leave them off there with sufficient coin to get back to England." He sobered in the next instant, asking, "How in the hell did you learn about

189

the Sherwoods?"

"I went to England to play cards with this famous card shark, Beldwin Sherwood, and then. . . ." He shrugged, at a loss for words to go on.

Tyrone wasn't surprised, for Big Jim disliked being bested at a game of cards. Then curiously, "You have seen Miss Sherwood before, then?"

"She was a spindly girl when I first saw her, but lovely even then. She hardly took notice of me when I went to game there, so crazy over horses and books was she. Very much like you when you were a youth."

Tyrone narrowed his gaze, remembering their bet. "Aha! You promised me you would discover the perfect little maid for me to wed, and I arrogantly informed you that if and when I should ever decide to take a bride, it would be for the sole purpose of obtaining an heir. But even at that, recall I warned you I would not forsake my old ways—not for *any* fluff in downy skirts!"

"And—isn't she perfect?" Big Jim asked.

"Sir, your message was, 'laying abed with bucks from Twickenham to Buckhurst Hill.' You call that perfect? Unsullied? Hah!"

"Ah-hh, hell," Big Jim snarled. "What have you done! I told my man, 'evading the bad, not laying abed!'"

"Damn me," he swore softly. Then, "It does not fall all on me, your blame. Caspar's memory has become befuddled with age and drink. Still, all in all, I won't believe this until I hear it from her own lips. But why would you have wanted me to know all this?" he asked, as an afterthought.

"Because, what I had meant was—take care of this virtuous treasure, see no harm comes her way," Big Jim said, his eyes dark as a shadowed forest.

Tyrone slumped low in his chair, feeling suddenly much older than his twenty-nine years. "Sir, do you know the young lady's name?" he tried.

"You haven't learned that by this time?"

Tyrone glowered impatiently. "Do you have it, sir!" he asked coldly.

"Ummm, I am sorry, Tyrone. The young lady's name

190

escapes me just now. I'm certain she will tell you soon enough, though. As you believe she will tell you of this other—umm— her virtuousness."

"Hah! You don't know Miss Sherwood, sir." Next he queried, hoping there was not something ugly in the Sherwood's closet of skeletons, "And, what of this manor, Stonewall?"

"I do not misread your thoughts, my son. Yes, there was an overabundance of liens against the place, but my gold was not turned down when finally all of the claimants came to collect. The only ones that did come forth who were eager to pay part of the Sherwoods' debts were young gentlemen who asked about Mademoiselle Sherwood's whereabouts. Bastards—they were reluctant to lend coin once they had knowledge of the overpowering circumstances that surrounded Stonewall, and that the young lady could not return to such poverty. There was not one soul wealthy enough to keep the Sherwoods from drowning. How was I to know that Beldwin Sherwood wasn't true to his word; that he had paid all his debts before signing the deed over to me—so he said?"

"So . . ." Tyrone said, waving his hand restlessly in the air as he spoke, ". . . not one of those aristocratic sonofabitches could supply them with funds. I'll bet the better part of the pack fled the doorstep well before the manor went up for sale. And the young gentlemen who straggled in, no doubt, were the bucks you had mentioned in your message—the young lady's lovers?"

Big Jim snorted. "What's the use. You forever condemn women for their shortcomings, even if they haven't any to speak of, you still put them all down as whores—sooner or later. Do you still hate your mother that much, even though she sleeps in her grave? I don't believe you do, you named your ship after her."

"Forget the name of the ship, it's a common name in Louisiana. Lord, doesn't it bother you to know that I saw her in bed with another man—that scene I witnessed long ago?" Ty grilled, his eyes brittle as winter leaves.

Big Jim sighed and said coldly, sadly, "It always ends this way, with you and I arguing about your dead mother. She was a

191

good woman, despite what you think or believe. She always sought your welfare, and she loved you very much, gave you everything you wanted."

Tyrone retorted mockingly, "Just like Jacinta gives me everything, only not material possessions."

Big Jim growled, "We'll not speak of her now. Jacinta is what she is and will never change. She has nothing to do with this conversation, anyway."

"Sure. Jacinta is not perfect. She is infertile, childless," he said, pouring one drink after another just as quickly as he could down them.

"Enough," Big Jim ended with finality.

With that both men fell into painful silence. Once more their conversation had taken a bitter turn. Father and son would continue to converse as the evening passed, but now with a certain noncommittal air between them. It was always like this; it was inevitable.

2

Straining their eyes for the first glimpse of the *Blacksails* riding the horizon, the crew and the native Baratarians whooped wildly when she was spotted. Now the black-hulled, black-sheeted schooner with the "bones on black" banner did sail triumphantly into the bay to the even louder, thunderous tune of raucous welcome lifting from the assemblage gathered there. A smaller figure stood watchfully on the other side of the pass on the tip of Grande Isle, hair blowing back like spun honey in the ever warming breezes. And her presence went undetected in the excitement, almost, but for one pair of dark green eyes taking in the lovely sight.

Captain Ty took his gaze momentarily from the schooner to Big Jim. "Tonight, sir, there will take place the most unhallowed of festivities in the western hemisphere. Wine, women, and song, all night long," he said poetically.

"Yes, so I've heard," Big Jim returned, his mind elsewhere, making plans, which included a bundle of feminine garments he'd brought with him.

When Big Jim didn't respond to the excitement, Tyrone turned to nudge Pearce Duschesne. "Well now, how many Spanish beauties will charm us out of our britches tonight, Pearce?" he asked, feeling his oats.

"Why, Captain Ty, I thought for sure you had your hands full already. Why the sudden interest in dark beauties, hmm?" Pearce wondered, blocking out the vision across the pass by standing directly in front of Tyrone.

"How many?" Tyrone repeated harshly.

Pearce challenged, "More than even you can handle in one night, *my friend.*"

When Captain Ty viewed the objects of their conversation climbing daintily out of the pirogues, he made adequate haste to swagger down to greet the somewhat peeved, dark-haired ladies. At his coming, the females suddenly were not so displeasured upon eyeing collectively this visage of carnal handsomeness. Too, there lurked about him a menacing fearlessness, given to men leading lives full of danger. Flustered giggles and much posturing took place amongst the gypsylike women when the tall captain moved among them, his warm hazel eyes divesting them of the full skirts and daringly lowcut white linen blouses. His lean fingers fondled boldly while he sampled some of the pear-shaped assets and curvaceous, generous behinds, all with their owners' quiet consent.

Now this was more like their old smuggler-captain, Ty's crew were thinking as they watched him boldly flirt. They chortled, encouraging the captain to roughly pull into his arms a long-limbed woman of approximately age thirty, with deliciously full red lips. The large amount of brandy he had consumed in such a short time, plus the many eager curves pressing dangerously close about him caused his temperature to rise feverishly high.

When Tyrone's armful began to pant and press her voluptuous body into him, he heard her begging him in Spanish to take her somewhere, quickly please. To her surprise, the tall captain holding her stiffened oddly and released her so suddenly that her dark head snapped back painfully. Replying with a brusque "later" in Spanish, the captain strode quickly aside to rap out an order to one of his crew. His man stood astonished at the sudden change in his captain, and bug-eyed, shaking his seaman's cap, he went to do Ty's bidding.

Big Jim had surveyed all this with thorough discontent, but would never let Tyrone know of this. His mind was on his own plans for the evening as he wondered how the lovely Angeline would like the dainty frock he had just lately ordered sent to her. Angeline would come easily enough when she learned that her mother, too, would be present.

Angel had watched the entire scene from across the pass, and it was apparent that Tyrone had not sighted her. She now strolled idly back to the lonely cottage. Not once had Tyrone glanced across to her as the tall stranger and Pearce Duschesne had done several times. She hadn't been able to make out the gray-haired man's features from that distance, yet there was something oddly familiar about his casual stance and his hazy countenance.

Angel kicked at the sand and the little stones shining orange-red in the settling rays of sunlight. It had become humid and hot, and she looked upon the cottage just up ahead with anticipation of its cooler interior. It was almost ironic that the brazier would still be sitting in the middle of the room, its kindling and peat long cold.

Angel couldn't help thinking that Tyrone had been deliberately cruel to that dark-haired woman in the gypsy outfit. Oh . . . no! Angel halted several feet from the cottage door. Could it be possible . . . possible that Tyrone had been Ellen's murderer? She spun about madly to see him and the tall stranger disappear in the distance behind a stand of oleanders. Will I be his next victim? she wondered out loud.

Inside, Angel paced the boards of the cottage floor. She chewed upon a thumbnail for what seemed like hours, slumping into the wicker chair, rising, plans forming in her mind, only to be discarded when they originated, over and over. He wanted her—true? He was indeed dangerous and she would have to proceed with caution. What did she have to lose?

"Yes, yes. I—I will play the str-strumpet for him." And

194

before long he would take her and Christine to New Orleans. He had said as much. She buried her small face in her hands to weep soundlessly.

Later, feeling somewhat refreshed, Angel rose from the chair and dashed away the burning tears with the back of her hand. She was about to tidy up the place when a bumping at the door gave her pause. She went to listen at the wood and the sound came again; she jumped, then asked in a tiny voice who was there.

A man's voice on the other side said, "Will you please open the door, miss? Can't hold this darn stuff all night, y'know."

Angel peered around the door at a small, dark man holding an armful of clothing. There were slippers, and some other items she could not yet identify. Stepping back to allow him to enter, she watched with calm interest as the hurried man bore the bundle to the cleared table, dropped the burden, and turned to go.

"Get ready, miss. There's a big cellar-bration tonight and you are supposed to come. Someone's gonna come get you in a few hours." He scratched his balding pate and added, "Oh, yeah, I'm to tell you that some lady called Christine's gonna be there, too."

After he had gone out, Angel sifted through the pile, but was mostly fascinated at the frock draped neatly on top. It was of a spring green shade and sprigged delightfully with tiny pink rosettes, making her think of an English garden in full bloom. The snug bodice was made for a yonger woman and she wondered suddenly about the person who had sent all these things. Would the captain send such a sweet, modest garment for her to wear at this so-called celebration? And, was he all through punishing her for her *misdoings?* Bah!

Nevertheless, she hurriedly tried on the frock and fastened slowly the tabs at the back, her mind flying hither and yon. She could almost feel the frock being ripped away carelessly by those cruel and lean fingers. That man did seem to derive a sadistic pleasure in spoiling almost everything he laid his hands upon.

Pleased that it would fit nicely after altering a few pleats in the bodice, Angel removed the frock to lay it methodically

195

upon the bed. She donned the robe next, and after searching the dresser for the cracked mirror she had seen earlier, went to perch on the edge of the bed with needle and thread in hand. She extracted the bodice's threads with the needle and her tiny teeth, stopping only once when dusk had fallen to strike flint to a thick candle.

Later, the frock altered and donned, her feet slippered, she proceeded to braid the glossy tresses of hair to fashion a princesslike coronet that wound snugly round her head. Studying the creamy crown in the cracked mirror, she swept low into a charming curtsy. She smiled, pleased at the reflection of softly slanting eyes and pouting pink mouth. She had pressed the crushed rose petals to her lips, knowing at once what they had been intended for; the rose petals had been sent along in a powder box. Whoever it was who had had these feminine delights sent her way, besides the lavender toilet water, must be an expert in the ways of women's toilets.

She didn't appear overdone or too fluffy; after all, it was only a smuggler's shindig. It would do Christine well, though, to see a reminder of the daughter her mother had known in the past. Yes, she appeared vibrant, glowing with health, as she whirled gaily from the dresser to seat herself upon the wicker chair, folding her hands in her lap demurely.

As she awaited her escort she could already hear drifting over to her the artless music and dominant male laughter bursting now and then into ribald song. Feminine voices answered back with some of the same, their high-pitched shrieks feigning outrage at being pinched or fondled too boldly. Suddenly she bolted from the chair. Someone had come for her—finally.

She was so happily surprised at seeing Bron that she hugged him right off. Embarrassed, Bron's eyes twinkled shyly as he stepped back to look her over closely.

"Little one. You like princess this night. Come, we must go."

Angel grabbed up off the chair the rose wisp of shawl and walked dreamily with Bron to the waiting pirogue. She asked Bron how her mother was faring, and he informed her that

Christine was doing very well, though she missed her daughter terribly. She was being kept busy helping Thelma with the children, and that he added, was the best medicine for someone who'd lost a loved one. Angel only smiled at that.

The pass would be crossed in only a matter of five minutes or so, and in that time Angel asked so many questions that Bron's head began to spin, but he chuckled deeply at her healthy interest.

"The boss and his lieutenants are all there," Bron mentioned of Lafitte and his crew. "What a bunch tonight. Much people from both islands, and some from far away. Like everyone in world, little one!"

Finally Bron was leading Angel up the beach toward the flickering bonfires that leaped out at the loosely interwoven throng of laughing, colorful people. Off to one side a group of what appeared to be gypsies made a small circle around a tall, long-limbed Spanish woman who began to swirl her red skirts and stamp with frenzied movements, tossing back a huge mane of unkempt blue-black hair. Her feet tapped wildly as she leaped to a cleared table, giving the pack of panting men surrounding her a delicious glimpse of leg and thigh now and then. The violinists and a lantern-jawed man squeezing a concertina moved closer to the group forming a rounded mass, painting a night scene that resembled a gypsy encampment.

The entire island seemed to be set on fire with the spirit of merriment, and Angel's late arrival went unnoticed. Bron led her directly to where Thelma and Christine hung back from the crowd, seated beneath a huge live oak and sampling some red wine and red snapper, the latter having been baked in leaves over an open-ground pit.

Christine exclaimed happily and rose from the blanket when she saw her daughter walking toward her. They stood clinging to each other a moment and then sank down to the blanket, talking in animated pleasure all the while. Angel returned Thelma's affectionate hug with genuine warmheartedness. They talked and talked, of the children and the night's festivities, until Christine turned quiet and contentedly drowsy from the food and the effects of the wine.

Jean Lafitte, Dominique You, and Renato Beluche stopped by to make amicable conversation for a time before moving on. Lafitte lingered, though, while the other rowdy two went off to search out women for the night.

"Ahhh, Mademoiselle Sherwood," Lafitte said, his smiling black eyes liquid. "A fairer maid I have never before seen. Would you care to dance? Listen, the musicians are striking up a slower tempo. Come—" Lafitte pulled Angel to her feet, "let us go where the ground is firmed for dancing. This sand gets in one's boots!"

They moved to the higher terra firma where much of the dancing was indeed taking place. The Black Falcon proved to be an excellent stepper, despite his holding Angel so close she thought she would soon be crushed to a nothing. As she danced with the most infamous pirate of the Caribbeans and the Gulf of Mexico, she thought she should really be filled with great fear, but she was beginning to realize that he was not the unholy terror of the seas that most thought him. In fact, she'd learned just this night from Thelma that Lafitte had only been to sea twice in his life so far.

How ironic, Angel thought, for the pirate-king of the century to be resigned to staying home tending his books and counting out his resources day in and day out. She almost had to giggle out loud at the ridiculousness of his frightful *nom de guerre*—Black Falcon, indeed!

Jean Lafitte was darkly handsome though, a ladies' man, and as most of the women present were waiting in line for a chance to dance with the man, Angel was left with a polite apology and the promise of another dance later. Not so tightly, though, she hoped, as she watched him glide away with a female Santo Dominigan.

She was just about to make her way back to the blanket when, with a gasp, she felt herself swept onto the terra firma once again, this time by Nikki.

"What are you doing here, princess?" Nikki asked with playful gruffness.

"Why, I'm here for the same reason everyone else is here, bold lad," Angel said with a twist to her speech.

"Not why, princess—*what?*" Nikki said, peering over her shoulder as if he watched for someone.

"What?" Angel repeated, then laughingly, "Dancing, that is what. Same as all these other silly marionettes."

"I am going to warn you now, sweet enchantress of the night. You'd better watch out for the black wizard! He doesn't know you're here yet, and for some strange notion all his own, he wanted you to stay put in the cottage." Nikki pressed the small, up-tilted nose with a forefinger, adding, "Probably not for long, though; someone would have come to fetch you."

Angel feigned a look of shuddering fear. "The black wizard, you mean of course—"

"Oh-oh. Don't look now, my dumpling. Please, look this other way. Here." Nikki twirled her deeper into the smash of dancing couples.

Curiously Angel leaned from side to side, trying to peer over and behind Nikki's wide shoulders, but he kept on moving with her in circles. Then she saw him. He was dressed totally in black, from his silk tunic down to his pantaloons and, finally, to jackboots that shined handsomely up to his knees. His dark beard had been trimmed neatly, too. He was standing next to one of the long tables laden with liquors and food. The tall stranger she had seen earlier was cast in deep shadow behind Tyrone. But what held her attention most was the disturbing vision of that voluptuous Spanish woman who had danced with more than a little sensuous abandonment, standing now affectionately close to Tyrone.

As Angel continued to stare between the couples, Tyrone suddenly tossed back his head at something the woman had said and he laughed loud with pleasure. All of a sudden his back stiffened noticeably and his eyes narrowed into slits as he cast a long searching scan over the shifting crowd, his gaze penetrating into the circle of dancing couples.

Angel didn't wait for those eagle eyes to find her, but begged Nikki to escort her immediately back to the blanket. Wending their way there, Angel felt as if she had been pierced with a sword after seeing Tyrone caress that woman's waist with a long, encircling arm. It was the second time this day he had sought that woman out especially. She should have been overjoyed to know this, but all she felt was a dull aching in her chest and a hollow feeling in the pit of her stomach.

It was only that her plans were going awry, Angel thought decidedly, nothing else.

Upon reaching the fringe of the crowd Angel was severely disappointed to find the blanket unoccupied. Christine was gone! She was just about to scan the mob for some sign of her mother and Thelma when Bron came over to inform her that one of the children had taken ill.

"Mum think daughter not return soon from dancing. She say Angel will not mind," Bron explained. "She say good night to daughter, and you understand." He belched loud and apologized at once. With that he took his leave and went to find his friends who were bragging fish-tales.

"Who in the world is Angel?" Nikki asked suspiciously. "Mmmm, she must have meant you, princess?"

Angel appeared dumbfounded and couldn't find the words to explain. The day was saved as Bron returned, weaving slightly. He was scratching his head and grinning sheepishly. Before Bron could open his mouth to speak, Angel had come to a decision and now looked off into the darkness beyond the edge of the firelight.

"I will go, too. After all, I have been informed that my presence is not desired here. I can be of help and stay with my mother then, as I can see for myself that no one shall miss me this night," she added strangely.

Before she could step onto the path leading to the cottage, Bron's hand gently restrained her and he shook his big head from side to side. Angel fixed her gaze upon the arm holding her, then slid up to meet bloodshot eyes. She frowned in puzzlement.

"You cannot go, little one. You must stay. I remember now, I have order to keep you from going," Bron said apologetically.

"B-but who?" she tried to fathom. "Surely not the smuggler-captain," she said, wishing it were true, but knowing inwardly this was not so.

"No, not cap'n. Cannot say. No question, little one,"

Bron cautioned.

Suddenly Bron saw something and then disappeared into the crowd, as if he had seen a horrible apparition of the night. Once again, Angel stood in bewildered puzzlement. She was becoming weary of this game. She felt Nikki watching her closely before he swore softly. Now she turned with a frown as Nikki peered up into the branches of the tree. He began whistling under his breath, as if unmindful of all around him.

"Nikki. What the devil is *she* doing here? I thought I ordered you to escort her to her mother's cottage. In fact, that was two hours ago!"

Angel stayed put, but felt Tyrone's anger close at her back. It prickled up and down her spine and her heart lurched bittersweet up into her throat at the nearness of his deep male voice. Now his harsh words dawned on her and she felt as if doused with a bucket of the iciest water. She wanted to stamp her slippered foot in outrage, feeling herself to be the leading dupe in an oddly planned conspiracy.

Why did her mother have to go and desert her now? And she thought Nikki was her friend—why hadn't he told her, instead of acting surprised to see her? Seeing Nikki's sheepish grin made her want to proceed with her earlier plans all the more. Nikki was no better than Tyrone.

"Golly, cap'n," Nikki apologized, "I completely forgot, slipped my mind till I saw the princess here and just now was planning to take her to the aforementioned spot." He was hoping Bron wouldn't get overly drunk and spill the beans. Also, he had forgotten to ask Big Jim how he was to explain her clothes.

Nikki saw the green eyes widen and the small nose wrinkle in distaste at him. But he said to Tyrone, "She just came here to see her mother, anyway. The lady was here but she's gone now with Thelma. What's—"

Nikki's speech was halted by the murderous glint in the hazel eyes and Nikki knew his cousin's black temper was dangerously near the boiling point. Nikki reached out for Angel's arm, but she stiffened at the contact. Still, he held it fast, not wanting to anger Tyrone the tiniest bit.

201

"Well now," Nikki quickly said, "I'll just mosey up with this angel here and take her to her mother." He saw her glare at him and he tried to smile.

Nikki was making to guide her past his cousin when the Spanish woman, Elena, sauntered over with swaying hips and breasts to stand close behind Tyrone. He glanced down into the liquid jet eyes, at the bold mouth that promised him much pleasure, and he knew in that instant there could be a full night in his bed pressed against naked generous flesh—if he wanted it. He knew even now that he would become thoroughly bored with Elena before the moon waned and the morning fully waxed. Still. . . .

Now Nikki had a thought: Even now should this English girl be clothed as a pauper, her unequaled beauty would blazon forth dramatically. This Elena appeared like so much gaudy tinsel next to the flawless young minx in their midst—truly, she was a match for the rarest of magnificent jewels.

"Eyes, like the first touch of spring blushing through the last shards of snow," Nikki said automatically while Tyrone at once caught and deeply pondered the prosy.

Angel's dark gold brows tugged upward and her lips curled in an unpracticed little flirt directed at Tyrone. Green fire danced hotly in her eyes and Tyrone did a double-take, feeling intoxicated all of a sudden as her eyes continued to entice, filling him with stabs of delight. He tossed down his guard and stared steadily back at her with his entire being kindled in passion's fire. He fought down the urge to snatch her up in his arms here and now and bear her into the wood. He wanted her more than before and it grew into a burning ache in his loins.

Unconsciously Angel's pink lips parted softly and her eyes misted over dreamily with the look of desire, a reckless want. She was caught up in her own clever deception to escape the island, and it was too late to turn back, as Tyrone had seized and captured the moment before it fled. The excitingly hot, magnetic current that passed between them left Angel all atingle and faint with expectation. She smiled saucily at Tyrone, exhibiting a dazzling facade of tiny white teeth. He returned the smile with a lopsided grin that curved his sensuous mouth, and his sparkling eyes hungrily devoured the sweet countenance.

Nikki's jaw had slowly unhinged and he felt the young woman beside him shiver with pleasure; he wondered what she was up to. Time hung suspended before Elena set forth to break the magical spell by stroking the captain's arm and speaking to his wooden figure beside her.

"Come with me, *si?*" she purred into his ear, the last foreign word inaudible to the other two.

Tyrone stared sightlessly at the colorful female beside him, muttering, "*Oui*—ahh—*si*, Elena. I told you, later, much later." When she continued to beg him, he gritted his white teeth and said roughly between them, "Damnit, woman, be still!" He was suddenly unable to concentrate and he was flustered like a green schoolboy; it was making him burn. Elena kept it up and he snapped, "Forget it, Elena. Not now—not later!" He didn't even notice her hurt expression.

Nikki pressed forward, taking up Angel's arm once again. She was reluctant to go and her steps lagged. Nikki grinned at his cousin and as he made to leave, he said, "Well, if you two will excuse us, I'll see the princess to her mama now."

"Prin-cess?" Elena queried, peering stupidly at the younger woman.

Suddenly a long arm shot out and strong fingers clamped tightly onto Nikki's shoulder, causing the younger man to wince. He was dragged roughly back, and his hold on Angel was released in the momentum of the gesture. Nikki stood inches from Tyrone, and that one grasped the chin before him firmly and pointed it in the direction of the frolicking mob that was becoming louder and wilder by the minute, intoxicated and bolder with the shrieking women. Tyrone said not a word but gave Nikki a little shove that he comprehended fully. Nikki flushed visibly, and then with a last smile of acknowledgement to the ladies, he shrugged impersonally as he sauntered off to find his earlier companion.

Elena smirked at the younger woman who now stood alone, staring meekly at the fireflies blinking on the fringe of cavorting shadows. Elena tried tugging at Tyrone's arm to get him away where she could better win his attentions. Elena wanted to tell the sexy-sweet, fragrant-smelling creature to get lost, but something about the smuggler-man held back her waspish tongue. She did the next best thing she could think of, and childishly stuck out her tongue at the other woman. Angel was speechless, for she couldn't remember witnessing such behavior since she was a little girl.

Tyrone fondled his bearded chin in indecision. Suddenly his eyes lit up when they riveted onto a nearing figure. Dominique You had latched *his* eye on to the Spanish woman earlier, but gave up ogling her when the smuggler captain had seemed to claim her as his own. He swaggered by just now most ungracefully, when something about Captain Ty caught his knowing eye. He lifted a brow, spun about, winked and nodded, to which Tyrone responded with a decisive nod of his own.

Suddenly and without warning, You whooped wildly as he lurched forward like a bull at full run and swept Elena off her feet and into his burly arms. Tipsily he bore her into the dark wood and Elena's outraged shrieks and Spanish invectives could be heard above the din of the musicians and drunken revelers.

Magically, there were just the two of them now. The music became as a distant murmur, the capering figures moved in blurred slow motion and the moon bathed the tall figure and the smaller, daintier one in a pale yellow aureole. Angel turned her back on the scene and fingers of hot breath from behind her burned the nape of her neck. She was turned gently about to come face to face with that warmth, but she looked shyly away.

"No, sweet, don't shy away from me now," Tyrone said low. Then, "Would you like to dance, *ma petite?*"

"Oh yes, please," she said eagerly, shining with that sweet smile he loved to see.

Cheers went up when the moon-silvered beauty and her tall, handsome captor began a slow waltz in step with the violins and concertina. Almost all joined in then and soon even the most awkward of couples appeared graceful in the flickering bonfires. Jean Lafitte glided by with Marie, and both winked boldly at the other two, who appeared oblivious that others were dancing, too.

A primitive atmosphere took over and just when Angel was beginning to relax in her partner's arms they were rudely taken apart. Angel was snatched up by Nash Mallory and Tyrone was whisked away by none other than Lola. A mad exchange of partners ensued, the tempo changed, only to relax again before it was struck up wildly again. Wine flowed freely as cups were passed and ale was sloshed about. Angel drank her share, surprised at one point to find herself in the arms of Pearce Duschesne, whose sluggard grin and practiced advances only caused inane giggles to erupt from her. She was feeling full of mischief and laughed out loud when Tyrone pranced by in exaggerated playfulness, wiggling his dark brows when he saw that her partner was now none other than Caspar, who rarely ever bended a knee when it came to hoofing it, unless he was earnestly spifflicated.

Angel danced with several of Tyrone's men, one of whom introduced himself as James Cordell, a newcomer to the smuggler's crew. He was wiry of frame and with blue eyes that devoured everything and everybody.

Satisfied at the outcome so far, the tall man with the ever-glowing pipe who had stood discreetly in shadow took his leave of the festivities, his going undetected by all but his son, and only he knew the reason for Big Jim's not joining in the carefree dancing; this was no time for disclosures that would cause Miss Sherwood disenchantment or suspicions. He would have to thank Big Jim for remaining aloof, but Tyrone truly did not know the full extent of this evening's conspiracies. He did wonder about the charming green frock and decided with a smile that Nikki was the contributor.

Much later Angel was deposited laughing gaily into Tyrone's long-awaiting arms. She was caught up in carefree abandonment, feeling more than a little dizzy, but happier than she had been in a long time. She threw caution to the wind, freely allowing Tyrone to press her dangerously close to his hard-muscled frame. It was like being thrust up against the bole of a sturdy oak, even though the other men had been less than

205

flabby, most of them being very well-conditioned. But Tyrone was all steel and taut flesh, and she was becoming like softened clay, yielding in his arms.

"You've had plenty of wine, I see," Tyrone said in her ear. "Have no more. I'll not have you intoxicated when the mid of night is here. And, judging by the moon and stars, we are close to the bewitching hour now, my little witch."

Angel smiled dreamily, toying with his silken hair. "And, sir, what happens at that darkest hour, *par example?*" she wanted to know.

"*Nous verrons, ma chère,*" Tyrone said, smiling down into the upturned face.

Angel blinked innocently, shrugged, and said, "I did not have much time in my studies to include sufficient French, so *pardonnez-moi,* monsieur. But that—what did you say?"

"Yes, I pardon you, my sweet. Although you seem to be doing quite well for all your so-called lack. What you do know of the language, I suspect that the Frenchman, Pierre Le Naisse taught you?"

"Some, *oui,*" she said simply, running a finger along his collarbone.

Tyrone stiffened, both from her words and the firing touch. "What else did he teach you about?" he asked ungraciously, watching her closely.

"Why . . . how to fence with randy pirates, of course!" she answered eloquently, a green twinkle sparking her eyes.

"*Touché!*" Tyrone quipped. "But randy, tsk, tsk. Such a word for reserved young ladies," he added with mock reprimand, as if ashamed of her verbal usage.

She lifted her chin a notch, asking, "*Nous verrons* . . . what does it mean, please?"

"It means 'it matters not,'" Tyrone finally returned, and, "*n'est-ce pas?*"

"It matters not what happens at the mid of night?" she asked, somewhat confused as she blinked up-curled lashes at him.

"*Oui,* for this is a night made for love, nothing else, and I'll teach you much French this night, whisper words that you never even heard of, *ma chère.*"

Angel trembled a bit, but emboldened herself to her resolutions and hardened herself to what surely would take place this night. She must not think of how much he had hurt her last time and how he had sought only his pleasure. It had been awful, and she prayed he would be gentler with her this time.

Tyrone had detected the slight quiver in her limbs and felt a temporary coldness come between them. He pushed back that same hot anger he had felt this morning in the cottage. By God, if he had to resort to rape again, he would do just that. Only this time she wasn't going to put him off so easily—he was going to make her feel that same hunger his body knew for hers, make her melt with desire.

"Look," Tyrone said, guiding her chin. "Already they are pairing off into couples, going to make love in the cottages, or find a secluded spot on the beach. Well, which do you prefer, sweet, a lonely strip of beach . . . or our cottage?" His arm tightened, jerking her to him as he studied her suspiciously in the firelight.

With an intake of breath she stuttered, "Our—our cottage? But—I thought that I was to join my—"

There was a blur of movement as his hand clasped fast over her mouth and she watched speechless as he shook his head slowly from side to side. They had quit dancing, their thighs brushed to a standstill. She could feel the thunderous pounding of his heart above where her full bosom touched. He lowered his head, cupping the back of her head in his huge hands while his mobile mouth covered hers in a silken, questing kiss. She was stunned at her own response, at the wildly disturbing languor stealing through her blood like satin fire. Her knees grew weak, and when she was certain she would swoon from the bittersweet ache he was creating in her middle, he lifted his head slowly to measure her reaction. Her lips, she knew, were parted and moist, her eyes glazed and begging for much more that she couldn't yet know the meaning and end of. He slid his hands to rest on her waist.

"Would you have me love you here? Tell me, my beauty,

beach or cottage?"

Slowly she gave her answer by gazing dazedly toward moon-shimmering Grand Isle. Tyrone nodded once in agreement, and taking hold of her hand he led her down to a beached pirogue. As she walked, her sore foot told her she'd danced more than she should have, but she daren't remove the slipper now and catch a small stone. Tyrone noticed her slight limping and at once swept her up into his arms to carry her the rest of the way to the water's silvery edge.

Crickets chirped, insects murmured, and the cottage facing the sea was hauntingly swaddled in a fine, drifting mist. The face of the moon peered down in awe at the couple entering the doorway bathed in its moonbeams. Angel was filled with a strange buoyancy when Tyrone struck flint to a candle, and walked unceremoniously over to draw back the mosquito netting on that temptingly huge bed. He unbuckled his belt next, and sitting down on the edge of the bed, unburdened himself of the long jackboots, drawing them off swiftly and dropping them with a loud thud.

Not sure of what to do next, Angel occupied her hands with the unbraiding of her long hair. Soon its length fell tantalizingly about her in tiny wavelets that rippled silkily down to her waist. She was seated in the wicker chair, not sure that she wanted him to speak first to break the deathly silence when, indeed, he did.

"Come here, my beauty." His voice was husky, masculine.

"Now?" she asked like a child too busy at play.

"Yes . . . now!" Tyrone demanded like the provoked adult.

As if her feet had a will of their own, they moved her soundlessly across the boards and halted unsteadily before the bedstead. She swallowed painfully, taking shy notice of him stretched out full-length and wearing only his pantaloons. His maleness was thrown into high relief by the candle and she beheld him as he had appeared just that morning—a huge and powerful animal naked from the waist up, his dark brows and beard a striking contrast with his tawny mane.

His unwavering eyes seemed to penetrate her innermost thoughts. Up to this moment she had possessed some courage, and, incautiously, she had not considered he would learn her game. A slow smile developed at the corners of his mouth, and whatever the meaning behind it, she cultivated the thought that he knew little or nothing of her sham, even though he possessed a quick and keen ability to discern one's thoughts.

In the next instant his hand reached out to move lambently along her arm, causing red-hot shivers to pass through her. Her cheeks bloomed with a scarlet hue and her mind became jumbled as her breath caught in her throat at the sight of his ever-growing desire. She tore her minute inspection from that unmistakable swell and sought to conceal her anxiety.

Bold as a lion, Tyrone reached up with both hands to pull her down beside him, his hands sliding up to her shoulders as he pushed gently to position her onto her back. She stared back unblinkingly at the hungry, lustful glint in his hazel eyes, and she prayed silently for some mild disaster to befall the island. Anything, to halt the inevitable. But it was not to be, for now he was working expertly the tabs at the back of her frock. She felt herself stiffen slightly as his lean fingers laid bare her back and began to tug the garment down to her waist.

"Relax, love," he breathed into her ear, "I'll soon make you pant and purr . . . you will see."

With a quick toss the frock was flung to the foot of the bed. Naked and shivering under his searching regard she watched as through a hazy cloud when he took a moment to peel off his pantaloons and tossed them too aside. When he crouched beside her bracing his arms on either side of her quivering shoulders, she dared to glimpse down past his torso. This time a gasp of panic tore from her lips when she saw fully the wealth of his naked manhood. For a female who had never before witnessed that phallic shape, it was just too much to bear all at once.

Never before, either, had Angel moved so fast as she did now. She slithered down under his arms, and like a scurrying rabbit, hopped from the bed and streaked with hair flying out behind her to cower in a far corner like some frightened, trapped animal. She huddled there with her back nakedly white and turned against his impatient and somewhat bemused glower.

That Tyrone had not even gotten to first base in his love-making was now clearly evident by the look of dark frustration that lined his handsome face. He cast a hooded eye in the direction of that sweet, feminine form; feeling half-wild in his smouldering ardor, readying himself once more for rape. He stood unclad and like a magnificent beast preparing to lunge for the kill. He dropped his head then and his gaze riveted to his own full-blown, throbbing display of desire. He damned himself silently as the full meaning of her strenuous fleeing act smote his brain. But, he would be damned if he was going to tolerate her impertinence this time and kowtow to her childish behavior.

"Hah!" he bellowed. "What has happened to the brave lady who defied me with a flash of a wicked blade and a wrath-filled sparkle in her slanty eyes? Where is she? Has she fled from the sight of mere naked flesh? Or—is it passion that frightens the woman-child so?" His patience had come to an end and a savageness seeped from within, making his countenance indeed barbaric.

Silence. An eternity seemed to pass and when she dared turning her face about, Tyrone was there above her, quietly watching and waiting. The look on his face was unreadable. He bent down suddenly and scooped her up into his arms and she struggled hard against him, pushing at his hard chest with her palms and waving her long legs in the air. He stood very still, allowing her to play herself out to his advantage. Feebly and at last her head rolled against his shoulder and the long mass of her hair trailed over his arm as he bore her to the bed without struggle. She thumped him futilely on the chest now and then, like the beat of a hummingbird's wings.

"You are cruel, Captain Ty. I hate you, hate you, hate you," she muttered breathlessly, and panted against his bare chest.

"We shall see," was all he said as he placed her gently on the bed and followed her down.

Tyrone slid his lean fingers through her hair, creating a blond cloud to spread aqueously about them as he lowered his tanned face to capture her lips in what began as a gentle kiss, but soon became forceful and demanding as his ardor grew apace. She labored with renewed strength, splaying her hands against the furred mounds of his chest. He lifted his head to grit his straight white teeth in her face. Her eyes widened at the feral gleam in the multiflecked orbs and the flat, angry planes of his countenance.

"You are through teasing me, mademoiselle!" he growled. "I always get what I want. Never forget that!"

Angel was reminded of the savage tales of Indians that roamed the New World in search of white victims to rape and maul, and Tyrone looked no less frightful at this moment to her. She arched her back to release his grip, but he imprisoned both her wrists and stretched them high and tautly over her head. This time when his mouth covered the gasping lips he pressed her back with his full weight, his free hand roaming over the mountains and valleys of ever-warming flesh, coming to rest between shivering white thighs. His kiss deepened and she could do nothing but whimper with pleasure as he seemed to guide her into a world of trembling passion, from which there was no returning.

Finally, every fiber and muscle afire, she lost all control of will in her awakening hunger. Feeling his mouth at her neck she heard him chuckle softly in her ear, a sound of bold triumph. His hot lips moved to the pulsating spot at her throat, paused then slid down to an auburn tip. He titillated the crest, his beard chafing the soft, burning flesh. He took his time in arousing her and when satisfied that she was filled with wanting, he released her arms and coaxed her with gentle words, telling her to use her hands. She grasped tightly at his upper arms, urging him to fulfill her destiny, her nails digging in his flesh. He groaned deep in his throat as he moved to poise himself above her, kneeing her thighs apart. A wave of remembered pain caused her to stiffen against his entry.

"I cannot . . . open your thighs for me, love," he groaned, wanting her to acquiesce.

His gently probing staff and his deep male voice inflamed her, vibrated her entire being so that, unafraid, she opened up to him like a rosebud coming into bloom. He lunged once, fusing them together and uniting them into one being. A loud cry of ecstasy escaped her lips when he moved with powerful silken strokes and laughed deeply with joy when she began to pant, naturally arching her back to meet each filling thrust. It wasn't long before ever-widening tremors shook his tall frame and he tossed back his head in his full-coming spasm of release. Breathing raggedly, he left her to lie on his back.

When she would have rolled aside, he pulled her possessively against his side. He listened to her hard breathing that blended with his own, both mingling with the rush of the moonlit tide rolling in. Her skin glowed with a pearly luster where he stroked it above the erectness of her breasts, and her long lashes blinked in deep thought against his bearded chin. He read her innermost wonderings and he knew from her bewildered and shaky manner that she had never before, not even yet, experienced that summit of womanly fulfillment.

"Tyrone . . . ?" she wondered in a husky voice that shook him.

"What is it, my love?" he asked readily.

"I—oh, it is nothing," she answered shyly, snuggling into the circle of his arms.

"Let me, sweet, answer you and show you what it is that you crave. Trust me?" he asked, lifting her chin to drink in her sweet wanting. He smiled at her nod, and said, "Ahh, good. You shall soon know that ultimate pleasure, my beauty."

Hypnotically moving, Angel again yielded and not once did she realize that tears were wetting her cheeks and rolling off to dampen already moist tendrils of her hair. The candle sputtered out and Tyrone missed the tears as his tongue probed into her mouth gently and he did his magic. She used her hands as he tutored her and she felt that powerful pressure enter her again, this time with a new speed that thrilled her, filled her to the wall of her aching belly. An exhilarating fire kindled there deep inside her and she panted with wild, almost painful need to burst that tensing bubble. She heard her lover whisper almost inaudible French love words into her ear that were mingled over and over with a name she didn't know. Suddenly she realized his intense longing for her to equal his desire in those words.

He said, *"Ma cherie amour,"* and her heightened climax

212

exploded into enormous, utmost, blissfulness that shattered every taut nerve and muscle into quivering ecstasy.

Somewhere outside in the pink streaks of dawn a wise little owl hooted, giving up his night stand to the crow of a cock. Tyrone continued to fill the young woman till she cried out no more, begging to be released from his demoniac possession of her body, soul, and life force. He withdrew reluctantly after the last full mounting of equal fulfillment, only to draw her close to him as if he feared she would vanish from his side. In deep contentment his wide chest rose and fell and his ragged breathing finally quieted. He knew she was wide awake as he was, and when he spoke his voice was emotionally deep in the stillness of dewy morn.

"When would you like me to take you and your mother to New Orleans, my sweet?"

"Hmmm—what did you say?" she asked, thinking she hadn't heard him right.

"I have to make the trip tomorrow, but I'm sorry that I cannot take you with me this time. It is much too dangerous with a full load. In a week's time I'll return and thereafter the decision will be yours. Immediately, if you like at that time?"

"Yes, Tyrone, we will be ready," she almost cried out, but held the tremors of her voice in check.

He kissed her eyes, one at a time, to close them as he murmured, "Sleep now. There is not much time before breakfast will be on its way."

When his steady breathing filled the room, Angel began to ponder the sudden decisiveness in the manner of his speech after their lovemaking. So, he had already had his fill of her. It came now as a great shock to her that he could so cruelly cast her aside, be finished and done after what had gone on this night. But then, perhaps he had indeed guessed her game and instead had softened to her desire to be away and intended now to release them. Just like that!

My God, what if she became heavy with child? What would become of her then? Penniless and carrying a babe. The smuggler's expertise in bending women to his lusty will had worked on her threefold. She was doomed to suffer forevermore. Where there should have been shame now, there was only a strange and bittersweet joy as she lay in the arms of this slumbering man her young heart could never forget.

A single forlorn tear slid down her soft, flushed cheek and soon a weary, troubled slumber overtook her and she dreamed once again she was drowning in a sea of passion, from which she would never return whole.

'Tis the strumpets plague
To beguile many, and be beguiled by one.
—Shaftesbury

Chapter Six

1

The fiery tropical sun rose to its midday zenith to beat down upon the backs and arms of the sweating bodies loading the pinnace that would, under the direction of Captain Ty, make the deliveries to the designated spots along the Bayou Lafourche and on up to Donaldsville. The tall smuggler-captain lit a slim black cigano, smilingly, as if he were recalling something extremely pleasant. His buff buckskin breeches molded nicely to his physical perfection as he stood staring in the direction of Grande Isle, almost expecting to see a picture of honey and cream come dashing down the beach to watch his departure.

Tyrone hated leaving without a parting word, but *She* had been slumbering so deeply that he took his leave silently, not wishing to awaken her. During breakfast he had been much too distracted to eat, and almost had to kick himself to make certain he was awake, was still not dreaming the evening past that made him now feel as if he dwelled in a bright new world. All that morning the recollection of the night before crowded his mind, and the awaiting skeleton crew wondered if their captain was going daft, staring stupidly into his untouched plate with a wistful air.

Now the small pinnace was heavily laden and stacked neatly with contraband goods, and one of the crew suggested to his captain that is was time to sheet the two masts and head for the winding waterways. Soon the pounding of the surf and the rustling of the palm trees became a distant murmur as the pinnace moved with the strong southern breezes, away from the bright archipelago and away from Miss Sherwood.

215

Tyrone's thoughts turned reluctantly to Captain Andrew Holmes, who had formed a company of dragoons, as directed by Governor Claiborne, to set forth in boats in the hopes of blockading some of the routes into New Orleans and Donaldsville. Tyrone had laughed with Lafitte. Even now smugglers in pirogues were stationed as decoys at the head of a dozen different routes. They would be searched, but in vain, Holme's party finding the pirogues loaded only with smelly fish. Ty's pinnace would pass through undetected while the crews, disguised as fishermen, some genuine, would lead Holmes's men away from him and into a merry chase toward Barataria. There, several cannon would greet the unwary pursuers and send them back to Holmes's camp, empty-handed.

Just this morning, Tyrone had said one of his several good-byes that year to his father. Big Jim had said: "And here you are, my fine latent gentleman, running swag and pampering those Cajun peasants you hold so dear. Lord, don't you know New Orleans is beginning to fear invasion by the British?"

Tyrone had shrugged doubtfully, but said, "Perhaps the English *will* take over Louisiana and that British flag will fly over the Cabildo. The British outnumber the American forces two to one. Still . . . you know Congress will not longer tolerate Great Britain's blockading American ports. Indeed, a state of war is bound to exist, as relations are becoming tenser by the minute."

"Yes, of course," Big Jim agreed, "and this is no place for the Sherwood women come this summer season!"

Without further ado, Big Jim had stalked off, leaving Tyrone to wonder what his father knew that he didn't. It was always the same, his father was for certain, a deeply mysterious man. Would he ever understand him?

The tired sun was lying heavily on the western seaboard to color the waters vividly in a flourish of crimson. It had been another clear, sparkling day, and looking to the west, Angel had sighted the third island in the archipelago—the Chenière Caminada—as she strolled on the tip of Grande Terre with Nikki and the hound. It was now the eighth day since Tyrone's

216

departure, and June was in its infancy.

Angel sat woolgathering, with the little owl just outside her window to keep her company. She had named him Morgan, for indeed he had been born by the sea, this little feathered creature. Angel had left her meal of thick gumbo soup, red snapper, and *bière douce* half finished. She was thinking ahead to this evening when she would, accompanied by Nikki, cross the pass and go to visit Christine and Thelma. Some evenings she would take the evening meal with them; some not.

In the misty-gold mornings before the sun grew unbearably hot, she would often sit outside the cottage door with Nikki. He would tell her about some of the past history of the Gulf, the islands, and Barataria. Angel learned that "Blackbeard" Edward Teach had terrorized and plundered the Gulf for many years before he was slain in 1718 by Virginian officers, and from Georgia to Virginia the colonists had rejoiced that he was finally dead. Since then there had been unknown privateers who preyed upon the increasing commerce of the Gulf, even before Lafitte was ever heard of. Then came the "letters of marque," and after the 1700s these privateers were entitled to keep prize plunder. Under the flag of his nation a corsair could have his prizes approved by courts of admiralty. War made it inevitable that these adventurers also received a pat on the back for capturing wanted prisoners. In New Orleans, privateers would pay their duty at the customs house and then sell their swag to merchants, while some preferred to smuggle and therefore scamp the law. There was even open approval of this smuggling, for the Creole residents of New Orleans wholly resented the Spanish domination and its customs laws.

At last, a new law was passed by Congress forbidding the importation of slaves from Africa to the New World. Lafitte was now firmly established and at once saw to adding this "black contraband" for his ever-growing list of buyers; and in a cotton and sugar country where blacks were constantly needed for the cultivating of the crops, Lafitte's list was endless. Yes, he was emboldened to smuggle, for Cartagena of his commission was a long way off. How much easier, Lafitte thought, to just smuggle them through the bayous and sell them. The slaves were sold first at the forge on St. Phillip

Street, then later, and after the Negro Insurrection, which New Orleans officials held Lafitte responsible for, he erected what was now called the *Temple*, where he auctioned them off to planters and merchants. They, in turn, arranged their own smuggling of the slaves through customs.

For the most part, Nikki remained mysteriously silent about his own past and Tyrone's. He did say of himself, though, that he was an orphan, and that after his parents had perished in a fire, along with all their earthly possessions and savings, Tyrone had taken him under his wing, so to speak.

"Sheesh! I never thought that I would become a smuggler, though," he said.

The sinking of the sun yielded to a melancholy purple that swaddled about the growing mists, and, by the time Nikki was rowing back across the pass, the inky water was shrouded in a dreamlike field of ghostly fog. The way up ahead seemed shoreless and their passage unending. With a puzzled frown, Nikki twisted and turned as he lifted the oars, holding them suspended in air while he peered up at the moonless sky and then studied the girl across from him who followed his trail of bemusement. A slight frown wrinkling delicate brows could be seen in the single lantern light.

"Are we lost, bold pirate?" Angel ventured.

"Aye, methinks we are, lass," Nikki returned, twisting about as he tried to seek out the shoreline. "Gosh, the shore from which we shoved off is gone, too."

Angel peered at him through a veil of drifting fog. "Do you think we are drifting out to sea? Or perhaps we have traveled into a lost world of mysterious enchantment from which we shall never return?" she ended with mock seriousness lining her darkened features.

Nikki half-smiled and began rowing again, this time back in the direction from which they had come. He squinted to pick up some sign of the shoreline, but couldn't see any.

"Maybe if we start all over again and keep rowing straight ahead we'll reach the other side. Whew! This never happened to me before, but then I was never distracted by a lovely sea-nymph disembodied in such strange vapors—the likes of which I've never before seen here in the pass!" Nikki said, to keep the mood light.

But Angel suddenly stiffened. "Look!" she shouted, pointing at a huge apparition that appeared out of nowhere and loomed like a sea-beast gone dead and still.

Nikki stopped rowing as they glided nearer the dark obstruction that did seem to be drawing them into its bulk. A warm, moist breeze brewed with an utterance that brought to mind long-dead sailors summoned from the depths of their watery graves, moaning as if they tried to communicate with the living. Angel shivered as she thought of all the pirates that might have perished right here beneath them.

"Great Caeser's ghost!" Nikki exclaimed. "It's the *Annette* —but how—how did we come this far, or. . . ."

Both were now mesmerized as the creeping, drifting fog poured out over the tall Indiaman's sides, and like ghostly forms, crawled up the towering masts to linger there like unfurled canvas. Timbers creaked and groaned and something went knocking along the hull to the beam ends.

"Oh . . . Nikki, please, let's be away from here. Good heavens, what is that! Up there on the deck—it looks like someone—or something standing there staring down at us. Please hurry . . . Nikki!"

Nikki gulped loudly as hairy fingers of fright crawled up and down his spine. He exercised the oars with facile hands and shoulders that moved swifter than ever to glide with sudden jerks away from the horrible specter. He glanced at the young woman who seemed as if under a spell as she slouched down low into the pirogue, sneaking peeks over her shoulder to see if the apparition treaded on the heels of their wake.

Nikki wondered madly if she had seen the hazy outline of a tall, handsome woman, standing rigidly straight, with frosted black, rippling hair streaming wildly out behind her, as he had. The name Annette made him wonder if indeed the deceased woman haunted her wooden namesake.

The pirogue seemed to skim the water in slow motion, as if in a nightmare. When finally they reached the shore, both breathed a shuddering sigh of relief as their feet touched blessed sand. This night Angel was certain to lodge with Christine, and Nikki would be satisfied not to argue the demand. He too, was going to stay put on Grande Terre till the morning sun shone cheerfully.

The haunting eve was forgotten. The pair involved in the scare would not speak of it in fear each would think the other unsound. Too, that night was now looked upon as an obscure dream, for in the dazzle of full day the *Annette* was tall and handsome with her spires reaching toward the cerulean skies as she rode at easy anchor.

Two more days passed and when Angel now remained with Christine in her cottage, Nikki, her protector, did not once object to the resettlement. Angel stitched with scraps of material discovered in old trunks by Nikki. She fashioned cooler garments for Thelma's babies, and in between, read for the first time Laurence Sterne's *Tristram Shandy*. Nikki had come across the hidebound first volume nestled in the bottom of an old oaken trunk as he had paused in his labors while clearing away some of the unsold junk in one of the thirty warehouses situated on Grande Terre. With these, Nikki also brought her a pack of yellowed stationery, and she spent her leisure time with pen and paper, wrote and rewrote letters to Uncle Stuart, until finally she had completed one, pleased it would not cause him to worry. Now the only problem was how to send it off. She would worry about that later, she told herself.

For now, added to these latest simple pleasures, Angel learned the procedure for "smoking" large pieces of meat over a slow-burning fire and how to "put up" early fruit yields, and how to make marmalades sweetened with honey that had been stored in earthen jars. When Bron's family ran out of soap and candles, more had to be made.

Angel carried to the spot outdoors one more bucket of grease and fat that had been saved from daily cooking. She wrinkled her nose as she joined Christine, who was happily scooping wooden spoonfuls of the dripping grease into a large iron kettle hooked over a pole atop an open fire. Bron bore a tall barrel full of wood ashes from the fireplace and placed it alongside a long wooden table, while Thelma brought the water buckets to pour over the ashes to make the brown substance called lye. When the grease bubbled, the lye would then be added, and under the women's watchful eyes, keeping the children well back, the brew came to thicken into a yellow substance of gelatinous soap. Before it had cooled thoroughly, Thelma ladled the jellylike substance into long rectangular wooden molds and added salt to make it harden well. Before the stuff had hardened fully, it was sliced into bars by pulling a wire clear through it.

Angel had a brainstorm while this was being done. The odor of the fixings was not pleasant, so she went to fetch the spray of wildflowers she had left to dry in Christine's cottage. The flowers were crushed and then added to the next batch of soap. The result was delightful and each of them had several bars of scented soap with the delicate colors of nature embedded in the cakes. Then Thelma had an idea, and following Angel's procedure, went to fetch a batch of powerful green mint leaves that she usually dried and crushed for use in her delicious herb tea. This second result was somewhat stronger, but the frosty shade of green matched Angel's lustrously smiling eyes. The sweet fragrance when they bathed in the secluded cove the next day made it seem as though they bathed in a wellspring of mint. The children sat in the wet sand and each played with his own pretty bar combined of scented pink, violet, and blue.

It was a scorchingly hot day and the women and children lingered, picnicking from the basket of goodies they had packed to bring along. After the lunch of smoked meat and garden vegetables, they stretched out under a dwarfed live oak while the children napped close by on their own separate blanket. The orangeade in the heavy pitcher was growing warmer by the minute.

"Cap'n Ty, he is late to come back," Thelma mentioned, her mocha eyes hooded. "Is it not so, An-gel?" She was ever delighted that the English girl had of late trusted her with her lovely name.

Angel rolled from her back to her elbows to sift the fine golden sand through her fingers. Her slumberous eyelids lifted and she let her wistful gaze roam to the Gulf and then back to her friend.

"Yes, I suppose he has been longer than the six or seven days Nikki said it usually takes." She sighed idly, wishing that Thelma would speak no more of Tyrone. She had often these days tried to push him from her mind, but their last night together kept invading her thoughts, making a flush rise in her young body.

"Tah!" Christine spat vindictively, causing Angel to take notice of her mother's screwed-up face. Christine went on. "That one! It would not surprise me in the least, my daughter, if the man is dilly-dallying in New Orleans at one of those gay quadroon balls!"

"Mama, I'm surprised at you. How could you know of such things, anyway?" Angel asked, brushing the sand from her calico frock with quick jerky movements.

Christine sniffed the air with a fine nose, saying, "Thelma has told me much about this New Orleans that is sixty miles upstream from here. A wicked sin city, no less. My Lord, do you know that Indians roam the streets freely?"

Angel gasped, "Indians?"

Thelma nodded, then smiled assuredly, saying, "All get along good, An-gel. All kinds of men come who trap furs, come to sell from far away. Rivermen and Jean and Pierre Lafitte, all walk together with Indians; men of 'free color' and planters, too. Most of men who own plantations are French-Creole and some American. I go there once with Bron when younger. I like to be here much better, much cleaner air. We both live here long, was born here."

Angel appeared puzzled as she asked, "Do you mean to say that Jean Lafitte and this Pierre who must be his brother . . . stroll boldly down the streets of New Orleans, out in the open? Pirates and smugglers?"

Thelma shrugged as if it was nothing, the proper thing for these infamous men to do. "They afraid of nothing!" she exclaimed. "Ty, him same way. Him born in Louie, folks been here long, too. No one dare to touch them, not even governor. Cannot prove them smugglers," she giggled, "cannot catch them. Ty, his beard hide much of handsome face and some folks of New Orleans who know him before, do not know him in his dis—dis. . . ."

"Disguise," Angel finished for Thelma. Then she said, "Tell me more, Thelma, like how do they get away with it." She had heard some from Nikki, but she wanted to hear more.

"Popu-lation buy nice things cheap from smugglers, pay no duty. Creoles do not like governor much and him charging duty. And Ty, him good to Cajun farmer and fishermen who make nothing much to live on. Cajuns live in swamps in small and dirty shanties with many children. They are not lucky to go to school if father cannot pay." Thelma smiled here, adding, "Ty, he gives things for them to sell and many go to school now, just like children who live in fancy tall houses not far from swamps."

Christine had fallen asleep during the conversation. Angel had not caught Thelma's last words for she was looking out to the bay where the *Annette*, that proud, haunted ship seemed now to beckon her, making her think of the spirit that lurked aboard her decks. Was it a woman's ghostly form she had viewed on that mysterious night? Or, had it been more a feeling that the spirit was like a sentinel, watchful that no harm came to her and Nikki? She at once chided herself for such foolishness. Heavens. She didn't believe in friendly spirits from the dead or, for that matter, unfriendly ones either.

Thelma rose from the blanket and gently shook Christine to tell her that it was time to be back to Grande Terre. Bron would soon be home from the upper swamp where he had gone almost every day now, awaiting Captain Ty's return. They sat in their pirogues, undiscovered, these fishermen, as if part of the Spanish moss that draped over them, watching the governor's gunboats patrol the Bayou Lafource.

"I am going to linger a bit more, Thelma," Angel said. "Perhaps even take another swim. It is so hot and I feel sticky all over again. You do not mind, do you? Mama?"

The lady and the native both answered "no," they did not mind, for they had a feeling the younger woman needed some time alone, for reasons of her own.

After they had gone, Angel sat with her knees tucked up under her chin. Her sparkling, freshly washed hair draped like fair moonbeams over her newly tanned shoulders and arms, trailing to her bare feet that were buried deeply in the warm sand. The swim she had taken earlier made her eyes dazzle like green ice as she took her gaze across the bay to watch, unseen, several more strangers filing into the warehouses. Nikki had informed her that they were merchants who braved the swamps and curving bayous to come and bargain for the contraband to be delivered later. Merchants from Baton Rouge and as far north as Natchez.

Angel did not see nor did she feel the pair of dark brown eyes that were raking her back greedily from not more than fifty feet away. The figure crept stealthily closer.

She was just about to drop the frock for another dip when a shadow fell over her, making her cry out in alarm. An arm reached around and icy fingers clamped tight over her mouth, stifling any further outburst she might have made.

"Shh, little spitfire. I will not hurt you. I only came to talk."

Angel's eyes registered first surprise then contempt as Pearce Duschesne allowed his hand to slide down from her mouth, coming to rest near the swell of a tender breast.

"If you don't mind, Mister Duschesne—" Angel plucked the sweating hand from her chest, "you are delaying my swim. It is unbearably hot and I would like to cool myself before returning to Grande Terre where my friends and my mother await me."

Pearce rolled his dark eyes up to the bright ball in the sky, then dropped them to that tender spot where his bold hand had rested only moments before.

"Ah, so it is another hot day, isn't it, *ma cherie?*" he said.

"I said as much," Angel responded sharply.

"But you have already been in the water, little mermaid. And, I must say that you are very beautiful with all your charms laid open to the observant eye. Where others are flabby, you are—ah—firm, longer of limb and more slender," he complimented effusively.

"*Oui,*" Angel mocked, pursing her lips as her dainty bare feet buffeted the sand and she glared up at him, adding, "And what a timely coincidence, Mister Duschesne, that you just happen to be the observant one. Do you always dally away the afternoon watching slender maids bathe in the raw?"

"I only noticed one lovely young maid here," Pearce said, his eyes sizzling with lust. "There is not another in all Louie as beautiful as you, *ma petite.* Even those golden-skinned quadroons with their *café au lait* eyes do not hold a candle to what I see here now."

"Perhaps, sir, you see too much and your eyes fool you," Angel said fiercely, preparing to leave as she bent to retrieve her hairbrush, soap, and towel.

He suddenly grasped her shoulders and spun her around to face him. For a long moment Angel returned his gaze unflinchingly, but where his was warm hers was cold as ice. She shoved his fingers away in disgust, but he only returned his hand to her shoulder. His brown eyes softened and she was startled at how gentle they could become.

"What must I do to make you mine . . . take you away from here? That could be arranged quite easily, as I have said before. I could borrow the *Tigre* and take you away this very night, *ma cherie*. We could travel unseen and be in New Orleans in a few days at the most, with Dominique's swift vessel," he lied of the latter.

"You cannot be serious. Dominique would never lend you his ship!" Angel breathed.

"Yes, yes, he would," Pearce muttered swiftly. "He owes me a favor, you see. I would take your mother, too," he baited.

Angel's head snapped up. "You—you would do that?" She watched him nod. It all sounded too easy and she said, "Oh, it wouldn't work. Captain Ty will come searching for us as soon as he returns. He thinks of me as mere property," she ended a bit sadly.

"*Mais oui*, you are but a possession of his, little one," he said in English this time, his voice deeply solemn and grave. Then, "Do you know where he is at this very moment?"

"How could I?" Angel answered, then stared at him in fearful anticipation.

"There is a quadroon ball at the St. Philips Theater and there he dallies this very night. Hmmm, I know this for certain. He would not miss it for all the Spanish coin in Barataria, and he is practically one of them—the Creoles—you know. He is very greedy when it comes to women, you know yourself, and his mistresses are many." He waited for some reaction from her.

Angel's heart pounded poignantly in her breast. So, her mother had predicted accurately about the ball. For a second her eyes misted over before she spoke. "I have forgotten, monsieur, the captain has promised to take my mother and me to New Orleans upon his return. I must trust his word. . . ." her voice trailed off in bewilderment.

Pearce was silent as with a decent gesture that belied inward intent, he lifted the puffed sleeves of her frock that had slid off her shoulders and pushed them back up into place. Like a gentleman he reached behind her and fastened the tabs, despite her protests that she could manage herself. When that was done she thanked him, her eyes yet bewildered.

"You see," Pearce began, "Tyrone is not the have-not he makes himself out to be." He wanted to reveal more of Tyrone's past but there wasn't enough time. Soon that young pup Nikki would come searching for her. He had to talk and work swiftly, must convince her that her life was in danger here. "The morning Ellen was murdered Tyrone was last seen coming from her cell. Her neck was broken and she had been ravished severely."

Angel stood aghast and her slender frame was shaken to the core. They had almost come as a physical blow, those words. How could this be? But then, what did she really know about Tyrone other than that he was a smuggler? Yet he *had* spoken most unkindly of Ellen, after her horrible death.

Pearce took up where he'd left off, softly saying, "Between you and me, there is, or was, a very beautiful Creole woman named Jacinta. She left him for another, impossible as it may seem, and after that he became thoroughly promiscuous, his character deteriorating to the point where he wreaks vengeance on all women."

Angel's emotions were at the breaking point. "Please, no more," she begged. Then, "When can we leave . . . tonight, really? There is really nothing for me to pack." A thought of great importance struck her next. "But, I have no coin and there is just no place to go when we reach New Orleans." She had thought about asking the governor to aid her and Christine, but surely *this* man could not take her there.

Pearce's smile was disarming as he said, "Rest, *ma cherie*, not so much worry now, about money and a place to accommodate you and—ah—your mother. I have friends in

226

New Orleans also, you see. There is a woman—ah—she has a big house and you will like her. She will give you and your mother a very comfortable room. After that, we will talk about your heart's desire, *non?*"

Angel nodded, feeling a strange excitement mingled with a terrible kind of gloom. At the moment all she could think of was getting away, as far away from these islands as possible.

Pearce shifted his gaze to a nearing pirogue, then back to her as he said hurriedly, "Now, look alive. Here comes your daring chaperone." His voice changed to a swifter tempo. "Make sure that no one learns of this, not even your mother. Not at first, anyway. Just get her down to the waiting ship as fast as you can. I will send you a message when it first grows dark. Then one of my trusted men will escort you there."

After a last look at her, Pearce strode in the opposite direction from which the frowning young man was coming as he swaggered up the beach.

"What did *he* want?" Nikki asked fiercely, glaring over Angel's shoulder at the departing figure of Duschesne.

Angel lowered amber lashes as she brushed idly at the sand on her skirt. She could feel Nikki staring thoughtfully and she hated herself for having to deceive him, but she was powerless to do otherwise. She felt a chill run all through her as Nikki continued to search out her thoughts. Just like. . . .

"Princess?" Nikki said, gently grasping her shoulder.

Angel squirmed inwardly, uneasily, and her teeth tugged her lower lip nervously. "Ohhh-hhh," she breathed a little laugh, "you know Pearce, he is always flirting outrageously."

"No, I don't know. Tell me, princess," Nikki said, eyeing the quivering lip.

"Please, leave it be, Nikki!" she snapped, and was all at once sorry. He was only interested in her being out of harm's way. She gave him her sweetest smile, brightening the afternoon that was beginning to grow shadowy. "I am ravenous . . . and hungry, too!" she giggled, showing him that all was well with her.

"Hmmm, if you're sure you are all right?" Nikki persisted, taking the proffered arm and pushing back his scabbard to make room for her skirt.

Angel walked jauntily, affectedly, beside him, matching his long strides as she unhappily glimpsed what she thought was to be her last view of Grande Isle. "Good-bye, Morgan," she said inwardly, and outwardly strove to concentrate on making her mood appear lighthearted, as she said out loud, "Silly Nikki. I never felt better!"

In the vast inky well of sky a heavenly body dashed, the comet leaving a vaporous tail as it curved toward its obliteration. Out in the bay a small craft slipped stealthily upon moon-dappled waters after detaching itself from between moored vessels. She headed in an easterly direction, and on the dawning of the second day out the craft entered the muddy green mouth of the great river.

Shrouded in a heavy, clinging fog as she stepped out of the tiny cabin, Angel breathed in deeply of this moister air. She was suddenly having qualms about this getaway. Christine had not taken to it well and was once again that distant, forlorn person she'd been before. She had been tossing fitfully on her pallet for hours, finally driving Angel to seek solace outside the cabin. She couldn't stand any longer the eau de cologne that Tessie and Peggy doused themselves liberally with. Besides, they were packed together like sardines in the cabin.

The strumpets had their own reasons for wanting to sneak away and take up residence in New Orleans, especially after what had happened to poor Ellen. They blamed Rollo for her death and, before that same fate saw them mangled, were readily thrilled when Duschesne asked them along, to be away from the murdering octopus Rollo.

Smuggler Duschesne was issuing orders to his motley skeleton crew when he noticed the young woman strolling in the wispy tendrils of fog that made her appear ethereal. The gray stuff followed her, swirled about the hem of the tattered madras and nestled like dewy diamonds in her moonbeam hair. She appeared deep in dreamy thought.

Mon Dieu, but she was a tempting beauty, even in that homely madras she wore. Pearce often had wondered, as he did now, what had befallen this garment she faithfully wore ever since her coming aboard. She had meant it when she stated she had nothing to pack! The snug bodice had been mended several times over a long tear, but the skirt bore several shapely patches of colorful calico, unique, but so ragged otherwise, he thought.

Feeling the lust-craving that the nameless girl awoke in him, Pearce decided to let her have her air in peace. Someday soon he would hear her name and possess her body, but for now, there was no place *here* to bed that delicate piece. He had lied about securing the flagship *Tigre*. It was but a small fishing schooner that they rode upon, and he had explained in his cleverness to the young woman that the *Tigre* had been just lately split in her hull. Dominique was a greater friend to Tyrone than he was to Pearce and Pearce wanted nothing to go awry before they reached New Orleans. Seeking to borrow Dominique's own ship would have aroused much suspicion among those swarthy pirates. To put it mildly, the many-gunned *Tigre* would have been welcomed with open arms by the forewarned militia.

Not that it was going to be an easy task as it was, not being sighted. It would be late night when they would finally slip into port and hopefully disembark unspotted. This was the only course, for if Captain Ty decided to run down his lovely captive, once he had set out to unearth the clues necessary to find her he would be like that sniffing old hound of his in quest of prey. By then, Tyrone would be back at the islands, while they would be just arriving at Madame Lulu's.

However, if Tyrone did learn that he had taken the young minx to Madame Lulu's establishment, then Pearce had no other choice but to kill him. He laughed harshly at the pleasurable thought of viewing that one in his last agonies as he floundered in his own dark red pool of blood.

First off and before they reached the brothel, he was going to have to get rid of that old hag Sherwood. She was too much trouble and would only serve a hindrance once her daughter was tutored in the ways of a whore. In anticipation, he licked his thin lips like a demented schoolmaster about to launch his favorite student into a prosperous career that would make his new life one of sybaritic ease.

As it happened, the luck of the devil was on Pearce

Duschesne's side, almost, for there was no ridding himself of the older woman now. They were stopped and searched only once after passing the Bayou St. Denis. After the armed militia had found nothing on the small schooner resembling contraband, one of the officers took Pearce discreetly aside. With a twinkle in his sky-blue eyes under the plumed helmet, the officer asked Pearce about the women, one in particular.

"Ahh, you see," Pearce began nervously, "have you not heard of Madame Lulu's establishment?"

The young and handsome officer in the dark blue uniform pondered for a moment. His eyes narrowed, and then at last he grinned mischievously as he exclaimed, "Certainly!" and instantaneously his voice lowered. "I don't know where the hell you come from or where you picked up such cargo, but I myself don't give a damn as long as you promise me here and now that I can bed that lovely honey-haired wench at Lulu's this weekend!"

Pearce gave the rakish officer a slight bow and said hastily, "Of course, sir!" as he smiled to himself at obtaining a customer so soon. He added, "You have my promise on that, sir!"

"Well then, ummm, monsieur . . . ?"

"Pearce Duschesne at your service, sir!"

The officer winced and snapped, "Cut the 'sir' crap out, Duschesne. To make certain that your shipment arrives on time we will escort you and the ladies the remainder of the journey, *non?*"

Pearce's dark eyes popped open at the irony of the situation, then he relaxed somewhat. "Whatever you say, ssss—" he began to hiss then dropped the title quickly.

"Good. Let's be under way then," the officer said, almost trodding on Duschesne's foot as he brushed by to give orders to his men. He turned back, grinding the butt of his musket into the deck as he casually relaxed his crossed hands over the bore. "Oh, by the way, Duschesne, my name is Armand Bujold— Lieutenant Bujold."

So, for the first time, a smuggler from Barataria was escorted into the Gulf's leading port by a party of dragoons—in morning light!

Angel's eyes were round as green china saucers when the ship rounded a great bend and the early morning skyline of New Orleans first came into view behind a forest of bare masts. From where she stood, hand resting on a ratline, the twin, gracefully round spires of the cathedral caught her eyes, seeming ablaze in the orange glow of morning. As they drew nearer the trading ships and flatboats she could see between them a large, iron-fenced square that overlooked the port; and solid ranks of red-and-tile-roofed houses huddled behind the willow-crowned levee.

"Civilization," she breathed. "Has it really been three months since I last looked upon a genuine city?" She hadn't realized she had spoken out loud until Tessie came to stand beside her.

"Indeed 'tis more than that, ducks." Tessie smoothed her blazing red hair. "First thing, O'im going to sink my arse in a hot bath then . .˙. why you name it, love!" she giggled.

Angel's eyes sparkled dreamily. "Mmm. It does sound too too wonderful. First off, I am going to send a letter off to my uncle, then Pearce will lend us money for passage back to England. He will agree when I tell him he will be reimbursed twofold. If he cannot lend the fare, for some reason, then I will have to make the money myself by cleaning house or situating myself as a governess for a time. Or there is always the governor to lend us the fare home." She clapped her hands together in joy. "Oh, why did I not think of it before, Tessie? I'm sure he will be more than agreeable."

Tessie had been blinking so fast she looked like a broken wood shutter flapping in a raging storm. "Say, ducks, I thought. . . ."

Just then the sloop with the party of dragoons was slipping by the schooner to take up the lead, catching the older woman's eye. Newly preoccupied, Tessie nudged her companion in the ribs.

"Ain't this something, being escorted by them 'andsome gents in them red 'n' blue uniforms? An' look at that, Lieutenant! 'E's ogling you again, you lucky duck. If 'e don't be as beautiful as that gorgeous smuggler cap'n who took up with you, O'il eat what's left of me petticoats!"

As the ship made its way north of the market place to tie up at the levee, Angel shifted her gaze toward the sloop, but Tessie's last words shocked her, ruining her newly found joy. The handsome vision of that smuggler who had loved her all through the night stared at her through the sparkling new day, with those flecked hazel eyes, searching, searing. Angry, loving. Loving? His face became part of the bustling port in front of her and she was so caught up in daydreaming that she failed to notice the pair of bright blue eyes measuring her dismal countenance as the sloop passed the schooner.

Armand Bujold had seen the little face, so lost, so sad, and it made his hardened soldier's heart go out to her. She was even more lovely in the light of day. But the clothes, the clothes. He had been so wrapped up in studying the winsome face when he'd first seen her that he'd failed to note the ragged state of her dress.

A tacky carriage waited patiently in front of a cafe near the levee to take the ladies up through the Vieux Carré, seen to only moments before by Armand Bujold. Christine and the two tarts were handed into the carriage by Duschesne and when he reached out for the younger woman's arm, his hand was restrained by a steely arm and a stiff regard from the lieutenant. The lesser man shrugged and swung himself up to be seated next to the wiry and foul-breathed driver.

Duschesne sat with smug satisfaction while Lieutenant Bujold spoke with the younger Sherwood woman, his red-plumed helmet tucked respectfully beneath his elbow. With the pressing crowd of shouting sailors and creamy-tan women milling about noisily, Pearce missed their conversation.

Angel had momentarily studied the young man in uniform. His blue eyes were fringed with bristly dark lashes, almost as long as her own. Bujold, on the other hand, had noticed her exquisite gait, which made him think of a Venus come to life. He had already been wondering what it would be like to kiss the pouting lips and sample her experience. Soon. . . .

"I am sorry, mademoiselle," Bujold was saying, "but under the circumstances this is the best carriage I could arrange, for the time being. You deserve better, and, between, umm, Lulu and myself, we shall arrange to have many gowns, very lovely, made especially for you."

Angel cocked her fair head in confusion, staring blankly at the uniformed man. "Monsieur, I do not understand. I—"

Armand interrupted softly. "Armand Bujold. Lieutenant. At your service mademoiselle." He bowed to kiss the small fingertips and was at once taken aback by the shy and surprised look. When he straightened to further measure her reaction, he asked, "And you are. . . ?"

"Just . . . Mademoiselle Sherwood, please." She drew back her hand as if he had burned it instead of kissing it with his expertly carved mouth.

He gave her a long, searching look that mesmerized her. "It would be a great pleasure, Mademoiselle Sherwood, to make a date beforehand to, umm, see you at Madame Lulu's two nights from this evening."

Confusedly Angel glanced down just then as a hissing black cat and a snarling mutt in hot pursuit sped under the belly of the carriage. Armand missed the chase, so intent was his gaze on the lovely creature before him, and he took the lowered head as demure affirmation of his proposition.

"Till then, adieu, mademoiselle," Armand said, and like a true gentleman handed this lovely piece into the waiting carriage.

The hired carriage jerked, then rattled, the horses' hooves clopping soothingly over the cobblestones where the open gutters that flanked the narrow streets were filled with stagnant water. Through open doorways of the foreign-looking buildings, Angel caught glimpses—not more than ten feet away—of merchants arranging their wares, and she was astounded at the quantity and quality of the rich silks and laces and colorful velvets that were piled high upon shelves. The streets hummed with activity, overpopulated with people of many nations. But chiefly, the tongue spoken here was French, patois, reminding her of someone she would rather not think of at all.

Tessie and Peggy craned their necks as the clop-clop-

233

clopping continued along the nameless streets. They liked what they saw, licking their lips as they passed tubs of cold water in which nestled *bière douce*. Even Christine was beginning to sit up and take notice of her new surroundings, especially when they passed a group of octoroon children squealing with delight before a pushcart of refreshments and that New Orleans' favorite candy, pralines, or the ever-popular gingerbread, *estomac mulatre*.

Endeavoring to hide her concern as they exchanged glances briefly, Angel noted her mother's sudden interest in the children as she twisted around to catch a last glimpse of the tots. It struck Angel then as she studied Christine that, even now, she herself could be nurturing a babe inside her own belly.

Oh God, she prayed, please let it not be so! Angel had not given thought to this the entire journey upstream, but now the disturbing possibility of her becoming a mother came to her in full force again. It was much too early to tell, but just the same an uneasiness crept over her as she wondered what the future would hold for her and Christine if it were to bring a wee babe into the midst of their disordered life.

Angel strove to keep her mind occupied with the gay and exciting crush of humanity all around them. At last the bouncing carriage halted before a wrought-iron gate, behind which a tall house of pink brick and yellow plaster wrapped around a huge, sunlit courtyard on three sides. The name Lulu and the conversation she'd had with the lieutenant invaded her mind and she hesitated momentarily when it came her turn to step down from the carriage. Pearce Duschesne waited for her to alight, a strange smugness about his countenance that rubbed Angel the wrong way.

"Come, mademoiselle," he said. "Madame Lulu is waiting to meet you. I told her all about you the last time I was here, just two short weeks ago."

Angel frowned, her body stiffening as she snapped, "So, how did you foresee at that time I would agree to return with you?"

Pearce shrugged. "Shortly after that little card party at Lafitte's, I made my way here, knowing that the next time you would be more than willing to accompany me. So, here you are and soon you will have all the gowns you ever dreamed of, and you will have picayune aplenty once you have become firmly established in your new position."

"New . . . position?" Angel wondered out loud.

"*Mais oui*. Now, no more questions. You will see, soon enough," Pearce said, taking her arm to follow the others through the courtyard bathed in golden sun.

Madame Lulu, with her elegantly high-piled coif, greeted the party at the main entrance. The introductions were made and she immediately led them into a green-and-yellow-papered parlor with tastefully appointed furnishings: French and Italian, the feminine and the masculine.

Miss Sherwood and Pearce Duschesne were waved directly to a gold velvet couch while the Madame positioned her generous frame onto a matching silk-cushioned settee. She pointedly ignored the youngest woman's state of dishevelment, actually increasing Angel's alarm as her eyes stayed riveted to the small face. Next the Madame clapped her hands loudly, and a fast-moving little blond maid arrived, standing expectantly, her eyes round upon viewing the pauperized occupants in the front parlor.

"Babette," Madame began authoritatively, "show the three ladies to their separate rooms on the gallery floor. *La petite* mademoiselle will linger for awhile longer."

Angel didn't like this one bit and she made to rise, but Pearce stayed her with a restraining arm. The gesture drew an oblique glance from Madame Lulu, and on viewing the girl's hands fluttering primly to her lap, her fair head down, Lulu's gaze narrowed in on Duschesne. He slowly nodded as his lower lip curled upward in an unuttered declaration of promise. So sure was he of himself and his ability to manipulate the poor girl beside him, Madame thought angrily.

When the trio were alone, Madame grabbed her chance to appraise the girl, whose eyes meandered about the room in detached interest, finally centering in on delicate bits of white furniture complimenting the bolder dark ones. Madame studied the young woman with a business-minded eye, taking in the swell of firm young breasts, the tiny circumference of her waist, and then, last but not least, the flawless complexion and the rich mass of flaxen tresses.

Ahh, but the eyes, Lulu perceived, like many-faceted green gems nestled in creamy, oval-shaped velvet. Many men would pay just to caress that sort of peach-and-cream flesh. Madame began to wonder what the girl would look like properly gowned, her hair styled in a fashionable coiffure. Ooh-la! All for only one man. Tsk, tsk.

Madame Lulu summoned the girl's attention. "Now, you would like to have a bath, a change of clothes? I think that one of the girls has something to fit. And then over dinner we will discuss—umm—things." She squinted a warning over to Duschesne.

Pearce didn't heed it, and snapped, "We will talk now!"

"A house of ill-repute," Angel breathed, her face vivid with enlightenment. Then, "I have never visited such a place, but I am not all that naive! And, Pearce, you must think yourself a very clever man indeed. Lord! How very ignorant you both must think me. Oh-ho, I must admit that up until a few minutes ago, before I had put two and two together, I must have fairly represented what most assuredly you house here, Madame. How sickening!" she groaned. "Ohh, and that man— that Lieutenant Bujold. He made a date to come here and . . . he thinks I'm a—a—" Angel stood as if shot from a pistol.

"Sit down and shut up!" Pearce demanded. "Of course, silly bitch. Bujold thinks you are a whore and he's coming here to get his money's worth—you!"

"Duschesne," Madame began disbelievingly, "did you say Bujold?"

Angel ignored the Madame and snapped at Pearce, "I am not a fallen woman, a tart, or whatever! I would gladly take the hand of death before I would ever sink so low as to sell my body for even a single night's pleasure!"

"You will, damn you!" Pearce shouted. "I have given up smuggling, everything, to help you escape, bring you and your wretched mama here. And how do you repay me?"

Angel shook her head, closed her eyes and bit her lower lip as she said, "Why did you not inform me of your bloody intent? I swear on all that is holy that his Majesty's navy could not have budged me off that island—for this."

His eyes gleaming wickedly, Pearce said, "Tah! Don't tell me that the horniest man in all Louie did not make you, mademoiselle. You are no damn virgin after you have lodged but once with Tyrone. I've a mind to tell you all about Tyrone's past and his mother—the whore!"

"Duschesne!" Madame Lulu hissed as she stiffened her spine. "Now, I must ask that you leave my house. You will not slander *their* name in my house."

Angel had fled to the buffet, hands clamped over her ears, where she was now choking on a lavish dollop of brandy she had helped herself to.

"Really, Madame," Pearce snorted. "Slander a fallen name in a brothel?" ·

Lulu's look was dangerous as she sashayed her silk-gowned hips over to the couch where Pearce remained, showing no sign that he was about to leave.

"You know nothing of *them*, Duschesne, and if you do not leave immediately I will have to send for George, my bouncer. How would you like for Armand Bujold to know what you are up to, hmmm? Wait! Let me finish." She held up her hand as he was about to speak, adding smugly, "You see, we have been awaiting your coming." Lulu saw his puzzled growth of frown and licked her lips in pleasure of what was to come.

Ruffled, Pearce snorted. "What 'we' do you mean, Madame?"

Lulu bent down close to his face and Pearce's gaze was glued to her angry, heaving bosom. She whispered with a deep hiss, "Tyrone. He is here."

Pearce swept his gaze about the room in horrible expectation, as if he would find Captain Ty crouched there in a corner, already prepared to spring upon him as lithe as a panther.

"Ah, not here in my house," Lulu said casually, "but close by, nevertheless. As is Armand Bujold. His home is just down the street and Armand and Tyrone are the thickest of friends."

She chuckled to herself as she thought of how Tyrone would react when he learned his friend Armand had taken a fancy to his woman.

"No. . . ." Angel had whispered in disbelief as she caught Lulu's last words.

Now Lulu was saying soothingly, "Yes, I am afraid it is so, mademoiselle." And to Pearce she explained, "You see, your journey here was a very lazy one. Tyrone arrived at his destination, only to learn you had swiped his woman from the island. He turned his boat around and preceded you back here by one day. Fast, eh? Finally, after searching for this young lady all over New Orleans, he came here asking if you had come. I related the conversation we had last time you visited me. Oooh, Armand does not know of this odd predicament yet, and when he learns this young lady belongs to his dearest friend, you will have two snarling hounds at your heel— monsieur!"

"That randy smuggler cannot do this to me forever. She is mine now. He snatched her from a ship he and his men plundered, and I snatched her from him. He cannot have her back! I will take her to a bordello far from here, Madame!"

Angel whirled into the center of the room, her eyes blazing green fire. "You are all lunatics, deucedly sick, for sure! I belong only to myself and I'm weary of having my life laid out before me as if I were some witless ninny. No man shall ever touch me again, I say. And, Madame, you can inform Lieutenant Bujold that his bold overtures are not to be granted. As for Tyrone, you can tell him *and* his dear friend to go to blazes!" She stuck her pert nose in the air and announced, "I am going upstairs now, to fetch my mother and we are leaving this blasted place. We are going home—" her voice cracked with emotion, "home, to England! Do you hear?"

With a flash of patched madras and a toss of a fair head she fled the parlor. In a few moments her flying slippers could be heard halting in indecision at the top of the stairs. From the window they could see the determined young woman race along the gallery of the second floor, searching for the room that housed Christine Sherwood.

"Now," Lulu warned Duschesne, "get your carcass out of here before I jostle the big lad in the back room who does my bouncing for me. He does not take kindly to being wakened during the day. He weighs two hundred plus and eats skinny-hindered men like yourself for dinner!"

Pearce hesitated, but had the feeling that she spoke no untruth. He had sighted a beastly man on his last visit who fitted this description exactly.

"Never mind, Madame, I am going!" he said and headed toward the door as premeditated murder shone in his eyes.

2

As if this were the next in a series of nightmares, Angel slumped into a plush chair as she waited for her mother to don a fresh gown that was actually unsuitable for day wear. But as there was nothing else in sight, it would have to do for now. Christine had bathed, brushed out her graying hair, and was looking a bit fresher, though there were dark circles visible under her eyes, as she glanced longingly at the silk-canopied bed. But only for a moment, as her daughter urged her to complete her dressing.

Christine set down the cup of tea she had been sipping, and whined, "My Angel, you are in need of a bath and some rest. Me, I am so sleepy all of a sudden. Why can we not stay for a time, have some decent fare and then be on our way?"

Angel stood and began to pace nervously. "Because, someone is coming here soon and I shan't be available for his evil plans. You want to go back home, don't you?" she asked hopefully.

Christine was just about to answer when a knock sounded at the bedroom door. It was Madame Lulu and beside her stood a huge man with his barrel arms crossed over his chest. His shoulders met the door frame on either side and his spread-eagled limbs were like huge boles of a tree. Angel stood bravely facing the woman and the gargantuan hulk. A hazy nimbus from the heat and light behind him made his appearance seem unreal. The Madame moved slowly into the room.

"*La petite,* she is fatigued," Lulu said sympathetically. "Please come with me. Babette has prepared a nice warm bath for you. There are frosted cakes, some mint tea and a comfortable bed waiting for you. For dinner we will have flounder stuffed with crabmeat. Sound delicious, eh?"

"I am not buying," Angel said ungraciously. "I know you have sent for him. He has made my life unbearable, miserable, and if not for him we would be halfway back to England at this very moment. I loathe Tyrone, can you not understand?"

"Ooooh," Lulu crooned. "I think I see why you are so unhappy. It is the way of a woman who feels she is being used. He does not hate you, does Ty, *petite amour.* I know these things. It is my business to know what makes a man want a very special woman. There is special magic between you and Ty."

"Pooh!" Angel returned. "Every woman is special to *that* one. He only wants me now because he has not apparently had his fill of me. . . ." Angel's voice trailed and her cheeks began to burn.

Nothing pertaining to surprise ran across Lulu's brightly painted face, only she held her tongue in this. She sighed in resignation and tried, "Let me help you then. Another course of action, perhaps?"

"I am sorry?" Angel said simply, with confusion.

"Simple," Lulu said, studying the carpet as she spoke, "When Tyrone arrives he will be informed that you have gone, vanished into the city."

"And then?" Angel asked, suspicious.

Lulu faced her squarely and her voice was gingery. "We will take it from there. If it is passage fare you need to return to your home, I will loan it to you." Here she held up her beringed finger, adding, "But, you must promise that you will send me the total sum back, immediately upon your arrival in England."

"Yes, yes, of course," Angel said, simpering, but shocked with joy. "I believe you and I will send you twice the total amount of fare, and pay you quite generously for the frocks we will need for the journey." She tilted her chin up, adding, "We are not without wealth, Madame, no, quite the reverse, and my father, bless his soul, has left his women well provided for."

"Good. It is settled then," Lulu stated firmly. "Babette is waiting outside the room to show you to the front bedroom. Whatever you wish, you need only ask Babette and it will be immediately yours."

Christine had fallen asleep in the plush confines of a chair during the conversation. Angel was indecisive now as to whether or not she should awaken her. The problem was quickly resolved when the Madame noted the girl's hesitation.

"Ahh, see. It is good that you stay, the poor lady is completely drained from your journey and needs a long rest," Lulu said, clucking her tongue. "I will see to her for you, loosen her gown a little, and George will carry her to the bed. When she awakens much later you can take your evening meal together, *non?*"

A few minutes later, Angel trailed the maid Babette along the gallery. They entered a room larger than the last. A lacquered tub stood waiting, shiny with soft tones of white and gold. With the help of the maid, the tattered madras was removed and Angel immediately sank down into the rose-scented water. Thankfully, the tension in her limbs abated as she scrubbed herself, washed her hair and sipped at her leisure from the mint tea set on a commode alongside the tub.

A half-hour later she donned a filmy pink thing and was shown into a plush bedroom, given some more tea and tiny cakes to hold her over until dinnertime. When the maid had folded down the counterpane and softly closed the door behind her, Angel slipped into the bed and slid her toes under the silken yellow sheet. Luxury. Wonderful.

Foggily she listened to the sounds of the city below her window until they became like a distant murmur. Her eyelids drooped heavily and her limbs felt like leaden weights. Strange. Soon she was floating on a sensuous cloud, and when she was semiconscious, a sweet longing stole over her as hazel eyes invaded her mind. A handsome visage drifted in the haze all around her.

"Tyrone, his mother a whore?" She tried to think, but she

241

couldn't, even if she wanted to. Then she slept, unaware that below her window the city was indeed just beginning to stir.

Late banners of yet hot sun streamed into the courtyard of Madame Lulu's establishment; its double-tiered fountain splashed softly as the covert Madame sat nearby on a padded bench to derive some comfort from the delicate cooling mist. The activity of the females rustling to and fro along the gallery, borrowing curling irons, rouge, and rice powder and various costume sundries, told her that it would soon be time for dinner. She and the girls would have to get down to business shortly thereafter. So, for now and at this time each day, the Madame set for herself a leisurely pace. Most lazy, in fact.

Madame did not even stir when the wrought-iron gate gave way to a low creak, then closed; now tall, highly polished boots strode the length of the flowered passageway into the somewhat cooler courtyard. In seconds, a dark-clad figure stood beside her, a brooding look on his otherwise devil-may-care countenance. The flickering sunlight glanced about his broad-shouldered frame, making his tan hair sway with golden highlights when he moved. It was disguised with its new shoulder-length growth, making one think of a tawny-haired Indian or an ancient Norse warrior. He was deeply tanned from his travels and his new thinness made him appear of even greater height.

Lazily shuttering her eyes, Lulu didn't bother to look up. She knew who was there beside her.

"She is here," she muttered abruptly.

"I know, it has just been reported to me. I came straightaway. Have you done as I asked, Madame?"

"*Oui*, Tyrone." Lulu glimpsed his immaculate attire, noting he had dressed with unusual care, but for the unfashionable hair. She said, "I followed your earlier instructions and gave her a mild sleeping powder. Babette has just informed me she is sleeping like a pooped child." She clapped her hands together, "Ahh, *la petite* mademoiselle is exquisite. Such feminine loveliness I have never before witnessed and I would be so lucky to have such uncommon

242

beauty in my household. Ah, well," she sighed reservedly.

Tyrone had quirked a dark eyebrow at that, roughly cleared his throat as he now said, "Watch her door closely, Lulu. Have George keep a lookout for Duschesne, just in case. I'll be back later to speak to her of my plans, after I have taken care of something and met with a man named Williams."

Of the young lady, Lulu said, "Ahh, that one, she will not like being told what to do. She has a will of her own and will not take to this conspiracy lightly, Monsieur Ty." She thought of something else. "And Jacinta, George says she has been searching for you. What if she comes here again tonight? The girls . . . I am not sure I can hold their tongues, they love to gossip."

A lopsided grin curved Tyrone's lips. "See that you do keep them quiet. Don't worry about Jacinta, I'll see her tonight—at the casino," he said, as if that explained everything.

"Just across the way?" Lulu asked incredulously, smacking her cheeks with both hands. "That woman, she will tear the girl limb from limb!"

Tyrone smiled comfortingly, thinking it the other way around. He turned to go, but was drawn back by Lulu's gasp.

"You must speak to Armand Bujold. He escorted that horrible man Duschesne and the ladies into port, I hear."

Tyrone grinned impishly. "So?"

"*Bon Dieu*, Tyrone. Armand wants to bed the petite mademoiselle. He thinks, you know, thinks she is a little lady of the night!"

Tyrone grinned even wider. "And, what does our lovely prisoner think of that?" he asked, as if he didn't already know.

Lulu spoke swiftly in French, relating to him the earlier incident in the parlor, leaving out her own heated argument concerning himself and his parent, but relating the girl's bitter retort, telling "Tyrone and his good friend to go to blazes."

Tyrone nodded when she had finished, the lazy grin never leaving his face until he glanced up along the gallery to the closed door that housed Miss Sherwood. He knew the room she occupied. Only now did he calculate that it had been over a fortnight since last he gazed upon that winsome face, recalling

243

their last night together as he stood here now in the pinkened sunset. It was not until one of the smiling, painted women waved to him from the gallery that he roused himself from his musings. He gave her a laconic nod and a wink before he strode off to see to his business, first at the Exchange, and then to meet with Bujold.

The sky had purpled and then it was dark when Angel walked the short space along the gallery back to her room after sharing a light repast with Christine in her own room. She did not wonder that they hadn't taken the evening meal with the girls in the dining room. She was happy to leave it to the discretion of the Madame.

Before Angel opened and closed the door to her room, she had the uneasy feeling that one gets when one is being watched. A pair of eyes that watched her every step. Someone big. Someone like that hulking bulk George.

Angel wore the lovely brocade gown that Babette had pressed and left for her to wear. It was the first thing Angel had earlier viewed upon awakening to the sounds of lively humankind in the hub of their night's diversions. This gown, a delicate shade of mint green, had been stitched so that the lace in the bodice spread out like an airy fan; the snug pleats pushing her breasts into a daring, cloven valley.

Angel thought: "All dressed up and no place to go."

Seated on the edge of the puffy feather mattress, she was almost wishing she *could* join the jollity below her windows. She stifled a yawn with the back of her hand, thinking that anyway she was so tired. She allowed her languid body to fall back upon the silken sheets, spreading her arms wide to delight in the delicious slippery feel of the bed. She was bored, all at once lonely and—she shook her head, so . . . very . . . sleepy . . . again.

A single candle held by an angelic china holder cast its yellow pallor upon the bed and the delicate female spread sensuously beneath the draping web of canopy. The painted cherub's round eyes studied, along with the tall, virile male standing there, the sleeping form. A warm flush tinted the

244

flawless cheeks and the sweet rosebud mouth was parted softly as if in yearning anticipation of a lover's kiss. The hem of her skirts was drawn up to her knees, giving her moonstruck audience a full view of curving limbs encased in white silk stockings.

Never before had Tyrone seen her so damn tempting and womanly-beautiful as she appeared to him now, laid out vulnerably, seminude as she was. His pulses quickened and he swallowed painfully at the sight that beckoned, dared him come taste love's joys. He started suddenly when she moaned and murmured something in her deep slumber and flung her small hand up to nestle among the spillage of loose waves.

That tiny, forlorn sound was all he needed to hear to realize that all was not well with her. There was something, a vital element, missing. It had nothing whatsoever to do with the sleeping powder, he knew. Rather, it was something latent he would have to uncover. . . .

"Please," she murmured again, rolling her head restlessly. "Please, just leave me alone," she groaned, and clenched her lids tightly.

He moved closer, wanting to touch her, love her, drive all her fears away. But still he stayed, listening, straining to hear every word as she rambled on:

"Why did . . . why did he do this to me?" she whimpered, making him flinch. "Mama—Christine—tell him—about the fire, the fall, so much blood. I am truly a—a virgin—the smuggler—" her voice became husky, "never be the same. Ohh—what if there is to be a child? No more—Mister Duschesne, I want to hear no more—" She was waking up now, "of it!"

Tyrone had groaned softly then moved quickly from the bed. The door opened and closed silently and the last words he heard as he went out were "never be the same."

"Who is there?" Angel questioned as she blinked sleep from her eyes, sitting up abruptly while her bleary eyes scanned the shadows beyond the confines of candlelight.

"There is no one here," the shadows seemed to whisper back to her.

"No indeed," she said to herself. "I—I must have been dreaming." She brushed away a tear that had squeezed out from the corner of her eye. And, why this sudden trembling, when it is so hot in the room?

She stood shakily, yawning sleepily as she stretched, halting suddenly with her fingertips resting upon her shoulders. She was feeling something like the lingering aura of a presence; the air charged with a stimulating quality that made her stretch out a hand tentatively, then draw it back. Then she shrugged at her silliness, while at the same time she couldn't shake the strange feeling that someone had stood here only moments before, watching her while she slept unaware. Perhaps it was only that it was so hot and she just needed some air. It really was stifling—there were none of the usual night breezes she had grown accustomed to back on the islands.

Lifting her hair from her sweat-dampened neck, she walked out onto the iron-wrought balcony that overlooked the narrow street below where much teeming activity was taking place. A prime carriage was just rolling to a halt before the iron gate. A man stepped out to disappear under her balcony, and while this first carriage was pulling away a second appeared.

Across the way, it was an assorted group she saw mingling there, and some of the colorful ladies in silks and brocades were being escorted on the arms of gentlemen, while some of each sex entered the gambling casino alone. A blending of strong perfumes and strong tobacco drifted up to assault her senses, reminding her of days gone by when her parents were wont to entertain.

Her mind drifted back. Soirees. Balls. Ladies' tea parties. Lazy jaunts into London on a blue sparkling morn. Stonewall. Green rolling hills. Echo . . . Echo. . . .

A second later she was brought rudely back to the present as her eyes riveted to that wiry frame of Pearce Duschesne pushing his way importantly into the lighted casino. There was grim determination in his stiffness and stride and she was hoping that he hadn't noticed her. She stepped back into the shadows of the curtain, her eyes never leaving the facade of the casino. She had a strong premonition that something horrible

246

was about to take place and her eyes were drawn there like a moth to a flame. This was very important, for some odd reason.

Here her worst trepidations were justified, for mere seconds later there sounded the ugly and loud retort of a pistol, snapping her nerves like popping fiddle strings all at once. Mildly excited voices called to one another, suggesting that this was not an unusual occurrence. The reactions below told her that this was the kind of society where murders, duels, and such were usually well hushed up, especially if the ones involved were important personages.

Heart pounding in her throat, Angel leaned out a bit further to better hear who it was they spoke so casually of as they flowed in and out of the casino to spread the gossip of the high point of the evening. Their voices swelled up to her:

"Monsieur Tyrone was very jealous, *non?*" a strident voice questioned another brightly garbed woman beside her.

"Was it really him?" a third wanted to know.

"Mais oui!" the second one answered both questions at once, and, "He has become very protective. Did you see the anger in his eyes when Pearce Duschesne approached *her?*" She tapped her fan on the first woman's forearm.

"But Duschesne drew a weapon first," a well-dressed young man piped up, his look somewhat incredulous. He shrugged in his waistcoat then, asking them all collectively, "What could Monsieur Ty do—stand by and let the man blow his head off?"

"What are they going to do with the body?" The first woman's eyes glittered like a greedy vulture's. "There was so much blood!"

Angel gasped out loud, backed up into the folds of drapery. Pearce Duschesne dead? And Tyrone, had he been wounded? She pulled the drapes against her forehead, and afraid, listened as they went on:

"There is most likely a fruit cart pulling up out back in the alley this very minute," the man finally answered. "The body will be concealed and taken out of town to where the river flows swiftly . . . you know the rest."

"Look," the second woman said, hiding behind her fan, "here they come now. Tyrone, Jacinta, and Armand. Ahh, we

247

have not seen the handsome threesome together for so long now. Where do you suppose Tyrone has been hiding himself? And, look at that beard. Why, he almost looks like a daring young sea rover."

"That cannot be him. Why the beard, the long hair . . . Tyrone Michael is a gentleman," someone said.

The informative man spoke up. "Some say he *is* a smuggler, but dare not speak it too loud. Shh, here they come now." He bent his elbow, saying, "Should we go inside now, mesdames?"

The gossiping trio nodded a greeting while passing by the other trio just coming to stand together beneath the light of a street lamp. All saw the tall, handsome man uninjured.

Angel, clutching the drape, peeked out from behind it to get her first full look at the woman aforementioned by the gossipers. Jacinta. Her golden-skinned arm rested possessively on Tyrone's forearm, her liquid jet eyes staring up with great solicitude into his face. His tawny head was bowed over the dark auburn head so that Angel couldn't catch the expression that the deeply tanned countenance bore. But the handsome woman, perhaps in her early thirties, was openly displaying her desire to be alone with him just now. She tugged playfully on both his hands as she backed up, but he muttered something while releasing himself from her grip, seemingly preoccupied for the moment with what had just taken place in the casino. He patted her hand, then turned from her to speak with Armand while the woman stood nonplussed by his gesture, her hands set on her generous hips, her eyes caressing his long and lean back.

Feeling like an eavesdropper, Angel stepped back cautiously into the room and let her shoulders droop after witnessing the scene of warm personal attachment among the three.

What hold did this Jacinta have on Tyrone? Why was she being so possessive? And, how could they appear so effortlessly congenial at such a time, after a murder had just taken place? It was unnatural, Angel thought. Yet, could it be called murder? Duschesne had drawn a weapon first, the man had stated.

Abruptly Angel came to a decision, disturbed by what she had just beheld. She would have to get away with Christine. It had to be tonight. Soon! For Tyrone was too close for comfort and she couldn't depend on Madame Lulu's remaining silent in this. No, not after hearing how admirable Tyrone's presence was in the public eye. They didn't even care, those who had recognized him, if he *was* a smuggler! He was too powerful a figure in this society, and Madame didn't fool her one bit—not anymore!

Then. Perhaps Tyrone had quit her and would leave her on her own, now that this handsome woman was here to monopolize his time. She certainly did seem to belong to him in some special way.

A disquieting thought struck her and her hands flew to her hot cheeks. Oh, God, no! Did Tyrone have her exactly where he wanted her? Him too, just like Pearce? *Strumpet!* Tyrone had said it himself—this was what she would become!

Tearing herself from her stance in the middle of the room and shaking from head to toe, she crossed the space to listen at the door. Enraged, sickened, and all at once brokenhearted, her hands shook like bloodless leaves as she fumbled with the cold knob. She peered out and saw a couple lingering on the gallery. She closed the door quietly so as not to attract attention and leaned her back against it to mull over plans of escape. Always escape. Would there ever be an end to it?

She would rouse Christine, and together they would slip furtively through the house, seek the back entrance and hopefully get someone to direct them to the governor's mansion. He was sure to help. He had to!

The figures of two women moved hurriedly along a noisy, smelly street where the open gutters gave off a nauseating odor of offal; it was worse in this section of town lined with dimly lighted barrooms where seamen and Kaintocks stumbled in and out of gaping doorways, bawling lusty ballads in hoarse, lewd voices. Painted women lingered here and there and called aloud to several groups of sailors who were passing by, examining the curvaceous merchandise.

It could be seen that the conspicuous pair of women, who were in a rush, one of a youthful appearance, the other middle-

249

aged, didn't belong here where corrupt violence and sexual immorality reigned. Still, they were there and had put themselves unconsciously in grave danger. All were unmindful of their passage until a burly, evil-looking sailor stopped to ogle them. He licked his thick lips when the younger of the two held up her skirts to step gingerly over a gutter filled with refuse. He threw back his head to chuckle and snort when she wrinkled a fine nose in uncommon repugnance.

"Eyyy!" he hollered across the narrow street, already making his way in a staggering gait toward the girl and the older woman. He slobbered, "What do we got here? Damn, but ain't you the purrtiest piece o' muslin. C'mere little lady and give us a kiss."

Angel tucked her mother protectively behind her and with icy aloofness turned to face the drunken seaman. He didn't frighten her one bit, for she was no longer a newcomer to his type. Nevertheless, she realized that here she and Christine walked without protection. The directions a man had earlier given them had somehow gone awry. A wrong turn perhaps down that last alleyway had led them to this place of sin. Actually, the only difference was that where this section was dirty and dingy, Madame Lulu's section had been a bit more refined. If you could even call it that.

"Suh," Angel began in an accent she'd heard earlier used by a Southern housemaid, "we seem to have got ahselves lost when we was out taking the night aih. Mah uncle, the govenuh, would be quite worried bah now. We ah from—umm— Virginia, wheah as you well know we Claibornes' hail from." She stopped, thankful that just this evening over dinner Christine had enlightened her on that bit of Thelma's eager gossip.

"Hrumphh. Are you for real?" the sailor sneezed as he gawked at her bobbing nod with bloodshot eyes. Then, "If you be who you says you are, then you know the gov'ner's at the Cabildo this time every night."

"Oh, but of co'us," she expired quickly, "ah'd forgot. Could you please, suh, direct us to the, umm, Cabildo?"

"You *ain't* for real, I can tell. C'mere puss," he mumbled

250

drunkenly as he reached out a grimy paw toward the fine girl's breasts.

Angel squealed and stepping back swiftly, whirled around to grasp her mother's hand. The two of them took flight like startled doves from the cote, never glancing back once to see that the seaman met the end of his stupor by tripping on a loose cobblestone that sent him sprawling to his hard bed. Seconds later his contented snoring filled the street.

Finally and after much walking they reached the Cabildo. They were fortunate enough to have found an elderly lady who was more than willing to stop and confabulate with them. Surprisingly, after giving them directions the Creole lady trailed along, eager for female company on this hot and humid night that had dared her to venture outdoors. So she said. They halted before the pillared arcade and the foreigners stared in awe at the massive architecture.

"It was built in seventeen-ninety-five by Don Almonaster Y Roxas," the kindly woman began, proud of her knowledge. "He presented it to the King of Spain. The name Cabildo in Spanish means Governmental Council."

Angel turned a smile upon the woman. *"Merci,* madam, but could you tell us where we might find the governor? The building is unlighted and no one seems to be stirring inside."

The woman canted her head that was bound neatly with a tignon. *"Oui,* there is not anyone here tonight, mademoiselle, only guards. The governor and his lady are gone for the weekend, up north to friends who are holding a fête on their plantation," she informed them with tongue in cheek.

Angel smiled feebly as the woman babbled on. She kept peering into the street as if she were expecting someone, and when Angel and Christine would have moved off, she held them back by begging endless information about their homeland. Neither did she care that the younger woman seemingly had other matters of importance on her mind and that her look was filled with utter consternation.

Christine nudged her daughter. "What a flibbertigibbet!" she whispered. "Let us go back to the Madame's. This is plain foolishness."

251

"Christine!" Angel hissed low. "She is sweet and just being kindly."

"Bah!" Christine exclaimed. "These people do not care a whit for us foreigners. We should get away—she has something devious on her mind." She suddenly noticed a light carriage coming toward them, and warned, "See, what did I tell you. Look at her smugness, she knows that carriage."

The Creole verified Christine's statement. "How lucky for you. Here is Monsieur Grymes. He is a good friend of Governor Claiborne's. He will help you. *Au revoir*, ladies," she sang airily.

With a single nod directed at the young gentleman already alighting to stride toward them, the self-satisfied woman took her leave of them. Angel flicked her regard from the woman's back to the stranger who came to stand at attention, as if he barred their way lest they should go around him.

"How do you do, ladies," he said pleasantly. "I am Mister Grymes. I noticed you standing here looking lost. May I be of some service, perhaps lend you my carriage?"

"Grymes? An American?" Angel inquired, at once embarrassed for being so forward. But her situation called for nothing less, she told herself next.

"Yes ma'am. John Randolph Grymes, District Attorney. May I?" He indicated the waiting carriage, holding out his other hand to them both, adding, "We will take you somewhere safe, from the night's danger."

"Of course!" Angel almost shouted for joy. This man had to be someone important, for his impeccable manners and dress told her it was so. Then, "Where are we going, sir?" she blurted out in a straightforward manner, blushing in the light of the street lamp.

"A town house, here in the Vieux Carré," Grymes said as he walked with them to his small carriage. Then, "I am sorry, I had completely forgot. My light carriage accommodates only two. Miss Sherwood, would you mind terribly riding with some friends of mine?"

Angel jerked to a halt and spun about to face the man squarely. "Strange, but I do not recall introducing myself to

252

you, sir," she said.

"Don't you?" Grymes asked tactfully, ignoring the girl's utter stupefaction as she stared at the walk, trying hard to remember. Quickly then, he waved his arm in a come hither motion down the street to where a bulky apparition loomed black beyond the light of the street lamp. "Here, they are coming now. I'll be taking your mother to the town house where we will all come together shortly. It's not far," he promised.

"Daughter," Christine whispered, "you are too trusting, I've always said. Do you think I should accept a ride from this stranger, and worse yet, go to a strange house alone with him? How about you?"

Angel shrugged, saying, "Why not? I think Mister Grymes is who he says he is and we have nothing to fear. I am certain he has met ladies in distress in this city before."

"Indeed I have," Grymes smiled after eavesdropping, a mysterious twinkle in his eyes.

Angel stared dumbly while the light carriage moved off, taking Christine and the mysterious Mister Grymes—District Attorney—with it. Suddenly she was feeling a bit lonely, but turned her head just as a high-sprung, elegant carriage came under the pale glow of a lamp. It was drawn smartly by two magnificent blacks with a high-spirited prance; tossing back flowing manes, necks gracefully arched, slender.

A golden family crest emblazoned the side, Angel noted, as it drew before her and the shrouded driver pulled his team expertly to a standstill. She had a moment of fear as she detected two black pits peering out from under the cowl. The driver looked away as the door swung wide and a deep male voice bade her enter while he reached out to gently grasp her arm and guide her to a seat that was velvet plush. There was a tap, then the carriage rolled away from the Cabildo.

Once inside, Angel found herself seated next to a warm and muscular frame. His hard thighs brushed against her own for a moment and she shivered at the shocking contact. There were two others besides herself, but she couldn't make out their features in the dark shadows above her shoulders, only their laps were visible. They both sat tall, though, and were both male—*very!*

Feeling at once shyly embarrassed, as if she was imposing, she nervously fingered the lacy fan at her bodice. She could see the high polish of the men's tall, handsome boots as they passed beneath a lamp instantaneously, then darkness blanketed them fully as they raced down a narrow alleyway.

It was a moonless night so far, and a cat screeched, the yowl pouncing on her tautly sprung nerves and stiffened spine. She started and the gentleman beside her shifted slightly, as if this bothered him. He placed a dark hand upon his knee, only a hair's breadth from her own. He was obviously as tense as she was.

When she was wishing that someone would break up the stifling silence, the man across the way cleared his throat.

"How are you this evening, Mademoiselle Sherwood?" he inquired, solicitude lining his deep voice as he leaned forward to catch the momentary flicker of light groping into the swiftly moving carriage.

Armand Bujold! She drew in a gasp, felt herself catch on fire as a thrilling shock flamed along her rigidly held spine. All at once she was acutely aware of who indeed sat beside her, his breath hot on her meagerly clad shoulders. She twisted her neck to face the warm, dark form, knowing he grinned mockingly at her bitter astonishment as his teeth flashed white briefly. All else was black.

"Good evening, sweet," Tyrone said huskily, wishing he could better see her reaction. All he made out was the glossy crown of her lowering head.

Before she could reply and move to hug the corner, the carriage was fluidly bouncing to a halt after rounding a sharp corner. Here the streets and the slate-roofed houses wore imposing facades and yellow light showered everywhere. It reminded her somewhat of Paris, as here and there lighted squares of window were beginning to blink off like retiring fireflies. These tall, narrow town houses were almost flush up to the cobbled street, with only a bit of walk in between.

As Tyrone was on the other side of her, Armand alighted

first and had the pleasure of assisting her down, leaving his friend to step out last. Angel's back was turned against Tyrone as she stared worriedly at the door, wondering what this was all about. Should she run? Silly girl, she chided herself. Christine would soon be along. But where were they? The light carriage was nowhere to be seen.

Her worries were short-lived for in the next instant the door was being opened in answer to Armand's knock and a sleepy-eyed footman looking dishevelled under the lighted sconces stepped back to permit entry into the foyer. He smiled openly upon recognizing Tyrone and was just about to utter a greeting when something about the man caused the footman to clamp his mouth shut, turn and scurry down the dimly lighted hall to go prepare a tray of refreshments.

Tyrone fastened his gaze on Angel's exquisite profile and looked her over from head to toe as the young woman remained indifferent to their presence, watching the footman enter a door at the end of the hall. Tyrone recalled how very lost and forlorn she had appeared as his carriage neared and stopped to pick her up in front of the Cabildo. If he hadn't gone to Lulu's for the third time this evening to see if she had awakened, he might never have found her. God forbid what might have befallen them on this night! He had dispatched several acquaintances in carriages to alert well-known Creoles and quadroons to be on the lookout for two English women fleeing from him, to be returned to Grymes or himself unharmed. It had been lucky indeed that the crafty St. Clair woman had discovered and detained them at the Cabildo.

Bujold noticed that his infamous friend seemed to be in a daze as he stared at the captivating young woman with whom he himself had almost taken up. Not that she would have let him, no, and he had a feeling that she wanted nothing to do with either one of them now. Well, perhaps Tyrone could remedy that, given a little time alone with her to become reacquainted.

Armand nudged Tyrone to bring him out of his trance, speaking in low tones. "How I envy you, man. Mmmm, but I'll just take my drink in the salon to the right, you and *la petite*,

255

the left." He started to move away but whirled back, warning, "Watch your time, my friend. It will not be long before you-know-who will be here."

Tyrone moved silently forward like a cat, already feeling her shrink away from him. Like a hungry beggar his eyes searched for a morsel of warmth from her, anything but this damnable remoteness she had placed again between them, reminding him of when first they met.

"Princess, look at me." He reached for her arm as she foresaw his intent and shied away. Then, "Damnit, girl. Are you going to begin that distressing crap all over again!" He tossed his gloves onto a lacquered black table.

"I am princess only to Nikki," was all she said. She winced angrily when he grasped her firmly by the hand and led her into a sumptuous salon where he at once closed the door with a reverberating slam and snapped home the lock. "Bloody damn," she whispered under her breath.

Angel dodged under the arm that was groping toward her, but she soon saw the folly of her gesture when he snatched her against his hard leanness.

"Keep away from me!" she yelped, twisting and turning against him. "I want no part of you, you snake in the grass!"

He held her at arm's length while she struggled to be free of him. He shook her once roughly and laughed harshly as he squeezed her chin around to face him while one arm continued to hold her immobile.

"You deserve the tongue-lashing, not I," he began sternly. "Although I must admit, come to think of it, it was I who wronged *you*."

She tried hard not gazing into those hazel depths, rather she kept her eyes trained on the broad turn of his shoulders, his well-tailored waistcoat. "I—I don't know what you mean," she lied as she fought for some composure, peering down at the hands that had murdered a man just this night.

"Yes, you do, *ma belle*." He bent his head over hers, delighting in the fresh, clean scent of her hair. "I have wronged you horribly and plan tonight to set forth to make amends. Ahhm, whether you know this or not—it is not easy for me—I . . . let's just say that you'll be very well-off, as your home will be here in Louie. I'll make you happy as a—"

"A lark!" she interrupted. Oh! She knew exactly what he meant. He planned to install her in a brothel in New Orleans where he could ease his lust whenever he felt the need of novelty, whenever he was not amusing his golden-skinned lover, Jacinta.

"Where is Christine?" she asked suddenly, looking primly to the door.

"She will join us soon. No more questions . . . for now."

"Please, just release me. I will never be happy again, ever. I—I am so confused and—and unhappy," she shamefacedly whimpered.

"I've knowledge of that," he said cupping the back of her neck with one hand. He gently tilted back her head and she was forced to lock gazes with him in the flickering candlelight that was threatening to sputter out. He drank of the strangely sweet pain he knew was sweeping through her, as it was him. He felt her go limp as a rag doll. His face moved closer, arrogant in the power he wielded over her.

"The cottage . . . the moonlight . . . the love . . . remember," he murmured.

She sucked in a deep breath and he smothered it with his eager mouth, his moist tongue at once thrusting, searing as it slipped between tiny teeth and sparked the inner surface afire. When she heard him make an inarticulate sound that rose from the depths of his throat, coming up to mingle with her own groan of heightening pleasure, he crushed her so hard she felt his swelling desire boldly against her belly. All coherent thought fled her mind in the next instant as a sultry flame blazed to fuse their clothed bodies together. His lips stayed as he moved his full length against her, pressing his loins ever closer until he feared he would surely shame himself where he stood.

Hotter and hotter and still they could not part. It had been so long, he thought agonizingly, since last he held her, purposely prolonging their passionate time together now. Pushing aside the fan of her bodice he fumbled at a swelling mound as he groped to free the sweet flesh from its confines. His lips left her clinging ones to slide hotly down to her throat and a savage joy coursed like molten lead in her veins when he urgently pressed his bearded mouth into the cloven valley, his fingers at the same time giving a freed breast to his lips. He teased a soft pink nipple.

"Oh! Oh! Oh God!" she panted as she hugged his head closer. Swaying on her feet, she tossed back her head to pant in ecstasy. She buried her fingers in his hair and felt at once the readying moisture begin at her thighs.

Still pressing her to him, Tyrone came up to whisper hoarsely in her ear, "I want to lie with you," taking such sweet pleasure in her abandonment to desire that he was unmindful of what he was saying. Then, "Ahh, not here, not now, my love." He pressed his face into the long silvery wavelets, murmuring, "A little later—alone—soon. Soon, you will be mine body and soul. I want to love you, fill you. Remember. God!" he growled softly as he pushed her gently from his aching thighs, "I can't . . . hold you any longer. Armand is at the door and I must go. Damn. . . ."

Angel almost sobbed in shameful wanting as she twirled away so as not to meet the lips and eyes she believed mocked her now. She fumbled to rearrange her bodice and brushed the back of a trembling hand slowly across her sweating brow. Her heart was pounding like a drum and she was filled with such sweet longing that she ached for him to complete what he had begun. It was lust and nothing more. She was no better than a shameless bitch dog, worse. Her mind decided for her, and at the same time her body cried total commitment to this man who was not even her fiancé.

At last the candle sputtered out with a thin blue curl of vapor rising to dissipate in the uppermost shadows. The salon was only dimly lighted now from the outside lights stealing in from the street. A shadowy figure moved stealthily past the open window as Angel turned just in time to see the salon door shut softly. He was gone. Her shoulders slumped dejectedly as she walked slowly about the room like one in a fantasy world.

What now? How long before this night's melodrama unfolded? She picked up a dainty China figurine with elfin eyes that peered up at her with mischievous innocence. Again she was reminded of Stonewall. Home. She would never again, could never, be happy as long as England was so, so far away. All she had held dear and longed for had vanished from her life. She felt disoriented in this land, refusing to acknowledge that something of much greater importance was happening to her young mind and body.

She was no longer a child in love with books and horses and saddle leather and mild flirtations. She was a woman with a woman's problem.

Madame Lulu, Armand Bujold, Mister Grymes, and even that sweet old Creole lady—friends all. Why, every soul she had encountered in this blasted city was in love and lock with Tyrone. Even his Jacinta, naturally.

Then. How about you, Angeline? Her heart took up arms against her level-headedness, leaving her with a dizzying sensation as it beat out a wildly sweet tune when she thought— Say it, say you love him! Want him!

"Oh, I cannot!" she cried, almost crushing the sweet figurine in her trembling palms. "It can't be, it is too soon to know."

"Yes, you can," an inner voice defied her wits. "Home is here, now, here with him, the one you cherish more than life itself." He had said—soon you will be mine, body and soul?

"No, no, he only wants me as his mistress," she argued.

Again the voice taxed her cruelly, "This is what you have waited for, yearned for, the reason for your existence. You were meant to love, Angeline Katrina. . . ."

". . . I can't seem to remember," Christine said nervously to the man standing before her in the gentlemen's salon.

Williams, in his dark, austere suit of broadcloth, straightened from the desk he had been writing upon with pen and paper and looked to Tyrone for aid. Tyrone shrugged as he took a deep breath, feeling the need of a potent libation to calm his unusual nervousness.

Armand noticed this and took his friend by the arm to go and stand before the long, open doors that opened onto the narrow path squeezed in between the tall town houses. In the gloom on this side of the house neither of the gentlemen noticed that a shadowy figure hurried away and went to the opposite side of the house.

"Fortunate for you and *la petite*, Tyrone, that Williams happened to be in town today." He accepted a cigano from Tyrone and lifted a candle to ignite the black tip of tobacco.

"Miss Sherwood will think otherwise, I'm afraid," Tyrone returned, blowing a blue spiral of smoke outdoors.

"Mmmm, yes," Armand looked thoughtful as he accepted a snifter half-filled with brandy from the footman.

"*Merci,*" Tyrone thanked the bemused servant, who bowed, then went to serve the other two occupants of the room a milder concoction.

"So," Armand began, "you are finally going to give up this smuggling business." The earlier statement was confirmed as he received a nod from the other. "Tah! If only Lafitte and Claiborne had knowledge of what they are, or I should say, *were* up against—" He shrugged, letting it lie. "My friend, is there nothing sacred to you?"

Tyrone stared past Armand's dark head. "This night—will be. I just pray the lady will recall her daughter's name before Williams gets impatient and decides to leave."

Armand looked doubtful but reassured his friend nevertheless. "You are just too damn lucky with the skirts, Ty. Don't fret, man. If anyone can make a lovely wench fall behind his booted heels, it is you." With a trace of jealousy nipping him, he added, "I should have tossed you in the calaboose long ago, *ami*. And tonight when you flew into a passion. Still, Pearce rang his own knell when he trained his pistol on you. I still cannot believe it, how fast you reacted."

"Nothing to it. Unkindness often reacts on the unkind person, *mon ami.*"

"Mmmm, yes," Armand murmured. "Considering the young lady, it was a very quixotic action. Neither will I ask if you had goaded him, or done the same had he not drawn on you—" he shrugged. "I was not there, remember? Come! We will question the Lady Sherwood some more."

With a chuckle, Armand clamped a strong arm about Tyrone's shoulders as they made to join the other two. Their handsome heads rode together, scheming. But inwardly Tyrone suspected that, as usual, her name would remain a mystery to him.

> The harp that once through Tara's halls
> The soul of music shed,
> Now hangs as mute on Tara's walls
> As if that soul were fled.
> —Thomas Moore

Chapter Seven

1

Jacinta Hunter née Villerne, with hard determination locked into her golden countenance, stiffly twitched her skirts, paused to cast a brief scan about the foyer, and next, bent to listen at the door that housed the young woman her Ty had brought here. When certain that the object of her current hatred was isolated in this salon, she turned the knob and with a quick slip was inside, pressing back with her lusty curves to shut the door softly. Her searchlight eyes swept about the room, coming to rest upon a delicate back poised stiffly in anticipation.

"Tyrone," Angel breathed to herself, putting the figurine hastily back in its place in the display case; when no answer came she turned slowly, her voice barely above a whisper, "Is that you, Tyrone?"

The huskily sweet voice made Jacinta's anger blossom twofold, but she stifled the urge to fly at the younger woman and mar the face so that when Ty looked upon it again he would cringe at the bloody scars. But no, that wouldn't do. It would only serve to hinder her near-future plans.

Angel heard the distinct rustle of skirts and she sighed in relief as she rushed toward the door, saying, "Oh, Mama, you have finally arrived. I was so worried. What kept. . . ." Her slippered feet froze and her outstretched arms dropped slowly to her sides. This was not her mother. It was the woman in the street—Jacinta!

"Hurry, you must come with me—immediately!" the

handsome woman began. "We cannot talk here. Out back, there is a carriage waiting in the alley."

"B—but, I don't understand," Angel stammered in confusion as she tried to read the woman's intent.

"I am sorry, mademoiselle. How stupid of me, my name is Jacinta. The last name is not important now," she said nicely. Rushed, holding out her hand to the younger woman, she added gravely, "I don't think—ahmm, Miss Sherwood?" Jacinta accepted the affirmative nod, then, "Yes, my man has told me all about you, poor girl, about to legally become one of his many mistresses."

Angel's eyes widened as she asked with astonishment, "Legally? I never—"

"Please let me finish," she interrupted, "but not here. You must trust me. What I have to tell you will make you want to leave here immediately," she whispered scandalously.

Angel shook her befogged head, trying to clear it. This scene was very similar to another . . . of course, Grande Terre, Ellen.

Angel thought herself a fool for possibly falling into a trap once again, yet there was something about this woman's simplicity and soothing tone of voice that made her follow this Jacinta obediently out to the rear of the house. While they were passing quickly under a lighted sconce, Angel had a moment of uneasiness when the woman's jet eyes obliquely swept her person, then snapped ahead.

Seconds later they were standing before a light carriage where the lazy driver at once drew himself upright from his restful slouch. Jacinta whirled to motion her inside the dark interior, but Angel hesitated, remembering something of great import.

"I cannot go with you . . . you see, my mother will be greatly worried if I am not here when she arrives."

Jacinta first stared hard, then sweetly at the younger woman as she said stupidly, "Your . . . your mother—" trying not to make it sound like a question. Swiftly she recovered as she recalled the older woman she had glimpsed as she hid outside the doors of the salon, listening. She had to think of something fast. The girls at Madame Lulu's hadn't mentioned another woman, but she tried this, "Ah, yes, your mother. I have already spoken to her of this—ahmm—matter, and she agrees with Jacinta that this is the only way out for both of you. I know more of your sad situation than you think and I want to help."

Jacinta tossed a hasty glance back to the house, then her eyes snapped warily back, "What do you wish, Miss Sherwood?" She left the bait dangling shrewdly.

Angel's eyes were wistfully sad while she decidedly announced, "I only wish to return to England."

Relaxing, Jacinta said, "Ah, good, just what I thought. You have made an intelligent decision, mademoiselle, and you will have your wish. But you must hurry now and don't fret about your mama. She will join you shortly. Please, get in, quickly, quickly, someone is slamming the doors in the house and shouting for Miss Sherwood!"

The last sound Angel heard was that of a booming voice echoing as the carriage lurched then careened along the dark alleyway. The bleakest of nights began, for she had left a part of her heart back in that elegantly appointed salon.

The hour was well past the bewitching stroke of midnight; the tall houses were silhouette-black. The pleasantly talkative woman seated next to Angel in the carriage related bits and pieces of her trying past with Tyrone. Angel's heart went out to the woman who, like herself, had unfortunately fallen in love with the bloody rogue. Jacinta added that, though Tyrone had been utterly cruel with her at times, bedding countless other women and taking himself away from her for long periods of time, she was not about to give him up. He loved her, Jacinta went on somewhat tearfully, though he sometimes had a strange way of showing his love.

Odd, Angel thought, that Pearce had told it the other way around—that Jacinta had jilted Tyrone. But then, Pearce had been a bold-faced liar on all counts.

"Now, tell me your story, mademoiselle," Jacinta eagerly asked. "We can take it from there and maybe put an end to my man's reluctance to give you up."

"He—he said that?" Angel sounded out, but with little hope.

Jacinta laughed nervously. "Oh, no, no. What I mean is, he would like to play with you for a time. A little last fling with a new mistress before we are to be reunited. You see—ahmm—Mademoiselle Sherwood, though Ty sometimes denies it, we are not to be separated by anyone—ever!"

Angel suddenly wanted to ask this woman the why and how of that horrible incident in the casino, but then Jacinta would learn that she'd eavesdropped, and she just wasn't up to hearing the gruesome facts tonight, anyway.

Instead, Angel burst forth to unfold the factual story of her turbulent journey to this end, leaving out nothing but the more intimate moments on Grande Isle. When she had finished she was thoroughly exhausted and sick at heart. Never once either did she reveal the devastasting love that had come to the fore this very night; it was growing more tangible in every passing moment, in every beat of her heart. She brought down the curtain by confiding in the woman her belief that Tyrone had been planning to install her this very night into a bordello to be used at his will.

"*Ma foi!* He told me just this evening that very same thing. Ah, but as before, I have snatched many out from under him, before the strutting peacock could break their poor hearts. Now . . . I'll be leaving you soon to my driver, Rafael, who will take you to a plantation a few hours more journey north from here. There was an ad just this evening in *Le Courier de la Louisiane* asking for a governess who can read and write English. I know the Gayarre people well."

Angel brightened. "I can do both quite well and have studied foreign languages somewhat. Oh! I can make the money on my own and in a month's time I will have the passage fare!"

"Ah, good. You are lucky to be so—ahmm—talented. Now, perhaps tomorrow I'll find time to send your *maman* your way. Do not worry about the Gayarres, they will welcome her too. The house is a big one and they could find work for her too, like mending and such." Jacinta grimaced at that.

Smugly satisfied at last, Jacinta pushed back into the plush seat. They had been going nowhere in particular; now she tapped, signaling for Rafael to take her back to the town house. She could return safely in the knowledge that Tyrone would be out—searching.

Gayarre was actually the last place Jacinta wanted to send this sad young woman. What else could she do on such short notice? She would visit Gayarre in a few days and speak with Wesley of her plans. How amusing were he to learn that at long last part of his grudging hatred for Tyrone would be avenged. Too bad, but this was to be solely her secret. Still—maybe later if need be. . . . For now her plans would merely be to make certain Wesley kept her at Gayarre and under no circumstances let the *poor sick* girl go. At least, not for several weeks, not until she had Tyrone under control as she believed she had had him once, long ago. Ah! but he could be hard-bitten!

Jacinta snickered to herself. How could this pathetic little fool beside her ever hope to earn the voyage fare in a month's time? Let her think what she would. One thing, she would never learn that the passage had come from Monsieur Tyrone's own reserves!

Under a half-moon the carriage jerked to a halt and its sole occupant almost tumbled onto the floor upon her startled awakening at the sudden jolt. Angel sat up to wearily rub the sleep from her eyes and peered out into the darkened shadows with bits of silvery moonlight playing about the grounds. Suddenly the door was snatched open and Angel shuddered when a leathery hand reached in to help her alight. Without actually looking at the man who now stood beside her, she knew somehow that he bore a hideous countenance.

Rafael bent down to pick up a large mesh bag that he growled was a gift, compliments of his employer. Something she would find useful, he added. He snorted under his breath: Rags his employer had forgotten to drop off for the beggars on the waterfront.

Angel was suddenly alive with apprehension as they stepped up to the pillared facade that loomed grayish in the diminutive light of the moon. The flicker of a candle moved about on the first floor of the house after Rafael applied his meaty fist to the knocker. Along the cavernous hall the glow floated toward them and stopped long enough to dip and lend flame to a wall-sconce. At the same moment that the door slowly creaked open, Angel heard the rasping sound that Rafael made as he called for his horse to be away. She was alone and she focused her eyes after blinking away the sudden glare of a trembling candle held up to her face.

Two great ebony eyes stared at her and a tiny voice asked, "Mamselle, can I help you?"

"I am terribly sorry. I know the hour is disrespectfully late, but—" Angel searched for proper words to admit her into the house, then she blurted, "I am here to apply for the position of governess. May I come in, please?" She felt foolishly like a beggar.

Saucer-eyed, the black woman glanced swiftly around the young woman to make certain she'd come alone. Satisfied, she stepped aside as Angel found the mesh bag and entered slowly. She stared around the bleakish entrance hall, hearing the massive clock strike three in the morning. She put down her bag.

"Who is it, Jenny?" a sleepy voice floated down from the top of the uncarpeted staircase as the white cloud of a nightgowned figure became discernible.

Still saucer-eyed, maid Jenny answered in a sing-song voice, "Doan know, Miz Hannah. Say she's here for the lady's job. Y'know, for Miz April?" She finally blinked once, lifting the candle holder higher.

The delicate figure drifted down now. "My goodness, at this hour?" A sweet brownette came to stand before the young woman, her pale gray eyes sweeping the green-gowned beauty. "Goodness gracious," Hannah breathed, "you're as young as I am, aren't you?"

"I am—" Angel bit off, turned a pale shade as she glimpsed the hall, and there lying atop a mahogany bench was the Good Book, giving her a sermon on truthfulness. She hated herself, but mostly she hated Tyrone for putting her in this awkward position. If it wasn't for him, she wouldn't have to speak falsely. "I am sorry. My name is Angel—Angeline Duponte. And, yes, I would so like the position as governess. I can read and write fairly well and have some knowledge of foreign languages."

Pleased, Hannah held out her small hand and Angel received

267

the warm palm into her own, feeling at once at home after the kind gesture. Hannah made no more mention of the late hour, and dismissed the curious maid after ordering her to ready the front bedchamber upstairs. She turned to the young woman shyly.

"I need to apologize, Miss Duponte. My name is Hannah McCormick. I live here with my half-brother Wesley Gayarre. Come, let's go back to the kitchen and rustle up some tea and cakes. All the servants are asleep, but for Jenny. She's the upstairs maid but sometimes suffers insomnia and rises very early to be about her chores. Wesley is away on business and shouldn't return till late tomorrow afternoon."

Angel dutifully followed the delightful, chatty girl down the almost barren hall and into an antiseptically clean kitchen where the young mistress of the house lighted candles and scrounged about the cupboards for the fixings. Hannah chattered all the while, enlightening Angel on the workings of the household, the few servants' names, and Wesley's only child, April Louise.

Angel sat silent as a church mouse while Hannah bustled about. This is horrible, she thought agonizingly. Here she was, partly under a false identity, and this young woman was being so kind. So far, Hannah hadn't bothered asking where she came from, her former employer's name, or if she even carried introductions pertaining to past employment experience and such things.

With admiration in her crystal eyes, Angel watched Hannah pour the steaming brew into dainty china cups, timeworn, with hairline cracks etched into the roses and leaves. On a platter Hannah set out tiny frosted cakes she said were left over from the evening meal. Hannah then sat down herself.

"May I call you by your first name?" Angel asked shyly.

"Oh, please do, Angeline," Hannah returned warmly.

"Is not McCormick an American name?" Angel wondered out loud, at once feeling like a snoop and chiding herself for it.

Hannah said in a tinkling voice, "It's all right, Angeline, please don't be embarrassed. After all, one applying for a position should also know a little about the people *she* is to work for. You were 'on' the moment I laid eyes on you. I might add, April will jump for joy after suffering the tutelage of grumbling, stiff-colored governesses what were ready to drop in their tracks after a session with my overly active niece!"

They laughed together for a few moments before Hannah became serious, toying with the rim of her cup.

"Yes, Angeline. My father, Jason McCormick, was of Scots blood and had arrived in America when he was but a wee lad. He chose the life of a flatboatman, like my grandfather before him." As she receded into her past, her eyes saddened. "Long before I came along, my mother, a Virginian by birth, married Paul Gayarre. He died of malaria and this plantation was left to Mama and my half-brother. Jason McCormick swept Mama off her feet and, of course, after they were married I was born, a year later. Papa lived here until he, too, passed on. But Papa never once felt he belonged here at Gayarre, Mama often said to me in a sad moment. You see, to him, Wesley was the rightful heir. They are both gone now—Mama and Papa." She added after pausing momentarily, "River pirates, so the rumor was, ended their life. Contrary to that, some folks say that Papa's boat was upset in a whirlpool and they both drowned."

Angel had drawn an inward breath at the mention of pirates, but Hannah had been so engrossed in her sad tale that she hadn't noticed the small sound. Recalling her own father's death and feeling again the pain of it, Angel spoke up softly, consolingly.

"I am sorry, truly. How awful for you, Hannah. I—you see—oh, it is nothing. . . ." She glanced away quickly then came back with a smile, as if that explained everything she'd been about to say. Hannah smiled back thoughtfully, though.

Angel had wanted to tell her own story, but twice in one night would surely make her break down, make a silly fool of herself. Perhaps tomorrow she would reveal how she had come to be here, leaving out the name Tyrone, naturally. As much as Angel would despise herself for twice deceiving her new friend, she could do naught else. This way, Tyrone wouldn't find her, and when Angeline Duponte sailed for England, he would be none the wiser if and when he tracked her to Gayarre.

"Our new governess is bone weary, I can tell," Hannah said suddenly and rose from her chair.

The upstairs bedchamber Angel was to occupy was shockingly bleak and smelled musty. Yet, to be sure, it was not so very different from what she had already seen of the sparsely decorated house.

"This was the music room before Muriel passed away. She was Wesley's wife," Hannah said and went on, "Wesley is not a lover of music like Mama and Muriel were, and against my better wishes he had it altered into this room for guests. As you may have noticed, Angeline, Wesley is a straitlaced man and cares little for frivolities. Only the barest of necessities must do. Well," Hannah said, expelling a breath, "I've chattered long enough. Sleep well, and tomorrow we will talk more."

Angel donned a white cotton nightshirt that Jenny had laid out on the bed for her. Staring at the black frame of the bed, Angel would have sworn that she had just been admitted into a convent, if not for the delightful presence of Hannah McCormick. Still, it was a good feeling to have a sturdy roof over one's head, she thought, climbing into the bed. She drew the gray coverlet up to her chin, shivering nevertheless. The house possessed a certain chill that matched the grays and blacks of the dark, austere furnishings.

She rolled onto her side and studied her tapered fingers resting on the hard pillow. Hannah's words had revealed something of her older brother's character and Angel suspected that Wesley Gayarre was a man who carefully saw to his own interests first. She slid her gaze to the short stub of a candle, mesmerized by the tiny golden flame. Suddenly it sputtered out and a chill raced along her spine. What had happened to Wesley Gayarre's wife, Muriel, she wondered as blackness surrounded her. Sleep well, Hannah had said?

Outside the morning shone but it gave only an infinitesimal luster to the cheerless bedchamber. Angel murmured softly in her slumber, dreaming the touch of warm and lean fingers caressing her back, making her feel as if she were made out of velvet. She whimpered in her semiconsciousness and heard a voice as from far off: "Never, Tyrone, never will I see you again."

Suddenly she was wide awake and remembering where she was. Not the cottage. Not Madame Lulu's. But the Gayarre

270

plantation. Worlds away from England.

Shortly she was seated on the edge of the bed, collecting her thoughts of the evening before, when Jenny's knock sounded once and then the cheery dark maid bustled in with a large breakfast tray, set it down and stepped back and bobbed her kinky head.

"Soon as you're done, mamselle, I be fixing your bath. Mistress Hannah will be here in a minute. She got a robe for you. Washroom's to the back up here," Jenny announced all in one breath. She bobbed again, going directly to draw the threadbare drapes and toss wide the long, multipaned doors. Golden streamers married with gray.

"Ummm," Angel murmured, nibbling a warm roll. "Very good, Jenny." She looked up, seeing movement at the open door.

With a soft morning greeting, Hannah, with cup and saucer in hand and a faded blue robe draped over one arm, walked in to position herself gingerly on the bed. While she waited for Jenny to make her exit, Hannah sipped her tea in silence with Angel.

Hannah was looking prettier than ever in the morning light with her fine-stranded, glossy hair catching the dusty rays of sun. Though her small eyes were a delicate gray shade, they sparkled with the same crystal-like intensity as Angel's own.

"Say, you *are* looking greatly refreshed this fine morning, Angeline. I only wish that I could appear as beautiful in the morning." Hannah smiled widely, showing her pearly teeth. She was unmindful that as she did this it increased her perky loveliness twofold.

Angel returned the warm smile and replied, "I was just thinking the same thing about you . . . Hannah. Your smile would best the grandeur of a royal palace, and I have always been envious of girls with sparkling gray eyes and warm brown hair like yours. Sometimes I feel like an outcast with my icy green eyes and my too blond hair, though Mama often tells me they are my better attributes." Angel cut here, recalling that she had failed to mention Christine the night before.

Hannah laughed in that tinkling voice, then said, "This is great, Angeline, already we are good friends, and we are going to have wonderful times—riding, long talks, and I will not be lonesome now anymore. With only an eight-year-old niece to keep my company. . . ." She shrugged, went on, "Oh, Angeline, I can see it in your eyes, you do understand, don't you?"

"Hannah, how very much you will never even begin to comprehend. I guess that it's writen in the book of fate for some to be a trifle lonely, then when that great moment of your life arrives—it will be great." Angel paused, and went on slowly, "That is, if nothing happens afterward to cause you to become lonely all over again."

Hannah's eyes grew wide. "Has that great moment happened to you, Angeline? Have you lost someone you loved very much? Is that what you mean?" she eagerly asked.

Angel met the gray gaze. "Yes, I have been in love, but that seems very long ago," she said, surprised at her own answer. "In fact, I just came to realize how much that man really meant then and now to me. But, when that love is not returned the pain is very great and one can do naught but flee to escape further hurt. He—he must not find me, Hannah."

"I think I see now why you have come, Angeline. But we shall not discuss that further, for now. I can see how much it pains you to speak of him so soon after . . . after leaving him." Hannah took in Angel's nod, went on, "You mentioned your mother. Do your parents reside in the Territory? Your name is a French one, am I right in saying so?"

Her head bent in thought, Angel traced the cotton flowers embroidered on the hem of the nightshirt. Hannah touched her friend's shoulder lightly, and asked softly, "What is it, Angeline? We are friends now."

"My mother, Christine, is to follow me here," Angel blurted. "Perhaps even now she is on her way. I'm afraid I have been overly presumptuous in this, Hannah. If it is asking too much, then we will leave as soon as she arrives."

"It's all right!" Hannah said, her voice lifting.

"It is—truly?" Angel asked and the other nodded reassuringly. "Oh, Hannah, I must be truthful with you on this—I have never once been employed as a governess."

"I know," Hannah returned. "At least, I had that feeling

272

from the first. This changes everything. Before you mentioned your mother, I had my doubts that Wesley would ever hire one so young. Don't you see? One has to begin somewhere if one wants to be a lady governess. What better way than to be chaperoned, so to speak, by one's own mother?"

"You are wonderful, Hannah!"

Hannah stood after handing over the robe to Angel. After it was donned, Hannah showed Angel the room where she would bathe. Angel turned back to Hannah before she entered, a tiny frown worrying her brows.

"Hannah," Angel started, "I don't know where to begin. You see, we—my mother and I—we shall not be staying long."

Hannah sighed. "I think I had knowledge of that also, Angeline. I also know that you have been trying to conceal your English accent." She heard the intake of breath. "Do not worry, it doesn't matter to me that you are hiding from this someone you love. I only wish that you could stay longer. But, we will have to work on that accent of yours before Wesley returns this afternoon. Keep saying to yourself that you are French, not English, *non?*"

"*Oui*, mademoiselle," Angel said, giving her a coy smile.

"Charming!" said Hannah, smiling brightly.

Somewhat sadly, Angel watched until Hannah entered a bedchamber just across the hall. As Angel bathed she was met with a new problem. In less than one day she had come to know Hannah as if they had been friends all their life. She was kind, pure in heart, and—what was it Hannah had said? 'I will not be lonesome now anymore . . . you do understand?' It was this—how could she go now that she had brought some happiness to a lonely heart?

After she had donned a cooler cotton frock given to her by Hannah, Angel found and entered the dining room. Hannah and her niece had not come down as yet, so she utilized this time in getting used to her new surroundings. As she moved about the room she thought again of the contents of the baggage Jacinta had left with her—as a gift. The baggy frocks, and colorless gowns of tabbied silk had been meant for a woman twice her size and age. Perhaps Jacinta had meant it as a cruel jest? Anyway, they smelled as if they had been quickly snatched from a discarded heap of rubbish!

"I just saw Jenny taking your baggage out back to burn, Angeline. Are you sure you wanted her to do that?" Hannah looked worried as she walked into the room.

"I'm quite sure, Hannah. They did not belong to me . . . I mean they were given to me and *phew*, they smelled terrible!" Angel pinched her nose.

Hannah giggled. "You don't sound too Frenchy—American perhaps. But then, one can never actually tell with the melting pot that has invaded Louie in the past decade. And now more, as we have those fire-breathing steamboats plying the river. Ugh! Give me a good old sailing vessel any day!"

Abruptly, Angel turned to gaze sightlessly out the window so that Hannah couldn't detect the sudden rush of emotion staining her cheeks scarlet. With a painful spasm in her breast, she wondered why it always had to be this way. Was there never to be a conversation without reminders of that smuggler? If this was what the poets called love—it was awful!

It was sultry but still a lovely summer afternoon to the two young women who decided to take a cooled pitcher of fruit-water and sandwiches out onto the lawn. They spread a blanket, sat, and had not taken two bites when a sing-song voice moved down from the porch, bringing with it a plump child with rosy cheeks and braids coming undone.

"Auntie Hannah, ain't you gonna introduce me to the new governess?" April Gayarre asked, smacking her lips loudly as she hoisted a powerful-smelling pickle.

Angel flinched first at the child's insolent grammar, then wrinkled her fine nose at the horribly wrinkled green thing the child was munching upon, licking first one finger then the other. Angel met eyes as disturbing as thunderclouds and when she smiled at the child she received a noncommital glare in return.

Hannah narrowed her eyes and her tone of voice was almost scolding. "Why didn't you come down for breakfast this morning, young lady?"

"I wasn't hungry," the child began, "and I ain't a lady."

"A truer statement has never been spoken," Hannah said. Then, "All right, April. This is Angeline Duponte and—"

"And I'm April Louise Gayarre," April interrupted as she polished off the green stub with a loud crunch. She raked Angel over from head to toe and with a pout she said, "Hmmph! I don't believe you're a governess. You are too pretty and I bet you don't even know how to read and write."

"April Louise!" Hannah scolded severely this time, making ready to rise, when the child whirled away, her pink tongue giving them both her last message. Angel watched the child skip away defiantly.

"I am sorry, Angeline! I really did think she would jump for joy. I guess I should have warned you ahead of time. April is spoiled rotten by her father and she gets away with everything, short of murder!"

Angel first quivered at the word, then said with confidence, "Never mind, Hannah. I was once a counterpart of that child and I believe that we should mix a bit of business with pleasure, that is all."

Hannah's eyes lit up doubly. "Say, that's a great idea, Angeline. How would you like to take a ride over the grounds tomorrow, see the entire plantation?"

"Oh! On horseback?"

"Mmm-hmmm," Hannah murmured.

A burst of excitement flooded Angel at the thought of again being astride a horse after so long. She was so thrilled she could hardly contain herself as she sprang to her feet, tugging at Hannah's hand.

"Take me to the horse barns now, Hannah, please?" she begged, her eyes asparkle like sun on sea-foam.

A walk of five minutes or so brought them to a whitewashed structure badly in need of repair. Angel noticed nothing else though, but the deep snorts of greeting, the delicious smell of oats and hay making her senses whirl with pleasure. On passing three mares, Angel stopped at the fourth stall to stroke a silky mane. She rubbed the mare's muzzle with gentle hands, wishing she had a treat for each and every one of the horses.

Hannah watched this mysterious young woman closely, mindful of her expertise in the handling of nervous creatures. This sport was Hannah's pride and joy and she realized Angeline's horsemanship would equal her own. When they reached the furthest stall, Hannah took delight in Angeline's reaction at what she found there.

"Ohh, aren't you beautiful, yes you are," Angel murmured, pressing her nose to the velvet muzzle of the bay.

Hannah reached over to pat the diamond forehead, saying, "This is Gypsy Girl. We purchased her from the younger Hunter, about five years ago now. She was only a skinny youngster then, but she showed high spirit even then. She is my treasure, but I'm going to give you the pleasure of having her to yourself on our first outing."

Angel peered askance at Hannah. A thoughtful crease lined her brow as she said, "Hunter." The name sounded familiar somehow, but where and when had she heard it?

Hannah's look became a guarded one. "Yes, Angeline— Hunter. You know the name?" she asked, cocking her head off to one side.

For a moment Angel pressed fingers to her temple, then she concluded, "No, I guess not. Either that or I have suffered a memory lapse between then and now."

Hannah's sigh was of deep relief. "Good gracious. For a moment there I thought maybe he was—you know—an acquaintance of yours, or more than that. God forbid if that rogue ever got *you* in his clutches!" She went on, "He lives north of here, or he used to. Anyway, Cresthaven borders Gayarre about half an hour's ride from here. That's riding astride—like the wind. Let's do that tomorrow—ride to Cresthaven. What do you think?"

"Oh my! What about the rogue?" Angel breathed, drawing a look of feigned fright.

Arm in arm as they left the barn, Hannah said, "Don't fret about him, he is almost a non-figure in this parish. So I hear and thank goodness!" she blurted lastly.

After the evening meal was cleared away by the servants, Angel and Hannah sat in the tiny salon, curled upon a windowseat. Angel watched the last sun rays melt away from the green lawn until the live oaks there were dressed in purple robes of twilight. Angel tried hard to camouflage the growing mask of concern lining her pale face and pricked her finger several times, until finally she dropped the prim and proper muslin she'd been mending onto her lap. Hannah, her own mind far removed from the tedious stitching, laid down her own work and stood to stretch.

"Well, Angeline, it appears as if we both wait in vain. Something must have detained both Wesley and your mother this day. Why don't we call it a day? I'm certain that tomorrow will find them both here by the afternoon meal," Hannah said cheerfully. Then, "Perhaps by the time we return from our jaunt we'll find them both chatting amicably and already well-acquainted. I'll leave word with Jenny in the morning to see to the introductions."

"Hannah, Hannah, I am not—my name is not Duponte," Angel said, not being able to stand the deception any longer. "Can I really trust you not to slip and reveal my true identity, to anyone?"

"Don't even tell me, Angeline," Hannah said, placing a finger on Angel's lips. "It is too easy to make a mistake. I know you only as Angeline Duponte so far, and if you like it will remain just so. And, don't worry your lovely head about your mother's coming. You know, you can always say you married hastily, then tell your mother the truth later?"

This partially pacified Angel. It all sounded too easy, and it seemed more likely that Hannah couldn't trust her brother to keep the secret. *Married.* Suddenly that hated word had a certain sweet ring to it. Marriage to a loved one. Would there ever be such a day in her life?

A single candle illuminated the salon window of the town house in the Vieux Carré. Inside, a man sat brooding and alone, his long legs stretched out before him. His unpressed, black trousers, and his white silk shirt opened to the waist were mussed as if slept in, though he had not seen a bed for two days. In his hand dangling over the arm of the chair was a half-filled snifter of brandy, having been sloshed carelessly onto the pale mauve carpet. His eyes glittered amber, mirrored the single flame of the candle in each dangerously staring eye. The glass was lifted to his sneering lips, stared into and then dashed into the cold fireplace where hundreds of shards twinkled on the Italian marble hearth and fine carpet.

The shards lay like his life, he thought with a snicker. Shattered. Irreparable, and damned, ever since he was a youth. A big, damned farce.

Tyrone stood, somewhat unsteadily, and went to the display case where an elfin figurine had caught his attention the whole of the time he had sat reclusive. He snatched it up, turned it over in the palm of his hand, and was at once reminded of *Her*. He muttered an oath. The considerable amount of liquor he had consumed was of no help; it didn't even make him forget her, not even for a moment. She was here, she was there, her image was everywhere. Everywhere but in the flesh.

An entire night and day Tyrone had searched until his mount was ready to drop, as he was himself, even though he was known to possess rugged strength and endurance. God, he must have alerted the whole damn city, but still no word; none came to give his torment ease. He was at his wit's end, unusually, and was just about to smash the dainty thing he now held in his hand, when a timid rapping at the door made him stride swiftly across the room. He wrenched the door wide and it slammed against the inside wall.

"Monsieur," the shy housemaid began, her eyes drawn to the figurine he clutched. Her gaze slid up to the dark glare. "Monsieur—" she tried again, failing to continue when she was mesmerized by the wild look she had never witnessed before in this man. He didn't come to the town house often, but when he did he was cool and aloof, not this crazy man she saw now.

Tyrone tossed the costly figurine into a corner where it shattered, causing the maid to start, and next to back up when she was certain he was going to strangle her for bothering him.

"Don't just stand there gaping like an idiot!" Tyrone bellowed. "What is it, woman, what is it?"

The octoroon's hand flew to her open mouth and she stammered, "Ah—ah—Jacinta—she—Ohh!" A flash of white apron and bow and cap fled down the hall, almost crashing into Jacinta.

"Why do I have to be announced into my own salon?" Jacinta asked herself. Then, "Why have you locked yourself in here, *mon cher?*" She entered the salon and closed the door.

"Damn, but I shouldn't have come here in the first place," a tired voice said from across the room, seemingly unattached to the tall man.

Her skirts rustling and her tongue clicking at the disarray of the elegant gold and mauve salon, Jacinta watched as slowly Tyrone turned and barely acknowledged her presence. He raked his fingers through his tousled hair and she moved slowly closer, swaying her generous hips. She placed a hand on his shoulder.

"*Mon cher*, if you keep this up you will become unwell." Jacinta puckered her full lips when he shrank back involuntarily. "So touchy," she said: "What is so bad about losing one lay? The slut must have been good, *non?*"

Tyrone's fingers bit unmercifully into her upper arms. "It wasn't like that, Jacinta." He looked the savage as he snarled, "Don't ever call Miss Sherwood a slut again. I'll not stand for interference in my personal affairs, you know that better than anyone."

"Ah, you are in love again, *mon cher?*"

"I've never been in love with anyone, Jacinta," Tyrone said with a beginning frown.

His fingers still bit into her flesh unconsciously and her eyes glazed over with lust. She loved every moment of the pain he was inflicting upon her. On fire, she tossed back her dark auburn head, thus pushing her hips into his hard thighs. When he finally released her, she followed close behind as he went to lean heavily against the mantel of the fireplace.

"You will forget her," Jacinta murmured huskily. "Come. Come upstairs with me, umm?" She traipsed a fingertip up his forearm to where the sleeve had been curled into a bunch carelessly. "It has been so long. I am on fire for you. You know I can make you forget other women. Our old room is waiting upstairs. It is yours, too. Come." She pressed her belly into his buttocks, clutching the muscled shoulder where her cheek rested now.

With a deep groan Tyrone turned to crush her against him while, insanely, his hungry lips met the waiting, upturned mouth. He kissed her long and hard, devouring the experience of the darting tongue. Though sentient, Jacinta couldn't believe this was actually happening to her. His searing kiss was deeper than ever as it twisted hotly and cruelly across her pliant mouth. Those magical fingers were moving down her throat and before long he would have her gown lying in a heap at their feet. His ardent procedure was not new to her and she panted in anticipation of a long night of sensuous fulfillment.

He totally surprised her next as he pushed her savagely away and said hoarsely, "We are finished, Jacinta. It was over long ago. You know that."

"*Merde!*" Jacinta hissed, almost stamping her hard slipper upon his stockinged foot. "You are drunk, Tyrone!" she said, wishing that was all it was. She would wreak vengeance on one winsome head, she swore inwardly.

Shaking his head to try clearing it, Tyrone muttered no apology for his actions but turned on his heel as he went to pull on his long boots and tuck in the loose ends of his shirt into his trousers. He hesitated a moment at the door before he turned back to face Jacinta, looking almost past her as he spoke.

"Do you know who in the city owns a light carriage with a nag favoring its right hind leg?"

"No, and how could I with so many carriages in the city," Jacinta lied, glad she had gotten rid of the nag just that morning, having Rafael purchase her another mare shortly thereafter.

"Be a dear, Jacinta, and take care of the Lady Sherwood for me, will you? Tell her that I will find her daughter—and soon!"

Jacinta clenched her teeth and half-shrieked, "Wha—?" Then at his unswerving gaze she tried in a quieter, meeker tone, "Oh, yes. I have already seen to the old woman. She will stay with me here for a few days and—"

"Good, good," he interrupted absent-mindedly. "Prepare a comfortable room for her upstairs. I'll send you whatever else you'll need."

"Some money . . . yes. The woman has nothing but what is on her back," Jacinta explained, mentally rubbing her hands together.

"You will have it," he said, and presenting his back to her, added, "Good night, Jacinta."

With that Tyrone left her staring icily after the closing door. She then stomped her foot repeatedly before throwing herself into a deep-cushioned chair to gnaw a long, buffed fingernail. She tossed a careless glance about the room she had decorated herself.

Jacinta's bosom lifted stormily as she thought: Ahh-hhh, yes, *mon cher* Ty, I will take care of them both for you. You are mine and you will return to me when I am finished with Miss Sherwood!

Under the high sun the magnolia trees bloomed fragrantly and the countryside reminded Angel somewhat of England. It whizzed greenly by as she spurred Gypsy Girl to even greater speed and the bay responded eagerly to the pressure of the gentle heel and the soothing tone of urgent demand. The weight of the new rider remained unchanged and Gypsy Girl flew like the wind as her nostrils flared wildly and her dainty hooves pounded the moist turf. Angel laughed in gay abandonment as the silky mane streamed back to tickle her pink cheeks and she glanced back quickly over her shoulder to see Hannah following close behind on a daintier but still quick, and darker bay.

Hannah veered off to the left and Angel followed rein as they neared a corner of strong fence that branched off to the west one way and the other to the south. Hannah was not slowing and when Angel saw her intent she, too, gave the horse her head, and leaning low, they cleared the wooden fence together.

There watching them from a light carriage in the fork of the road was a lone spectator, observing the breathtaking sight of young womanhood astride, looking as wild and free as fair-haired gypsies, the show of pink and white petticoats blowing back away from trim, cracked leather boots.

"*Bon Dieu*," said the observer as she leaned forward to get a better look and her high-piled hair caught the sunlight to glow a deep reddish brown.

Jacinta muttered a vile oath, snapped hard on the reins and sped up the lane, doubly vexed, for Rafael had gone on a drunk the evening before. In her vexation, Jacinta failed to note the dust cloud of yet another carriage that was now nearing that same fork in the road.

Wesley Gayarre noticed though, and he urged his driver to a quicker pace so that he might meet his guest at the front entrance. With gaze riveted he never noticed Hannah and the mysterious governess who had entered his home when he had stayed away on business.

Some distance away now, Hannah and Angel halted atop a small rise to rest their mounts for a time. Here they could view the great river below that dazzled and blinded them as it caught the bright rays on its rippling current. Shielding her eyes with her hand, Angel twisted in her perch to follow the winding river flowing southward to a point of haziness. She brought herself back around and suddenly wondered at the expectant look written upon her friend's little face. Hannah's smile stretched mysteriously as Angel searched the hillside copse for the reason for Hannah's strange behavior.

Then she saw it. A great sprawling white mansion looming high above the river, like a world in itself. She stared awestruck as the place seemed to beckon her, and mesmerized, she followed Hannah back to the winding road that would take them to Cresthaven.

Shortly, Angel found herself on a wide, winding lane bordered by orange, magnolia, and pecan trees that led up to the great house, the majestically gothic edifiace with its white pillars supporting the second-floor gallery that stretched the full length of the house. She could make out dense woodland in the backdrop as she slowed her mount to trot beside Hannah.

The sunlight caught the coruscation of tall, gleaming windows, and Angel breathed, "How very beautiful it is, Hannah." Her eyes misted over. "But it looks forlorn, the grounds neglected—why?"

Hannah nodded. "Mr. Hunter, a big Yankee of the best stock, presented it to his son on his twentieth birthday. The rogue, remember?" After Angel's nod, she went on, "I don't think he ever comes here anymore, though. All the plantation hands have been long gone, all but for Della. The housekeeper runs the place and keeps the interior fit as a fiddle. There are some gardeners, I have heard, but not sufficient for such a great plantation as this one."

282

Angel cocked her head to one side. She felt a definite sadness envelop her as she asked, "What happened? Why does this Mr. Hunter's son neglect it so?"

Hannah sighed. "The details are unknown to me. Young Hunter disliked living here alone for some reason, I guess, even though it's a short distance from the city." She peered askance at Angel's shocked expression. "What is it, Angeline, you look as if you have just seen a ghost?"

Angel stared ahead as if she had indeed spotted a familiar apparition drifting weightless about the grounds. She felt the same weirdness of the night in the pirogue with Nikki, but said, "Oh, it is nothing, Hannah," and then, "Would Della, this housekeeper, mind so very much if we visited?"

"Of course not. In fact, I would suppose she is quite lonely with only a few other servants besides herself."

No sooner had they dismounted than a thin, elderly black woman appeared upon the spotless porch. Her black eyes lit up in recognition as she ambled forward, dropping her hands to wipe them on a fresh white apron.

Della licked her thick lips, saying, "Lordy me, is that you, Miss Hannah? Been such a long time since you been visiting. You was just a child then, and look at you, all done grown into a fine lady." Her watery eyes took in Hannah's companion. "Who you got there with you, Miss Hannah? Never seen her before, and she's as pretty as a ripe plum, too."

Hannah smiled her agreement. "This is Angeline Duponte, Della. She is April's new governess."

Della shook her head, looking a bit lackluster as she recalled, "That's right. Heard Old Saul mention something about Wesley having a little girl. Sure was bad news when I heard her mama fell off a horse and broke her sweet neck, just like—" she quit, altering, "Muriel Gayarre, Lord rest her soul."

Hannah groped for words as she wondered at the same time what indeed had summoned her to bring Angeline to Cresthaven. It was too late now, anyway, as Della was already leading the way indoors.

"I just made up a batch of hoecake and just awhile ago finished waxing ever'thing. It smells mighty good inside. Don't worry none about them horses out there, I saw Old Saul

283

coming round to care for them just now."

Despite Angel's preoccupation with the housekeeper's troubling words over the deceased, she found the house invitingly cool after the long ride. She stood transfixed as her eyes wandered over the grand appointments gracing the huge, spotless hall. This room had been painted a champagne color, with French tables and polished chests standing elegantly above an inlaid, dark oak floor. She had never before witnessed such immaculate and studied care; even back at Stonewall this much dutiful attention had not gone into the house.

"I don't think Mr. Hunter will mind if we borrow his parlor for a spell," Della began. "After all, you ladies is just as much his company as mine."

Once inside the tall double doors of the parlor, Angel suddenly halted before an ornately gilded pier glass mirror and stared at her reflection. Her softly slanted eyes were now wide with wonder—and something else. As she continued to look into the mirror her own reflection blurred and a great portrait hanging over the mantel came to life.

"That there mirror has never been moved. The late mistress left orders to leave it be," Della almost sighed.

As if a moving force propelled her, Angel whirled and crossed the room to go and stand directly below the portrait. Paralyzed, she studied the stunning oval face, and kindly brown eyes returned her perusal. Angel felt that indeed the canvas breathed life. Time stood still for her in these hypnotic moments; somehow the two women seemed to be communicating with each other.

A blurred figure came to stand beside Angel, but still she remained motionless and spellbound. Della's eyes traveled from the enchanted girl to the portrait and then back again.

"This here was Mistress Hunter," Della said sadly, but her eyes were filled with love. "Cresthaven belongs to the boy now. He—he's away for a spell," she ended in a rush of emotion.

Hannah came to stand beside them, deeply moved by the reverence that strangely filled the room. She was just about to speak when a movement from Angeline caught her eye. One hand had fluttered to her forehead and Angel now swayed unsteadily on her feet. Hannah was reaching out for her when

Della, alerted first, caught the swoon with a thin arm supporting the young woman's tiny waist. Greatly concerned, they helped the fainting girl to a long divan where Angel was put to lie back with her feet upon a small pillow.

"Lan' sakes, child," Della murmured, taking hold of a wrist. "You's shaky as a newborn foal. Here now, don't you move an inch. Miss Hannah, you watch the poor miss." Wringing her hands, Della shuffled out of the room and into the hall where her surprisingly booming and strong voice hollered for a maid.

Angel tried rising but was met with gentle hands pushing her back down. Angel argued with Hannah that it was really nothing to worry about. When questioned if she had finished her breakfast that morning, Angel shamefully answered that her excitement had overwhelmed her need for food. Only a cup of tea had she downed, she added.

When Della hastily returned with a tray of foodstuffs, Angel was already sitting up despite Hannah's protestations. A maid followed with a basin of cool water and some linens. After she set them down, Della shooed the curious maid out of the room, and with arms folded across her chest, came to stand before the divan. Clucking her tongue, Della shook her turbaned head at the pale girl who insisted that she was fine now. The tea was poured and a plate of buttered hoecake was placed into the trembling hands.

"You sure you feeling better, Miss Angeline?" Della asked with a doubtful frown.

Angel nodded firmly as she took a sip of tea. Hannah and Della exchanged duplicate looks of worry. The young lady was sure pale and shaky, Della thought, then motioned to the door with a discreet quirk of her head, and Hannah caught her message. Della then excused herself politely and went out the door to await Hannah in the hall.

"Angeline, will you be all right if I leave you for a few minutes?" Hannah inquired, setting down her cup on the highly polished table.

"Of course, I am fine now," Angel said, and to put Hannah's fears at rest, nibbled daintily at a hoecake.

Alone now, Angel set down her half-finished bit of cake, and closing her eyes, leaned fully back into the plump cushion. She could still feel the portrait staring and for some odd reason when she reopened her eyes, could not bring herself to look upon it again. Instead she was actually seeing the huge room she was in for the first time since entering. She stood, strength flowing into her limbs once more as she studied the elegant appointments.

Bright and cheerful, the parlor was rife with furniture and rich with textures of no small splendor, from the abundance of voluptuous Chippendale sofas and chairs to the extraordinary velvet wall-hangings. The moldings and niches were all a rich dark oak, and mauve marble columns at the room's entrance were topped by the same hard wood. Rust velvet balloon drapes were drawn up over delicate veils of white curtain that permitted the outside light to enter, and the rolling vastness of the plantation could be viewed. The symmetry of the high-ceilinged parlor reminded her of a European *palais*, but despite the grandness of the place, Angel felt it remained cozy and intimate.

Just outside in the hall, Hannah and Della had come to a decision concerning the young woman. Miss Duponte appeared to be in a state of sheer exhaustion and needed a few days of bed rest; after that she would be fine. With mental reservation Della agreed this was so, while Hannah was none the wiser. One thing was certain—Angeline Duponte would not return to Gayarre astride.

2

One of the several well-cared for Cresthaven carriages was hitched up and Old Saul was proud to be once again of service. It had been a long time since the still robust mulatto man—named *Old* Saul since he turned eighty, and now nearing a young ninety—had driven the team of powerful chestnuts to transport guests to their destination. The two bays from Gayarre were secured by a length of rope to the back of the carriage, and Old Saul, decked out in his fine red and gold livery, waited out front stiff-backed as a general.

Unhappy though Angel was that she was not permitted to

286

return astride, she finally but reluctantly agreed with Della and Hannah that her state of health came first. She waved farewell to Della after thanking her for her hospitality, and yes, she would return for a visit. With a sigh of resignation Angel sat back to watch the countryside roll on by.

Somehow the eerie night in the pirogue and her first glimpse of the grounds of Cresthaven and the portrait of the stunning late mistress of that mysterious plantation were all linked oddly together. She shivered, allowing her thoughts to take a different turn. What Wesley Gayarre would think when learning that the new governess would be indisposed, bedridden in her room for a few days, she couldn't help but wondering. Too, there yet remained the problem of Christine's coming. She was now seeing the gathering of rain clouds out her window and thought how appropriate the weather was to her situation.

By the time they reached Gayarre, a light drizzle had indeed begun to fall. Hannah thanked Old Saul as they alighted with the help of his weathered hands. He turned down Hannah's invitation to share a spiked cup with Morice, the cook, and smiling toothlessly from under the wide brim of his hat, he climbed back aboard. He waited until the women were ushered inside by the footman before beginning the longer than usual journey back to Cresthaven. He would have to make haste, for the roads would become perilous muck, impassable by the time darkness settled in.

Once inside, Angel grew apprehensive upon hearing Jenny tell Hannah that her brother had arrived. That was all, Jenny added, except for one visiter who had not stayed long on business with Wesley, and had left shortly before their return.

"You go upstairs and get yourself into bed, Angeline," Hannah said after Angel left off staring at the closed parlor door. "I'll speak to Wesley before you meet him. And, don't worry about your mother. It is possible that the smell of rain kept her driver from delivering her here. Who knows, she might even arrive by flatboat before the evening meal. If not, then hopefully tomorrow."

Angel climbed the stairs like a mechanical doll. After Jenny had helped her remove the muslin frock and given her a robe,

Angel sat on the edge of the feather-tick bed. Jenny promised to return soon and went downstairs to await further orders from her mistress. Angel swallowed painfully, fearing something horrible had befallen Christine. She curled up on the bed but no restfulness came. She listened to the forlorn patter of soft rain falling against the eaves. Sometime later she found herself standing by the window and gazing down the lane that was already turning into red muck.

What if there had been an accident and Christine never did reach the town house that night? Had Jacinta been sincere in promising that her mother would soon join her? Well, all she could do was to wait, but it was wearing on her. Soon she would be forced to tell this Wesley Gayarre the truth if Christine did not arrive within the next few days.

Much later, Jenny knocked softly once then entered, saying that dinner was ready now. "I can bring it up, if you is wanting to eat now, mamselle."

"Thank you, Jenny, but I would rather go down and join the Gayarres," Angel said, moving toward the clothes press for the muslin. There were several simple frocks, all prim and proper, hanging there now, yet Angel longed for the feel of silks, velvets, and tiffany gowns.

It was shameful to desire such luxuries at a time like this, Angel scolded herself, but being of noble birth she couldn't help feeling the way she did. Perhaps in the near future she would find herself garbed as was her wont. For now she would have to be content with what little earthly pleasures she had, at least until she was back home.

Jenny pursed her thin lips. "Lor' no, mamselle, you got to stay in bed like Miss Hannah says." She went to pull out a drawer and remove a fresh nightshirt. "I gonna fetch your dinner now, you eat good, den the Gayarres's coming up to visit."

Feeling like a lonesome child with the pox, Angel donned the nightshirt, ate lightly of the meal brought up on a bed-tray, and then sat back with propped-up pillows to await Hannah—and Wesley Gayarre.

Drifting off, lazily content after the plum pudding and several cups of hot tea, Angel did not even stir when the door opened ever so quietly. Languidly she opened her eyes and with a start she saw Hannah standing beside a man of medium girth and height, with sandy-colored hair slightly graying at the temples. His pale gray eyes were studying her face closely, as if examining the flawless skin for some slight imperfection. Wesley Gayarre was astonished that not even one tiny freckle tinged the beauteous cameolike complexion, and the eyes— like chips of green ice!

Angel sat up stiffly, feeling conspicuously on observation. She slowly dragged the sheet up to her chin, noticing the man grinning slowly. A pleased expression of lifting brows followed, passing over the long, squarish face; everything about the man was that shape, even his widespread shoulders. She read at once that here was a man who possessed a mind turned in upon a single-minded purpose in life. She shivered as she pondered momentarily just what that might denote. Though he did not resemble Pearce Duschesne in the least bit, the air about him was coming across to her like the dead man's equal.

"*Soooo*," Wesley began, "this is to be our new governess. Excuse me, I should say my daughter's youthful tutor. I hear that you took slightly ill today while visiting our oft unseen neighbors." He shot his half-sister a sidelong look of disapprobation.

Hannah stood stoic in her demeanor though, and watched him turn his full regard back to the embarrassed girl in the bed.

"That is right, monsieur." Angel tried smiling, but the greeting did not reach the suddenly paler hue of her eyes. "But please do not think too badly of me, as I shall be up and around in no time at all." And then I'm going to get the blazes out of here, she silently promised herself. But there was Hannah, Hannah smiling with such sweet concern for her. God! What to do?

Closely Wesley watched the long lashes curtain crystallike eyes and discreetly studied the rise and fall of luscious mounds beneath the sheet. He began to ponder why in hell Jacinta Hunter wanted this sickly but beautiful Angeline out of the country, when it was Jacinta herself who had sent her to be engaged in his household in the first place.

"Tomorrow, my dear," Wesley began to the young woman,

"we will talk some more. Sleep well now, Mademoiselle Duponte."

With those parting words the squarish frame made his exit, leaving his sister and the new governess to talk awhile before they, too, bid each other a good night. The subject of Christine's nonappearance had not arisen and Angel was relieved to not dwell on it. For the time being, anyway.

Downstairs in the parlor, Wesley Gayarre sat, idly flipping through the newspaper, revolutionized newspaper, the *Louisiana Gazette*. He sipped not a drop of liquor of late, nor did he pleasure himself with a smoke or take stimulating liquids such as black coffee or tea. He folded the sheets neatly on a table, then flicked at a speck of lint that had caught his attention on his dark gray trousers. His colorless eyes rolled upward where he pictured Angeline Duponte slumbering temptingly in the old music room.

Wesley turned back the pages of time. In his mind's eye, Muriel sat at the pianoforte, a gay and lovely woman. That was before the unfortunate accident that had claimed her life. The overly jealous woman had caused him much grief, with her sad eyes and weak-kneed manner. Wesley stood suddenly, like a swiftly released spring. Damn! What's done is done!

He turned to less troubling thoughts, as he reflected back. The sugar plantation had seen him hard at work for most of his thirty-seven years. But now the extent of his toil consisted mainly of riding the plantation, shouting orders to his hands, seeing that the bordering fences were not neglected. He didn't want to lose any more precious land than he had already.

It irked Wesley that the north plots which should rightfully have been his were now going to seed. He had given up the gaming tables years ago when the elder master of Cresthaven finally procured the northwest sections from him, now in the possession of that man's son. Damn that estranged lad for pulling up the fences several years back and relocating them, thus cutting off prime planting fields from him. Young Hunter didn't hold any proof that the sections belonged to him, as there were no legal documents proving ownership.

A wry smile twisted Wesley's lips as he went to pour himself a glass of water from the sideboard. There was no way that young Hunter could keep those sections from him anymore, and he planned next week to weed those damn fences and get that border back where it should be. Who would know or even care. All that remained of Cresthaven's workers were an old woman, a handful of household servants, maybe a few gardeners, and Old Saul. Who knows, perhaps someday he could even snatch up Cresthaven and its many-thousand acres for little or nothing. Then all would be his. Yes, his and Angeline Duponte's—Angeline Gayarre—for he had come to a decision this very night when first he laid eyes on that winsome face. She would become his bride. To hell with Jacinta and everyone else!

It was on the third morning of her confinement that Angel finally realized that something was horribly amiss. Christine had not yet arrived and this obviously had to be investigated. She made up her mind to speak to Wesley Gayarre as soon as she had put on a fresh frock and done something to the unruly state of her hair. Without the maid Jenny coming to her aid, her trembling fingers could never have completed the task of braiding the thick mass of freshly washed hair into double loops, one on either side of her head. At last she pinched her pale cheeks and went down to find the man of the house.

Wesley was in the hall, just about to follow Hannah and April into the dining room for breakfast. He looked up as she descended the stairs attired in a demure white muslin.

"Charming, charming," Wesley exclaimed. Virginal, he thought, marveling at her swift recovery. "You are looking much better, my dear. Shall we go in?" He made to guide the governess inside but she hung back.

"No, I must speak to you—alone," Angel said, watching the man's brows lift in wonder. "I mean—it is about my mother and I wanted to ask if you could—help me. I need a carriage and a driver," she blurted finally.

"Yes, Hannah has told me all about your mother. We can talk freely at the table. Come, we will be delighted to finally have you join us. April will be thrilled, won't you, sweetheart?"

"Yes, Daddy, I will keep my mouth shut," April promised, content that her father was in such a good mood today.

The maid served them a light breakfast of bacon and eggs, toast and honey. The meal was taken for the most part in silence and April was quieter than was her usual wont. It was not until Hannah and Angel were sipping their tea that Wesley turned to the new governess.

"Mademoiselle Duponte, now you must tell me about yourself," he said as he sat back waiting for her to begin.

Angel opened her mouth to speak and found that all at once the words would not come.

Wesley cleared his throat, helping, "You look to be from a family of some importance. It is in your features, your bearing and . . . there is a touch of English breeding in you, *non?*"

"Yes—I—my mother is English," she said taking a deep breath before going on, "We, my mother and I. . . ." She halted, not being able to mention her father's death, and something warned her not to mention him at all.

Wesley shifted uncomfortably in his chair. "Please go on," he said simply.

This time Angel found the courage and her mind whirled as she felt herself painfully transported into the past. "Just this spring my mother and I set out from England to visit America. We sailed, amongst other passengers, on a Spanish merchantman bound for Puerto Bello. I mean, the *Fidelia* flew the Spanish flag . . . but this is a long story in itself that I won't get into just now. After the Fair we were to then board a ship bound for the Gulf but before we even reached Puerto Bello, we were set upon by—pirates." She halted this time because of the incredulous gasps that surrounded her.

Hannah did gape at this new disclosure while Wesley leaned far back, as if thoroughly enjoying this tale. April peered at the governess with a new respect on hearing the thrilling word "pirates."

"Mmm," Wesley murmured. "Quite interesting. Ahh, then what, my dear?"

Angel gulped a bit of tea to moisten the sudden dryness in her throat before she went on. "We were taken aboard this—this smuggler-captain's truck-ship and then proceeded to a chain of islands where we were held in captivity, but remained unharmed."—Here she suppressed the urge to smile ironically. "After a time, in opposition to his own kind, a smuggler helped us to escape. Upon reaching New Orleans, we found that there was not a soul we could depend on for further help, not even the smuggler." That was enough of that! Angel thought, and went on. "We were penniless, my mother and I, and you can see why I sought employment." She prayed Wesley had no knowledge of Pearce Duschesne's death. She wondered too if she had revealed too much and he had guessed who had held her captive? In the next moment though, her fears were put somewhat to rest.

"Mademoiselle Duponte, your secret is safe with us," Wesley began. "Have no fear that you have said too much. I know of these pirates and smugglers of whom you speak. There is not one person in all Louie who does not have knowledge of the Black Falcon and his ruthless, marauding band of filthy pirate followers—plundering, murdering, and raping helpless women." Here he halted to measure her mood, but it remained unchanged and he was half-satisfied that she was unrobbed of her virtue.

Unseen by Wesley, Angel had indeed flinched for a split-second, but at once breathed easier when his eyes bespoke his hatred for the outlaws. She began to feel that perhaps she could disclose the true nature of her plight and so do away with the alias Duponte. Not just yet, her mind warned. Wesley may also be one of Tyrone's many acquaintances and merely hiding the fact from her. She had to be sure, very sure.

"Now, Angeline," Wesley said, feeling he knew her better. "Your mother's first name is. . . ?"

"Christine," she blurted, unthinkingly.

"Mmm, it is Christine Duponte then," Wesley said.

"No!" she answered too quickly. Then, "I—I cannot say her last name, sir."

"Well," Wesley released a quick breath, "How can we discover her then? I must know her full name, for New Orleans is a big place—full of many nationalities, my dear."

Angel glanced around the table, feeling cornered all of a sudden. "Please, no one in New Orleans must learn of this," she said, and when he assured her they would not, she went on, "Her name is Sherwood. Christine Sherwood." Oh God! Why

293

was she being so stupid.

"Hmmm, I begin to see. Your mother is hiding perhaps from her second husband—an Englishman to boot—and we must not mention this name Sherwood. This could be the reason you fled England together?" He couldn't think of another reason; too, this was not an uncommon happenstance in the brawling city where crimes of passion took place every now and then. He smiled shrewdly and asked, "Am I correct in this?"

"Yes, yes!" Angel wanted to scream but merely said, "Somewhat." She was overjoyed that he had solved the torturing problem for her, as the constant devising of lies was beginning to wear on her. And, for the most part, it was not untrue, only reversed, and not a husband *she* secluded herself from.

Wesley did not ask what the "somewhat" included, but rather thought he had hit upon the young woman's problem. An amusing thought struck him suddenly. It could just very well be that Jacinta's newest lover had gotten an eyeful of this tempting piece, and so Jacinta's haste to send Angeline packing was quite understandable. He patted himself on the back for the second time this morning. He could deal with Jacinta when the time came. For now. . . .

Wesley stretched out a hand and patted Angeline's arm in solicitousness. "First off, let us have a description, my dear, and come morning I will see some friends of mine."

Angel's eyes widened when he said "friends," but Wesley held up his hand, saying, "I promise, no last name is to be mentioned. At least not to any Englishman or—" He laughed here, "smugglers known to be searching for a beautiful escapee. Tell me, where was your mother last seen?"

There was little time for Angel to ponder much else during the busy week that followed the nerve-shattering breakfast. For her time was well spent in the schoolroom opposite her bedchamber. First off, Angel tutored April in literature and cursive writing, since the child knew well how to print. April's language improved considerably and she began to look forward to these sessions. When she did her studies well, her tutor would reward her by teaching her how to embroider on swatches of cloth or tell her classical stories of old. April especialy relished the romantic tales of princesses, queens, and kings, and handsome knights in shining armor.

Finally the word was out and it rang from New Orleans to plantation to bayou: "The United States has declared war against Great Britain!" Angel felt the traitor, living in the midst of her country's enemies. But soon, soon she would be going home.

The southern nights on the plantation were alive with Negro voices humming low from house to field to garden's end. Soft dusks found Angel strolling through dewy grass, pondering the rose-hued clouds, wandering, dreaming of what might have been. The early springtime spent on the islands seemed sadly haunting to her now, like autumn leaves falling after summer thunder was but a fading memory. But it was midsummer, and vanishing somewhat during the heat of afternoon, these bittersweet memories returned when shadows lengthened and she sought succor in her bedchamber.

Relief was not forthcoming. Visions of the little cottage and Tyrone's handsome bearded face took shape before her weary eyes and again she felt his lean lover's fingers caressing every inch of her, his hard body painstakingly drawing her out of her lonely shell and into a world of ecstasy.

One dreamy moonlit night found Angel pacing like a restless shadow in her dismal sanctuary. The air was sultry and she was feeling restless yet heavyhearted as she crept downstairs quietly and slipped out into the dark shadows of the garden. As she strolled beneath feather-tipped and veiny branches here and there, the light of the silver moon touched her youthful countenance. In her loneliness she appeared vulnerable, while in her breast she yearned for one man's touch to satiate this hunger that tormented her day and night. Shamelessly she would welcome his advances this night and give herself wantonly to that smuggler.

The larger trees beyond seemed to stretch out to her and beckon her to come run wild and free without restriction or thought to where the morning might find her. A slight breeze bringing the scent of the river lifted wispy tendrils from her sweat-dampened cheeks and she thought painfully that a deep, familiar voice called her name. She knew it wasn't so, it couldn't be, and yet as she stood there the sound grew louder, then mournful, like a beast crying for its mate. She fled to escape the unhuman howl that followed her up to her room where she threw herself down upon the bed and sobbed into the hard pillow. It was not that she doubted her sanity, but rather that she felt a sadness and a definite oneness with the poor creature that searched for its mate somewhere out there in the night.

Morning found Angel lying across the bed on her belly with her arms upstretched over her head. She gradually awoke and groaned. The same nausea that had threatened her the morning before came back full force. She struggled limply onto her back to stare up at the gray ceiling, while she drew a trembling hand across her brow that was wet with moisture. She must have eaten some bad fish several nights back to—but that was impossible. No one else was. . . .

All at once it hit her with staggering impact—her time had not come this month! She hadn't counted the days since the last flow, but realized she was late. This sudden shock did make her stomach heave and she flew off the bed to go relieve herself in the basin. She returned raggedly to the bed on shaky limbs, and, when she sat, she hung her head to weep miserably. A short time later she tossed up her head and dried her eyes to squarely face her quandary.

Perhaps it wasn't so. My God, she prayed, let it be just the anxiety of the past weeks and her mother's disappearance. Yes, that could very well be, for Wesley's journey into the city to search for her mother had led him nowhere. No one seemed to fit the description she had given him, and the town house she had described was clearly unoccupied, but for a few household servants, Wesley had sadly informed her.

After she had splashed lukewarm water onto her face, Angel went to don a fresh frock and rake a comb through her tangled hair. She was feeling a mite better when she slipped down silently to breakfast alone, thankful that the Gayarres had not risen yet. After sipping her tea she cautiously bit into a warm buttered roll that the maid had set out before her as soon as she seated herself. As she chewed, she stared vacantly at the dust-motes drifting aimlessly in the sun's filtering stream.

Later when Angel was closeted in the schoolroom with her pupil, Wesley took Hannah aside just when she had been planning menus for the week with Morice. It was a matter of great importance, he said. And now he confronted her in the parlor, seated opposite her.

"Hannah, I am afraid Angeline is . . . slightly ill," Wesley said pointblank.

"Oh! We'll send for Dr. St. Clair immediately then," Hannah said gravely.

"Ah, no, Hannah. It is nothing all that bad." He shifted his squarish frame, explaining, "You see, she is suffering from this minor illness." He saw Hannah frown, but went on, "But can't you see, dear sister, she has lost her memory, that is all."

Hannah lowered her head. "Lapse of memory"—Angel had mentioned it herself the day they had visited the horse barn. To Wesley she said, "Why, I think it's true. But, I never thought of it seriously until just now when you brought it to mind."

Wesley leaned forward. "Now, listen closely. You must not permit her to leave Gayarre, under any circumstances. Even if she begs that she must go search for this Christine Sherwood. Trust me?" His colorless eyes grew cold as marble, making Hannah draw back at his expression.

"Yes—I understand." Then her eyes were filled with concern for her troubled friend as she asked, "But what about her mother?"

"I have already delved into that matter. Listen, I have reason to believe that either this Christine is nonexistent, or that perhaps Angeline most unfortunately witnessed a horrible scene involving her mother—" his voice lowered, "like death at the hands of those ruthless pirates. This would cause Angeline a mild but temporary insanity, *non?*"

Hannah flinched at the thought of Angeline's witnessing a horrendous murder take place—especially her own flesh and blood!

"Yes, yes, that could be it—just so," Hannah agreed. "She does seem in a daze most of the time, and I just know this is not her usual nature to be so—oh! I just don't know, Wesley," she finally ended, confused.

Wesley left her with that, dismissing himself from the parlor. Hannah's hindsight told her maybe she should have disclosed Angeline's heartbreaking love affair. But that was odd in itself. What man in his right mind would fail to return the love of such a beautiful and intelligent woman as Angeline? He should have married her, she thought angrily. Unless, yes, unless the man was already married to someone else?

Daybreak gave way to a blue-and-white-marbled sky, and with noon nearing, Angel picked up the book of Poe she had been reading earlier in the solemn hush and resumed at the mark where she had left off:

> Thou wast all to me, love,
>   For which my soul did pine—
> A green isle in the sea, love,
>   A fountain and a shrine,
> All wreathed with fairy fruits and flowers,
>   And all the flowers were mine.

. . . By what eternal streams. She finished the last verse and stood to stretch, peering out the window over the grounds of Gayarre. Dropping her arms in a bored gesture, she took up watching the fieldhands just coming in from their drudging labors to enter the whitewashed cottages that stood in a neat row beyond the line of live oak. From this distance the dark men were the size of miniature dolls. Their skin glistened blackly in the late July sun as they gathered around turbaned women dipping tin cups into wooden buckets to quench the thirsts of their men.

Interested now, Angel leaned through the window as one tall, well-formed youth pulled a willowy girl against his side as he drank greedily from his cup. The shy girl squirmed to get away as he tossed the cup aside and snatched her to him to kiss her lustily on the lips. As the also well-formed girl continued to vainly struggle, Angel recalled a like scene and tore her gaze from the young lovers.

Only minutes later, Angel entered the muggy parlor to pick up the sewing she had left there the evening before. As she sat upon the settee her fingers began to work the needle and thread in and out of the soft rose brocade that reminded her of dawn, the color subtle and yet arresting to the eye. She had ordered the bolt from the store's catalogue as Wesley had been generous in the past month when paying her for tutoring his daughter.

Would she continue to be a governess now—now that things were about to change? Would Wesley continue to *pay* her—or what?

Generous, yes; for this gown would be special, Wesley had said. For she would wear it at this weekend's festivities. He wanted to make sure that she would be gowned appropriately for the occasion that would bring neighbors from far and wide to Gayarre. The only thing now left to do was for her to give Wesley her answer—that she would become his bride.

Angel ran a hand over her yet flat belly. She was positive she was with child, however, and stabbed the needle into the rose brocade. No doubt that smuggler could spit blindfolded, so to speak, into a troop of naked ladies and meet fertile ground. How many had grown big with his children, and how many more would follow with big bellies after her? Nothing more than ripe watermelons in a patch to that one!

When Wesley entered the parlor, Angel had come to a decision. But he appeared so smugly sure of himself that she almost faltered. Indeed, he'd planned the upcoming affair as if he already had her answer.

"Wesley—I appreciate all you have done for me, but—" she began and broke, unable to decide where to truly begin.

Wesley's lips twitched and his voice was cold. "Well, let's have it," he demanded impatiently.

She went ramrod straight. "I am, as you say in French— *enceinte.*" She stared boldly at him as his face loomed with

299

cynicism lining the squarish features.

"I see," he uttered with sarcasm. "But are you sure that you do not arrive at this conclusion prematurely?" He watched the crystallike eyes glisten with unshed tears.

"I am sure," she said quietly, glancing away now.

Wesley sighed. "How long?"

"Two months. Perhaps more, perhaps less, I cannot be exact."

Wesley clenched and unclenched his rawboned fingers. This was the only part of him that was lean, all else was the copy of a huge wooden soldier in civilian garb. Without formalities he began, "I am far established in my way of life for this sort of thing, but this does not change anything between us. I still want you for my wife."

Angel felt as if a great burden had been lifted. On the other hand, she was filled with apprehension toward the future, a future with a man she could never come to love. Already she had been familiarized with her mission in life as she realized this somber man would dominate her days till she was laid to rest in the bowels of this earth. How swiftly and cruelly the pages of her fateful life turned, she thought tragically.

"Yes, Wesley," she breathed finally, for she saw no other way out, "I consent to becoming your wife. But I must tell you that I am not in love with you, nor will I ever be—I'm sorry."

"Love?" Wesley ground out harshly. "Who ever mentioned anything about love? I want a faithful wife, someone to share with me all that is mine, not a bride of passion. Although, *mais oui*, I expect you to be there in my bed when I need carnal release We can drop the niceties now, for it is apparent you are not green as far as sex goes. Don't worry overly much, as those times will be few and far between. You see, Angeline, I want my bride to be prim and meek, not a demanding harlot."

Angel's eyes would have widened at his bold words, but she was gladdened in this, that much would not be expected as far as the marriage bed was concerned. She could never again yield to a man fully; rather she would turn her mind aside when performing the duties of a wife. She was lucky in this, she told herself. And yet, a part of her would always crave that sweet fulfillment that only one man could awaken in her. She knew this to be so, for she had vowed to never love again, ever.

In the days that followed Angel's commitment, she saw a change in Wesley. He uncloaked his true nature, and his manner was full of cruelty to his cringing household servants and sugar-slaves, and anyone else who might tempt his anger with the slightest infraction. Angel began to wonder what she was getting herself into by marrying this overbearing man who would probably see fit to punish her own child when he grew to the age of mischief. True, Wesley was overly lenient with his own daughter, but would he be so kind to one not of his own flesh and blood? Still, he had promised to continue the search for Christine. For now, what more could she hope for?

Wesley wasn't bothered in the least that he had deceived his bride-to-be about searching widely for her mother. The truth of the matter was he never had intended to discover Christine Sherwood. There was nothing in it for him, so why should he? Moreover, he was certain that once the Englishwoman appeared at Gayarre, Angeline would up and leave him. Too, he planned to be rid of the brat immediately after the birth. No filthy pirate's bastard would find comfort in his house!

A new problem cropped up for Wesley Gayarre the day before the engagement ball. His plans to remove the log fences had been minced. He was in a foul mood, and Hannah and his as yet unofficial fiancee received the brunt of his heated tirade as he paced back and forth in the parlor.

"Damnit anyway," Wesley cursed, taking his sister by surprise. "All of a sudden there is a mighty coming and going of laborers and craftsmen over at Cresthaven. The overgrown gardens are being raked and cleared; hammers going night and day repairing cottages. *Bon Dieu!* You can hear them darkies singing and their rip-roaring laughter carries all the way down to the northwest border. What in God's name is going on?" He snatched up the newspaper to scan it for advertisements that would perhaps give him a clue.

Hannah smothered a giggle, but her brother caught the beginning of it and whirled to glare at her. "And what is the matter with you, have you gone daft?" He slid his regard to

Angeline, who at once resumed her stitching, wishing to be left out of the conversation.

"Now Wesley, stay cool," Hannah began, repressing the urge to giggle again. Then, "Didn't you know? Young Hunter is back, and from what information Jenny has obtained from servant leakage—he is back to stay!"

Wesley groaned and paled visibly as he sank into a deep-cushioned seat instead of his usual chair. *"Ma foi!* I never would have thought—and what a dunce! Do you know what I did—out of conventional neighborliness and politeness?" he asked both the young women who blinked at him innocently.

Then Hannah remembered something, and said, "Of course, dear brother. Recall, you had me make out the invitations, and *he* was number one on the list. Goodness gracious, he will never show, so why fret?"

Angel looked from one to the other, and finally couldn't hold her tongue any longer in this. "Is this young man so very bad? Why, one would think you had something he wanted, Wesley," she said, trying to be sweet, and not too obvious.

Wesley's face bloomed scarlet nevertheless. "Bad?" he said, then repeated himself, "Bad! He is worse than that! Why, my darling Angeline, he is a devil disguised as Lord only knows what all—politician, (onetime), devil-gambler, scandalmonger, whoremonger—"

"No disguise," Angel interrupted. "A real Mephistopheles by the sound of it!"

"Mais oui!" Wesley sounded passionately. "And, ahh, yes, I do own something he believes is his alone, but my plan is to repossess all that is mine."

"Wesley!" Hannah said, blanching. "I do wish you would forget about the land. What's done is done. Why can't you let it lie? You know his reputation, and he might even kill you if you press too far. He has been known to be utterly ruthless. Why, just a few months back when I shopped in New Orleans I learned that the infamous smuggler Tyrone and he are—" Hannah cast aside her sewing to rush to Angel's side, begging, "What is it, Angeline, aren't you feeling well?"

Angel had cried out on hearing the name, and following a sob

302

she weaved suddenly to her feet as Wesley rushed forward to intercept the swooning form. Hannah, on the other side, aided her brother, beginning to fear that Angeline was given to frequent spells of fainting. But Wesley, on the other hand, thought he knew full well the reason for Angeline's weakened state. *So*, he thought to himself, this was the reason for her being indisposed so shortly after her coming. It was plain to see that pregnancy did not suit her delicate frame, and there would be no more becoming *enceinte* for her, he decided firmly.

"Please, don't fuss over me," Angel groaned, steadying herself. "If you both will just excuse me, I will go outside and take some air."

The day was overcast and a gray haze shrouded the lands of Gayarre as Angel ran blindly, fast as her trembling limbs would carry her, toward the barn. Hannah and Wesley had been reluctant to let her go alone at first, but both finally consented to her needing some air. Besides, the housemaids came in to draw their attention to the final arrangements for the weekend's festivities.

In a daze, Angel found herself just outside the barns, where the horseman was leading Gypsy Girl outside for some exercise. When Jacques saw her he nodded politely and the Girl snorted a greeting as Angel walked forward to pat the silky mane. The graceful neck arched toward her and Angel turned to Jacques as if she had just thought of something. She smiled at the lad.

"Jacques, I will exercise the Girl, ride out, if you don't mind?"

"Do not know, mademoiselle. Thees mare is so frisky today. I have order from Monsieur Gayarre that mamzelle should not ride alone," he said, the Adam's apple working convulsively at his throat.

"It is all right, Jacques. Wesley does not mind, and I shan't be out long. Saddle her up for me?" Angel pleaded hastily, displaying her most winning smile.

The horseman stuck a finger beneath his cap to scratch his head and then most reluctantly led the Girl away to do the governess's bidding.

*   *   *

An old cabin stood somberly halfway up a hillside and just above the great winding river. It appeared long ignored and unused. It was here that Angel rested her lathered mount after pushing the Girl to her greatest speed. The ride had been exhilarating for a time, but now a feeling of bitter emptiness returned as she studied the lonely sight before her. Age lines grappled about the cabin in the form of moss and vines struggling their way through wide, weathered cracks in the boards. There was a strange disquietude and something foreboding about the mist-enveloped place. She jerked hard on the reins, whirling the Girl from the gray haunted sight.

Above the hazy river the high bluff led her along its edge and after a time she unconsciously slackened her hold on the reins, giving the Girl free roam. Angel gave no thought or care to where the horse was leading her. Her head sagged dejectedly as she pondered her sorry state, and the man who had caused her so much pain. An unusual hatred for men, one in particular, began to grow apace and she permitted it to eat away at her until she was at the point of bleak despondency.

The Girl became her pathfinder and Angel cared not a whit that the beast trod dangerously close to the edge of the precipice. The Girl grew nervous with the unfeeling weight and the limp hands that led her nowhere. The slightest note from a songbird and the horse would stumble in the rock outcropping before her, thus unseating the rider to tumble headlong over the edge. Miraculously, Angel was startled out of her deathly trance as she caught a flash of black through the trees, and suddenly she was sawing hard on the reins, saving herself from a welcome but horrible death.

Guiding the Girl away from the danger and into a copse of pines, Angel watched between the veiny lower branches as a tall rider mounted astride a huge apparition of black passed several hundred feet before her. Seen intermittently between the tall trunks, the masculine rider drove his mount to top a higher rise where, if Angel hadn't been impelled to move away, he would immediately have caught sight of her. The distance between them, plus the haziness clinging to the air, made it

304

difficult for Angel to make out the rider's features, but he was a big man, ramrod tall in his saddle, and menacing, from what she could discern of him.

Suddenly she was alive again and gulping hard. Hunter. It must be, for Hannah had mentioned that the man had returned to Cresthaven. She recalled next that Hannah had been about to reveal that this stranger and Tyrone were good friends. She must flee before he detected her presence, but before she could set spurs to her mount, she was seeing him reining about to gallop in the opposite direction from his home. He seemed pressed for time all of a sudden as he spurred his huge black to an even swifter gait, and, emerging from the pines, sped across the short distance to the road.

Fallen cones and needles crunched beneath the Girl's hooves as Angel ducked through the opening of green needles upon reaching the pine's edge. She hung back, and poked her head forward watching the tall rider jerk his horse to a sudden halt. Angel held her breath as he stood high in his stirrups as if sensing something, then resumed the faster pace when he sat back easy. She breathed normally once again.

Angel was shaken upon seeing this man who no doubt knew where Tyrone was at this very minute. Would the mere thought of him ever continue to lay waste her heart? First love and last.

"Ohh, Tyrone, why didn't you love me, too?" Her tears mingled with the soft rain that had begun to fall without her knowing it. Neither did she know where the Girl was taking her again. She was a blob, a nothing.

She rode unseeingly, for how long she would never know. Suddenly Angel lifted her tear-stained face and was struck with awe, as once before. Cresthaven loomed grandly above her, as she was all but at the door. It was not the front entrance but the back, and a door was opening now with a deep moan of hinges.

It was Della, gaping as if a white specter had arrived at her pantry door. "Lan' sakes, child, wher'd you come from all a sudden? You gave this old heart a mighty scare. You all right, little gal?" With a worried frown the housekeeper rushed toward the youthful governess.

Angel peered down from her mount dazedly into the anxious brown eyes of the black woman and permitted her to help her dismount. The thin but strong arms wrapped around Angel and she thought her heart would burst at the loving, warm contact of the older woman. So unhappy, Angel was not totally aware of where the housekeeper led her, but soon it was warm and cozy and Della's voice was soothing, even when she yelled back through the door.

"You out there, Sam-boy?" A prompt answer revealed that indeed the horseboy was near. "Good. Take that there mare and rub her down easy now. It'll do her good. Hear?" Della cocked an ear outdoors and when the "Yes'm!" came she gently went to push Angel into a chair near the hearth. Della hooked up the smoke-blackened kettle to brew some tea. She stoked the coals and a nice warmth seeped into Angel's chilled bones.

"Now, li'l missy Angeline, you tell ole Della what's bothering you. Is something, sure. It's plain to see even with these ole eyes of mine. That man Wesley didn't beat you none, did he?" she asked, her voice rising, and, "I knows he beats his slaves sometimes. Them niggers done tol' our niggers."

Angel felt she could trust the kindly old woman and she desperately needed someone to talk to just now. She shook her head sadly and poured out her misery as she told of the upcoming marriage, how she had agreed to become Wesley's wife—but not everything. . . .

". . . and now I cannot back out. Oh, Della, what shall I do?" Angel cried in frustration. "Life is so unfair. Our marriage shall be a farce. I do not love Wesley, and he has made it quite clear that his feeling is mutual."

From the kettle, Della poured the hot brew into two cups as she hashed this problem over in her mind. Her face went blacker as she placed one bony hand on her hip, and said, "Ain't no problem, a'tall. You don't have to marry that mean old man, you sweet li'l angel. Don't you know that? You is your own woman and not even Wesley can make you do something you'll regret the rest of your life, honey chile. Jest think hard afore you make a big mistake." Her voice rose and, "It'd be different if you was gonna have a wee one. . . ." She let it hang then.

Angel sipped the tea, feeling its warmth settle in the hollow pit of her stomach. Again this morning she'd forgone breakfast. Never again, she told herself. From now on the baby came first. Suddenly this mite in her belly was becoming very dear to her—he would be a boy, look just like her lost lover had the last time she was with him. Handsome, virilely exciting, and with a sardonic twist to his lips when he was grown. For the baby's sake she had to wed Wesley, and Della's last words made her see that clearly.

No, she could not confide in Della. She was this Mr. Hunter's housekeeper, and *he* was a friend of Tyrone's. No one else must learn that she was *enceinte*.

It went unnoticed by Angel that Della had departed the kitchen until she now returned with a man's dark-wine silk robe draped over her arm.

"I plumb forgot you was all sweaty and cold," Della said. "I been so namby-pamby lately. Here. You go back there in Della's room and take off that soppin' thing you got on and put this here robe on. The master won't mind no bit. He keeps this one downstairs and hardly ever wore it but once or twice. He got twenty more like it in different colors upstairs in his highboy."

Angel tentatively received the silken garment into her arms, delighting in the slippery-rich feel of it. "Twenty?" she asked incredulously, eager to hear more of the wealthy man, yet at the same time prompted to go, lest he return early from his visit, for he had headed in the direction of Gayarre. She was glad she was absent from there just now, though.

"Yup, jest ask me," Della said proudly. "Mr. Hunter's one of the richest young men in all Louie, honey. A real nabob. Tee-hee. Cresthaven is biggest and best of the sugar cane kingdoms," Della said, her eyes misting over momentarily, adding, "Was, honey. Will be again, too, now that the Mister's back. I only wish he'd bring someone smart and pretty like you home someday."

Angel blushed and Della's eyes twinkled mysteriously as she

307

studied the young woman over from head to foot, thinking to herself: Yessir, a sweet little wife like this Angeline. Out loud she said, "Hurry on now, honey, you been in that wet frock too long now." Della ended on a cheerful note, humming as she went to pour a second cup for her company—this time with just a dollop of the Mister's best-stocked brandy to warm her good.

Angel stripped off the clinging frock and slipped into the jumbo robe that wrapped around her nearly twice. Her senses immediately took hold of the masculine scent of its folds, enveloping her in a world of dizzying warmth. She felt so good now, strangely secure, and she began to wonder what this Mr. Hunter really looked like. She had only glimpsed him from afar at first, then watched from the pine's edge as he expertly manipulated the huge and powerful black.

Della chuckled to herself as the youthful beauty entered, rubbing her pinkened cheek against the huge cavity of the draping cuff. Della watched closely as the girl sipped the laced tea and the fresh dewiness of her face glowed in new contentment. Della, too, was feeling good about this unexpected visit as she draped the frock over a chair near the hearth to dry.

"Mmm, I do feel much better," Angel murmured, feeling a delicious peace of mind. "Thank you, Della. I feel oddly as if I have always known you, and you me. About this house—I feel as if—oh—this is silly of me," she admonished herself, taking another sip of the brew.

Della shook her turbaned head. "No, honey, you ain't silly. I know just what you mean. You feel like you belong here, now don't you?"

Angel murmured, "Yes," she did, just as the grandfather clock in the hall *bonged* one time, upon which she immediately set down her cup and stood. She feared the master of Cresthaven would soon return to his home.

"I'd almost forgotten the time and that I need to add the finishing touches to my gown. I must be on my way. Is the frock dry, Della?"

Della fetched up the dried garment tenderly. "Sure is. Now

you go put it on while I get that boy to bring around your horse." She peered out the door, saying, "Ain't this wonderful! It's clearing, and Old Sol is peeping out his yellow head. Going to be a fine weekend. Jest fine, indeedy."

Sam, the boy, had gone back to his task of pitching hay, whistling a merry tune when his black eyes grew as big as shiny marbles and he dropped the huge fork with a heavy thud. Across the greensward he could see Miss Sherwood just coming out the back door, preparing to mount the mare he'd just cared for. He stood dumbstruck, gaping as the girl mounted then bent over to take Della's hand for just a moment, whirled her mount and galloped away. Woodenly he came to stand beside Della with his mouth and eyes three perfectly round circles. They watched the fine girl ride under the lifting mist that drifted high now like lemon-yellow clouds. She vanished.

Samuel's mouth worked convulsively before he said, "Why'd you let her go, Della?"

Della turned to Samuel. "What's the matter with you, boy, ain't you ever seen a pretty white gal afore?"

"Doan you know that she's Miz Sherwood and Mistah Hunter's been lookin' for that gal a long time now?"

Della was just about to scold and correct him when the sound of pounding hooves entering the back gate drew their attention.

"I swear I done tole the truth, Della," Samuel pleaded. "She's—"

"Hush up you mouth, boy!" Della hissed low.

Hunter, astride the huge black, thundered into the yard and trotted his beast as he slowed to dismount just outside the stables. He cast a glimpse over his shoulder while handing the reins over to Old Saul. His countenance was brooding and dark to the mute twosome in the few seconds that they saw his face. Samuel took a step in that direction and was stayed as a hand fell heavily upon his lean but muscular shoulder. A low whisper warned in his ear.

"Don't know what you talking about, boy," Della began, "but this no time for him to go off chasing her. You let me

309

handle it." She thrust out her sagging bosoms.

"What the devil is going on around here? And why are you two standing there gaping like complete idiots when there is work to be done?" Tyrone bellowed as he strode with a long gait toward them, a muscle working furiously in his cheek.

Della and the new laborer Tyrone had brought back on his return to Cresthaven exchanged dumbfounded looks and shrugged in unison. Tyrone's menacing look bore holes into two pairs of black orbs that stared innocently back at him.

"What the hell! You two look as if you've just been zapped by lightning—or worse!" His hazel eyes slid back and forth between them. "Well then, answer me this . . . who was that furious-paced rider astride Gypsy Girl?" he demanded.

Della nudged Samuel and he painfully said, "Ummm, that there?" He did point into the direction that Angel had taken, then fell silent.

"Damnation!" Tyrone ground out. "Yes, that! That fleeing apparition that raced as if all the demons in hell were in hot pursuit of its tail!"

"That there was . . ." He turned to Della for aid. She said something for his ears only, and Samuel drawled, "Umm, Yassuh, that there was Angel-ine Du-ponte. Her horse done throwed a shoe and I done fix it for her and that's what I did and that's why she come, ummm-hmmm." He looked conspiratorlike as he glanced to Della for approval. She was head lady around here, and he didn't want to displease her none.

Tyrone frowned suddenly, stroking his clean-shaven chin thoughtfully. There was something mighty fishy, more than met the seeing eye, around here, he thought as he spied the swinging pantry door. As if it beckoned him, he strode swiftly to it, turned and all but collided with Della who was padding behind taking up the rear, as her hand whisked back and forth behind her skirts to shoo Samuel back to his tasks.

"Of course," Tyrone muttered as an afterthought. "The governess Wesley Gayarre plans to wed—the invitation." He paused, and, "Hmm, what the devil is the respectable old bag doing astride the Girl and racing madly across the countryside? She must be as much a lunatic as her husband-to-be," he declared with waggery.

Della held back her tongue. The outer door slammed shut as she followed Tyrone into the warmed kitchen. She saw her master in the foulest of moods she had ever seen, except for that last little quip. Mr. Hunter had been back almost come a month now, drinking that potent brandy heavily as he sat up into the wee hours of the morning staring broodingly into the cold hearth and hardly ever speaking two words to anyone. His once again great household staff saw him coming and going in the waking hours as if he was driven by that chief evil spirit himself.

Della thought: Jest could be that pretty little thing had something to do with it? Must be, she determined, cause Samboy said hisself the master was looking for that sweet Angel peach.

In the past, Tyrone Michael Hunter seldom ever—since he was a boy—used the pantry door and Della knew his curiosity was at its height as he walked slowly about the kitchen as if sensing something amiss, his nostrils flaring like a beast's. He espied his robe draped carefully over a wooden chair and went directly to pick it up, holding it up now to his nose while his eagle eyes rolled about the room in bewilderment. He clutched the robe tightly and whirled on his heel to face his housekeeper.

"You goin' to the Gayarres' shindig tomorrow, Mr. Hunter?" Della drawled, seeing the look of wonder turn into amazement, then one of dawning sheer joy. He appeared like a small boy who had just recovered a valuable he'd thought lost.

"No, I had not planned—" Tyrone bit off, his eyes searching Della's watchful regard of him. "Della, tell me, what does this *old bag* Angeline look like?"

Della rolled her eyes heavenward. "Ummm, all old bags look the same to me, Mr. Hunter." She pursed her purplish lips thoughtfully, at length. Then, "You know—if you sees one old bag, you sees 'em all." She chuckled deeply at her own humor.

Tyrone took two steps to stand directly in front of the old woman he had known since he had frolicked in this her kitchen, constantly tugging at his knee britches. But now, he was a grown man, and there was something savage yet wonderful in the air all about this changed man.

Now ... he was smiling down beseechingly into the housekeeper's gentle brown face, gently pressing a hand on either side of her sloping shoulders. "Tell me, sweet old woman. Tell me all you have learned of this Angeline Duponte."

O villain, villain, smiling, damned villain!
—Shakespeare

Chapter Eight

1

Wesley and Jacinta were just emerging from the parlor when Angel spun around the door to make her untimely entrance. Wesley strode to her side, taking the chilly hand into his, not questioning her overlong stroll. His mind was too taken up with the weekend's festivities and what he'd just discussed with Jacinta.

Wesley announced, "Here she is, my bride-to-be!" as if Jacinta didn't already know. "You have met Jacinta Hunter, my dear? Oh, but how stupid of me. Of course, you would not be here if not for Jacinta's delivering you to us. I have her to thank for that." He shot *her* a meaningful look.

Wesley's suddenly nasal voice droned on and on, but Angel wasn't hearing anything but the name "Hunter"—Jacinta Hunter. So . . . Jacinta was their neighbor's wife and . . . Tyrone's mistress. Why had her husband stayed away so long, and why did Jacinta reside in the city?—Or, did she truly? Oh my, this was all very confusing, Angel thought and realized a sudden cold chill next when Jacinta smiled broadly, as if with malicious amusement.

With tiffany skirt and crisp petticoat rustling, Jacinta stepped closer, her dark eyes raking the younger woman's deshabille. "I am certain Wesley will make you a very happy bride, Angeline. This could not have happened to a nicer girl." Jacinta made emphasis on the latter as she turned haughtily on her high-heeled slippers, leaving Angel with her mouth agape, about to reply.

"Why of course, *cher*, we would not miss it for the world," Jacinta was saying to Wesley at the door.

Her heart hammering in her breast, Angel's mind stuck on

313

one torturing thought. Who had Jacinta meant by "we"?

Wesley was left alone to his dark ponderings after Jacinta had departed, and Angeline went up to rest. Damn the Hunters for intruding on his life once again! And Jacinta—what would be her next move? He would soon find out, perhaps when she arrived tomorrow with her husband.

After securing the door and with determination in her stride, Angel crossed her room to search for her shears. She realized then that she had forgotten to ask Jacinta about her mother.

Gradually the dense blackness of the night thinned and lightened, then the sky became ever brighter, as the awaited day finally arrived, bringing many to the doorstep of Gayarre. Angel prayed this night would bring many answers as well, troubling though some might be. She stood now before the long looking glass, fussing with the altered bodice that fit snugly beneath her of late fuller breasts. Goosebumps ran up and down her arms as she eyed her profile with its daringly upthrust display of creamy white flesh. With her shears and long into the night, she had fashioned a square-cut bodice, creating a dangerously low cut. She prayed Wesley would not demand its removal after all the pains she had tediously taken. She had slept some, though, and well.

Jenny fashioned the pale hair into an elaborate coiffure of high-piled sausage curls, permitting some to cascade down the slim back while tiny wisps coiled just in front of her ears. The gown hugged her tiny waist and, as Angel didn't show yet, there was no cause for alarm. At last Jenny added the finishing touch of the lagniappe that had been packaged with Angel's rose material; delicate silk roses sewn to burgandy grosgrain ribbons. The maid arranged them here and there in Angel's glossy tresses, and finally stepped back to admiringly observe her handiwork.

"Ooohh, Miz Angeline," Jenny crooned, "you look jus' lak one of dems fairy-book princesses and you go'in to knock 'em dead tuhnight. Especial dem fine gents. You sho doan need no sparkly jewels like all dem fine, snooty gentlewimmens wear. Unh-hunh!" Jenny left then, saying she must help Hannah complete her toilette now.

Indeed Angel wore not one piece of jewelry, and, if she secretly wished for a gem from Wesley as a wedding gift she might as well have wished for the moon. Wesley thoroughly disliked any sort of sparkling adornment on a woman. When Angel would have chosen a pale velvet or tiffany for her gown, Wesley had intervened, well pleased with her second choice of the dusky rose bolt of cloth.

Hannah stepped into Angel's room for a "last minute chat," she said, but Angel knew better. Hannah planned to plead again with her about whether she was certain about this forthcoming marriage with her half-brother.

First off, Hannah squealed, "Angeline! You're gorgeous! If you were not my very best pal I should be hard put to hide my greenest envy!"

Angel hugged Hannah close then leaned back. "Shame on you, Hannah, you are just trying to heighten my confidence, knowing I'm terrified at receiving all those guests downstairs. And look at you, you are ravishing in that green brocade with its gray ribbon trim. It brings out the sparkles in your eyes. Why, a handsome prince would fall to his knees at first sight of you and beg your hand."

Hannah cast her lovely gray eyes downward. "Umm, no chance of that ever happening," she murmured, then squared her shoulders. "How about you, Angeline, are you very certain about this announcement tonight?"

"Oh yes, Hannah. I have already given my troth." She thought about something before adding, "Whatever else happens, I want you to know that you will forever, by my truest word, be my best friend, Hannah McCormick."

"You have taken the words right out of my mouth, Angeline," she said, and a bond between them was sealed. As if to punctuate this, Hannah revealed, "The downstairs maids mean well, but their ears and mouths come in great sizes!"

Angel realized that Hannah had learned of her pregnancy via the grapevine. She had meant to tell Hannah before, but had been reluctant to until this night, when she'd been about to reveal her condition to her friend.

Reading Angel's mind, Hannah sighed. "I would have done

the same were I you, Angeline. Anyway, Wesley meant to have you—baby or no. He said hotly this morning that he will never let you go." With another hug, this one ending the conversation, Hannah went down to greet the latter half of the guests.

Deepening purple shadows created moody images along with the fog that, like uninvited creatures, stole from the great river to slither across the now hardened road and up the lane leading to Gayarre. This new, moist air was sweetened with the scent of deep summer blooms mingling with smoke curling from open pits where delicious meats were being turned and basted. Angel stood alone on the gallery just off her bedchamber to watch from the shadows as the last trickle of guests arrived.

Some came by horseback, some by conveyance, and a few trod uphill with servants and lanterns that wheeled light before them, after having disembarked from planters' boats. They had been arriving since noon, while Angel lingered in her room at Wesley's request. He wanted her to make a grand appearance when the last of the guests had settled in to make the walls near to bursting.

Shrouded in shadow, Angel searched the visages of each and every couple as they passed under the torches that shed light upon the platform and into the hall. Only a few were familiar to her, but for the most part they were unrecognizable.

Would Jacinta blatantly arrive on the arm of that randy smuggler? Ah! The name Duponte would be useless to her now, but how could she drop it at this late date? He would see right through her game, but still, it was going to give her much satisfaction to play it this night. He might even assume she truly hated him and leave her alone. At any rate, he could not make her play his whore. No, never again; she would ignore him at every possible turn, or else those beautiful eyes would mesmerize her instantly and melt her into a blob of feminine fluff.

"Angeline?"

She started for a second before Wesley came up behind her, stood close and began to rub the back of her silken arms. It was the first bit of warmth he had displayed during their short relationship and the roughness of his hands hurt like a frigid chill on her flesh, especially after her dwelling on another, whose lean hands were a lover's silken caress.

She moved just enough away to break the contact, saying, "I could not help myself, Wesley, I had to see. What are those people doing over there beneath the trees with the large tents?" she asked, merely to make conversation.

Wesley regarded the lawn with a landlordly eye. "Pitching them, my dear. You did not expect them all to sleep inside, did you?"

"No, I guess not."

"Listen, you can hear the musicians striking up a waltz. Surely, you can dance?" His words belied his thoughts, for he hated music and dancing with a passion.

"Yes, I can waltz. I can fence, too, you will have to survey my stance sometime. I have perfect form!" she ended excitedly.

"Ahh, good. What . . . fencing? No wife of mine shall be caught dead doing that! You are to be a lady at all times, Angeline. Do I make myself understood?" She nodded demurely and he went on. "All of the prosperous planters in our territory will be present this night. You will make the acquaintance of a few artists, and politicians, and I do hope Governor Claiborne will come. Oh yes, Major Milton and a few of his regulars, and General Wade Hampton, instrumental in ending that black slave rebellion. They are here now—"

Angel realized that he was rambling and she listened half-heartedly as she gazed up at the silver crescent of moon, wondering what the night would bring. Crickets *chrrruupped* and katydids sang *Katy did, Katy didn't*.

"Well, let us go down now and greet our guests. Ready?" Wesley asked as he took her arm to guide her into the bedroom.

"Not just yet, Wesley. I have suddenly developed a slight headache. It shan't be long before—"

Wesley spun to face her blackly. "If you are having last minute regrets about our forthcoming marriage, put them out of your head. I have gone to great lengths with my pocketbook and my time!" He sneered at her soft countenance, pulling her roughly along. "Anyway, you will crush your gown if you lie down. Come now, I despise weak-kneed women. And try to

317

sound French, will you?"

Angel endeavored to beef up her courage and tried on a smile when they descended the stairs arm in arm. She unconsciously searched the line of guests pushing forward to greet their host and his beautiful ethereal companion. Wesley beamed above his stiffly starched collar of serviceable threads as General Hampton stepped up to bow deeply over Angel's hand, pressing a warm kiss into her palm.

"Why, you old fox, Wes," General Hampton said as he straightened, his sly blue eyes lingering on the square-cut décolléte. He listened raptly as Wesley made the introductions. "Duponte?" Hampton inquired with a quirked brow. "Why, one would assume that you were of English background with the delightful accent and all."

Angel smiled into the merry eyes. "I am, sir. My mother is English and one of her forebears was of French descent." This was the truth, but why, oh why did she have to be reminded of Christine just now? It distressed her so.

The general was just about to ask about her father when he noticed Gayarre's angry glare dipping into the bodice of Angeline Duponte's gown. Consequently Wade Hampton coughed under his hand, but loud enough to distract the mute man and halt him from embarrassing this lovely creature. To further stall Wesley's intent, a young man in uniform strutted up to salute his superior, at once requesting the honor of a dance with the mademoiselle. When the militant general nudged Wesley smilingly, his host shrugged in concession.

Angel moved nimbly to escape the stiffly formal atmosphere that surrounded her fiance. She relaxed to the jubilant mood of the young officer who guided her through the hall and into the no-frills dining room that had been set up for dancing; tables had been pushed back along the walls, and as no formal dinner had been prearranged, the guests could nibble at their leisure from the platters of meats, breads, and hors d'oeuvres— translucent sea-gray shrimp nestled atop bowls of steaming rice, and green turtle soup. The latter two were kept heated by a servant, ready at a moment's notice to be spooned out from a large dish that sat atop flickering candle flames.

As Angel danced with the young man introduced as

Lieutenant Parker, her gaze roamed over the flamboyantly gowned quadroons who stood meekly against the wall, their mamas watching them like a hawk does a chicken. Angel had heard that they were uniquely beautiful and now she witnessed it herself. She constantly scanned the crowded room, her glance snagging every so often on the doorman out in the hall.

One dance led to another and another, each arm different, until she was left breathless, and still she was begged unceasingly for just one more waltz. Wineglass after wineglass was thrust into her hands until she had to decline even a noggin more. Soon she was left dizzy and her stomach queasy. She couldn't even look at the food, much less try and put some into her stomach. She really should eat something, she told herself, but it was so hot and the odor of rich foodstuffs, liquors, and sweating bodies made her seek fresher air.

Amused and interested glances fell her way as she tried gliding away from the crowd but tripped most ungracefully into the warship bulk of a matronly servant she'd never seen before. This was considered most humorous by the guests and was greeted with a burst of guffaws.

"Lawd a-mighty!" the black servant said to her offender, then seeing who she was, the servant helped the flushed young woman escape out into the moonlit garden. "I got tuh make haste an' see to dem brats dem wimmin drug me here ta watch over. If'n I don't get out to dem tents, dem chil'en goin' ta bring 'em down lickety-split. Ain't yo' lonesome all by yo'seff?"

"No, I am fine," Angel said, peering up at the moon, and when she turned the servant was huffing across the lawn, saying, "I has to go, I has to go."

Angel shook her head, smiling. The old woman with her shiny, puffed cheeks and guttural voice had been the high point of her evening, so far. Angel was feeling much better now and she walked alone, sedately. Filmy vapors seeped through every bush and tree and rounded the corners of the house. The tendrils swirled around her skirts as her feet wandered aimlessly. She paused to contemplate the radiant sickle moon.

Would he still come? And would he dare dress like a rake-hell pirate, in full black beard and sideburns, that earring twinkling, swinging from his ear? Maybe he would even sport a long, wicked sword dangling from a wide leather belt, or a bright sash wrapped around his lean waist.

"Mademoiselle Duponte? You aren't making sense. You're speaking of pirates and smugglers and a lean waist and hips. *Hiccup.*"

Angel whirled to see Lieutenant Parker peering at her strangely, while he wavered where he stood, grinning stupidly. He had far progressed in his cups since she had first waltzed with him.

"I was just thinking out loud, that is all. Shall we go back inside?" Angel said as she made a move to glide past him and take the lead into the house.

"But . . . I wanted to tell you something," Parker said happily, almost drooling at the pale sight drenched in moonlight.

Angel's mind was elsewhere, other than on this lad who was handsome in a youthful sort of manner. She wondered if she would be missed if she slipped upstairs and into her room. She was going to do just that when he stepped close, and moving all too quickly, encircled her sweet form, surprising her by kissing her full smack on the lips before she could even protest. The kiss was somewhat sloppy and too warm, but executed with experience. Compared to another's it was callow, Angel took time to think before she protested beneath his lips.

"Lieutenant Parker! Release me!" Angel hissed as she exerted force upon his chest and thrust him madly from her, causing him to stumble back a few paces from her.

"Angeline, is that you?"

Angel concealed her highly strung vexation when Wesley strode upon the scene unexpectedly. He raked the young lieutenant over suspiciously, then with an ugly scowl watched his fiancee smoothe a tendril unconsciously back into place.

"Hmm, I see. Did you enjoy your stroll in the moonlight, my dear?" Wesley asked in a nasal voice. He didn't wait for an answer, but turned on Parker instead. "You may leave us now, *Mister* Parker," he snapped meaningfully.

With a shrug of tousled forelock and bold shoulders turning, the young man marched away, telling himself he wasn't through here yet. He tripped across the threshold and made a beeline for the table nearly groaning with wines and liquors. He tossed off a noggin and thrust his cup out for more, then leaned back to watch the door.

Wesley grasped Angel firmly by the elbow and drove her in that same direction Parker had taken only moments before. She flinched in pain as Wesley cruelly pinched her when she faltered in trying to keep up his furious pace.

"Wesley, stop it! You are hurting my arm," Angel cried, trying to shrink away, but he spun her about to face his ugly leer.

"I do not give a damn about your arm, my dear. I have been searching for you for over half an hour to make the announcement. And where do I find you? Huh!"

Wesley said no more but pulled her along, right into the center of the activity where he called out and clapped his hands together at once. His voice boomed across the assemblage to draw them as near as they could crush. Angel felt those same eyes upon her that had witnessed her accident with the harried servant, as Wesley's arm snaked about her waist now.

"Ladies and gentlemen, silence please. . . ." Wesley droned on then as he introduced his sweet little bride-to-be.

Angel wasn't listening, for two figures across the room had caught her eye. First her line of vision rested upon Jacinta, not daring to go further. The full-blown figure was draped in yellow tiffany of the sheerest kind and was fashioned à la Josephine; Jacinta was on the arm of—a stranger! Angel began to breathe easier, indeed, she almost swooned with relief. *He* wasn't here.

Immediately after Wesley had ended his speech, the mob piled toward them with well-wishes, hearty pats on the lucky fellow's back, stifling hugs and squeezes that made Angel feel as if she were being smothered and crushed to death. Jacinta and her stranger straggled over to congratulate them. The gray eyes beside Angel lit up at the latecomers. The Creole woman was the first to speak.

"Angeline, kitten, you look charming in that homespun creation. I am sorry, you did make it yourself, *non?*"

"Yes, I did, Jacinta," Angel replied simply, feeling all at

once gowned shabbily in comparison to the sunshine-yellow gauze of silk that floated before her eyes. She was suddenly reminded of the "gift" Jacinta had bestowed so charitably upon her—Ugh!

Jacinta fingered the gauzy veil beneath her breasts, sweeping the thing out in front of her as her dark eyes slanted over the simplicity of the younger woman's rose-colored gown. She rested her gaze on the softly swelling breasts, but smirked in the knowledge that her own gown was more fashionable, being the very latest Empire cut.

"*Bon Dieu, petite*, how can you stand the homey drudge of laboring over a needle for hours and hours?" Jacinta questioned tartly, then answered her own question most insultingly: "It is beyond me!"

Angel smiled mischievously. "My grandmama quoted often that idle hands are the tools of the devil, Madame Hunter." She pointedly eyed the rosy aureoles beneath Jacinta's meagerly clad bodice as she continued, "I might add—you would do well in employing the art to add to the lack of lining in your own gown." Angel's retort was saucy and she rested easier in watching the arrogant smirk go to pieces.

Wesley reddened profusely, but the stranger only lifted his bushy gray brows as Angel watched him conceal a lazy grin beneath his mustachios. He asked to be introduced personally then. "After all, I have heard your name spoken, but you do not know mine, mademoiselle."

"Ah, permit me," Wesley chimed in. "Angeline, you have met Jacinta, now meet her father—Monsieur Guy Villerne. Likewise, Angeline Duponte, my intended."

The last word was as if stricken from his lips, barely heard by the foursome, for just moments before the front door had been swept wide, and the soft breeze that billowed the draperies seemed also to have deposited Satan himself. Low murmurs spread, and everyone near the entrance gaped awestruck at the tall, menacing figure in black that doffed his matching cloak lined with scarlet silk.

Angel's mouth quirked at the corner and she ignored the intruder who was more than a little tardy. She fastened her eyes instead upon the mantelclock just chiming out that

322

bewitching hour, bringing painfully to mind a moonswept isle. The whoever was obstructed from view and Angel disregarded the ladies congregating in that direction. Soon Wesley too excused himself, and with a frown he went to see who this rude arrival might be. Jacinta and her father curiously followed their host, leaving Angel to stand alone.

"Lawd a-mighty!" Angel mimicked the funny servant she'd met earlier and at once whirled to find the long table where she ladled out for herself a glass of punch, this time free of inebriants. She suddenly felt a bit tipsy again, but this time she couldn't fathom why. It had been a long time since her last glass of wine.

Suddenly Angel stiffened when a body brushed against her, and turning her head cautiously, relaxed at once when Hannah smiled obliquely at her.

"Oh, Hannah, where have you been?" she beamed as she touched the slim, white arm lightly.

"I might ask the same of you, dear girl," Hannah returned. Glancing back over her shoulder, she added scandalously, "Imagine that Mr. Hunter breezing in at this late hour! Do you want to meet him now?"

Angel almost chocked on her punch and replied quickly, "No, not really. Perhaps in awhile and after his audience have done with him." She bent to slip a finger in her slipper. "Oooh! I will just have to get used to high-heeled slippers, that is, if I ever don the blasted things again."

Hannah chuckled. "I know just what you mean. Come on, let's try to sneak into the salon before the midnight madness begins. I've had enough dancing for one night and a soft divan sounds mighty tempting to me at this moment!"

As they made their way unnoticed into the hall, Angel was relieved that the center of attraction and his company had moved into the front parlor. Folks ambled in and out, and on passing the open door, Angel caught the drift of some conversation.

"*Mon Dieu*, what a prince of a man!" a wealthy planter's wife whispered to her female companion.

"Dawlin', don't you mean prince of the devil himself? Lawd! He gives me the shivers with those distuhbing eyes dartin' heah and theah!"

"*Oui*, I know," the first woman answered. "But is he not also villainously handsome? And some say that he is. . . ."

Angel missed the latter comment as she trailed Hannah into the only vacant room on the first floor. Hannah closed the door to the salon and lighted several tapers, then plopped down into the nearest divan, kicking off her slippers. Angel positioned herself gingerly upon the settee, spreading out the dusty rose brocade while she rubbed an instep with one unslippered foot.

Hannah began to chatter away about all the officers and young bachelors she had danced with, "None of whom I would particularly care for as a beau, if the occasion should so arise," she added, almost wistfully.

Angel only half-listened. She experienced an almost irresistible urge to flee to the refuge of her bedchamber. Something was about to happen—she just knew it. This same odd feeling had come over her earlier when Hannah had suddenly appeared at her side. It was growing stronger and more tangible. . . .

Out in the hall, Angel heard footfalls scuffle up and halt just outside the door—the knob turned. The sound jolted her nerves and her spine stiffened, before she dipped forward hurriedly. Her back curved as she ungracefully fumbled under her skirts for the lost slipper.

"Ohh, where is it," she whimpered softly to herself and bent even further until the glossy coils of hair swung forward to hide her distressed face.

". . . and here she is. Angeline, I want you to meet Mr. Hunter. What *are* you looking for, my dear?" Wesley questioned, his eyes riveting on the bold display of her all but spilling bosoms. "Straighten yourself, Angeline!" he demanded.

Disconcerted, Angel stayed as she was while her eyes rolled up an inch to view Wesley's serviceable brown shoes and a pair of highly polished black boots step up before her. The neighbor bent down and instantly retrieved the slipper out from under the settee. Angel watched as the lean and beringed hand reached under the hem of her gown to encircle her silk-stockinged ankle and fit the slipper onto her foot. The contact

324

caused wildly wonderful sensations to course through her limbs, and her eyes widened in shock as they flew upward to meet the lazy grin she knew so well.

The eyes were the same, the amber flecks glowing in intensity, and the sensuous lips were the same, the strong features, the hair with soft lights. This was. . . .

Hannah's words of the day before flooded back to her: The infamous Tyrone and he are—the same! Tyrone *Hunter!*

There was no time to dwell on it further, for in the next instant Tyrone unbent, gently pulling her up with him. They stood so very close and their eyes locked and held for what seemed an eternity to both. Angel thought surely her knees would give in to betray the emotions she was feeling at this moment. Indeed, he was more handsome clean-shaven than he had been as a bearded smuggler. He was thinner though, but still moved with an easy catlike grace, she noticed with starved eyes.

Wesley intruded with a loud emphatic cough. "I am sorry, Hunter, but my intended is not herself this evening. Please excuse Angeline, would you?" He lastly glared at her.

"Angeline—hmmm?" Tyrone murmured softly, menacingly.

"*Oui,*" Wesley said. "Angeline Duponte. But not for long."

Boldly Tyrone reached out to grasp the trembling hand in his own larger, warm one. His eyes caressed the dainty fingers as he turned them over and, drawing the hand to his lips, his kiss lingered in the palm while he peered up, his eyes never leaving her sweet face. As he brought his hand still grasping hers to his chest, she could only stare mesmerized at the shining white-hot diamonds, set in purest gold, dripping from several fingers. He straightened when she detached her hand brusquely, as if he had scorched it with those jewels flashing blue sparks.

Inquisitive guests began to tumble in, followed by the footman bearing cordials. Jacinta too, swept in and Angel found a seat on the divan next to Hannah, their quiet time interrupted. This room too, was soon a busy hive, and the women were separated from the men, each group gossiping, but desiring company as a whole.

Angel heard Hannah whisper behind her hand. "He is staring right at you, Angeline. He looks as if he would dash over here and pounce on you at any moment. I must warn you, though he may appear the dashing gentleman, he's a cunning rogue right down to the core."

"Rotten core," Angel hissed under her breath. Then, "Hannah, excuse me, but I have a clandestine tryst in the powder room."

Feeling the effects of her cordial, Hannah giggled. "All right, puss, see you later then. That is, if you don't meet up with a rogue on the way back."

On her way out, Angel tossed a sidelong glimpse over her shoulder and noticed Jacinta standing intimately close to Tyrone. Why not! They were husband and wife! Angel thought miserably.

Her insides tied themselves into knots and she seethed inwardly. Tears of frustrated rage carried her on up to the convenience. The sickening thought of Tyrone having used her so callously shook her violently. She felt no better than one of the strumpets at Madame Lulu's.

Tyrone was so wrapped up in the ravishing sight across from him that he neither saw nor felt Jacinta rustle up to loop her arm into his. He ogled Angel's posterior as she rose gracefully from the divan and her skirts swished. He could see her reflection above the mantel as she strolled to the door with a gentle sway of her hips, casting a pert glimpse in his direction, totally unaware that he spied on her in the mirror.

"Angeline," thought Tyrone, "Angel in the mirror." He finally had her name. Now. . . .

With a debonair flick of a tanned wrist he straightened his collar, then helped himself out of Jacinta's possessive grip. He was drawn into the wake of undulating rose brocade, and Jacinta pursed her lips in vexation as she called after him.

"Jacinta, *chère*," Tyrone shot over his shoulder, "you will catch your death if you don't acquire a shawl before the morning dampness settles in."

All but hopping with rage, Jacinta stomped her foot. "Pah!" she shouted to the vacant portal to save face.

Across the room, Hannah placed a finger to her chin.

"Hmmm, very interesting," she murmured.

With the music ceasing, voices muffled down the now emptied hall as the guests retired to either the salon for a final libation or, if they chose to, the dining room for a snack to hold them over till the morning meal; the latter was but several hours away. Angel paused halfway down the stairs to meet this inactivity, hearing nothing but Wesley's voice droning above the others, firmly established in a bull session. She lingered there inconspicuously for a moment, then shrugged wearily. She didn't think she would be missed, so she turned to go back up and retire.

Midway up the stairs, a hand reached up from behind to cover hers, halting the next placement of her foot. Angel slowly turned to see who held her fast. It was the young lieutenant and he weaved unsteadily as he leered dumbly into her wary countenance.

"Again, Lieutenant Parker, you are hurting my arm. Release me now, I say!"

"Angeline, you make me wild with desire," Parker said inattentively. He then became emboldened as his last potent beverage took hold, and he slurred, "Be my mistress. Meet me later—tonight!"

Bending over her, all atremble with male heat, Parker tried pressing a wet kiss on the tempting curve of neck. He was as strong as an ox, even in his inebriety, and Angel wondered frighteningly when her wrist would snap from the pressure of his hold. He crushed her to the balustrade, and somehow they had almost reached the top of the stairs. Angel was thankful for one thing—that no one was watching the entanglement from below. Though she very much disliked his drunken, amorous advances, she knew if caught Parker would be in for demotion. She would just have to frighten him into awareness.

"Parker," Angel warned, "I shall cry out for Wesley and he will murder your bloody carcass if he catches you fondling me. Not to mention what will happen if the general learns of your misconduct. You will be in a bloody pickle, that is what!"

"Aaah, c'mon, Angeline. You know you want it as much as I do. I can tell by the scent of you, by the way you sashay those soft skirts of yours. Ever'one can tell you're hotter than hell. I got something here you won't soon forget," he dared to mutter in his inebriety.

Parker would not be dissuaded. Growing weaker by the minute from her struggles as she was, at this pace the lieutenant would soon have her upstairs behind a locked door. She prayed for something to put an end to this loathsome scene when, in the next instant, she saw that a larger, jewel-encrusted hand covered Parker's entirely, squeezing, crushing, until something audibly snapped and the young man groaned as if dying.

Behind Parker, Angel could make out the black-clad figure of Tyrone, even though the staircase was dimly lighted. The tall smuggler spun Parker around to face him as he whispered a warning, so low that even Angel couldn't hear.

"Now . . . I am going to escort the lady to her room. You go down like a good lad and get a long breath of fresh air. If you bother mademoiselle again, I shall personally make certain that you will never again be able to please a woman. Comprehend?" He punctuated that by bending a knee threateningly.

Parker gulped, cowering before the big man he'd never seen before. He nodded rapidly then whirled to stumble down the stairs, as fast as his wobbly legs could carry him. He was lucky to still have use of them, besides his manhood, for two of his appendages were broken and he would have a hard time explaining this to the company surgeon.

Angel stood silent until she finally found her tongue. "Thank you, Mr. Hunter! Now, if you will excuse me I shall bid you too a good night and continue to my bedchamber."

She had not gotten far when she noticed that he had tracked her, his lean hand hovering near her waist. She spun about, breathing a weary sigh while pressing her hands toward his broad chest to bid him come no further.

"As I've just informed that amorous lad . . . I'll keep my promise and escort you to your room, Angel-ine," he said mockingly.

"I am quite capable of that now, Mr. Hunter." Moving down

328

the hall she tossed back, "Again, good night!"

Still, Tyrone saw the rose brocade down the poorly lighted hall, until she paused in applying her trembling hand to the knob. Suddenly he was behind her again, his arm snaking around as his fingers encircled her wrist gently but firmly. He could easily crush her hand in a moment's notice as he had done Parker's. She could only stand breathless now, sensing that leashed cruelty in him. But his hand only slid up her arm and the blood rushed through her veins hotly as he turned her slowly about to face him. Above his lionlike eyes his dark brows shrugged in that maddening manner she knew so well.

"The beautiful rose has blossomed and the bud is lost, yet the thorns remain to prick the one who would dare caress it." Suddenly his face grew hard and a muscle twitched ominously along his jawbone. "Does Wesley Gayarre feel this need that tears him hither and yon when he touches you, sweet Angeline? Does the mere nearness of you set his heart to beating a rapid tattoo?" he questioned hoarsely.

"Blast it!" she hissed into his handsome smirk. "How would I know that? He wants me as his wife—that is all!"

"All?" Tyrone drawled, tickling her arm with traipsing fingers. "Ah, surely, Angel-ine, he has revealed his love to you, otherwise a marriage is but a farce, merely a bit of parchment. Of course, there is always that other kind, but that soon grows sour in the morning light, after the initial passion wears off. For us it would be for—"

"All of a sudden you are again an authority on love?" she interrupted sharply, tugging at the hands slipping beneath her armpits. She could feel the iciness of his diamonds and the warmth of his fingers at the same time.

"I do not claim to be an expert on anything, but I do know this—that you do not love Wesley. No, be still. I surveyed you downstairs, whether you knew it or not, and your pale eyes displayed to him none of that fiery spirit you used to show me—" pulsating fingers trailed lightly across her breastbone, "like now," he breathed, feeling her heart pound hard and fast.

"Lust-crazed beast!" she said truculently and slapped at the increasingly familiar hands.

329

"Who is Duponte, my sweet?" he asked, a low chuckle following.

"You know very well I made that up!"

"Did you now. Are you truly Angeline then?"

"Yes . . . Angel! Now, lay your hands off, or I shall scream!"

"Ho!" he exclaimed in feigned fright. His voice deepened then. "And I would have to smother your lips with a kiss . . . Angel." He tried out the name, liking the sound of it very much; it fitted her to a T.

Suddenly she was brought fully against his hard frame. One arm encircled her waist and his smiling lips crushed down on the pouting mouth, angrily then sweetly probing with his tongue. He pulled her twisting hips up tight against his starved loins. Angel could feel his desire growing, agonizing her quivering thighs as he all but lifted her off her feet. The kiss deepened. The dark walls revolved around them. They were wrapped in a spinning vortex of wild pleasure. A dampness came to her cheeks and she wondered momentarily if she wept.

Such sweet madness. Aaaah! Tyrone! She became submerged further in this wild desire as she felt herself melting; her arms crept up unconsciously to wind about his neck. Tyrone moaned low as his lips moved to kiss the soft, moist cheek. He paused, tasting the tears. Suddenly his fingers twined about the plump coils of hair and he cupped the back of her head, nestling the damply flushed cheek tenderly against his shoulder.

"Angel . . . Angel. You are mine, *mine*, and I'll never let you go now that I've found you again." He bent to kiss her ear, hugging her fiercely to him. "You will have everything . . . your heart's desire," he breathed.

His words sank in; again, no word of love had he muttered and it hit her with a sudden clarity that wrenched her insides. He belonged to another. He only lusted after her, as the lieutenant had done such a short time previous. True she carried Tyrone's poor babe within her, but she would never reveal this to him—never!

"How dare you preach your cheap words then fondle me!" she rasped, swiping away tears with the back of her hand and wrenching aside. "Stay off! I hate you, hate you! Don't you understand that I need no more of you and your lust-evil thoughts. You cannot hurt me anymore, smuggler. You shall not snuff me out as you did Ellen, and yes, my dear mother . . . I've no doubt!" She stepped back, hating the hurt look that had deceivingly entered his eyes. "Who—are—you—really? What—are—you?" she said with drooping eyelids.

Tyrone raked his fingers through his neatly trimmed hair before he reached out like lightning to grasp her shoulders, his fingers hurting. His breath was released in a ragged, rasping sound that made her start. His face grew increasingly saturnine as he spoke with seemingly great effort.

"Ahh, Angel. You know that I had nothing to do with Ellen's death, and your mother—" He shrugged confusedly. "What can I say—she disappeared not long after you fled the town house. I have unceasingly sent out search—"

"Promises!" Angel interrupted, glaring at him with renewed hatred. "Do not ever, I mean ever ever touch me again!"

With that she tore from his grip with unwomanly strength, opening and closing the door with but a few violent movements. Once inside she tossed herself onto the creaking bed and sobbed out her anger and frustration, and a vow that she would wed Wesley—happily!

Tyrone Hunter stared at the forbidding dark wood, and, but for those still lingering downstairs, he would have ripped the thing from its hinges. Feeling at a total loss as to what to do next, he spun about on his heel and made his way downstairs.

To those trickling into the hall to find their beds for what remained of the wee hours, Monsieur Hunter appeared like a frightful apparition, his eyes likened to amber marble, his dark brows drawn together in a brooding scowl, warning all who regarded him shrugging into his cloak to keep their distance. The carnelian-lined cloak billowed out behind when, without assistance, he yanked the door wide, and a flash of black was sucked into the void of that darkest hour before dawn.

Monsieur Villerne closed the gaping door and turned to enter into the hushed conversation of those who were left.

"*Bon Dieu!*" he exclaimed. "That my daughter Jacinta ever married a Hunter! It is good she stays at the town house." He was about to add more, but Jacinta had come to stand just then in the frame of the door.

Several of these folks snubbingly filed out the door, mortified at the wagging tongues. When in residence, either in Vieux Carré or Cresthaven, Tyrone was a regular Sunday worshipper. These acquaintances showed their respect for the man Hunter by ignoring others who spoke ill of him this eve. Guy Villerne suddenly found himself standing alone, his daughter shrugging across to him.

The crest-emblazoned Hunter carriage careened wildly down the lane, the partial darkness eddying by as a faint crimson loomed up in the east and pinkened the shivering dew that clung to the bearded moss of the silent wood. Tyrone did not welcome the dawning that would soon disturb his dark solitude and check the emotions that rode his countenance hard. His face was set in grim lines and his knuckles were stressed whitely between the leather straps that drove the black team relentlessly along the roadway.

"Aaahh," he growled out loud. "Green-eyed witch, that I ever set eyes upon your sweet shape, your winsome face . . . Angel. I should have guessed you were Angel. You have turned my life into a living HELL!"

He turned his thoughts instead to his work to avoid that angelic vision. Yes, there was much planting of the dirt fields to be done, old accounts and new ones to be drawn up, plus renewing, or rather becoming better acquainted with his neighbors. His financial skills were abundant and he would welcome the seclusion to set them into full force. He was going to be very busy indeed.

The dawn-swaddled clouds drifted lazily in an easterly direction; a cock drowsily cleared his throat then crowed somewhere in the distance to pierce the slumbering air while Cresthaven loomed up ahead like some ancestral castle born out of a mist-shrouded isle. The stately columns glowed a morning welcome to the dark conveyance sweeping grandly up the winding lane, high spokes singing smartly above pitch. The full-length French windows had been opened to gracefully accept the morning, taking in yellow bands of fresh light that Tyrone knew already glanced upon the Aubusson carpets.

The weathercock atop an outbuilding spun madly, halted, then pointed the way home to the weary traveler. Tyrone Michael Hunter had indeed come home to stay, his infamy a thing of the past.

2

Early upon an August morn, Angel found herself again pacing up and down the well-worn tapis in her bedchamber. Morning, noon, and night, her fears trod rampant upon her brain. The wedding date had been reset for the following week. But most troubling was that that smuggler-gentleman, that filthy rich plantation lord, was to be her neighbor.

A soft knock summoned her to the door and she continued to free her hair from its ribbon bindings as she went to answer. Jenny, her eyes all agog, stepped into the room with a short respectful bob.

"Ooooh, Miz Angeline! Two big trunks just come for you. A big man with beetle brows, he says they yours. The boys's bringing them up now." She beamed like a brown coneflower.

Angel released her hair as the familiar arched trunks were heaved into the room. Angel's gape was incredulous. The maid waited for her to open the mysterious bulks after the boys departed, Jenny wondering what they contained.

"Oh . . . Jenny!" Angel shrieked while kneeling beside them, rubbing one lovingly. She could see, even before lifting the lid, the volumes of Whittier and Emerson and other belles-lettres nestled between her white lisle mitts and the blue tiffany frock. She would have wept thinking of Christine, if Jenny hadn't spoken next.

"That's what the man said, for Miz Sherwood." Jenny's eyes twinkled happily for the sweet lady kneeling on the floor like a beaming child at Yuletide.

Angel's head rose slowly, her eyes boring the wall. She

whirled to face Jenny then. "What—did—you—say?" She searched the unblinking face.

Jenny clamped a brown hand over her mouth then dropped it to wring it with the other. "Oh! Oh! Shut mah mouth," she chided herself.

Angel rose slowly, but spoke unalarmingly. "Jenny, you spoke that name as if you've known it all along."

"Yes'm, my beau tole me," she blurted after a moment's indecision. "We gonna be married, Miz Angeline, Sam and me."

"Hmmm, I see. And, does this Sam reside and work on the Hunter plantation?"

"Cresthaven. Umm-hmm, he sure do, and he's Mr. Hunter's best hand. Sam's 'telligent and strong," she said proudly, digging into her white apron. "Jest look at what he give me. Gonna have a marrying ring made just like white folks, Miz Angeline. Mr. Hunter's a kindly man, sure."

Angel's eyes had widened at that mysterious, twinkling earring that Tyrone had worn at the first, and now. . . .

Preoccupied, Angel sighed. "It is not fair that all but Hannah and Wesley know the truth now. Well! I think it's high time to lay open with the Gayarres. Fetch Hannah for me immediately, Jenny." Angel whisked the back of a hand across her sweating brow.

Jenny had bobbed, now frowned. "Miz Angeline, you all right? I know you been sick couple a times."

"Oh, that is all over with now—" Angel broke to peer at the maid closely. "What do you mean . . . sick?"

Jenny wrung her hands, looked about the room, then shrugged.

"Come now, out with it!"

Jenny shied, "We all know you gonna have a wee one and—"

"I'd forgotten," Angel snapped, almost reprimanding the girl as she went on, "News travels fast around here. Who do you mean by *all*? Samuel? The housekeeper Della?"

At first Jenny cowered, afraid to speak. "Mmmm-hmmm. Sam knows, Della knowed a long time. She said she knowed when you come to visit at Cresthaven first time. She doan know whose baby—no one does."

Angel moaned, then softly ordered, "Forget about Wesley and Hannah for now, Jenny. Run down and have Jacques saddle the Girl for me."

"I doan know, Miz—"

"Do as I say!" she snapped, then softer, "I must go visit Della. Tell no one what you are about." She glared at the hesitating maid. "Now!"

Jenny fled the room, saying to herself, "Lawd! That lady could scare the whiskers off a dawg today."

Angel brushed back a straying lock of hair with the back of her hand as she lifted a cream-colored frock from out of the trunk. One of her favorites, it had been a trifle large in the bodice, but it would now be a perfect fit. She smoothed out the wrinkles in the soft muslin as she hunkered back on her heels, looking thoughtful.

First the earring, now the trunks. Pure evidence that Tyrone wished to remove every trace of her from his mind—and his presence. She was not so certain he would just as easily wash his hands of his own flesh and blood. If he learned she was pregnant, he needed only calculate the time span to realize whose seed she bore. She could always say she had lain with another? God Forbid—not another lie! No thank you. She was just not up to it.

"I must get to Della and beg her to remain silent in this!" Angel said frantically to herself.

Hastening, Angel ripped off her robe and yanked the cream frock over her head, disregarding the wrinkles. A hasty brush was applied to her loose hair before she twisted it into a demure knot at the nape of her neck. Her pale reflection stared back at her and she pinched some color into her cheeks. Standing sideways, she searched for a bulge of tummy, but none gave evidence yet that she was with child. Good.

A sudden vision of Jacinta popped into the mirror, mocking her and laughing cruelly at her downcast appearance. Jacinta herself appeared in swirling emerald silk, as usual gowned to the hilt of Paris fashion. Her sultry eyes bespoke her

335

possessive nature—Tyrone belonged to her, and if need be, the child Angel would bring forth, also.

"Over my dead body!" Angel spat at the vision, threatening it with her hairbrush, to which the Creole woman vanished like a slithering green snake.

"Angeline, what on earth—?" Hannah strangled her words as she almost vaulted over a spilling trunk in her hasty entrance.

"Please, no questions now, Hannah. But listen, I shall tell you all when I return from Cresthaven." Angel tapped her chin with a forefinger. Hannah had been more than kind. She could repay her now. The garments would be a perfect fit for the smaller woman. "Everything here is yours for the keeping, Hannah. I would keep only the belles-lettres, and this frock, nothing else. A small token in exchange for all that you have so generously bestowed upon me—especially your dear friendship," she ended softly.

"Angeline, wait. I don't understand—"

"Hannah, you may call me Angel. Angel Sherwood," she said, and spun out of the room, leaving Hannah staring around dazedly.

Still sporting his casual swagger, the tall, young man with crisp dark hair joined his yet taller cousin out back of the sun-kissed mansion. A healthy hound loped easily alongside, cutting didoes around the chuckling man who tossed a stick high into the air.

"Fetch it, Noble!" Nikki called watching the hound spring into action, stretching long tendons to retrieve the bit of wood that had fallen among a colorful profusion of summer coneflowers.

Tyrone shook his head slowly, his white teeth bared brightly at the playful antics of the newcomers to Cresthaven, arrived two days previous. He bent to the job at hand as he clouted, hammer steady in hand, a peg into a section of split-rail he was repairing. He spoke in a mumbled tone between a mouthful of pegs, his bare and tan back flexing in his labors.

"Damn!"

"Yeah, I know, diddle-diddle," Nikki chuckled, bending to assist his satirist cousin in hiking up the rail to steady it. "You thought I came to help build up the plantation. Really, I did. I just can't get used to this new way of life and all this hea-vy labor," he grinned. "Wow! There's so much to see and do. Is this really all yours, cousin? Hell, I wouldn't know, our parents hardly ever visited. I never even met Aunt Annette!"

Avoiding the last comment, Tyrone answered the question. "It better be, else I'm in a heap of trouble resting my butt on someone else's estate. Have you made up your mind about staying on, Nik?"

"That I have, Ty! I've no home—" he shrugged, "no kin but you, and I must admit the enchanting islands were very lonesome and dull after you'd gone. Even chasing dark gals began to bore me."

"And Caspar?"

"Really—yes! The flock shall follow their leaders, cap'n. Even saltbottom hisself!"

"Just remember. We will slave just as hard as my men. No dallying till we have worked this place up to its former grandness and brought the land back into full production. Cresthaven is going to yield the best cane in all Louie again, Nik."

Nikki grinned sheepishly. "What the devil are you going to do with all those rooms? Ah! There must be fifteen in all, front and back, up and down."

"Dear long-nosed cousin, you must have gotten yourself lost during your excursion through my house. There are twenty, in the central house, that is. Not counting the servants' quarters naturally, where I'm certain you discovered prying in on their private domains was a no-no."

Nikki first crowed over the mansion's size, then blushed red over the latter verity. That black housekeeper shooed him out proper good with a healthy swat on his lean behind with a flat straw broom.

"There is also," Tyrone continued, "a small happy community up yonder where my freshly bought slaves—yes, Nik, I did purchase them—work together, copulating and

337

living very comfortably on abundant supplies, and are free to hunt my northern woods."

Nikki hunkered beside the rail, peering around at the bordering gardens where several gardeners just now were trimming, raking, and weeding out the overgrown beds and bushes, and sweet pink- and yellow-eyed creepers now climbed freshly painted trellises.

"All those bedrooms," Nikki clucked. "No children to fill them, I mean—do you have a lady in mind to—uh—you know?" He dwelled thoughtfully on a certain fair-haired princess.

"No," Tyrone replied tersely, his look brooding.

Suddenly the tall door to the stable creaked wide as Samuel burst out into the sunlight. "Beauty is goin' to foal, Mistah Ty!" Samuel hollered. He had been stationed at the mare's stall since dawn, prepared to summon Tyrone when Beauty showed signs of full labor.

Shortly inside the stall, Tyrone stroked the silky mane. "Ea . . . sy, girl. It won't be long now," he spoke soothingly.

Caspar arrived just then and stood in the background with Sam and Nikki, all eyes intent on the mare showing signs of difficult labor as she stiffened, nickering softly while lifting her fine head and then relaxing as Tyrone murmured soft words to calm her.

Tyrone caught the presence of Caspar and as their eyes met Tyrone received a curt nod, indicating that Caspar had done his task, delivered the trunks to Angeline Sherwood.

"Sure 'nough," Samuel chuckled. "That young'un is goin' to be as big 'n sassy as Beast hisself."

In the stall directly across the way, Tyrone's raven Beast tossed his huge head to whicker as though replying. He was a great grandchild of the colts Tyrone had left behind when he had first left Cresthaven. Proud Beast, with hay trailing from his velvet mouth, seemed purely unconcerned at the birthing of his offspring and went back to masticating his lunch. That is, until a flash of green silk interrupted him and he blew at the intruder.

Jacinta sashayed upon the scene, easy to look at in her

stunning and flowing green fashion, the perfect representative of Empress Josephine's daytime wear. Her composure dissolved though when Tyrone tossed a quick scrutiny her way, glared, then demanded harshly that she be on her way.

Jacinta smirked to herself as she took her leave, hearing the deep chuckles follow her out into the bright saffron day. She snatched up her rustling skirts to cross the greensward, almost dry now after the rainfall the evening before. She cursed Tyrone's companions, the threesome, always in his presence. She disliked Caspar and black Samuel, both of whom she'd just met, and that dislike she knew was returned twofold by them. Nikki? Well . . . she could charm that one into liking her.

As much as she detested using the back entrance, she had to to avoid the red mire of the drive at the front. She had forgotten that on the other side of the house a gate opened to a flagstone path that ran the entire length of the house to the front. Once seated in a silk-cushioned, double chair in the parlor, Jacinta relaxed after pouring herself a small sherry. She glimpsed the room as she sipped the red liquid. This elegance was the essence of life. Sure, she dressed magnificently, her town house was no *pied-a-terre*. But her funds were dwindling and soon she must beg for more, as much as she hated doing it.

Jacinta still felt unsatiated, even after the lusty bedding down with a City Guard the evening before. He had been handsome enough in his deep blue uniform, a polished gentleman, but comparing his to Tyrone's lovemaking, the City Guard was an amateur.

There was no need to send Angeline packing off to England anymore—Wesley had seen to that. Even better, Tyrone wanted no part of *la petite mademoiselle* now. A blind fool could tell that, by the manner in which he had rushed those trunks off just this morning. She had just arrived when Tyrone had ordered that titan Caspar to hustle them off to Gayarre. And dismissing the barn incident, she just knew by the distinctive gaze in his lazy-lidded eyes just this morning over cafe, that this evening promised much pleasure with that stud tumbling her on that huge four-poster of his. She could hardly wait.

Jacinta was just about to turn away from the window where she'd wandered in her musings, when she caught sight of a lone rider clipping at a neat pace up the lane, the frisky bay churning up clods of red earth as they approached the house. Jacinta clutched the marquisette curtains and almost rent them in her irritation at seeing Angeline dismount to tie up the mare at the corner split rail. Jacinta picked up her skirts to get to the door hurriedly before Della could be summoned from the kitchen by the brass knocker. It was a good thing it was the footman's day off.

A roundlet of sunlight played on the visitor's unswerving countenance as the door was swept wide. Angel had an uncanny feeling seeing Jacinta standing there in duplication of the earlier experience with the looking glass.

"What do *you* want?" Jacinta asked ungraciously. "Tyrone is very busy and cannot receive visitors. Comprehend?" She put on a sleepy face as if just roused from bed.

But Angel wasn't fooled one bit, for Jacinta's impeccable appearance belied her words. "I did not come calling on your husband, Jacinta. My business is with the housekeeper Della," Angel explained.

"Oh?" Jacinta narrowed her dark eyes in suspicion. "Well, she is not here, so it might be wise for you to leave. My—uh—husband especially does not want to see you."

"Not here? Where else would Della be if not here?" Angel asked, as if Jacinta had not mouthed the last sentence.

"Visiting one of her kind in the slave cottages," Jacinta replied as hastily as she could think up the lie. Then an idea came deliciously to her. How angry Tyrone would be if Angeline popped in at the crucial moment of birth.

"Well then," Angel began. "Tell me how I might reach the cottage, and I shall be on my way."

Her mouth slashed into a red smile, Jacinta said coolly, "Oh, how silly of me. I have just remembered that Della is in the biggest barn—ahh—feeding the chickens."

Angel's brow lifted in puzzlement. "But, is that not the stable for horses? I thought—"

Jacinta interrupted slyly, shrugging, "They keep them both

340

together here. Now, go outside to the right of the house, then follow the drive to the back. You can't miss it.''

The mansion being situated on the east bank of the great river, that same Mississippi Red mire was rampant there. Taken unaware, Angel was halfway through the deceptively softened mire when she stuck fast. She tried making it to the fence; it was useless and she thought of going back to fetch the Girl, when she noticed Jacinta's wide grin at the window.

Gritting her teeth in determination, Angel snapped up her muddied skirts. A soft hide boot held fast and her next step left her legs spread so wide that she lost her balance, flopped over and splayed her hands in the mire. A troublesome fly landed smack on her cheek and she brushed it madly away, leaving a smear of Mississippi Red on her now hotly flushed cheek.

Jacinta, roaring with uncontrollable laughter at the hilarious mien that the younger woman presented as she peered up with smudged cheek, thought how she would love to see the look on Ty's face when this filthy urchin strolled in to make him even more furious at a second intrusion.

Very unceremoniously Angel tugged first one leg and then the other out of the boots. Clutching them in her hands she held her chin at an audacious angle as she tiptoed out of the mud and onto the greensward. Suddenly another problem greeted her, in the person of Noble, barking and galloping over to sniff out the stranger. Angel prayed that Tyrone was not about; he would chuckle at the mess she had foolishly made of herself.

Noble skidded to a rocking halt before her with his tail skipping back and forth as he caught the familiar scent and remembered the dulcet tone of her voice.

"Now, be still, Noble." Angel patted the rearing head when he whined and barked a greeting. "Yes, hello, now go lie down like a good boy—please,'' she said low, not wishing to attract attention if Ty was about.

Noble took his favorite spot in front of the stable, his pink tongue lolling out between his long fangs, cocking his canine head when the young lady gave a hip against the tall doors and lifted up the latch that opened from either side. The creaking door swung wide and cast a spreading swatch of light into the sweet vastness. It was antiseptically clean, smelling of freshly cut hat, harness leather, horses; and everything was in tiptop condition. It was three times larger than the stable at Gayarre and everything here was neatly in its place.

Standing silent, Angel listened for chickens, but not even a solitary contented guggle could she detect. Probably out back in a fenced-in yard, she decided as she tiptoed toward the sound of soft neighing and muffled voices. Softly and tentatively she called Della, but no answer came, only fine horses turning great heads to roll liquid brown orbs, snorting at her presence. She turned this way and that along stalled corridors to follow the murmur of voices, until she stood before a huge bin of sweet-smelling hay. She stepped around the obstruction, then reddened profusely and gulped hard at the scene before her.

Tyrone was hunched over a mare Angel knew was just about to foal. She gave a start when Tyrone growled harshly over his shoulder at the skirt's hem he saw. She almost dropped the boots dangling limply from her hands when he fully turned.

"Damnit, Jacinta! I told you to stay the hell out of—" His frown riveted to the muddied face, then he blinked over her in a thorough search before he turned back to the task of easing the foal into the world.

Old Saul ambled over from another stall, and with the other three men, he regarded the young woman anxiously for a moment before seeing what Tyrone had—that she was unharmed and only quite dirty. Angel was left with the sinking feeling that she must indeed look a fright.

Angel forgot everything else then as she became thoroughly fascinated by what she beheld. The hindquarters of the foal were beginning to emerge and somehow she felt this part should not be born first. The laboring mare was having a hard time as she blew and groaned. She could almost feel the rich timbre of Tyrone's voice as he spoke.

"Easy now, girl. Ah, yes, he—*he*—is coming."

Caspar piped up, "Look at that, just as black as Beast, Cap'n Ty. No wonder she is roughing it. Look at the size of him, backing out and ready to buck already!"

Nikki chuckled, saying, "A brand new one for the Hunters' fine collection of steeds."

Angel felt strangely atremble watching this man who had made love to her so passionately. As with a stud, it only took one or two joinings and she was caught with a growing belly. She was delicately boned and smaller in the hips than most women her age, and it would likely be hard labor for her to produce his offspring. Angel couldn't take this anymore, had to get out of here—now!

Tyrone was urging the mare back down when he glanced over to see Angel taking steps stealthily backwards, as if to go as quietly as she possibly could.

"Stay!" Tyrone ordered. "You are making the mare nervous." Then, "Ah, the foal is almost—here now—done!" he shouted victoriously.

Mare Beauty let out a shuddering moan and cheerful approval was expressed from the four men upon seeing the slippery newborn. Tyrone hunkered back on his heels, emitting a gladdened sigh of relief as he brushed the droplets of sweat off his brow with the back of a hirsute forearm. The rest was up to the mare now. She reclined for a minute then saw to the cleaning of the black beauty that rested already proudly erect with spindly limbs tucked under fawnlike. Tyrone grinned widely with the other men when from across the way, Beast shook his flowing mane and whinnied proudly at his robust offspring.

"Look at him," Nikki said, "he knew what was going on all the time!" He laughed with Tyrone.

At last and painfully, Angel bloomed a bright shade when the five men slid their regard to her rather amusedly. All those smiling eyes upon her dishevelled countenance. It was more than a girl could stand. They no doubt realized she had found the mire not as impenetrable as it had at first seemed to the unwary eye. She had to say something quick, something to break the embarrassing silence, even if it seemed stupid now.

"I—I was searching for Della. Jacinta informed me that I could find the housekeeper out here—feeding—the—chickens."

"Chickens?" Caspar and Nikki chorused.

"Wha . . . t?" Tyrone followed, a dark brow arched. He caught the others concealing wide grins behind their hands, even Old Saul. "Hmmm, I see. That woman will stop at nothing to create a stir of excitement," he said almost apologetically as his eyes scoured the mud-stained frock.

Angel murmured a little "Oh" and realized she had been the object of a mean and spiteful joke. There were no chickens—of course!

The men suddenly became busy in the back of the stable and Tyrone caught the sparkle of a tear in the green gaze that centered on the newborn. The colt unfolded to hoist himself up on wobbly limbs that appeared somewhat crooked. But Angel smiled a little when the frisky tail whisked back and forth. Suddenly she could feel those measuring eyes on her and she decided to make a hasty departure, when she was brought up short by the gruff question in the man's voice.

"Angeline . . . why do you search for my housekeeper?" He put on his shirt.

Keeping her back to him, she said, "I—The last time I visited—there is something I borrowed from her and—and yes I came to return it," she fibbed, hating herself. She glanced over her shoulder to see Tyrone roll up his sleeves to wash; she wondered why he'd put it on to do so? A gentlemanly gesture?

"That's right, you have been here before, haven't you?" he stated as he bent to splash clear water up over his arms from a bucket.

Feeling the caked boots growing heavy in her hands, she murmured, "I'll just go find her now, if you do not mind." She moved and again was held back by the stern note in his voice.

"*What* do you return, if you don't mind my asking?" He quickly stepped around to block her going. He toweled his furred arms, then flung the thing aside.

"I—I left it in the saddle pouch." She stuck out a foot to go around him and he halted her, this time taking the boots from her to clean them briskly inside and out with a rag.

"That is not what I asked you," he said, as he finished cleaning the boots. He handed them over to her, staring hard.

344

"Well . . . what? Is it so personal that you must clam up?"

Angel sat on bunched hay to pull on the long boots, saying, "Yes, I am afraid it is. Personal, but not important. Just a thing."

"I don't believe you, Angel Sherwood," he ended mockingly.

"Ohhh! I do not have to stand here and answer to you—no sir!" she snapped. Picking up her muddied skirts, she whirled and stomped away as she made a beeline for the tall doors.

Halfway across the greensward, Angel spun about in indecision. She tugged at a lower lip with her teeth. Tyrone, painfully handsome in the outdoors, virile in all-revealing breeches molded to lean, strong thighs, strode boldly toward her, no question as to his abundant manhood. He noticed at once where her gaze lingered momentarily before it dropped shyly, and his eyes grew heavy-lidded. He stood tall before her.

"If you would have but noticed the secret gate, you could be away now, if that is what you wished. And, my house is your house . . . anytime, Angel." He smiled into her flushed face meaningfully.

"Thank you, but I shall choose the gate today—Mr. Hunter."

Tyrone shrugged. "Come along then. I'll show you the way, my sweet."

While he was closing the vine-covered gate that led to a flagstone path behind them, Angel whirled, hastening her steps until she was halfway to the mare. Suddenly Jacinta appeared smilingly beside the Girl, as if to bid the odd-looking company adieu. Then she saw Tyrone, his face set in sinister lines. His regard was cold, and Jacinta wondered if she'd done the right thing by sending Angeline to the stable.

Tyrone leaned indolently against a pillar, watching Angel busy herself at the saddle as she shifted it, seemingly preoccupied in a search. She lifted her eyes to see him standing a few paces from her and the Girl. Now what? Well what to do? she asked herself. She paused there, scarcely breathing. All she could think of was she'd have to return someday when he was gone from the plantation. Jenny would help find that out from

Samuel for her.

"Fine mare," Tyrone remarked as he came to pat the Girl's long nose. "She was once part of the Hunter collection. Like a good fool I let her go—" His eyes shone mysteriously, "slip out of my hands."

"Yes, I know," Angel murmured, letting her gaze slip down to the tip of his scuffed boots. "I—I see that I have forgotten the borrowed item," she managed, noticing his wife sidling up behind him. "I will return tomorrow perhaps, with the thing, but now—"

Suddenly Tyrone reached out with oddly shaking fingers to brush at the caked mud on her cheeks. Their eyes locked for a painful moment before she brushed back a straying lock of hair, at the same time warding off the thrilling touch of his fingers. He untied the reins at the post and gave her up onto the mare's back, his hands encircling to linger at her yet small waist. She was staring down at the clean-shaven face she longed so terribly to caress, when Della appeared at the entrance and smiled widely when she saw Angel for the first time that day.

Angel spread a smile, once quickly, and when Tyrone turned to see what she smiled at, Angel spun about madly and spurred the mare, at once lurching into a headlong gallop down the lane.

"What the—!" Tyrone half-exclaimed, almost losing his balance when the mare's hindquarters brushed him. "Angel . . . come back, damnit!" he bellowed after the blur clipping toward the fork in the road.

Della came down off the porch, clucking her tongue. She gave the haughty Jacinta a quick, hostile perusal before she took up watching the dust cloud rise to the tall trees beyond the lane.

Her brow furrowing with even more lines, Della inquired, "What's the matter with the honey chile, Mr. Hunter? Why'd she go off like that?"

"Why, *mon cher*," Jacinta said, disregarding the housekeeper's presence, easing herself between the two of them, "couldn't you see how terribly embarrassed the poor thing

346

was?'' She smirked rudely at Della, adding, ''How funny she looked with—''

''Be still, woman!'' Tyrone snapped. Then to Della, ''Do you suppose you could tear yourself from your chores long enough to have a chat with me, old woman?''

''Sure 'nough, Mr. Hunter,'' Della said. ''Sure 'nough.''

Jacinta stood very still on the front lawn, staring after them as they entered the house. She turned her head back in the direction Angeline had taken. At first her eyes narrowed evilly, then she stomped her slippered foot in defeat, gritting, ''Ohhhh! Ohhhh!''

Angel tugged the stained frock over her head, heedless that she had ruined the tabs at the back. She kicked it aside into a heap, making a mental note to have Jenny burn the disgusting thing first chance she got. She wanted never to be reminded of this humiliating day again. She tugged a brush through her long hair, pondering the dancing web-patterns on the gray walls that the sleepy, filtering sun made. It was hot, and the tepid breeze did nothing to alleviate her sticky feeling. Too, there was still caked mud on her cheeks and legs.

It was some time later when gloomy darkness crept through the house like huge gray beasts that Angel emerged from taking a leisurely bath Jenny had prepared for her. Her stomach growled noisily with hunger, mingling with the echo of voices drifting up to where she paused in the hall. Wondering at the whiny, complaining voice, she edged over to the balustrade and leaned out to hear April's complaint drifting up the stairwell.

''Yes, Daddy. She hasn't been in the schoolroom with me for two days now. She's been up in that room of hers walking back and forth,'' April paused to sniff loudly in that disturbing manner of hers. ''This afternoon I saw her ride off—toward Cresthaven. And Ha—Ha—Hannah, she's sleeping again, ''Da—da—daddy.'' April hiccoughed after whining of her day's lonesomeness.

Wesley's murmured answer was inaudible to Angel. She chided herself first for neglecting the poor, lonely child, then worry crossed her features as she became curious about

347

Hannah's lassitude of late. Poor, sweet Hannah, with nary a suitor to come calling and make her laugh and be merry like a girl her age should be. Wesley went his own selfish way, caring not a whit for his family's happiness.

Angel heard signs that Wesley was quitting the salon. Galvanized into quick action, she could already hear his footsteps coming up when she shut the door to her room. She cast off the old robe to find something presentable to wear to dinner. She had packed the green gown she'd worn to Gayarre that first night, meaning to have it sent back to Lulu, so she couldn't wear that. As Hannah hadn't taken the trunks to her room yet, Angel reached nervously for the first frock she spied. It was a snug fit, an immature brown holland, and she was at once sorry for choosing it. The thing hung on her like a limp, wrinkled rag.

How did the old thing ever come to be in her trunk? She thought for certain she had tossed it out long before the fateful voyage. Too late now—Wesley was at the door hollering as he rattled it with a thunderous quaking that caused her to flinch.

"Open this door immediately, Angeline. Why have you locked it?" Wesley demanded.

Angel went to open the door she'd locked to give herself time to dress. She stepped back, just in case any blows should come her way. She wouldn't put it past him now, not when she viewed his raging face as he burst like a mad bull into her room. She stood with frock unfastened as his colorless eyes roamed over her boldly. He backed her up to the edge of the bed. She noticed the hungry glint in his usually cold and unemotional eyes. Clutching her frock closed with one hand behind her back, she stared hard as he reached out to cup her chin roughly, digging into her soft flesh on either side.

"Your insolence annoys me, Angeline. Where have you been . . . off to see your lover?" He noticed the filthy, ravished frock lying in a heap on the fraying tapis. "Hunter has been under your skirts, ummm? Do not think I did not notice him ogling you at *our* engagement party!"

"Wesley, I've done nothing to make you ashamed of me. I— I just went for a ride and—ouch! You are hurting me. Leave me be!" Angel cried, her eyes diamond bright with tears.

"It is time I taught you a lesson, my dear, pregnant or not. We shall be wed in New Orleans tomorrow without anymore stalling. For now . . . I have waited too long for this."

Forgetting that the door gaped open, Wesley grabbed a handful of damp hair to pull her roughly against his surprisingly hard frame. He kissed her unexpertly, brutally bruising her unyielding mouth with hard wet lips. She hammered his chest with balled fists, but his free hand snatched the brown holland down over her ivory shoulders. Her bosom heaved in revulsion when he applied his square fingers to a rounded breast. She was weak from not eating since dawn and she panted to catch a breath, causing Wesley to mistake her breathlessness for sluttish passion. Unable to withstand the attack of wet lips and seemingly numberless fingers any longer, Angel swooned against him. It was his turn to catch his breath at her womanly softness that nourished a starving flame in him.

"How tender. The Angel and her amorous bridegroom. It couldn't have been timed better if I planned it myself. In for a night of sport, Wes?"

The familiar voice came to Angel as if a pail of water had been dashed into her burning face from the doorway. His desire blatantly visible, Wesley released Angel and stiffly turned to watch Tyrone push himself from the jamb, sauntering into the room unannounced. An arrogant sneer on his lips made him no less handsome.

"Hunter!" Wesley croaked. "What is the meaning of this intrusion upon our privacy!"

"Sorry, Wes, but your footman seems to be out for the evening, so I just helped myself to your hospitality," Tyrone said coolly, watching Angel self-consciously arrange the frock over her thin chemise. His regard left her then to rest upon the ugly shade of red choking Wesley into speechlessness. "Wes," he went on maddeningly, "you must excuse us, but it seems that—mmmm—the lady, if you wish, and I have something important to discuss." He nodded toward the open door, indicating the other to make use of it.

349

Hands clenching and unclenching at his sides, Wesley said, "You mean you and Mademoiselle *Sherwood* have something to discuss, don't you?" He disregarded the audible gasp behind him, snorted, then went on, "It is practically old news, from Donaldsville to New Orleans."

Tyrone studied his precisely cut diamonds before he took up staring around at the gloomy walls and the three shadows occupying them. Angel felt Tyrone was aware of her every movement, even though he seemed to ignore her as she struggled and finally fastened one of the tabs behind her back.

"So," Tyrone began after giving it some thought, "she has finally yielded that truth to you. How nice of the foxy little bride. I had almost given up hope for her, as she seems to be very adept at keeping secrets—employs special methods undreamed of by simple-minded maids."

Uncertainty crossed Angel's features as Tyrone frisked her once quickly with his eyes before his gaze slid away. She had witnessed this calm and collected manner of his before and knew it spelled danger to its victim.

Wesley went one further. "Didn't you hear, Hunter? I said it was old news, but I have been waiting for Angeline to tell me herself."

Angel glanced up from her nervous fingers. "I would have, just this night, but. . . ." Her small voice dwindled down to nothing, and Tyrone couldn't help wondering what had become of the brave hoyden who once dueled with him.

Hand Napoleon fashion, Wesley walked slowly around Tyrone. "I also know what a horny devil you are, Hunter, and that Angeline has been to visit your home on several occasions now. These visits will cease for we will soon be man and wife—tomorrow, in fact—and you have no business with her tonight. Do I make myself perfectly clear?"

"Noooo!" a shriek rent the bedchamber as Angel scurried to the portal where she was met by the lightning speed of that tall frame grasping her by the shoulders to spin her about.

"Hunter! Release her this instant!" Wesley shouted as he came up behind the two grappling near the door.

"Let me out of here!" Angel spat the words at the face

glaring down upon her. "You are both insane. I'll not be subject to any more of this inane chatter. Come morning I shall take my leave of Louisiana Territory and somehow, some way, I am going to find my mother and secure passage back to England!"

Wesley laid a hand upon Hunter's shoulder to restrain him and at once was sorry, for he was grabbed by the collar and thrust away with such force that he stumbled backwards, dazed, and would have landed hard on his back if he hadn't splayed his hands out to keep his balance. He watched aghast as Tyrone spun back to Angel as she was backing up to the door, fear apparent in her eyes as she worried about his intent.

"Keep away from me . . . smuggler!" she cried. Then, "What do you want from me? No—ooo!"

Swiftly a rending tear sounded in the room and the brown frock came away, open down to Angel's belly, all with the fleetness of a panther's swipe. While Angel worked furiously to cover her near nakedness, Tyrone stepped behind her. To still her movements he twisted one hand about her shoulder and with the other reached around and pressed gently, caressing her quivering belly. Angel stilled under the warm touch burning through her thin chemise and relaxed like a weak kitten, back against his chest.

"Please . . . please don't hurt me," she begged and felt Tyrone at once stiffen. His head lowered and his breath closed in on her as he was about to murmur something, when Wesley stepped up, but held his distance warily lest Tyrone should again thrust him back.

"*Bon Dieu* . . . what do you think you are doing, Hunter, raping my woman right here in front of me?" Wesley demanded, pop-eyed, then retreated a bit at the murderous glare in the other's eyes.

"First, monsieur, I will answer Angel's earlier question." He bent to whisper in her ear, "What do I want, my love?" He laughed scathingly at her slight quiver, then spoke louder. "This, my child that you carry within your slightly rounded belly."

"*Your* child!" Angel shrieked, kicking back at him, but

351

impeded from harming him by her heavy skirts. "I will never let you take him from me!"

Tyrone only chuckled low, saying, "I'm happy to hear that you are in whack as to the sex of the unborn child. A son meets with my approval also, love," he ended mockingly.

Flabbergasted, Wesley sputtered, "*He* is the father. . . ?" But he was not heard as the two ignored him fully to converse heatedly about gossiping servants.

"Of course," Wesley answered his own question. Angeline had called Hunter "smuggler." Just the other day an acquaintance of his had mentioned a certain freeboater with a vile reputation and murderous temper who was seen in the casino when a man named Duschesne was murdered. The description was: Garbed like a gentleman, but with thick, burnished locks, sporting a full black beard; he had escorted a Creole woman in broad daylight through the gutters of New Orleans. He wore a pirate's ring in his ear, the man had mentioned. Yes, Wesley could now see the tiny slit where the ring had pierced Hunter's earlobe.

Tyrone pulled up what remained of Angel's frock to cover her, saying, "Now, you will come with me . . . to my home."

Angel slapped the offending hand away, and realizing the implication of his words, said, "No. I'll not give up this child—nor will another woman mother him!"

"Another woman?" Tyrone peered at her. "What?"

"*Ma foi!* This is insane!" Wesley shook his head, deciding to back out, for now. He strode out the door to go find himself a stiff potion, for the first time in several years.

"Yes—" Angel finally answered, looking very small and pauperized in the brown holland, "and you know very well whom I refer to."

Growing impatient with her, Tyrone flicked a tanned wrist lined with silken cuff. His puzzlement grew, and whatever he was about to say was quickly prevented by Hannah's appearance at the door, sleepy-eyed, her gaze going from one to the other.

"Angeline?" Hannah began, "is everything all right? I mean—I passed Wesley in the hall and he appeared greatly

352

disturbed about something."

With temper flaring, Tyrone lashed out at Hannah viciously, "And so he should be, young lady!" Without further explanation he turned to Angel and said, dangerously soft, "Our conveyance is waiting outside with Caspar . . . shall we?"

"Now? Tonight?" Angel couldn't believe this was happening and she shook her head to clear it.

"Of course . . . tonight. Did you think me so foolish as to leave you again, to have you flee in the night, once more having me scouring the countryside like a madman to find you?" he asked all in one breath.

Angel opened her mouth to speak but no words would come. He took her silence for permission to proceed with his plans.

"Then it is all settled. I'll await you below while you make yourself presentable to Cresthaven. Della is waiting to do your bidding with two personal maids who will at once settle you into your own private rooms, apart from mine so my peers need not gossip of improprieties. Added to the army of chaperones, a couturière from New Orleans' finest shop will be arriving day after tomorrow. She will be in attendance for several weeks to come. Mimi will be introduced into your private salon where you'll be fitted for gowns and whatever suits your needs—and fancy."

"Oh, yes. You would keep me around till the babe is delivered to Cresthaven, then rub me out of your life. No! No! No! I'll not be your upstairs whore in waiting while you sit below with your haughty wife. What is it, Tyrone, is Jacinta barren?" she asked after a volley of protests.

"Wha . . . ?"

"Angel," Hannah interrupted, "can't you see? Mr. Hunter is asking you—" she laughed lightly, "*demanding* that you become his wife. And why not, when you seem to be carrying his child, I understand?" Hannah looked to Tyrone for validation, and, somewhat befuddled, he gave her a curt nod. He continued to look thoughtful but listened as Hannah went on to say, "And what is this about Jacinta? Good heavens, Angel, she is his stepmother!"

353

Tyrone reddened somewhat at those words, but Angel just backed up to the bed with eyes and mouth perfect circles of astonishment while she sat, gingerly, as if the bed were made of eggs she didn't want to crush.

"So . . . that's it!" Tyrone shouted. Then, more laughingly, "My stepmother and her nasty little games are well known by everyone in Louie." As on several occasions before, he felt the urge to snap that golden neck of Jacinta's.

Tyrone went on as if the conversation hadn't taken a turn. "Without banns, there will be this week a hastily planned wedding performed by Marrying Squire Williams. Nothing will stop this joining now. The babe is mine and no one will find cause to name him a whore's son."

With that remark Tyrone went downstairs to await Angel's coming. Angel glanced about the room wild-eyed while Hannah regarded the brown holland with surprise and mild distaste. She had never seen Angel look so untidy and beggarly; she could have been a simple housemaid but for her aristocratic beauty.

Angel hesitated in donning a fresh, simple frock she'd altered. "Hannah, I have not eaten since early this morning, and I fear I shall faint from hunger."

Hannah realized Angel was stalling. She chuckled, saying, "Don't worry, love, he'll catch you if that occasion should arise, and upon your arrival at Cresthaven you can fill your belly to your heart's content. Cresthaven boasts haute cuisine when he is in residence, I've heard."

"But . . . Hannah, just when I began thinking I knew him— oh, I must start from the beginning. Come, help me with my toilette while I tell you the entire story. There is not much time."

And so, leaving nothing out, Angel revealed all that had taken place since she had left her home, with much animation over the better parts and with just as much low spirit over the lesser. When Angel was finished Hannah fastened the frock and held Angel at arm's length.

"You are as much an enigma as Mr. Hunter is himself, and you love him, Angel." Hannah paused. "I'm not certain, but I think he's in love with you too, and doesn't realize it himself yet."

"You heard him, Hannah, he cares only for the child that I shall bear him. Nothing of love has he ever mentioned."

Hannah carried slippers to Angel, worried at the same time that her friend might do something foolish, like try to leave Cresthaven once the child was born. She shuddered, picturing little Angel the wife of such an infamous rogue, even though he was the wealthiest man in all Louisiana Territory.

Angel took the desired items from the trunks to arrange them neatly into a portmanteau, along with the serviceable frocks she and Hannah had altered to fit her. Next she searched her mind for something that would leave Hannah untroubled when she was gone from Gayarre.

"Hannah, we will still see much of one another, and I demand you visit Cresthaven as often as you can."

For the first time in days, Hannah giggled, "I'm sure you won't be lonesome, Angel, with such an interesting man to keep you company."

"Oh dear, I just hope Wesley can find it in his heart to forgive me," Angel said, but then thought that *she* could never forgive him, though, for trying to rape her earlier.

"Yes, Wesley is put out, and I'm afraid the Hunters have outdone him again. Tyrone's father easily duped my brother in a game of chance. It was Wesley's land-greedy nature that lost him the northwest plot when he played it against Hunter's west woods—Cypress Haunt."

"I'm sorry, Hannah, to play a part in it . . . indirectly," Angel murmured.

"Bosh! Now you need not fret that Wesley will attend the wedding, but you will send *me* a message when the nuptials will take place?"

"You can count on it, as you will be the very first to know, Hannah," she said at the same moment Jenny peered bug-eyed around the door to inform her that Mr. Hunter was becoming impatient. "Inform Mr. Hunter that I shall be along in a few moments, Jenny."

The portmanteau with Angel's few personal belongings was now folded shut and one of the servants entered to tote the large bag down. Hannah slid her gaze toward the arching trunks and opened her mouth to speak.

"Hush! They are yours now, Hannah," Angel said smilingly. She patted her belly lightly. "Besides, in a few months I would have to part with them anyway."

With that Angel drew a deep breath, making her way downstairs to meet her destiny.

I have you fast in my fortress,
And will not let you depart,
But put you down into the dungeon
In the round-tower of my heart.
—Henry W. Longfellow

Chapter Nine

1

Tyrone paced back and forth like a caged leopard and halted only long enough to put out his smoke in the steadily growing tray of half-smoked ciganos. Black fury glowered across Wesley's hooded lids, watching the object of his malcontent, a devious plan taking root in his mind. He could not prove to Claiborne that Tyrone had been a smuggler; Tyrone's father, having been a City Guard, would only cover up for his son as in past times. Tyrone's influence in the city couldn't be denied, as there was a penchant for miscreants and mischief there. Whatever would be, for now, he still wanted Angeline and he meant to have her back one way or another. He would tread cautiously, for his enemies would always be just one step ahead of him. Silent and defeated for the time being, he slouched down further into his chair to await the inevitable.

By the time Angel descended the stairs, Wesley was well on his way to being pie-eyed as he drained his glass for the fifth time since coming down to the salon. If he had exchanged two words with Tyrone, it would have been a miracle. Tyrone waited in the opening with his back to Wesley, a muscle working along his jawbone, and he stood taller, almost at attention, when that first bit of proper muslin appeared and her full length came slowly down into full view.

When Tyrone made no motion to either speak or move forward, Angel began to fret that her appearance didn't meet with his approval. His eyes raked her slowly, like daggers recognizing their target. She halted midway, then went on until she reached the bottom step. She felt a chill like rime at her back when his steady gaze riveted on her abdomen possessively. She placed a hand to her belly to break the contact.

"Is something amiss, sir?" she questioned to break the embarrassing silence.

"It's about time you came down," Tyrone snapped, causing her to flinch at the bitterness of his voice.

Without another word to either Angel or the man in slouched stupor behind him, Tyrone strode swiftly to open the door himself, snatched up the portmanteau, then gestured with a nod for Angel to proceed him. Before she went out into the night that was much like another that had lighted her path to Gayarre, she cast a glimpse over her shoulder to where Hannah stood at the top of the stairs looking small and forlorn.

Outside, tendrils of late summer fog clung to the elegant equipage and the ominous shape of the attendant unfolded, coming alert from his slouched position. He yawned widely and called down a greeting to the night travelers. Tyrone grunted in reply and Angel followed with a softly spoken "Hello" to Caspar.

Angel felt a lingering quiver in her limbs as she settled herself back into the plush cushions after Tyrone's warm hands had connected with her waist securely to guide her inside. He came down beside her while one arm reached out to pull the door shut with a click. The carriage started fluidly into motion as Caspar steered the mighty mares down the winding lane to the main road. Angel stared straight ahead to avert her gaze from the pale ray of lantern light spreading across their laps and the lean fingers resting casually upon well-tailored knees, so near her own.

Silence reigned and her senses began to swim from the reek of brandy mixed with tobacco and the warm body pressed too close for any comfort. Unconsciously she began to toy with her tattered reticule. Tyrone seemed highly perturbed and again it crossed her mind that he thought her appearance unsuitable for presentation to Cresthaven. As plainly dressed as she was, he most likely was having second thoughts about bringing her into his beautiful home. Too, she wanted to die each time her stomach growled like a ravenous lion on the brink of starvation.

Presently Tyrone snapped his head around so swiftly that Angel started. She peered up at him and though his features were somewhat obscured she could make out the harsh, set lines of his jaw and the angry scowl drawing together dark brows above glittering eyes.

"Give me that damn thing!" he growled into her face.

"What?" She was at a total loss as to what he wanted from her.

He continued to glare at her as his hand reached into her lap and grasped the tattered reticule she had been worrying with nervous fingers. He tucked it swiftly on his other side and bent his head to watch her own droop momentarily before her chin lifted and she stared outside at the questing moon that tried dappling the fields of night here and there.

"I am sorry, Tyrone," she began timorously, "that I annoyed you so, but I am slightly weary and totally famished—" she bit off in embarrassment.

His quick temper flaring, he asked, "What has that got to do with your jitters?" He waited for a reply but none was forthcoming. "Never mind. We are almost home now," he ended gruffly.

Home. Angel tried not thinking about where her heart yearned to fly; not here, not with this unfeeling man, did she want to put down roots. She fell silent, cherishing the stillness for the time being, and tried disregarding the tension of nerve and sinew beside her. She couldn't believe that this day had not yet ended.

The carriage seemed to move on the last stretch at a snail's pace. A tempest raged within Tyrone as his conflicting emotions involved every facet of his being. When the wall of hedge was reached, marking the last mile to Cresthaven, he was feeling thorough disgust at himself for having treated Angel as if she were a captive once again and no better than a scullery maid. He couldn't name his anger that caused such a turmoil in his innards, but he yearned to touch her, please her, and make her laugh that mellifluous sound he loved. He wanted to be gentle and understanding, but damn, his male pride got the better of him, wouldn't allow him to crawl on his knees to any woman, least of all to this one, who spurned him every chance she got.

What did she think he was anyway—a eunuch white with age? Or so blind and stupid that he couldn't see her naive gestures and sense her overweening disgust at his advances? He would be damned if he was going to press himself upon her anymore, upon a woman who detested him. For it was plain to see that her thoughts dwelled upon another. She was mooning, no doubt, for a lover awaiting her return in England, or, perhaps it was Wesley Gayarre she regretted having to leave. In any case, she was going to be *his* wife, and that gave him plenty of time to do what must be done.

Splashed with pale moon and from a distance, Angel noticed for the first time three lighted dormers protruding from the roof atop the sprawling mansion. Peeper frogs noisily guarded the placid pond that bordered the drive, and bearded live oak reminded her of a frightful scene in the Baratarian swamp. Had she really visited Cresthaven earlier in the day, that house built on a rise at the end of the lane curving back toward the river? Her head bobbed, her eyes blinked drowsily. Yes, she thought she had.

The carriage halted and before Angel knew it, she was being swept down by strong arms that encircled her waist, very gently, and made her feel secure. In her drowsiness she failed to notice it was Caspar, not Tyrone, who helped her to alight. Blinking away the brightness spilling from the house, Angel made out a thin frame coming toward her.

"Miss Angeline, so good to see you again," Della said cheerfully. "C'mon, honey-pie, right on upstairs with me now. Maids Daisy Mae and Sarah was waitin', but they're pooped out. Bein' an old night owl myself, I don't sleep till the house is bedded down proper. 'Cept for Mr. Hunter, he's a night critter too." She chuckled. "You must be plumb tuckered out by now, honey."

Uncaring where Tyrone had taken himself to, Angel followed like a weary puppy treading behind the housekeeper, on up the grand staircase, where at the top they turned left to follow the long hall to a massive front bedchamber. Della

360

gestured toward the now dark windows, reflecting the candles' glows.

"You can see the Old Devil river from up here, dappled by moon at night 'n shimmerin' in day by Ol' Sol," Della said.

A generous repast of tender squab from the pigeonnier followed, swept into the room upon a large silver tray carried stiffly by a gaunt, middle-aged man. Angel surveyed the lovely, dainty appointments cast in subdued light, the four-poster with coverlet folded down invitingly to display creamy silken bedding and plumped pillows fat as brooding hens, in relief.

Della waited for footman Joseph to be gone before she informed Angel that this bedchamber had been occupied by the former mistress, Tyrone's sweet mother, God rest her soul. Della hovered about while Angel attacked the delicious fare with much gusto and drank greedily of the cool lemonade. She watched contentedly as Della proceeded to put away her meager belongings from the portmanteau that had somehow occupied the room before she had herself.

After she had hung the few frocks in the wardrobe and filled but one small drawer in the chiffonier with undergarments and such, Della brought the solitary nightshift and coarse robe to the bedside. Though she stared at the poor garments she remained silent, laying them across the bed while Angel began disrobing immediately. The housekeeper's eyes twinkled merrily at the glorious sight of the naked little tummy bulge that housed the future master of Cresthaven.

A man child, yessir, Della thought to herself. Then, proudly: After all, it was she who brought this little girl where she truly belonged; and that had come, that secret, after much probing from Mr. Hunter. And him, he had gone off to Gayarre like shot from a mighty cannon. Seeing that, there was no doubt in Della's mind as to whose seed little Angeline bore. That man had ordered the front bedchamber swept, aired, bed made fresh, and a delicious repast prepared for her coming. He had even sent a boy off posthaste in a light carriage, with more than enough persuasive coin to fetch that roly-poly redhead to come stitch up some new glad rags for his bride-to-be. She shook her head. The little girl sure needed them if she was going to be *Mistress of Cresthaven.*

Sweeping back the fine gauze that draped the bed, Della shook her head thinking that Cresthaven sure had its share of mysteries, past and present. She waited while Angel climbed in to settle herself comfortably. If this little lady had knowledge of the conspiracy between herself and the Mister, she sure was keeping it to herself graciously. Pure and kind, just like the past lady had been, Della mused. If only Tyrone shared her thoughts on the subject of his dead mama.

Hunger satiated, and dreamily floating upon a sensuous silken cloud of sheer luxury, Angel could barely murmur to return the housekeeper's "Good night," as she went out the door, closing it softly behind her. Angel snuggled the downy pillow close and sighed, "Be gentle with me and my unborn child, Cresthaven." She fell fast asleep to the echoing cry of a forlorn whippoorwill somewhere outside her window.

Giving their tuneful morning benediction, gaily twittering birds drew circles about the upper half of the house, stirring Angel in her silken cocoon. Coming awake, she stretched full length and curled her toes into the slippery bedding, yawned wide, and breathed deliciously deep of the yellow jasmine wafting in through open french doors. She felt dreamily misplaced as she sat up to rub her eyes, opened them wide, then stared around in awe at what she'd missed fully seeing the evening before.

The slender elegance of the furnishings caught her eye first. On her left was a dainty dressing table occupying the space next to the marble fireplace, and skimming her eyes down the bordering, polished dark oak flooring, directly across from her, she saw a high rosewood chiffonier. A long wardrobe of the same wood took up the most part of one wall. Her scan riveted to a pair of tall, slim doors which, no doubt, led to a sitting room. Plenty of time to explore later; right now she continued her perusal of the room.

French doors stood open on either side of a corner window seat and Angel, wondering why so much window space, swung her bare legs over the bed to get up and investigate. She delighted in the plush pile of the rich Persian carpet beneath her feet as she went to see what could be so interesting as to

362

warrant such extravagant construction.

Moments later her curiosity was rewarded twofold by the most breathtaking sight ever imaginable. Looking down from the window on the great winding river on such a fine day made her heart soar like a bird in flight. In such elegant surroundings she felt much like a cherished princess in a tower chamber of some great castle. She strolled through the doors leading onto the gallery and leaned out over the railing.

Cresthaven indeed was a vast dreamworld all its own. And she was to see just how true this was, when later she would wander the seemingly endless halls that led into room upon room of unbelievable spaciousness.

Cocking an ear, Angel whirled about abruptly to the sounds of a husky female voice followed by a more youthful, timorous-sounding one.

"Mademoiselle?"

"Mamzelle, are you here?"

Coming in from the sunwashed gallery she was confronted by three pairs of searching eyes, two servile, the third politely studying the dainty frame she saw. The two girls bobbed a curtsy, each in turn as they introduced themselves as her personal maids. Angel gave the girls a friendly "Hello" before her regard slid to the middle-aged woman who still seemed fascinated, speechless. Angel waited for an introduction, becoming slightly embarrassed in her nightshift that left her slim legs bare, as she wondered at the same time who this dumbstruck woman could be.

"Ah! I am sorry *petite*, but you are s*ooo* lovely, so clean, so fresh—and young," she crooned. "I am Mimi, and M'sieur must not have inform you that I come a day ahead to begin to outfit you in complete new wardrobe. Oooh—" she crooned again, her eyes twinkling merrily, "A wedding gown that will be pleasure for Mimi to create for such perfection." Then Mimi clucked her tongue. "It is too bad you have only a parlor wedding, M'sieur say to me this morning over breakfast."

Angel's eyes widened in surprise. "He told you that?"

Mimi tossed red curls winding up into a tower above her head, and laughed. *"Mais oui.* And he say the gown must be the finest I have ever stitch for him," she said without thinking,

363

for her mind was preoccupied; she was anxious to begin her work. "Now, I go to get my things and we take measurements after you have bath and breakfast, *non?*"

Angel had overslept horribly, she realized, and her afternoon was well taken up after she'd bathed, been served a delicious meal in her room, turned this way and that as she was fitted for the wedding gown, frocks, silk brocades, chemises, chemisettes. She had only to ask for "whatever else your little heart desires," Mimi said, echoing M'sieur.

"Oh, Mimi, I shan't ask for more," Angel told the seamstress. "I am afraid I've far overspent his pocketbook already."

"Never!" Mimi merely said, and Angel fell silent.

It was nigh onto the dinner hour when Mimi and the maids finally left the young woman to lie down, and the quiet spell found Angel slumbering peacefully, so peacefully in fact that when Sarah returned to announce the evening meal, she had to tiptoe out, not wishing to disturb the weary mistress.

As the lavender-splash sunset sank lower Angel finally stirred in the huge, canopied bed. She rose refreshed, donned a serviceable green frock, brushed out her squeaky-clean hair, and drew it into a glossy knot, with stray tendrils hugging her cheeks. She lingered at the dressing table, wondering what was expected of her for the remainder of the day. She wasn't hungry yet, not tired, but suddenly bored, so she decided to roam the upper half of the house, hoping at the same time she wouldn't run into Tyrone.

If Tyrone would mind her wandering through his house, she could not guess. She hadn't seen him since he strangely disappeared the evening before and left her to the servants. Well, she couldn't very well stay locked in her room like a timid mouse, and the very idea of Tyrone's minding if she roamed in what was to be her home, too, was preposterous.

The decorous door leading supposedly to a sitting room was locked, so she slipped quietly into the hall and stood for a moment contemplating the heavy double doors directly across from her room. Still, as she crossed the short distance she couldn't shake the feeling that she was some thief in the night, snooping about. Her hand went tentatively to the knob and then she gave the door a shove and entered.

The morning-room was gray in late day, but the lacy curtains took in a little light, enough for her to find and scratch flint to light a slim taper. In moments the Aubusson carpet and Gobelin upholstered chairs, Egyptian lounges, and tapestries all glowed with mellow light. Angel exclaimed in childish delight when she fixed her meandering gaze upon the satinwood china closet and went immediately to examine the Commedia dell'Arte housed behind the curving glass doors. She beheld Meissen-style flower sprays and porcelain figures of Harlequin, Pulcinella, Pantaloon, and Scaramouche. Here she laughed lightly, recalling Pierre Le Naisse and his naming her a female Scaramouche.

"How lovely," Angel breathed as her fingers hovered near the reflecting glass. She didn't dare touch for she had no desire to leave smudges there.

"Window-shopping?" A deep but youthful voice sounded with a touch of humor.

Angel whirled about in surprise, then smiled at once. "Oh! Nikki! How wonderful to see you, and just when I was feeling quite alone and melancholy."

Nikki grinned impishly. "Oh, you were, were you? And who was that I heard chuckling and exclaiming over bits of porcelain, then?"

Angel's laugh tinkled gaily. "Ah, Nikki, you have always made me feel greatly distracted and relieved from a bevy of worldly care. Your presence is always an especial enjoyment to me. Please come and sit with me for a spell. I have been beset with excited, giggling maids the entire afternoon and feel much like a human pincushion. Though Mimi is a sweet soul, she is the most talkative woman I've ever come across."

Angel continued to chatter aimlessly until Nikki held up his hand in a limbo of male distress. "Whoa, princess," he said, taking her hand to guide her to a plush sofa. She sat and he occupied the violin-backed chair across from her. "Sounds like the yammerbug has bitten m'lady also. Now, you tell Dr. Nik everything, 'cause I know something is bothering you—Angel. You know, Angeline's a very lovely name and shame on you for keeping it from us all this time."

"I'm sorry, Nikki, but—" she bit off, then shrugged with a deep sigh.

"Begin somewhere, princess," Nikki tried.

"Oh, Nikki, here I am preparing for my own wedding half the day and I don't even know when it will take place, who will attend . . . nothing. I am treated like a pampered queen, then a mindless adolescent who is not allowed in on a deep dark secret. When I questioned Mimi and the maids they were closemouthed and deflected my questions with trivia. And—" she sniffed, "neither hide nor hair have I seen of the groom since last night when he deposited me into the hands of the servants. Not that they were unkind, mind you, but. . . ." Her voice trailed as she ran a slim hand down from her waist lovingly. She shrugged, unable to say what else was troubling her mind.

Nikki, catching the gesture, cleared his throat and lifted his gaze from her lap to meet her preoccupied stare sheepishly. "It's true then. You *are* having a baby," he said all too hastily.

At first Angel was shocked, then her laughter bubbled at the ludicrousness of his words. One minute she was giggling and then set to weep the next. Could this moody shift be part of being in the "family way?" she wondered.

"So true, Nikki, and the whole blasted Territory no doubt is by now aware of it! Therein lies my grievous situation," Angel said, her eyes drawn to a Greek urn atop a marble stand.

Nikki gently pulled her face around to face him. "You mean you are a little afraid that Tyrone has cruelly invited half the country here to gawk at the poor girl he got breeding?"

"Yes . . . but I pray he has not, Nikki, for I would die of shame." She hung her head. Had Mimi mentioned that it was to be a parlor-wedding, or had she only dreamt it this morning?

"Is that all?" Nikki drawled, actually believing there was more that she was not telling him.

Angel nodded slowly. How could she tell Nikki of her worst fear? That Tyrone would grow tired of her presence, perhaps even whisk away the babe the moment it was born? Why would he need the babe's mother? Wet nurses there were aplenty in the slave cottages, she had learned. If only she could measure swords with Tyrone as she had done before when equipped with courage. Bah! A lot of good that had done her afterward!

"Oh, Lord, how weak kneed I've become," Angel groaned inwardly. All for the love of one man, a man so handsome, so magnetic, with an air of elegant simplicity that made her heart ache in desire to be with him, hold him close to her breast, run her fingers through that tawny mane of hair. But it would not, could not, be thus, for she would hold herself in check until the day to go dawned.

"I'll let you in on a little secret, princess. It's going to be a very slim line of guests to arrive at Cresthaven's doors. I know my cousin and crowds are one of his pet peeves—"

"Devil take!"

"Hey—what's wrong, princess?"

"Did—you—say—'cousin'?" Angel hammered out slowly.

"Aaaaaawww, Angel, don't take it so hard," Nikki drawled with a grin. "We were—I mean I was going to tell you tonight, but you didn't give me the chance to wait."

"And why, Nikki, did not Mr. Hunter tell me long ago? It is just not fair! How could you both hold out on me this long?" she asked, half angry, half laughing.

"Tut-tut, Angel. How could *you* hold your name from *us* this long?" he tossed back in a velvety voice.

Angel suppressed a giggle behind her hand, then her smile grew wider and wider until she burst out in a fit of laughter.

"Forgive me?" Nikki begged when she had calmed.

"I suppose so," she said, looking thoughtful. "Only if you do something for me?" she cajoled.

He grinned with boyish charm, saying, "You just name it."

"I greatly wish that my very special friend be present at my wedding, so would you be so kind as to fetch her when the time is come, dear Nikki?" Angel said, peering up at him from her russet-gold lashes.

"Your wish is my command, m'lady. Now, just tell me who she is and I'll personally see that she gets an invite and a ride here in my grand carriage," Nikki chuckled.

Suddenly Angel's eyes lit up and smiling mysteriously, she said, "Her name is Hannah. Hannah McCormick. She is Wesley Gayarre's half-sister. She lives on the bordering plantation with him and his daughter."

367

Nikki only shrugged. "I'm green in this parish of Louie, but if it's the plantation I saw on my way here, that should be very easy to find." He took her nod for affirmation of that. "Well . . . is she pretty?" he finally asked, curious.

"She is . . . indescribable," Angel said, cocking her head thoughtfully. "You will have to see for yourself, Nikki. To me she is the most wonderful lady in the world, besides my— Chris . . . Christine." Her voice fell and her chin sagged forlornly.

Nikki stood brusquely and went to examine the Greek urn Angel had studied only minutes before. He kept his back turned to her as he spoke.

"We are still working on it, Angel. The crew of smugglers search for your mother day and night, taking shifts, not to mention Tyrone's many acquaintances. She'll turn up someday . . . soon," he said, as he turned halfway around. He shrugged, adding, "I just know it."

Angel bit down hard on her lip to keep from crying. She glanced longingly at the french doors, feeling the need for some air to revive her from her gloom. Nikki intercepted her glance and went to swing the doors wide, breathing deeply of the blistering night air commingled with the breath of fragrant moon-yellow jasmine.

Not a leaf stirred in the motionless air that smelled of rain from where they stood on the gallery. Angel watched the ripples on that timeless river, like a great black serpent slithering on its belly. She shivered despite the heat. This sweet longing was leaving her weaker each day, especially now in his home, so close to him yet, worlds apart. How was she going to face him on their wedding day? Furthermore, how was she going to depart Cresthaven and leave her heart behind?

Below them a dark carriage suddenly wheeled up to the house and careened to curve around to the back.

"Who was that, Nikki?" Angel questioned curiously.

Nikki shrugged disinterestedly. "Probably just one of the servants, maybe Old Saul returning with supplies. Or Tyrone's new manservant, James Cordell, finally showing."

But Nikki kept his face averted so that she couldn't see the hateful twist of his lips. His smile reappeared as he turned to engage her attention on something that should interest her.

"You are not without a confidant as long as I reside at Cresthaven, princess," Nikki said simply.

"Nikki! How wonderful. Cresthaven is to be your home, too?" She smiled genuinely.

"It's big enough for a company of dragoons. But I'll only stay here until I earn my way and can build my own little home up the river apiece. My only problem is finding the right woman to share it with. Until then if you should need conversation, my room is down the hall from yours. The first east-facing bedroom. Tap once and I'll come to meet you in the morning room. . . ."

Unknown to them, a shadowy figure moved stealthily just inside the doors and then was quickly gone.

"Now tell me this, my confidant. Have you learned something I should know?" She peeped up at him.

"I thought you'd never ask. Yes, I have." Here he halted, recalling just this morning how he had overheard Mimi's gasp as his cousin demanded that the wedding gown be finished in seven days, no later. Tyrone, saying he could count on someone else to meet the deadline, withdrew a weighty purse from out of his breeches pocket to count out a goodly sum in coin. Enticed, Mimi's eyes riveted on the purse, and she replied with haste that she would send for her girl immediately to aid her. Excused with that, Mimi had rushed up to meet the bride with Sarah and Daisy Mae in tow. Nikki came back to the present, saying, "You will become a blushing bride the first part of September. By then all should be in preparation for the nuptials and feast afterward."

"I shan't see the groom till then?" Angel asked dejectedly.

"Not a chance. Believe it or not, Tyrone is a bit old-fashioned, so don't be put out if he pointedly ignores your presence till then. I must caution you—his bedroom is on the other side of the sitting room. So be watchful yourself, he's been a bear the last few days. His daytime domain is the study below to the back of the house, and when he's not there he's out riding with—ah—with Beast, his favorite steed."

"Thank you, Nikki, I shall be cautious," she said, moving with curiosity renewed as she remembered the carriage.

Nikki shuffled to block her from going that way and she peered up at him questioningly. "Nikki . . . let me pass?"

"Ummm, where are you going?" Nikki asked, leaning casually against the wall of the house.

She scanned the length of his extended arm, then faced him, saying, "This gallery wraps around the house, I noticed today. I want to see what is out back." She tossed her head jauntily. "That's all."

Nikki dropped his arm reluctantly and eased a finger into the unusual stuffiness of his shirt collar. He allowed her to pass then, following the determined young woman with a heavy tread to the back of the house. The sky in the distance quaked with the premonition of rain.

"Angel, I don't think—" Nikki began then quieted when the handsome twosome below became visible in the flooding light from the house.

Suddenly Angel was wishing she hadn't been so bullheaded as to come this way. It was too late now. If she moved but an inch forward or back, her presence would be detected by Jacinta and Tyrone, for they had shifted their position and now faced the gallery, directly below where Angel stood paralyzed with Nikki close behind. And Nikki had become just as rooted as she was; he groaned inwardly when Jacinta lifted her eyes, momentarily catching the two standing motionless. Her susurrant voice drifted up to them.

"*Mon cher*, I have missed you and our daily rides," Jacinta said, sidling closer to Tyrone. "But you will continue tomorrow, *non?*"

An indifferent air played about Tyrone's countenance and when he answered low his words were inaudible to his balcony audience. Still, he could be seen to gesture toward the house where his study and library linked together. His ruffled hair and manner of dress could give one to believe he'd been hard at work there before being interrupted. Angel read it differently, though.

Seeing her chance, Angel inched back to press herself against the wall of the house when Tyrone studied the sky behind him. She breathed a sigh of relief, but lingered in shadow to make sure she could slip along the gallery and into her room without being sighted by him. She listened as this time his deep voice resounded loud and clear.

"Yes, yes, I'll ride with you tomorrow. Now go before someone comes snooping along and sees you here with me," he told Jacinta gruffly.

Angel smothered a gasp as her knees trembled horribly and her heart thumped painfully in her breast. She twisted her head this way and that in search of Nikki, but noticed only a strange new gloominess about her. He had gone and left her alone. The moon and stars had drawn in and the heavens were robed in ominous billows. She'd learned by now how capricious the Louisiana climate could be and a distant roll of thunder underscored this as she stepped forward cautiously to peer below. Jacinta was just climbing into her carriage, this night driven by her ominous driver. Tyrone was nowhere to be seen.

Jacinta's carriage left as quickly as it had come. Angel was unaware that her tears mingled with the first drops of rain as she passed blindly by the recently closed doors of her own bedchamber. She almost passed, too, by the morning room, for it was swathed in total darkness. She spun a half-turn, stepping inside the morning room to close the doors securely against the stormy elements.

Catching her breath in little sobs, Angel leaned back against the doors, unconcerned with the dark, the house, and the maids who, no doubt, searched her out for the evening meal. Above and below she heard mantel-clocks and grandfathers chime out the hour of nine almost in total unison. Alerted, she shook herself mentally from hearing again and again the coldly harsh words Tyrone had muttered from below.

Already nine of the hour, Angel thought numbly. She must have lingered upon the gallery longer than she thought. The evening meal would have been put away hours ago. She daren't ask for something to tide her over till morning.

The hastening rain pounded against the roof as Angel, steeling herself against the hurt in her mind, made her way to go search out the doorway. Halfway across, lightning flashed to illuminate the room instantaneously. She froze, bumping into a piece of furniture in her nervous trepidation. Someone was in the room with her! Someone tall and. . . .

"Nikki . . . ?" her voice quavered, ". . . is that you?" She called as she clutched at a fine piece of Worcester porcelain to keep it from toppling to the floor.

She was answered by a scratch of flint before a taper flared and cast light upon an imposing stranger. His eyes bore into hers as she stared in helplessness at this night visitor standing across from her in the circle of most potent light. At once she felt faint, her mind racing back to the events before leaving Stonewall, boarding the *Fidelia*.

"You!" Angel said, breaking the silence.

"You remember," James Hunter stated simply, his deep voice flat, his jeweled eyes fixed upon her. He manipulated his lithe frame around the table to come and stand before her. He smiled amicably to put her alarm at ease.

"Hunter," Angel breathed, ever so softly. Then she shook her head and said louder, "What! Hunter! You are . . . Jacinta is—"

"Yes, Jacinta is my—ah—wife," he said almost distastefully. "And as you may have already guessed . . . Tyrone is my son."

"But why—why did you visit Stonewall? What did you have to do with *my* father?" She wanted to know.

"Business," he said simply.

Confusion reigned in her brain. "Business—with—my—father?"

James sauntered over to pick up the urn that Nikki had studied earlier. Angel waited for him to answer and when he remained silent, she spoke with a trace of vexation in her voice, "Sir! You are avoiding my question. What was your business with the late Beldwin Sherwood?"

"I was sorry to hear about your father's accident, my dear," James said, putting the urn back. He faced her as he explained, "Beldwin was a good sort, very clever in a game of cards. Quick and shrewd; his name got around." But not clever enough to know when he had been bested, he wanted to add.

Angel pursed her lips thoughtfully. So . . . that was their *business*. Many had come from far and near just to be closeted with Beldwin and his cronies in Stonewall's famous Gold

Salon. All the way from America to England—true. Strange, she thought, how fate twisted its gnarled fingers to intertwine lives together—but she couldn't help thinking there was more afoot than this mysterious man was telling her.

The trauma waned and her curiosity grew. "But, sir, why do you steal into your own house like a common thief in the night?"

"I have my reasons, my dear. You see, this is not my house. I left Cresthaven to Tyrone on his twentieth birthday." He shrugged. "He was heir any way you look at it," James said as he studied her from under hooded lids.

Angel missed the quick perusal of her midpoint when she asked, "If you do not mind my asking, sir, where do you live then?"

"I travel a great deal of the time, that is, when I am not in residence at my town house in New Orleans. Actually . . . my wife Jacinta lives there," he said cryptically.

"Yes, I have been there," Angel said, her slow smile brightening the room like flooding sunlight. Her eyes twinkled mischievously. First she had learned that Nikki and Tyrone were related, now, here stood Tyrone's father.

An enchantress, James Hunter thought to himself. Just as he remembered her that long ago night in her white nightgown and robe, asking for a glass of water in her father's salon.

"Now," James began, "I have something for you you must keep hidden . . . for a time anyway. A wedding gift." He drew forth from his silk vest a heart-shaped ornament dangling from a fine chain, buffed gold in the candlelight.

Angel stared in awe at the costly lavaliere he pressed into her palm. He took his tanned and freckled hand away, then gestured for her to open the heart. She did so, and a glossy curl sprang up lifelike before her eyes, winding around her tentative fingers, as if possessed of a will all its own. She lifted her head to search his face for some meaning of the strange but lovely gift.

"It belonged to Tyrone's mother—a Kent heirloom," he said simply as he began to inch back slowly.

"Oh, sir, I will treasure it always," she said tearfully. "Thank you a million times." Handling the lavaliere lovingly and studying it, she asked, "But how did you learn of the wedding, there were no banns published?" Then she shrugged lightly, answering her own question, "Of course, I should have guessed. News travels fast around . . ." Her voice trailed, for when she lifted her head he had vanished, just like he had vanished off the deck of the *Fidelia* that day, now seeming ages ago.

Angel did have her evening meal, delivered on a huge tray by the ghostlike footman, where it exchanged hands at the door to be placed at Angel's disposal by Sarah. Angel only nibbled at the roast beef, tiny buttered vegetables, and freshly baked bread. Sarah bustled about the bedchamber to put things in apple-pie order. When the Cajun Sarah took up the half-finished tray, the black maid, Daisy Mae, exchanged places with her. As Daisy Mae brushed out her lady's long hair, she informed Angel shyly that much had been accomplished that day in the careful cutting and basting of her trousseau.

Angel drifted dreamlike through the following days. She lingered mostly in the upper half of the house and strolled the gallery for fresh air. It continued to rain intermittently and when the sun peeped out occasionally and the rain halted, Angel stood out on her perch to delight in the feel of the rain-sweetened breezes. There was no time to be lonely, for the softly chattering maids surrounded her almost constantly and Mimi floated in and out with her assistant for fittings. When she was alone for short periods of time, her thoughts dwelled on the night visitor, James Hunter. She wanted to see him again and learn more of Cresthaven's history and Tyrone's life as a youth here. It might help, she thought, for her mind to be occupied otherwise. She had been self-absorbed for too long now.

Tyrone lingered in his study after Caspar and Nikki had gone to their respective places of lodging. The downstairs maid had long since removed the trays of food that the three men had partaken of. Strewn about the heavy-duty workbench and his desk were leaves of scribbled-on paper, old ledgers and accounts, and a drawing on a separate leaf for a special keelboat and a "trader." For the latter he would have to take the final plans to Baltimore sometime in the near future to have it built. Too, he wanted to put the Indiaman up for sale; she would bring in a tidy sum and right now, in time of war, she would be ideal to sell.

Tyrone and his cronies were hard at work reviving on paper the lay of the land for next year's sugar crops. They planned the leveling of a sapling section situated in the north wood that would serve two purposes: additional planting ground, which of course meant the backbreaking task of removing young but obstinate stumps, and an abundant supply of firewood to warm the hearth of Cresthaven for several years to come.

In his leather chair, Tyrone stretched out his long legs before him and crossed them upon a matching footstool. He totally disregarded the by now warmed liquor in his glass and became pensive, staring at nothing as he reached over to fiddle with a pen on the desk top. His thoughts raced back and forth between his work and his bride-to-be, and though he tried to leash his emotions and dwell on the first, the latter crept in with silken arms twining about his neck. He flipped the pen aside with a fierce movement, gritting his teeth against the uncontrollable pendulum in his brain.

So. Certain articles necessary to run a plantation would be hard to come by now that a state of war existed, and here would be where the keelboat would come in handy between Donaldsville and New Orleans. He and the tradesfolk could each in turn supply to one another those things needed. . . .

Angel. Fathomless green eyes. The blush of youth yet on her flawless cheeks. Angel in the sun with her lustrous hair unbound, gently rocking hips, softly moving breasts under a sweet, feminine frock. The blighted rose!

Curse me! Ruthlessly robbing her of that sweet, untouched purity that was hers, hers to give when the time became ripe. He spoke aloud and his voice was harshly bitter. "Now we are to be man and wife, and she wants nothing to do with me. Well, we'll see about that now, won't we, dear lady!"

He went out into the hall to take the stairs three at a time, then halted before her door, running a hand through his thick hair. What was he doing? Just what in hell was he doing, he wondered wearily. He clenched his hands into tight balls as he went into his own room where he stretched out full length, fully clothed, on his bed, where he then slept like a man drugged.

Angel steered clear of the lower back part of the house where she knew Tyrone worked, often late into the night with Caspar and Nikki. When the sound of the master's footfalls treading the stairs fell upon her ears, she would turn tail if she chanced to be traversing the hall at that time and flee to the safety and seclusion of her room. She had yet to view the huge library she knew was situated alongside the master's study, plus the many other elegant rooms yet unseen. She had already been in the front parlor while visiting with Hannah the day she'd looked upon the beautiful portrait hanging there. She could hardly wait to delight in its perfection once again.

On a cool gray morning several days after her arrival, Angel, knowing the master was out riding the fields, beseeched Della to give her a tour of the lower floor. An hour sped by fast, and after she'd gazed at length upon the portrait, they stood in the formal dining room where the wedding festivities would commence. The immense spaciousness and sparkling chandelier with serenely glowing tapers made Angel feel as if she'd entered a great and solemnly hushed cathedral. If only she could enjoy all this, Angel thought to herself as Della finally snuffed out the tapers.

That night after dining with Mimi and Nikki in the smaller dining room, just as elegant as the formal one, Angel sat propped up in her downy bed with an old gothic novel chosen from the library. Glancing up from the scary passage she'd been half-absorbed in, she retraced her steps to when she'd stood before the ornate double-doors of the library. She recalled running her hands longingly along the leather bindings of the vast collection. Halting her hand, she had spied one among many she had never even heard of. Plucking the gothic novel *The Castle of Otranto* from the endless rows of lovely books, she looked to Della for approval of her borrowing from the master's collection.

"Fiddlesticks! You go on right ahead," Della had said, "don't you let Mr. Hunter worry you none, honey chile.

What's his is going to be yours too, any day now."

Now Angel thought to herself as she had earlier—and what is mine will be his also. Of flesh, that is, for of worldly goods here she really had none. Now England, that was an entirely different story. Much inheritance awaited her and the son she would bear. There she would ultimately go someday to claim it, and her husband would never discover her. She would leave with but a few old frocks tucked away in the tattered portmanteau, and her child, when he could withstand the rigors of a long voyage.

This was her sole secret, and if she could have found a way to go immediately, she would have. But traveling alone and pregnant would be risky indeed. She could even miscarry crossing the unpredictable seas.

"If only Christine was here," Angel said to the high-ceilinged room as she plumped her pillow. She pressed back into it, sighing deeply.

Angel reflected all the way back to when such dreams of the future with a love to hold, a husband, rosy-cheeked children aplenty, and a happy home, hadn't meant much to her. But now she would have been a faithful wife, a loving mother, yes, and if Tyrone loved her now just a teeny bit she would have made him proud as a peacock to see her fill the position honorably.

Angel gazed longingly toward the tall door that separated her bedchamber from his with only a sitting room between. No, she couldn't. Only a frown of disgust would she receive if she foolishly went to pour out her heart's love to him. Then again, he might just take her to his bed with lust foremost in his mind, and her heart would sink emptier and hungrier than ever before.

With the patter of rain outside to lull her to sleep, Angel dreamed of haunted and mist-shrouded gothic castles, the book trailing in her fingers. She awoke in the mid of night as the full moon sat on its midnight throne, and she felt her thin nightgown sticking to her in the muggy night air. Rain long ceased, the stars came in with a new warm air blowing, moving across the carpet indolently to barely stir the fine gauze draping her bed. Slippery and damp in the new lawn nightgown

377

Mimi had given her just that day, Angel, for comfort's sake cast the thing off, and in the raw, drifted back into deep slumber. She clutched the dainty lavaliere until it loosely draped over her fingers. The Kent heirloom; it belonged to her now.

2

A humid haze hung over Cresthaven the morning of the wedding. Not a leaf stirred outside, but inside the household had awakened early to the tune of frantic haste as one and all did their parts in last minute preparations. Delicious odors of meats, sauces of every kind, cakes and desserts wafted in through the open windows of the mansion, trailing from the bake-house, where Cresthaven's brand-new cook, Melvin, whipped up his culinary feast. The slaves, too, were not without their own gay liveliness, for in every cottage preparations for a little feast were in order to celebrate the joining of the master and his new mistress.

Lantern-jawed Preacher Williams and his wife Hilda preceded the trickling in of folk who had been arriving since noon from upstream and down in keelboats, while some preferred to arrive in carriages, rented or owned. Indeed, the number did not exceed that of fifty-some folk, and it would be discussed for some time to come as a very small wedding they had attended, especially being that of one wealthy groom, Tryone Michael Hunter. Discussed yes, but politely, discreetly, never causing eyebrows to lift, for these were the chosen few Tyrone had elected to do business with. Too, the wives of the menfolk were of the elegantly meek sort, and Tyrone had made their acquaintances several times while attending Williams's parish in the past.

Armand Bujold, in striking blue uniform, sauntered in with a petite brunette on his arm. Jacinta Hunter, her lips pursed haughtily, auburn curls piled *à la Grecque* atop her head, accepted the hand of a planter who helped her alight. She had donned her best in jewels and gown this day in hopes of outshining the blushing bride. But the truth of the matter was that Jacinta had overdressed to the point of garishness. Nikki

Peroune escorted Hannah McCormick through the few gathered below in the hall. She smiled timidly up at him before he released her arm and she ascended to look in on the bride upstairs. Again, Nikki's dark frown returned as he watched the lovely girl mount.

Several hours before the wedding a message had been relayed to Angel. Her smile became more radiant, if that could be possible. Hannah was to be one of the witnesses, as was Nikki, to stand alongside the bride and groom as they exchanged their vows.

But now, Angel sat before the mirror frowning at what Daisy Mae and Sarah were doing to her hair. They were securing the mass of it around her head and pinning curls this way and that, with no particular style whatsoever. Angel cocked an eyebrow in puzzlement as they continued to create flattened curls about her head, allowing tiny tendrils to hug her warm and suddenly pulsating temples. Over her head, the maids exchanged mysterious smiles as their mistress's jaw dropped lower and lower and her eyes grew rounder at the non-hairdo.

"Now see here!" Angel said and was about to scold them further when Mimi swept into the room with a flowing creation held up proudly high in her hand.

As the maids hung silently back, Angel turned to stare amazedly at the seed-pearl-embellished headdress fashioned of the same fine lace as the flowing veil. Mimi, with a triumphant look plastered on her wearily smiling face, came forward to gently arrange the headdress on Angel's head. The low, turban-style piece wound snugly about her hair, leaving the tendrils of hair to peep out at her cheeks and temples. Other than these few wisps of hair showing, her crowning glory was concealed completely. The total effect in the looking glass was exotically classical with her tiny face framed thus, and the long sweep of her dark lashes was especially noticeable in the stunning profile.

"Ahhh, pièce de résistance!" Mimi crooned as she leaned back to glow proudly over her handiwork.

Angel brushed a single happy tear aside and stood to hug Mimi in momentary thankfulness. Mimi had slaved long hours into the night to complete her trousseau, Angel realized.

"Now, I will crush your gown, sentimental girl," Mimi cried with glad tears as she held Angel at arm's length.

Together the maids spun about the tall pier glass mirror for their mistress to observe herself full length. The empire-waisted cream silk gown was stitched in simple but elegantly slim, flowing lines. The only bit of embellishment on the gown was the sprigged design of tiny seed pearls sewn into the snug, uplifting bodice and the flared sleeves that draped femininely to the elbows. The dewy-eyed bride in the mirror stared back at her with fixity, the impression of poise belying the turbulent pounding in her chest and the quaking of her limbs beneath her flowing skirt. There was a radiant cast on her face, and a tentative smile full of hopes for the future.

A shadow of doubt blurred the beauteous vision in the mirror for but an instant before the young bride smiled brightly once again. She was determined to make the most of this day, to spoil nothing for the guests who had come from far and near, and, especially, for the man downstairs waiting, who would promise to love, honor, and obey till death us do part. Angel prayed silently: Please God, let it come true.

Then quietly, Mimi and the maids hastened from the room, stepping back to allow Hannah to enter and closing the door behind her. Hannah silently watched her friend for a moment before she made a move forward. Angel's lace-turbaned head was bowed in what appeared to be quiet meditation as she waited for the signal of music that would soon summon her to go stand at the top of the stairs. Her head lifted then and she stared wistfully out the window to where the haziness gave a primeval cast to the grounds.

"Angel," Hannah said tentatively, "you outshine the golden rays of the setting sun."

With an effervescent laugh Angel whirled, took up her skirts in both hands, and, on slippered feet, rushed to greet her friend with flushed and glowing cheek pressed against Hannah's for an instant. Angel took time to compliment Hannah on the lovely lavender-blue of her new gown and Hannah blushed with speechlessness, thinking that her friend always gave of herself graciously, never greedy to receive compliments as most women were wont to do.

"Oh, Hannah, I am so breathlessly excited that I'm afraid if I so much as utter a word my voice will come out slurred, as if I've sipped wine in my room all day."

Hannah kept one side of her face averted as she spoke. "Stuff and nonsense! You are doing fine right now. Don't worry, it'll be you who will intoxicate the others, not the wine *they* will consume this afternoon."

Della entered, clucking excitedly. "Glory be, ain't you like the first blossom of spring, all peaches and cream and honey." Tears sparkled in her eyes and she dabbed at the foolish things with her apron, adding, "And young Mr. Hunter, cocky as a barnyard rooster in all his finery and flippin' out his timepiece every other minute." She cocked an ear. "Music's started. Time to go down now, honey bunch."

Before Angel knew what was happening, Hannah had planted a light kiss on her damp brow and disappeared. The violins reached Angel and she set forth mechanically, placing one satin slipper in front of the other as she went to stand at the top of the stairs. She peered down shyly at Nikki who waited, standing erect as a starched young general with his arm bent to receive hers. His soft brown eyes sparkled suspiciously of moisture. For good luck Angel had pinned the Kent heirloom to the bodice of her chemise, next to her heart.

The front parlor had been adorned with Angel's favorite flowers—white mums and yellow roses, fresh from the greenhouse just an hour beforehand. All the french doors stood wide to hopefully catch some breath of air from outdoors, though not a lace curtain nor a velvet balloon drapery stirred. Everything had the air of quiet expectation; lacy fans held by ladies halted on cue when the bride and her handsome escort paused a moment, framed in the doorway. All eyes were riveted on the picture of bridal perfection.

Smiling sweetly, Angel's eyes scanned the room in that instant to take in the womenfolk with their heads tilted dreamily, the men looking uncomfortable in their starched collars and dark suits of brocade. Yet all smiled upon Angel in a friendly fashion, making her feel these invited guests were amicable and warmhearted. All but for one. Jacinta's dark eyes were bitter pools of careless jealousy and her tinted red lips above her fan disfigured her otherwise handsome countenance. Her eyes flicked from Angel's dainty frame to Tyrone's broad back. The groom turned then to look upon his bride, and if he displayed any emotion, no one was the wiser, for his countenance was cast unreadable, even to Angel. Jacinta smiled with smug determination and lifted her chin a notch, the bones at her neck strained.

Angel paled cowardly for an instant before Nikki's comforting arm stirred then ushered her down the makeshift aisle between the guests lined straight up to the hearth where Tyrone and Hannah stood waiting before the austere Williams. Feeling him beside her but not seeing anything but the dark blue sleeve of Tyrone's fine cutaway, Angel bowed her head when the Marrying Squire began to speak.

"For this day—" Williams began, "God has granted us permission—to use this parlor—as his—holy place to join this couple . . . together . . ." he paused to glance up at Tyrone from beneath his horn-rimmed spectacles, ". . . in holy matrimony." He glimpsed the quirk of a smile at the groom's mouth.

Now a hushed silence fell, and for all the deep reverence that came over them one and all, they could have been in a great holy cathedral. There was only one unexpected measure of rudeness—a woman could be heard to cough out loud, insultingly.

Williams cleared his throat and began, "Dearly beloved, we are gathered here. . . ." and continued until the vows were to be exchanged.

Angel heard Tyrone's deep voice saying, "I do," and then her own pledge, seeming to come from afar. Plain gold bands were exchanged as Nikki caught Hannah's eye and a glow emanated from his. Angel felt warm fingers, steady, sliding the ring onto her finger, and finally she peered up at her new husband. A spark of tenderness glowed in his eyes and Angel confusedly thought she detected a look of triumph flood his face.

"Mr. Hunter," Williams interrupted, "you may kiss the bride now."

Tyrone needed no coaxing as he suddenly bent over her with

his lips parted to seal the vows. He pulled her up with the flat of his hand at her back and she had to stand on her toes. She flushed and trembled at the ardor of his kiss bruising her mouth, and drank in the clean, male smell of him. Tyrone grew bolder before his surprised audience as he pressed her swell of bosom against his chest. Someone coughed again, and the moist, clinging lips of the newlyweds parted reluctantly, their eyes locking for but an instant. Much to Angel's surprise, Tyrone kissed her cheek, her moist brow, then turned with her to present his flushed bride to his much relieved guests. They had sweated the possibility that the amorous groom had been about to consummate the marriage here and now.

Congratulations with hugs and kisses were in order. With a ruddy blush Caspar dipped a finger into his starched collar as he went to plant a shy smack on the bride's burning cheek. Armand Bujold was next in line with his pretty brunette. Tyrone, in a jovial mood, would have none of it when the girl Nancy stuck out her hand to congratulate him. He pulled her to him and grinned wolfishly when his wife watched him, then surprising everyone, he planted a fatherly kiss upon the girl's brow.

Angel, in response to her husband's playfulness, tossed her head back merrily and her soft laughter and twinkling eyes mesmerized those about her. She sobered abruptly when Jacinta swished up to Tyrone and waited in demure affectation while he took the time to straighten his muffling cravat, one of fine white muslin beneath another of white silk. Angel tore her gaze away from the couple about to embrace and watched Joseph enter with a tray laden with several bottles containing bubbly champagne, followed by two more servants bearing trays of daintily stemmed wine glasses.

Suddenly Angel stared hard at Hannah, seeing what Nikki had seen earlier to cause his dark frown. Despite Hannah's cosmetic efforts to conceal the bluish-purple bruise on her cheek—the brand of a domineering and perniciously spiteful man—Angel could make out the imprint of a squared fist. Angel was now thankful Wesley Gayarre had not acknowledged the invite sent off to him and she cared not about his losing face in the Territory. Still she could not allow hatred to enter her heart for the man, nor anyone else for that matter, not even Jacinta, who now leaned recklessly against Tyrone, her bosom pressed intimately into the crook of his arm.

Again Angel sought interest elsewhere, thankful when Joseph came to pour a glass of the bubbly for her. Before tilting her glass to sip the pink liquid, she found herself gazing up at the portrait of Tyrone's mother. It was remarkable—the stunning woman seemed alive again and smiling at her with pleasure, and as if with appreciation over all she viewed from her place above the mantel.

From across the room Tyrone beheld his wife just about to sip from her glass. His powerful voice rang out loud and clear as he strode swiftly to her side before the rim of the glass met her lips. His voice gentled now as he chided her.

"My dear wife, don't you know we must share together our first sip and drink a toast for the morrow?"

Angel smiled sweetly up at him. "I am sorry, Tyrone," she apologized and held her glass out to meet and clink with his.

The crowd gathered around as Tyrone sipped from hers and she from his. They stood together in the middle of the room and Tyrone's eyes leisurely touched every corner of the sweet, oval face. She was totally unaware of how sweetly seductive she appeared this day. Tyrone felt the start of a quickening in the midst of his six-foot-three frame. When he spoke at last, his voice flowed out huskily as he quoted remembered lines.

"A green isle in the sea, love, a fountain and a shrine. . . ." His voice trailed to a halt, wondering if she recalled their island night of full, mutual, passionate ecstasy.

He gazed down at her intensely, so wrapped up in drowning himself in the crystal-green pools, that Angel prayed for a moment his interest might be genuine and not merely born of lust. Just then Jacinta's voice sounded from behind them.

"How sweet, Ty, you really should have been a poet, *mon cher*. I have never heard such poesy. Is it the brandy or the bride?" she laughed.

Angel snatched the moment fast and continued the stanza her husband had begun. ". . . All wreathed with fairy fruits and flowers, and all the flowers were mine," she ended as Tyrone lifted a brow appreciatively.

Jacinta glared at the trim back as if the bride had whacked her a healthy one in the face. Dinner in the formal dining room was announced by Joseph just then and Nikki grinned widely, leaned back on his heels and whispered words for only Jacinta's ears.

"I'm sorry—ah—Jacinta? Ahh, yes, Jacinta. But all your acclamation must go to Poe, not the groom. And, it is the champagne, not the brandy, madame." He left her brusquely then to loop his arm into Hannah's to follow the guests into the dining room.

Jacinta twirled an aperitif in front of her scheming face after she had seated herself at the huge table directly across from the bride and groom. Nikki and Hannah were seated respectively one on either side of the radiant couple. Caspar sat with his back to the sideboard and tugged his cauliflower ear thoughtfully. It went like this:

Wonder of wonders, Cap'n Ty, that you should fall into the lush cradle of this English lass and make her with babe. This truly being the strange part; no other lass had taken and ripened his seed. Plenty there were, too, and as many as an ardent lord would take to his bed and cast aside the same morn, never this man to blink an eyelash in the direction of their going. Surely now, the hoyden is vanished, now a graceful swan glides fully gorgeous and grown under the endless warm look from that sweet male trumpeter.

Toward the end of the plate dinner, Tyrone made an announcement to all, especially to his wife. "Melvin has prepared us a special surprise for our final course," he said, wiping his lips with a dinner napkin.

On cue, a call went along the hall and a shuffling ensued. A huge white frosted wedding cake was hoisted high over the head of the proud cook and delivered to the center of the hastily cleared table. Melvin hung back as one and all observed the delicate artwork of sweet icing that pictured a likeness of Cresthaven and in the center two tiny dolls of a bride and groom shoulder to shoulder.

Like the old Captain Ty, the groom winked recklessly in the direction of his wife and she smiled gaily in return. Her one glass of champagne was relaxing her considerably and her

385

happy heart thumped a wild tune in her breast under his warming gaze. The sparkling chandelier was mirrored in the already crystallike eyes as she stared mesmerized at the sugary confection.

Greatly piqued, Jacinta slammed down her glass so hard that the pink stuff splashed upon the delicate frosting of the cake. Rising abruptly, she smirked at the damage she had created and took herself speedily to the door.

"Oh dear, Oh dear, just look what that woman has done to my lovely masterpiece!" Fluttering cook Melvin rushed to repair the damage, dabbing lightly with a napkin until the wine was almost soaked up. The result was that a delicate pink pond was constructed right where, bordering lane and cedars, the original one existed out front.

"Oh, look, Tyrone!" Angel breathed. "The pool is settling, is it not beautiful? And right where it should be." She gazed around at the smiling faces, then down to her lap, suddenly embarrassed at her animated outburst.

Tyrone's sensuous lips curled in pleasurable amusement. He too, studied what Jacinta's flare-up had wrought and he took up the small hand from the satin lap, bringing it to his lips for a light reassuring kiss.

"Aye, Mistress Hunter, 'tis surely a sight to behold and it pleasures mine heart threefold to see my lady so lighthearted and gay," he said in his best Old English accent.

Angel glowed from turban to slipper as he eased himself up behind her, and handing her the knife offered by Melvin, eased her up from her chair, crossing his large hand over her own. Leaning with her to the cake he pressed her hand tenderly, making a generous slice of the cake. She was acutely aware of the male hardness of chest and thighs molded against the back of her. All present watched closely as the couple partook of the sweet wedge, already forgetting Jacinta Hunter and her bitter curse.

"Here, Master Hunter!" Angel said, releasing a giggle as she smushed the wedge to his mouth.

Tyrone, with cheeks full as a chipmunk's, had allowed her to stuff the cake in as he had foolishly opened wide. The gathered assembly broke up with wanton laughter. Tears of the same coursed down Hannah's cheeks, and two giggling maids on the other side of a matronly woman each passed a handkerchief down the line to the young woman. A neighbor by the name of Gar Saville dried his sparkling dark eyes as he stood to hail the merry couple.

After swallowing the mouthful, Tyrone made a lunge at his wife to swing her full circle, but she evaded his grasp and with a squeal of delight, took herself to stand just inside the doors. Tyrone took several swift strides before she halted him with a sudden pained expression and a hand upon the headdress. Her other hand was stretched out to bid him stay.

"I'll not be long, sir. I must surely go upstairs and remove this thing, otherwise I shall swoon and embarrass our guests," she explained, directing a sweet smile around the room.

A short time later, Angel entered the ballroom, still draped in her wedding gown, but now her crowning glory—thanks to Sarah's nimble fingers—waved close to her head in front while the mass of it was drawn up in back to cascade down her back in a waterfall of ringlets.

The guests were enchanted as beneath the twinkling chandelier the tall, virile groom swept his bride into a nimble waltz when the musicians started up. He whirled her in time to the music and Angel grew bedazzled by his enduring charm this night. He was the attentive husband and she felt secure and wanted for the time being. She desired greatly for this evening never to end. But suddenly she was filled with apprehension, for there was something of import she'd forgotten in the day's haste and excitement. Midnight. Just like on the island. It struck her awake like a fire bell in the middle of a London night. All weddings end at midnight and after that. . . .

The dance ended just then and Angel was grateful when the others joined them on the floor. She couldn't look up at him now for she was afraid he would read her innermost torment yet lingering on her face. They were gliding dreamily again and Angel cast a frantic perusal about the room in search of a clock. Swirling gowns and dark suits obstructed her view. Then she spied it—an ormolu clock adorning the mantelpiece above the fireplace. It was set too far away for her to read the Roman numerals on its face, but she knew too soon time would run its course and meet that bewitching hour.

They switched partners and danced and danced. Angel's trepidation was forgotten for the time being when she caught sight of Hannah. The bruise on her cheek was nearly erased with the new pink flush glowing there. Her dashingly covetous suitor swept her around the gilded ballroom and Angel watched over the shoulder of her partner as, together, Hannah and Nikki strolled outside through the french doors, their fingers laced as they went.

Angel heard it then, during a pause in the music. The grandfather clock chimed out the hour just before midnight. She stood trancelike near the long table clothed in fine white linen, where Tyrone had steered her to quench their thirst from the huge crystal bowl of rosy punch. She sipped the sweet liquid slowly, feeling nothing else but the silent force of his unswerving gaze drinking in her profile. Suddenly she shied from him and his lean fingers pressed upon her satin-clad shoulder. Gently yet firmly he turned her to face him and his look of unuttered passion exploded in her veins and stabbed at her heart.

"It's become quite hot in here and some of the others have drifted outdoors," he said with a suggestion implied.

Angel blanched as she recalled the wild evening spent dancing on the island—he had said very near those same words. She had no desire to be alone with him and revisit that scene. She must win at this game of hearts and flee, otherwise she would be left with nothing but a broken heart.

"Shall we?" Tyrone went on impatiently when she hesitated, voicing no acknowledgment of his words.

She lifted a delicate brow, pretending to be engrossed in the social chitchat going on at the refreshment table. Someone piped up behind them:

"Umm, yes, this war has almost halted the movement of people flowing into the West."

Angel turned quickly to the ruddy-faced man, unwisely ignoring her husband, as she said, "But if peace is made the movement will begin again someday. I have read much literature on Yerba Buena and the seven hills. I should love to go there someday and meet some of the old hardy pioneers who

conquered that vast wilderness. I hear they are still there. . . ."
Her voice melted flat when a dead silence met her remarks and all nearby eyes were riveted on the dark face with dangerously narrowed eyes behind her.

"Angel."

She bit down on her tiniest nail, then squealed in surprise when Tyrone swooped her up in his arms and bore her unceremoniously out into the night. With no word of his intent, he carried her to the suspended swing on the front porch where the latticework hid them from view of the guests out taking air. He sat down with her settled atop his lap. The swing creaked along the porch romantically and Angel squirmed to rise from him, but he held her pinned. He chuckled at her futile efforts and she stilled, mesmerized by the look of him as the moonbeams squeezed in through the wood screen. He had long before removed his dark blue cutaway and her hand now rested upon his silver-dappled chest. Beneath the silken feel of his fine shirt she could feel his heart beating a strong tune. The contact made an ache of longing brush the pulsating tips of her breasts.

"We have guests, sir," she tried scolding, but her voice lacked strength.

"And so we do, love. But, you failed to note the encouraging smiles that fell our way as we departed." He shifted slightly and she jumped. "Damn! Don't be so skittish. You are my wife now," he murmured almost harshly in her ear.

She tried sitting gingerly as she breathed, "Please, Tyrone, couldn't we go inside now? I have a horrible thirst in this heat."

Looking deeply into her eyes, he returned, "So do I, love, but it can wait . . . for awhile, anyway."

She glanced aside, his meaning quite clear to her.

He moved then, bringing something out from beneath his belt. "Here," he began, "my wedding gift to you, madame."

A soft velvet box rested in her lap, and with nervous anticipation she lifted the lid. A very daintily cut emerald drop necklace with tiny earrings to match sparkled in the spotlight of moon. She was totally unprepared for this, but fascinated nevertheless by the extravagant and lovely gift. She sighed raggedly when she lovingly fingered the eardrops.

He frowned. "Is something wrong with them? I selected those especially to match your eyes, but if you'd rather, I will exchange the gift for something—"

She interrupted softly, "No, Tyrone, I love them and thank you, but it's just that—I'm afraid I cannot wear the beautiful eardrops."

His shoulders drooped. "And why not?" he questioned sternly, but his face soon lit up as she explained.

"I meant to have my ears pierced several times, but I had been informed by a few classmates at that time of the pain involved. Not only that, but there is always the danger of infection, they said. Why, one girl even told the tale of someone who had her earlobe removed because of festering." She shuddered.

"Hah! An old wive's tale, Angel, and they were no doubt extremely jealous of you adding to your beauty." He chuckled low when she dropped her lashes in embarrassment. "Listen, I did my own with a bit of numbing and a dollop of alcohol. There isn't much feeling here of pain." He pressed a dainty lobe between his beringed fingers and she lifted her chin expectantly.

His look was troubled when their lips brushed slightly. He sighed and leaned back into the shadows so that she couldn't read his face.

"Will you do mine, Tyrone?" she begged earnestly. "I would love to wear—" She halted. When the day came for her to go, she could not take the emeralds with her. She would only take his son away from him. Suddenly she felt very sad.

"Of course, madame. I will do it this week for you, in fact, and I promise there will be no pain, my love."

A twinge of nostalgia made her heart skip wildly when he murmured those two words that linked her possessively to him. She jerked her head up to peer into his eyes desperately.

"I feel just terrible, Tyrone. I have no gift to give you." She was going to add that she only had saved a few coins from her governess's job, but she daren't. She would need them when the time came.

His eyes sparkled mischievously. "Ah, but there you are

wrong, madame," he said huskily.

His double meaning was crystal clear when, torturous for her, he slowly reached down to caress the small mound of her belly. The tips of his long fingers ached to slide lower, and Angel shifted back, wishing next that she hadn't. Her undersides now pressed down dangerously into his loins and she could feel him full-blown through her gown.

Angel closed her eyes as the heat seared through her. He didn't utter a single word or make a move and she painfully began to wonder if he was regretting Jacinta's hasty departure. This was all very strange and different of him, to desire her and not attack her with warm, roving hands, and hot, probing kisses. He seemed, too, to be waiting for something to happen.

She wanted to beg: Love me, oh, love me, Tyrone, now and forever. But instead she took the cowardly alternative. It must be, or soon she would be upstairs in his bed, allowing him to have his way with her. And that, she determined, she must never allow to happen.

"Should we not go in, Tyrone? We are being awfully rude, seated alone out here like a randy pirate and his mistress." She was at once sorry, for he chuckled deeply at that and drew her closer. "I am serious, Tyrone, you needn't chuckle. Let us go in," she begged, pushing back from his chest.

"*I* am serious, Angel," he murmured low, "and I like that scene you just mentioned. It has a familiar ring and brings to mind very pleasant memories of a green isle by the sea."

Take care! her mind screamed. He is making you feel again. The hour of midnight draws near. Beware!

With affectation, she said bitterly, "Not to me, sir. I would like to forget what took place there, and I shall, in time!"

He tightened his grip on her arms, snarling, "Tell me you didn't find pleasure in our lusty love-making that night! Tell me!" His voice rose as a cloud passing over the moon darkened his features to wicked black.

"I did not!" she lied hotly, wanting to wound his male pride. Yes, yes, it was true. All he desired was to possess her body for a time. This, and the child she would bear him. The reason for his husbandly attentiveness was made quite clear to her now. Again, there had been no mention of love—only lust! A very cute play he and sly Jacinta had put on this night—even his amusement when his whore flew to the door in a rage had been an act.

"You shall not have that which you most desire from my loins!" she whispered hotly, causing him to flinch. She didn't care. The babe was to be hers. Not his whore's!

"What . . . !" he asked incredulously, pinching her arm hard.

"Exactly!" she exclaimed, trying hard not to flinch from the pain he inflicted upon her soft flesh. "Oh, you look so surprised, Tyrone Hunter. I know now why you carted me to Cresthaven. It is this—you only want one thing from me, and let me repeat . . . you shall never—"

"Be still!" he snapped, drowning out her words.

Tyrone couldn't believe what he had just heard, and yet, he had feared the entire day this evening would climax in disaster. He stared at her hot and hard, for what seemed an eternity. His look was of such total loss that Angel read it as his wanting the child so very badly that he was obviously afraid she would flee from him again.

Angel listened downcast as he began his inevitable, hurtfully bitter tirade.

"I must compliment you on your performance several months back in the cottage. You really had me fooled, you know." He snorted through his long nose. "Never before had a woman displayed such intense passion and such utter wantonness and complete surrender to me. You should have been in the theater, madame."

"Ooooh! Lust! Lust!" She had risen from his lap and now she spat down at him, "You are abominable, Mr. Hunter! You are the one who raped me first. I only played your whore expecting you to tire of me, as is your wont with hapless women. I even believed you would release us once you had your fill of me!"

"I realized that from the first, but neither did you deny me a full night of passion!"

"Oh-ho! Deny! And next you will inform me that if I deny you your husbandly rights, you will ease your insatiable lust on another's loins—like your own beloved stepmother. If you haven't done so already!" Angel was totally surprised at her own venom, and she had only asked for what came next.

"I will and I have," he said matter-of-factly, snatching her back savagely when she would have fled. "Wait, there is more, my ice-queen. Where you have been, there will come another and yet another. And life won't be sweet for you at Cresthaven, and where *you* will be my devoted, faithful wife, I in turn will treat you as merely a cool and aloof brother . . . *if* you are lucky and heel to my every command . . . discounting the bedchamber. You shall not see me as charming, kind, pleasing, affectionate, or harmonious, as far as you're concerned. You see, I don't really need you the way you think I do, my dear. Now! I strictly demand one thing—no, actually three! You will sit beside me when I order you to do so; you will most properly attend church services with me in our parish; and by my side you will present a devoted mien at the social affairs given by these guests here today."

"Is—that—all—sir?" Angel gasped out between stiff lips.

"No, there *is* one more thing," he continued ruthlessly, "steer clear of my bedroom, for if you stumble that way you may be in for the shock of your life. Comprehend?"

"Horribly!" she hissed as her hand shot out to slap the coldly handsome face, but he snatched her hand just an inch from his cheek. "I loathe you, and one day you shall find out just how much!" she hissed maliciously, feeling for now that she'd spoken the bloody truth.

"What does that mean!" he demanded.

This cold stranger grasped her arm to spin her back, but she wrested it aside and in that instant the hem of her gown caught beneath a heavy heel. As he stayed her from stumbling headlong off the stone-surfaced porch, he quaked for a moment when his palms unwittingly molded the delicious swell of breasts beneath her armpits. She mistook the placement of his hands for fresh attack, but then witnessed the angry frustration as his hands clenched and dropped to his sides and he spoke with a cruel twist to his lips.

"Never mind. Say goodnight to your guests. Plead a sick headache . . . anything, and go to your room like a celibate nun. My room, as you already must know, adjoins yours . . .

393

but don't fret, madame, as I've no intentions of consummating our marriage this night . . . or any night, for that matter," he ground out with harsh finality.

Her husband let her go to do his bidding while he proceeded to the sideboard to get thoroughly and devastatingly saturated by drink. The tall clock in the hall did chime out the hour of midnight as the fragment of a bond was shattered at the onset.

Sweetest li'l feller, everybody knows;
Dunno what you call him, but he's mighty lak' a rose.
—Frank J. Stanton

Chapter Ten

1

Torrential rain continued to sweep over Cresthaven and lifted the muddy level of the Old Devil River. Just so, the weather cleared, took up again with light misting clouds, then abated with a peek of sun now and then in October, banking the tide of events up to late and soggy November.

At first, and true to his word, Mr. Hunter had civilly escorted his lovely though somewhat pale bride to the many functions in the homes of his friends. He was right by her side to lend assistance in and out of a carriage, even though she professed she didn't need any. They traveled by keelboat or planter's boat, as did the others in the parish, when the thick mire made the roads a sea of slush, ill-suited for travel by any carriage. But now that Angel's sixth month of pregnancy had passed, Tyrone often went off alone or in the company of Nikki and Gar Saville. Monsieur Saville often stayed on at Cresthaven now that the cutting of the rain-soaked lumber had begun. When rain fell too heavily for that job, the sugar-house demanded time for restoration. Tyrone worked himself fanatically, not only at restoring his own sugar plantation, but often went with Saville to help fill in the swampy lowlands of Mystic Marsh, hopefully to transform the black marshland overgrown with young willows and alligator grass into productive land.

Caspar, having been a woodcraftsman in his much younger days, erected a nursery between the main upstairs bedrooms, removing an old storage closet, and still there was enough room for it to remain part sitting-room with folding doors to shade the spot where the crib and dresser would stand. Tyrone helped put in a window, and the folding doors would be opened on warmer days to catch the breeze in through the window.

Out of the ordinary was the visit of a General Humbert one pleasant evening. Angel listened with rapt attention over dinner while he spoke of his being exiled after a heated quarrel with Napoleon. An old soldier who had fought diligently in both Europe and Santo Domingo, he was a wartime hero of Napoleon's army and now sought to retire and spend the rest of his natural days in New Orleans.

When at home Tyrone ignored his wife at all turns and treated her at social times with a casual fleeting regard, the latter equaling the attention he lavished upon his toilers. In fact, it was well known that Mr. Hunter smiled upon his cronies and servants with more benevolence than he did his own wife. *When* he smiled, which was not often these days.

Jacinta's visits to the plantation were not rare and oftentimes, when Tyrone had a free hour or two, the mistress would see the two ride astride, cavorting out across the grounds together. Not gloomy and despondent at these times, Tyrone's deep laughter drifting back to Angel was enough to make her heart wrench horribly. She hadn't been allowed her favorite sport and Tyrone made it quite clear that if she dared ride, she would suffer the consequences. What could be a worse fate than what she had endured up to this point in her life at Cresthaven, she often wondered.

Angel became bored, listless with the weight she bore, and she was very lonely. It was in this frame of mind, after a lengthy bath one day, that she stared at her naked body in the pier glass mirror. As she slid her hand down over her belly she marveled at the growth of new life. By degrees the miracle she housed had astonished her, and her soul crept longingly to that day soon when she would first hold him in her arms, cradle him to her bosom.

One golden December morning, Indian-summer-like, with clean white clouds strung across the sky like wash on a line, Angel had awakened early to go downstairs to have her breakfast alone. She loved the hush of the early morning hours when she could sip her tea at leisure, then roam through the house without fear of meeting up with her husband, for he had been absent the entire week. She stood at the top of the stairs about to descend when the front door opened and Angel, still wrapped in her robe, backed up in case it was a neighbor come to visit.

"Oh, m'sieur," Sarah began, just traversing the hall at that moment. "I will tell missus you be back."

"Yes, Sarah, you do that," Tyrone returned tersely as he passed her and his boots could be heard to stride the length of the hall back to his study.

Dejectedly Angel returned to her room to dress. Now that her husband had returned she would tread cautiously once more.

It was by horseback that Tyrone had gone just the week before, for it was quicker than by conveyance, this way taking only close to two hours to reach New Orleans. It took less than that this time because his friend, Jean Lafitte, along with his brother, Pierre, had been officially charged with smuggling. Added to that, the American merchantman *Independence* of Massachusetts, had been attacked by pirates in the Gulf. After feeding and sheltering his horse, it was to the crowded Place d'Armes that Tyrone finally hastened to meet with District Attorney Grymes after he had been closeted with Governor Claiborne and survivor Williams the better part of the day. When Grymes made out the wording of his official reports, Mr. Hunter was the first to read them before they appeared in the newspaper.

Tyrone related the outcome to avid listeners as he strode the streets till he reached the Hotel de la Marine. The tale, he said, would be forgotten within a week, for the pirates of the Gulf appeared not once in the report. Lafitte triumphed and was a more popular figure than ever—a hero in the public eye. The formal charge against the Lafittes had not been recorded.

"Ahhh-hhh, Lafitte! *Magnifique!*" The café houses, the cabarets, and the numerous colorful establishments whispered.

Tyrone Hunter put in an appearance at General Humbert's birthday party that evening. He conversed for a time with Jean and Pierre, and planter St. Geme, then took his leave after wishing Humbert a happy fifty-sixth birthday. There was in the dining room of the hotel an impending air of something akin to a riot and Tyrone didn't want to be present and included when the taut silence erupted into a madhouse. It was not like him to steer clear of trouble, but then, Tyrone shrugged—nothing was like him these days.

Outside the hotel, Tyrone was just about to fetch his mount when a pretty, golden-eyed quadroon with café au lait skin plucked at his elbow. At first he was angered at the intrusion upon his musings, then he flashed a charitable smile down into the creamy, uptilted face.

"*Mon cher Ty, amour,*" she murmured, an excited gleam in her eyes. She went on in French, "Where have you been keeping yourself? Tell me it is not true you have married?" She took in his fawn-colored trousers molded skin-tight.

Tyrone's voice was rich with the French patois as he answered, "Collette, you are lovelier than ever." He bent over her to whisper in her ear and her eyes grew round, bemused, and then confounded. Alerted, he straightened to full height. "By the way, Collette, where is your husband this night?" he asked, this time in English as his eyes narrowed to a darkened doorsill where a figure lurked momentarily then disappeared behind the door.

"Husbaan?" Collette tried in English, then resumed her French, "*Oui, oui,* he is at Thiot's, but—"

"Never mind," Tyrone interrupted, pressing cold objects into her hand. He turned her to face away from him, patted her on her curvaceous behind, then climbed onto the Beast, that the pickaninny had brought around for him. "Good night, madame," he called over his shoulder as he turned into the street.

Behind the pane of glass the watcher wondered if that was payment for later. He whirled from the window, but not before he noticed the young woman's gesture of frustration as she eyed the coins nestled coldly in her smooth palm. His square frame disappeared out the back door of the place.

Collette stood silently under the lamplight and paled a lighter tan. It was true that her husband was a good-for-nothing, drunk all the time, but still, he loved her. She had to

398

earn a living somehow, otherwise they would starve to death. But the infamous Ty had never paid her before and she hadn't cared one bit, for he was *magnifique* in the bed. Was it true then what he had whispered? That he was madly in love with his wife? Only she would suffice in his bed? Oh! He had not been serious. Not him!

Collette sighed pensively as she tucked into her skirt the coins she had done nothing to earn, and went to find a customer who hopefully would give *her* some pleasure this night.

That same day her husband returned, Angel visited her favorite haunt of late. She wandered along the riverside, kicked idly at the ruby earth, the turgid turf, steering clear of the wetter parts, as she pondered the fortnight of chilly dampness, not unlike the winters she had experienced in England. With one exception: that the winters had been warm with love from her parents; and from the mare Echo she could go out and talk to. The horse would respond by rubbing her velvet muzzle against her cheek. Whereas now she felt unloved, unwanted by her husband—but not totally without friends in need of her companionship and she of theirs. Like Hannah and Bonita Saville. But she saw very little of either nowadays.

Now ecstatic, Hannah saw more and more of Nikki, and either she visited Cresthaven in search of that lad, or he went to court her discreetly at Gayarre. Either way, they were an almost constant twosome and to all onlookers very much in love.

There was something essential amiss in Angel's own life and she knew it was the lack of the love of a man. She had to admit it, and only to herself, that it had been wonderfully passionate that long night in the cottage, and, even though the afterglow had dissipated, the memory still hung on.

The air was growing steadily chilled and when she had almost reached the start of the long white fence, she halted in her tracks. Her heart thumped with renewed anguish. Tyrone and Jacinta were just returning from a ride, their mounts lathered with sweat, giving evidence they had ridden far into the wood. Angel watched her husband glance about him as he rode, straight and tall, tearing his gaze from that golden womanly form as if he detected someone indeed surveying them from somewhere. Suddenly Jacinta whipped her mount to race around to the back, and Tyrone followed at a slower pace.

Hidden now and then by the oaks, Angel hastened to the rear entrance where Della, inside, was busying herself. It was nigh onto the dinner hour and Melvin, just coming in from the bakehouse the same moment Angel swept in, greeted her warmly. Melvin enjoyed seeing her there, but at times wondered why she left the menu planning solely to her husband's choice. She acted not like a mistress should, but instead comported herself often like a housemaid.

"Where you been, honey?" Della chided, noted the overly pinkened cheeks. "You shouldn't be out there roaming about every day in this chill, you're goin' to catch your death, and you in your delicate condition."

Angel thought the housekeeper couldn't know the real reason for her high color. But she did feel a bit feverish just now. It was only because of what she'd seen, she told herself.

She had missed the dark eyes studying her rounded belly that had dropped of late lower. "But just now the air has chilled, Della." Angel tried on a merry face. "This day has been like the first hour of spring, so warm and beautiful and golden." She had always loved this season of the year.

Della pursed her lips to an even greater thickness. "But now it is as chilly outside as it was yesterday, honey." She halted, seemingly waiting for something to happen next, as she placed her hands on her hips.

When the mistress would have sat down into a hard-backed chair, as she was wont to do of late in the kitchen, Della padded over this time to gently take Angel's arm. She guided the mistress firmly to the door leading out into the long hall.

"You jes' can't be helping around like a servant, and sittin' back here all the time, mistress. Yeah, hear, you, *you* mistress of Cresthaven, honey," Della murmured gently, tears sparkling. She cocked her turbaned head and almost choked, "Whatsa matter with you, honey?"

When Angel didn't answer, Della graciously fell silent, and sad, for she knew there was something dreadfully amiss with her and Mr. Hunter; for a long time she'd had knowledge, as did the entire household, that they kept separate bedrooms, and in the daytime saw very little or nothing of each other.

"It just ain't right," Della mumbled to herself after her mistress had gone upstairs. "But nobody's business, neither," she added gruffly, turning to Melvin. He just nodded, going back to the bake-house, forgetting what he'd come to the kitchen for.

Della stared long and hard at the door leading to the hall. "It's gonna be okay when the baby's here—" she sighed deeply, "Lord, I sure do hope so, and by the look of that belly, it's gonna be any day now."

Angeline Sherwood raced across the open fields with Echo pounding the turf beneath her. Angel perched high to catch the breeze, the fresh, sweet wind whipping through her swirling hair. Whizzing past her was the dewy English countryside, verdant and lush in the springtime morn. Billowing out behind her and in the height of fashion, was her brand-new, dove-gray velvet riding skirt. Matching ribbons fluttered like silver streamers twining about the lustrous mass of undulating hair, vivid against the blue English skies. She had just turned sixteen that season, and life was full of golden days, elegant gowns of creamy chiffon, tinkling parties, and just being a girl was a pleasure in itself.

Angel murmured softly in her sleep, rolled her head from side to side upon the silken pillow. But she did not waken.

England again. Falling rust- and amber-colored leaves. She was strolling through Covent Gardens near the theater on Drury Lane.

"Fire! Fire!" Trapped. Run. Run. Skirts are on fire!

"Watch out! Look there—she tripped on a loose one!"

"Hurry, wet the girl's skirts—she is afire!"

A large man bent over her with a worried frown. He was garbed in a shiny-wet slicker.

"My legs—" Angel sobbed, "in the back—they hurt—burn."

"The danger is past, miss. The fire is out. Here now, your parents are coming."

"'Tis a burn on the back of her legs."

"Oh, Mama, there is blood!"

"Hush love, you are alive. That is all that counts."

A soothing voice. A black bag snapped shut. The salve helps some.

"Ahem. Angel is fortunate to have escaped with only minor burns, Lady Sherwood. But as for the loss of blood . . . the hymen may have been ruptured slightly."

"Here, love, drink this. It will make you sleep."

The murmuring voices drifted to the far corner of the bedchamber and snatches of conversation broke through the fog in Angel's brain.

". . . embarrassing situation later?"

"Not so, Lady Sherwood . . . the absence of it does not always denote sexual activity. . . ."

The door shut quietly. Christine came to stand before her bed. "Mama, I am a virgin . . . say I am, Mama?" The last word resounded in the room and swirled in her brain like a heartbeat.

The voice changed and strong hands shook her gently, saying, "Wake up, Angel. No, you must not sleep. You are tossing with a bad dream." A hand pressed her forehead. "Yes, she has a fever, Della. Fetch me cool water and linens, immediately."

"Yes, Mama, we will not speak of it again, I really promise. I believe what . . . you say. . . ."

The deep male voice again. "Can you wake up now? You must, Angel."

Dark lashes fluttered open to reveal tiny slits of crystal but feverish green. "Tyrone . . . is that you?" her voice came out weakly.

"Yes, love, I'm here," he answered, frowning at the bulging expanse of belly.

Della came to stand beside Tyrone. A cool cloth touched her forehead like a feather and Della left only to return again. As Angel peered up into the haze, she saw her husband again as she had the week before he left for New Orleans, his hazel eyes brooding, riveted to her belly. Did he think she looked fat and ugly? Is that why he frowned again? He didn't look like that when Jacinta was around. No. . . .

Was that Christine standing behind her husband? "Mama . . . have the scars gone away? Please look . . . I want to know," Angel muttered.

"Scars?" he asked, his voice going deeper then. "Oh, yes, the scars. I will look for you, love."

Angel felt hands unlike her mother's roll her onto her side, then her nightgown was sliding up, up. . . .

"There is nothing here but a few little—" he paused. Then, "God, not this! It is not time yet for the water . . . ruptured. She is just into the eighth month." The voice was grieved.

"Not time, Mama. Not time for what, Mama?" Angel felt her damp gown being removed over her head; several pairs of hands seemed to be lifting her gently.

"Oh, Lord. Lord. The honey chile. I should've known, her dropping low like that, and her with the chills now, too."

"No woman drops like that in her eighth month. How could it be time? Unless. . . ."

"Unless you was thinkin' of another time afore that, Mr. Hunter?"

Tyrone raked his fingers throughout his hair, mussing it, and securing his robe about his waist. He flushed red, groaning, "Ahh, but there was only a few days in between our—our—you know, Della."

Tyrone grew much redder when Angel began again to mutter, but it was an angry hue that Della missed as she went to fetch the new manservant, Cordell, to bank the fire up in the mistress's bedchamber, and to wake only Sarah and Daisy Mae, no one else.

Angel mumbled, "Please . . . please come again, James. I've so very much . . . much to talk about . . . with you . . . I love. . . ." Suddenly she began to thrash about, her upper body glistening with sweat.

Tyrone's countenance loomed thunderstricken. "James? Who the hell is . . . James?" he fiercely questioned the young woman in the bed who was supposed to be swollen with *his* child. He stared around himself helplessly. Was she really having his baby? And did he really know this woman, his wife, at all? Hadn't she said while sleeping fitfully from the sleeping powder as he stood in the bedroom at Madame Lulu's that he had been the first? Or, had she indeed? There were many who went by the name of James in Louie; even his own father, who was often called Big Jim. But Angel had mentioned *love*.

"James!" Angel's eyes flew open, but unseeing in her fever. "Please help me. Take me away from here. I have the locket you gave me . . . always near my heart. Here. . . ." Her voice dwindled, her lids fell heavily, as her hand reached up to rest on her breast covered by a sheet.

Della had returned with Cordell following at a sleepy pace. She stared hard at Mr. Hunter standing before the bed like stone, and the mistress drenched with beads of perspiration. Like a ghostly being, Tyrone turned to the housekeeper, whose eyes had grown big, blacker, and round like saucers. Della disregarded what she had heard Angel mutter while Tyrone bent to snatch up his wife's damp nightgown.

"She won't be laboring for a few hours yet, Mr. Hunter, but we got to keep that fever down," Della said quickly, taking up a cloth and dipping it into the cool water in the basin. "Maybe false labor, too, but ain't too likely, 'cause of the water coming." Della busied herself at the bedside.

Moving stiffly, Tyrone unpinned the lavaliere from the nightgown and, upon opening the locket, stared hatefully at the lock of hair. Whoever had given her this would surely die for messing with what was his, namely his wife. He would skin the fool's hide, inch by inch.

Tyrone trudged heavily into his wife's morning-salon where he slumped carelessly into a green-and-white-striped loveseat. His countenance was laden with murder, cast into the infernal regions. Angel. Just like his slut of a mother, Annette. He fingered the thin scar on his forehead and grimaced, recalling the pain. She had done it—his mother. He still harbored hatred in him for her indiscretion.

He had been just a lad then, and in one of her fits of anger she had whipped a heavy boot at him when he found her in bed with a stranger. She had scarred him forever. He grew to a man, hating her kind, using them cruelly over the years. He should

404

have destroyed her portrait long ago, and someday soon he would go downstairs and burn the thing.

Tyrone hissed deeply, "Poor little untainted Angel. Curse!" Then he thought: Woe be to the fellow who would try taking her away from him! His eyes burned like fiercely glowing embers. When had it happened with Angel and her lover? Not New Orleans. When! When!

Hours must have passed when a loud shriek brought him bolt upright and he tore through the open doors into the bedchamber where Angel was straining, moaning, and clutching the pillow above her head. Her face was as white as the hair that streamed wildly about her. Another whimper and her eyes flew open with pain-filled wonder. She didn't speak a word now, only panted hard. She rested momentarily and relaxed, looking up hazily to see Tyrone with an unreadable expression. Her brow furrowed with worry and fright.

Della and the two maids seemed to float from afar, coming through a hazy mist, lingering behind her husband. The fever had subsided somewhat, though, and her speech made more sense.

"I am sorry, Tyrone," Angel breathed. "I should not have been out walking every day and caught this chill. The baby— he is coming, isn't he?" She grimaced, knowing another contraction was on its way.

"Be still now, Angel, save your breath for the birth," Tyrone heard himself mutter tersely.

A kettle of water boiled above the grate; Della dropped string into the water. A pair of scissors wrapped in linen waited on the commode, having been boiled beforehand. There was now sufficient warmth in the room for the baby.

Della mopped Angel's brow, then turned to Tyrone. "The fever's down. You go fetch more fresh linen, Mr. Hunter. And you gals, one of you get the mistress a fresh nightie, the other the antiseptic. Hurry on now, time's gettin' close and we can't lose none and be fetchin' later."

The housekeeper watched the tall frame stride through the doorway and her old mind swept back cobwebs to when she had eased his tiny, pink person into the world. When she looked back to Angel resting peacefully in the bed now, Della wore a very toubled frown, making her appear older than ever.

Tyrone returned shortly and looked down upon his wife. Her eyes were shut and she wore a fresh nightgown. Her face was whiter than ever, and he gulped hard, wondered with sickened dread if he was going to lose her. The baby didn't matter anymore. Her lover didn't matter anymore. His thoughts rested solely on Angel and nothing else was important—for now. He went to confide in Della who was preparing the crib in the nursery for the infant soon to be born.

Running his fingers through his ruffled hair, he asked in a rasping voice, "She is going to be all right, isn't she?" He felt drained of life suddenly.

"What?" Della turned to see him standing there. "A'course she is, Mr. Hunter. That youngster just made up his mind to come a bit early, that's all. From the size of her belly, he's gonna be a big one, too. Almost like a full-term babe."

A muffled scream summoned Tyrone and the housekeeper back to the bedside. Angel bit the back of her hand to still yet another scream as she arched her back high. Tyrone bent to stroke her forehead with the cloth and her tongue darted out to lick her dry lips. Tyrone straightened and hung back as Della bent to Angel.

"They're comin' more often and stronger now," Della began. "Won't be long now, honey." She peered askance at Tyrone and her eyes bulged. "Mr. Hunter, what you think you're doing, rollin' up your sleeves! It's time for you to shoo now and go take a long ride on that Beast of yours, or get drunk like most menfolk do at this time."

Angel came alert as her neck strained in his direction. "Oh, yes, Tyrone, Della is right—" she halted to whimper, "you must go, go and do as she says. It is not natural for a man to witness the birth of his offspring."

Tyrone shook his head, having made up his mind. "It is natural, Angel, and it has been done before, long before you or I ever came into being. You, Della, were much younger when you eased me into the world. I'm not leaving, in fact I'll stay and be of some assistance." ·

"Ohhh!" Angel screeched right into a knifelike pain.

Tyrone cast a glance at the white figure in the bed as he went to wash up his arms at the washstand. "After all," he said, "it can't be all that different from mares when they foal."

"A breeding mare . . . that is all I am to you!" Angel panted. "Out, Mr. Hunter, get out of my—Ooooh!"

"You will not be rid of me so easily this time, madame. I'll see this through whether you like it or not." He turned and his eyes dared Della and the two gaping maids to defy him. "Well?" he said gruffly, "Don't just stand there. Get those warmed linens, antiseptic, and cotton to the damn bedside!"

"Yessir," Della beamed. "Look at that curly head a-comin', big and round as a nine-monther. Any more growin' in the cubbyhole and he would have been a whopper."

When Angel should have screamed for all she was worth, now she just smiled triumphantly, weakly, and pushed harder. Her husband's course of action had put her greatly at ease. He seemed to naturally know what to do for her to make it normal and easy. He gently demanded of her one more great push and shortly the full length of a male child was delivered. Despite his earlier belief that this child wasn't of his own flesh, he smiled widely and proudly, but then frowned, for the infant did not breathe or cry immediately as it should have.

"It's a boy!" Della announced to her weary mistress, then hushed up suddenly when she noticed what Tyrone had, that the babe didn't let out a squall or breathe normally.

Angel felt the tense expectancy in the air and struggled to rise to her elbows. Her eyes cast about the waiting faces wildly and her face contorted with a new fear as they rested on Tyrone who stood with the babe in his hands. He appeared indecisive about something.

"What is it, Tyrone?" Angel cried. "Why is he not crying?"

Tyrone stared mesmerized at the bundle, so tiny in his big hands, as Della swiftly went to fetch the boiled string, scissors, cotton and antiseptic from the commode. A clean and warmed linen was placed on the bed by Sarah to receive the new life— hopefully.

Angel went whiter than ever as her husband rubbed three fingers up and down the baby's back. He stopped, again wearing that strange, somber expression.

407

"Mr. Hunter!" Della cried. "Don't be afraid to hold that baby up and spank him. C'mon now. What you waitin' for?"

Tyrone hoisted the babe up by his feet and gently spanked the pink buttocks. Nothing happened. Della pulled out her handkerchief as tears sparkled in her brown eyes. The two maids were holding on to each other, staring at the lifeless tiny form.

"Tyrone, please, oh, please, do something for him," Angel cried, without force. "He is alive, is he not? Make him cry, make our baby live, Tyrone. Make our baby live. . . ." Angel fell back to the pillow sobbing, drained.

Galvanized by the single word "our," Tyrone held the infant boy up and rubbed him vigorously and spanked again several times. The tiny chest heaved once, then deflated.

Tyrone whacked once more, saying, "Cry, my son—live!"

As if nourished by those sweet words, the wee limbs flailed, the lungs filled, and with great gusto a loud squall pierced the deathly silence. Relief immediately overcame them all, and, as if storing energy for this moment of applause, the babe soon brought down the house with his loud, angry yawps. Without further ado, Tyrone handed over the noisy bundle to the joyously weeping housekeeper. He went to brush a kiss on his wife's brow, surprising Angel with his brusqueness as he strode over to the washstand and busied himself there, as if nothing out of the ordinary had taken place the long night.

After Della had completed what was left to do and Angel lay resting peacefully, a door opened to shed morning light into the room. A pretty face appeared around the jamb of the door, and a cheery voice inquired, "Goodness, what's all the noise about up here? Nikki came to fetch me in such a—" She peered around with round eyes, then entered, "The baby? Heaven be praised!" Hannah rushed to the bedside, taking up Angel's pale hand, and peering down at the wrinkle-faced bundle. "A boy?"

Angel nodded weakly as her gaze followed her husband to the door. She called out his name but he was already closing the door when her voice reached the wood and volleyed back with a hollow ring. Angel felt her aloneness even though Hannah congratulated her on the good size of the infant and Della and Sarah crooned as they took the fussing bundle to the table set up for the bathing.

Soft murmurs and much shuffling of footsteps from the hall floated about Angel's head. She soon found blessed restfulness after being soothingly washed by gentle Daisy Mae and given a warm cup of broth to sip. She slumbered deeply until late that same morning when the sun was already high, shining brightly on the grandness of Cresthaven.

Mid-December arrived. But for the birthing event, things had not changed much at Cresthaven. Tryone still remained cool and aloof, and was gone much of the time, while his wife gained back her strength in a week's time, keeping to her room while the rumble of wheels below and the rattle of horses' hooves came and went. Often she could hear the husky laugh belonging to Jacinta and she would look away from the window, biting her trembling lips.

Angel searched high and low for the lavaliere she'd somehow lost while giving birth to her son. She couldn't question the maids or Della about its whereabouts, and anyway, if found by one of them it would have been brought to her attention by now. As she waited for James Hunter to make a second appearance, she began having second thoughts about leaving Cresthaven with her son. Even though Tyrone continued to shun her and the babe, she kept hoping that a miracle would happen. So disastrous had their wedding night been, that Tyrone's anticipation over the coming event had left him completely cold, even to his own flesh and blood. Now he didn't want anything to do with either one of them, Angel thought ponderously.

During the next week nearing the Yuletide season, Jacinta continued to visit. With her superior smugness held in check, she thought at last she had a hold over Tyrone. As his wife never seemed available to entertain him, she went out of her way to do so, prattling on endlessly and flirting coyly as they rode out together. This was one such morning, when they were just returning from a brisk ride and Jacinta's gay laughter and Tyrone's deep voice filled the hall as they entered.

"Well, who in the world would want to murder you, *mon cher?*" Jacinta questioned breathlessly.

"This is the second attempt, Jacinta," Tyrone returned, slapping the braided leather of his riding quirt against his thighs. "The first time was several weeks back when I was returning from New Orleans. Whoever it was, he followed me for quite a distance out of New Orleans. I was lucky it was dark, too dark in fact for even the American rifle to find its mark—me. I know how very accurate the rifle is that my tracker carried and fired, for I own one myself. Lucky for me again no attempt has been made to increase the speed of loading one of those things. From now on, believe me, I'll be carrying a weapon on my person."

"And you say that the second time was yesterday, when you were returning from the Savilles?" Jacinta tilted her head, tugging off her riding gloves.

Tyrone halted abruptly in striding to the parlor doors, and turned to glare at her. "Did I say that?" he questioned, tossing the quirt onto a table of delicately carved maple.

"*Oui, mon cher.* When we were riding through the woods a short time back," Jacinta returned quickly as she followed him into the parlor after he had tossed the doors wide.

Again Tyrone's steps halted, this time inside the portal, when he viewed the scene before him. It was like a family portrait, with Angel and Nikki seated a few feet apart, the old freshly painted white wicker cradle swinging softly before them. Above the low rim a tiny fist waved once in the air, then dropped, as Nikki continued to gently rock the babe to sleep. In her black velvet riding outfit, Jacinta smoothed back a dark strand and went to stand next to the cradle to peer down.

"*Mais oui*, Tyrone, no wonder you carry on about his size," Jacinta purred, lifting a dark brow at the mother's surprise. "He is—ah—very well-constructed for a premature baby."

Nikki coughed, saying, "He is not a piece of furniture, dear Jacinta. You should say instead that he is a robust babe for an early comer."

"Whatever," Jacinta said, waving a hand in the air as she went to plop down onto a sofa directly across from them.

Tyrone had stood silently in the middle of the room, and now he strode to the sideboard to pour himself a stiff brandy. "Anyone else?" he asked, waving the bottle.

410

"*Oui*, a sherry," Jacinta piped up to him over her shoulder.

Nikki declined, saying it was much too early in the day for him, and Tyrone didn't even have to ask his wife again, for she hardly ever finished a glass with her meal, in fact. Jacinta leaned forward after Tyrone had handed her a dainty glass over the back of the sofa.

"So, *maman*, what are you going to call him?" Jacinta directed her question to Angel.

Angel thought for a moment, then mimicked the maid's words of several days before, "Daisy Mae said 'he's mighty lak' a rose', but of course Rose is a feminine name, and I love the name Brian. So . . . seeing as he does resemble a perfect flower, this gave me an idea, and I came up with Brian Ross." She looked to her husband for approval, but he only turned brusquely to pour himself another noggin of brandy.

Jacinta merely shrugged both her brows and her shoulders. "Pour me another too, *mon cher*," she said as she handed the glass back over to him.

Contrarily Nikki smiled at Angel and patted her hand comfortingly, but she remained calm, cool, and collected. Her cheeks glowed with health and she was gorgeous, electrifying in pale turquoise. It was a brocade silk with simple lines, long-sleeved, that she wore this warmer December day, and her youthful beauty enhanced the plain garment ninefold.

Angel bent to the cradle, exhibiting part of a full and very much rounder breast that rocked sensuously when she moved to fuss with Brian's blanket. She caught her husband watching her and her eyes tilted up to him and shone. Tyrone, made punch-drunk by the delightful sight, moved around the couch and the sherry was thrust recklessly into Jacinta's outstretched hand. Green eyes widened at the inevitable and Angel curbed a soft giggle when the damage was done.

"Ohhh!" Jacinta screeched, leaping to her feet, struggling with the spilling glass. "You have filled my sherry to the rim! Here, get me something to wipe off my habit before it is ruined completely."

Nikki chortled gleefully as his cousin fetched a gold-embroidered linen from the sideboard and handed it over to Jacinta. As she dabbed at her soiled skirt, she glared narrowly at the two across from her, obviously enjoying this scene immensely.

"Habit?" Nikki rubbed it in. "Has my cousin's stepmother become a member of the religious order?"

Tyrone's eyes darkened like nightfall. "Nikki, your tongue has become so dulled that your words fail to entertain anymore. Why don't you go and find a dreary little room on the top floor and amuse yourself . . . like the attic, for instance."

"It was just a playful remark, without significance," Nikki said, winking at Angel as he stood facing away from their company.

Angel tossed her head airily and her drawn-back hair rippled sinuously over a shoulder to trail down to her breast. "No matter, Nikki," she dared, despite the scowls that came her way.

Angel's spirit, too, quickly dampened when Nikki had quit the parlor. She supposed Tyrone had good reason for being singed by Nikki's playful spite directed at him and his stepmother. He had meant it more for Jacinta, but somehow it had evinced his dislike of their togetherness of late. It, too, moiled on her heart more than she cared admit to herself. But what could she do? This was no primrose path she had come to walk.

For a moment Tyrone smiled secretively to himself behind the rim of his tall glass. But Angel still blushed hotly whenever he was nearby, recalling to mind his midwifery. His attire today, as usual, was immaculate, unwrinkled, right down to his fawn-colored riding breeches, the tight cut of which left nothing to the imagination. Again, he was resplendent with diamonds, making her wonder if he ever removed them at all. Reluctantly she pulled her prying regard from that lean physique and her eyes again caressed the sleeping infant.

"How was your ride, my husband?" Angel inquired to break the stifling silence that had reigned since Nikki's departure.

His probing eyes found her lifted ones and she was at once sorry for having asked the question that now rang in her ears as a bit presumptuous-sounding. Her intentions had merely been to make conversation; there was interest involved, too, for she looked forward to the day when she would be allowed to ride astride.

Tyrone shrugged broad shoulders. "As usual, a break from the daily routine, but monotonous just the same, like everything else in life," he said dully, then drained his glass, and tilted the thing thoughtfully and peered into emptiness.

Jacinta's response came quickly. "Why, *mon* Ty, you did not tell me you rode out every day. I thought you were much too tired, when you burn the midnight oil every night. You work too hard, *mon cher*," she cooed.

"That's the name of the game," Tyrone said tersely as he went to put his glass aside.

Systematically Jacinta turned back to Angel. "My how you have filled out, *petite mignone*. She looks cute, doesn't she, Tyrone. Rosy cheeks, pinkish ribbons trailing down her back . . . and that delightful—ah—frock. Did you make it yourself, child?"

Angel respired deeply before she spoke, sounding weary all of a sudden. "Mimi keeps me well-stocked with the latest creations, Jacinta. Besides, the duties of motherhood keep my hands full, to say the least." She glanced at Tyrone, but he had turned his back to them to go and stand at the window.

Jacinta felt suddenly saddled with that green-eyed monster. Nevertheless, she waved a hand indicating the cradle. She tried, "What drudgery, and I suppose you have to wear a tight bandage now, to restore your girlish figure back to normal. What a pity! How uncomfortable it must be for you, child."

"Not a chance, Jacinta!" Angel volleyed. "You see, I am not wearing one, nor do I intend to. I believe that a tightly applied abdominal binder results in more harm than good. Anyway . . . I've no need of such binding, for my figure remains much the same as before concep—" she halted abruptly, peering down with a sober expression.

Suddenly Tyrone turned and put his back to the window. It was hard to read his expression with the light behind him, but Jacinta's nostrils flared when he continued to gawk at his wife's back, as if waiting for her to go on. Angel blushed hotly, feeling him there behind her. Jacinta tried again, with a new twist to her lips.

"Madame Hunter, you have forgotten to lace up your bodice when you last fed your son." She waited for the younger woman to color more, but Angel only smiled indifferently. Confused by this, Jacinta went on hotly, "The way you abuse your horny husband is a shame, madame. Can't you see he has been drooling for an hour now?"

Angel perked up, bored no more. "An hour! Oh, my goodness, it is time for Brian's bath," she said busily as she disregarded the one breast partially exposed, looking aside to her husband. "Tyrone, would you be so kind as to fetch Sarah for me now, please?"

Her sweetly mouthed plea took him around the sofa and, with her eyes feasted upon him, he turned from her confusedly to go and summon the maid. His mouth suddenly split in a wide grin. He had been enjoying this game of genuine female wit. Horny! And damned well he was! He had felt the grinding pressure in his loins all this hour as indeed he did drool and gawk like a dumbstruck lad with green balls.

He yanked the bellcord with butterfingers, feeling much like a volcano about to erupt. Sarah finally appeared, breathless, at once knowing what was expected of her. She bobbed around the tall human structure who was rooted and not about to go anywhere at this moment of embarrassment. Curse these tight breeches! he thought.

Tyrone had checked his widespread emotions by the time Sarah came toward him carrying the wakened babe. The maid smiled shyly up at him and Tyrone felt a twist in his gut when the infant burbled softly as Sarah walked slowly around him. He checked himself from reaching out to caress the healthy pink cheeks. He studied the near-emerald-tinted eyes as Sarah paused an instant in indecision, but noted next that Mr. Hunter remained untouched by the sight of his wonderful son. With a perfunctory nod from him, Sarah took the babe upstairs for his midday bath.

When Tyrone turned back to the room, Angel had calmed herself after witnessing his disinterest in their offspring; it had been repeated often in the last few days. She stood brusquely while lacing up the loose flap of her bodice. She tied off the bow with a jerk and made to sweep past him with a mulish set to her jaw. Her elbow was caught in a viselike grip and his tall frame allowed no passage to the portal. Resistless to do otherwise, Tyrone leered down at her and suddenly she did the unexpected.

Jacinta watched with mouth aslack as Angel tossed back her head flirtatiously and ran a finger across his chest in a playfully naughty gesture. "Did you wish something of me, sir?" Angel purred, slanting her eyes up to him.

Tyrone heartened at this new sport, but held steadfast with former resolution. She had done this act before and he was on to her now, though her motive this time was ungraspable to him. This was much bolder of her, sensuous, and very much to his liking.

"Angel, you'll not take your meal in your room again tonight," he said, trying to look stern, but a lazy grin hedged around his lips. He continued a little hoarsely, "You are not that indisposed—ah—ill. I mean—from now on you'll come to the table. I don't relish the idea of eating with the men again— or alone. I would like having my wife where she belongs, not hiding away like a hermit all of the time." Lord, it was growing hot in the room; Tyrone sweated.

Crystal orbs twinkled impishly and she curtsied as far as his grasp would allow. "Yes, master, I shall do your bidding from now on and with good grace come to dine with you this eve. Your wish is my command, master. Now, if you are done with me, may I be excused to go ready myself for our evening together . . . at the table, master?"

Tyrone felt half-witted, tetchy, and without a reply. He was spared when Jacinta arose with much ado from the plush sofa, a ho-hum expression lining her face. This flirtatious family affair was beginning to nauseate her and she could do with another drink before she made the trip back to the city, made pleasantly shorter this time by a comfortable cabin owned by a burly captain who waited on her with his barge. She made a racket at the sideboard as she clinked glasses and such and when she was done, she was well pleased.

Tyrone had released Angel's arm in the commotion and was now watching her go. With his back turned to Jacinta, she missed the prurient gaze riveted to the gentle sway of turquoise skirts. Similarly, Tyrone missed the evil eye that followed his wife out into the hall.

2

Seated at the dinner table, Tyrone and Nikki immediately rose when Angel entered the room. As usual, she appeared ultrafeminine, her hair done up this night in soft waves hugging her cheeks and cascading ringlets that bounced saucily over her shoulders. Mimi's newest creation, a deepest blackberry brocade minus lines boasting the usual simplicity, plunged low, inset with a sinuous curve of lined lace that thrust her breasts high. Tyrone stared down agog at this eye-opener as he held out a chair for her to be seated.

"I'll have to have a talk with Mimi," Tyrone said somewhat gruffly, taking the seat beside his wife.

Angel turned to him, taking in his attire, which had obviously been donned with special care this night. "Why is that, my husband?" she wondered sweetly.

He coughed behind his hand. "I much prefer Mimi turn out gowns for my wife of a more—" He groped for words, colored unusually. He cleared his throat. "I will have to instruct her to lift the line of your bodice in the future. This one, madame, is not decent, it displays too much flesh for a married woman."

Angel hadn't realized her revealing dinner gown would affect him this much, but then, that was definitely what she'd had in mind as she'd dressed for this quiet dinner. She swept a hand around the room now.

"What damage, sir? We are at home with only your eyes, Nikki's, the servants', to survey my—umm—immodesty, as you call it." With a new sense of daring she went on. "And, what of your couturier, Tyrone? He, too, could take a looser stitch in your trousers . . . like your riding breeches for one." Her eyes slanted up under her lashes as she sucked in a cheek.

Tyrone spewed out a mouthful of white wine he'd been sipping, and he coughed, almost gagging. Nikki roared with mirth as he slapped his thighs and took in Angel's heartless smile. He held up his glass to her.

416

"Should we drink a health to the new mother?"

Tyrone raised his reddened face, and said in a silky-soft voice, "Shut up, Nik." He then turned to his wife. "You have made me appear more foolish than a heap of dung on the carpet, my sweet."

Her eyes grew round. "What is a—heap—of—dung?" she wondered, her curiosity aroused.

Nikki chuckled. "That, my dear cousin, is really out of place here, and not so foolish actually. Just a thing out of place," he repeated.

"For some reason this dinner has gone wayward from the start," Tyrone announced. "Let's start all over and speak no more of garments and heaps and such."

"Suits me, m'lord," Angel teased, feeling her oats now that she had won an advantage over him.

Tyrone sat back broodingly as he wondered what other malice aforethought his wife had in mind for him. He had a hunch that she had England on her mind this night, perhaps would even beg him to take her and Brian there in the near future, on the contrived surmise that Christine Sherwood had possibly found her way back there? But he knew better, as should she, that the slightly demented woman most likely yet roamed the streets of New Orleans in search of her daughter. Was she alive or dead—no one really had knowledge of what had become of the wretched woman.

Biding his time, Tyrone turned the conversation to the likewise dangerous topic of war, as the first course was being served: a delicious beef potage with generous chunks of vegetable, brioches, and French bread that only Melvin could bake to crusty perfection. The meal was rolled in on a cart by Cordell, tonight serving not only as manservant but footman, as it was that man's night off. Tyrone buttered a hunk of the bread as Nikki took up the conversation.

"If Jefferson had asked for a declaration of war in 1807, the country would be to the guess of many united in support much more than it is now." He laid down his spoon, warming to the subject. "Peace-minded Jefferson asked Congress to pass what was to be called the Embargo Act, forbidding cargo ships to leave American ports for foreign countries. With both France and England blockading the other, plus attacking American shipping, trade was made difficult, though the American merchants preferred the risks rather than sitting still in her commerce, and so . . . the Embargo was repealed two years later, after failing full enforcement."

Tyrone waved a butter knife in the air. "And now, even stranger, New England, which has both sailors and shipping does not want war, even though Madison stated this war is about defending sailors and American vessels. Again, these merchants prefer the risks of neutrality rather than facing certain losses by warfare."

Angel couldn't contain herself any longer. "What's more, nothing is being gained in this war as far as territory goes. For one . . . Detroit has been surrendered to British troops. After that defeat, the New York militia sat on their bloody behinds, watching the British drive the soldiers under Captain Wool back to the river in Canada where the American troops were forced to surrender." She paused when two pairs of dark brows raised, but went on hotly. "Pray, what victory does America hope to gain by this simple-minded war?" she begged ungraciously, fending for her sod.

Tyrone hid a smile beneath his napkin. "My dear wife, I didn't know you were such an intellectual on such matters. But then again, I should have recalled our lively political discussions on board the Indiaman with the smugglers and privateers of Barataria." Again he smiled before he went on. "You seem to have missed the gist of our conversation, my dear. What is hoped to gain is an end to the British attacks on American shipping. Detroit and Canada are but two of a series of defeats at the hands of the British. True . . . but you didn't let me finish before. Even now, sea battles are raging and several American victories are amazing the British, as four of their own ships have been captured and one destroyed so far. All with a handful of our well-executed ships against a hundred or more of the British."

"Yes, I've read something of it, of the war at sea spread out in the pages of Le Courier de Louisiane," Angel said with aplomb, "but what good is victory if nothing tangible is gained by either side, I still want to know. The dead and mortally wounded are a high price to pay for such foolishness between men who are supposed to be mature and intelligent adults. Had I but met this Thomas Jefferson I would have sided with the peaceable man fully!" she said in a peppery voice.

In her agitation, Angel suddenly lost the spoon into her stew. Tyrone and Nikki exchanged lazy glances of amusement as she bent stiffly over the deep bowl trying to spy the drowned spoon. Feeling the pair of eyes regarding her distress, she slowly lifted her chin a notch but soon bloomed scarlet. She emitted a feeble chuckle and waved and shrugged, then sat back with a face like marble. She peeked over as Tyrone stood, gallantly coming to her rescue as he fished for the silver spoon with two forks.

"Ah-hah! Here it is," he announced with much ceremony, pulling the dripping utensil to the surface. Then, "Hmmm, this will never do. You just sit tight while I ring for Cordell, sweet."

Cordell arrived at once and fetched a fresh bowl of potage ladled from the tureen and a fresh spoon. He swept it down before Angel in a grand fashion and his bright blue eyes rested on her momentarily before he nodded to her respectfully. Cordell left the room and the two men waited for her to pick up her spoon.

"Hummph!" Angel snorted, wrinkling her nose at them both. "You are poking male fun at me just because I claim the right to speak for my beloved country and the hundreds of maimed lads on either side."

Tyrone realized, as was befitting a mother, that she thought of her son. He sat silent now, closed to the subject that was drawing closer and closer to England. Nikki relieved them all by bringing the conversation to a close.

"It has been said that nobody ever really wins a war, princess," Nikki explained.

Angel nodded. "Mmmm, yes. I suppose you are right," she conceded. "But—"

"No more, please," Tyrone begged, holding up his hand. "I don't wish for another war to intrude upon our lovely dinner."

Angel finished up her potage, taking a sip now and then from her glass of white wine, while Nikki talked seriously about getting hitched up with Hannah right after Christmas.

"Single blessedness is not as exciting as it used to be. Besides—" he sighed deeply, "I've never met any girl as wonderful as Hannah McCormick."

Tyrone grunted. "And I suppose Wesley Gayarre approves of this match," he said curtly.

Nikki sipped his wine thoughtfully before answering, "He hasn't been around Gayarre much these days. Either he's out riding his land or he's imbibing at his old haunt in the city. I don't care much for the likes of that man and I almost got into it with him once. I had to back down, though. That man is strong as a bull and twice as mean. We'll marry despite what he says," he ended on a final note.

"I shall be very happy for you both," Angel said quickly. Then steering the conversation away from Wesley, she asked, "Where is Caspar? I haven't seen him about the grounds today as I usually do."

Tyrone said, "He left early this morning for New Orleans to send a letter off for me to—ah—England." Hang! Tyrone suddenly cursed himself for a big mouth.

Angel's heart fluttered in her breast as Tyrone peered closely at her while she toyed with the long stem of her glass thoughtfully. She seemed to have been baiting him all along, and now Tyrone would have it out.

"Are you missing England so much, Angel?" he asked offhandedly.

"Oh, yes, Tyrone," she blurted, turning to touch his arm lightly. "I would love to return—for a visit, and perhaps—just maybe Mama has found a way home and is there waiting for me."

"But she would have sent a message by now, my dear," Tyrone said, his anger heightening. Suddenly he was being reminded of a man named James. He stared straight ahead, sipping his wine. "Did you know that Stonewall was put up for auction and released to the highest bidder?" he hurled the question at her, indulging his annoyance.

Angel gasped and paled visibly. "What?" She stared around, feeling as if she were disintegrating into nothing. "How—how could I have known? I have been away over a year now."

Tyrone ignored the warning from his cousin that he had

gone too far. This was going to hurt, and Nikki was thinking that at least Tyrone could have picked a more peaceful evening than this one to lay open the bare facts. His cousin seemed driven by demons and there was no stopping him now.

"You see, wife," Tyrone began cruelly, "Stonewall was put up for sale months before the *Fidelia* sailed for Puerto Bello. Your Uncle Stuart was left in charge of drawing up the final papers, on your parents' parting request that he do so."

"So that is why Beldwin had a word with Winnie shortly before we sailed," Angel breathed almost to herself. Then, "But why wasn't I told?" she asked no one in particular.

Tyrone shrugged and Angel shifted to face him, searching his brooding countenance for an answer. He blinked, somewhat startled at her catching him studying her so intently. Her scent was intoxicating, stimulating every nerve end and warming his cold blood as no potent drink could. His muscled limbs felt like molten lead as her hand rested softly on his arm again and burned clear through the silken sleeve of his shirt. She was a whisper away and it was all he could do to restrain himself from reaching out to caress her. He summoned up the vision of a young hoyden scowling in readiness to do battle with a score of armed pirates. The vision blurred and he was delivered back to the present and her beside him breathing heavily.

"And how do you happen to come by all this information?" she asked, prettily angry.

"There are ways of finding things out, my dear wife," he said mockingly. He was nudged by the thought of her entwined in the arms of her lover, and he went on more cruelly, "Did you perhaps have knowledge that your beloved parents were in dire straits before your departure?"

"I—yes, I had wind of it, but my thoughts centered on its being mainly because of the voyage," she said abjectly.

Ungently Tyrone began, "The voyage to Puerto Bello was to be their last adventure before settling down right here in Louie—" He gave her the chance to gasp, then he went on as if he hadn't paused, "where your father had procured a job of sorts beforehand. There was not a soul who would lend Lord Sherwood another farthing. His gambling debts were well known in London and the surrounding areas—by all who came into contact with the man."

"You really discover who your friends are when a financial crisis arises," Angel breathed. She suddenly realized there was not a bloody soul back in England she could call friend. And poor Winnie, he would now be friendless and alone. The lares and penates of the household would all have been sold by now, the proceeds divided up to pay off Beldwin's mountainous gambling debts. She was a pauper now, and at the mercy of her own husband.

Her distress was making itself felt. Marching into the room, Cordell delivered thick slices of pink ham and steaming vol-au-vent stuffed with chicken. The huge platters were placed on the table, and Angel felt suddenly ill looking at all of the fine, rich fare displayed palatably upon the long table. She stared unseeingly. All this grandiosity surrounded her and suddenly it didn't have any meaning anymore.

How would her husband use her now that he had her cornered with no place to run and hide. Was he perhaps one of that breed that sired children by the dozen only to prove his manhood, then ignored his offspring like a herd of cattle put out to pasture? Was that what he had in mind for her? There was nothing left for her in the world but her son. No place for her to escape to. There *was* one way left open to her. Uncle Stuart. . . .

As if Tyrone had read her thoughts, he ruthlessly took up his narrative again. "Your uncle is well taken care of though, I've heard. Seems that some kindly soul has seen to his medical bills and he lives on quite comfortably now in Cornwall." He halted momentarily to fork some steaming ham onto her plate. His eyes narrowed significantly. "Ahh, I might add, Stuart has all he can handle just caring for himself and his own needs."

"That ramshackle ship . . . unfit for dogs!" Angel blurted out strangely. "No wonder every bit of clothing was packed and servants so solemn during our departure. Why, oh why, didn't they tell me! And Winnie, I cannot believe he was in on it, too. I should have known. How naive of me!"

Tyrone shrugged, then went on with more care, explaining, "They most likely wanted to spare you any suffering over the

422

loss of your home. In all due time I'm sure your parents would have broken it to you, gently."

Grimacing at the food, Angel pushed her plate back. How cruel this man beside her, her husband, could be. *He* hadn't spared her feelings one whit. But then, he didn't love her as her parents had. If only she didn't love this man so much, she could return hate for hate. Couldn't she?

Nikki rose from the table suddenly, dismissing himself with the excuse that he must go see a man about a horse and would return shortly. When he was gone his words hit her like a ton of bricks and she moaned.

"Horse! I suppose they had to sell Echo and her colt, too. My beautiful mare, Echo. I shan't ever see her again or even know what Prancer looked like."

Tyrone, almost choking on his vol-au-vent, peered askance at her, asking incredulously, "You named the foal before you ever saw the beast?"

Angel colored with rage. "Beast! And I suppose you know just what became of them also, Sir Know-It-All!" She shifted to glare hotly at him.

"That I—ummm, know nothing, madame," he answered nonchalantly. "Here, eat now. You haven't had anything but the potage, and I like your figure the way it has nicely filled out. Never cared much for scrawny women."

"Nothing escapes your eagle eye, does it! It is utterly remarkable that you have not a trace of knowledge about who has Echo and her colt. How is it that you are so unerring in everything but that tidbit of information?" She tossed her napkin down and fairly glowered. "And . . . how in God's name did you unearth what you did? I never even told you where I lived!"

Tyrone made himself more comfortable as he sat back grinning while he clasped his lean fingers over his silk shirt and tapped his firm chest. Hazel dusk met cool green and when he finally answered, it was maddeningly slow.

"From England to America news travels faster than in the past, and information can be obtained in a month's time—and other transactions can take place, too, I might add," he explained, marveling at the manner in which her eyes turned a

423

frosty shade of turquoise when she was upset or angry. His eyes rested on her untouched plate and he tried, "Aren't you hungry tonight, sweet?"

"Ooooh! Always mocking, you are. What you need, Tyrone Hunter, is a simpering maid who will say, 'Yes sir! No sir, I wouldn't do that! As you say, sir!' and give you everything you desire in a snap!"

"Sorry," Tyrone chuckled. "I couldn't have suitable respect for a woman who was overly simple and easy to manipulate. I relish the adventure of often discovering new facets in my—ah—life-mate's character." He quirked a brow, adding, "I much rather would enjoy the delights of a woman clothed in mystery and intrigue." He smiled to himself, thinking that she had not been a woman but a little hoyden at first.

Nikki returned just then and, endeavoring to break the strain of the moment, passed by a cart and brought with him a tray bearing crystal-stemmed glasses and a decanter of after-dinner cordial. He twirled the tray atop his fingertips, and swooping it down onto the table, performed with a polished half-bow.

"Madame?"

"I've had really enough, Nikki, of everything . . . for one evening. Thank you just the same. Now, I shall go upstairs and read for awhile before I retire. Good night, gentlemen."

Tyrone made to get up and help her from her seat, but she pushed him back down the few inches with the palms of her hands, saying, "Please, sir, do not trouble yourself, I am not the invalid you make me out to be. I would like to be alone now, for I've much to ponder this night."

When she was gone, Tyrone sat sullen, staring into his glass. He hated the stuff. He rose to go to the sideboard and pour himself a shot of his favorite brandy. When that was done he stood in back of his chair, ignoring the congealing food on his plate. Nikki was scratching his head and finally he couldn't stifle his question any further.

"Read? Ponder? Is that how your gorgeous wife occupies herself before bedtime?"

"How would I know?" Tyrone replied tersely.

"Really, Ty. You are retarded, old man."

"Shut up, Nik. There is only a matter of eight years between you and myself—puppy."

"You really did it this time, cousin. What in hell are you trying to do . . . make Angel thoroughly despise you?"

Tyrone grunted. "Had I but known that, I would have been the perfect gentleman this night," he said mockingly. "Hah! Don't kid yourself, Nik, that was accomplished several months ago. She hated me before I ever opened my fool mouth at this table tonight. Angel still thinks of me as a blackguard and I can't blame her for that!"

"To be sure! Your actions around here lately are not unlike that of an unfaithful husband, randy pussing about the countryside with Jacinta. Angel most likely thinks that you lay the bitch several times weekly in the woods. Damn. What do you see in that slut when you possess the most delightful woman man ever laid eyes on?"

"Possess! That *is* a laugh, Nik. Maybe in name only, not in flesh nor spirit. And Jacinta, that one trails after my butt wherever I go, like a horny she-dog!" Tyrone paced the length of the table, stretching his long legs and Nikki watched him for a space before he spoke.

"You could tell her to get lost and not bother you?" Nikki suggested.

Tyrone stopped his pacing. "Don't think that I haven't already tried that. I swear that woman just lies in the brush waiting for me to take Beast out, then follows me jabbering into the woods and all the way back. What a Jezebel, she can't seem to keep her hands to herself. If it was not for her begging me till she was blue in the face, I wouldn't have that white devil in the stable, kicking down her stall every day. How she ever persuaded me into carting that fool horse here, I'll never know."

Nikki cleared his throat loudly. "Yeah, I'd like to know that myself, old man," he wondered, lifting a brow until Tyrone fairly smouldered.

Tyrone ignored the unspoken accusation, and went on, "What a fool! I thought she showed good bloodlines. And white! Jesus! I swear that the mare is moonstruck!"

Nikki chuckled feebly, at the same time asking, "How do you do it, Ty?"

"How do I do what?" Tyrone stared around at Nikki as if the younger man was demented.

"Switch the conversation from Angel to horses, that's what."

"How do I do anything?" he questioned, and Nikki shrugged.

"Life has no rhyme or reason," Tyrone said oddly. Then on the brighter side somewhat, "Let's go out to the old barn and see what havoc that white bitch has wreaked this day. I swear someday I'm going to ride that one to her death," he said.

"Hmmm," Nikki had a thought and said it aloud. "One minute hot-tempered, the next brooding, and then grinning stupidly. What's gotten into you?"

"Hell if I know. I'm a mess!"

"Hmmm," Nikki pondered, "must be you're in love with a fair maid . . . very much? No one else will do?"

His face mottled suddenly, Tyrone looked unraveled when he retorted, "You mean have I bedded another since Angel?— No! Now does that answer your question quite sufficiently?"

"Sure and it does!" Nikki mimicked Caspar's brogue.

Cordell, with a tray of rich sweets, met the two men just leaving the dining room. He took in the unfinished fare as he wondered what to do with the dessert. Tyrone glanced the length of the table over his shoulder and then came back to the tray of nutted tortes.

"Take them back to the kitchen, Cordell, and indulge yourself," Tyrone told the man. "Have the maids help themselves, too. Yes, you can have Ranae clean up now," he added, answering the question in the man's eyes.

Cordell shrugged as he went back to the kitchen to fetch Ranae. Without his beard, James Cordell wondered how long it would be before the old captain of the smugglers recognized him, even at that.

After Angel had donned a lacy nightgown she fluffed her pillow, then stood staring at the white emptiness of the bed. Dismissing Sarah, she had sat at the white and gold dressing

426

table, brushing out her hair herself as she pondered her dilemma. Now she wasn't sleepy one bit. The room had been stuffy and Sarah had left a long door open a crack to air out the place. The cold moon beckoned, and as if hypnotized, Angel donned a warm robe and went out to stroll the gallery, keeping an ear out lest Brian begin to whimper.

From where she stood bathed in pale moon, deep male voices drifted up to her and she could make out two misty forms just making their way to the back of the house. The back of her husband's tawny head glistened with the dew and he appeared to Angel as one unreachable, having no rival to his towering lean height, his sensational good looks. A terrible urge to run down after him and brush her fingers through his hair and hug him close struck her.

Consequently Angel whirled about, flushing with the want of him. It was just no good what was happening to her inside. Tyrone thoroughly despised her, had made it quite clear to her only this night. He wanted to hurt her, make her suffer time and again. The past was like withered leaves blown away; her parents were gone, Stonewall had a new owner, and all she had left was her son to cling to.

Outside the air was crisp and the Yuletide season was upon Cresthaven. Yule logs had been cut beforehand and piled up high against the side of the house while they waited for the Christmas Eve fires. Inside wood floors were finished being scrubbed and waxed till they shone with a deep nut-brown luster, smelling nicely of lemon and beeswax. Every piece of fine furniture glowed afresh; carpets were brushed up; brooms and dustmops were kept busy as maids circulated throughout the wide expanse of the mansion the entire week. Not a corner had been neglected by the time the small party burst in out of the bracing air of morn as they returned from the early morning church service.

Tyrone, in high spirits, smiled at his wife's healthful glow as he was helping her out of the new fox-lined velvet cloak. Angel was dressed in the colors of a summer sunset—cloak, smart bolero, and slippers all in a deep, swirling purple. The pinkish-mauve, Paris fashioned velvet gown was cut with a scooped neckline and a slim, long skirt, and several lawn petticoats edged with pink frills peeped out below the skirt when she walked or sat. Her husband was just as grand, in his dark brown, skin-tight pantaloons and matching frock coat. His tobacco-brown silk vest matched his tall hide boots. He was a sight that would set many a maiden's heart to thumping.

Angel reluctantly let her husband relieve her of the silver-fox muff that had kept her hands toasty warm during the long ride back home in the carriage. Arm in arm, Hannah and Nikki led the way into the brightly lit parlor, while Angel and Tyrone followed with Caspar at their heels. The latter had grumbled all the way to church, mentioning something about never having been inside one before. Now the huge Irishman looked forward gladly to a tot of rum to warm his insides as he settled his bulk before the great crackling fire.

"I swear, Caspar, with that massive bulk of yours between me and the fire, I'm surely going to find no warmth," Nikki chuckled and smiled at Hannah beside him.

Caspar grunted. "Shouldn't cuss right after church, lad. Sure and God will hear you, and you won't be getting frostbit where you're bound."

"*Touché*," Nikki returned with a deeper chuckle this time. "Your jokes are getting better every day, large man. I guess you've got your life cut out for you now, and even that little kitchen maid has caught your rheumy eye. Yet, isn't she a mite too old and scrawny for you?"

Caspar blushed mightily and the light banter went on. Hannah and Angel helped Della trim the tree with colorful wood characters, real candy canes, and bits of colorful velvet ribbons tied in pert bows. As Angel carefully lifted a golden-haired angel out of a box that had been stashed away in the attic for years, her mouth formed a delicate O. It was so beautiful. She caressed it lovingly as she wondered at the same time if Tyrone's mother had fingered it last and had packed it away in the layers of straw herself.

Tyrone took notice of the tender moment and broke away from the men to come stand beside her. He peered down at the treasured item of his youth, recalling the very last time his mother had trimmed the tree with it. It was the Christmas before she had passed away, seeming an eternity away now. His visits had been short both times.

"That was Annette's favorite," Tyrone said quietly as his soft eyes caressed the up-tilted face. "It had been in her family for generations. I'll always treasure this piece of the joyous season. It's very fragile, the head is made of glass."

"Annette?" Angel breathed the question softly. She felt suddenly as if the angel burned her hand as she recalled the name of Tyrone's ship.

"Of course, sweet. My mother . . . Annette." He frowned a little, bemused.

Angel blushed profusely, as her bitter words back on the island came back to her all too painfully. No wonder he had been angered when she blurted out that he probably had named his ship after some painted strumpet. How awful of her to have said that!

"Forgive me, Tyrone. But why did someone not tell me before? All this time I have been living here admiring the portrait, and all that I knew her by was the late Mistress Hunter," she said poutingly.

Realizing the mistake now, the frown left his brow and he chuckled down to her ear. "You are even more beautiful when you pout, do you know that? And fie on you, madame, *you* never informed me of your fond interest in portraits. We will have a sitting soon of the new Mistress Hunter, would you like that, sweet?"

"Yes, I guess I would like that very much. . . ." Her voice blew away with her gaiety.

She felt his long arm slide about her waist and she trembled from the contact. The only other time he ever touched her was when she rose from the table, or like this morning, when his hand had ridden possessively at the back of her waist, causing thrills to run along her spine. She blushed with love at his mere sweet presence.

Tyrone, on the other hand, mistook her little quivers for revulsion at his familiarity. He brooded once again, as he was in the habit of doing lately. Reluctantly he let his arm drop back to his side. He nodded politely before going back to join their guests. He was only there a short time when, turning back

429

to glance in her direction, the sight that met his eyes signaled him like a red flag waving. Angel tottered precariously on her perch of a pillow-piled chair, fumbling with the angel but failing to reach the higher altitude to plant the doll at the top of the tree.

"What the—" Tyrone exploded.

Swiftly he was beside her as all eyes in the parlor turned just in time to witness him reaching up to lift his wife clear of the danger, setting her down beside him as if she were a mere feather. She had felt herself being swooped down, with the angel still clutched tight in her hand and Tyrone's arm wrapped securely about her waist. She stared round-eyed at her distressed husband, who ended by mopping sweat from her brow with a handkerchief. He found his tongue at last and his face was drawn tight.

"Damnit, Angel! If you ever do anything like that again, I'll—I'll—I don't know what the hell I'll do to you!" he said with acerbic tongue as his fingers raked his hair.

Angel frowned in confusion at his mean outburst, then peered down at the doll, before thrusting it at him while tears sparkled crystalline on her lashes. She turned with a vicious twist and only a swirl of pinkish-mauve could be seen going out the parlor door. Tyrone gritted his teeth in passing the doll to Hannah and followed in Angel's wake. When he reached the foot of the stairs, she had already fled to her bedchamber. He heard the door slam, but nevertheless, took a wooden stance as he bellowed upwards loud.

"Damnit, Angel! Come back down here at once!" He waited for a response but none was forthcoming. Finally he tossed his hands toward the high ceiling in a helpless gesture, wheeling about to come face to face with Della.

"Well . . . what do you want?" he snapped into the brown face.

"She's stronger than ever, and she won't break. She's not a dumpling, Mr. Hunter," Della informed him in a cautious manner, for he was like a volcano about to erupt fire and lava.

"Hell you say!" He worked the muscles in his cheek furiously. "A moment more and she would have crashed to the floor, tree and all. She could have broken her back . . . or some other part of her body!" he added foolishly.

"Maybe," Della came back, half accordantly. "Leave her be now, Mister. Anyway, she's got to nurse that hungry youngster of yours just now."

Tyrone frowned darkly. "Of course, the boy . . . again." He strode back into the parlor, looking for all the world like a mean ogre.

Della clucked her tongue as she watched the tall form with shoulders fashioned rigidly. She slid her gaze to the top of the stairs and thought with compassion:

"Poor honey chile. She thought Mr. Hunter was mad 'cause of that fragile doll maybe breakin', not herself. Lawsy, when are them two gonna understand each other? They both tense as two folks can get."

Della shook her turbaned head slowly, and as if on command, the footman ushered Jacinta and her father into the vast hall. The housekeeper wrinkled her shiny brown nose as the flashy woman tossed her red wrapper at the footman and swept into the parlor, as usual like she owned the whole darn place.

Jacinta looked like a demimondaine in a red silk gown that revealed every curve, throwing into relief her more generous portions. Hannah took a moment to study the sparkling diamond necklace and ear-drops that must have painfully drained her budget. Jacinta's gems reflected the red and orange flickers from the hearth, but not with the same pure intensity as did the diamonds that encrusted their host's fingers. Jacinta noticed this also as Tyrone greeted them with a preoccupied air and a wave of his hand to a sofa. After the coolness of the greeting, Jacinta neither was appeased when next her stepson strode casually over to Hannah McCormick and took her by the arm, gently guiding her over to the portal. Bending over the brown head, Tyrone spoke for her ears only. Hannah was seen to nod, to wink with conspiring air across to Nikki, and then she excused herself politely to all before she went to do as bid.

After completing the task Angel had set out to accomplish with the Christmas decoration, Tyrone left the tree and found a seat upon the sumptuous yellow sofa. He lounged there, oblivious to the conversation Guy Villerne was monopolizing among himself, Nikki, and Caspar. The host's thoughts rested solely upstairs, but it was not long before his peace was interrupted, when Jacinta eased her silk-clad form down onto the cushion beside him.

"So, *mon cher*, where is the happy little *maman?*" Jacinta purred the question like an imperious cat.

Tyrone cocked an eyebrow, contemplating her nearness. He shifted his lean frame to bend an arm up over the sofa to better watch the entrance. With his one shoulder shielding her view of that portal, his answer came slowly.

"I'm thinking she will be down shortly," he answered tersely, unexcited by the arrival of his uninvited guest.

Just then the footman entered with a tray of hors d'oeuvres, followed by Cordell who bore another of the same. The latter appeared taken aback slightly when he spied Jacinta sitting there next to his employer. He swept the tray down onto a low table between the sofas, then turned without further ado, and Jacinta, with a squint of dark eyes, watched the wiry form depart the parlor.

The woman and her father attacked the light fare as if they hadn't seen food for several weeks. Tyrone kept his eye peeled toward the open doors, unmindful of the delicious tidbits, and bored thoroughly with the conversation and Guy's idle chatter. Pressed against his hip was the gift he had ready to present to his wife. It was Christmas Eve and he wanted to surprise her with another trinket. He shoved the thought of the costly old lavaliere out of his mind; his gift would outshine it and any others the mysterious lover could come up with.

"Well, Hunter, what do you think?" Villerne had posed a question to his host.

Tyrone twisted about. "I'm sorry. Come again, Villerne?" he offered.

"This war with England. Sugar! Trade will no longer be possible into Europe or in the eastern part of America. Does this not mean something to us planters?" You a rich, me a poor planter, he kept to himself.

"Ahhh, yes," Tyrone said after stifling a yawn. "Relations seem to be getting a mite rigid. We can take up with the sugar transportation once the war is ended. Now why worry, Guy?"

432

"But all major ports will be blocked. Does this not trouble you, monsieur?" Villerne blustered.

"Blockaded? Mmmm, I'm not troubled overly much, Guy." He took up measuring the frame of the portal again with his eyes.

Villerne glared at the back of Tyrone's brown silk vest, more often than he cared to. He tried again, "Your mother was daughter to one of the wealthy Southern planters, *non?*" His eyes always shone when money came into the conversation—usually by his introducing the subject.

"Ummm, yes, as a matter of fact she was. But she had English ancestors, too. You recall my wife is an Englishwoman, also. Care for another oyster, Villerne?"

Villerne sat back, realizing his host had cut the conversation of war and "who's who" short. All of a sudden Villerne remembered he was in the home of a man rumored to have been a smuggler. A very wealthy one at that, he smiled to himself. He daintily helped himself to another fried oyster as he popped the delicious morsel into his mouth, then licked off his fingers one by one. He pleasured himself with a brandy, of the finest stock, and began to think about his daughter's suing her husband for divorce. Rumor had it that Big Jim Hunter had moved all his belongings out of the town house, leaving Jacinta a sparse few furnishings, the clothes she had on her back, so to speak, and the low-quality gems she now wore. Villerne also knew that Jacinta had sent this man Cordell to seek employment here not long ago. His daughter had something up her sleeve that was any day due to slip out, and Villerne hoped it spelled m-o-n-e-y.

"Wonder of wonders!" Nikki spoke up from his position at the tall windows. After sighting a carriage and horse at the bend of the long lane, he let the drape fall back into place. "Cresthaven seems to grow in popularity this holiday. We have another visitor and I'm thinking I know who it is," he announced, tapping his chin decidedly.

Hannah and Angel were just descending the stairs, equally surprised to see who it was that the footman, Cordell this time, allowed in the front door. Wesley brushed off his coat and handed it over to the young man doubling again as footman and manservant. Wesley looked up to see the pair of young women just coming to the last step, and he disregarded Hannah's look of apprehension as his colorless gaze rested on the radiant mistress of Cresthaven.

Hannah had finally persuaded Angel to come down, never telling her that Tyrone had put her up to it. She had just emphasized that if Angel kept herself locked up in her room to sulk, it would spoil the holiday for the rest of them. The Christmastide would be ruined without the mistress present, Hannah murmured. Angel had finally capitulated, not one to rob others of pleasure when it was up to her to conform to the occasion, like in past years when she would have much preferred to be out riding Echo to aiding Christine with tea parties and such. Angel felt much better now and her hurt tears had been long dry.

Wesley walked right up to her now to plant a cold kiss into her palm. He peered up, still holding onto her hand, saying, "You are looking lovelier than ever, madame." He couldn't bring himself to add that motherhood agreed with her, and left it at that.

"Thank you, Wesley. You are looking fit yourself," Angel returned, withdrawing her hand when he seemed reluctant to let go of it. She noticed a flash of gray muslin behind him. "Who do you have there hiding behind you, Wesley?" she wondered, cocking her head off to one side. Then she realized it could only be the child.

"April?" she urged. "Ah, come on dear, do not be so bashful. I know that it has been awhile, but you remember your—your—" she faltered upon feeling an immobile presence close by. A very powerful one at that.

"Governess, love," Tyrone finished for her, mocking a bit, leaning indolently against the polished doorpost.

Angel gave him a feeble smile as he was pushing himself away from the frame to greet Wesley and his shy daughter. The handshaking over, Tyrone bent to the blushing child.

"I don't think I've ever had the pleasure of meeting this young lady before. Your daughter I presume, monsieur?" Tyrone asked, amiable enough.

Wesley made the introductions while April colored under

434

Mr. Hunter's gaze at her pudgy face. As he straightened to lead her and the grown-ups into the parlor, April was thinking how young and handsome this tall neighbor was. She thought surely he would have been closer to her father's age. But she had overheard while snooping in on the servants' conversation that he was rumored a tawny-haired devil with multiflecked eyes. They had said there was a narrow scar on his forehead, but she hadn't seen any with that lock of hair falling over his brow. They gossiped of him as being a tall, menacing figure, ever in black. They hadn't fibbed one bit, except for one thing; he was dressed in rich browns on this occasion. April liked the color brown and she liked Mr. Hunter, too.

Tyrone, passing by the child on his way over to be seated, winked boldly at her. April reddened even more, and, catching a peep at those skin-tight trousers, for the first time in her girlhood experienced a wonderment of the male human form. He possessed an aura reminding her of how she imagined the robber knights of the Middle Ages she had studied about. She couldn't take her young gray eyes off him.

Soon all were seated comfortably about the hearth, but Tyrone damned the situation mentally. Somehow Jacinta had contrived to seat herself next to him again, this time on the rust-and-cream sofa. Her hand was cradled in the folds of her red silk gown and brushed Tyrone's hard thighs. April wanted to giggle when her former governess, seated directly across from the host and his stepmother, studied Jacinta's hand hypnotically.

With Angel on one side of him and Villerne on the other, Wesley rambled on and on in his resonant voice with Villerne vying for second place in the conversation. Wesley was looking more squared out than ever, robust in health, though he seemed ill at ease, as did Cordell, who flitted in and out to replenish trays of hors d'oeuvres and brought decanters of sparkling red and white wine to whet the appetites for the main meal.

Angel tore her gaze from that sluttish woman's straying hand and took up watching the fire that blazed magenta, crackling and shooting hot blue sparks onto the hearth. She wallowed in that old fear until a growing anger took form.

435

How dare he flaunt his mistress here in her home! Stepmother—hah! Angel thought waspishly. Then, for the second time that day, tears burned her eyelids, but she wasn't about to create another scene, especially with Jacinta goading her to do just that.

Tyrone caught his wife visually when she replanted her gaze onto Jacinta's hand that was becoming bolder than ever, fingering a thin fold of the brown trousers. He grinned his pleasure when Angel lifted her eyes in horror at his catching her off guard. Tyrone was bewildered by this new side of her, but Angel, on the other hand, thought he mocked her cruelly. When the footman entered, Angel missed her husband's gesture of plucking Jacinta's hand up and patting it to stay on the red silk lap. Jacinta would not glance his way and only pursed her lips in a disgruntled manner.

Joseph cleared his throat and announced, "Dinner will be served at the seventh stroke. How many will be partaking, sir?" He looked to Tyrone.

"Why, everyone is staying, Joseph," Angel piped up emphatically. "Have Ranae set service for nine, would you please."

No refusals to dine came her way, and with a servile bow Joseph set forth to do as he was bid. Tyrone again saw his wife in a new light and decided it suited her well, indicating she was gracefully slipping into her role as mistress of Cresthaven. That she could slip into his arms as easily he wished as he rose to go and stand before the fire, his long, lean back to his audience.

"I'm not unlike a lovesick lad," Tyrone groaned silently within. "I am wild with the want for her. Day into night and night into day, and noonday dreams of passion. Me, onetime prince of smugglers and lover of many. Not anymore. Dreams of possessing her haunt me and damn! But I shall win her love and none shall challenge my will, not James, not her!" Broodingly he gazed into the flames. God! How he must have made her feel the whore at one time. His love-making had been savagely ardent back at that cottage, and, he just could not fathom it, she had given herself to him in complete abandonment, matched his passion, thrust meeting thrust and . . . could he do it again? Would she warm to his lover's skill this time?

Suddenly Tyrone's loins grew warm, but with a different kind of heat than that emanating from the hearth. An idea nudged him and he wondered if it would work. It would have to be effected when the excitement of the holidays wore off. They would have to be alone. In his bedchamber somehow? A week from now? Perhaps two? After the theater, he decided firmly. A place away from home.

> *Who knows not Circe,*
> *The daughter of the Sun, whose charmed cup*
> *Whoever tasted, lost his upright shape,*
> *And downward fell into a groveling swine.*
> —Milton

Chapter Eleven

1

Angel fastened her eyes upon that length of brown-clad male perfection silhouetted against the hearth. So wrapped up in studying him was she that she failed to notice the pair of gray eyes that pored over her gentle beauty from head to slippered toe. All she had eyes for was her husband: the way he pondered the licking flames as if he sought something of interest between the sides of the marble facade; the neat way in which his darker hair at the nape of his neck waved; long and lean but strong fingers braced against the mantelpiece. She thought him wonderful and a delicious warmth began spreading through her woman's network of sentience. She wanted him to come near her, touch her, speak to her, but not hurt her anymore.

As if seizing upon her silent plea Tyrone turned about, wearing a roguish smile that grew wider when Wesley vacated the cushion next to Angel's and went to stand at the window where the darkening skies, as gray as his own eyes, peered back at him. Tyrone came down beside her so swiftly and yet so gracefully that Angel smothered the hint of a giggle at his haste. Suddenly she was borne to heaven when, casually, he eased his arm up over the sofa and brushed her shoulder, resting his arm there in that fashion. In the next instant he had cause to damn Joseph silently when the man stood in the doorway announcing that the crab gumbo was now being served as the first course.

The guests filed out hungrily, dogging the footman like a

pack of ravenous beasts. No one had even noticed that Tyrone stayed his wife with his hand, gently pressing her forearm. Questioning eyes turned upon him and he smiled secretively as she colored at his thorough perusal of her.

"Sir?"

"Yes, Angeline Hunter. Did you wish something of me?"

"I?" she asked simply, next felt something rest in her lap. If he was getting fresh now—"Oh!" she gasped in surprise.

It was a tiny box with gold filigree meshed over royal-blue velvet that he had placed there. Benumbed, she just stared until his fingers nudged her hand to the waiting gift. She opened it and her breath sucked in as he slipped the daintily-set emerald ring onto her finger. With much animation she studied the square-cut jewel, with fine, costly diamonds that darted with blue-violet fires dancing around the larger, flaming green stone. The jewels appeared as priceless as his own.

Angel was so thrilled that she gave no thought to the fact that there might be a reason for this gift: a whim, perhaps, to fatten her up for the kill, she was to think later. Just when she was getting used to her philosophical way of life, he came and made her confused all over again.

"I am speechless, Tyrone, and I've never owned anything as grand as this," she murmured against the fine material where she had leaned against his broad shoulder. Her cheek left off caressing his arm, for she had grown quite familiar unconsciously, and now she held her beringed hand high to view the treasure.

"You can thank me by thrilling me also . . . with a kiss," Tyrone suggested huskily, warmed by her affectionate gesture.

With a forefinger he lifted her chin and was about to capture her lips when Nikki sheepishly interrupted from the door with, "Ahem. If you two are going to make love, I'll just go and keep your gumbo warm. Sorry."

When Angel shot up off the sofa Tyrone gritted his teeth in frustration. Interruptions, always interruptions. He heard Angel telling Nikki to go fetch the large package under her bed.

"You know," she reminded Nikki, "the gifts I had you purchase for me when you last visited the city?" Angel snapped her fingers in front of the young man's dazed look. "Nikki?"

One side of Nikki's mouth quirked as he was taking in the murderous glare coming his way from the angry fellow seated on the sofa. "Sure, right away, princess," Nikki murmured and backed up out of the room to spin up the staircase fast.

Chattering as she seemed to float dreamily back to the sofa, Angel explained with embarrassment that it was all she could afford. "I mean, it will seem petty in comparison to your fine gi—"

Tyrone interrupted swiftly, "Angel, whatever are you jabbering about?" He waited but she now hung her head. "Hmmm, I think I see. You purchased a gift and it was all you had left, it took all your savings from your governess's job?"

"Yes, yes. But how did you know?"

"I know more than you realize, sweet. But never mind that now. From this day on you will have your own money to spend. Don't worry about gifts for everyone else, I've purchased them all beforehand. Della will soon put them under the tree."

Tyrone was never so pleased with a gift as he was with the fur-lined leather gloves, and when he opened the package that contained new-fangled waterproof boots, he beamed with pleasure over her wise choice of serviceable items. The two combined were just what he needed when he worked long hours out in the chilly, damp weather of late. With Della coming in to ask if they were ever going to join their guests, Tyrone never received the kiss he wanted. He had to be content with walking into the dining room with his wife, his hand pressing her waist.

Rain began to fall about the house like a light sigh as inside the cozy warmth of the dining room, the fine regalement was laid out with no limit as to quantity or quality. There was savory wild rice nestled in deep majolicas, roast turkeys and chickens stuffed with pecans and raisins, red fish cooked in white wine sauce, peas and onions smothered in creamy white sauce, and waiting on the sideboards and carts were puddings of every flavor, nutty tortes, and steaming hot chickory coffee.

By the time the party arrived at the dessert, the drizzle had transformed into a surly rainstorm that pummeled against the tall french windows in large gray sheets. The feast had progressed smoothly until now; but as if the storm was a harbinger of discord, the harmony was broken as a slight disagreement broke out between Messieurs Gayarre and Hunter. It was the self-same crusade with Wesley. Land. He had been sitting upon nastiness the entire evening and now, pressing his luck too far with suggestive remarks dealing with the ownership of the northwest lands, Tyrone's composure departed and an argument was hatched.

Tyrone glanced around the table, then said decidedly, "Ladies, I'm sorry, but I'm thinking we gentlemen should take our discussion into the salon with our brandy. I'm sure you ladies can entertain yourselves for a time in the parlor?"

As the feast was near completion, with only April finishing up her pudding with full scoops to her mouth, Angel nodded her assent but wore a troubled frown when she led the way into the hall. Jacinta swept grandly ahead, her eyes narrowed covertly. She had studied her hostess's hand during the whole dinner, taking in the sparkling gem that hadn't been there before the meal. Jacinta looked nothing less horrendous than a flesh-eating wolverine now when Tyrone halted his wife to request something of her.

"Madame, this downpour has already made the roads impassable. Have Joseph and Cordell put up our guests for the night. Not even Gayarre can be reached with that muck ankle-deep out there. Would you, sweet?"

"Yes. I'll see that the maids freshen the beds and that Cordell and Joseph bank up the fires for the evening," she said, catching an overstuffed April yawning widely in the doorway. "And Della will see to April shortly."

Tyrone gave a sideways glance at the pudgy child, smiled to his wife, nodded, then took himself reluctantly to the salon. Angel held out an arm for the child to come into the half-circle of it, and together they went to find the housekeeper.

Christmas day dawned chilly and damp. Later Angel stood pressing her palms against the cold panes of glass in her room. In sober thoughtfulness she watched the rain as it continued to fall before her eyes and far away. The chambers were toasty warm, comforting the guests who had stayed on. The rain had ceased for an hour or so, then methodically took up again.

Angel had no idea how long the men had isolated themselves in the salon the evening before, for after an hour's time, Joseph came to relay the message that the gentlemen would be closeted for quite some time yet. Weary from the day's activities, Angel had retired, along with Hannah. That left Jacinta alone in the parlor sipping her sherry, as it was her wish to await her father, she stated.

But was it truly all Jacinta waited for, Angel wondered as she nursed her son, rocking in her favorite chair. Somehow Jacinta's mood had seemed linked with that matter to be settled behind closed doors. Just this morning there had been a stiff silence at the breakfast table, though Wesley had chosen to take breakfast alone in his bedchamber. Tyrone had been easily irritated when his eggs were not done to his liking. He had gone back to the kitchen to chew Melvin out thoroughly, his deep voice thunderous as it bellowed down the halls.

Angel sighed pensively as she closed her bodice and carefully rose with her sleeping son so as not to awaken him. She passed into the nursery, her silk mauve dressing gown and petticoats rustling as she bent downward and gently placed Brian in his crib. She stood back, amazed at the growth of her healthy son. Their son, Tyrone's and hers. She wept in her heart for the boy then. Tyrone hadn't held him once since he was born. It was ironic when she thought of how he had whisked her from Gayarre, anticipated the birth, and was there administering when the moment arrived.

Angel went back into her room and sat before the hearth, observing the magenta flames flatter the dark oak flooring and the fringe of the Persian carpet beneath her slippered feet. The small coffer stood open upon the dressing table and the costly gems her husband had lavished upon her winked with green and violet lights as they played with the flickers from the fireplace. She smiled reminiscently then, of the afternoon two weeks ago when Tyrone, with Della as worried onlooker, had pierced her ears. She still wore the gold posts but without the weight of the emerald ear-drops. They rested in the case with her other gems.

Angel touched a studded ear, barely remembering the tiny pinches. Giving her easy courage, Tyrone's beautiful eyes had

442

peered down into her face each time his gentle and steady fingers pierced a lobe with a post. He had been most gentle of late, almost loving, but for the angry outburst the morning before when he had flown at her in a rage, fearing that the Christmas angel would be dropped and broken. And she had learned that Annette was his mother. Annette Hunter née Kent. It had been her lavaliere that James had presented Angel with.

"Ah, James," she said softly, staring into the fire. "I am indeed sorry that I've lost your lovely gift—" She sighed. "If only you were here, I believe it would make a world of difference. Where are you, James Hunter?" She wished she knew, and fixed her gaze on the gallery doors as if he would suddenly appear. All at once she felt goose pimples on her arm and spun about in her chair, feeling a presence close by.

"Sorry, ma'am," Cordell said, appearing surprised at seeing her there in the chair. "I did not see you with your back to the door. I came up to inform you that dinner will be served shortly, ma'am."

Angel stood brusquely, saying, "Thank you, Cordell. And, next time you wish to see me . . . knock! Even if the door is ajar as it is this time, I would appreciate it."

Cordell nodded aslant. "As you wish, ma'am," he said as he backed around the door, closing it softly behind him.

Angel shuddered. The young man gave her an eerie feeling with his prying and piercing blue eyes. He seemed constantly just lurking around some dark corner, giving her a start oftentimes in the hall as he stepped out of the shadows, seemingly preoccupied at some task. Besides being Tyrone's manservant, Cordell took upon himself tasks without number. He hadn't been at Cresthaven very long as an employee and this brought her to thinking of the lost lavaliere.

In the next instant Angel was beside her jewels sweeping the coffer up. She snapped the lid shut, and tucking it under her arm, passed into the nursery where she hunkered down to hide her treasures in a bottom drawer of the blue bureau under a pile of blankets. With that done, she checked to see if Brian had awakened at her entrance, then went to ready herself for dinner.

Wesley was again absent from the table. Guy Villerne was rambling on about how beastly the weather had been for the holidays, keeping a running conversation with Nikki about it and whatever else happened to pop into his head. Nothing was mentioned of the heated discussion the evening before, and during lulls in the conversation the room dragged in each tick-tock of the hall clock. Tyrone's ill-temper was renewed; his mood was out of humor, weighing heavily upon Angel and depleting her own spirits. Too, with Jacinta casting sly glances in her husband's direction, Angel hardly noticed her full plate. Tyrone noticed her though, and her strained look, and his callousness suddenly vanished. He rose at once to stand behind her chair.

"It seems that everyone is finished here. That new stock of brandy and liqueurs has just come in this week. Let's go into the parlor and sample them, shall we?"

Tyrone pressed himself into a cheerier mood and for Angel he played the gallant host, plying her with a bit too much peach liqueur. He was soon happy with the results though, as she giggled tipsily when Nikki, the Merry Andrew, stood up and began to quote the beginnings of Charles Perrault's tale of the cinderwench. He added before he began that though this tale was intended for youths, it was still one of Hannah's favorites, and didn't everyone have a fairy book when they were small?

Hannah wrinkled her nose playfully at Nikki, but Jacinta grimaced while Guy eased back in his seat, waiting for the young man to make a fool of himself. But still the older man enjoyed himself and was soon laughing along with the others. Nikki faltered when he neared the part where the king's son was about to give a ball. He screwed up his face, trying to recall the dialogue.

"I know," Tyrone spoke as his face lit boyishly and a tawny wave fell over his forehead, "the tale of the family drudge whose fairy godmother sends her to a ball at which a handsome prince falls madly in love with her."

"Hush!" Nikki chided, shaking a finger at Tyrone. "You're giving it all away, man. Let me see—ah, yes. A ball was in order and the poor cinderwench was aiding her ugly stepsisters along with Mademoiselle de la Poche." His voice took on a feminine high pitch as he said to the cinderwench: "'Cinderella, would you not be glad to go to the ball?' 'Alas!' said she, 'you only jeer me; it is not for such as I am to go thither.' 'Thou art in the right of it,' replied they. 'It would make the people laugh to see a cinderwench at a ball.'"

Nikki came to the part where the cinderwench fell a-crying in the far garden, then halted, saying, "I know, Hannah, you be the fairy godmother, and Angel, you be the cinderwench and—Jacinta, you be the evil stepmother," he ended, lifting his brows humorously when the latter narrowed dark eyes at him.

"Pah!" Jacinta retorted, "count me out! I have never heard such silly nonsense, and I never read anyway. It's a waste of time."

Tyrone stood and bowed elegantly, and as if sweeping a cape out behind him, said, "And I shall be the—umm—handsome prince." He aided the cinderwench to her feet and she giggled, a bit wobbly.

Guy Villerne took up with the comedians. "Should I be the fat pumpkin?" he offered.

"Grand idea!" Nikki cried. "When Hannah strikes you—" he chuckled warmly at that, "with her wand you turn into a splendid gold coach. Too bad Gayarre isn't down here. He could be the mouses."

"Mice!" Angel corrected and fell into giggling again with Hannah.

Nikki stepped up to Angel, then halted thoughtfully. "Say, wait a minute, I've forgotten me. What or who shall I be?"

"The idiot! naturally," Jacinta snapped as she spun about from the sideboard with a fresh drink in her hand.

Hannah, with one hand pressed to her forehead the other to her stomach, fell upon the sofa in a fit of choking giggles. She, too, had had her fill of the peach liqueur.

"*Bon Dieu!*" Jacinta spat, staring around the room. "You are all drunk, even you, father!"

Nikki stretched out a finger and wagged it at her, saying, "Ah, now Jacinta dear. It is you who are intoxicated, we are just having a little fun. If you change your mind, you can always be the mouse-colored dapple-gray horses."

Haughtily Jacinta tossed her head and whirled about as the

play began. She harkened though, as Hannah told Nikki to play the godmother because he remembered the lines better than she did. "Anyway," Hannah added, "I forgot to bring my wand."

More laughter abounded and Jacinta sneered. She turned back to watch, her curiosity gaining the upper hand, indeed more tipsy than the rest as she wavered where she stood, smothering a hiccough with the back of her hand.

"All right, Angel, do your stuff," Nikki said.

Angel sobbed, peering up at Nikki from her bent position. Nikki quoth: "'What is the matter, dear child?'" in a perfect godmother's voice.

"'I wish I could—I wish I could—'" She was not able to speak the rest, being interrupted by her tears and sobbing.

This godmother of hers said to her, "Thou wishest thou couldst go to the ball, is it not so?"

"Ye—es," cried Cinderella, with a great sigh.

"Well," said her godmother, "Be but a good girl, and I will contrive that thou shalt go." Nikki took her by the arm. "Run into the garden, and bring me a pumpkin."

This fair cinderwench chewed on her tiniest nail as she contemplated the pumpkins, and when she spied a sizable one—Villerne—she went over to pluck it up and brought it back to the fairy godmother. Jacinta expelled her breath in a huff as her fool father stood for the nonsense. Soon there was a splendid coach drawn by six beautiful horses, footmen of the same number, and a fat, jolly coachman, who Nikki portrayed excellently—all seen in the mind, naturally.

The fairy then said to the cinderwench:

"'Well, you see here an equipage fit to go to the ball with; are you not pleased with it?'"

"'Oh, yes!' cried she. "'But must I go thither as I am, in these nasty rags?'" She indicated her dress.

Nikki only just touched her with his wand, and the cinderwench spun about, whirling, whirling, lifting her heavy tresses high off her neck as she did so. Halting her spinning, she transformed herself to a glittering princess, lifted the hem of her gown and stuck out a dainty toe to indicate her pretty glass slippers. Everyone smiled wide when she curtsied gracefully and Nikki went over to pick up an old fiddle leaning against the wall. He began to scratch out a waltz melody, somewhat tunelessly, as the handsome prince moved elegantly across the floor to take the transformed cinderwench into his arms.

The mirror reflected the couple as they glided, whirled, and dazzled all in the room, but for one, who continued to snicker at this play. Tyrone held his back ramrod straight as he continued to lead, his head bent dreamily above Angel's. She smiled up with lips parted, the pink moistness of her lower lip tempting him. Tyrone considered the possibility that this might very well be the night, the night of love he'd anticipated for so very long.

Angel's heart throbbing, aching, no stranger to pain, now burst into the sweetest song of all songs. My love! My love! My love!

Hanging back and still scratching on the fiddle, Nikki was very pleased with what he had brought to pass, and there loomed, Hannah noted, a wicked smile in his eyes. Hannah realized what he had done as no one else did.

Moving smoothly, but shaken, Tyrone, the tall prince, bent down to whisper in his partner's ear, his voice a husky murmur. "You are more lovely, more beautiful than ever, my Angel. I must tell you now, that I—I—" He glanced up and suddenly frowned.

The tall clock did strike out twelve times out in the hall then, and almost everyone fell to soft, curious laughter at the perfect timing that now brought the dancing couple to a standstill. Feeling slightly disappointed as she stood in the middle of the carpet with her husband, Angel tried on a smile, peering up at the brooding face. Her heart gave a twist as she wondered painfully what he had been about to tell her. He appeared awfully tense, so she bent down to loosen a slipper; new high-heeled ones she hadn't worn much yet.

"Ouch!" she exclaimed, carrying a slipper and limping up and down to the couch where she at once sat. Tyrone tagged along and loomed now above her, his eyes unreadable. She explained, "I've said it before and I'll say it again . . . never will I get used to these blasted things. They may very well have

447

been glass for—"

Tyrone's brow darkened, but it wasn't for her. He had sighted Wesley in the portal, and now watched the square back of him as he moved back into the hall and up the stairs. No one else had spotted Wesley, and Tyrone was curious as to how long the man had lingered there silently contemplating the scene.

Once again the gay mood of the holidays departed as Tyrone, wearing a thoughtful frown, went to find his half-emptied glass. Jacinta was just moving away from the table where his brandy had sat warming. He snatched up the glass, swirled the contents and grimaced as he tossed off half of what remained, then appeared surprised as he peered into the powdery dregs. He looked as if he were trying to remember something, blinked his eyes wide, then shrugged. He began to feel odd and presently a strange languor stole over him.

Tyrone was lounging upon the sofa when everyone got up to retire. He hardly noticed his wife as she paused in the portal to glance back at him with a worried frown stitching her fine brow. Tyrone cursed under his breath when finally he did look up, seeing that last bit of pinkish-mauve vanish out into the hall. He stood, weaved to and fro, then lurched forward as he groped his way up the stairs to find his bed.

"Lord, am I soused," he mumbled as he fell into his bed. He was fully dressed and fully aroused, but could not rise to seek what he desired most.

Outside in the hall two shadows merged together to speak in hushed tones and then detached to go their separate ways.

The fire lazed upon the hearth and sent ghosts dancing along the walls. Angel couldn't have been asleep for very long when a soft tapping sounded at her door. She struggled drowsily to her elbows, still feeling the lethargic effects of the peach liqueur. The tapping came again, ever so softly, but nevertheless audible.

"Who is there?" she called out softly, sleepily.

The response came as a single rap, and alarmed, Angel rolled off her bed dragging on her cream faille robe as she went on bare feet to listen at the door. She tossed the waterfall of bright

448

hair over her left shoulder and bent down with her ear at the crack. Silence reigned, and curious, she tried the knob, then spied the folded bit of paper at her feet. Snatching up the note and rising to open the door, she gave the hall a thorough scour, then went to read the paper before the fire. Feeling afire and faint her hands shook as she read these words:

Madame. If You want to know what has been Going on Right under your nose go into your Husband's room immediately. You will then See for Yourself.

The note was unsigned and scrawled crudely. It fluttered to the floor as Angel clutched the back of her wood rocker, her knuckles stressed white in high relief. Paling before the fire she felt as if she had been belted a heavy blow. Her heart thudded beneath her robe and she knew a sick, bilious feeling. She choked it back and stiffened her spine resolutely.

"No. I shan't go in there. I daren't. It is just a mean prank," she said, trying to convince herself. But who would do such a thing . . . Jacinta? Then, it may have been Wesley's doing. He still meant to have her, she had read it in his face the day before when he had kissed her hand and held it possessively.

A miniature fear nudged her next, and though she tried beating it aside it grew to colossal proportions. Perhaps her husband was ill, and she was standing here dumbly, afraid of a little piece of paper. Could it be that Tyrone drank himself into a stupor each night, but just now some kindly person was letting her know?

A stub of candle upon the bedside commode wavered and glowing-white logs crackled in the cavern of the fireplace as Angel stepped cautiously into the alien bedchamber. Nothing seemed amiss and there was only a slight movement in the huge four-poster that was only three feet shy of the sixteen-foot-high ceiling. She drew closer, then halted, solidified in horror. At her feet the red silk gown was strewn carelessly among her husband's own articles of clothing. She stared, sickened, reminded of their wedding night and Tyrone's words of warning to her: "Steer clear of my bedroom, for if you stumble that way, you may be in for the shock of your life."

Angel's head reeled as she choked back a whimper. Her mind screamed; how could he have waltzed with her in that amorous fashion earlier while at the same time ignoring his mistress so thoroughly? They both had to be mad for each other; there was just no other explanation for what she now saw.

Angel made to flee the room when a rustling from the bed brought Jacinta sitting up, gasping in outrage upon finding the younger woman there. Angel stood frozen by the lustily handsome look of the other woman.

"What do you think you are doing here!" Jacinta's words hissed hotly across to Angel. Jacinta permitted the silk sheet to fall to her waist, boldly displaying pendulous, pear-shaped breasts with deep auburn tips that stood eagerly erect.

Now uprooted from the spot, Angel smothered a cry with the back of her trembling hand. She backed up to the door slowly and groped behind her for the brass knob, then gasped audibly when Tyrone rolled drunkenly to his side, trying to see his bed companion.

"Wha—" he began, then fell back mumbling as he snatched Jacinta close. "C'mere, you, vixen," he growled lustfully, then sighed deeply as his head rolled back, his eyes closing contentedly.

Jacinta moved away from him then as she kicked the sheet down to her feet, this time permitting the stunned intruder a view of their thorough nakedness. Angel's eyes rolled away, sickened by the lewd scene, as she caught at the knob. For an instant when her knees betrayed her and almost buckled under her she stumbled, bringing a hiss from the mussed bed.

"Get out now, bitch, before my lover awakes and sees you here." Jacinta flared at Angel's back.

On hearing Tyrone giggle deeply as if tickled, Angel whirled out the door and sped along the hall, gaining her room to close the door and lean back against it, standing there breathing heavily, for how long she would never know. All she saw in her mind's eye was Jacinta's and her husband's limbs interlaced, their nakedness a white imprint in her mind.

Jacinta had taken great pains to divest Tyrone of his clothing a half hour before. He had been at the height of passion after

450

unknowingly tossing off the philter she had put into his glass, and she'd almost gotten herself raped before she did what had to be done. After wrestling with him for a good fifteen minutes in the dark, he'd finally fallen back to the pillow in a drunken stupor. Jacinta had procured the potion from Mamma Mandisa, a *cunjer*, who brewed every kind of potion and worked from her shadowy cellar on Madman's Street.

Having had a second end in mind while obtaining the philter, Jacinta now lowered her head to find Tyrone's warm but slackly moist lips. Her body followed and she found his hands, bringing them up to press them to her hardened nipples. She grinned victoriously when she found him yet hard with desire and her breath rushed out fast when he growled low with pleasure, and, rolling with her, tossed her onto her back, moving with savage intent.

"*Mon* Ty, *mon* Ty, come to me now," Jacinta murmured, feeling a delicious ache deep in her belly.

"Help me, my green-eyed vixen," Tyrone mumbled. "My wife, my Ang—el," he crooned, then relaxed completely, letting his breath out in a *whoosh*.

"You are blind, you oaf!—Arrrghhh!" A strangled sound escaped her and she could barely catch her breath with his full, dead weight upon her. Too, she was spitting mad after those endearments she'd heard. And now . . . he was losing it! He was snoring lustily!

Tyrone halted his ruckus for a moment to babble something, and what he said of his wife caused Jacinta to struggle dementedly. Finally, after heaving with all the strength she could muster, she maneuvered him off and rolled him onto his back. Her desire vanished, and like a whirligig she spun off the bed to snatch up her rumpled gown and oft-mended chemise.

Jacinta stomped into her gown in such a tantrum that she made a clean rip in the red folds. Muttering a crude verse she glared at the topsy-turvy bed where Tyrone was splayed out like a dead soldier, his noisy overture merry as a barrel of crickets. As she paused in the open door, Jacinta had it in mind to slam the door behind her loudly, but that would only awaken the house and foil what she had in mind next. She must not undo the damage she'd already created between the married couple. The little slut would no doubt leave her cozy home within a fortnight after what she had beheld here this night.

Jacinta's lips curled insanely. The philter had done its job nicely: perhaps a bit too nicely though, for she'd missed her chance in bed with Tyrone and had waited too long. Jacinta wasn't done here yet—not by a long shot.

"Mistress, honey. You open this door now, hear? C'mon now, you can't sleep all day. I ain't going away this time. You hear me?" Della persisted, rattling the knob.

Feeling weak as a sick kitten, Angel rolled over in her bed, still wearing the robe she'd hastily donned before creeping into her husband's room the night before. She had fought down the overwhelming urge to be sick and finally, not being able to hold it back anymore, she had sunk down to the floor holding the porcelain basin in her lap. She had given up all, even her heart, she believed now.

Last night had marked the beginning of the end of her life, she thought now as she saw that the room was filled with bright rays of noonday sun that did naught to cheer her. She sat up, sweeping her legs over the bed's edge to search out her slippers.

"Coming, Della," Angel called out cheerlessly, plodding over to unlock her door.

"Why'd you lock your door, mistress?" Della wondered, concerned over the pale countenance. Setting down a tray of biscuits and hot tea, Della again wondered out loud. "You all right, honey? You look as if you been up most the night."

"I was—very restless and could not sleep most of the night," Angel repeated, going over to peer into the looking glass. She wouldn't tell Della why she'd locked her door; she hadn't relished the thought of having someone like Jacinta come in to gloat over her wretched sobbing.

"Sarah brought Brian in this morning?" Della queried, buttering a warm biscuit for the mistress.

"Ummm, yes. She used the hall entrance into the nursery and brought him in here at the crack of dawn for his feeding. He's still asleep?"

Della grinned. "Not now, he ain't. Sarah's givin' him a bath, and Lawsy! I thought that there boy was a-snorin' this morn.

Wasn't him—no—it was Mr. Hunter a-snorin' down the walls and halls a few hours ago. Sheesh! Never heard that big lad sleep so sound. Must be he had a long night—too?"

Angel whirled. "Della, please go and—and take the tray with you, as I have no hunger for food this morning. I only wish a bath. Please see that a tub is brought to my chamber and filled, as I shan't be leaving my room until—until I feel better."

Feeling as if she'd just had a tongue-lashing, Della padded over to lift the tray. She hoped she hadn't been too nosy, but on her way to the door, Angel touched the housekeeper's arm gently.

"I've been taking my edginess out on you, Della. Forgive me." Angel felt much better when Della smiled and patted her arm consolingly.

At the door, Della paused then turned back thoughtfully to Angel. "All the guests is leaving today 'cause Old Sol is shining. He's gonna be around all day and harden that red clay good by nightfall. Wesley is done gone and good riddance to that old troublemaker." She made to exit then paused again, adding as an afterthought, "Mr. Hunter's been askin' 'bout you. Says for you to come down to his study when you wake and done primpin'."

Angel drew in a deep breath and issued forth with, "He . . . he is awake?"

Della cocked her head, saying, "A'course. Always is this time of day. Sure did sleep long, though. It's noon, honey. Don't you worry none, he won't bite. Not today, he's lookin' fit as a fiddle!"

Angel gritted her teeth, thinking: Naturally! Then aloud, feigning disinterest, "Where—umm—where is Jacinta?"

Della popped her head back in when she'd almost gone. The mistress's strange behavior was puzzling to her, but she answered, "Think she's down there, too." She thought for a moment, and, "Sure, her and the Mister come down together. Anything else now, honey? Sure wish you'd eat something."

"That is all, Della," she said, trying on a smile before the turbaned head nodded and disappeared.

While her bath was being readied in her room, Angel strolled the gallery where the sun shone, the air was crisp, and clean white clouds chased across a wintry blue sky. Her knuckles whitened as she leaned over, clutching the railing. Taking in a deep breath of nippy air she began to feel invincible, as she had once before. It had been a time seemingly long ago when she had stood in expectation on the deck of the *Fidelia*, watching, waiting, for the inevitable to happen. This time, however, whatever would befall her, she was going to equip herself with a stand of arms, prepared to meet the worst foe, though her armament be invisible.

She spun about, leaning back far to gaze up at her house. *Her* house! Yes, this was her home now, and she would be bloody damned if she was going to leave it!

Taking a hasty scented bath, Angel stepped out and Daisy Mae came forward with a fluffy towel. After she was dried, she sat still while Sarah did her hair in waves and saucy curls midway down her back. Next Angel chose a long-sleeved, sea-green frock with a line of emerald embroidery running down the skirts vertically at intervals. An emerald-shade hussar vest went over her head last. She excused the maids and lingered at her dressing table, peering into the glass at the sad but determined young woman who was prepared to fight for the love of her man. Yes, for herself, but mostly for her son. God willing, she would win, too.

Tyrone, just fixing the last tab of his fly, stepped out of the downstairs convenience and so brusquely he almost collided with the housekeeper. The untouched tray tottered in the old woman's hands and his long fingers swept underneath to keep it from falling.

"What's this?" Tyrone demanded, snatching up an uneaten buttered biscuit.

Della's eyes rolled like brown marbles. "Why, you know what dat is, Mr. Hunter . . . it's a hobbyhorse," she chuckled warmly.

"Ahem . . . Della."

The housekeeper peered up, up into the hazel eyes. "She won't have any. She ain't hungry now and—" Della let her sentence drop when she spied Jacinta in back of Tryone.

Jacinta glanced briefly down the hall before she spoke. *"Mon*

454

cher, let us get our business done with. Father is waiting for me in the salon and the flatboat is due to come by in an hour. Do you mind if we leave our carriage and horses for a day or two more?"

Tyrone frowned at the housekeeper before dismissing her, then followed Jacinta back into his study. He thought so hard on something that he failed to notice the flash of sea-green coming along the hall. He left the door ajar and went to lounge in his leather chair, placing his feet upon a low table. He almost reached for a cheroot, then remembered he had quit the nasty habit the week before. He waved Jacinta into her seat as he'd done earlier.

"You did not answer my question, *mon cher*," Jacinta said smilingly, as she recalled she had been pressed to his lean body the evening before.

"Yes, yes, Jacinta. Saul will see to the carriage and horses. Now, what was it that we were discussing?" he asked, his mind actually elsewhere.

As Jacinta had positioned her chair to face the door, she now caught a movement there and began to speak quickly. "You were angry, Tyrone. Her Majesty?" Now she stood, her back to the door.

Tyrone took up from where he'd left off. "Ah, yes. I will kill her myself, strangle her and bury her in the barn six feet under!" he ground out.

The female voice was pleading, "Oh, be good to her for a while longer, *mon Ty*."

"Ah, yes, Jacinta. I'll bow and scrape to Her Majesty until she is broken. I'll pet her and pamper her, cajole her, and then I'll break her damn fool neck. The bitch!"

Outside in the hall Angel felt like screaming in anguish, "No! No! Anything but this." Again his beloved voice drifted out to her and her knees gave way like the evening before, but she stood her guns, supporting herself against the wall.

". . . I should have never brought her here in the first place. But it was all your idea . . . recall? Now you'll just have to help me be rid of her. She is causing too much trouble in the—"

Jacinta interrupted. "But, *mon cher*, I thought you wanted her. You said she was beautiful, no?"

"Hah! Beautiful! Not now. She disgusts me, just like a white ghost with those big sad eyes," he said, pouring forth his annoyance.

Jacinta's skirts rustled. "You are just angry, *mon cher*. Give her more time. You can use her for the—ah—little ones you want, just for a few years, then get rid of her."

Leather creaked as Tyrone stood. "I'll not discuss this anymore this day as I've something important to attend to now," he said, watching Jacinta pause at the door. He added, "One more thing, Jacinta. You'll have to limit your visits here, I'm thinking that this upsets Angel and. . . ."

Angel didn't hear the rest. She was galvanized into trembling action, then noticed there wasn't time to make it down the long hall. She backed up cautiously and slipped into the library. Closing the door, she pressed her back against a wall, hearing them enter the hall just then. She pinched her eyes shut and gulped hard. Her weapons were beginning to desert her.

KILL HER! Tyrone wanted to be rid of her—now! How ironic that Jacinta should pose as her defending angel. She almost laughed hysterically before hearing the front door open and close, Tyrone's resounding footsteps retracing the hall.

There came a low whisper and the hair on Angel's arms stood up. She pressed her fingers to her temple upon hearing a voice and jerked her head around expecting to see someone standing there. But all she saw was rows upon rows of leatherbound volumes. Was she going mad indeed? Then she heard it again, this time clearer, giving her a message she couldn't fathom. Not yet.

In the next instant the back door flew open and Angel peered around her door as an angry wind blew in, screaming like a banshee, feeling out every corner of her muddled brain. She pressed her hands over her ears and before she knew what she did her limbs had taken her into the hall, where she ran smack into Tyrone. He caught at her arms as she tried whirling away.

Tyrone chuckled at his good fortune, "Ahh, here you are, my love," he murmured then peered at her closely. "You look as white as a ghost and you are trembling all over." He noticed the back door standing open and banging against the wall. He pushed back a strand of her loose hair, saying, "You shouldn't

456

be out walking without your shawl, Angel, you will catch your death."

White as a ghost! Death! Angel tried not to swoon and stilled her tremors enough to try, "Did you not hear it, Tyrone?"

He gripped her firmly but gently by the shoulders. "Hear what, my sweet? And why were you scurrying as if something had frightened you?" he asked.

Concealing her wild eyes from him, she dropped her long lashes and explained, "It was nothing, Tyrone. I—I just thought I'd heard a ruckus outside . . . that is all." She stood so near him, so frightened, and yet so much in love with him.

Tyrone tossed back his magnificent head to laugh as his fingers slid up to cup her chin. "Indeed you did, Angel. My slaves are gathered outside near the stable, awaiting their Yuletide gifts. Wait here and I'll fetch you one of my warm cloaks so you can accompany me outside."

Samuel and Jenny were there among the smiling blacks. Angel greeted them warmly and they did likewise, Sam beaming proudly with his arm snug about the tiny girl's waist. Angel cast aside her fear and trembling suspicions for the time being and shared with her husband the genuine friendliness he felt for his slaves, whom he referred to as his "men."

Awe-filled over this mysterious man who was her husband, Angel watched silently as the blacks passed around a weighty jug of cheer while the master of Cresthaven doled out serviceable shirts and tobacco for the men and bright calico dresses of strong thread for the women. Also, there were sweets for the tots who milled about shyly as the tall master gave them each a bagful.

Way out back to their white-washed cottages the well-pleased slaves strolled after the distribution of gifts. Delighting in the masculine scent of the cloak, Angel, rose-cheeked now, hugged the huge garment tighter about her slight frame. The odd fear was still present, and it was sharper yet when Tyrone strode over to rejoin her. She trembled a little when, taking her by the arm gently but possessively, he led her back to the house.

"Cold?" he asked as he hugged her against his side.

"Ummm, a little," she returned, at the same time exhilarated

457

and terrified by his nearness.

Just before entering the house something caught them by surprise. Caspar rounded the corner of the house, mounted on a tall chestnut mare, and skidded to a halt. Tyrone pressed Angel's arm, asking her to wait, then went to speak with Caspar. Angel tilted her head as she thought how ridiculously large the man appeared astride, for she had never seen him on a horse and—suddenly she was reminded of the arrogant stranger she's seen astride the black by the river cottage. Mr. Hunter—her husband.

The two men blurred before her eyes. It just couldn't be. Tyrone couldn't be thinking of putting an end to her life. Then visions of Ellen sprawling with neck broken loomed before her, then the scene in Tyrone's chamber the night before, and more. She began to fear for her sanity, for she'd already been hearing voices.

Tyrone returned to her, appearing dismayed about something, but whatever it was he kept it to himself. Again they were interrupted as they made to step forward, this time by a loud whinny then a snort blowing across the yard. Angel spied the huge white head of a mare nodding arrogantly from out the stable doors. She froze.

"Tyrone," she began, "I've never seen that mare before. Where did she come from?"

"That, my dear, is Jacinta's ill-tempered mare. I am thinking of shipping her out very soon, though. That is, if I don't succumb to breaking her lousy neck first!"

Angel placed a hand over her heart, asking quietly, "Does she have a name? I mean . . . what is she called?"

As usual this afternoon, Tyrone frowned a little at his wife's strange behavior and speech. Then he replied, "She is, mistakenly, named Her Majesty."

2

James "Big Jim" Hunter showed up at Cresthaven several days later when the roads had hardened sufficiently for travel upon them. The new year's air bore a smoky smell and the trees all appeared ash-brown against an orange and purple sunset that cast its low rays into the morning-room, setting the elegant appointments and its occupants aglow with rosy hues. It was directly after dinner and Tyrone could have murdered his own father in cold blood for what he had interrupted. . . .

A subtle perfume floated up to Tyrone's nostrils where he lounged upon the fluffy rug before the hearth with Angel and the babe. Her recently washed hair spun like heavy silk down over the pale mauve robe that barely concealed the ivory mounds of flesh. Her rich, husky laughter filled the room as she played with Brian Ross, making him coo, and casting a spell over her attentive husband. His eyes caressed the softly rounded shoulders peeping out from the robe, crept up to catch the bright halo of her hair, her tan-and-amber lashes, the petal softness of her lower lip, then on down again, below the slim column of her throat. An uncontrolled, rampant fire burned in him and his long-drawn-out celibacy bordered his mind on madness. It was an exquisite form of torture he experienced.

Angel gazed into the multiflecked, golden eyes and felt herself begin to melt before the flames of desire she again saw there; for many days now he had courted her, she realized. Feeling feminine and warm after her bath, and feeling, as well, a new joy these last few days—discounting the bedroom scene—she lifted her face, allowing her lips to part softly, invitingly. Then he drew her to him. The moment was short-lived, for Sarah entered to take the babe and prepare him for bed.

Tyrone growled up at the maid, "Next time knock!"

Sarah cautiously explained that the door had been left open. Before her husband could snap back at Sarah, Angel placed a hand on the sleeve of his smoking jacket to check his nasty temper. While Sarah backed out with the bundle, Tyrone gestured for her to close the door behind her, and stayed Angel when she made a movement to rise. Unafraid, she smiled languidly and rolled her head to snuggle her face in the hollow of his neck. Suddenly she was shy. His elbow slid out until both were spread full length, side by side, her face now close to his.

Tyrone cleared his throat hoarsely, raised one eyebrow questioningly. "My good wife, will you tease me again, then leave me panting?" He took up a dainty hand, turned it over and pressed a kiss into the palm, all the while searching her face. Unbeknownst to her he worked at his fly.

Angel lost herself in little flecks of green and gray swimming in a sea of amber, then, surprising him, she smiled wickedly and traipsed a tapered finger across his wide chest to play with the chestnut mat at the peep in his jacket. He caught her hand swiftly, and drawing it downward gently but purposefully, pressed her small fingers over his bold erection. He delighted in her shocked expression of his white-hot passion and groaned deeply. Suddenly he was a singleminded, thirsty flame that sought to consume the lips his now closed over, his tongue darting into the moist sweetness of her mouth, drawing a whimper of desire from her throat. Soon she felt the crisp mat of hair that tickled her bare, upthrusting breasts as he peeled back the robe and his long fingers performed magic along her inner thighs. He moved from her momentarily to labor in jerks to remove his already unbuttoned pantaloons. In those few moments Angel came awake from the haze of passion that had surrounded her.

"No, Tyrone," she panted, "Not in here . . . please."

He laughed deep and devilishly in his throat, and said, "Ohh—nooo, not this time. I've come this way before and this time you'll not escape me, my little green-eyed witch."

She squealed as she tried rolling from him, but he was down and on her, snatching her back. Her thighs yielded when at once he mounted to penetrate that first morsel. Touching, they both gasped in shivering expectation.

"Mr. Hunter, you in there?" Della inquired, an excited catch in her voice behind the door. "We got company! Your papa! Big Jim's come home to visit!"

"Ahhh . . . damn!" rasped from within and a muffled giggle followed.

Tyrone shot Angel a murderous glare and she cowered. He had jumped to his feet like a young boy caught in his first act of sexual activity, and he stood now with legs wide apart, peering down upon Angel until she properly veiled her eyes with her lashes upon seeing him shrivel slowly. He bent down and with vicious jerks pulled up his pantaloons and buttoned his fly. He strode brusquely over to snatch open the door, then turned back with his eyes narrowed in on his wife dangerously.

"Later!" he promised, going down then to greet his father before she could reply.

With drinks in hand, Tyrone and his father drifted from the salon into the parlor, where Angel awaited them after she had donned an aqua gown and descended. Her green eyes shone diamondlike as she took her pondering gaze from the lovely portrait to the men just entering, followed by Joseph bearing a tray of meat sandwiches, and tea for the mistress. When Tyrone made the introductions, James silenced Angel with a look she recognized immediately; he pleaded with her not to reveal his last visit nor the lavaliere he'd given her. Suddenly she was sorry for having lost it, deciding to resume her search tomorrow and scour every inch of her chamber. It had to be there—somewhere.

A frown etched itself on James's face for a second before he erased it, and said, "I have had the pleasure of meeting Angeline before—ah—actually quite briefly," he added the latter when Tyrone's head jerked up.

Thinking his father meant the island, Tyrone cleared his throat gruffly as he thrust the tray of sandwiches beneath his father's nose. "You must be famished, sir, why don't you stuff—umm—eat something. This roast beef left over from dinner is quite delicious—cold."

Peeking up at her husband, Angel flushed hotly under his scrutiny. She was still under the influence of what had almost taken place a short time ago and at this time could barely think of anything but that. Her head bowed and she missed the thoughtful look playing over his countenance. Tyrone bethought himself of the pact made between himself and his father several years ago concerning James's finding him a suitable wife. If it was mentioned now, Tyrone would have two reasons this night for strangling the old man.

Tyrone smiled grimly as he sat across from them. How would she react upon learning that James in England, like a vulture, had been ready and waiting to snatch up Stonewall at the flick of a pen, then presented the deed to his son, satisfied that he had won the day? Too, James would no doubt add that Tyrone had married only to obtain an heir. Tyrone groaned inwardly at that.

Tyrone took up watching his wife conversing softly with James, and permitted his eyes to linger upon her hungrily, like a half-starved man. He swallowed some brandy and it went down like hot stones. Angel would realize this wasn't so, wouldn't she? Anyway, why should he fret, James would only destroy what he set out to accomplish from the beginning by telling her. He himself was just not ready to reveal who owned Stonewall to Angel; the stakes would be too high to lose the game at this point. He must play his cards right and have Angel settled down comfortably in a state of connubial bliss first.

"I should be in Charleston this time of year," James said out of the blue, turning to acknowledge his son.

Tyrone appeared startled for a moment, then quipped, "And, sir, why aren't you?"

"Why, I came to see the new Mrs. Hunter and meet my grandson, didn't you know?" he returned, tamping tobacco into his curling pipe.

"Well then, sir, why don't you just go up now and see him. Brian is still awake, I'm sure," Tyrone replied coolly, taking note of the startled look his wife suddenly wore. He realized why. This had been the first time he had spoken of the boy using his given name. There was something else. For the first time since his father's coming, he was acutely aware of the color of James's eyes, so like Brian's. Dark jade. Could he have been mistaken concerning the lover?

"Where are you going?" Tyrone wanted to know when Angel rose from the sofa with his father.

Angel returned with a question of her own: "Would you like to come up with us, Tyrone dear?"

He snorted as he waved them away, sitting back to sip his brandy. His father paused in the doorway, turning back with Angel at his elbow. James asked, "The land—how did it go with you and Gayarre?"

"What big and long ears you have, sir," Tyrone remarked in his dark mood. Then, "You should know by now that I never release what is rightfully mine. That is, only that something I place a value on would I hold fast," he explained, looking pointedly at Angel. "You won the land fair and square, you know," he added, and his hands made fists, "but I almost had to pound it into Wesley's square head!"

"So you reiterated and he dropped the subject?"

"Naturally. But old Wes is a land-greedy man, and I really don't think I've heard the last of it, at that—not by a long shot!"

James shrugged, dropping the subject, eager to meet his grandson. When they were gone, Tyrone stared moodily at the portrait of Annette, wondering what she would have thought of all this. What did he care about the woman, anyway! She was cold in her grave! Suddenly hearing a clink of glasses, he whirled about.

"Cordell!" Then he demanded, "How long have you been busying yourself there, man?"

"Been here all the time, sir, replenishing the liquor cabinet," the servant answered, putting the bung on a bottle busily. He then came around the sofa to remove the tray of half-eaten sandwiches.

"Damnit, man, you are supposed to be my manservant. Get done and off with you!" Tyrone swore next, snatching a quarter-filled brandy decanter off the tray as Cordell swept hurriedly by.

Upstairs in the pretty blue and white nursery, James held out his arms, longing to feel his grandson in them. "May I?" he asked his daughter-in-law. She handed the boy over and James chucked the green-eyed lad under the chin. He smiled at her, saying, "What have you named him, madame?"

"Brian Ross," she said proudly. "Altogether it means 'powerful steed'." She would not explain that the manchild had first reminded her of a rose.

James nodded his approval. He said, "My dear, Tyrone must be very proud, cocky, wanting more exactly like this one?"

Angel colored but James had caught the vital flame burning in her eyes. He dismissed the last question by asking another: "You love him very much, don't you?"

A hand flew to a flushed cheek. "Oh! I did not realize it showed that much. He is my everything, as is Brian. But without Tyrone I would wither away and die. Indeed I love him more than mere words can express. Even now, after all that has gone before, I clutch him dearly to my heart."

James placed the sleepy child gently into the freshly painted blue crib he remembered so well. He turned back to her, saying a cautious few words. "You are very forgiving, my dear." He studied this flawless beauty beside him, her eyes tenderly locked upon her son, who yawned in wide spurts. James tried, "May I ask you if—ah—Tyrone returns this love? You needn't answer though, I'll understand if you don't."

Angel's eyes slid over to the blue faille drapes drawn back at the small casement window. Tyrone had constructed the window himself before the birth to keep the nursery aired properly. Something gnawed at her insides and the answer to his question came hard for her, especially the truth. She relived the unfettered love-making that had been interrupted just a short while before and her heart thudded hard.

Believing what she did, Angel finally answered, "He does, in his own way and it must suffice for the time being."

"I see," James said simply.

Angel knew how a willow branch must feel in the wind, for that was how she felt—as if she swayed to and fro in a forceful, meandering breeze. True, Tyrone had as much as confessed he valued her a short while before. Did he perhaps love her just a little . . . or was it lust again that had influenced his tongue?

Brian's black lashes fluttered open just then and he peered guilelessly up at the grownups. He chuckled and crowed upon seeing them still at his cribside. Angel shifted her gaze from the babe to his grandfather and the room again grew hushed as Brian ceased his cooing to stare unblinkingly. James nodded slowly, smiled, then took his leave quietly as he slipped out the door. Mother and child watched him go.

After the arrival of the senior Hunter there was little time for Tyrone to be closeted alone with his wife. He found his father nerve-wracking and Brian Ross no less trying. Big Jim took it upon himself to program Samuel in the responsibilities of overseer for the sugar slaves, then spent his leisure time with Angel, either discussing London society endlessly, the history of the wicked city of New Orleans, or just chattering idly about the rainy weather. To complicate matters further, every time Tyrone would tiptoe into Angel's chamber at night, the child would wake immediately and be set to howling. To top it all off, Angel had taken to securing the door leading into the hall. Quelled by all this, Tyrone finally gave up and again kept long hours in his study with Caspar and Nikki, and often Big Jim would join them.

On the night they were to go to the Orleans Theater, Angel, standing in only her chemise, gazed impatiently at the gown of deep cherry velvet that would display the alabaster perfection of her shoulders. She was waiting for Hannah to cut her hair in the latest fashion that had breathed a sensation from Paris to America. Propped against perfume bottles was *La Pamphilet* from France. The etching of a flirtatious coquette smiled from out of the page, her hairdo cropped, with tiny waves hugging the sides of her dainty face while the back was in short, tight curls.

Hannah appeared indecisive. "But, Angel, the change will be a drastic one. You are very fortunate to have hair like thick silk, and not everyone can wear their hair as long as yours and still look gorgeous, even in the morning light. It's a shame I say. And Tyrone, what will he think?" she asked, a little frightened at the thought of his coming down hard on her.

Angel waved her hand, saying, "He does not care how my hair is arranged, long or short, he never notices it."

When Hannah still hesitated Angel tapped a slippered foot upon the carpet impatiently. Hannah sighed then mumbled to herself as reluctantly she went to fetch the scissors from out of the drawer where Angel kept them.

Downstairs, already garbed in their finery for the evening's entertainment and awaiting the women, the men were left sipping their brandy as Tyrone went up to see what was keeping his wife. Her door was ajar and his hand hung suspended in air where he would have knocked. Feeling a bit high after several noggins of brandy, he paused as these words drifted out to him:

"Hurry, Hannah," Angel was saying, "cut it short all over, just like in the picture."

Galvanized into quick action and before a lock was snipped,

Tyrone swung the door wide, demanding, "What is this! Ah, no, you don't. Cut one fair lock on your head, woman, and I'll shave me bald!"

At first ruffled by the intrusion, then shocked by her husband's threat, Angel whirled around to face him. "But—but, Tyrone," she pleaded, "it is the new look. Every belle in New Orleans is having it done."

"I've been an observer of this new look, and you are no belle, my dear, you are my wife. I won't have my woman tripping about the countryside looking like a featherheaded chicken!" Suddenly he softened at the sight of her *au natural*, and a virile, wicked gleam leaped into his eye. Tugging at his pocket watch he grinned wolfishly, and said smoothly, "Get finished now, sweet, but leave your hair as it is. We'll soon be leaving for the theater."

Angel noticed his thickened voice, chiding, "Tyrone, you have overindulged in your cups!"

But he'd already shut the door and was making his way downstairs. He whistled softly to himself a sprightly melody, cocksure that when the day expired he would score a success.

Hannah was walking around her friend in the bedchamber, smiling. "Long or short, he never notices it," she mocked in a singsong voice.

"Take care, Hannah McCormick!" warned Angel, and a giggle followed.

The elegant equipage drew up before the St. Philip Theater on St. Peter Street, the most fashionable rendezvous of the city since 1808. The theater could accommodate seven hundred persons and this night the two rows of boxes and the parquet below were packed to capacity with the melting pot of humanity. The lights were just dimming when the party of five scuffled tardily to their curtained box on the first level.

The dramatic performance was done in French by refugees from Santo Domingo, but Angel's mind was only half centered on the play. She pondered the quizzical glasses that had turned their way upon their entering and the French tongues buzzing in the crowded theater, seemingly making their party the center of attraction. The women in their see-through taffetas and velvets and laces had stared openly at her husband. No wonder, she thought, he was certainly dashing in his single-breasted suit, creamy silk cravat at his throat, and silk ruffles at his wrists, the darker attire complimenting his tawny hair. Angel felt the scythe of jealousy nip her.

"As deep as the sea," Tyrone had murmured mysteriously into her ear when alighting from the carriage. Angel wondered about those few lovely words now too.

What Angeline Hunter didn't realize was that she lacked not in admirers herself, for when the first act abruptly finished and the great chandelier was lighted, the door at the rear of the box opened and several young bucks beat their way in to meet the fair beauty they had seen from afar. Hannah suppressed a giggle behind her fan as Tyrone allowed the young men to pay court to his wife. There was so much loud chatter around them that Angel barely had a chance to open her mouth, much less reveal that she was not spouseless.

Angel leaned to her husband, rebuking, "You are obviously enjoying this little game, sir, but don't you think you play it out a bit?" As his lips curled up on one side, Angel had to hide a smile behind her lacy fan. She chided, "Don't be cruel, Tyrone, tell them."

James leaned from his seat to whisper in his daughter-in-law's ear. "Didn't anyone ever tell you that my son has a sadistic nature, madame? And if you should show signs of affection to anyone else, your marriage will end immediately?" he ended playfully, but Tyrone had overheard that last bit and he glared at James.

Tyrone was just about to introduce Angel to the young men (as his wife) when the door swept wide and Jacinta, never seen escorted by her husband, glided in on the arm of a tall, dark, gypsy-eyed man. James's face registered sheer disgust for the woman, and she, in turn, completely ignored him. Jacinta sported the new hairdo and Tyrone glanced horrified at the shorn locks before his regard slid back to his own wife's bright head, done up in a tastefully coiled upsweep. He only smiled. But Angel decided the snugly waved fashion was gorgeous, especially with Jacinta's natural auburn glints.

Jacinta made the introductions and the young man with her

467

at first grew restless, then relaxed a bit when James Hunter didn't seem to care at all that he escorted his wife. When Beau St. Clair bowed over Angel's hand a flame leaped into the somber depths of his eyes. The young bucks filed out upon learning the fair-haired *mignon* was wife to the tall, superior-looking man holding her arm possessively. Their eager smiles vanished along with them, but St. Clair's perusal continued to dine on the honeyed beauty he saw.

Just this day Tyrone had presented his wife with another of Annette's costly jewels. Each week he gave her another piece, taking immense pleasure in doing it this way. This one was a delicate necklet with a single red ruby centered at the throat, enhancing the glamour of the cherry-red velvet she wore tonight. The flowing gown was graced by a small train spreading on the floor immediately in back of her.

Jacinta gave a sidelong sneer to Angel when St. Clair acknowledged Tyrone with "Sir, I must compliment your wife, and of course, you, on your good taste in women. She stands out like a rose in a bed of white lilies of the valley."

"Monsieur St. Clair, are you implying that I do not belong in this crowd?" Angel asked, but there was a trace of soft humor in her voice.

"On the contrary, madame. You are *ravissante*, a belle, no less," he answered, wishing her husband would suddenly expire on the spot.

Tyrone hid an amused grin behind his hand when Angel lifted an eyebrow impishly at him. Jacinta's face reflected the green of her gown, and when Tyrone thought she would surely boil over with envy, she took her escort by the arm, making a hasty exit.

When the final act was over the curtain jerked together with a loud swish. The lights came on slowly as the crowd stood collectively, then buzzed their disappointment as a roll of thunder rumbled along St. Peter Street, the rain already pelting the wooden planks and gutters outside. The streets would soon become impassable by conveyance, and those who had come from afar would have to stay on with relatives or seek their refuge in lodges for the night. While others damned the storm Tyrone mentally applauded it; in fact he'd foreseen it with his seaman's weather eye.

"Bad weather," Tyrone observed when his party stepped outside.

With hat cocked on one side, Tyrone drew Angel's cloak about her and with the others following, helped her first into the waiting carriage. The wheels slipped in the greasy loam and then they were off, Caspar taking long detours to the town house, avoiding the poorest thoroughfares. Oil lamps barely lighted the way in the heavy mists of rain as they swung from projecting arms nailed to wooden posts, and everywhere people rushed to be cozily installed for the night, their shoes and silk stockings drenched, carrying their own personal lanterns lighting the planked streets before them.

Somehow Jacinta had beat them to the house, opening the door herself and as if she'd been expecting them. Slightly out of breath, Jacinta stood snootily below a lighted sconce, her muddied skirts telling the tale. Nikki, Hannah, and Big Jim alighted, beating a path into the cozy and dry warmth.

"Au revoir," Tyrone chanted, closing the door of the carriage as the others looked out from the hall in surprise. He then slid aside the window to call up to Caspar, "To the hotel, my friend, and make haste!"

Caspar shot Jacinta one of her own disdainful looks from his lofty position, then shaking raindrops off his huge slicker and hunching forward, clicked to the mares. Tyrone sat back with a sigh, peering at his wife out of the corner of his eye as the carriage first slid then rolled onward to its destination.

"Hotel?" Angel finally asked with a quizzical brow.

"Would you rather I take you back to the town house, and sleep there with a house full of guests?" he asked, his eyes glittering in the pale lamplight stealing into the carriage.

"Yes," she answered simply, suddenly frightened of her own husband.

"Madame, I'm sorry, but I just can't do that."

Angel fell silent, believing he meant what he said.

The carriage drew up in the lee of a two-story wooden building boasting a magnificent dome. Angel paused when Tyrone climbed out then held out a hand for her. He asked, "Coming? Or would you rather spend the night in the carriage?

Caspar will see that you have warm blankets, my—"

"Oh no! I'll not sleep outside in this foul weather, even in a carriage, you cad," she sniffed, ignoring the proffered hand and sweeping right on past him and up to the door.

He crossed the short distance, coming to stand beside her. She turned her cheek aside when he made a motion to wipe away the droplets that had dribbled there from the protruding shelf above the door. He made a pained expression, feigning hurt.

"Oh, Tyrone, you look so silly when you do that. Stop it!"

He bowed from the waist then opened the door, making an arc for her to pass under with his long arm. Once inside they shed their outdoor garments, Tyrone handing them over to a stooped man who had recognized the patron at once and had come to serve him.

"Is my room ready, Rafe?" Tyrone asked him, handing over several coins into his palm.

"*Oui, oui,* always waiting for you, monsieur Ty. I 'ave it cleaned and air just today."

When the man went out back to see about sending up a late meal to their room, Angel mimicked, "Is my room ready, Rafe?"

"Well, one never knows when it will rain, does one," he stated rather than asked.

As they made their way across the black and white marble floor, several women lingering in the lobby gave the striking couple a thorough looking over. These well-dressed women watched discreetly while the pair made their ascent up the winding stair. Angel had caught their first perusal though, for once inside the totally ornate, red-velvet-and-dark-wood room, she turned to him just as he was closing the door.

"Do you come here often when in the city? You must, otherwise that man wouldn't hold a room for you," she answered her own question, shivering despite the fire crackling in the fireplace. Indeed the room had been prepared well beforehand, she decided.

Briskly Tyrone strode over to close the window that had been left open by a negligent maid. When that was done he turned, looking thoughtful about something. Suddenly it dawned on him. She was jealous! Jealous of his stepmother, jealous of those women downstairs he'd never even given more than an indifferent glance to. He wouldn't ask her if she would rather he stayed at the town house while James was not there—which was why he took this room while in the city, so he wouldn't have to go there. But tonight was special, and Rafe *had* been informed beforehand.

Angel glanced shyly at the solitary bed in the room and almost gasped upon seeing a diaphanous peignoir and nightgown spread there. Before she could ask who it belonged to, a young buxom maid entered, bearing a huge tray with an elegant repast of oyster patties, ham and potatoes, plus bouillabaisse and, to top it off, cordials of *le petit gouave*. Rafe followed and proceeded to pull over two chairs while the maid was setting down and arranging her burden on the table. They went out, leaving the couple to face each other across the room.

"It is very nice, Tyrone," Angel said sweetly, but then felt nervous again, "and very romantic. What are we celebrating?" She peeped over at the filmy nightwear upon the bed, then dropped her lashes.

"Us." He became very busy next as he pulled out a chair for her and she sat while he spread a napkin on her lap with much ceremony before he went around to seat himself.

The meal was taken in golden silence, and when Angel thought she would surely burst from all the delicious fare, Rafe knocked, then entered with a tall bottle of wine of a rare vintage. Rising, Tyrone followed the man to the door, spoke to him momentarily then secured the door for the night. Angel watched him return to the table, conscious of his every move, from the all-powerful male sinews that stretched beneath his trousers when he walked to the long fingers that curled about the wine bottle when he opened it and poured a glass for each of them. As his glass clinked with hers in the quiet room, she felt a quickening deep inside her. She knew how this evening would end, for she'd felt the tension growing all along.

His probing eyes burned into the frostiness of hers, melting them into a soft green blur. He murmured, "To us, *cherie*—" he smiled and her heart caught in her throat, "and the beginning of many long nights like this one."

Panic rose in her at the bold expression in his eyes. It had been so long since that night on the island and out of nowhere came a terrible fear. Would she be able to please him? Please him as Jacinta no doubt had many times?

"It has been a long time, love," he said, duplicating her thoughts. He reached out to close his long fingers about her small hand, and asked in a thickened voice, "Are you afraid?"

Again he seemed to read her innermost thoughts, but she tried hiding this fearful feeling from him as she said in a small voice, "No."

"No?"

"Yes, yes I am," she confessed. Then, "You once told me that there will come another and yet—"

He wouldn't let her finish. "Never mind what I said on our wedding night. All you need to know is that it never happened, that I never even meant to bed another woman after you. Believe this or not, Angel, but it is truth . . . there has been no one since you."

Angel was stunned by this outright lie. She had caught him abed with Jacinta and it hadn't been just part of a dream she had. He could not have been that drunk, at least not in the morning when they had awakened to go downstairs together. Della said she saw them, so it must be true. In her heart she had already forgiven him, but this new deception was more than she could bear!

In a fit of hot temper she rose, almost upsetting the table in her haste to go and stand across the room, trying to get as far from him as she could. Making a decision, she whirled to face him and the incredulous look that was spreading across his darkened countenance.

"I want to go back to the town house. Now!" she shrieked, unafraid, and hating him for the liar he was.

Where she hadn't upset the table, he did so now as he stood, spilling the remainder of the wine. The china clattered across the carpet to the wood floor and his voice exploded above the noise.

"What the hell do you mean? Damnit, Angel, I demand an

explanation for this silly-assed outburst!" He stood clenching his huge fists against his sides, muscles in his cheeks working furiously.

"You randy bastard!" she shouted, stomped her foot, and faced his terrible anger squarely. "I'll not stay here another minute with you—don't you ever touch me again!"

A timid rapping came at the door and Tyrone strode over to viciously snatch it open, almost wrenching the door from its hinges. Rafe popped his eyes at the mess on the floor, then asked if everything was all right.

"Of course everything is all right," Tyrone said mockingly after he'd glared at the man first. He poured several more coins into the man's hands, asking him to clean the floor up as fast as he could.

While Tyrone paced the carpet and Rafe bent to his task, Angel inched her way to the door, intent on going downstairs to fetch her cloak and find Caspar. She never even touched the knob, for Tyrone swiftly barred her way, grasping her painfully by the shoulders.

"And just where in hell do you think you are going?" he gritted out between his teeth.

She waited while Rafe took up the mess in the tablecloth then went out, closing the door behind him as best he could. Tyrone paused a moment then kicked it shut the rest of the way. It slammed loudly.

Now she answered, "I have told you I'll not stay—"

"Shut up!" he snapped, shaking her roughly. He bent down close to her face and breathed, "Would you like me to seek my amusement elsewhere this night?"

"Please do! You will be doing me a great favor. And you can take your fluffy nighties with you!" she spat back at him, sweeping a hand toward the bed.

He released his grip on her. "If that is the way you want it, madame. There are many lovely quadroons in this city, not one identical, or alike in charming a man, not one that would refuse me as roommate this night, or any night for that matter," he said truly, without conceit.

"You should know," she retorted. "And wasn't it you who said you delight in mystery and intrigue? I'll just bet those

473

love—ly quadroons are full of it!" She broke away, beginning to pace the carpet. She flung over her shoulder, "Conquests. That is all women are to men like you, nothing more than a physical exercise. Charming, fascinating, romantic, yet cool and aloof. Promiscuous . . . yes, you should know!"

"You are my wife!" he shouted in exasperation.

"Oh, don't say it, that my being your wife is a different story altogether. What do you think I dwell in—a storybook land? That you would lay me here tonight, and spread my legs once home for a week, maybe two, then we go our separate ways when you tire of your *wife* and go back to all your love—ly quadroons . . . Jacinta? A fine marriage outlook indeed!"

"That is just about enough!" Tyrone demanded, amazed at her tantrum.

"Then go about your business, Tyrone Hunter!" she spat back, just as forcefully.

"You amaze me, Angeline Hunter. You are a most unpredictable woman. Umm—I believe you are jealous?" he prodded.

"That is totally untrue. You have gotten the wrong impression, sir," she said, trying not to look at him.

"That is just what I thought—you *are* jealous," he said decidedly.

"Why don't you go! I'm certain Jacinta awaits your pleasure, is just panting to toss up her skirts for you, as she did just a few weeks back. And you just could not resist the temptation!" she snarled, truly feeling the green monster at her back.

"Confound it, woman! That does it, you've gone too far!" he bellowed, snatching up his vest and striding to the door. He paused to turn around at the door and look at her, but she was ready with another retort.

"Go then!" she hissed. "I shall stay here for the night, but do not expect to come crawling into my bed later with the smell of a whore on you!"

The gilded daggers of her eyes spoke irate volumes after the coldheartedness of her words. Then he was gone, the door slamming in her face.

474

*   *   *

Slowly waking, slowly gazing about the room, Angel came back to the vacant pillow beside her. Morning. Feeling drained of emotion, she forced herself to rise and cross the room on icy feet to stoke the few glowing embers that remained, the heap of dead ashes beneath all that was left to remind her of a night that should have been one of enchantment. She was feeling something close to physical pain, but the bitterness she'd endured during the wee hours of morning was now gone, replaced by the agony that Tyrone had taken his pleasure elsewhere. That he had lied to her meant nothing now, but it was too late to regain what she'd lost. All of a sudden she couldn't imagine a loveless life. The future looked dismal indeed, for that was exactly what she'd set the stage for.

Hunkering before the growing flame in only her chemise, Angel stood to look out the window. Already the world appeared very empty to her. A tear slipped down her cheek and wetted her bosom. After a time she splashed cold water onto her face from the basin and donned the cherry velvet. She had left her reticule in the carriage, so she raked her fingers through her loose hair and pinned it back up into a sleek knot. She was ready to go down and inquire as to how she might find the Hunter town house, when a knock came across to her. She almost tripped on her skirts dashing to answer it, praying it might be Tyrone.

It was Hannah. For a moment they only stared at each other, then Hannah, looking a bit sheepish as she spied the diaphanous nightwear draped carefully over a chair, informed Angel that Caspar waited outside to drive them to the waterfront where they would make the journey upriver by keelboat. The rain had ceased early in the morning, she added, but the trip by carriage would have been slow and lumbering, to say the least.

Giving one last glimpse to the filmy garments, Angel dejectedly followed Hannah out the door. She didn't ask of Tyrone's whereabouts nor did Hannah offer any information. Hannah was unusually quiet, only mentioning that Rafe would fix something for them to eat on their journey—cold ham, just-baked bread, a jug of hot cider tea, and black coffee for Nikki and Caspar. Not once did she mention Tyrone.

While they were waiting downstairs for the food, two men stumbled in sideways, at least that's how it appeared until they turned about with their human burden. Between them a dishevelled gentleman hung limply, with tousled hair, he who was singing in melodic embellishments of a young man pining for his lady fair. His hat was more than cocked off to one side and his pockets were all turned out, displaying his misfortune at the gaming tables, yet he didn't seem to mind this a bit, for his mouth was split wide in a ludicrous grin that showed he was feeling no pain.

Angel turned to see what all the commotion was about and why Hannah's mouth hung open in astonishment. "Tyrone," Angel breathed, turning her head from the inebriated figure before he noticed her.

The man, drunk as a lord, rolled his eyes then focused them momentarily upon the women standing at the back of the hall. He bellowed across to them, watching his steps, "Good evening, your ladyshilts—ah—ladyshlips, I mean. Pardon if I don't dine with you, but my lady fair waits for me—" he shook his head, hiccoughed loudly, "so mad, she's gonna be *soooo* mad, madder than a wet wet hen. Sq*uaaaaak!*"he ended, with a fairly good imitation of an enraged chicken, for all his inebriety.

After he was half dragged up the stairs by the two river gamblers, Angel picked up her skirts to follow, but Hannah reached out to gently restrain her by taking an arm.

"Hannah, I must stay and help him. And those men, they might harm him. When he wakes up—"

"No! You shouldn't, Angel. It'll be best if he doesn't know you saw him in this devastating condition. It will save much embarrassment now and later on . . . for both of you," she explained.

"I do not care, Hannah, he needs me," she said with finality.

Sighing, Hannah went along to possibly be of some help. Meanwhile, Nikki, upon seeing Tyrone enter between the two burly men, hastened inside lest the two decided to divest him of the shirt on his back. Nikki couldn't help smiling to himself, though. He had never seen Tyrone in such a pickled state.

Tyrone's late evening of drinking had begun at the town house after leaving his wife at the hotel. Nikki had warned his cousin not to go out when the clock had then struck one time. But Tyrone had danced merrily on his way, sure he would discover a gambling corner where no one would recognize him in the dead of night.

The two ruffians chuckled on their way down just as the ladies reached the door that was slightly ajar, enough for Angel to peep in and determine her husband's mood before entering. She was bent over spying on him when suddenly she stiffened her spine, jerking upright at what she had viewed. Her cheeks colored profusely. With tab open, Tyrone had been relieving himself in the chamber pot; he faced her, but with tousled head bowing thoughtfully, a stream meandering on either side of the pot. Now he snorted as the bed creaked under his weight, bold four-letter words tumbling from his lips, unfit for ladies' ears.

Gulping, Angel whispered, "I think you are right, Hannah, let's be away from here before he notices us!"

In their haste to descend the stairs they met Nikki face to face. Hannah's fiance, trying to conceal a grin, said, "Big Jim will come later in the evening to nurse the poor lad back to health. He'll sleep most of the day, anyway. Ready? The keelboat is waiting with a warm, comfortable cabin to accommodate you ladies."

At Cresthaven the weeks rolled by swiftly, and still there was no sign of Tyrone or Big Jim. Angel was subject to despondency after the first week of her husband's absence from the huge house, so Hannah stayed on as companion to the lonely mistress of Cresthaven. Too, Hannah felt a sense of freedom being away from Wesley and his lately cruel tongue. April, being so young and naive, escaped the censure of her father, and she always had Jenny to pamper her and distract her from Wesley's ugly moods. Hannah and Nikki postponed their wedding for a later date when everyone would be there to celebrate it.

Brian Ross was Angel's chief mainstay these days. His growth was rapid, his little limbs and mouth constantly on the move. Angel began to worry that he would never get to know his father, for Tyrone had hardly acknowledged the wee lad's presence, but for once—the day when they had lain together as a family on the rug and Tyrone had allowed Brian's little fist to close about his thumb.

When Angel woke from an afternoon nap one day early in February, she donned a frock over her chemise and went down to find Hannah for some company. She was just about to enter the parlor when Hannah's and Nikki's voices drifted out to her. Angel's skirts swirled about her ankles as she came abruptly to a standstill.

"How could he work both ends against the middle, being both a smuggler and a politician? His loyalties must be scattered like dry leaves to the wind!" Hannah was saying, a trifle hotly.

"Let me tell you," Nikki began. "Time and again Tyrone left the smuggler's settlement to stay at a town house on Rue St. Charles, fully equipped with an army of faithful servants, many of whom were the very beautiful and talented quadroons, educated from an early age on how to pleasure a man, to say the least."

Angel's shoulders drooped at that. She knew she was eavesdropping, but she couldn't tear herself from the spot. She had to hear the rest.

"Let me see," Nikki paused, then went on. "Oh, yes, he even attended church services regularly and became respectable for a time. He visited the governor's mansion to become familiar with the political situation. So everyone thought. Claiborne's wife is one of the most beautiful and sought-after women in all New Orleans, and it was by her request that Mr. Hunter was allowed to come and go as he pleased. Tyrone finally realized that Claiborne did not fully understand the population, the Creole residents. Smuggling relations have long been a way of life in the community and the city's growing commerce would have suffered greatly if Claiborne had succeeded in preventing smuggling. Tyrone, along with others like him, overcame the

478

unpopular restriction.

"Tyrone finally went back to the absolute independence of a smuggler's life. Those who knew him best called him a maritime Robin Hood, though he joined forces with the rapidly growing smuggler's colony and held Cartagenian letters of marque on council of Jean Lafitte. In other words, he was free to prey on Spanish vessels."

"You mean he took from the rich so to speak and gave to the poor?" Hannah was heard to ask.

"Yes. Even Lafitte didn't know . . . then. With his own share Captain Ty transported his riches to those poor Cajun inhabitants in the swamps, made them very comfortable while he kept nothing for himself. Further on up the line, many of the merchants and shopkeepers in the city who possess very little conscience were more than happy to purchase the prime booty for very little coin. The merchants made a large profit with the superior wares and New Orleans' commerce still continues to grow under illicit traffic; has since the old French Colonial days."

There came a long silence before Hannah finally asked, somewhat sadly, "Do you know why Tyrone didn't live on at Cresthaven?"

"Too many bad memories, I guess. There is more to it than meets the casual onlooker's eye. All I know is that Tyrone hated his mother, my aunt, and she was supposed to have given him that scar on his forehead. . . ."

Angel would hear no more and fled the hall. Dusk was falling when she was still perched on the edge of her bed. She barely heard the banging of shutters being closed for the night, so engrossed in thought was she.

One afternoon in late February, Caspar returned from the city with the message that Tyrone and Big Jim would soon be returning from Charleston, where they had gone several weeks before on business. After Caspar had gone out back, Angel paced up and down the carpet in the parlor, letting loose a well-aimed kick of a slippered foot to a fine chair leg.

"Not one word until now!" she said sharply, releasing her

pent-up tensions. So, he was good to his poor friends—but what about his wife and son! Her small white teeth nipped her lower lip. "I wonder how many brazen whores will follow and come to camp on the doorstep when he returns. He bloody may well even invite them into his bedchamber!"

Hannah's gray eyes grew wide. "Angel! I've never heard you speak this way before. What is it that is troubling you? I realize Tyrone should have sent a message sooner, but maybe . . . just maybe you had words with him? That is why he returned to the town house several hours after leaving you at the lodge, and why he hasn't let you know his whereabouts all these weeks?"

Angel spun around, her ears pricked up. "Wait a minute, Hannah. You said Tyrone returned to the town house. What did he do then, after that?"

Hannah giggled. "First, as you already know, he got thoroughly pickled and stayed that way till morning. Then he proceeded in all haste to go out and find game."

"What kind of game?" Angel asked with narrowed eyes.

Hannah sighed in exasperation. "Angel, I can't believe this is really you talking to me. Didn't you see him when he entered the hotel? His pockets were turned out, and, tell me how in the world could he have done a woman justice in his condition?"

Angel snorted, "He has done it before. Right in this very house, under my own nose!"

Completely baffled, Hannah breathed, "I don't believe it. *Who?*"

"Jacinta, his stepmother. That is who," she cried. "I saw them, naked as jaybirds after receiving a message in the dead of night, summoning me to his bedchamber."

"Lord, how awful it must have been for you," Hannah replied. She was thoughtful for a moment, then a look of enlightenment crept slowly across her pretty face. "Angel, I should have told you this before, but I'll have to speak openly now and without reservation. Nikki filled me in on the happenings of the night Tyrone returned to the town house. First, it is well known by everyone that Jacinta has wanted her stepson ever since—since—"

"Since he bedded her the first time," Angel said, then at a nod from Hannah she begged, "Please go on."

"Well, from what I understood, Jacinta was after Tyrone again that night. Angel—" Hannah breathed shockingly, "she was almost nude when she entered the salon where Nikki was trying to press black coffee on Tyrone. All she had on was a transparent blouse that only reached to the top of her thighs and her cropped hair was turbaned in a flowing red scarf." Here Hannah giggled before she went on. "Nikki said she looked like a barefoot gypsy with her dark eyes shining unmistakably with lust. Huge gold loops swung from her ears when she sashayed over to Tyrone and bent over him . . . rubbing his thighs. He mumbled something about Big Jim and she said not to worry, he was sound asleep upstairs." Hannah paused in indecision as to whether she should go on or not.

"Tell me, Hannah. I must know everything. It is very important to my—our happiness. Tyrone's and mine."

Well, why not, Hannah thought, and continued. "Uncaring that Nikki looked on—because I gathered she was as drunk as Tyrone—she lifted her blouse high, straddled him with her nakedness right there in the chair and began to—umm—undo his fly. Soon she was—ah—pumping on him furiously, when Tyrone threw back his hand and groaned. Right then and there, Nikki thought it was a wise move to make exit when, swiftly, Tyrone stood suddenly and dumped Jacinta right onto the floor, legs spread, and with her womanhood displayed for all to see. She didn't seem to mind a bit that he'd done that. She kept on writhing shamelessly on the floor, asking for it. Guess what happened next?"

Seated on the edge of her chair, Angel shook her head, shrugging at the same time, impatient for Hannah to finish.

Hannah licked her lips. "James Hunter walked in! He glanced about the room, saw Nikki and his son at the sideboard pouring drinks, thoroughly ignoring the panting figure snaking on the floor. Big Jim said she wouldn't need her voodoo medicine, philters, for several weeks to come after he finished with her. He told her he was going to toss out all the vials she'd acquired of late from the *cunjer* she'd been visiting.

481

So you see, Angel, if Tyrone wasn't interested in a dalliance with one of the most talented-in-the-bed Creole women, he wasn't wanting for anyone." Hannah smiled, adding, "But for this . . . he wanted you that night, Angel. Nikki said so. Why—"

"Philter," Angel breathed curiously. "Hannah, I may have something here, relative to the night I walked in on them. Hmmm, it could have been Jacinta herself who scribbled the note, but, did she deliver it under the door, or did someone else? Tell me, Hannah, about these—ah—philters."

"Potions. Love potions, I would guess. Jacinta takes these potions herself lately. Nikki says she always carries a vial with her, but if you ingest too much, you won't be able to even see who you're with, much less perform if abed. Especially if there's a notable lapse of time since . . . Angel, what is it?" Hannah looked her friend steadily in the eye and it dawned on her what the other was concentrating upon—"Oh! Angel!"

There has been no one since you, since you, since you . . . Angel floated on Tyrone's words, knowing in her heart it was true. She acted much like a fluttering schoolgirl with her first crush, walking the halls of Cresthaven like one in a gauzy dream. She had dispatched Caspar speedily to Mimi's establishment, ordering several new gowns in jonquil colors, pale lavender, and spring-green tiffany, taffy- and peach-colored frocks of jaconet embroidered at the bodice in hues of spring, along with petticoats in lawn, bastiste and mull, short of waist with slim, long skirts. She had shawls for spring, in handwoven lace, and a few of cream-colored chiffon. Added to these, she already owned several nightgowns of the sheerest gossamer silk that she'd never even taken out of drawers. Now she planned to do just that!

Of her list sent to Mimi, Angel was surprised when everything was delivered a week later. Mimi sent along a note saying this had come as a surprise to her, that strangely enough Monsieur Hunter had put in an order several weeks before his wife's that almost duplicated hers, knowing as he did what colors and fashions best suited her. A veritable rainbow, along with the soft naturals, graced Angel's wardrobe by early

March. A bewitching black dressing gown accompanied a wicked nightie of the same color—Mimi's lagniappe to the young madame. Such an extravagant gift, but perhaps it was because of the large order. Angel wondered, but did not dwell on it.

Angel was in her heavenly realm all that week, waiting for her husband's return home. She didn't have long to wait.

That something still
For which we bear to live or dare to die.
—Pope

Chapter Twelve

1

Angel woke early one glorious Saturday morning to the golden sparkle of sun invading her chamber, the smell of bacon and eggs making her nose twitch curiously. Who would be up at this hour having breakfast? With heart pounding she slipped from bed and hurriedly snatched up a robe, going to listen just outside her door. Voices drifted up to her from the bottom of the stairs. It was Della she heard first, then James asking if he might see his grandson. This meant Tyrone was downstairs having his favorite breakfast. He was home!

Awhile later, Tyrone stood motionless in the parlor, giving no outward sign that he was affected by the fair vision gliding in just now to greet him cheerfully, but inwardly he was staggered by the mere sight of her after two whole months. There developed a certain electric charge in the air, and he wasn't certain which one of them gave life to it—perhaps both. Still, something warned him to retain his self-possession and stand aloof.

"Good morning, my dear. Della tells me you have been well, and Brian Ross also," he said as she came to him.

Tyrone pecked his wife lightly on the forehead, avoiding the upturned lips presented to him. Immediately after the fatherly kiss, Angel opened her eyes to see the broad back moving slowly away from her. Disappointment made her face fall miserably as he strode over to the window to light a slim cheroot. He had begun using tobacco again, she noticed, and he was much leaner, but it did not detract from his handsomeness. If anything—her cameo complexion flushed—he appeared more virile than ever. But his remoteness stung and she longed to run to him, pour out her love, but her feet proved stubborn. He was still angry with her, then. She had been a shrew at the hotel, so what did she expect?

Angel hesitated but a moment, then indomitably, walked over to seat herself prettily upon the sofa, spreading the peaches-and-cream frock of jaconet about her like an opened fan. She began to chatter about the goings on at Cresthaven during his absence, telling of Brian's rapid growth, Sam and Jenny's wedding and—oh—the singing and merrymaking that had swelled from out back, keeping her awake one night last week till early morning.

"I did not mind, though," Angel continued. "It is not every day that such a happy event takes place."

Tyrone had been quietly studying her mannerisms, but now lifted a sardonic brow as he asked, "You gave them the presents I left for them?" After her nod, he went on. "Good. Now, you'll have to excuse me, my dear, but I have a letter to get off to Charleston. There are a few pieces of equipment I forgot to order while I was there."

Angel wanted so very much to inquire about his trip and show her earnest interest in his lumber and sugar business, but he was already striding briskly out to the hall.

Dash it! How she wished she could be more like Jacinta at times. That would never do, of course, because she couldn't bring herself to do the wanton things Jacinta had done to try and gain her end. Angel smiled suddenly, quite wickedly. But then, Jacinta wasn't *married* to her husband, either.

Darkness cloaked Cresthaven and Angel wore black. She was seated at her dressing table when she dismissed Sarah for the evening. Sarah had brushed her mistress's hair one hundred strokes and the silvery-blond hair shone with a lustre all its own. Angel's cheeks were rosier than ever but Sarah hadn't mentioned this to her mistress; she only smiled at the hint of deviltry in the green eyes.

Alone now, Angel waited for the familiar footfalls that would come upstairs and go into the bedchamber on the other side of the nursery. Her second glass of white wine since dinner sat atop her dresser and she sipped it now at her leisure, waiting,

waiting. He should be ready to retire early after his long journey, Angel thought, but the bongs out in the hall told her it was already the tenth hour. She couldn't wait any longer.

In his study, Tyrone glanced up from a sheaf of papers he had been going over when a timid rapping sounded at the door. Nikki stood up to answer, while Big Jim and Caspar exchanged curious glances. With his back to the others in the study, Nikki gulped in astonishment upon opening the door. Then his nose twitched curiously. He could tell the fumes for what they were, for he hadn't imbibed this evening at all.

"Angel, what—?" he began, then shielded her from view with his tall frame, shutting the door behind him as he stepped out into the hall with her.

"Nikki, I want to see my husband," the entrancing woman said, then giggling, "Come now, step aside."

Nikki noticed at once that she wasn't really intoxicated, just mildly tipsy. Still, she was draped seductively, the filmy thing peeping out from the slit in her dressing gown, both meant only for the boudoir. He couldn't allow her to enter like this. Tyrone would surely be embarrassed, possibly even angry with her in this half-dressed state.

Keeping his eyes averted from the black thing, Nikki pleaded, "Go upstairs, now, princess, like a good girl before—"

The door was snatched open before Nikki could finish his sentence. "What the devil?" Tyrone began. His eyes riveted on the almost sinful sight and he stared as if hypnotized, his eyes dropping lower, lower, before he snatched them up to measure the flushed face. "Angel," he said huskily, "what is the meaning of this?" He recognized the black ensemble as the one he'd chosen especially for her.

Nikki intervened. "Cousin—" he shook his head, "Boy, are you stupid!"

As Nikki went back into the study he cut them from view by closing the door swiftly after him. Angel, at once sober and slightly ashamed, hung her head as she picked at a ribbon on her dressing gown with nervous fingers. She would not look at him. Her courage had dwindled after one dark look from him.

"Madame, I'll walk you to your bedroom door," Tyrone offered, taking her by the arm. "Then I shall bid you a good night, as I have work to get finished."

On the way up, Angel allowed herself to lean heavily against his arm, her breast pressing boldly into the silken shirt. His sleeves had been rolled up to his elbows and the coarse hairs on his forearm tickled the underside of her wrist deliciously. Her breast tingled where it touched and a hunger began to throb in her belly, setting her afire for him. He released her abruptly at the door, but lowered his face. Her lips waited for the kiss, and then, all he did was sniff. He straightened and her hopes died.

"Wine? You shouldn't drink alone, madame," he warned. He let his eyes roam down the revealing nightie between the gown, and he said coolly, "You mask your true feelings when you go searching with wine in your belly, my dear. How do you feel now?"

"I feel—" she halted, sensing he played a game with her. Hiding a smile she went on, "I am quite sober now, Tyrone. Anyway, I only had two small glasses. One with dinner and then Sarah brought up another."

"I'm sorry I couldn't dine with you this evening, but we had this work to get done. I promise that tomorrow I'll join you, though. Good night, my dear," he said in a silken voice, turning away.

His back was slowly moving away from her, so slowly in fact, that he barely seemed to be making progress along the hall. He halted and glanced over his shoulder to see her rooted in the same spot. Her open hands slid down her thighs, worrying the silk. He seemed to be studying the wall for a moment, then, avoiding the stairs, he went directly to his chamber, closing the door softly. Even so, the sound was like thunder to Angel's ears. He had been acting indifferent since his return, but this last gesture was gelidly executed. Angel pouted. He hadn't even given her a kiss, not even a fatherly one as he'd done earlier in the parlor!

A small fire crackled at the hearth when Angel entered the bedchamber tentatively. She saw his bed was vacant and peered about, searching out the shadows for that tall frame. Her heart beat like a wild thing as she closed the door carefully behind her, wondering if he had gone out to the gallery for a night stroll. Turning about, her heart caught in her throat.

487

Tyrone stood there, bared to the waist, with a strange expression molding his face in the firelight.

"Are you looking for someone, my dear?" he asked, his eyes searching the frightened face.

He didn't wait for an answer, but to her utter amazement sauntered right by her to seat himself on the edge of the bed where he began pulling off his tall leather boots. He halted there, and, but for his aloofness, acted as if this was all perfectly natural; as if they had enacted this scene a hundred times before. She relaxed, but only a little.

"Come here, my dear," he said unalarmingly, unmoving.

She moved to the bed as if on air, wondering why he had taken up calling her "my dear." He used to utter warmer endearments, and she didn't know if she especially liked this new slant of cool respectability he used with her. It made her deathly afraid for some reason, but of what she'd only tasted, and not yet fully determined.

Tyrone emitted a half chuckle. "You're as tense as a snared bunny. Here," he said patting the bed with a hand, "lie down and I'll rub your back for you. Would you like that?"

"Yes, Tyrone. I would . . . very much," she answered in a frail voice.

"Good. First, take your dressing gown off. I'll stay just the way I am—my dear."

At first the meaning didn't catch, then she realized he meant to keep his trousers on. While she was removing the gown, he crossed the room to his dresser and returned with a vial of something in his hand.

"What is that?" she questioned softly.

"Just some oil I picked up while in Charleston. It's—ah—very relaxing when rubbed into the skin."

While she climbed into the bed with her backside to him, Tyrone's eyes gleamed like those of a snake in the grass. Ever since this morning when she had sat prettily upon the sofa chattering away at him, he had known of her urgency to mate. There was only this underlying fear of hers he had to deliver her of.

The oil was slippery in his palms as he peered down upon the softly curving buttocks illuminated beneath the gown. He would have groaned with his quickening need but covered it up by saying hoarsely, "I can't. I'll ruin the precious nightgown you're wearing, Angel."

"Why did you not say so," she murmured, slipping it down to her waist before she lay back down to stretch flat upon her stomach.

He had caught a glimpse of the perfect globes, and his knees gave way naturally to the bed as he bent to apply the musk oil to the flawless ivory back. The slippery warmth of his strong hands massaging her back made Angel relax completely. Only then did he lower his head to brush his hot cheek against hers and nip at an earlobe gently. He felt her quiver once but paid it no mind, driven only by an overwhelming passion to love her. His fingers had been warm, then hot, now they were red-searing into the naked flesh that became pliant under his fingertips and palms, traveling lower and lower, manipulating her slowly as he rolled her onto her side. The throbbing she had known before inside her returned twofold, but when his fingers slid down her belly she cried out as if pained.

Tyrone straightened brusquely to glare down upon the oval face turning to him, noticing the little beads of sweat that moistened her upper lip. Her eyes were heavy-lidded.

"My dear, or, my love," he questioned almost harshly. "Which do you prefer, Angel?"

Knowing that worst fear once again, Angel came up to meet him with a sob catching in her throat. "My love! My love! Tyrone, love me—now!" Her voice became softer, murmuring, "Love me now and forevermore."

In unconscious shyness she had crossed an arm over her breasts. As he came to her, one of his arms encircled her back while his free hand held hers fast between them. He bent to brush his lips with hers, then the kiss deepened and he removed the offending arm that shielded his chest from meeting hers. Soft breasts melted under the hard chest before her quickened breath attested to her readiness. He left for a few seconds to be free of the trousers. When he twisted about on the bed he noted with great pleasure that the nightgown had been discarded, and her arms opened invitingly to him. First his eyes feasted themselves upon her full nakedness, gleaming sensuously from the applied oil, then he joined her, murmuring against her ear.

"Motherhood agrees with you, wife. Beautiful falls short of describing you, my love. But if you live up to your namesake this night, I'll have to beat you, thrash you within an inch of your life," he said, ending with a deep chuckle.

She answered him by pulling him down to meet her softly parted lips. In the cloud of passion that enveloped her, she wished fervently to learn the better how to please him, so that she might emerge fully satisfied from this night in the knowledge that she had accomplished her best sexually.

"Teach me, Tyrone, teach me all that a woman should know," she breathed hotly, sweetly, into his ear. Then, "I want to know all of love's joys . . . tutor me along the way to please you?" The question was shy.

"Lord!" his voice was a husky groan. "I am fully aroused now, my sweet—feel." He guided her to himself. Her small hand closed about the hard shaft and he shivered in unhumanlike heat. Her thighs fell apart under the urging of a knee. "Angel, you do please me! You inflame me!" he groaned in urgent passion.

Tyrone raised his head from kissing her throat, and, as she arched her back, breathed a soft stream of pleasure against her lips. He filled her. With a cry of ecstatic joining, she received the fullness of his silken thrust like a glorious flower unfolding to receive the sun into its stamen. With his hands lifting her buttocks he strained to go deeper. Filmy-eyed, Angel panted under the bittersweet pressure, the tension that was building apace from his rhythmic pounding. She became wild, no more gentle motions as she abandoned herself in meeting thrust for thrust, rocking her hips as if she couldn't get enough of the fire searing into her belly.

Later she would wonder if he had truly repeated over and over that he loved her, in French, but for now she was so wrapped up in what was happening to her freshly awakened body that everything became a hazy blur. He was a tan-haired lion, leaping, lunging, then halting as she cried out his name, then one last surge brought them as one to the ultimate in ecstasy.

Angel saw him gazing down upon her, his white teeth flashing in the dimly lighted room, smiling like a triumphant warlord exulting in his final victory. His tawny head tossed back as he rolled onto his side to relax, bringing her with him, still joined.

A little later her world was spinning as finally he brought her back down for the second time to earth and settled her softly, rapturously, into a bed of down. He was her tan god, her golden beast that preyed upon her heart and won it again and again and for time boundless, feeling the trip hammer of his heart thumping against her swollen breasts as her own did a rapid tattoo.

Angel sighed deliciously in the crook of his arm as they nestled and rested. Her heart brimmed with love, but still in her shyness she couldn't mouth the words. Yet, had she during the height of ecstasy? Had *he?*

"I am so terribly happy, content right now, Tyrone, I feel it's a sin. I have never felt so completely a woman as I do now. Did I please you? Was I an apt pupil, Mr. Hunter?"

"Please me!" Tyrone chuckled outrageously in her ear. "Mistress Hunter, you drove me insane with pleasure as no woman has ever done before! As for your second question— yes, you are a natural, my love, born to receive love and give it. But, dear charm, there is more. . . ."

He rolled over with her and they tumbled on the silken sheets. In the following blissful hours Angel was alternately shocked and delighted in what he did to her quivering body, and what he gently persuaded her to do to his. The fire burned high as they tumbled about on their playground of love until she was rendered insensible and had to beg him to cease.

Sometime in the wee hours of morning, Tyrone whispered at the nape of her neck, "My bewitching angel-woman. I've worshipped the ground you walk on ever since you fearlessly lost that blade to me, and I learned you were not a rosy-cheeked lad but a lovely young woman." He swallowed the catch in his throat, murmuring, "I'll never have my fill of you, sweetest heart, you are my life . . . Angel?" But she was sound asleep. He smiled at the profile in childlike repose. "Yes, I've done you in for the night, my beloved. Dream on, Angel." He rolled to

491

his back and slept, his fingers yet laced with hers.

Rosy spikes of dawn stabbed between the folds of the motionless drapes. An early spring was heralded with a sweet chorus from birds that circled the rooftop and perched on the eaves with breasts proudly puffed. A new wind was softly blowing as morning waxed and Angel slowly awakened, sinking down further beneath the silken coverlet to stretch sinuously. Meeting a bare flank and a naked hip, she blushed under the covers right down to her toes, recalling with an unmaidenly smile the long night shared making passionate love with her lusty husband. She felt like one reborn with new mental fiber; and new muscle, even though some were definitely sore.

Tyrone was indeed a master in the art of love and she knew this without the consciousness of an experienced woman of the world. He had fully exercised this talent with the mindful expertise of a connoisseur as he tutored her in love's joys. Angel found no shame in full-blown passion nor would she ever again, and as long as he desired her she would remain content as a babe, asking for no more.

Rolling her head on the pillow, Angel's dancing green eyes viewed the slumbering form of her husband. He was stretched out full length and the coverlet on his other side reached only to his thigh. Sitting up ever so cautiously so as not to wake him, she studied the lean but strongly muscled form, thinking him some magnificent beast of the wilds, with his tawny mane of hair and the darker thatch growing on his rippled chest and . . . She tore her glance from between his legs. Lord! but he is hirsute, she thought.

With breasts pointed sensuously, she raked her tapered fingers throughout her long fair hair to comb out the tangles, then flung the silken mass over her bare shoulders. In the next instant glancing downward, she gasped at the throbbing, eager erection. Multiflecked golden eyes flew open and a rakish grin surprised the little face above him. Seeing her shocked expression he emitted a lusty chuckle while displaying those straight white teeth.

Angel drew a mock-serious expression, saying, "Naked blade! You were not asleep at all and only bided your time to catch me off guard!"

492

Rolling quickly from him, Angel was snatched back at the edge of the mattress. He pulled her beneath him while she protested with a shriek. He straddled soft thighs with a hard knee placed on either side of the long limbs. He came down to nuzzle her neck, the fires in him yet unquenched.

"You are wrong there, madame. I awoke just now to the delicious sight of you preening your feathers."

"So! I am a bird, am I?" she asked imperiously. "And you, Tyrone Hunter, are an unslaked rogue!" She flirted from beneath dark lashes.

"Ah, but you, my love, you are a tempting hen for a horny cock to behold in the early morn." He clucked his tongue at her, demanding, "Where is your modesty and your shame, madame? Ogling a naked blade like a bold, painted actress." He pressed into her softness, smiling. "But, you are on again in a moment, as the fourth act is about to begin."

She blushed in the new light. "Tyrone, it is morning, and I am hungry—famished!"

"So am I, love, so am I." He drove his point home as she cried out first in outrage then in full receiving joy.

Angel woke for the second time. It was noon. Someone had drawn back the drapes and the beauteous day shone ever so brightly. Scanning the vast, high-ceilinged room, Angel decided that Tyrone had most likely gone down to his black coffee, bacon and eggs. She felt at her leisure in getting bathed and dressed, for she had given Brian Ross his morning nourishment before blinking wide and climbing wearily back into her husband's big bed. She had slept like a rock after that.

Bounding from the bed now, feeling fit as a fiddle, but for some spots that hurt, Angel embraced the lovely springlike day, going to the gallery to throw the doors wide. She hugged herself tight, listening to the hubbub of feathered creatures greeting her. Her silvery laughter rang free and she suddenly didn't want to stay inside and miss the sunshine that beckoned.

Galvanized into action, she whirled and raced stark naked into her own chamber to wildly search her wardrobe for the pea-green riding outfit and soft hide boots. She twirled gaily, clutching the garment to her bosom, having already decided to ride today. Perhaps she would even pick the wild one—Her Majesty!

By the time Angel had wolfed down a hasty breakfast fetched by Daisy Mae, bathed, donned the pea-green, she looked more radiant than ever, like a bride reliving the night past. Even though her cheeks needed no pinching, Brian did so anyway, chuckling when his gorgeous mama laughed at his antics. More giggling reached her ears, coming from her husband's chamber. Angel thought: The maids should have tidied his room by now. What could be keeping them from moving on? She placed Brian back in his crib and went to stand at her husband's door, watching the busy bees.

"Daisy Mae. Sarah. What on earth are you two doing with my clothes?" she questioned the maids who rushed in and out of the hall with armfuls of negligees and various articles of her clothing that had been folded in her dresser only minutes before.

The maids halted, exchanging sheepish looks with each other. At last Sarah spoke up, the quicker to obey. "Mr. Hunter tole us to do it. He say to bring all your things to his room, 'cept some gowns and frocks. He say there's plenty of empty places for them—" she giggled then added gleefully, "He say you tired of marchin' back 'n forth for this 'n that."

"Oh he did, did he?" Angel demanded but hid a secretive smile from them.

"Mmmm-hmmm," Daisy Mae and Sarah hummed in unison.

Angel mastered the recalcitrant white mare her first time out. But after several outings she was finally found out, even though she stealthily saddled up herself, while Old Saul seemingly snoozed in the hay. Her husband stood glowering darkly at her one fine April morning when she thundered from the north into the greensward, all pink and pretty from her long jaunt into the woods. His visage was so stern that he frightened her momentarily as she reined up.

Angel tried smiling into the angry hazel orbs. "I know I should have asked, Tyrone, but I just couldn't help myself, even knowing what your answer would have been. She reminds me so much of my own Echo but for the coloring. I can handle her, as you can see for yourself. All Majesty needs is the firm gentleness her former master so carelessly overlooked and—" she smiled with much brilliance, "a little sugar for her sweet tooth."

"Former master! I'll not have—" he began then cut it short as he rebuked her. "Damnit, Angel! I was just about to saddle Beast and come searching for you myself. You haven't seen the worst of Her Majesty's temper. You could have been thrown— killed! You have been lucky thus far, that's all." He reached up to help her off the blowing mare that refused to quiet for him, sharp hooves almost trodding upon his boots. "Bitch!" he ground out, at the same time squeezing Angel's waist hard to sweep her out of harm's way.

Angel appeared hurt. "Tyrone. How could you!"

He softened at once while pushing back a straying lock of fair hair, saying, "I wasn't referring to you, my sweet. But if you disobey me again by riding this one with the mean streak, I'll have to resort to spanking your bottom roundly!"

His rebuff was severe, but he made hungry, passionate love to her again in the middle of the night, waking her from sleep after leaving his study, as he had done almost every night since their reunion, except for when her time of the month had come in March. He had been owlish, and when she was done his humor restored once again.

One morning Angel confronted him in his study, choosing the worst time to do so. There were times when his work must not be intruded upon, and this was such a day.

"Tyrone," she tried sweetly, all dripping with honey, "please may I ride Her Majesty today? I promise to be very careful and not ride out too far. You could come with me?" she implored, running a finger along a paper's edge.

He glanced up from a ledger he'd been going over, and with a preoccupied frown, gave his full attention once more to the column of numbers, saying casually, "I've already given my answer on that. There's no reason for us to discuss it further."

"Majesty is not the demon you say she is. All she needs is a bit of handling, then she will be as good as Beast or Beauty," Angel explained, hell bent on having her way.

"Ride Beauty," he replied simply, ignoring her. "She's as good as your old English mare. Better . . . she's Louisiana Breed."

That did it! "As you say, master," Angel said meekly, but flounced to the door. She snapped back over her shoulder, "You southern planters, you are all anti-British!"

Now he looked up, but just in time to catch the bit of green velvet flicking around the door. "Now what is that supposed to mean?" he asked around the room, but the ledgers and strewn papers had no voice to aid him. He tossed his pen aside and snorted, "Women!"

"Men!" Angel breathed huffily, unconsciously trodding upon a lovely bed of wildflowers on her way to the stable. "Down, Noble! Down!" she ordered the hound springing up from his resting place. She whirled about before entering to saddle up Beauty. "Horny humpback!" she yelled back to the house.

Standing at the open window, Tyrone tossed back his head and roared with mirth upon seeing his wife shake her small fist at him, hearing her mild invective. He thought to himself: Horny for you, yes, my love, but you have the hump in the wrong place. He went back to his work, all the while wishing for her company. He couldn't ride with her just now, but when the planting of the sugar was initiated, he would accompany her about the fields and show her the lay of the land.

April changed her gray and brown wardrobe for May's more colorful one. Tyrone's visage lately was more brooding than not, and justifiably so. A change had become apparent in his wife, ever since she had taken to riding off by herself into the north woods. Sometimes she wore a faraway look when returning. But that, he thought, could be because Christine Sherwood was still missing. He had almost given up with sending out search parties, but Angel still cherished the faint hope that Christine lived, and so the search went on day in and day out. Lady Sherwood had not returned to England, for his man had only come back from there last week to divulge that information to him.

The lavaliere and the mysterious "James" Angel had spoken of while in her delirium kept him curious and wondering. If

496

there was such a man and he happened to show, it wouldn't be long before a new hole would have to be dug in the parish. The locket was ever with him, though he never gazed upon it. One thing did mellow his gloomy ponderings, though, and that was the startling moment several days back when for the first time he'd really studied Brian Ross. With tawny hair and limbs of considerable length, he was certainly beginning to show signs of becoming a chip off the old block! And the eyes—Hunter's Jade—Big Jim's grandfather had called them. Every other generation had the same.

The sun hung suspended like a white-hot ball over the river, creating a blanket of twinkling diamonds to wink up blindingly at Angel and Tyrone as side by side they rode the crest. They made a handsome picture indeed, with her daintily seated upon Beauty, Tyrone tall and proud on the Beast. Soon they were galloping across the river road under clear skies, heading north toward the cultivated fields where the blacks were already planting in the rick black earth. The couple reined up before the exact, orderly rows where the blacks labored, with Sam overseeing the work to be done. Tyrone noticed his wife's interest and helped her down after sliding from his own mount.

"How is it done, Tyrone? I mean, could you tell me how it becomes sugar," Angel waved a hand across the fields.

"I thought you'd never ask," Tyrone teased. Then, "Through the smiling summer months the cane will grow tall, and when it is ready they will fall the stalks and haul them out back in wagons to the sugar house, where the kettles will have been put to boil beforehand—" he pointed to the tall chimney of the sugar house beyond. "The blacks will crush the cane under rollers, then boil the extracted juice until it begins to thicken. Before the thickened syrup crystalizes completely it is sent to the cooling room; purged, diluted with lemon juices and vinegar. The hogsheads are then suspended to allow the molasses to drip out into vats. We then have a small fortune in brown sugar. That is, if the granulation process goes well."

Angel faced him, asking, "Could I come out and watch the procedure, maybe even stir a kettle or two?"

Tyrone watched the clear green eyes slant in anticipation and smiled as he remembered himself asking his father that very thing as a child. "Yes, you can come with me to the sugar house. But I promise you one thing, you will sweat like a monkey in no time. That is, if the smell doesn't assail your senses first." He chuckled deeply.

Angel's laughter pealed across the warm earth like a silvery bell. Her husband gave her a hand up and she was off before he could mount, racing off toward the tangled woodland in gay abandonment. Wanting the wind to race through her hair, she tore the pins from the sleek knot and, giving her head a shake, tumbling it about her shoulders wild and glorious. Seeing this, Tyrone mounted the Beast speedily.

"Hallo!" cried Tyrone and the chase was on.

"Halloo!" whipped back as Angel urged the mare to greater speed.

The smiling blacks paused in their labors to watch the young sugar king in hot pursuit of the beautiful mistress. And Sam, after waving to the lighthearted couple thundering across the untilled section, bossed the blacks into bending back to their task. Sam smiled to himself, glad for the sweet mistress, glad for the first time in his life that the world was finally a good place to be.

Their senses were stimulated by the scents of pine needles, damp moss, musty wood, but mostly the presence of each other was wildly exciting. All atremble in anticipation of making love as they had in the outdoors on the island, slowly they melted to the dry ground beneath a huge live oak that spread its natural canopy over them. Kissing, they parted, breathless, taking it slow this time, wanting to etch in memory how lovely it was just being together, lying fully clothed, hugging, kissing, petting.

"Hold me, hold me tighter, Tyrone!" Angel whispered in his ear.

Tyrone chuckled back. "Why whisper, sweet, we are the only ones here. The horses won't mind if you speak a little louder. Be free!" he said, then doing as she had asked, gave her a long bearhug.

Soon his silky tongue was slipping into her mouth, then out and lower, lower, while a warmth began where his weight pressed between her legs. His tongue left off drawing circles on an ivory mound of flesh, and this time he whispered something in her ear—a question.

"What!" Angel exclaimed, but her heartbeat quickened.

"Ah, sweet love!" Tyrone hugged her tighter. "You are a delightful naivette. Yes, it feels good and it doesn't hurt. Most women find it wonderful, ecstatic," he informed, stroking her velvet-clad belly with one hand while tugging up her skirt with the other. He muttered, "I want to taste every part of you."

"No!"

Suddenly she had bolted upright, slapping down her skirt and smoothing the folds with shaking hands. Tyrone's passion shriveled as he leaned his weight on a bent arm, peering at the full profile above him.

"Why, Angel," he murmured, half questioning, half hurt.

"Why not? I will tell you why not! Women. Always other women!" she began, preparing to launch a tirade of resentment on his past lovers. She opened her mouth and suddenly he had her by the arm.

"Come here, sweetheart. I'm sorry, I truly am. Never again will I bring up those women that didn't mean a thing to me. Forgive me?"

"Well . . . all right," she capitulated, snuggling back into the circle of his arms. "Mmmm, this is nice, Tyrone. Is it all right if we just lie here like this? It is so peaceful and I don't want anything to spoil it."

"Of course!" he said, liking the idea himself. "More important things can come later when we are at home. That is, if you don't object?"

"I am willing to try anything once, sir," she said shyly, looking forward to what would come later that night.

His eyes closed and he dozed with her against his chest. He was weary, for he had stayed up most of the night before, finishing up the drawings he would soon take to Boston, accompanied by his father.

Angel pondered the veiny, leafed bower above. For two months now she had shared a bedroom with him, and several times she had almost poured out her heart's love to him. They certainly gave all when lying entwined in each other's arms, but what she'd desperately hoped to hear had not escaped his lips yet. It was all too good to be true, this happiness, so she would rein her heart until that day when she learned she would forever be the only woman in his life. Was it too much to hope for? Oh, God, she prayed, let me always be the one first in his heart. Let me be woman enough for him.

Tenderly she reached up to touch his cheek, trying not to wake him as she ran a finger along the thin scar on his forehead. His eyes opened suddenly and she smiled into them caressingly.

"How did you come by the scar, Tyrone?" she asked softly, wanting to know the story behind it and if his mother had truly given it to him.

At her question his eyes narrowed, and his whole body stiffened. "Don't ever ask me that again! It's none of your business," he snarled as he brushed by her roughly to rise to his feet.

Angel was hurt and all the way back to the house a sour silence reigned. As she rode beside the cold stranger she wondered: Was her husband truly a misogynist, a hater of all women, even her? He had to feel something for her when he made passionate love to her at night. But could he distinguish between lust and love with all that hate in him? He had been deeply wounded by his mother . . . but why? Would she ever learn the mystery that surrounded Cresthaven?

From that day in the woods until Tyrone was to leave for Boston, everything changed and the new relationship that had developed consisted of stony silence. Their love-making had come to an abrupt halt, for no longer did he wake her in the middle of the night, but crawled into bed in the wee small hours with liquor on his breath. She kept to her side of the bed, away from that lean body she craved and loved, and cried silently into her pillow until sleep claimed her once again.

On the morning that he was readying to leave, Angel entered the hall where Tyrone was just setting down his briefcase and valise next to the door. His mood was dour when he turned to see her there, his look saying he hadn't expected her to see him off. He made no move toward her and an overpowering anger seized hold of her, making the deep hurt of the past week lessen.

"Perhaps if you stay away long enough this time, you might even forget what your wife and son look like, since doubtless you shall not miss us much and should be able to entertain yourself easily enough!" Angel hissed on impulse more than anything else.

"Angel!" Tyrone's voice was bewildered and half angry, "that was entirely uncalled for, and you know it. In fact, it was downright shrewish. You know I must make this trip and have had a lot on my mind lately."

"You forget awfully easy, my dear husband. This shrew, as you call me, accepted your apology in the woods if you remember correctly, but you, sir, gave me no chance to beg forgiveness of my discourtesy to your sensitivity."

"Angel, I—" Tyrone began, but just then Big Jim came along the hall, toting his own bags.

Angel was mindful that Tyrone stepped forward to brush a gentle kiss on her forehead, but she felt cold as ice, inside and out. He stepped back and turned, going to tuck a bag under each arm.

"We shouldn't be gone more than two weeks," he said between stiff lips, his back ramrod straight.

"At the most," Big Jim piped up. "Take care of my grandson, Angeline. Tell him I love him every day, will you, my dear?"

Angel slanted a smug look over to her husband, saying sweetly, "Of course, father. Brian Ross will always know just how much we *all* love him around here!"

With that, Tyrone watched her snatch up her skirts and heard the silk of her dressing gown rustle as she turned majestically to mount the stairs. He breathed out as if it was his last breath, then dragged his feet heavily out to the waiting horses. Turning one last time to glance up at the house, he felt a strange sense of foreboding steal over him. He studied the ground thoughtfully a moment, shrugged mentally, then mounted the Beast.

The sun came up, went down, and the days and nights were long; most were dreary ones for Angel. She had long talks with Hannah, but the lingering echoes of her last conversation in the woods with Tyrone came back to haunt her, alternating with images of lovers entwined in their private little worlds of passion; so for the most part Hannah did the talking. But every time Angel heard the front door open and close she would dash to the top of the stairs if she happened to be upstairs, or if downstairs, rush out of the parlor in hopes Tyrone might have arrived earlier than calculated.

It was the twelfth day since Tyrone's departure and the house was silent as a tomb. Hannah had left for home early; and Nikki had accompanied Della and Melvin to the city to pick up some needed staples and dry goods for the household. Just that morning Caspar had ridden out on the tall chestnut horse, his destination unknown to her. She dismissed Sarah and Daisy Mae early so that they could go out back to the cottages. A baby shower was being held for Jenny, and they didn't want to miss it.

Jenny had fled Gayarre after Wesley found she had married up with one of Cresthaven's blacks. He had beaten her till her bare back bled, but the evil man hadn't bothered searching for her; anyway, he saw no need to have another mouth around to feed, and April had a new tutor, a bony, wheezy man by the name of Brookwood, Hannah had mentioned offhandedly.

Afternoon gave way to ashen nightfall, the silence in the halls of Cresthaven unbroken. After having taken her dinner in silence, given Brian his evening nourishment and tucked him into his crib for the night, Angel found herself again standing below the portrait of Annette Hunter. Moving back and forth as she pondered its loveliness, Angel saw it from right and left angles, the soft eyes ever following her. Suddenly Angel started. Did she hear the front door open and close? Yes, yes, someone was stirring in the hall. Tyrone! It must be!

"Tyrone!" Angel cried ecstatically, entering the hall.

She had missed the blurred shadow dashing away and she halted suddenly, her skirts held high above her slippers. She froze, only her head twisting and turning. Taking a few steps forward she peered along the hall, calling into the shadows, "Who is it? Is—is someone there?" She slanted her head for some moments in bewilderment. Then, "I could have sworn I heard—" she stopped, noting a folded piece of paper beneath the lowboy a few feet from the door. It must have blown there after someone. . . .

502

Angel rushed to snatch the paper up, feeling eerie fingers of apprehension ruffle her spine. She unfolded it and as she read her hand flew up to cover her thumping heart. Reading further, her fear fled and an excitement such as she'd never known before flooded her being.

"Christine, Christine! Mama, they have found you!" She whirled to dash madly up the stairs, the paper fluttering to the floor behind her. Then, as a thought came to her halfway up the stairs she spun around, and went to fetch Ranae.

Angel ushered the downstairs maid into her bedchamber, telling the woman to keep an eye on Brian while she was gone. She ripped through her wardrobe until she found what she sought. While she was donning the velvet riding outfit, Ranae stepped back into the chamber after quietly checking on Brian.

"Where you going, mistress?" the downstairs maid questioned, her dark eyes wide as saucers. "It'll be dangerous for you to be out riding in the dark, unchaperoned. Anyway, Della told me the Mister left strict orders for you not to go prancing about on horse—" Ranae smothered a hiccough.

While Angel argued with the maid, downstairs in the parlor Cordell tore up the note and put it to burn in the fireplace. As he watched the edges turn black and curl up into nothing, he thought of what must be done, and his loins warmed with desire as he thought of the woman who had brought him to this dangerous course of action. Hearing steps coming down the stairs, he moved from the hearth, pressing back into the gray shadows. When the front door opened and closed, Cordell left his hiding place and stealthily crept up the stairs. He wanted to make sure Ranae had passed out.

Cordell knew the mistress had stationed Ranae in her bedchamber, but what the little lady didn't know was that Ranae had been sipping hot toddies with him in the kitchen for several hours. As usual, it wouldn't be long before Ranae snored gustily in the chair, her stupidly smiling lips flapping with each noisily expressed breath.

Out in the stable Old Saul, too, had earlier been plumped up with toddies, pressed on him easily by the young servant, with much conversation of the "good old days" and an attentive ear. Cordell had been careful with watering his own cups down real good. Now Old Saul slept like the dead when the tall doors creaked open and the slight woman entered to go quickly about her business.

Angel raced Beauty as fast as the mare's legs could carry her. Her Majesty had appeared spooked, wild-eyes glowing, so she gave up any thought she'd had of taking her.

The night was chilled, though late spring, the shadows along either side of the road seeming to reach out and oppressive with the feeling that at any moment someone or something would leap from the bushes and snatch at her skirts. Swirls of river fog creeping across the road intermittently blinded her, but she drove on, her destination the southernmost border where the tall hedges grew.

Suddenly two cloaked figures loomed up ominously in the road, concealed in hooded shrouds of black, their mounts one on either side of her. Beauty reared up, pawing the air, her nostrils blowing as she spooked. Angel patted the mare down gently, until she pranced before the intruders, backing up and gentling under the soothing hands. Angel began questioning at once.

"You said you worked for my husband. Why did you send the note and not come to the house in person?"

The smaller of the two only grunted in reply.

"Can you not speak? And what is all the mystery? Where is Christine . . . my mother? You said you could bring me to her." Angel fired questions at the two, who seemed reluctant to speak.

"Ahhhh!" was heard from the smaller one.

"Shut up!" the other snapped in a deeper voice, muffled by his hood.

"So—" Angel began, "you have brought me here on false pretense. Who are you people and what do you want?" she demanded, then shouted, "Let me pass!" She kneed Beauty in trying to escape.

The larger of the two spoke low, saying, "Come with us. Do as we say and you will not be hurt. We will take you to your mother."

"I do not believe you!" Angel almost screamed. It touched her mind that these two meant to do her harm.

The more Angel protested the meaner the smaller one became, laying a vicious quirt to her thighs, making her wince, but she would not cry out to let them know how frightened she was. They had maneuvered her about and pressed her toward the river, one on either side of her.

Even though her two abductors spoke low and indistinctly, Angel thought their voices were somewhat familiar. Try as she might to be brave in this, she felt her heart pound painfully and her limbs weaken as they ruthlessly led her on like a prisoner, through the tangled wood and on down a washed-out ravine to the small cabin she remembered having seen before. Though it was darker than dark here, she knew it to be the very same place where she had seen Tyrone astride the black almost a year ago.

Now she could hear the mighty river flowing, knowing it was not more than eighty feet below from where the two men halted before her. They dismounted before the gloomy bulk of the cabin, quickly demanding her to do the same. The smaller man shoved her jerkily through the door, and once inside pushed her down unceremoniously onto a hard chair. Without further ado, he then went to spread his thin fingers before the warming heat of the crudely built, ancient hearth. The larger man lighted an oil lamp but turned it low, standing all the while with his back to the room.

Angel gave herself a moment to look at the interior. It appeared to be an old planter's cottage and was surprisingly tidy and clean. A hastily prepared meal of barest necessities was left uneaten, as if the occupant had retreated like a rat to some dark corner upon their arrival. A quick glimpse to her right revealed a curtained alcove, possibly a bedroom, and she gathered that there the person or persons had fled to hide. Whoever lived here hadn't done so for very long, for there were patterned webs in the corners here and there.

Would they soon kill her? she wondered shudderingly. Toss her body in the river afterwards? Or worse yet, rape her, leaving her here to die quietly under the torment of filthy vermin. Tyrone would never know what had become of her. Though the thought of someone's coming in time to rescue her was almost an impossibility, she prayed desperately for just that to happen.

Angel shut her eyes tightly against the black-clad figures who seemed to be contemplating their next move as they spoke in hushed tones, for the moment avoiding her. Because one of them, or both, might very well have a concealed weapon, any thought she'd had on making a sudden move to escape through the door quickly left her.

"Tyrone, please help me," Angel implored silently, "find me and take me home! Please come to me before it is too late!" It was just no good, for he was far away and she would never gaze upon his handsome face again, and now he would never know how much she truly loved him. She had found her heart's place in Cresthaven, and had too late discovered that it was where she wanted to live and love for the rest of her natural life.

Suddenly she found this gave her a new determination. She would find means of escape . . . even if she died trying. At least she would go knowing she had fought with every breath to the end.

Angel had just begun making plans for escape when the cowl was wrenched away from her smaller tormentor's head. The golden face was smugly contorted and Angel knew it well. "How . . . Jacinta. You! Are you mad?" Her eyes slid to the other, wondering, horrified, as Wesley Gayarre pushed back his own hood. "You are both insane!" Angel hissed, then, "What in God's name is going on? Why have you brought me to this place?" She waved a hand around the room.

Wesley's colorless eyes glistened with something curiously akin to hot revenge. Jacinta detached herself from his side, and coming to stand before Angel, appeared to derive a sadistic pleasure in what she was about to disclose.

"You really don't know, do you," Jacinta hissed in a feline voice, adding, "You poor little thing, misused orphan. Bitch! How I hate you! You and your icy-green fox eyes and your ivory skin. Silly slut. You still haven't realized Tyrone does not love you . . . never will! He hates all women, but *I*, only *I* have a special hold on him. A young man never forgets the first woman he made love to, especially if she taught him everything there is to know about complete fulfillment. We are two of a kind, Tyrone and me."

506

Unable to further withstand the hurt Jacinta was inflicting upon her, Angel said with acid tongue, "The fulfillment you speak of, Jacinta, is nothing but pure lust—and I mean animal lust! You know nothing of true love, that all-consuming emotion that goes on forever and turns two people into one. For the past several months, my husband and I have shared a beautiful and magical experience—together. I just know he loves me, if only half as much as I do him, it is enough. I only wish to God now that I had told him before this night made me realize how foolish I've been to hold back what is in my heart."

Jacinta grunted. "There, you see! He has not told you he loves you, and he never will, fool. He only intended using your body until a new plaything comes along. Pah! He only married you because he thought that mewling brat was his, so he could have an heir. Don't look so surprised, you know yourself Tyrone thinks different now. Yes, you see, you spoke of a James while you were delirious in your sickness. Cordell heard you mention the name time and again and reported to me everything else that happened after. He is not loyal to you . . . only me. Stupid fool Cordell! He thinks I want him, am ready to go away with him. Pah! He is a pup compared to my Ty. Now, what Cordell doesn't realize is that when Tyrone arrives home this night and discovers him sneaking off with your jewels, Cordell will be accused of siring the brat."

"Tyrone . . . coming home tonight?" Angel repeated breathlessly, almost to herself. Then, "What do you mean about Cordell? What in the world are you planning to do?" she all but sobbed in confusion.

Jacinta smirked, leveling her dark eyes to the shining green ones. The older woman seemed to purr as she said, "I will not give you the satisfaction of knowing what will happen next, bitch. All you need to know is that Tyrone will believe you an adultress, a whore! Someday soon there will be only Tyrone and Jacinta. James Hunter will leave everything to an already wealthy son when he dies. James has given his own wife nothing, not even the town house is in my name. Not one picayune does he intend leaving me in his will. So, it is up to me to see that I get what is rightfully mine. And you, your brat, *nothing* will stand in my way to get it!"

"Madness!" Angel shouted, went on incredulously, "You cannot mean what you are saying, Jacinta. You will destroy all with your greed. Even if you plan to murder me, Tyrone will never have you—ugh!—how could anyone! James Hunter must have been mad to take you for his wife. You are evil, to say the least," she ended softly.

"Don't fool yourself, chit," Jacinta said, her hatred for the lovely young woman flaring up again. "You know Tyrone will need me when you are gone. He has always thought of me as his only *maman*. I suppose you have learned how much he hated his true mother?" The barb struck vulnerable ground, causing Angel much mental pain.

Grinding his teeth together, almost salivating, Wesley stepped between the two women, facing the older one. "That will be enough now, Jacinta! We have not come here to discuss love and these silly matters of money. Angeline wants to know why she is here and I, for one, am eager to have this thing over and done with. Go, Jacinta, and tell the other—ah—to come out here now." He rubbed his hands together, whining in a smaller voice, "Hurry now. We don't have that much time left to do what we must."

The man is entirely mad, Angel thought agonizingly, as she watched Jacinta take her own sweet time going to the curtained room. As Jacinta's mind evilly relished the scene that was about to take place, Angel's heart pounded up into her throat as she wondered what horrible apparition lay waiting behind the material divider to devour her.

2

The wind soughed mournfully through the hillside trees and about the cabin as the soiled curtain was finally drawn to one side. Angel all but swooned where she stood, gaping incredulously at the old crone, trembling too, as if she had surely caught the ague. The woman standing there garbed in nothing but a filthy, stained rag looked so different, so much older and horribly emaciated.

Angel barely trusted her voice, muttering, "Mama! Chris-

508

tine . . . is it truly you?" Angel choked in outrage. "They have starved you!"

Her eyes terribly frightened, Christine nodded once, weakly. Instantaneously Angel's flying limbs carried her across the splintered boards, and with an inarticulate sound escaping her, her outstretched arms enfolded the frail woman close. Weeping soundlessly, both mother and daughter caressed each other's sweet face, searching with tear-filled eyes to be convinced this moment was real. Angel gently etched a finger along the wizened cheeks and mouth, smiled then, reassuringly, realizing she had more to live for now than ever.

Somehow, Angel vowed, she would get them out of this danger alive, and safely back home to where love awaited them both. Home. Yes, *home!*

Weakened by the reunion, Christine gestured for her daughter to help her to a chair. Christine held both her daughter's strengthened hands to her cheek, clutching them as if fearing Angel would vanish if she didn't. Then the older eyes narrowed as she peered contemptuously across the room to her hated tormentors. They had delivered her here months ago to follow up with this evil plan worked out between them. From behind the curtain, Christine had heard her beloved daughter's voice, but had been ordered beforehand not to move until summoned . . . or else!

"How sweet!" Jacinta spat, then whirled back to Wesley, demanding, "Let's do get this over with. I can't wait to see Tyrone's face when I inform him that his sluttish wife and her mama are dead. Hurry Wesley, he might be out with a search party at this very moment!"

Rooted to the spot with a deranged gleam in his colorless eyes, Wesley appeared to have progressed into devastating madness in the short time that had flown by. The laugh that rang out now was indeed not of sound mind, ending in a horrible cackle, his face bearing resemblance to a grotesque mask.

"Mine, mine," Wesley cackled. "I will have my land back now. More! No one will ever know how Cresthaven burned to the ground in the night while everyone but my sweet Angeline slept inside." He peered around the room slyly, adding, "We

509

must make certain James Hunter is there, too."

A wild shriek rent the cabin's musty air as Angel detached herself from Christine's terrified grip. She faced her tormentors squarely. "You will never get away with it . . . I shan't allow you to do this!" Changing her tactics, she stared hard at the man she'd almost wed, trying, "Wesley, you need help immediately for this sickness of yours. Think, Wesley! Think about what you are doing. Blast it! A number of lives are at stake. Please, try to think through the haziness of your mind!"

Jacinta swiftly drew forth a slim dagger from beneath her skirts, pointing it directly at the younger woman's heart. Angel blanched, backing off. Jacinta sneered at her hated rival with a wicked shine in her dark eyes, her golden face distorted. Wesley only smiled at Angel sweetly, like a little boy who cherished something.

"Wesley," Jacinta commanded, "tie them up with the ropes and then I will gag them so they can't scream. Cresthaven will not burn, but *this place will*—with Angel and that scrawny nag in it."

Going to the smaller room, Jacinta returned with an old sheet. It shredded easily enough as she ripped it into strips for gags. Wesley considered her actions for a moment, then the words seeped into his addled brain. He lunged across the room and caught Jacinta by her wrists, surprising her and making her cry out in pain.

"That is not what we planned, you conniving bitch!" he grated. "I have reunited Angeline with her mother for a reason. I think . . . *yes*, I *promised* her I would do this. They will stay here for now. I will have Angeline forever, and my lands back. As we planned earlier . . . remember?" He blinked at his partner in crime.

Becoming impatient with him, Jacinta blurted, "For what! So you can do away with them as you did Muriel and Annette?"

Wesley looked frightened, then wild, dropping to his knees on the boards as Angel choked back a scream. She prayed in a low voice, "Please God, this cannot be happening. It is all some bad dream, please let it be so. Tyrone—" she whimpered, "please help us."

But Wesley confirmed the worst himself and with self-accusation cried, "Muriel! Annette, my lovely! Forgive me!" He crawled on his knees, snatching for the velvet, saying beseechingly, "Angeline. I will be forever good to you. I will not hurt you," he whined and pleaded.

Angel inched back horrified, then all at once seeing her opening, lunged at Jacinta with clawed fingers. Though Jacinta was the larger and stronger of the two women, the Creole was amazed at the well of strength Angel opened up. She squeezed the weaponed hand, digging sharp nails into Jacinta's wrist, forcing the dagger to fall clattering to the boards, then kicked the weapon neatly out of sight. Continuing to wrestle, Jacinta easily overpowered the younger woman and flung her into a crumpled heap on the floor. While the old woman knelt beside her daughter, Jacinta at once whirled about in frantic search of the weapon.

Surfacing from his daze, Wesley crept up stealthily behind Jacinta, and swinging her about, clubbed her smack in the face with a closed fist. An ugly welt grew and purpled the handsome woman's face at once. Jacinta reeled from the blow as she clutched for the wall, her eyes daring to dart low in search of the weapon.

Angel's mind ticked fast in indecision while Wesley snatched up the ropes intended to bind them. While the house slept he was going to murder those Angel had come to know and love so very much. Tyrone might escape uninjured while the house blazed. But, her baby! Oh, dear God—Brian! She saw him in her mind's eye burning to death in his pretty blue crib.

Angel peered at her mother then. She was suddenly torn between fleeing by herself to warn those at Cresthaven and staying to face whatever happened with her newly-found mother. For it was plain to see that Christine was in no condition to try a hasty escape; only a careful pace could she manage in her weakened state.

All this time Christine was awakening to what was going on around her, and even though her dear husband was gone she realized her will to live on was great. While they had embraced, Angel had mentioned that she had a beautiful son and that she loved the smuggler-man who had abducted her. He was good to her and the babe, Angel said. Christine wondered now if she would ever gaze upon this grandson of hers, and her heart was with Angel, standing defeated for the moment beside her. Christine was prepared to relinquish the sorrow she'd dwelled in for so long and bask in the sunshine of the future. If there was to be one.

A terror-filled scream ripped through the cabin and spilled out into the night just before a slim and well-aimed blade caught the firelight as it lifted then sliced down into flesh, piercing, lifting again, stabbing, hacking, blood flying, over and over.

A pale new moon westered as Tyrone raced the Beast frantically, scoured the wood and crossed and recrossed the boundaries until his mount was lathered and driven mercilessly. Driving in blind desperation he had passed on by the very cabin in the black murk that hid his mate, only hearing the river murmur his anguish and despair back to him. With the Beast's tail into the wind, Tyrone pressed forward to meet the visible form of horse and man just emerging from a stand of live oaks. Big Jim's worried frown matched Tyrone's own under the pale light rising. Tyrone muttered a few foul invectives upon learning his father had found nothing out.

"Tyrone, you are running blind and you will kill the Beast if you don't stop back home for a fresh mount," Big Jim said. "Let's try the house again and see if Angeline has returned there. She is not at Gayarre. I've just returned from there, and Hannah will be here anytime now."

Tyrone had been silent, deathly so, but now, not meaning to, questioned his father harshly. "Has Wesley Gayarre returned yet? How about Caspar, has he returned to Cresthaven?"

A negative reply to both fired questions was heard before Tyrone surged his mount forward, the huge head with its direction-wise eyes steady on the path to home. Pounding hooves churned the turf, following while Tyrone drove on ahead like a crazed man. Tyrone was totaling up the hours since his return and finding his wife gone. Three hours! Earlier, a drowsily recovering Ranae had told him only what she knew, that the mistress had ridden out when the sky was moonless and there had been no stopping the determined lady.

512

After that, Ranae said sheepishly, she had fallen asleep in the chair.

The Beast shivered to a halt with slick sides heaving, flared nostrils puffing out streams of warm moisture, flecks of white foaming from the mouth. Tyrone lifted up from the saddle to scan the grounds, his gaze settling upon the glowing squares of the mansion up ahead. Big Jim ate up the distance the anguished man had put between them, and before his mount could rock to a halt, Tyrone was off again, driving the poor horse as fast as the trembling legs could carry his master.

At the house, he leaped down, clearing the stone platform and threshold in several powerful strides. He slid into the hall, trying to decide which direction to take first. No sound was to be heard but the tick, tock, tick of the clock.

"Angel!" he bellowed, and again. He turned to mount the stairs.

Alert to the slightest movement, Tyrone felt more than saw the people merging together from the salon, coming to stand deathly pale and quiet in the portal. All but one evidenced frightened concern for the mistress. Joseph, Hannah, and . . . Jacinta. They watched as the master of Cresthaven settled his gaze upward. He realized with utter dread that she was not up there in her room with Brian.

In the funereal silence Tyrone took in the ugly purpled cheek marring the otherwise handsome face of his stepmother. She flashed to his side, picking up his hand, and he brushed her fingers aside roughly, then grasped her painfully by the shoulders. He stared hard and ruthless, reading her look.

"You know something," he began fiercely, "you know where she is . . . tell me!"

"Tyrone—my Ty," she whined piteously, "look what Wesley has done to me. Don't you care?"

He shook her roughly then, causing the auburn head to snap back and forth like a whip. He leaned over her, slowly gritting out, "Answer me, woman, or it will be the very first time in my life that I break a woman's neck!"

A minute crawled by slowly as Jacinta reasoned with her hurt, thinking there might still be a chance for her in the future here. Once the shock of losing Angel wore off, things

513

would get back to normal around here. Yes, before Tyrone went off to join the smugglers they had known lusty good times together. She knew all there was to know about her stepson, for she had paid her informers well. Even though her husband lavished not one picayune on her already depleted coffers, there were other ways an experienced woman could reward her men—men like Cordell, for instance. For now she just kept hoping the fire she'd set back at the cabin was blazing well. With Angel and her mama tied up and Wesley dying from severe lacerations, there would be no one alive to tell the tale.

Tyrone was shaking her urgently once again. Time. She had to stretch it out. She set forth to play her part well, affectedly weeping, wailing, and finally emerging from her pain enough to speak.

"I—I was just coming to Cresthaven to beg some money from Big Jim, when I noticed Wesley in the road with Angel. Something was wrong, I could tell, because he snatched up her reins and was pulling her along with him, I—I followed them to the old planter's cottage near the river, remember, *mon cher*, the place where—"

"Cottage!" Tyrone shouted. "Damn me for not checking it out! Go on, go on," he snarled hurriedly.

"I was so afraid that Wesley would harm your wife because he seemed terribly angry with her by the sound of his voice." Here Jacinta flinched at Tyrone's contorted sneer, but went on in spite of it. "When they entered the cabin, or cottage, I went around to peek in the window through the blinds. That is when I saw Angel with an older woman. They—they were hugging each other—"

"Christine," Tyrone breathed deeply. It couldn't have been anyone else. He wanted to believe Jacinta now, as she seemed to be telling the truth. Hope sprang up in him as he pressed, "Well, what else?"

"Wesley began tying them, I think. Yes. That is when I noticed a blade lying on the floor beside him, with—umm—Angel eyeing it. Then and there I decided to go in to help your wife and mother."

"Wait! How do you know it was Angel's mother?" He was noticing the blood spattered on her bodice now.

"Don't you remember, *mon cher?* It was I who cared for the lady at the town house until Wesley got hold of her. At least, I would think after she disappeared it was he who imprisoned her at the cottage," she lied expertly, having had the woman hidden herself up until several months before. Jacinta went on, "Angel must have stabbed Wesley with his own dagger, because when I finally got enough strength to heave the furniture he had piled against the inside of the door, he was bleeding all over the place while he continued to tie them up. He had the bloodied dagger then. When he finally noticed me, he socked me and I passed out. I—I suppose that is how I got Wesley's blood on my clothes. The place was burning when I came to. I—I don't know how, there must have been a struggle. I could not see Angel and her mother for all the smoke. That is when I came here for help."

"Fire!" Tyrone shouted, shaking the haze from his brain. "Devil take you! Why didn't you tell me immediately!" He sped toward the door, without further ado.

"Wait! There is more, Ty. I haven't told you what a traitor your wife is—" She hid an evil leer. "Was."

Tyrone hadn't heard her. Unsprung, he had shot like lightening by Big Jim who lounged against the doorjamb and had taken the entire conversation in. If looks could kill, Jacinta Hunter née Villerne would have been a dead woman by now.

"Bitch. You'll soon get your comeuppance," Big Jim snarled in a lethal tone of voice before he followed in Tyrone's wake.

Old Saul plodded around from the back of the house leading Her Majesty and two more fresh mounts. When Tyrone saw that he would have to take the white mare—swifter than the two chestnut mares—he muttered an oath, but snatched the reins up anyway. Big Jim drew Tyrone's attention before he had fully mounted up.

"Look!" he shouted while pointing to a dark apparition.

Just then a huge and wildly beautiful mare thundered into the light pouring from the house. The moonlight struck sharp hooves, wickedly slashing the air as she reared up. All gaped in awe as she came down, ducking her magnificent head to charge, then shook it out while lurching forward at a neat gallop. The flowing blur of blue-black mane whipped back as

515

she sped by her audience and down the lane.

Tyrone's eyes lit in enlightenment while the mare came to a skidding halt near the pond, then turning about, pranced back in a showoff manner to come stand unbreathlessly and paw the turf directly in front of the master of Cresthaven.

Puffing and cursing, Caspar emerged from the shadows at the side of the house. He said apologetically, "I wanted her to rest, cap'n, even though she's in the pink of condition. I wanted to wait and surprise you and the lady in the morning. I only returned an hour ago with her and look at—" Suddenly Caspar had noticed the crestfallen faces of the Hunters, and now he queried, "Sure now, something is amiss. What is it, cap'n?"

But Tyrone wasn't listening. Angel's Echo. She has finally arrived, to be reunited with. . . .

Tyrone's eyes were damp with unshed tears as Echo tossed back her midnight head, looking curiously fresh after her long journey from England's shores. There wasn't another precious moment to lose, so he reached out to stroke the velvety nose, letting her get to know his feel, murmuring soothing words, and she neighed softly in return, as if she knew she belonged here with this man. Nudging him, Echo's dark eyes were mysteriously aglow, and Tyrone knew she was ready to fly. She still wore her bridle but was without saddle. Tyrone left the white mare to Caspar and swiftly mounted Echo bareback, racing off down the lane with her as one.

"Go—Go—*Go!*" Tyrone urged, for precious time was wasting.

He had left everyone staring after his haste to be away until they, too, mounted to follow. Caspar joined the search, handling Her Majesty with little or no trouble once he was under way. They had left the extra mare for Nikki should he arrive yet this night. Old Saul waited with the mare, finally wilting against the side of the house, dozing with one eye out for the master's cousin.

Jesus! She flies like the wind, Tyrone thought, getting used to the powerful tendons that stretched beneath him. With singleminded purpose, man and beast rumbled as one across the fields and then between black veiny branches that twisted and twined and threatened to arrest their flight. The man's eyes burned wetly, but the moisture was not due to the wind. His companions were left in the dust, but reined up suddenly with a start after the raging howl that shivered back to them. They then proceeded with caution, wondering all the while what dark monster prowled the dark wood in front of them.

A section of rotting timbers ignited, sending sparks of red, magenta, and ochre into the chilly night sky as orange-black billows of acrid smoke boiled forth from the cabin as if pursued by ghouls. The glass items in the larger of the two rooms shattered now in loud crashes, stirring Angel. She choked awake, feeling the throbbing where Jacinta had laid the butt of her vicious quirt upon her head . . . only minutes before? Her nostrils burned and her lungs felt nigh unto bursting; her eyes streamed tears, blinded by the heavy shroud of black smoke that was drawing her life to a close—and Christine's. The heat beneath her body told of boards beginning to smoulder. She tried moving, to roll over onto her belly, but fell back to the boards in a choking heap. She spun down, down. . . .

Tyrone. Captain Ty. Angel could see him now. He sported his tan breeches, blousey tunic, and tall black pirate boots. A glossy dark beard covered his chin, and a mysterious gem twinkled in his ear. He smirked sardonically into her face, showing those straight white teeth. His cutlass gleamed wickedly in the sunlight as it slashed into the air. He claimed his prize. A green isle in the sea, love . . . New Orleans; Gayarre; Cresthaven. Behind the portrait, behind the portrait. . . .

Suddenly the door burst wide as if kicked open from the outside, creating a raging inferno that sucked the worst part of the blaze upward. Angel had been delirious, overcome by smoke and flames, but now a cleansing river breeze brought her to her senses. At once she slithered across the floor like a serpent, going to her mother's lifeless form. She breathed! Thank God, Christine was alive!

Angel chewed, chomped, and spit at the tight rag until her mouth and chin chafed. She tossed back her head in sobbing agony, then rejoiced when the thing slipped down to her chin.

517

"Mama! Wake up!" Angel hollered and pleaded as she bumped against the thin frame. She squirmed closer, and with her teeth, pulled the smothering cloth down. "Hurry, Christine! We have to get the—get out of here. Crawl behind me. Try, yes, that's it, try as hard as you can!" she shouted to keep Christine alert and moving.

A bloodcurdling scream ripped through the smoke and Angel soon realized it was her own. Almost reaching a bucket of water, she had come upon Wesley lying in steaming pools of his own blood. Had Jacinta stabbed him after he had finished tying Christine and herself up? Jacinta must have done it after she herself had passed out from the blow. Wesley now stared at her sightlessly for a moment. Angel reached out to him and it was as if a spark of recognition flared up begging her forgiveness, then slowly his eyes widened as blood gurgled from his mouth. His horribly ragged breathing ceased. Wesley Gayarre was dead.

A fired timber floated crazily to the floor just behind Christine and she screamed, waking her daughter from a dazed state. Angel slithered back to the burning piece of wood. One end of it glowed orange-red and she plied her binds to it, almost burning her hands in the process before she was freed. Working next with frenzied movements, she got the ropes away from her ankles. She stumbled once and fell before finally reaching Christine to free her also.

After wetting their skirts down well with a bucket of water heated from the fire, they fell against each other and made it outside just in time. Taking in great gulps of refreshing air they stood safely away from the fire, seeing the walls collapse suddenly like so much paper. While Christine wept after their timely escape, Angel looked to the red and black heap of what had once been a ramshackle building and was now Wesley Gayarre's charred grave.

Angel shook her head with a definite sadness for the dead man, but after this night the memory of him would be forever wiped clean from her mind. He had meant to take her loved ones from her in a most horrible and sinful way. Though he had gone mad at the end, it had been the foremost plan in his mind well before this night.

And Jacinta. What evil web of deception would the woman be spinning back at Cresthaven? She no doubt had made up a good story to relate to Tyrone as to why the mistress had gone gallivanting into the night. Would Tyrone believe his beloved stepmother, or herself? And Cordell. What did he have to do with all this? What might make Tyrone believe Cordell to be Brian Ross's father? Heavens!

Consequently Angel's eyes widened in shocking speculation. No! It could not be! But a new and horrible thought that came to mind spurred her into action. Yes—it might very well have something to do with Cordell's first name, connected with the Kent heirloom somehow, indirectly.

"Beauty, come Beauty!" Angel called into the surrounding trees, fearing the worst—that Jacinta had taken the mounts back with her, or that they had shied from the fire and bolted off into the night.

Suddenly Angel smiled faintly as Christine came walking from beyond the glow of rubble, leading Wesley's mount. The daughter saw through her mother's frailty a new, strong-willed woman. Lady Christine Sherwood of England was going to be fine, indeed. Next, Angel held a trembling breath, for brave Beauty trotted out into the open, shying from the smouldering rubble, yet trusting enough to answer the call of her gentle second master, she pranced to her side.

Angel offered a hand to Christine. "Everything will be all right now, Mama," she said softly.

"Yes, my daughter, by the grace of God," Christine returned, "and, let no man say we women are weak and helpless." She tried a laugh with happy tears.

Disregarding the pastel carpet, Tyrone trudged with ash-covered jackboots into the luxurious salon and slumped into a chair of green and white silken cushion, hanging his tawny head in utter despair. Presently he rose to go and stand before the mantle with torso bowed forward and hands splayed on the warmed Italian marble. A small fire had been lighted below him and he fixed his gaze blindly into the crackling hearth, feeling no warmth, only stabbing desolation at his loss. He saw again in his mind's eye the smouldering rubble of the cabin and a mournful animal sound ripped from his throat, ending in a deep masculine sob, as he smashed a right hook into the stone, feeling no physical pain from his bruising knuckles.

"Curse me! What a damned hero I am," he cried out loud, "I passed my love right by when she needed me most and now she is gone, perished, consumed by fires—like she was in hell! Nothing left, nothing. Ah Lord, why? Why!" he asked around the room, disregarding the movement behind him.

"Why what, Tyrone?" Jacinta asked, rustling into the room. "You have nothing to grieve for, *mon cher*."

With a deep growl Tyrone spun about on grinding heels to glare at the woman who had intruded upon his time of soul-filled bitterness. He believed he hated everyone at this time, even his beautiful wife who had perished in the blaze, leaving him a heartbroken man. Their fleeting time of happiness had been close to his heart, and now . . . now there was nothing left for him in the world. There was one important thing he must do now, though, and that was find the man James who had given his wife the lavaliere and—kill him.

With a fixed stare at nothing, Tyrone said, "Go away, Jacinta. Go away and leave me alone." He sauntered off down the hall and into his study, never even noticing that she had followed him.

There came a scuffling of feet along the hall and Jacinta appeared, saying, "Not yet, *mon cher* Ty. First you must see for yourself what that sweet little wife of yours had planned." She gestured to the open door as she blurted, "Come in gentlemen, and bring Cordell with you—*James* Cordell!"

Caspar and Joseph didn't need to be told and disregarded Jacinta entirely while they held Cordell imprisoned between them. A white-faced Cordell had ceased his struggling by now and he sneered over to Jacinta who returned his look with an imperious one of her own. Caspar eyed Cordell with hate before his huge arm unfolded and he held out Angel's small coffer for Tyrone to see.

"What is the meaning of this!" Tyrone thundered as he

closed the distance between them in two easy strides.

"Sure and they're the lady's jewels, cap'n," Caspar assured. "We caught this clod sneaking around in the stable trying to get himself a mount."

"She told me to. Her!" Cordell cried in outrage, watching the one mentioned look at him archly.

"He lies. Do not believe him, Tyrone. He is—"

"Shut up, Jacinta," Tyrone bit out furiously.

His visage was stony and dark, making his scar visibly white as he plucked the coffer from Caspar. Tyrone snapped open the lid and the gems he had lavished upon his wife seemed to twinkle mockingly up at him in his present twisted state. Golden orbs narrowed dangerously as he plucked the lavaliere from out of his breeches' pocket, his gaze riveting upon Cordell's ashen face for his reaction.

Tyrone's voice came out low and his first words were concentrated into a fierce directness: "What were you meaning to do with my wife's jewels . . . James Cordell! James, yes, I know you now. You were one of my men of the crew. And what about this—you bastard?"

Cordell just stared hazily at the locket, shaking his head at this confusion Jacinta had erected between him and the Hunters. He couldn't realize Hunter's meaning, and so he blundered, "I'm not entirely without blame, sir, but I'm a damned fool for believing Jacinta was in love with me. We were going to go away together, she said."

"I see," Tyrone said simply, but his voice was deadly. He tucked the lavaliere away.

"I will tell you myself, then." Jacinta swept forward. "Cordell was going to take the jewels and run away with your wife. He has twisted it around. She and James have been lovers for quite some time now, haven't you realized that yet?" She delighted in the manner in which Cordell's eyes widened in utter disbelief at what she said.

Tyrone grasped her by the arm, hurting. "What about Wesley, you told me Angel was with *him!*"

"*Mais oui.* He was very jealous when he found out that she was to meet James at the cabin, the very same place where

521

Wesley had the old woman hidden, and he was just going there himself. I tried to tell you, I heard all the conversation before Wesley hit me."

Cordell elbowed Caspar and Joseph aside, and they, knowing what would ensue next, hung back. Tyrone was spoiling for a good battle, his hatred a driving force. It was in his eyes, it was inevitable. Before Tyrone helped himself out of his riding jacket, he heard Cordell curse Jacinta.

"Lying bitch! Why'd you do this to me? You had it all planned, me joining the crew to spy for you, coming here to be employed, sneaking around and getting information for you. Me, and I'll bet a hundred others. You and I, as planned, were going to go away with the jewels. Tonight, you said."

Jacinta shrieked, "He lies, my Ty. You know he was a smuggler, one of your own men. He followed Angel to New Orleans after first bedding the tramp! He is the sire to that brat!" She dared a swift glimpse to the door before going on. "He gave Angel that locket and told me she had lost it. This is all true, I swear," she ended, almost on a sob.

"Bitch!" Cordell shouted, "you even had me leave that note at the front door for the lady!"

Tyrone shook his head but it wouldn't clear sufficiently for him to think rationally. His roar and his motions were like a raging mad bull as he moved to toss his jacket onto the floor in a crumpled heap. As long long ago, he saw red. Blood. The scar. He gave no time to ponder the motive behind Angel's wanting to leave him, he only wanted to damage something or someone.

Cordell was just as angry, for Jacinta had deceived him, set him up. He was by no means weak or unnerved and had kept himself in shape, even though his job of late meant not having had to lift the heavy crates and chests of contraband as he had done on the island. His muscles were stringy, stood out like taut cords. He was well-matched with the master of Cresthaven, excepting that he was a slightly younger man.

Tyrone, with fists held high in front of his face, advanced upon his ready opponent and they began to circle each other like expert prizefighters. Tyrone took the first punch at the younger man and it landed to connect squarely upon his chin, snapping back Cordell's head with the mighty impact, and with a surprised look going to Tyrone as his head righted itself. Instantaneously a right flew at Tyrone and he ducked it swiftly, and coming up, Tyrone duplicated the servant's right and ground a fast blow that would have otherwise crushed the other's nose had he not jerked his head abruptly aside. Still, the servant took it on the side of his head and reeled dizzily.

Soon they began to breathe heavily and perspiration trickled off brows as the two continued to dance around each other. A flash of white apron in the portal caught Tyrone off guard and his opponent slammed him one on the chin, making a dull sound in the room.

"Lordy. *Lordy me!*" Ranae cried; seeing the upturned chairs and the blood trickling from the corner of Mr. Hunter's grim mouth. She saw the blood-spattered servant in worse condition and hesitated only a few seconds longer as the fight continued. Ranae shook the dust off her feet, and throwing her hands widely splayed in the air, went to climb the back stairs as fast as her shaking limbs would allow.

"Didn't he know the lady has come home with her mama and is upstairs with the babe now?" Ranae talked to herself, shaking the hot toddy fuzz from her brain. He must have missed her by only a few minutes. She had to hurry, else the master would beat that man to death!

Taken unaware, Cordell's eyes widened before he folded over from the blow directly under his ribs, causing his breath to escape him in a huff. He barely had time to recover when Tyrone clasped his forearms together and crashed them down onto the man's shoulder while a knee came up next to catch Cordell under the chin. Blood flew from the fleshy gap and Cordell was flung back from the next impact, hitting the wall behind him hard. A set of books toppled then fell, scattering across the blood-spattered floor, and Tyrone struck him again and again. A bone snapped in the younger man's face. His nose was broken, split wide.

Pale blue eyes clouded, his face twisted with pain, Cordell begged, "Enough, please, enough!"

Tyrone was driven as if by demons at the sound of the man's

voice, and he continued his brutal attack, snatching Cordell by the blood-red shirt front as he drew back his arm like a deadly strung bow. Cordell's eyes cleared long enough to witness the visage before him, contorted with blood-lust, prepared to pound him into a bloody pulp. This next one would surely put him into an early grave.

Directly behind them and with a savage glint in her eyes, Jacinta shouted excitedly, "Kill him, Ty, kill him! Oh *yesss*," she hissed, "kill him. You and I can have it all then. Angel was no good, just like Annette. Do it to wash away the memory of your mother and Wesley—they were lovers, too!"

Tyrone froze and his balled fist lagged. Crazed by the sight of so much blood, Jacinta went on, now shrieking, "Kill your wife's lover!"

"Wesley?" Tyrone asked belatedly, still staring at Cordell. He shook his tousled head to clear it.

Jacinta went on ruthlessly, "Wesley told me, he was with Annette when you found them upstairs, when she gave you that scar on your forehead. It was him, just like now this man is the little slut's lover."

It all seemed to fit together somehow, like a crazy puzzle in Tyrone's befuddled mind. He turned on Jacinta, and, never letting go of the limply sagging form, spoke in a deadly menacing tone. "Never, Jacinta, but *never* call Angel a slut again! I've warned you before. Whatever was between her and this man—she was not that!"

Cordell choked, "Your wife—she meant nothing to me. I'm sorry—sorry. She was kind—beautiful—and I never—meant to do her any harm—" He couldn't go on as he clutched Tyrone's blood-stained shirt, trying to make himself understood.

Tyrone, taking the man's meaning the wrong way, demanded truculently, "What are you trying to say? And, what about the lavaliere you gave my wife? Speak man, or I'll finish you off now!" He bounced the already reeling head off the wall paneled in dark oak as he shook him savagely.

"God, no, Tyrone! Leave the man be!"

The strong but dulcet tone reached his ears and Tyrone spun

about like one in a slow-motion dream. He stared wonderstruck across the room. Angel stood there, looking incredibly fresh, whole, but with her lovely hair singed along the entire length. Bruises and scratches, but nothing more serious, colored her fair skin in purple and pink here and there. A miracle! He thought this sweet vision betrayed his mind and senses, until she spoke again, indeed looking and sounding like a celestial being.

"Tyrone, help him. Don't hurt him anymore, you will kill him," she cried, her eyes pleading mercy for the brutally beaten man who slumped against his shoulder, blood oozing from nose and lips.

Though her reaction was not one of joy, Jacinta was as stunned as Tyrone at seeing Angel alive and whole. She was about to step between them when Big Jim entered, his green eyes sweeping the room that lay in shambles and the battered servant slumped against Tyrone like a broken doll. Big Jim lunged forward just as Tyrone slackened his hold on the servant. Big Jim caught and eased Cordell onto a cushioned bench and dabbed at the bloody cuts with a handkerchief. Joseph knew what would be needed and went to fetch the items to doctor Cordell.

"Angel—" Tyrone's voice was hoarse with emotion, a mixture of wonderment mingled with a soft caress. "Come here, little love. Lord, let me hold you to be certain you are alive and sound."

Gathering up the skirts of her dressing gown, Angel flew into the waiting arms that at once held her fast, full of joy that she was indeed unharmed; and she kissed him back, tasting the blood on his cut lips, unmindful as he was that a pair of hatefully jealous eyes slitted at them.

"Ahhh," Tyrone murmured with pleasure as her sweet breath rushed into his mouth, making him minimize the dreadful events of the evening and forget for now that so many questions yet went unanswered. "You were here all this last hour?" he wondered, seeing the fresh gown.

"Yes, Tyrone, upstairs shedding our smoke-stained garments."

"I died a thousand deaths thinking you perished in the blaze," he said.

Angel wanted to put her blond head on her husband's shoulder and weep. Maybe all this was meant to be, for she realized home was here with him, but she couldn't voice this just yet.

Jacinta interrupted, jouncing over with hands on her generous hips. "*Mon* Ty," she hissed low so that Big Jim couldn't hear, "doesn't it sink into your thick skull that these two are lovers?" Her hand indicated Cordell and Angel in one sweep.

The reality of the night's events crowded in on Tyrone, and he remembered Jacinta's earlier, crushing information that Angel had meant to leave him. For now, he couldn't fathom that his insanely jealous nature blinded him to all truth. His usually tanned face suddenly drained of all color, making him appear saturnine. Feeling the womanly softness beside him, he couldn't believe Angel capable of murder or infidelity, but he desperately needed some special words of reassurance from her now.

Angel wanted to pour out her heart's love to Tyrone, as she had promised herself back at the cabin to do immediately if she was fortunate enough to be spared and at home with him again. But this was neither the time nor the place, she told herself. She had to be alone with him for that. Too, all Jacinta had spoken of earlier flooded back to her in a horrible rush and she was at once afraid. She didn't have to look at Tyrone now to know he was growing tense. It was in the air and it made her fear the worst—that he believed the evil, conniving woman who was his stepmother.

Big Jim, frowning darkly, joined the trio after Caspar had carried off the battered man to his room in the servants' quarters. For a moment Jacinta was afraid her husband would spoil the seed of distrust planted in Tyrone's mind. But she could see Ty was having second thoughts about Angel. The tenderness he'd shown her minutes before was melting into an icy remoteness as he surveyed her every move. The tempest was about to commence.

"James Cordell will live," Big Jim began, "but will have a hard time moving his mouth for a few days, to be sure." He shot a black look to Jacinta and she stuck her nose in the air.

"James," Angel breathed the name almost like a caress as she recalled the troubling thought she'd had earlier. "James Cordell," she repeated, then blinked out of her daze.

Tyrone's countenance paled further and now as if half-alive he moved away from his wife. He went to stand at the window, dismissing any further discussion on the night's events. His silence was more than Angel could bear, but she suddenly realized her mistake. That was all he'd needed to hear to think the worst—two damaging words that would make them forever strangers. She was thoroughly exhausted, unable to think clearly anymore this night, and what she had just muttered could not be retracted and explained away with ease. What Jacinta had destroyed here would take weeks to correct—maybe even a lifetime. That is, if Tyrone even allowed her to stay at Cresthaven. He had condemned his mother for her dalliance with another man—Wesley! So how could she hope to be an exception when she was already guilty in her husband's eyes?

Oh yes, it was all very clear to her now, Angel thought wearily and was suddenly angrier than she'd ever been in her life. By presenting her with the heirloom James Hunter had started something; Jacinta had made ruin with her knowledge gained by her informer and lover, James Cordell; and Tyrone thought her faithless, thought she had presented him with Cordell's bastard, and was not to be trusted.

All she had to do now to be proven guiltless was to ask James Hunter to reveal who had given her the lavaliere. But no, she wasn't about to do that. Tyrone had to see the light himself, first believe her free from all these blemishes he had assumed true without sufficient proof.

Blast it! How could he make love to her as he had and call her his little love, it was an insult to her dignity and made her no better than a whore. Jacinta wasn't wrong when she had stated that Tyrone and she were two of a kind!

In silent fury Angel strode to where Tyrone stood. When he

detected a presence behind him he turned slowly about, only to meet a hearty slap on his cheek. His expression, first one of hurt, quickly altered to one of derision. The side of his face flamed with the bold imprint of her hand and his scar went livid.

"For your lover I presume," he said sarcastically, cocking an eyebrow before brushing past her.

Angel was at once sorry for hurting him for she still loved him, more now than ever. "Please—don't go," she begged, but he had already strode into the hall.

Jacinta tittered softly before she, too, left the room. That left only Angel and James in the study. He walked over to her, and placing a gentle arm about the trembling shoulders, said in a hushed tone, "My dear, let's talk. That is, if you are not too tired?"

Angel smiled up at him a bit sadly. "I would like that very much and perhaps it will help me to sleep better, for I am much too pent-up inside just now to fully relax."

After Big Jim had fetched a pot of tea from the weary and shocked housekeeper who had just recently returned home, he joined Angel in the parlor where she awaited him. The tray almost clattered to the floor when James took in the sight of Angel tottering on a chair she had pulled over beneath the portrait of his deceased wife. Angel turned ever so slowly about to meet his startled gaze, and in her shaking hands she clutched an unopened, yellowed envelope. James rushed over and caught her just as she was making a careless descent.

Angel began softly. "It says here, 'To my son: Tyrone Michael Hunter.'" She handed the envelope into James's care and his eyes didn't leave hers as she added, "She—she was staring down at me again, as if trying to tell me something with those beautifully sad eyes." Again Angel had heard the haunting voice in her mind, but this time hadn't ignored its urging.

The first faint streaks of eastern dawn-pink swaddled the sky when the young Mistress Hunter wearily sought her bed, graciously leaving James alone to open the envelope and pour over its contents.

It was sweetly written, in the neat hand of Annette Hunter née Kent, to a son she had loved more than life itself. In fact, her loyalty and protection of the tawny-haired lad had cost her her own happiness. James Hunter realized this, and what a blind fool he'd been. His shoulders slumped forward after reading the letter and his sorrow for his lady came forth in dry, wracking sobs.

With noon breaking Angel tumbled guiltily from the bed after noticing the vacant pillow beside her. When she had crept softly into bed that morning Tyrone had been sleeping fitfully and had reached out for her once. She had returned the caress and snuggled closer to him and had soon fallen into a deep sleep, never knowing if he had tried speaking to her. Had she mumbled in her tormented, nightmarish sleep?

The air was soft and sweetly smelling of Cherokee roses when it breathed gently into the room. As she had fasted for twenty-four hours an extreme hunger made her dress swiftly, hoping that lunch was being prepared. She had learned it to be imperative to nourish one's strength in times of tribulation.

Dying of curiosity, Sarah entered and at once set about to correct the damage done to her mistress's hair. She held her silence as she applied eau de quinine and wielded a trusty scissors, finally forming new gypsylike wavelets and curls to cascade down past Angel's shoulders. Angel smoothed the creamy yellow frock she wore with slightly trembling fingers, trying hard not to dwell on the day before as she went to check if Christine stirred in the guestroom down the hall. The recently occupied bedchamber was vacant, so she went downstairs to a silence that made her heart thunder in her breast.

Angel heaved a sigh of relief upon entering the dining room. Everyone was there but Hannah and Nikki. They most likely had gone to Gayarre to settle matters there and see to the child, she determined. Jacinta's face fell when Angel, gliding into the room, looked like the fairest creature on earth, a new and sweetly seductive air about her. Tyrone gasped with pleasure seeing the small face surrounded by haloes of bright hair. He

529

decided this chic look complimented her new maturity.

"Here you are," Angel tried cheerfully, going to Christine who perched Brian Ross on her knee, feeding him bits of a dainty cake.

"Oooh, such a handsome prince of a lad he is, daughter," Christine cooed proudly, already looking as if some pink had entered her cheeks. "And now he is already taking cow's milk with a bit of corn syrup, and has eaten well this morning. Could I take him up and put him down for his noon nap, daughter?"

"Please do, Mama," Angel said, chucking her son under the chin. "Mama is nigh onto starving, yes I am," she told the lad and he chuckled happily.

Pah! Jacinta thought, screwing up her face, "She acts as if nothing out of the ordinary has happened, but I will soon put an end to her pretentions!"

Tyrone rose, pushed back his chair and went to stand beside his wife and mother-in-law, who was just making to rise with the child. He held his arms out to her. "Mother, permit me to hold my son for a minute first." A secretive smile played about his mouth as Angel's brow lifted in puzzlement. He went on, "I haven't seen much of my son the past several weeks. It's not often that we two get to have a man-to-man talk, what with all these females clucking about us. Ouch!" he exclaimed as Brian reached up to smartly tug a hank of his hair.

"Besides being handsome he hefts a strong hand," Christine chirped.

Tyrone cleared his throat. "A woman of good judgment is your grandmama, and his good health attests his mother's care," he added to his glowing wife.

Jacinta gawked at Tyrone as she wondered at his sudden change of heart. Angel too was very much surprised, but her spirits rose to the occasion and her silvery laughter tinkled in the room as James stood up to join in admiring the child. Then, all too soon, Brian was brought up to bed as he whined his tiredness. The gay atmosphere became as gravely serious as it had been the night before.

Shortly Angel began to feel a certain clamminess and her forkful of dripping gravy and beef was checked in mid-air as

Tyrone continued to watch her every move. She couldn't read his expression and the silence hung heavy. As she was the only one eating now, she pushed her half-full plate aside, not hungry anymore. Besides, she didn't like the idea of eating alone with so many eyes snagging on each mouthful she took. What was everyone waiting for?

Jacinta rose and twitched around the table. "Well, isn't this nice and cozy," she smirked, stopping directly behind Angel's chair. "Angeline, you will become skinny and sickly if you do not eat." She sneered, then turned to Tyrone. *"N'est-ce pas?"* she said to him.

"Rather I would have her svelte than attractively plump," he said as he pushed from the chair-back he'd been leaning upon.

His downright answer left no doubt as to what he truly thought. Jacinta narrowed her eyes as Tyrone pulled out his wife's chair for her after inquiring if she was done. Without further ado he ushered Angel into the parlor. Jacinta compared her generous curves with those of the retreating slim shape, before her gaze settled on James. He smiled tauntingly at her, even though his mood didn't match the gesture.

"Pooh!" Jacinta exclaimed before she flounced out of the room.

Tyrone pulled Angel down gently beside him and they made a handsome picture of contentment seated together on the loveseat. Jacinta noticed this upon entering and made herself at home by choosing a fat armchair near the couple. She regarded her stepson flirtatiously and he returned her gaze passively. She was so engrossed in weaving evil webs that she failed to note James coming to stand beside her.

"Jacinta, it is time to go," James informed her, all the while keeping his eyes glued to the portrait of his beloved lady. He must have been crazy to have married a bitch after having had the best. His gaze fell to the dark head below him. "You are making a fool of yourself, Jacinta," he hissed, but she made no move to rise. "Can't you tell when you are not wanted?"

Jacinta shot up out of the chair, her dark eyes glinting wickedly. "I know what you are up to," she sneered. "You

531

think I murdered Wesley Gayarre."

"You said it, not I," James returned, but he knew it for the truth it was.

"Well . . . you are wrong," Jacinta began. "It was—"

James had snatched for her, but he caught the air. "Let's go, Jacinta," he warned dangerously. "The carriage is waiting and so is Caspar. I want to have some time alone with Tyrone and Angeline . . . so if you will be so kind?"

"Never!" Jacinta snarled. She tried wrenching away as he again reached out for her. Her fingers clawed the air like talons. "Leave me be, old man!" She spat some French gutter-type invectives in his face. "You always loved Annette—never me. You only married me after she died to own a good piece of fluff, a beautiful woman on your arm to show off at your gaming tables. Pah! How I fooled you, Big Jim Hunter. Tyrone had me long before—"

"Shut up, bitch!" James ground out as he caught and dragged her screaming and kicking toward the door.

James tried clamping a hand over the gnashing mouth, but Jacinta swiftly avoided him by whirling about, ducked out of his reach. She hopped on one foot as she had lost a high-heeled slipper. She found a safe place behind the sofa and continued her tirade, directing it to the young couple in the room.

"Look at them, so enamored of one another. Pah! They do not give a damn who is bedding who. It was you yourself, Ty, who swore you would never marry any woman, but—" she flared here—"I know all about your bargain with Big Jim. You stated you would only consider marriage for the sole purpose of obtaining an heir! Only then would you settle down like James wanted you to!"

Angel lifted her downcast eyes to gaze into those hazel depths and for a painful moment she thought he struggled with the truth before he chose his words carefully, slowly.

"First, Jacinta," he began, his eyes resting solely on Angel, "I have married not just any woman, but rather a very special one, who bore me a son who is equally special." His regard left off caressing his wife and slipped to Jacinta. "You know as well as I do, Jacinta, that my plan was to make Angel my wife the night you so expertly carted her away. Ah, yes, it was your carriage I saw pull away from the town house. At that time Angel's pregnancy was unknown to me, nor do I think she herself knew she carried my seed till she had been employed at Gayarre for several weeks."

Angel's countenance softened at the revelation that he had intended to wed her. "If only I had known, Tyrone. I was afraid you only desired me as a mistress, nothing more. I wanted to put as much distance between us as possible and I even left Christine behind in my foolish haste. But I was torn between being hurt and leaving my heart behind . . . with you."

He bent close to her ear. "I realized the disgrace I had brought to your good name. Yet I wanted you, loved you even then, but like a fool I was blind to the fact, afraid that you hated me. I had it in mind to court you, woo you once we were wed. I made a mistake by trying to communicate the language of love with bold gestures and sly caresses, rather than with words. My sole aim was to make you fall madly in love with me, as I was with you," he ended, with a question in his soft hazel eyes.

"Oh Tyrone, you did that expertly, long ago, and more fully than you realize—" She halted here, afraid to ask what had been troubling her. His bitter words of the evening before still hurt. But, oh! He loved her! He *loved* her!

"Yes, I believe in you, Angel," he answered her unspoken fear, pressing her arm tenderly. "Angel, my Lady, my Wife, my little Love, my Heart, and mother to my beautiful son," he murmured, as his hard cheek met her soft, flushed one. "Forgive me for being a jealous fool, my love."

"Pah! Pooh!" Jacinta spat. "Love! It will not be long before you will be bedding another, *mon cher* Ty. You toss women aside as fast as a horse leaves its droppings!"

"We're talking about real love, Jacinta," Tyrone began, warming to the subject. "Sacred as well as physical, a steady and honest giving of oneself. No one can break the fused bond between Angel and myself. I know that now as I shall twenty, forty years from now."

"I say that brat is not of your blood, Ty!" Jacinta spat vindictively, but she had already felt the heavy hand of defeat.

James stepped up to her. "Brian Ross is my grandson, I can vouch for that, Jacinta. What other man in all of Louie has eyes the color of bright jade?" he said proudly, opening his eyes wide to remind her. "Brian has them, besides being a chip off the old block—he looks just like Tyrone!" He knew she couldn't contest the fact.

Before Jacinta could open her mouth again James went after her, reaching out a long arm to snatch the cropped hair. She screeched and hollered like a taunted crone as he pulled her along out into the hall, where he spoke in a dangerous tone of voice. Angel and Tyrone exchanged glances, she wondering what James had in mind to punish her. Tyrone nodded knowingly as he listened.

"It's high time you eat crow, Jacinta. I'm taking you back to the town house immediately, but too bad it will be such a short visit before the authorities come for you. You'll never set foot back here again to harm these people, for I'm going to make certain you are tossed into the calaboose for the murder of one Monsieur Wesley Gayarre!"

"Pah! You should thank me for doing in your dead wife's lover. Didn't you know, Mr. Hunter?" Jacinta said in a whiny, taunting voice.

A painful slap answered her before James shoved her at Caspar. The big man had been asked beforehand to escort Jacinta to the waiting carriage and Caspar delighted in this task, for he'd never had any love for the Creole woman. She struggled, but the old pirate overpowered her swiftly.

James returned to the parlor where Tyrone was just in the process of asking his beloved spouse a question. James hung back, not wanting to intrude until they finished.

"Why did you go to the cabin in the first place, Angel?" Tyrone was asking gently as he stroked her forearm.

"I received a note at the front door, with news of Christine it said, and that the writers worked for you," she answered.

"Jacinta . . . and Wesley," he said thoughtfully.

Angel recalled just now the scrawl of the note she'd received one other time. Someday maybe she would mention the night Jacinta had slipped the philter into his drink, but not now.

James came fully into view when they glanced up after staring into each other's eyes with something close to worship. Fishing into his pocket, James came up with the yellowed envelope meant for his son. Tyrone paled visibly, recognizing the handwriting. He peered at his father questioningly before Angel took it upon herself to explain, her voice strangely hushed.

"I found the letter behind Annette's portrait, Tyrone. Last night after you had gone off to bed, as I waited for James to bring the tea into the parlor," she said, making an emphasis on the name, watching Tyrone closely for his reaction. He looked slightly puzzled, so she went on. "I'd had a form of presentiment, and not just once. I should have heeded it the first time but I thought myself foolish for hearing such things. It came to me again as I woke in the burning cabin, but I forgot it until later when I sat quietly, trying to unwind in the parlor."

Tyrone had been silent, but now a queer tremor shot through him as he noted the pained expression his father tried unsuccessfully to conceal.

"Angel, have you read this?" Tyrone asked softly and received a negative shake of her head.

"Tyrone," James warned, "I think Angeline might not want to be around when you read this, she might hear some pretty foul language and even be in danger of some flying objects."

Angel graciously made to rise, but Tyrone held her back with a restraining hand. "No. Stay, Angel. She is part of me and whatever this contains, no matter how provoking, she's free from danger here," he told James.

Angel stayed, but her eyes were solicitous as he pulled the stationery from the envelope, the frayed edges telling of the passage of years.

"Wait," James again halted. "Before you read that I need to explain that this has to do with—ah—Wesley and Annette. No—" he said holding up his hand, "don't look that way, Tyrone, it's not what you're thinking." He paused, collecting his thoughts. "You see . . . I, too, condemned Annette, whether you knew it or not. Unjustly yes, I know that now. But

535

for that reason I stayed away from Cresthaven so much when you were growing up, for Annette always seemed nervous, concealing something from me, and we couldn't talk for it. That was where I made my biggest mistake. You were all-knowing for one so young, but even the most intelligent of beings sometime read into things what's truly not there.

"We should try to confirm what we suspect and give the person the benefit of the doubt, but we don't always do it when we feel wronged, when we think that someone had been disloyal and has hurt us." He peered pointedly at Angel, and for the first time ever in his father's presence, Tyrone reddened. James went on, "I love my lady even now as I did then, there will never be another like her—" he ended on a choke of emotion, "for me."

Tyrone was beginning to understand. His father must have worshipped Annette, for he had always tried to explain, though somewhat ironically back then, that she was a good lady. Tyrone himself had remained indifferent to James's words, as well as personally to Annette. His father must have felt in his innermost heart that she could not have committed an act of unfaithfulness.

James sighed deeply, shaking his graying head sadly, then he suddenly clenched his fists in frustration before striding out the door. "I only wish one thing could be possible now . . . for Wesley Gayarre to return from hell so I could make him suffer—ever so slowly—for the pain he has caused this family. So . . . there is one other of his kind I must deal with now."

After his departure the parlor was silent as a tomb, with only the rustling of a page now and then. Curiously Angel watched her husband, afraid to say a word to disturb him. His tawny head was bent studiously and his strong features appeared saturnine. All of a sudden Angel jumped with a start when he stood and moaned out loud.

"Lord, what a fool I've been all these years. My own sweet mother was afraid of that bastard Wesley and what he would have done to her. That sonofabitch blackmailed her into silence, said he would murder her only son if she breathed a word to anyone that he had raped her. *Me*, he meant *me!*

Another time he said he would inform her husband they were carrying on an *affair*—if she didn't let him. Either way, she was caught in the coils of that madman. Damn! He forced Annette time and again in her own bedroom while my father was stationed in the city. I must have been stone-blind not to realize it!"

"You—you were so young back then, Tyrone," Angel breathed.

As if he hadn't heard her, his handsome face twisted into livid fury as he fingered the slim white scar that marred his forehead. "She didn't give me this scar—" he yelled in turning to Angel, and she quailed at the crazed look of him, "that bastard Wesley did, and I only pray that he rots in hell for the corrupt deeds of his life!"

Tyrone tapped a page loudly. "It says here he even threatened to set fire to the house while we slept at night with James away!" he shouted.

Angel gasped at that, but he went on as if he hadn't heard the sound. "While I was here, at that, yes, helpless, too young to comprehend what was taking place in the house that was to be mine someday. Then one day I finally did realize what was going on—the dark shadow of a man in her bed, ramming into her. The day he threw that boot into my face—*Wesley!*"

Angel drew back a little, but could now understand why Tyrone had lived with heartache, then bitter, haunting revolt toward his own mother when he had finally gone away to sea alone. She could just see him as he shunned every gesture of motherly love that a boy should otherwise accept eagerly, hold dear forever in his heart when she was gone from this earth. No wonder he had hated women, used them. Angel just hoped and prayed it was not too late for him to truly learn to love, to forget what hadn't been there in the first place. The scar inside him was far worse than the one Wesley had given him on his forehead. True, Tyrone had already taken a step forward a short time ago by admitting his love for her.

Angel's heart went out to him as he poured out his frightening grief, his wrath taking up again where it had first played itself out upon the servant Cordell. Angel felt as if her back was a taut violin string.

"And Muriel Gayarre, no wonder she followed Annette to her grave. Wesley murdered his wife by breaking that once lovely lady's heart." He clenched his fists into balls of steel. "Lord, I truly wonder if Annette wasn't being pursued by that animal when she tumbled off her horse. Now—now I know who tried taking my life twice, most likely took Annette's," he said dangerously low. "Ahh, how I too wish him back . . . I would fillet the scurve!"

Hurrying over to him, Angel took gentle hold of the tense arms. "Oh, Tyrone, love, please do not think that way. What's done is done and there is no summoning back the past or . . . Wesley Gayarre," she breathed. She couldn't reveal that indeed Wesley *had* been Annette's murderer. Wesley had said as much in the cabin. What good would it do anyone now, in fact it would only hurt Tyrone and make him hate all the more. She would leave it be.

The room became silent now as Angel's gaze swept the portrait. She could just see the beautiful Annette crawling from her deathbed to write the letter—or maybe she had done it even before the fall, knowing Wesley was indeed going to race her to her death. Whenever she had written the revealing letter and snugged it behind the portrait, Angel just knew that somehow Annette had contacted her from her grave.

Peering down into the worried little face, Tyrone brushed back a tendril of fair hair. "Who gave you the lavaliere, sweet?" he asked gently, pulling it from his breeches' pocket.

Her eyes widened. "You have it? I thought all this time I had lost it, or someone had stolen it." She leaned against him. "Tyrone, Tyrone, it belonged to Annette . . . the Kent heirloom. Your great maternal grandmother's own. Your father presented it to me right before our wedding. I didn't tell you then because I promised secrecy to James."

"James . . . James . . . *James.* Oh, Lord, I am ten times a jealous fool, my sweet Angel." His long loving gaze was worth more than a hundred endearments as he reached behind her and clasped the lavaliere about her neck, where it belonged.

"Let's go upstairs and get on with our life. I have a great need to hold you and love you just now. Of this day what remains unanswered can be threshed out for the rest of our lives together." There remained a question in his beautiful eyes, though.

Angel hugged close to her husband's side as he wrapped a long arm about her waist. "I choose not to, Tyrone," she murmured. "Not ever again."

"My love . . . I was hoping you would say just that."

Epilogue

"Della said just this morning—if you sweep the feet of a child with a broom, it is a sign he will walk early," Angel informed Tyrone as she tried to look serious.

"And did she?" Tyrone wanted to know, hiding a grin.

"You mean did she sweep Brian's feet?" Angel said as they strolled in the gardens.

"Mmm-hmm."

"Heavens no!" Angel exclaimed. Then more softly, "I wouldn't let her."

Tyrone chuckled. "The plantation black has superstitions pertaining to just about everything, like cats and dogs, rats and mice. Like: To keep a dog at home, you must cut a small piece from the end of his tail and bury it under the front steps."

Angel shook her head in mock seriousness, saying, "Poor Noble. Have you noticed his tail getting any shorter?"

They laughed together gaily and the flowers nodded with answering gladness. Happily they strolled for a spell while the sunshine fell upon their heads warmly and the music of the wind was light and airy.

"Come," Tyrone said suddenly, "Let's walk to the stable as I have something there that will please you immeasurably—as well as myself, when I see your little face light up."

Angel tilted her head in wonder, but Tyrone only led her silently over to the fenced-in yard beside the stable. He hoisted her up onto the rail, then whistled twice. Old Saul peeped his kinky, charcoal head from inside the huge doorway then disappeared behind the frame. Angel waited entranced, like someone in an audience waiting for the curtain to rise.

Suddenly there appeared a flash as black as jet and Angel

could scarcely breathe when, like a thunderbolt out of the blue, Echo made a repeat performance of the night before when Tyrone had watched the fiery mare in awe. He chuckled happily now, and it warmed the cockles of his heart to witness the tears of unspeakable joy stream down Angel's dewy cheeks. He took in the glad reunion of woman and beast as the midnight mare pranced over to sniff out the gay young woman calling out softly.

"Echo, my beauty, my own," Angel murmured pressing her cheek along the velvety nose. The mare snorted at the young woman scoldingly.

His elation matching hers, Tyrone caressed the huge jaw, saying, "She will need some taming down after her long journey from England. Also, she seems a mite peeved at your having left her for so long."

"How, Tyrone, oh how did you get her for me?" she wondered, barely able to contain her excitement at this moment.

Tyrone cocked an eyebrow, dismissing her question by asking one of his own. "Aren't you forgetting something, sweet?"

Angel first studied him and then the mare. Next she emitted a joyful screech as an unfamiliar almost full-grown colt bolted from the stable, wild in its freedom to run. Almost blue, the slender colt reenacted the scene the larger horse had executed. The colt reared up, then, coming down, kicked out his hind legs to stretch them; bucking, he rocked his peach-fuzz mane. Angel didn't have to be told that this gorgeous youngster was Prancer—Echo's own colt.

Her effervescent laughter tinkled in the late afternoon as Beast's younger colt careened at a gallop from the stable to cavort with the other youngster. Tyrone helped Angel down from the fence and stared deeply into the green eyes that shone like evening stars.

"We'll have to keep these two upcoming studs apart when their minds turn to courting the same lady of the season," he murmured close to her ear, tickling it.

"Yes," Angel began, "and by that time Brian's brother, or sister if you will, shall have a mount of his or her own to ride," she answered mysteriously, waiting for his reaction.

Tyrone gulped. "You mean . . . you don't mean—?"

"Yes, I do!"

He snatched her up from the ground and twirled her round and round, his warm hazel eyes sweeping over her as she slipped her arms about his neck to hug him and tossed back her head in gay abandonment. He brought her down and kissed her deeply, with a definite hunger. Soon she returned kiss for kiss, embrace for embrace, and the flame of love grew between them. Tyrone stopped suddenly and lifted his lips from the ones that clung to his. He cupped her chin between long fingers.

"I love you, my lady," he murmured, then louder, "and if you don't stop teasing me I shall have to press you to the ground, toss up your skirts, and give those two youngsters watching us something to look forward to."

Angel blushed hotly, his words reminding her of the old Captain Ty. All at once she went into the security of his long arms. "I love you, Tyrone," she softly said against his broad chest. "Always love me as you do now. Never change, for I would be lost if you stopped loving me all of a sudden." The frightening thought shook her.

"You have echoed my own thoughts, sweet love," he breathed against her newly washed hair, no further explanation needed.

Angel lifted her chin to peer into the passionate gaze. "Echo. That reminds me. Aren't you going to tell me, Tyrone?" she begged.

He stepped back holding her at arm's length. "Why, of course. I had them shipped first class from my home in England," he answered, with a mysterious gleam a-sparkle in his eyes.

"You—" she breathed, "you own Stonewall?"

He bowed gallantly, lavishly. "I do, and have for . . . let me see, is it a year now? Yes. James presented the estate to me while I pleasured myself with the company of my beautiful and young captive on that isle."

"Oh! So that was James Hunter's business with my father," she said, feigning anger. She placed one hand upon a temptingly curved hip and her dainty nostrils flared defiantly. "Why did you not tell me sooner, sir?" She sauntered toward him while he backed up, smiling.

"Now . . . Angel, don't get your hackles up. It's not good for a gentlewoman while *enceinte*," Tyrone explained, raising a hand to ward off the accusing finger wagging in his face.

"So—" she began, hiding a smile, "now I understand fully. James struck a bargain with his son that was—if he discovered a suitable wife for his infamous son, he in turn promised to be a good laddie and raise a family. But! that did not include falling in love with her, did it now?"

"No," he said confessedly, "no, it didn't. But I chased you and see . . . *you* caught me," he chuckled arrogantly.

"And, my darling husband—how is my Uncle Stuart?"

"Ah, well," he began sheepishly, then rushed on, "A great physician has seen to him. He is almost cured. Isn't that swell?"

"Swell," Angel repeated, still tracking as he continued to back up. "And, some kind soul saw to his welfare also?"

"Indeed, as he sees to everything that has to deal with his lady love," he replied, as his glittering eyes roved over her boldly, insinuatingly.

"Tyrone Hunter! You are no gentleman—still a randy rogue!"

Chuckling deeply, he saw his chance and whirling, broke out into a playful romp across the greensward. They cavorted about the huge house like happy children, giggling, screeching aloud, playing hide-and-seek until, at last, Tyrone fell rolling upon the turf under a spreading magnolia with draping Spanish moss. He reached out a long arm, snatching her gently down with him upon the matted grass when she would have sped past to escape him.

"Again, you have caught me—" he muttered breathlessly, peering up into sparkling green orbs, "and captured my heart forever and ever."

Angel pressed down intimately on his hard length. "Aye, Captain Ty, forever and ever, till death us do part." Her sweet breath mingled with his.

Lying together upon the crest, their two profiles met,

silhouetted as one against the clouds' pink lattice. Here the sun shone softly, and thrushes and cardinals and mockingbirds cooed love songs and sang of twilight nigh, and the nascent magnolia flowers bloomed fragrantly, and the sweet breezes whispered to mingle with Negro voices drifting up mellifluously. A contented sigh settled over Cresthaven at long last.